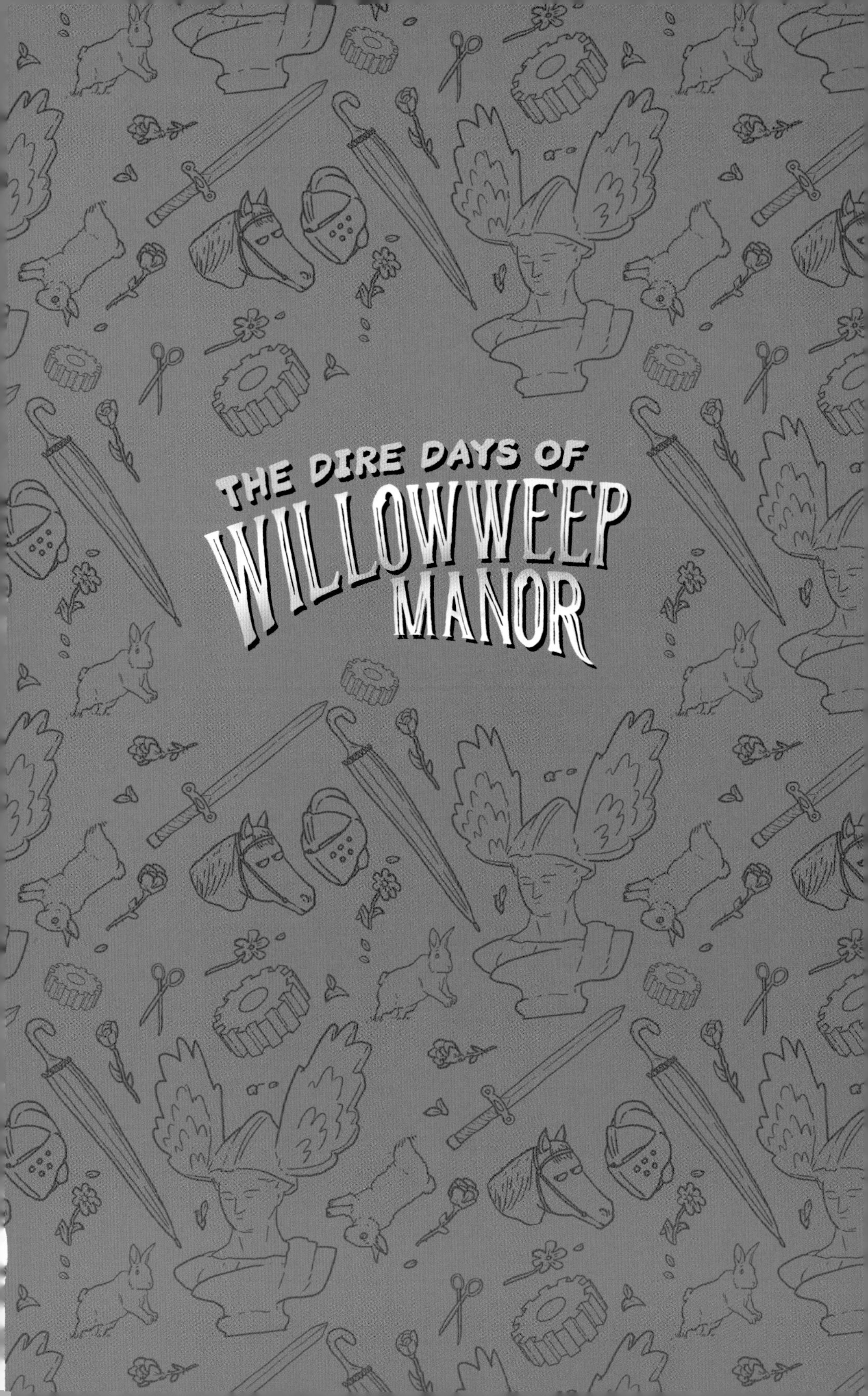
THE DIRE DAYS OF
WILLOWWEEP
MANOR

For Andrew, my parents, and Daniel Pinkwater
—Shaenon

For Cedra
—Christopher

MARGARET K. McELDERRY BOOKS · An imprint of Simon & Schuster Children's Publishing Division · 1230 Avenue of the Americas, New York, New York 10020 · This book is a work of fiction. Any references to historical events, real people, or real places are used fictitiously. Other names, characters, places, and events are products of the author's imagination, and any resemblance to actual events or places or persons, living or dead, is entirely coincidental. · Text © 2021 by Shaenon K. Garrity · Illustrations © 2021 by Christopher John Baldwin · Cover design by Karyn Lee © 2021 by Simon & Schuster, Inc. · All rights reserved, including the right of reproduction in whole or in part in any form. · MARGARET K. McELDERRY BOOKS is a trademark of Simon & Schuster, Inc. · For information about special discounts for bulk purchases, please contact Simon & Schuster Special Sales at 1-866-506-1949 or business@simonandschuster.com. · The Simon & Schuster Speakers Bureau can bring authors to your live event. For more information or to book an event, contact the Simon & Schuster Speakers Bureau at 1-866-248-3049 or visit our website at www.simonspeakers.com. · Also available in a Margaret K. McElderry Books paperback edition · Interior design by Christopher John Baldwin and Karyn Lee · The text for this book was set in Baldwin. · The illustrations for this book were rendered digitally. · Manufactured in China · First Margaret K. McElderry Books hardcover edition July 2021 · 2 4 6 8 10 9 7 5 3 1 · Library of Congress Cataloging-in-Publication Data · Names: Garrity, Shaenon K., author. | Baldwin, Christopher, 1973– illustrator. · Title: The dire days of Willowweep manor / Shaenon K. Garrity ; illustrated by Christopher John Baldwin. · Description: First Margaret K. McElderry Books hardcover edition. | New York : Margaret K. McElderry Books, 2021. | Audience: Ages 14 up. | Audience: Grades 10–12. | Summary: After she saves a man from drowning, Haley wakes up in a pocket universe that appears as a gothic estate and helps three brothers whose job it is to protect her world against a penultimate evil. · Identifiers: LCCN 2020042104 (print) | ISBN 9781534460874 (hardcover) | ISBN 9781534460867 (paperback) | ISBN 9781534460881 (ebook) · Subjects: LCSH: Graphic novels. | CYAC: Graphic novels. | Multiverse—Fiction. | Good and evil—Fiction. · Classification: LCC PZ7.7.G394 Di 2021 (print) | DDC 741.5/973--dc23 · LC record available at https://lccn.loc.gov/2020042104

THE DIRE DAYS OF WILLOWWEEP MANOR

Shaenon K. Garrity
Christopher Baldwin

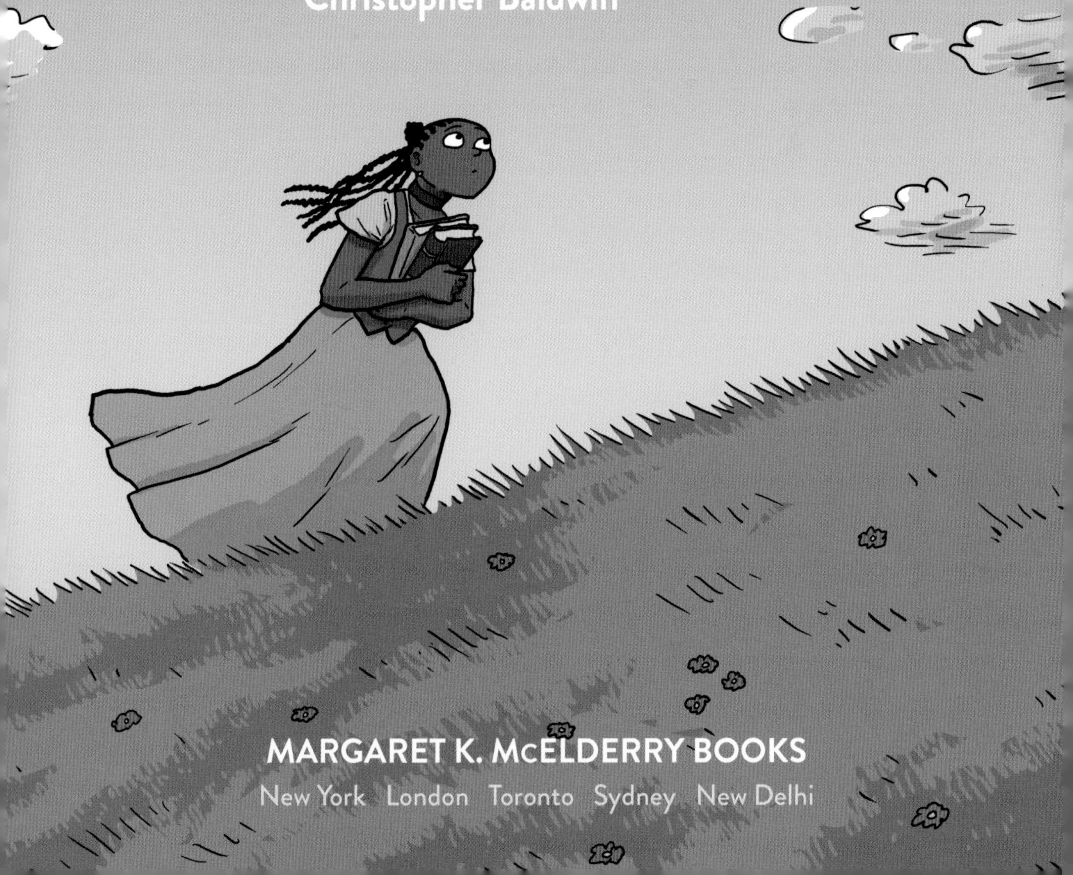

MARGARET K. McELDERRY BOOKS
New York London Toronto Sydney New Delhi

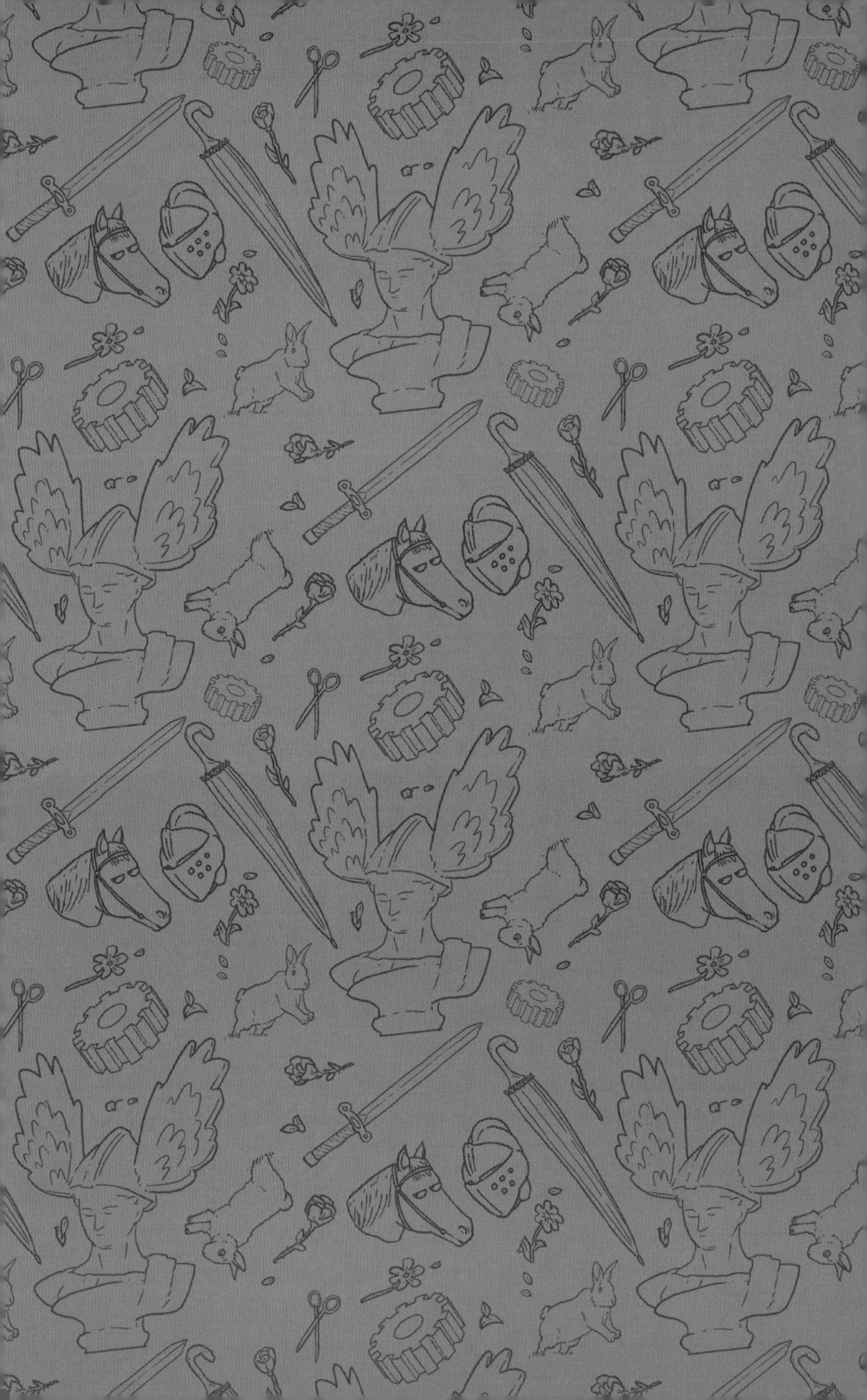

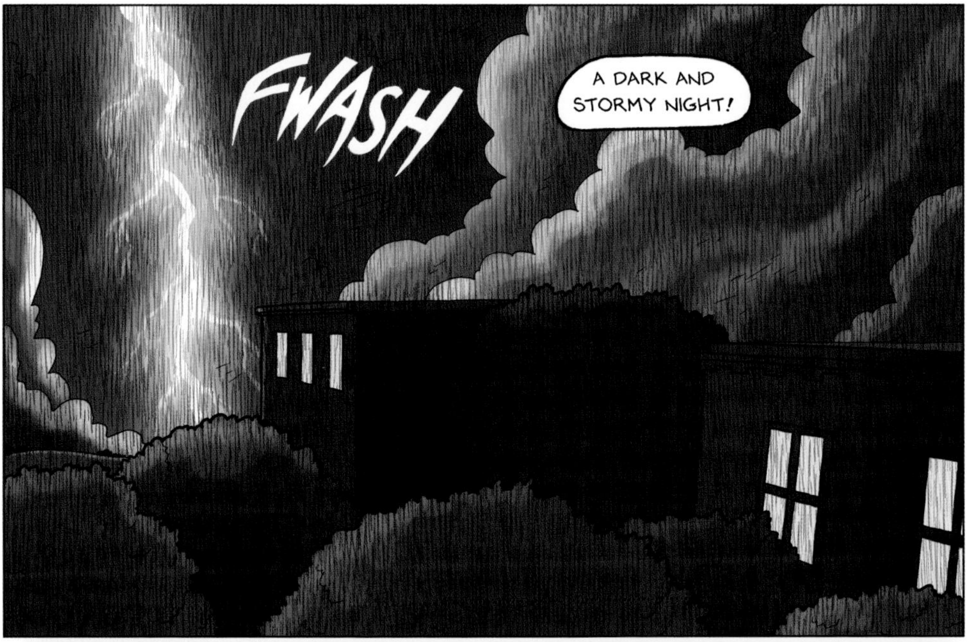
FWASH
A DARK AND STORMY NIGHT!

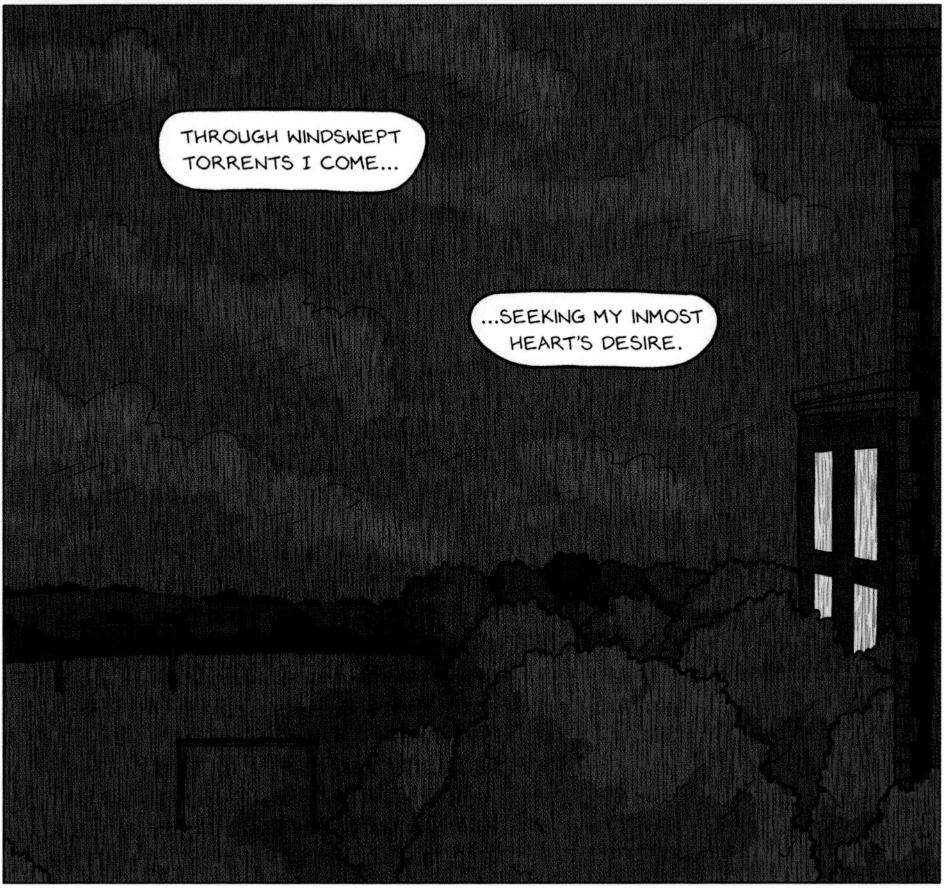
THROUGH WINDSWEPT TORRENTS I COME...
...SEEKING MY INMOST HEART'S DESIRE.

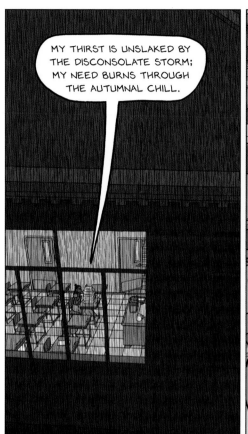

MY THIRST IS UNSLAKED BY THE DISCONSOLATE STORM; MY NEED BURNS THROUGH THE AUTUMNAL CHILL.

PLEEEEASE CAN YOU RECONSIDER MY GRADE?

READ

HALEY, THIS IS YOUR FOURTH ESSAY ON WUTHERING HEIGHTS.

AND...?

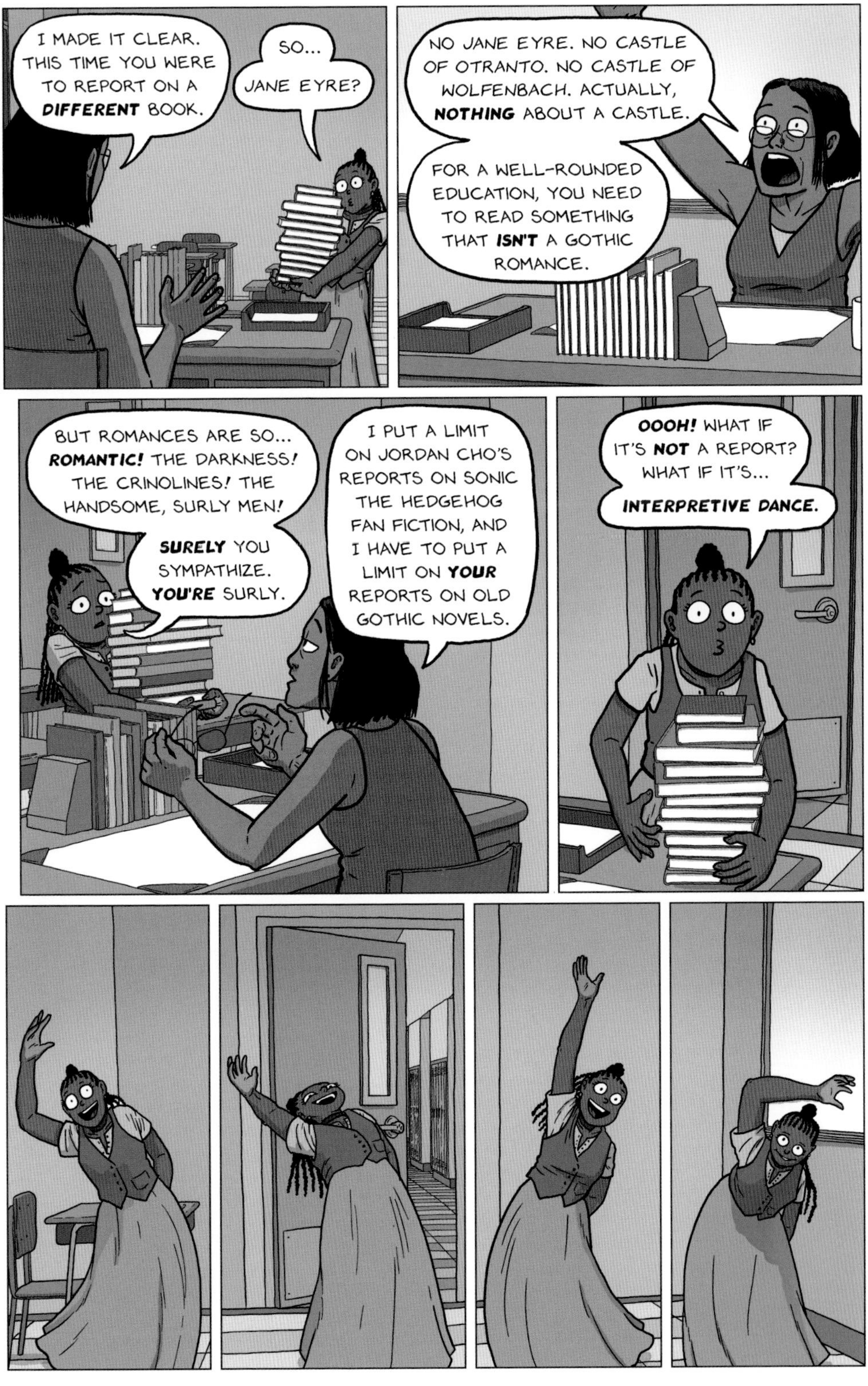
I MADE IT CLEAR. THIS TIME YOU WERE TO REPORT ON A **DIFFERENT** BOOK.
SO... JANE EYRE?
NO JANE EYRE. NO CASTLE OF OTRANTO. NO CASTLE OF WOLFENBACH. ACTUALLY, **NOTHING** ABOUT A CASTLE.
FOR A WELL-ROUNDED EDUCATION, YOU NEED TO READ SOMETHING THAT **ISN'T** A GOTHIC ROMANCE.
BUT ROMANCES ARE SO... **ROMANTIC!** THE DARKNESS! THE CRINOLINES! THE HANDSOME, SURLY MEN!
SURELY YOU SYMPATHIZE. **YOU'RE** SURLY.
I PUT A LIMIT ON JORDAN CHO'S REPORTS ON SONIC THE HEDGEHOG FAN FICTION, AND I HAVE TO PUT A LIMIT ON **YOUR** REPORTS ON OLD GOTHIC NOVELS.
OOOH! WHAT IF IT'S **NOT** A REPORT? WHAT IF IT'S...
INTERPRETIVE DANCE.

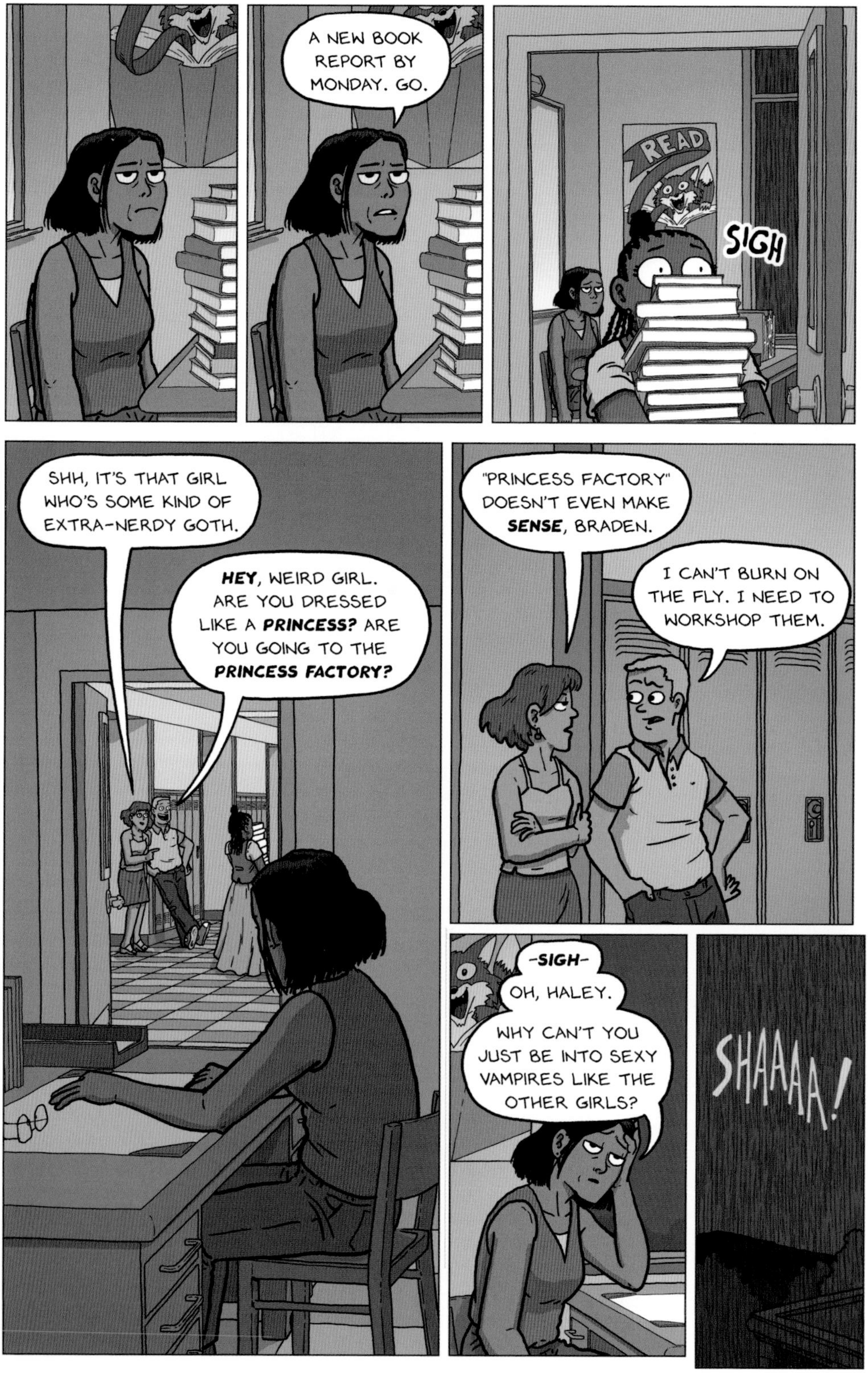
A NEW BOOK REPORT BY MONDAY. GO.
READ
SIGH
SHH, IT'S THAT GIRL WHO'S SOME KIND OF EXTRA-NERDY GOTH.
HEY, WEIRD GIRL. ARE YOU DRESSED LIKE A **PRINCESS?** ARE YOU GOING TO THE **PRINCESS FACTORY?**
"PRINCESS FACTORY" DOESN'T EVEN MAKE **SENSE**, BRADEN.
I CAN'T BURN ON THE FLY. I NEED TO WORKSHOP THEM.
-SIGH-
OH, HALEY.
WHY CAN'T YOU JUST BE INTO SEXY VAMPIRES LIKE THE OTHER GIRLS?
SHAAAA!

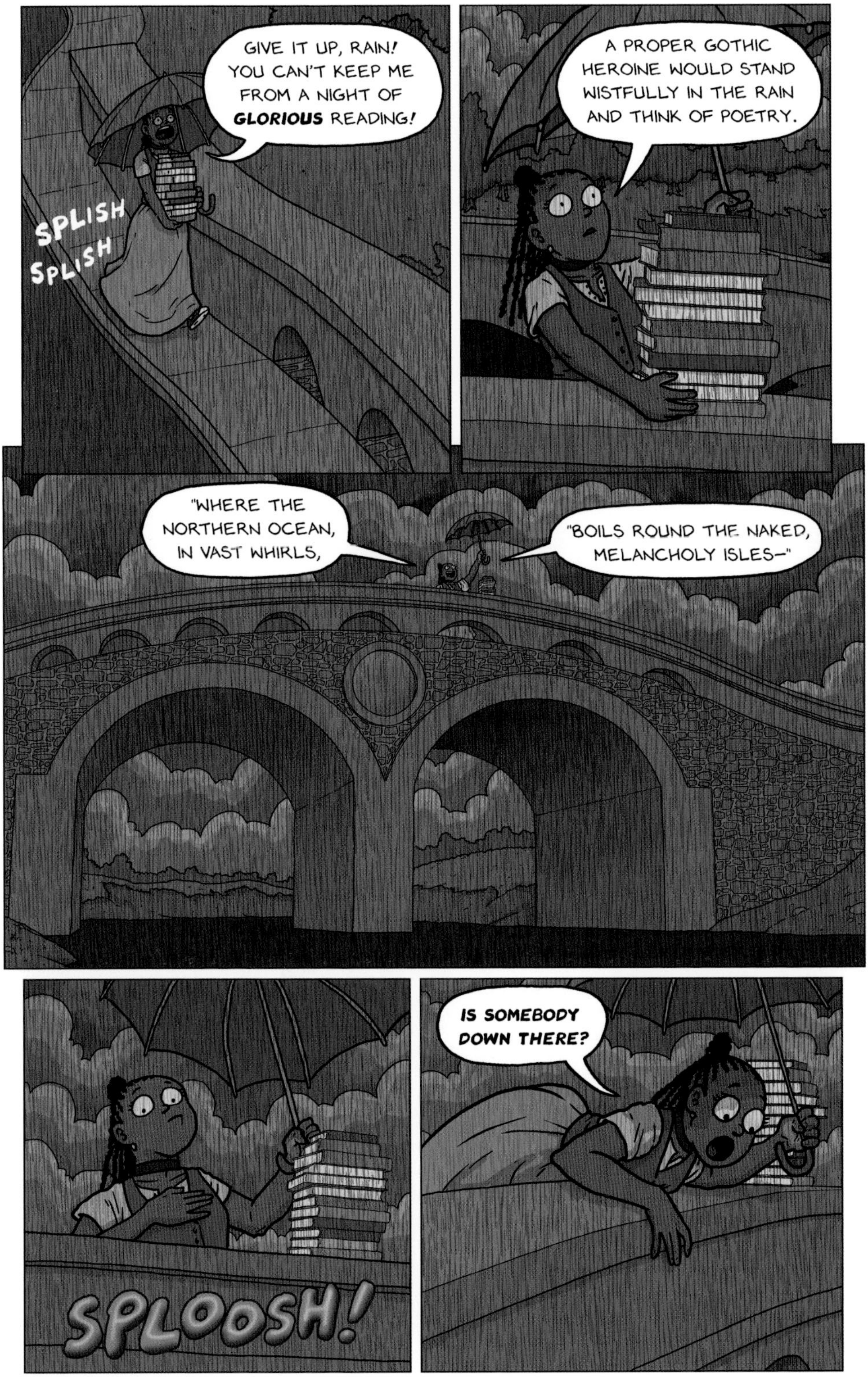
GIVE IT UP, RAIN! YOU CAN'T KEEP ME FROM A NIGHT OF **GLORIOUS** READING!
SPLISH SPLISH
A PROPER GOTHIC HEROINE WOULD STAND WISTFULLY IN THE RAIN AND THINK OF POETRY.
"WHERE THE NORTHERN OCEAN, IN VAST WHIRLS,
"BOILS ROUND THE NAKED, MELANCHOLY ISLES—"
SPLOOSH!
IS SOMEBODY DOWN THERE?

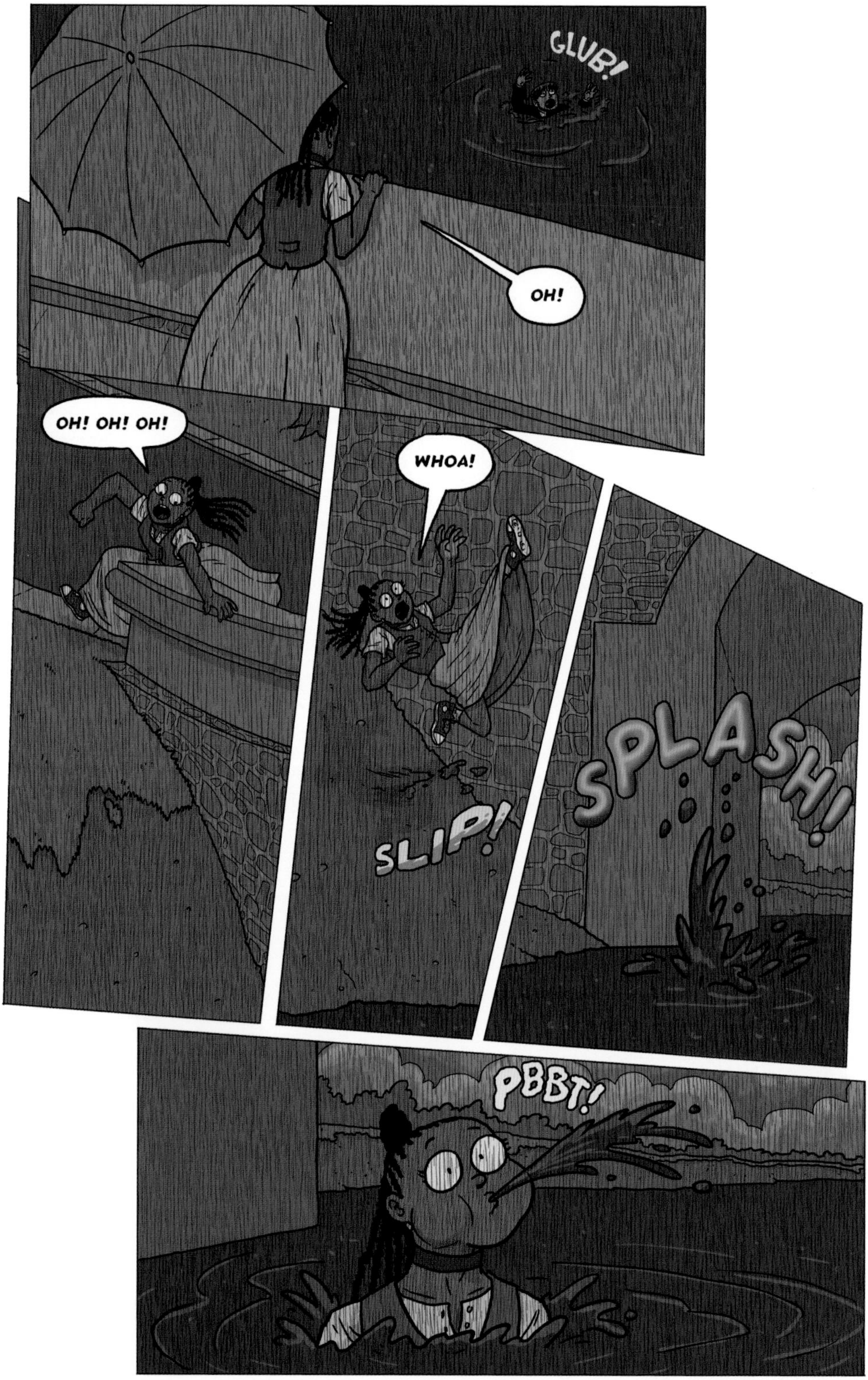
GLUB!
OH!
OH! OH! OH!
WHOA!
SLIP!
SPLASH!
PBBT!

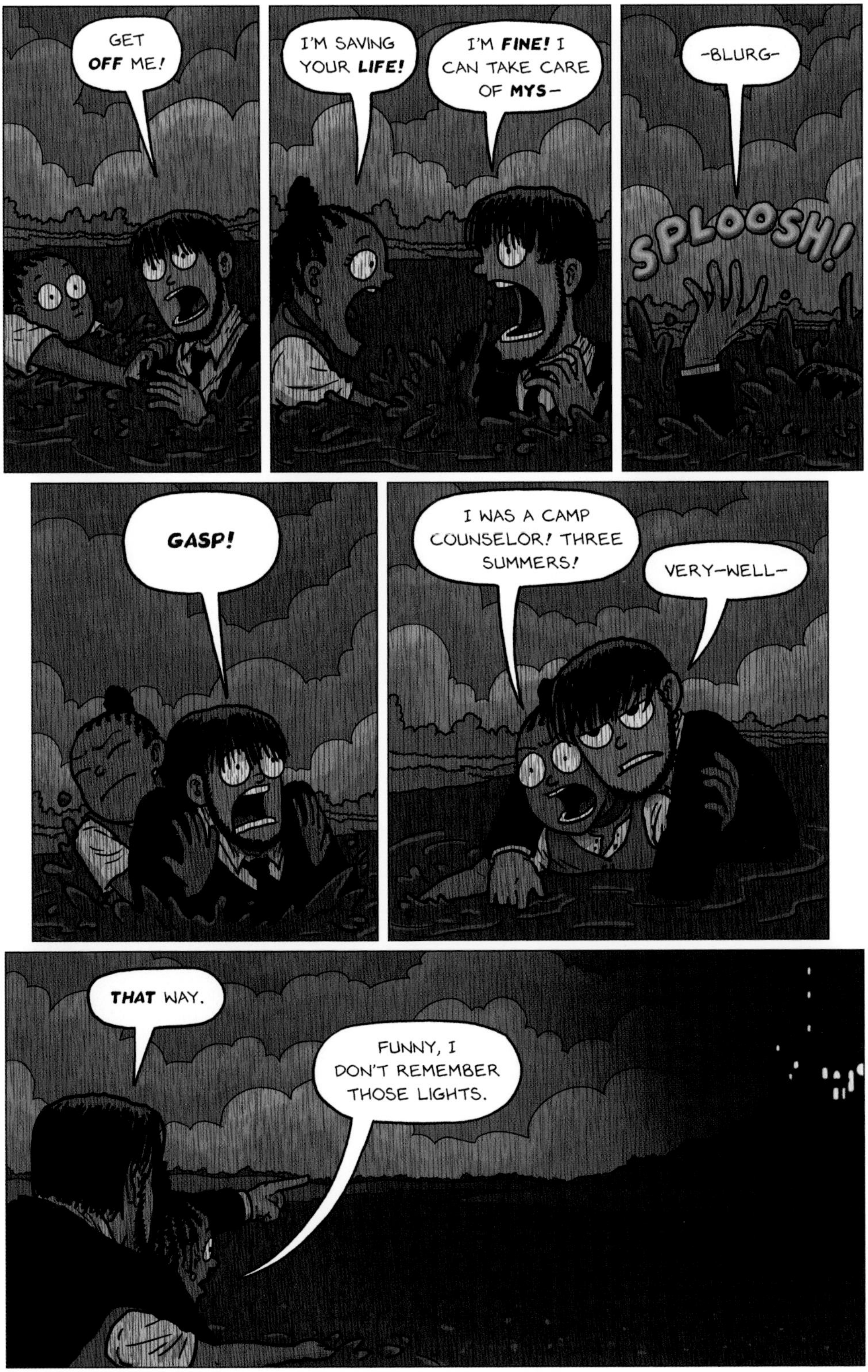
GET OFF ME!
I'M SAVING YOUR LIFE!
I'M FINE! I CAN TAKE CARE OF MYS—
-BLURG-
SPLOOSH!
GASP!
I WAS A CAMP COUNSELOR! THREE SUMMERS!
VERY—WELL—
THAT WAY.
FUNNY, I DON'T REMEMBER THOSE LIGHTS.

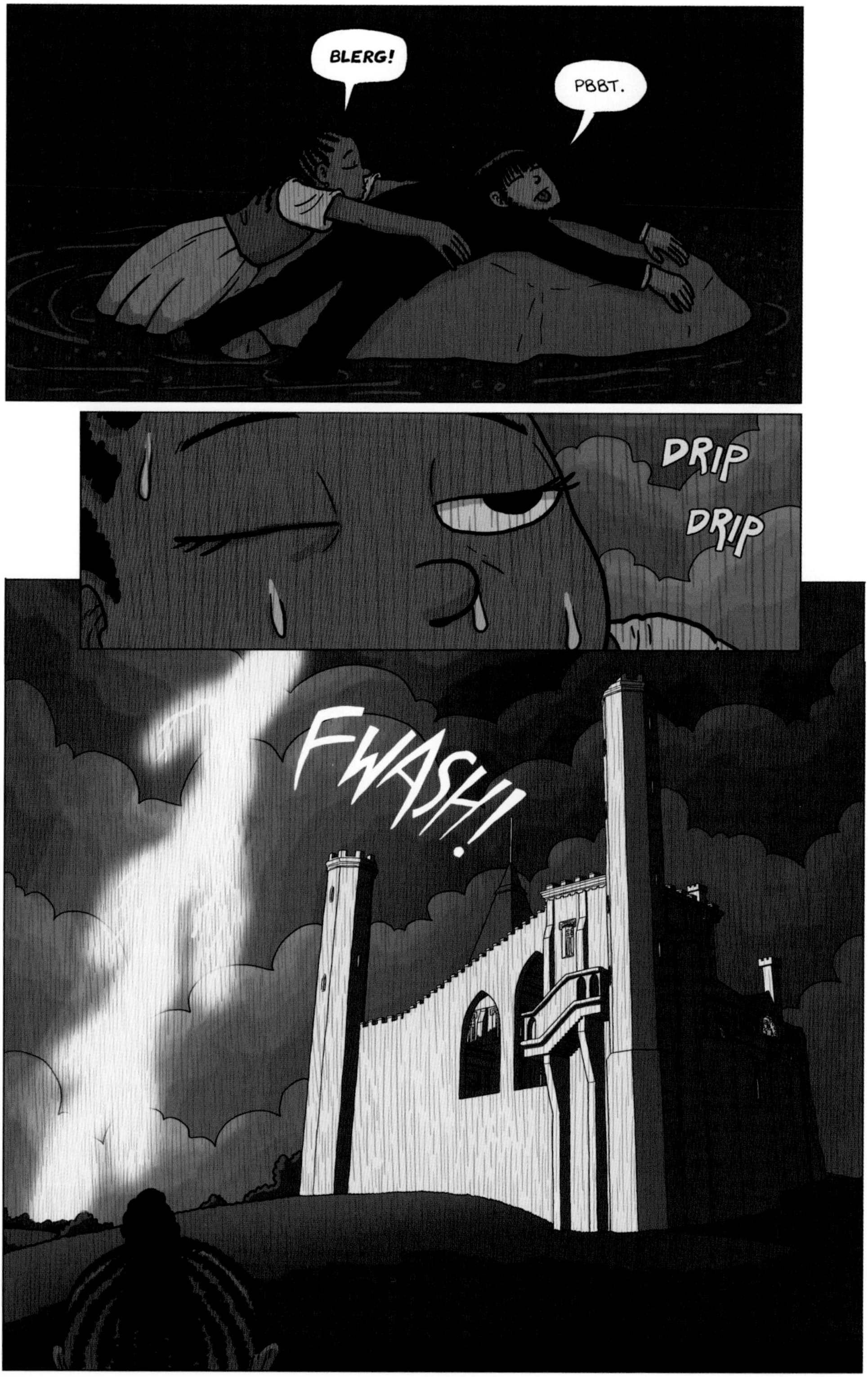
BLERG!
PBBT.
DRIP
DRIP
FWASH!

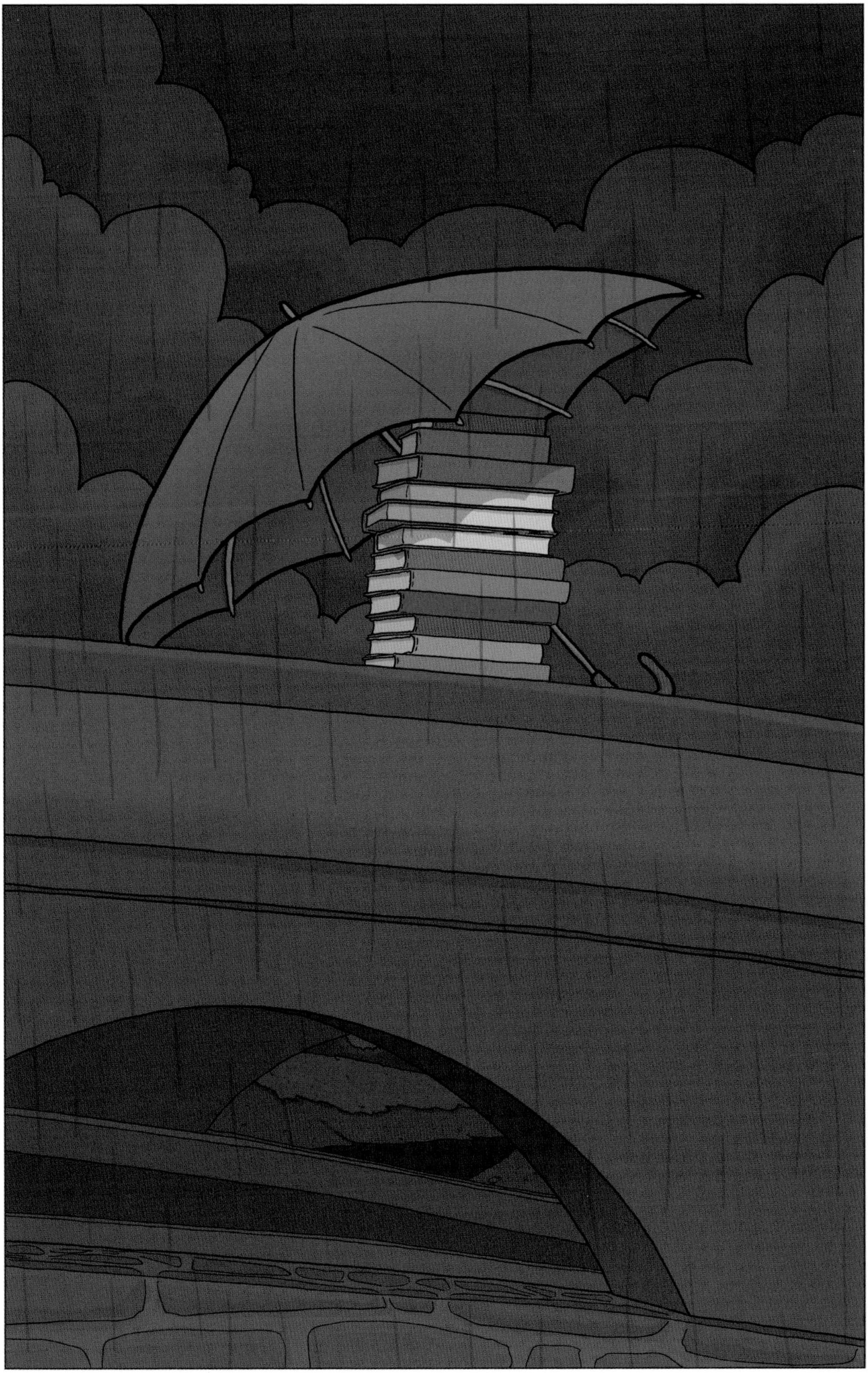

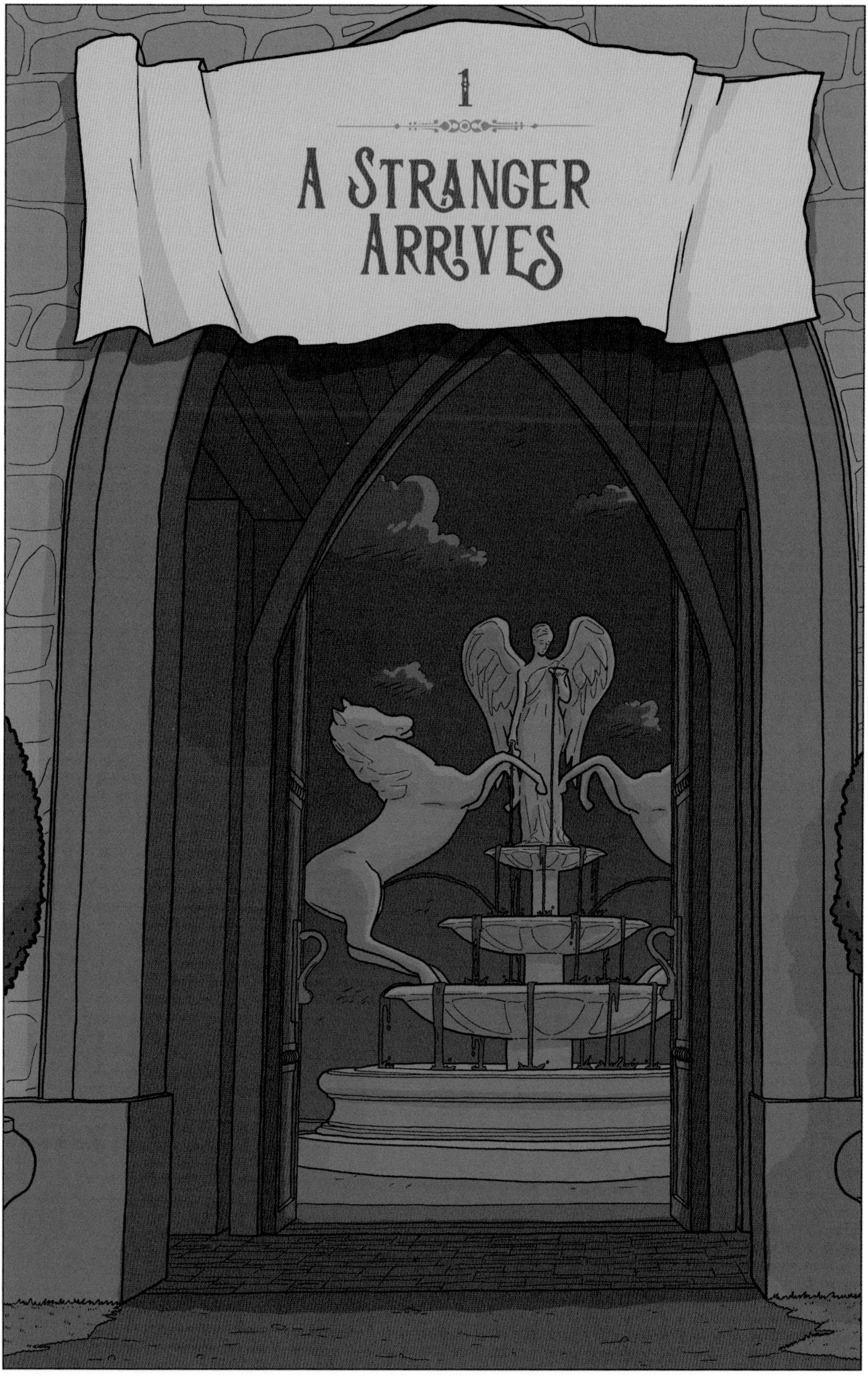
1
A Stranger Arrives

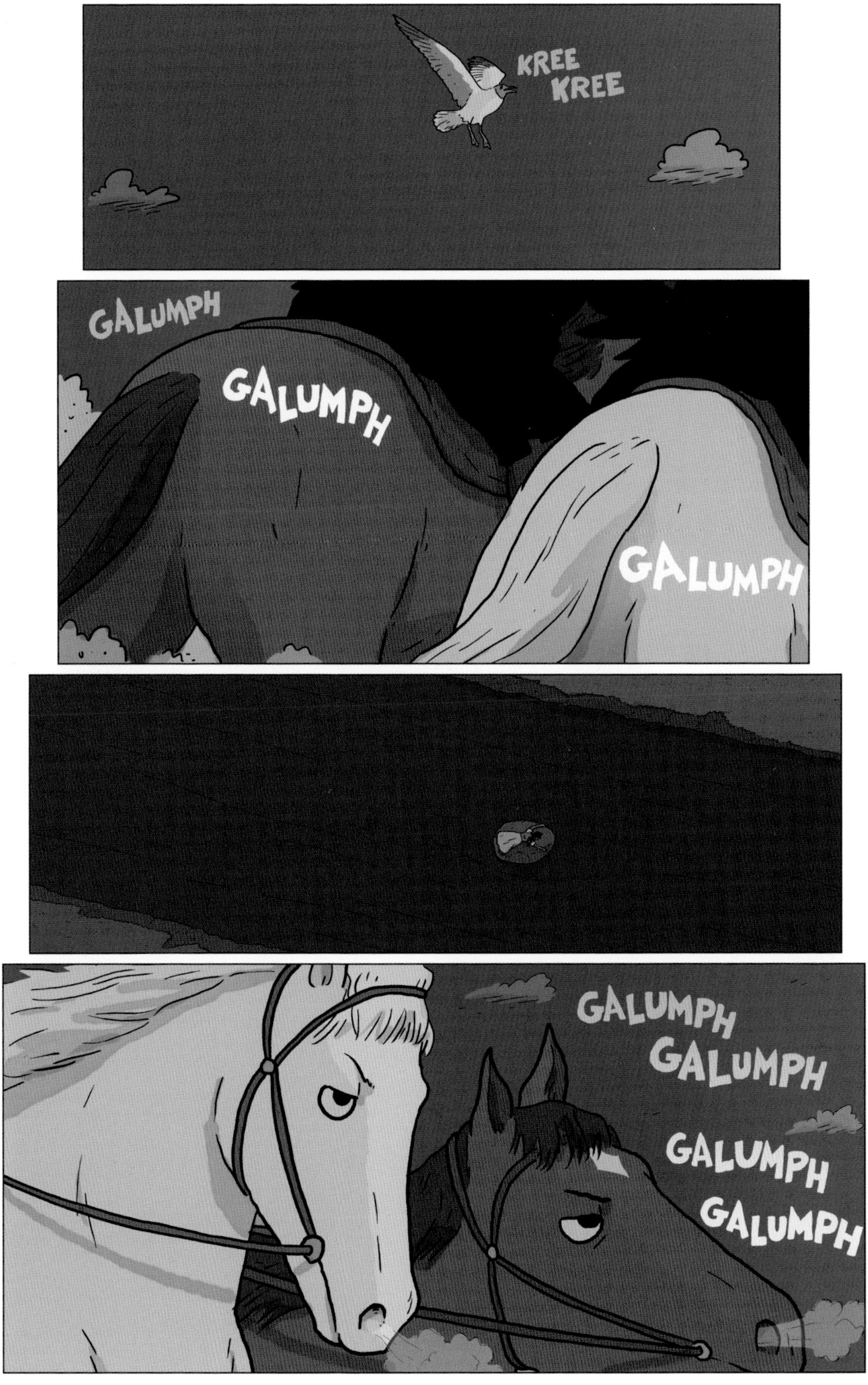
KREE
KREE
GALUMPH
GALUMPH
GALUMPH
GALUMPH
GALUMPH
GALUMPH
GALUMPH

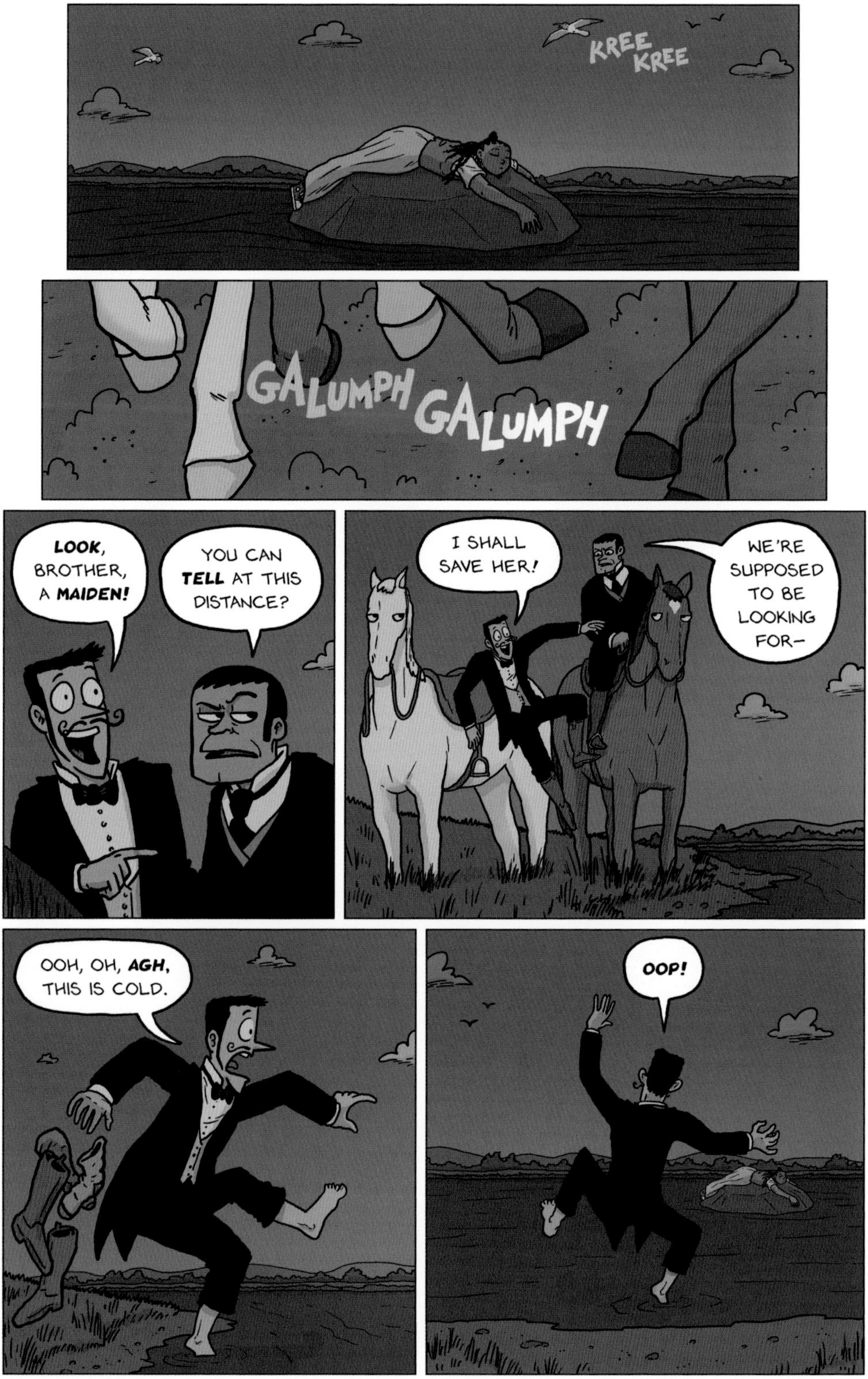
KREE
KREE
GALUMPH GALUMPH
LOOK, BROTHER, A MAIDEN!
YOU CAN TELL AT THIS DISTANCE?
I SHALL SAVE HER!
WE'RE SUPPOSED TO BE LOOKING FOR—
OOH, OH, AGH, THIS IS COLD.
OOP!

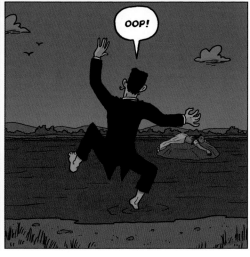

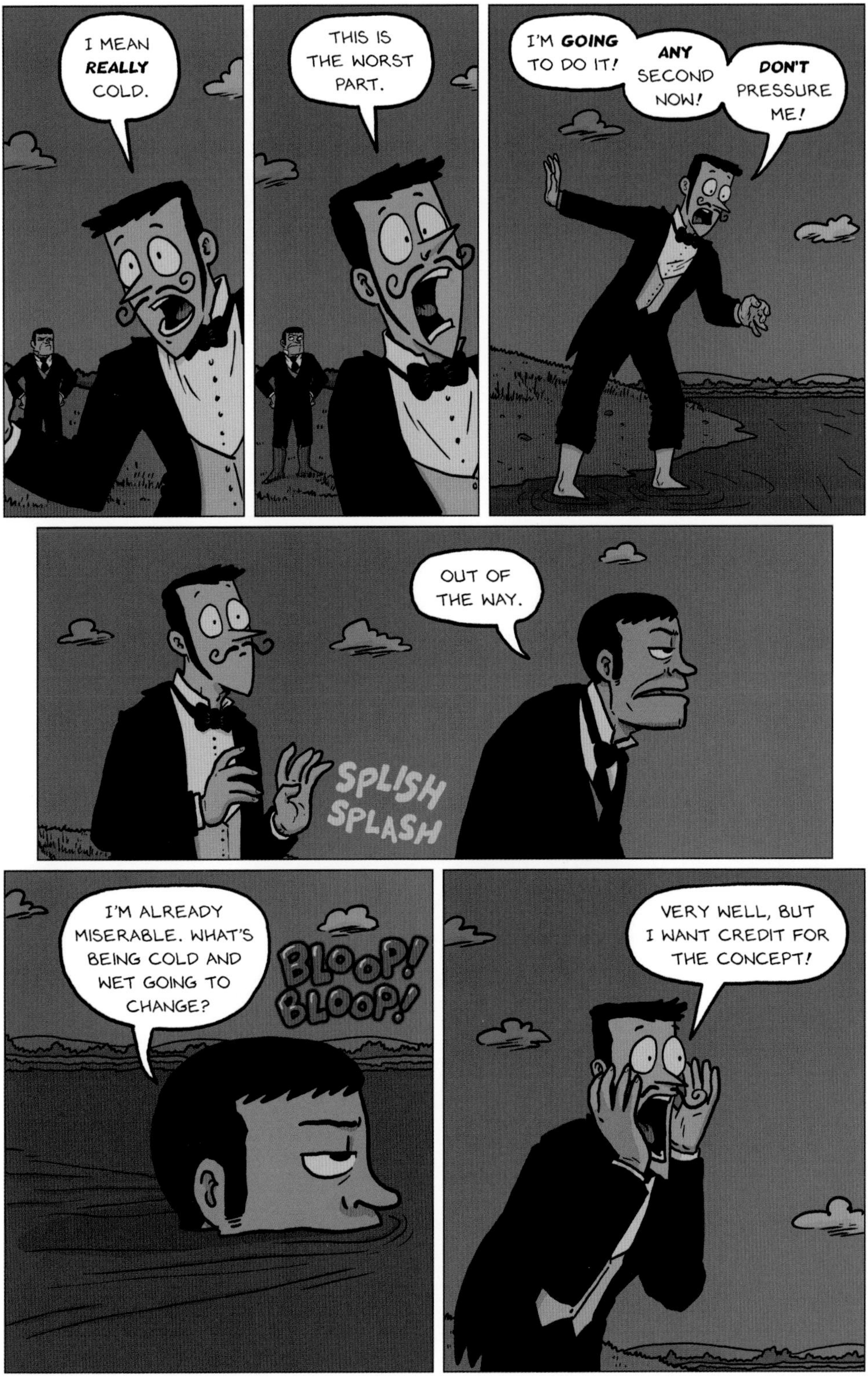

I MEAN **REALLY** COLD.
THIS IS THE WORST PART.
I'M **GOING** TO DO IT!
ANY SECOND NOW!
DON'T PRESSURE ME!
OUT OF THE WAY.
SPLISH SPLASH
I'M ALREADY MISERABLE. WHAT'S BEING COLD AND WET GOING TO CHANGE?
BLOOP! BLOOP!
VERY WELL, BUT I WANT CREDIT FOR THE CONCEPT!

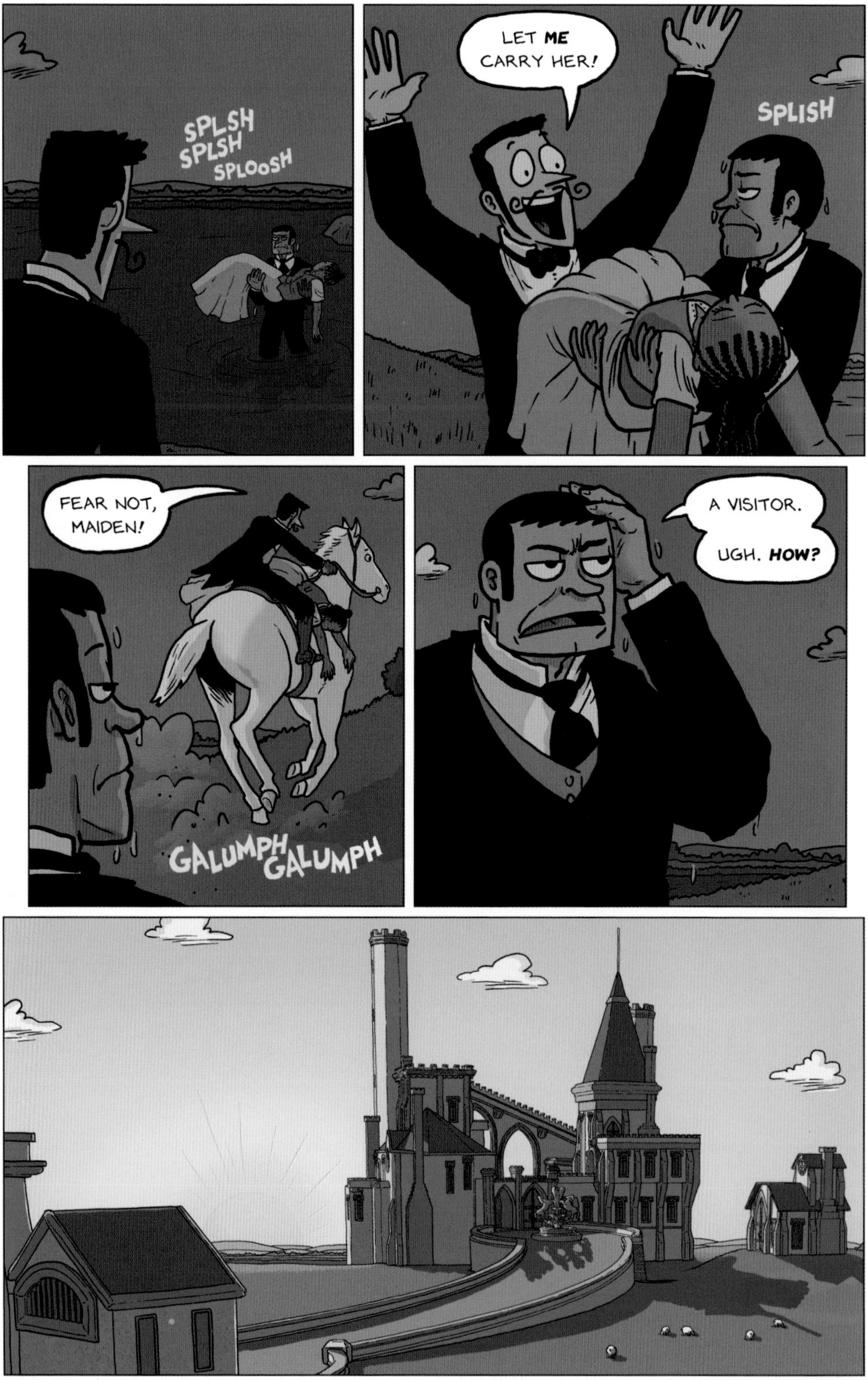
SPLSH
SPLSH
SPLOOSH
LET ME CARRY HER!
SPLISH
FEAR NOT, MAIDEN!
GALUMPH GALUMPH
A VISITOR.
UGH. HOW?

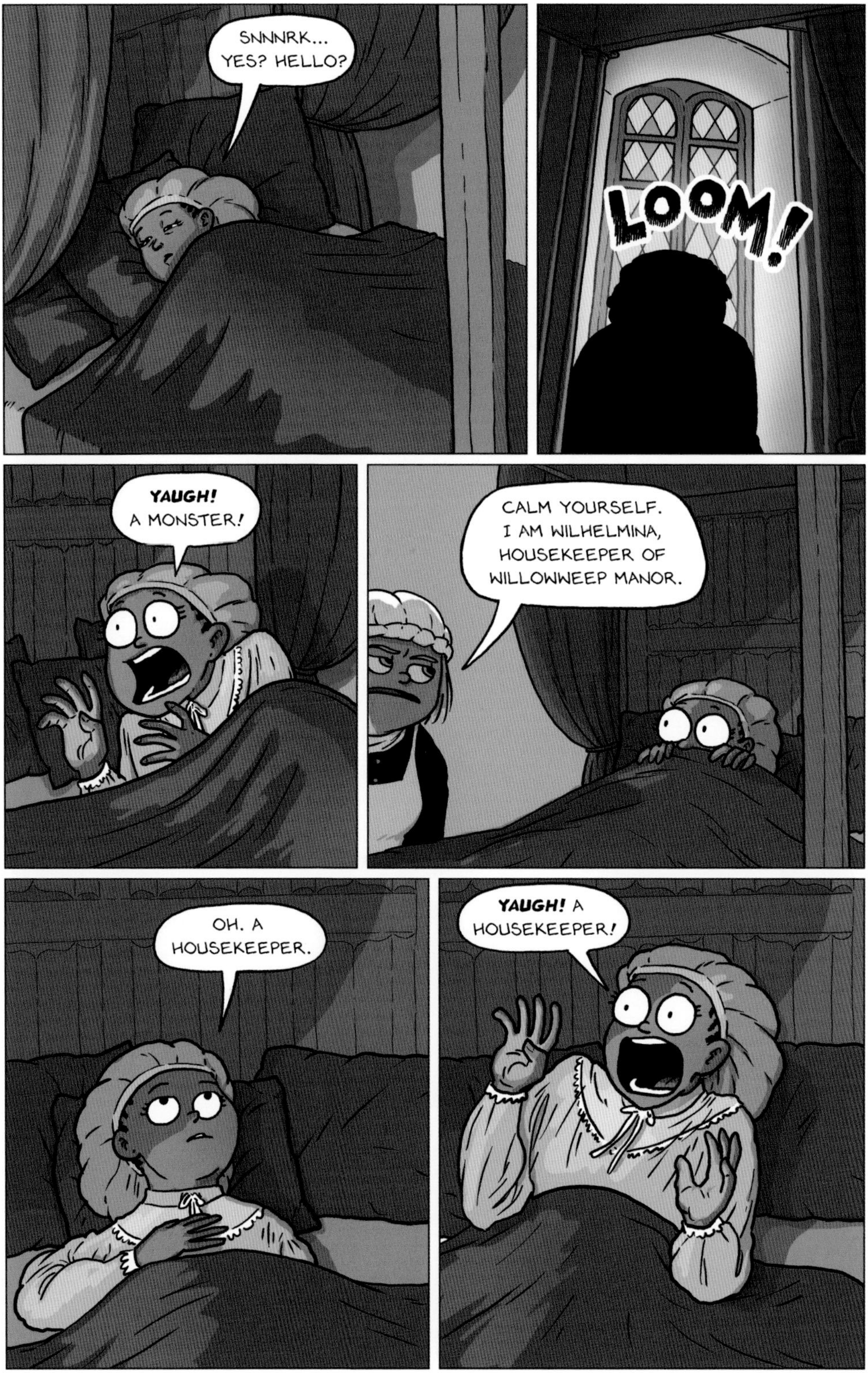
SNNNRK...
YES? HELLO?
LOOM!
YAUGH! A MONSTER!
CALM YOURSELF. I AM WILHELMINA, HOUSEKEEPER OF WILLOWWEEP MANOR.
OH. A HOUSEKEEPER.
YAUGH! A HOUSEKEEPER!

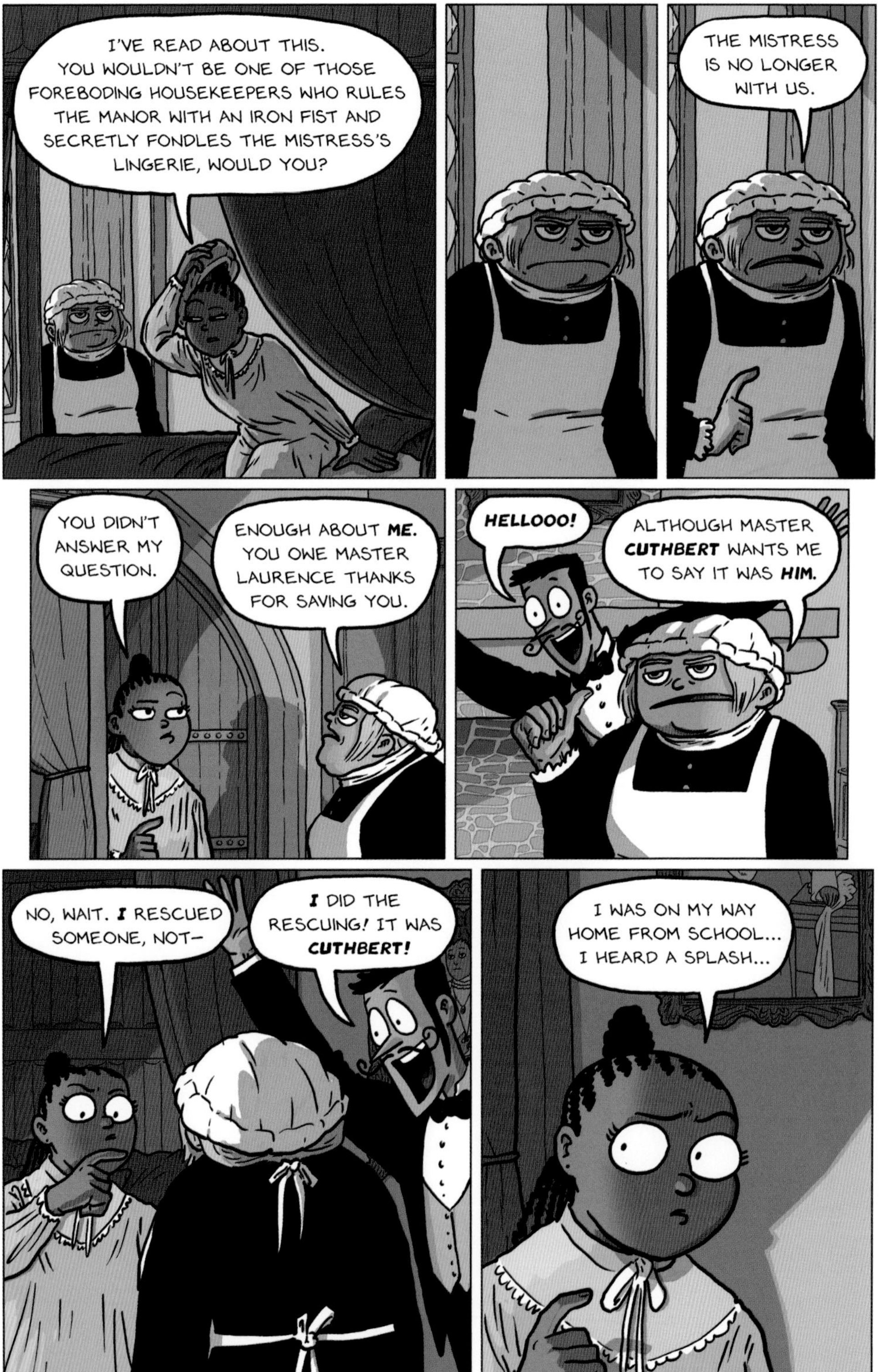
I'VE READ ABOUT THIS. YOU WOULDN'T BE ONE OF THOSE FOREBODING HOUSEKEEPERS WHO RULES THE MANOR WITH AN IRON FIST AND SECRETLY FONDLES THE MISTRESS'S LINGERIE, WOULD YOU?
THE MISTRESS IS NO LONGER WITH US.
YOU DIDN'T ANSWER MY QUESTION.
ENOUGH ABOUT **ME.** YOU OWE MASTER LAURENCE THANKS FOR SAVING YOU.
HELLOOO!
ALTHOUGH MASTER **CUTHBERT** WANTS ME TO SAY IT WAS **HIM.**
NO, WAIT. ***I*** RESCUED SOMEONE, NOT—
I DID THE RESCUING! IT WAS **CUTHBERT!**
I WAS ON MY WAY HOME FROM SCHOOL... I HEARD A SPLASH...

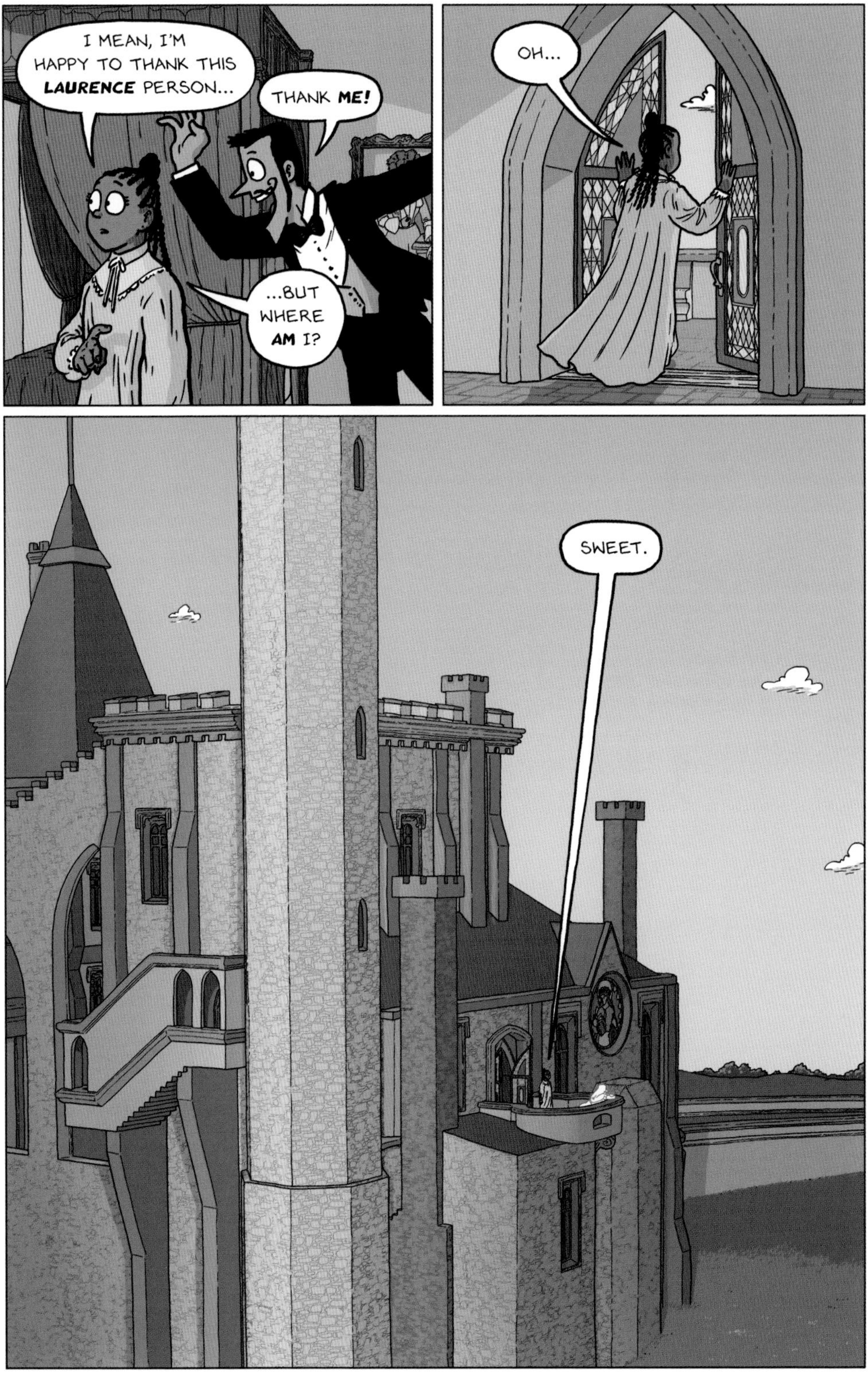
I MEAN, I'M HAPPY TO THANK THIS **LAURENCE** PERSON...
THANK **ME!**
...BUT WHERE **AM** I?
OH...
SWEET.

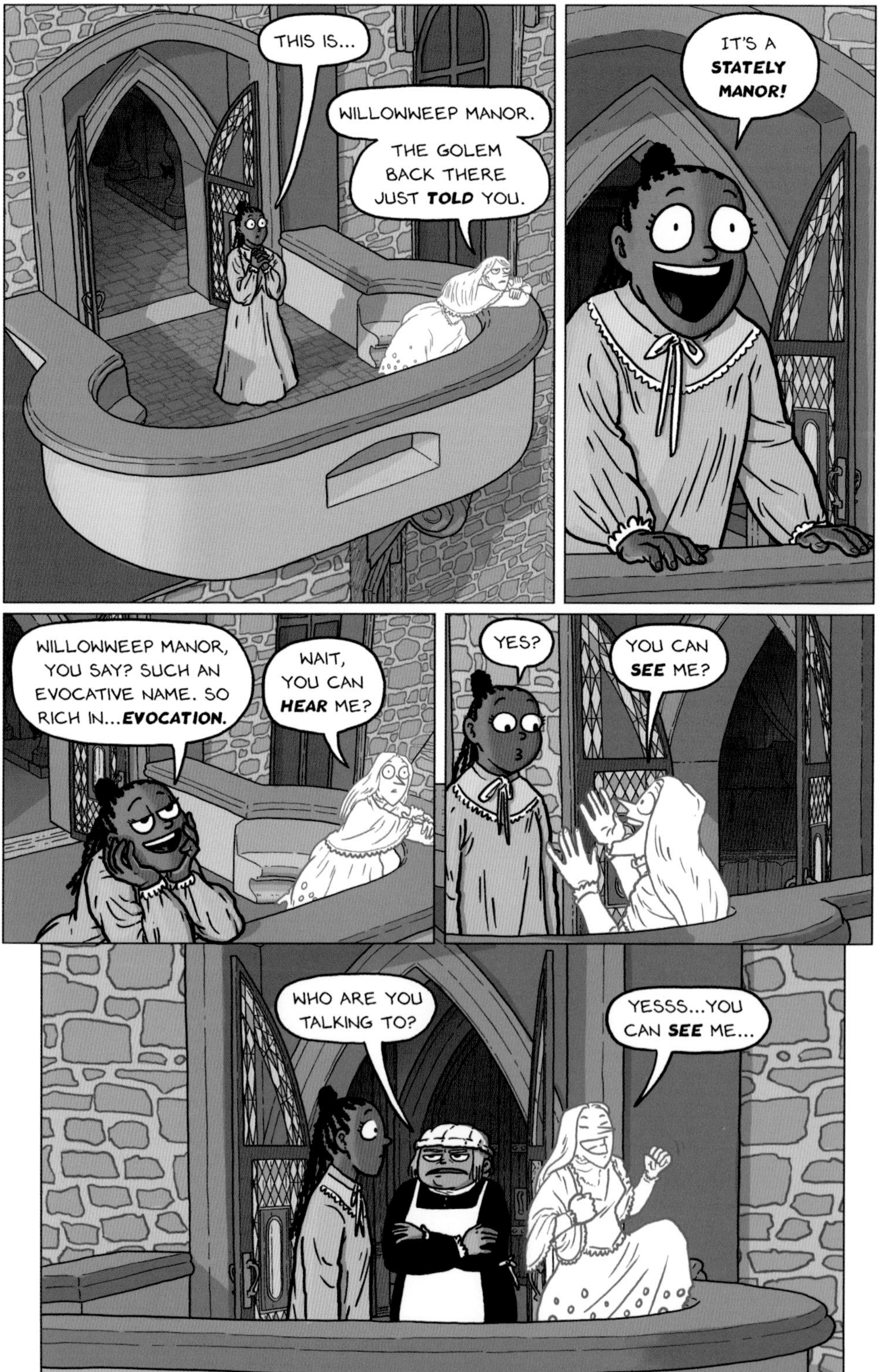
THIS IS...
WILLOWWEEP MANOR.
THE GOLEM BACK THERE JUST **TOLD** YOU.
IT'S A **STATELY MANOR!**
WILLOWWEEP MANOR, YOU SAY? SUCH AN EVOCATIVE NAME. SO RICH IN...**EVOCATION.**
WAIT, YOU CAN **HEAR** ME?
YES?
YOU CAN **SEE** ME?
WHO ARE YOU TALKING TO?
YESSS...YOU CAN **SEE** ME...

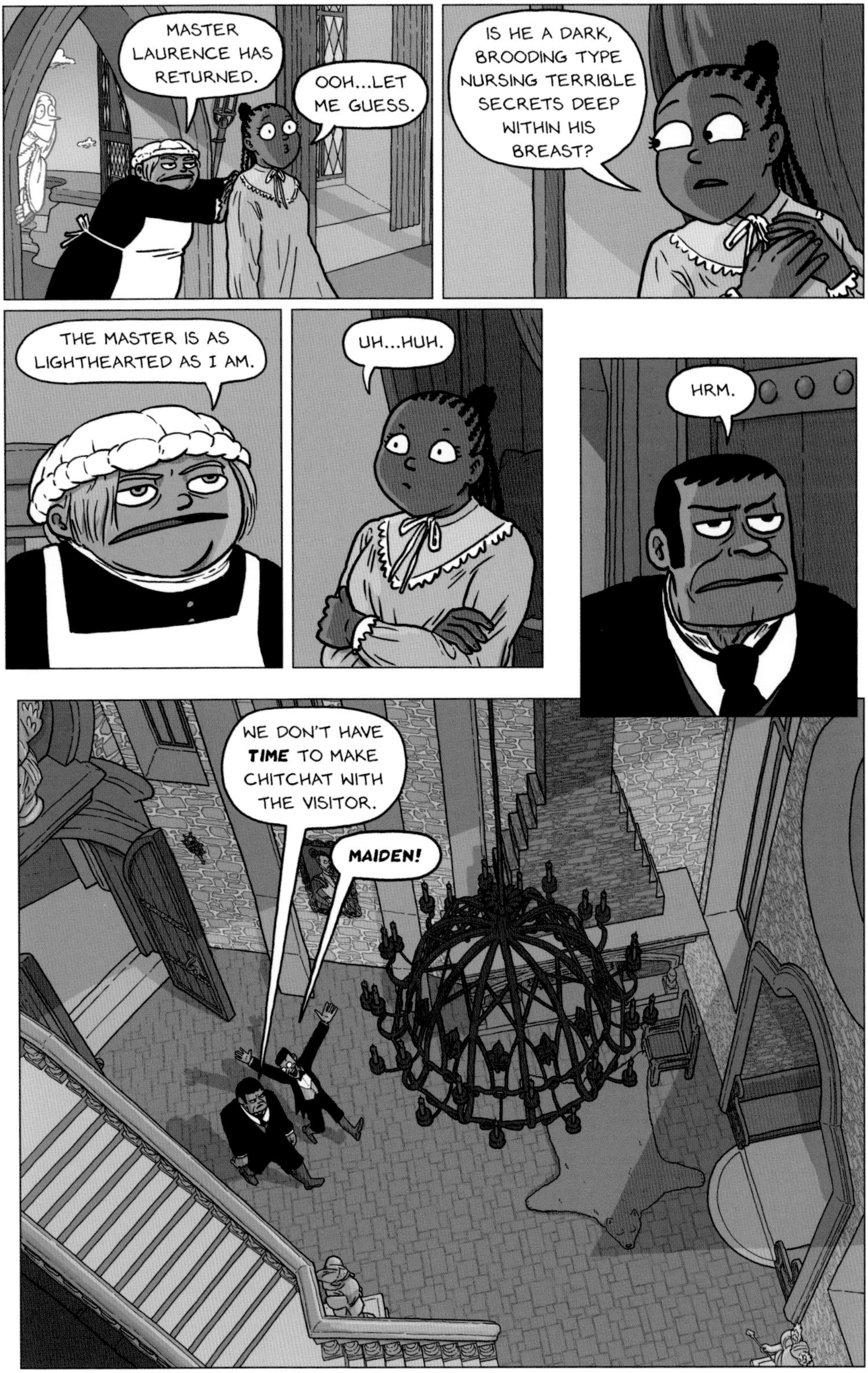
MASTER LAURENCE HAS RETURNED.
OOH...LET ME GUESS.
IS HE A DARK, BROODING TYPE NURSING TERRIBLE SECRETS DEEP WITHIN HIS BREAST?
THE MASTER IS AS LIGHTHEARTED AS I AM.
UH...HUH.
HRM.
WE DON'T HAVE **TIME** TO MAKE CHITCHAT WITH THE VISITOR.
MAIDEN!

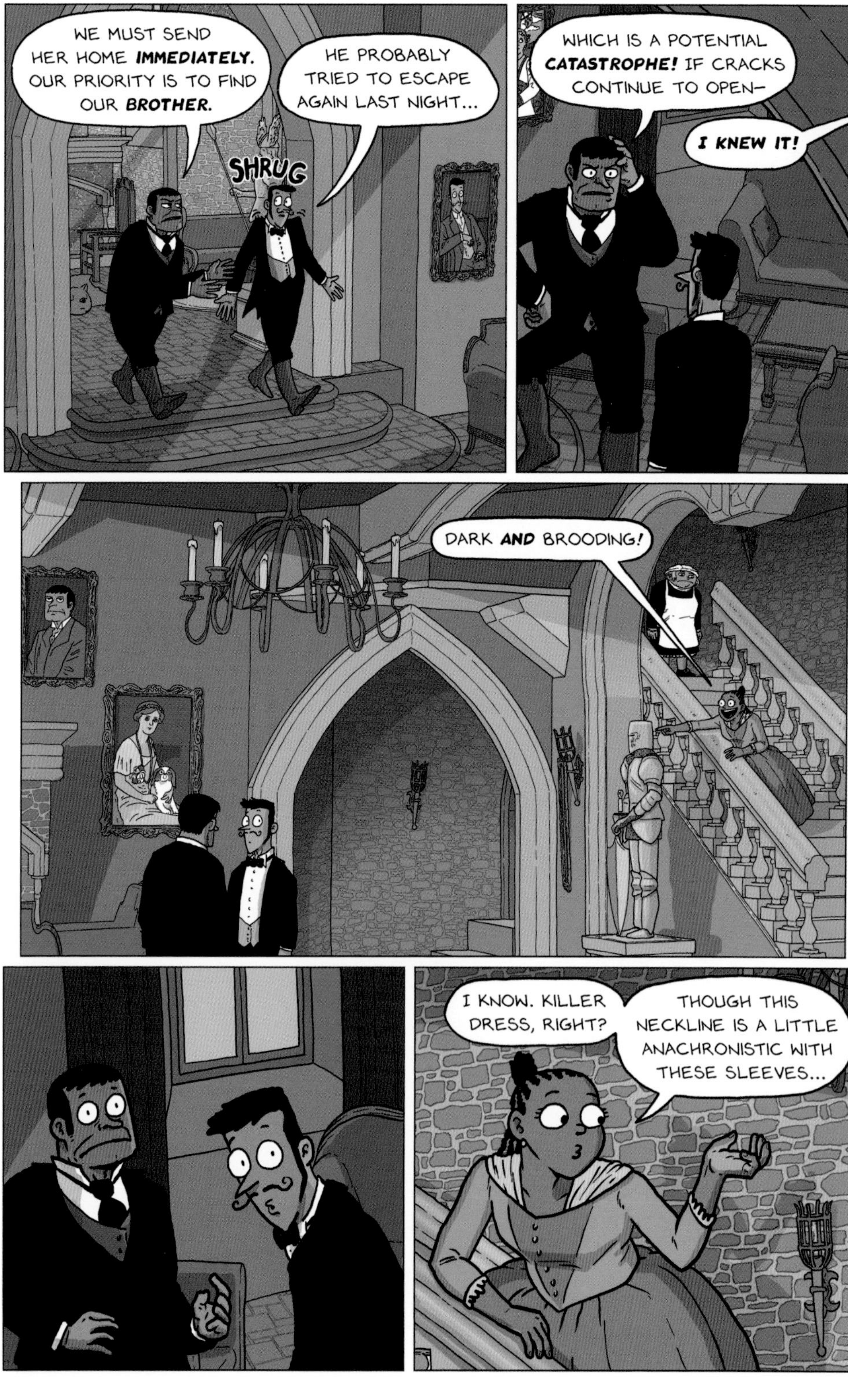
WE MUST SEND HER HOME **IMMEDIATELY.** OUR PRIORITY IS TO FIND OUR **BROTHER.**
SHRUG
HE PROBABLY TRIED TO ESCAPE AGAIN LAST NIGHT...
WHICH IS A POTENTIAL **CATASTROPHE!** IF CRACKS CONTINUE TO OPEN—
I KNEW IT!
DARK **AND** BROODING!
I KNOW. KILLER DRESS, RIGHT?
THOUGH THIS NECKLINE IS A LITTLE ANACHRONISTIC WITH THESE SLEEVES...

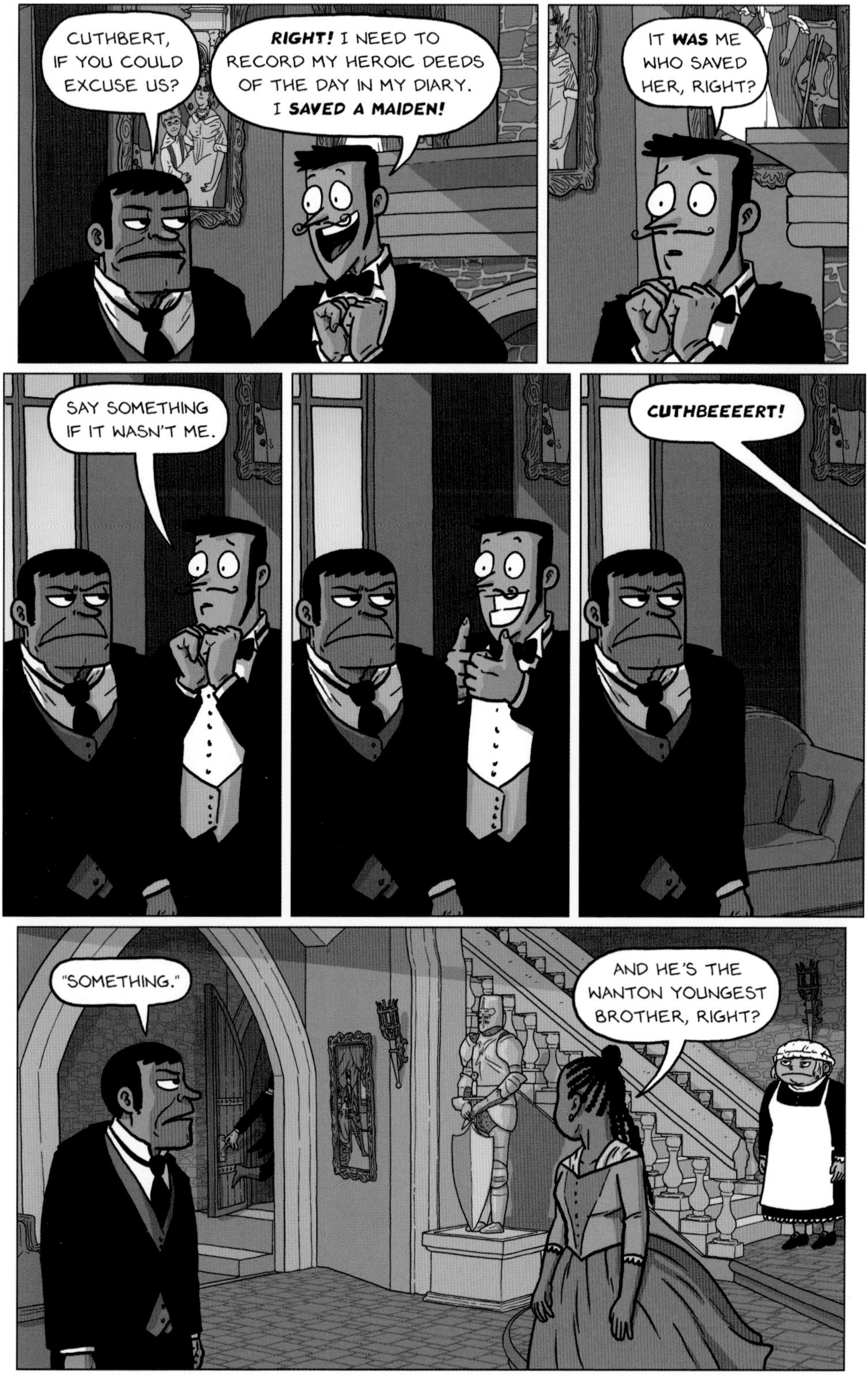
CUTHBERT, IF YOU COULD EXCUSE US?
RIGHT! I NEED TO RECORD MY HEROIC DEEDS OF THE DAY IN MY DIARY. I SAVED A MAIDEN!
IT WAS ME WHO SAVED HER, RIGHT?
SAY SOMETHING IF IT WASN'T ME.
CUTHBEEEERT!
"SOMETHING."
AND HE'S THE WANTON YOUNGEST BROTHER, RIGHT?

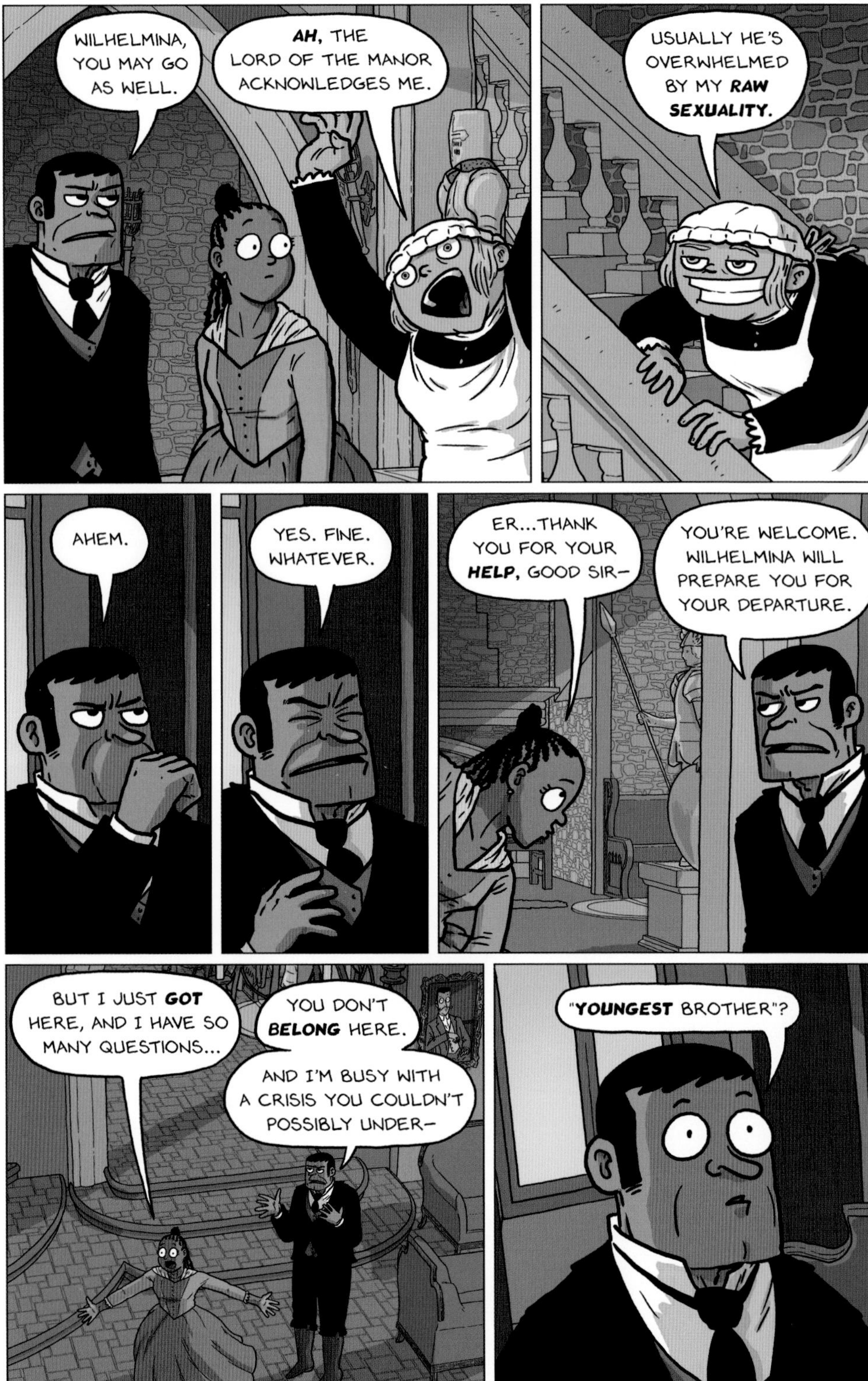
WILHELMINA, YOU MAY GO AS WELL.
AH, THE LORD OF THE MANOR ACKNOWLEDGES ME.
USUALLY HE'S OVERWHELMED BY MY RAW SEXUALITY.
AHEM.
YES. FINE. WHATEVER.
ER...THANK YOU FOR YOUR HELP, GOOD SIR—
YOU'RE WELCOME. WILHELMINA WILL PREPARE YOU FOR YOUR DEPARTURE.
BUT I JUST GOT HERE, AND I HAVE SO MANY QUESTIONS...
YOU DON'T BELONG HERE.
AND I'M BUSY WITH A CRISIS YOU COULDN'T POSSIBLY UNDER—
"YOUNGEST BROTHER"?

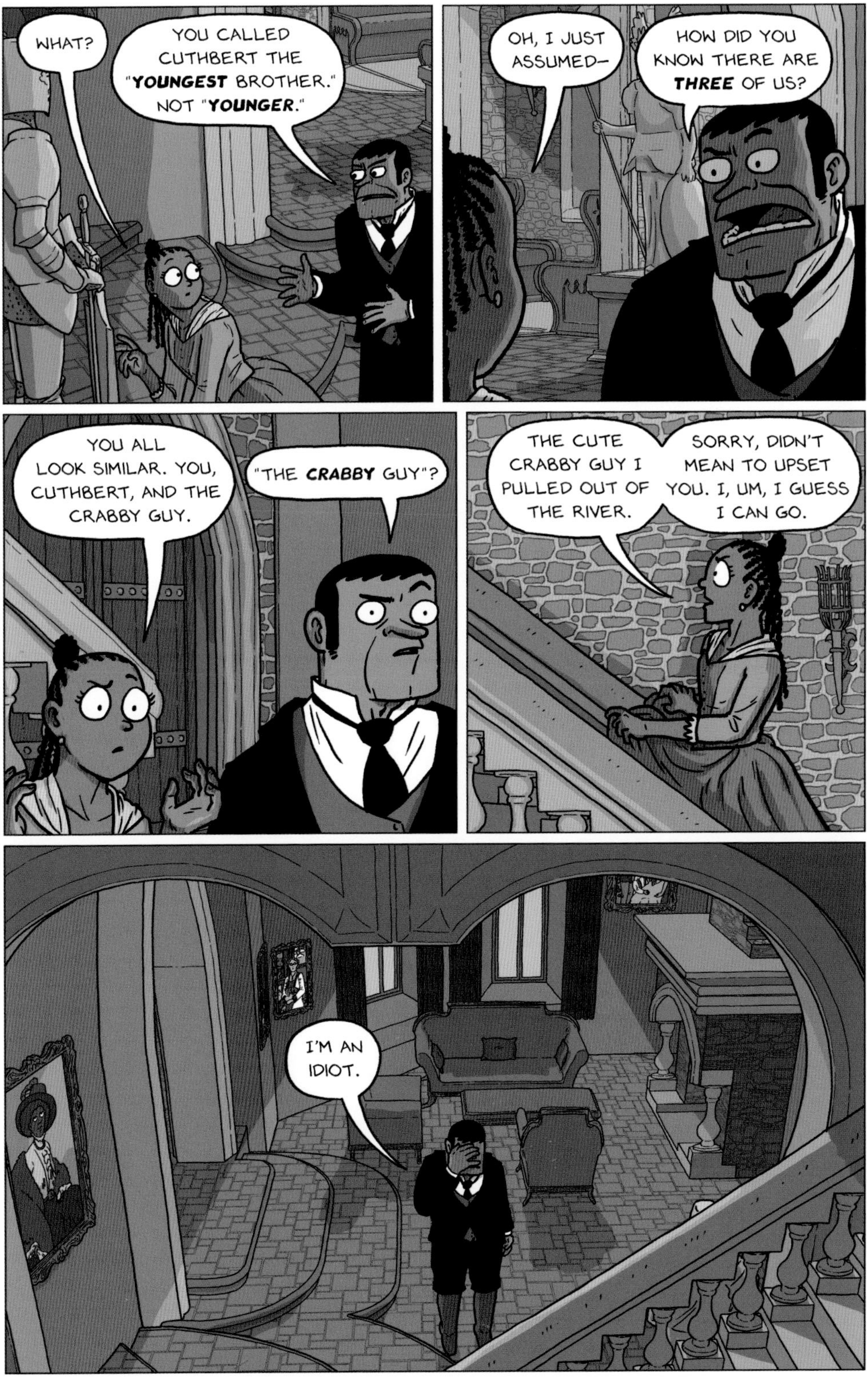
WHAT?
YOU CALLED CUTHBERT THE "YOUNGEST BROTHER." NOT "YOUNGER."
OH, I JUST ASSUMED—
HOW DID YOU KNOW THERE ARE THREE OF US?
YOU ALL LOOK SIMILAR. YOU, CUTHBERT, AND THE CRABBY GUY.
"THE CRABBY GUY"?
THE CUTE CRABBY GUY I PULLED OUT OF THE RIVER.
SORRY, DIDN'T MEAN TO UPSET YOU. I, UM, I GUESS I CAN GO.
I'M AN IDIOT.

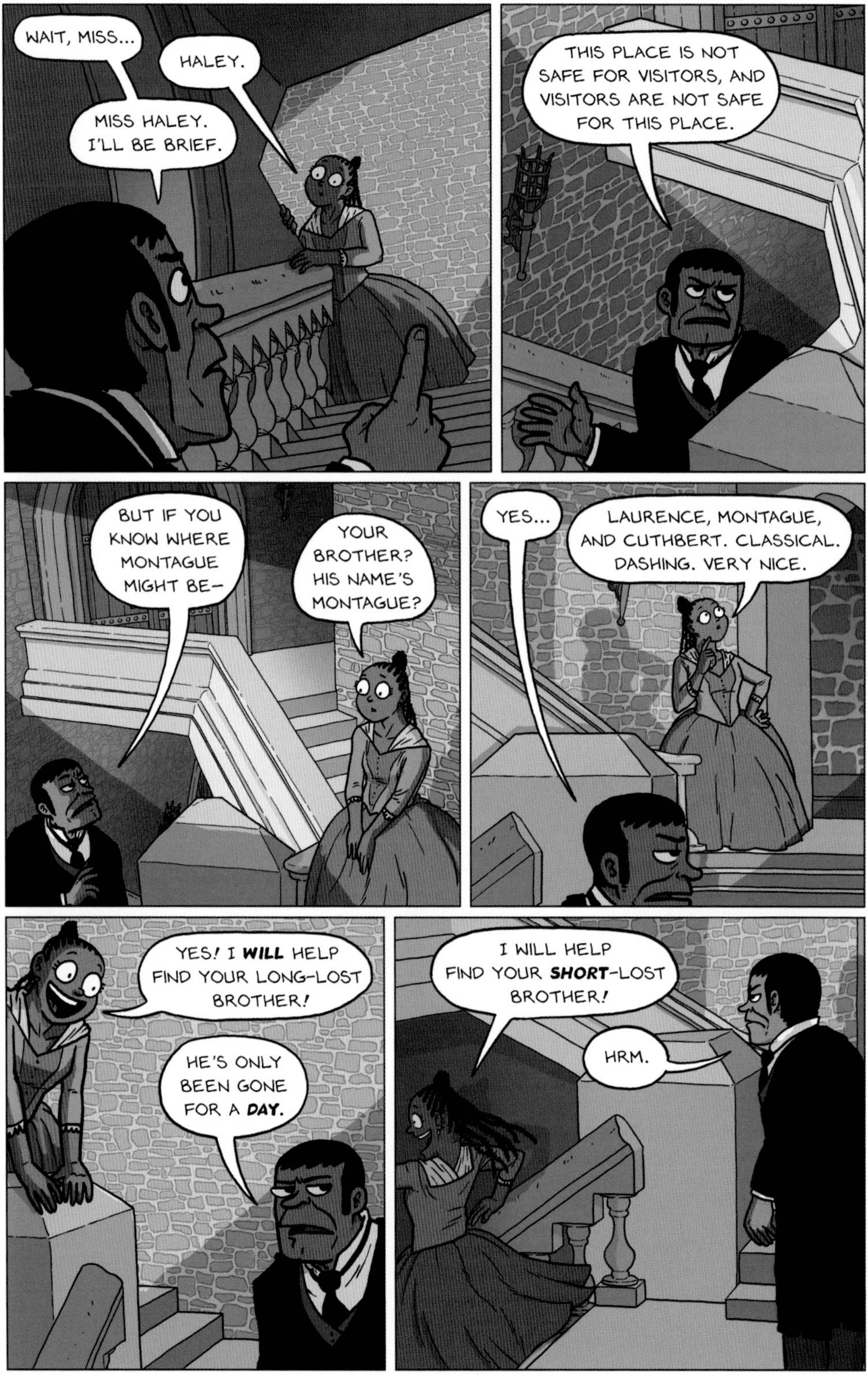
WAIT, MISS...
HALEY.
MISS HALEY. I'LL BE BRIEF.
THIS PLACE IS NOT SAFE FOR VISITORS, AND VISITORS ARE NOT SAFE FOR THIS PLACE.
BUT IF YOU KNOW WHERE MONTAGUE MIGHT BE–
YOUR BROTHER? HIS NAME'S MONTAGUE?
YES...
LAURENCE, MONTAGUE, AND CUTHBERT. CLASSICAL. DASHING. VERY NICE.
YES! I **WILL** HELP FIND YOUR LONG-LOST BROTHER!
HE'S ONLY BEEN GONE FOR A **DAY**.
I WILL HELP FIND YOUR **SHORT**-LOST BROTHER!
HRM.

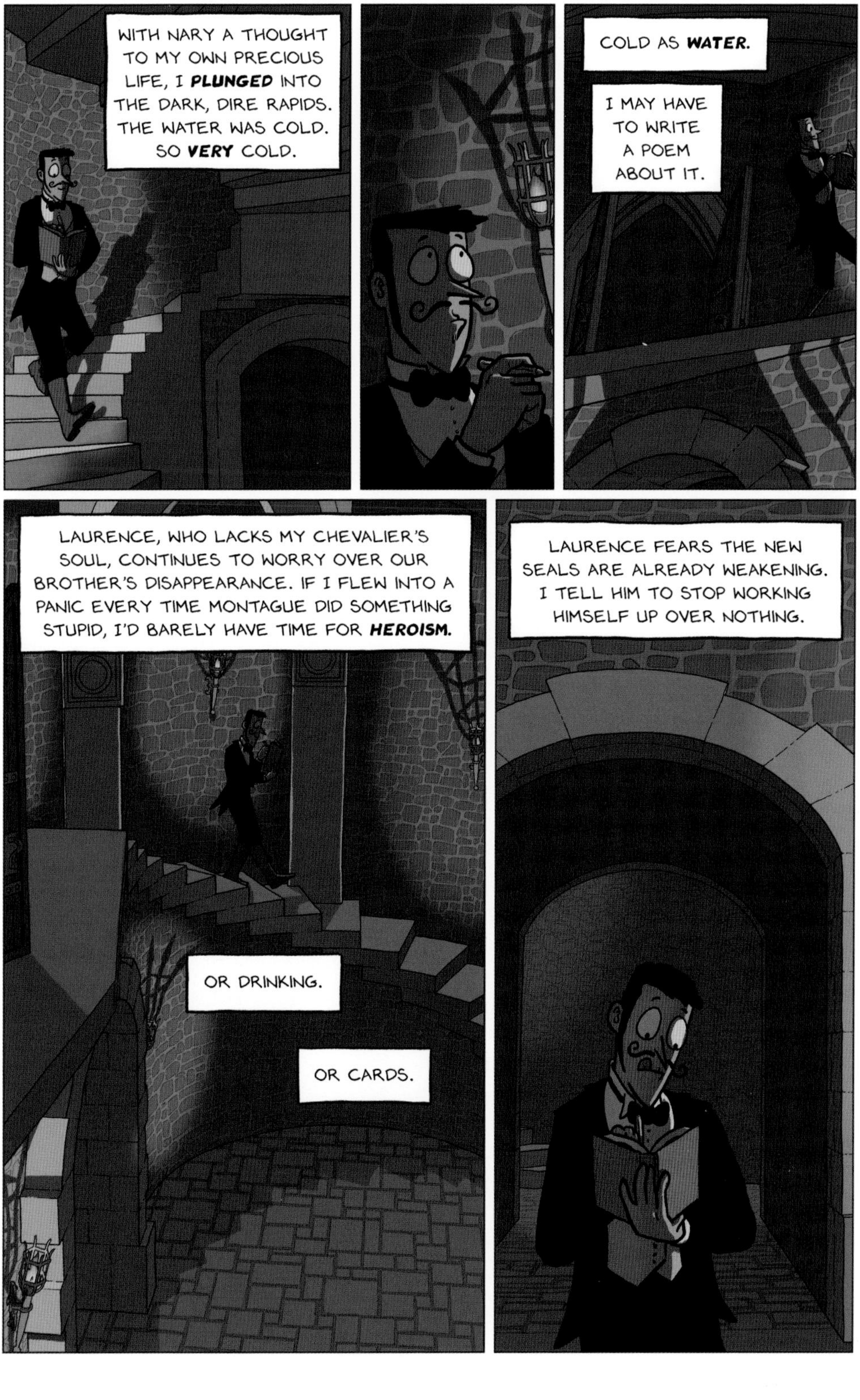
WITH NARY A THOUGHT TO MY OWN PRECIOUS LIFE, I **PLUNGED** INTO THE DARK, DIRE RAPIDS. THE WATER WAS COLD. SO **VERY** COLD.
COLD AS **WATER.**
I MAY HAVE TO WRITE A POEM ABOUT IT.
LAURENCE, WHO LACKS MY CHEVALIER'S SOUL, CONTINUES TO WORRY OVER OUR BROTHER'S DISAPPEARANCE. IF I FLEW INTO A PANIC EVERY TIME MONTAGUE DID SOMETHING STUPID, I'D BARELY HAVE TIME FOR **HEROISM.**
OR DRINKING.
OR CARDS.
LAURENCE FEARS THE NEW SEALS ARE ALREADY WEAKENING. I TELL HIM TO STOP WORKING HIMSELF UP OVER NOTHING.

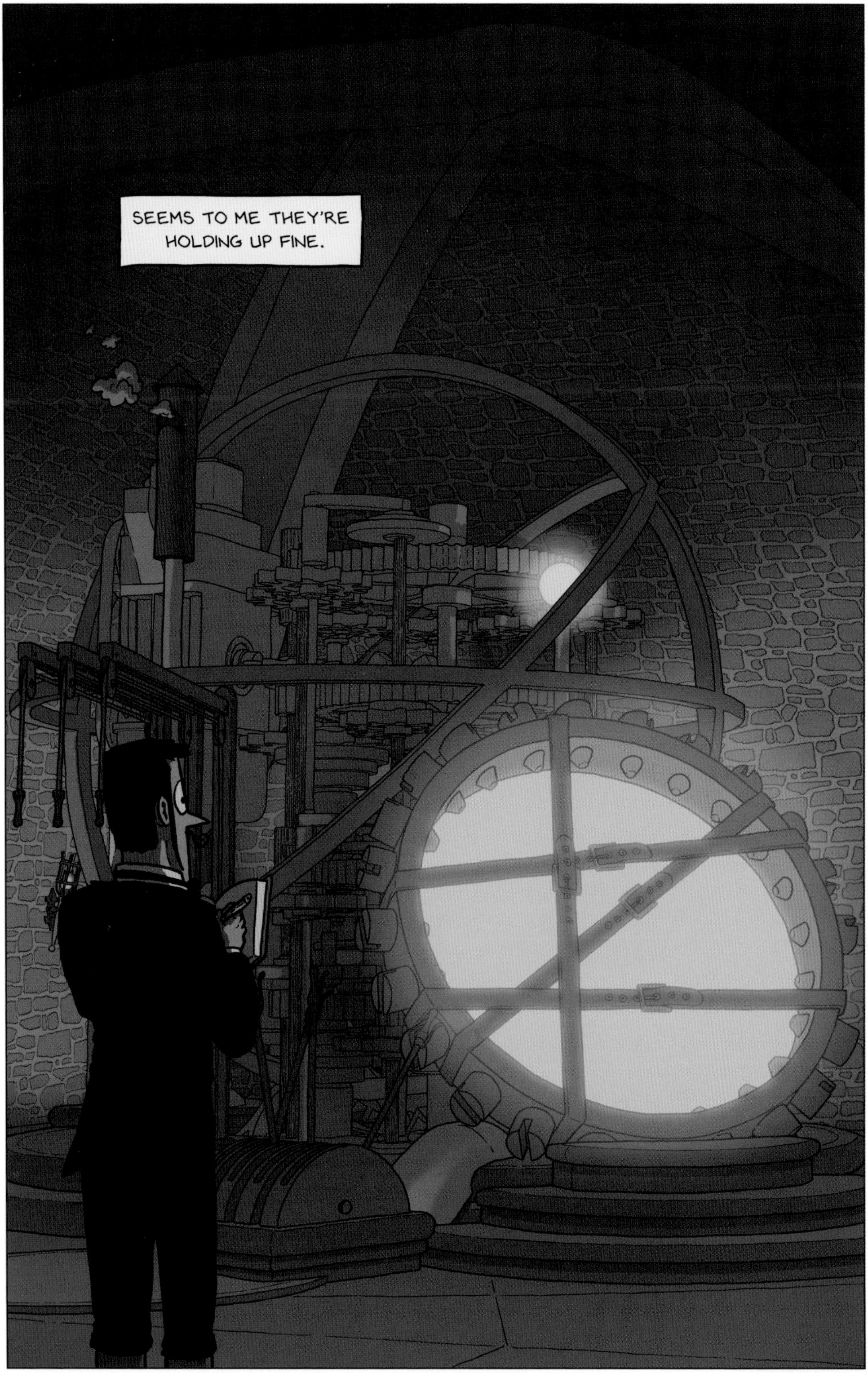
SEEMS TO ME THEY'RE HOLDING UP FINE.

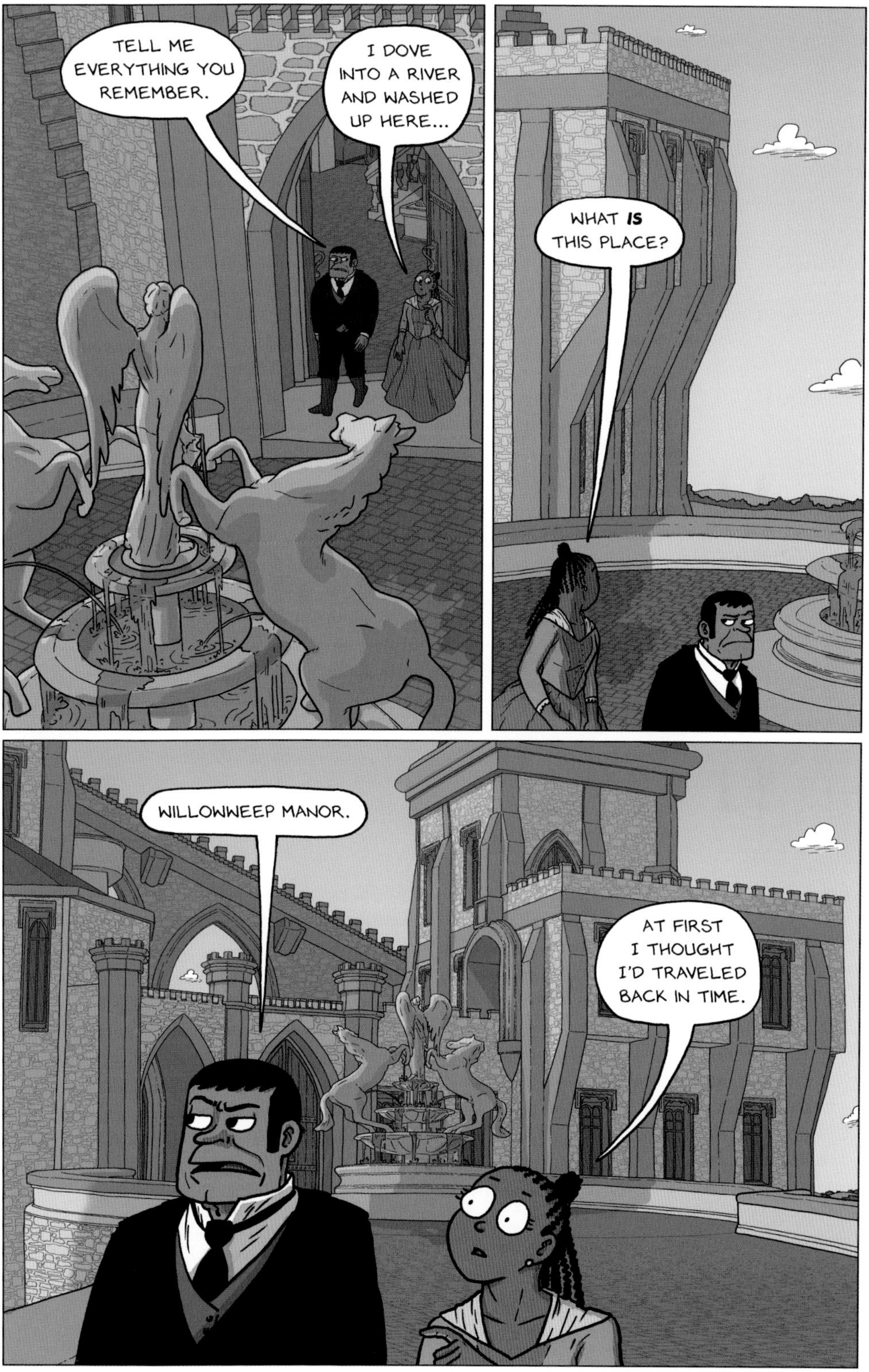
TELL ME EVERYTHING YOU REMEMBER.
I DOVE INTO A RIVER AND WASHED UP HERE...
WHAT **IS** THIS PLACE?
WILLOWWEEP MANOR.
AT FIRST I THOUGHT I'D TRAVELED BACK IN TIME.

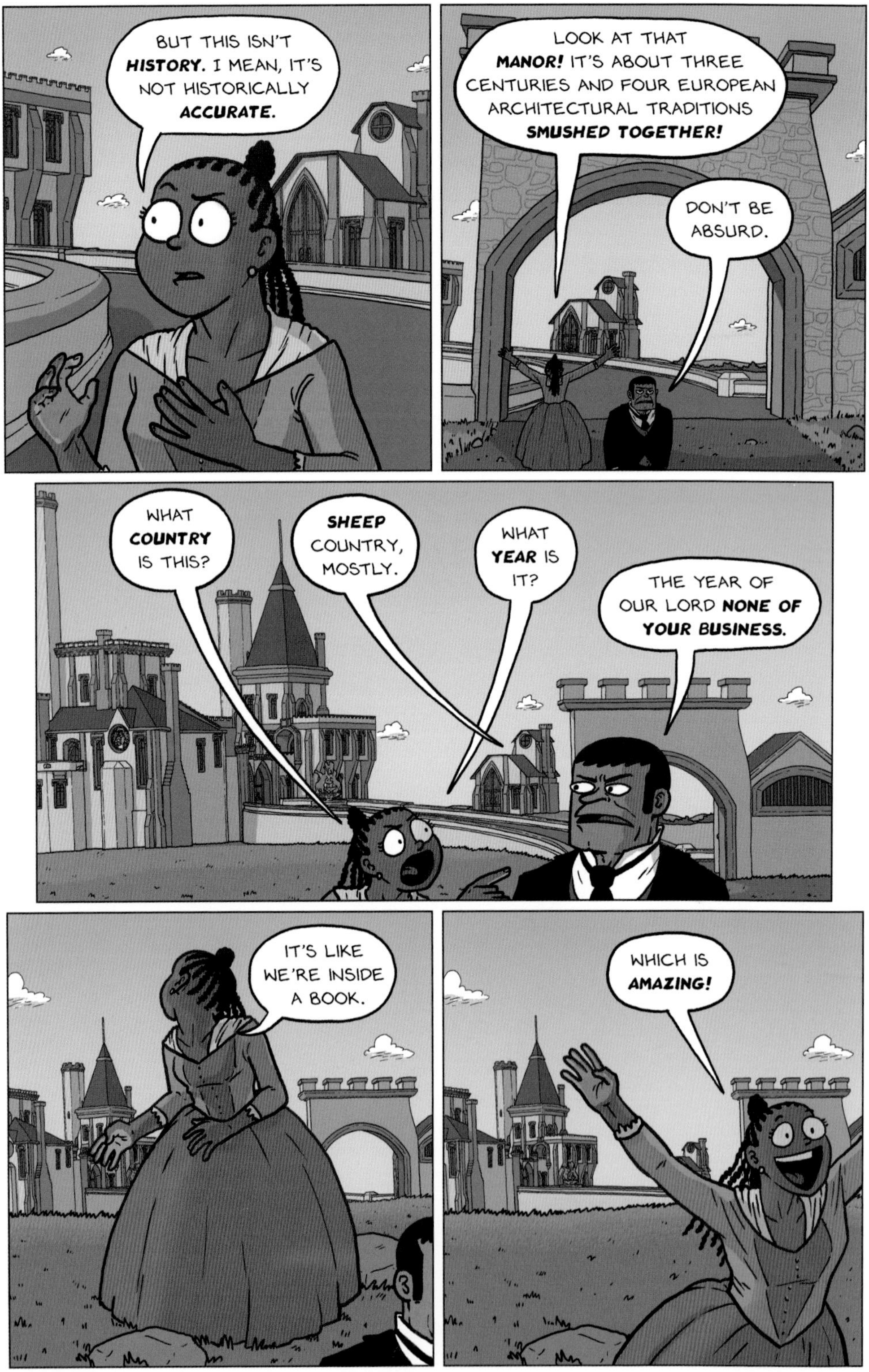
BUT THIS ISN'T **HISTORY.** I MEAN, IT'S NOT HISTORICALLY **ACCURATE.**
LOOK AT THAT **MANOR!** IT'S ABOUT THREE CENTURIES AND FOUR EUROPEAN ARCHITECTURAL TRADITIONS **SMUSHED TOGETHER!**
DON'T BE ABSURD.
WHAT **COUNTRY** IS THIS?
SHEEP COUNTRY, MOSTLY.
WHAT **YEAR** IS IT?
THE YEAR OF OUR LORD **NONE OF YOUR BUSINESS.**
IT'S LIKE WE'RE INSIDE A BOOK.
WHICH IS **AMAZING!**

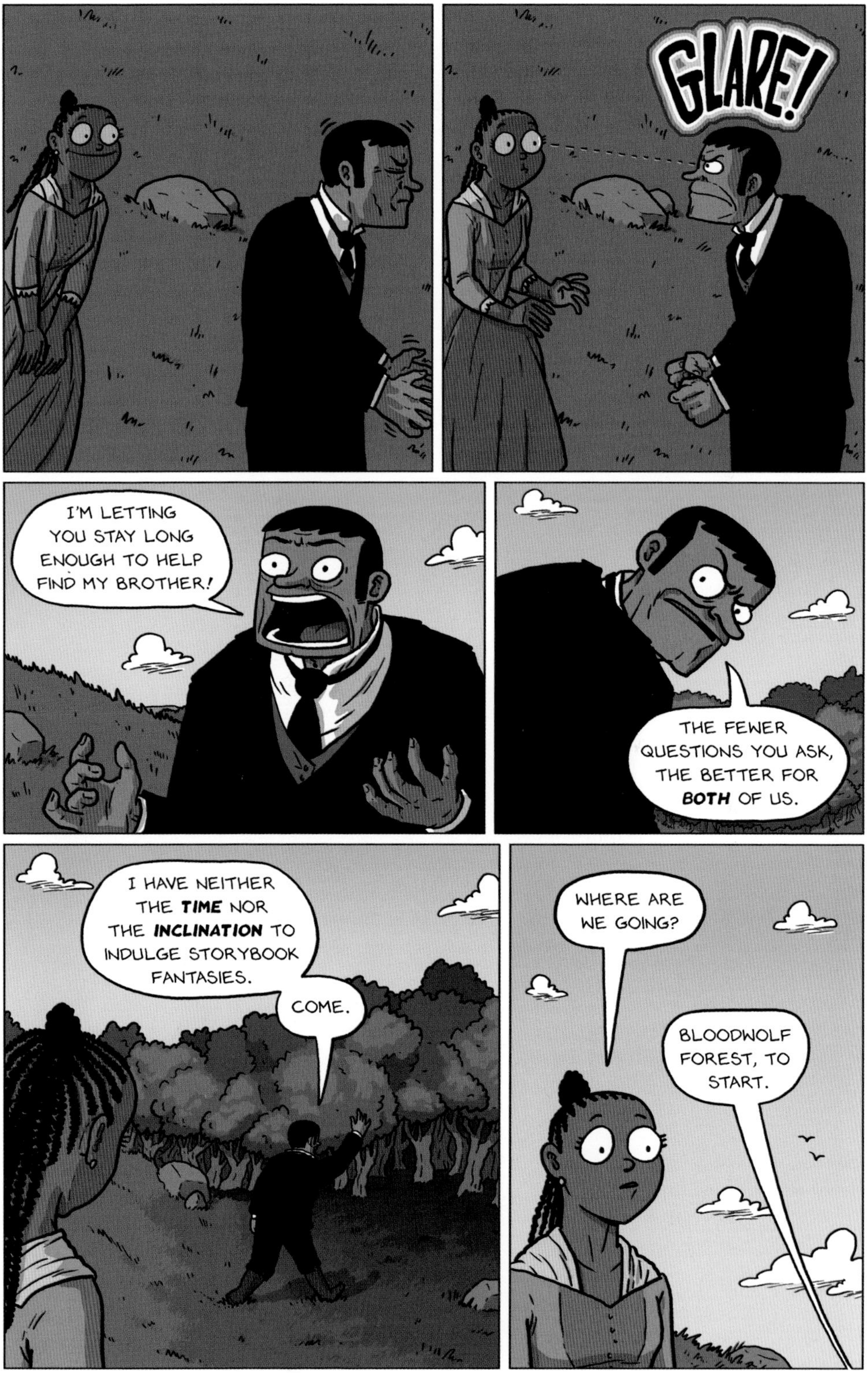
GLARE!
I'M LETTING YOU STAY LONG ENOUGH TO HELP FIND MY BROTHER!
THE FEWER QUESTIONS YOU ASK, THE BETTER FOR **BOTH** OF US.
I HAVE NEITHER THE **TIME** NOR THE **INCLINATION** TO INDULGE STORYBOOK FANTASIES.
COME.
WHERE ARE WE GOING?
BLOODWOLF FOREST, TO START.

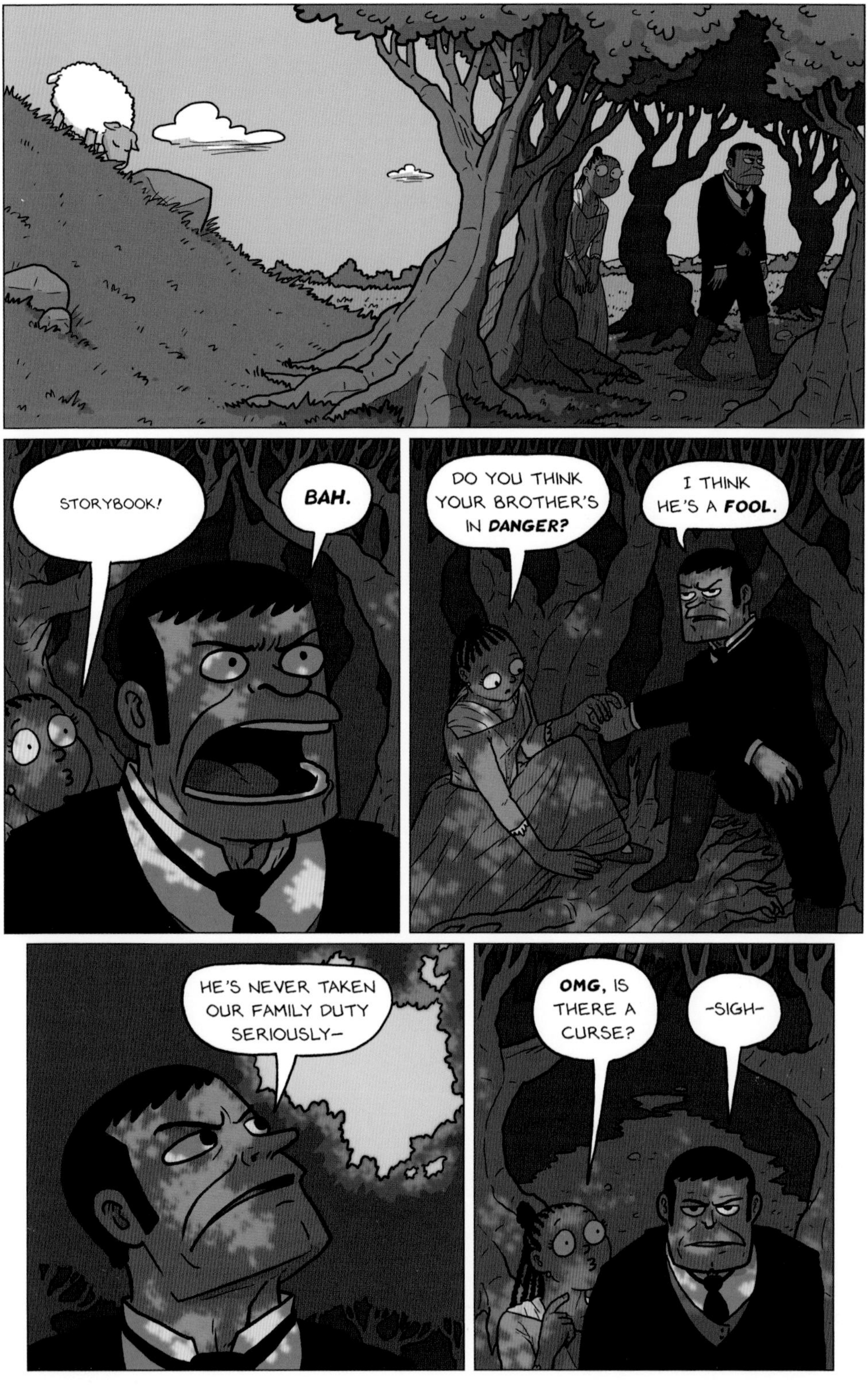
STORYBOOK!
BAH.
DO YOU THINK YOUR BROTHER'S IN DANGER?
I THINK HE'S A FOOL.
HE'S NEVER TAKEN OUR FAMILY DUTY SERIOUSLY—
OMG, IS THERE A CURSE?
-SIGH-

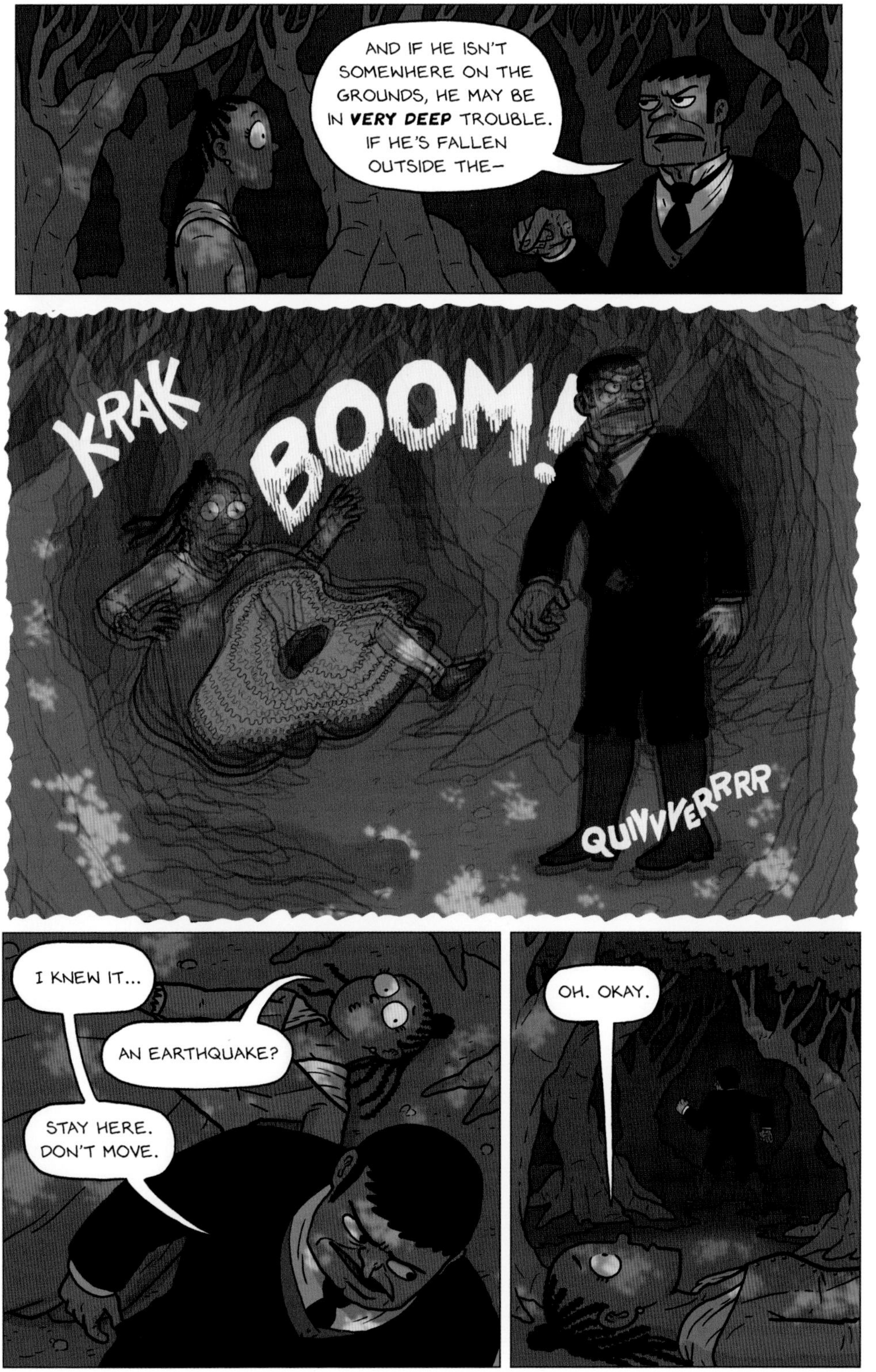
AND IF HE ISN'T SOMEWHERE ON THE GROUNDS, HE MAY BE IN **VERY DEEP** TROUBLE. IF HE'S FALLEN OUTSIDE THE—
KRAK
BOOM!
QUIVVVERRRR
I KNEW IT...
AN EARTHQUAKE?
STAY HERE. DON'T MOVE.
OH. OKAY.

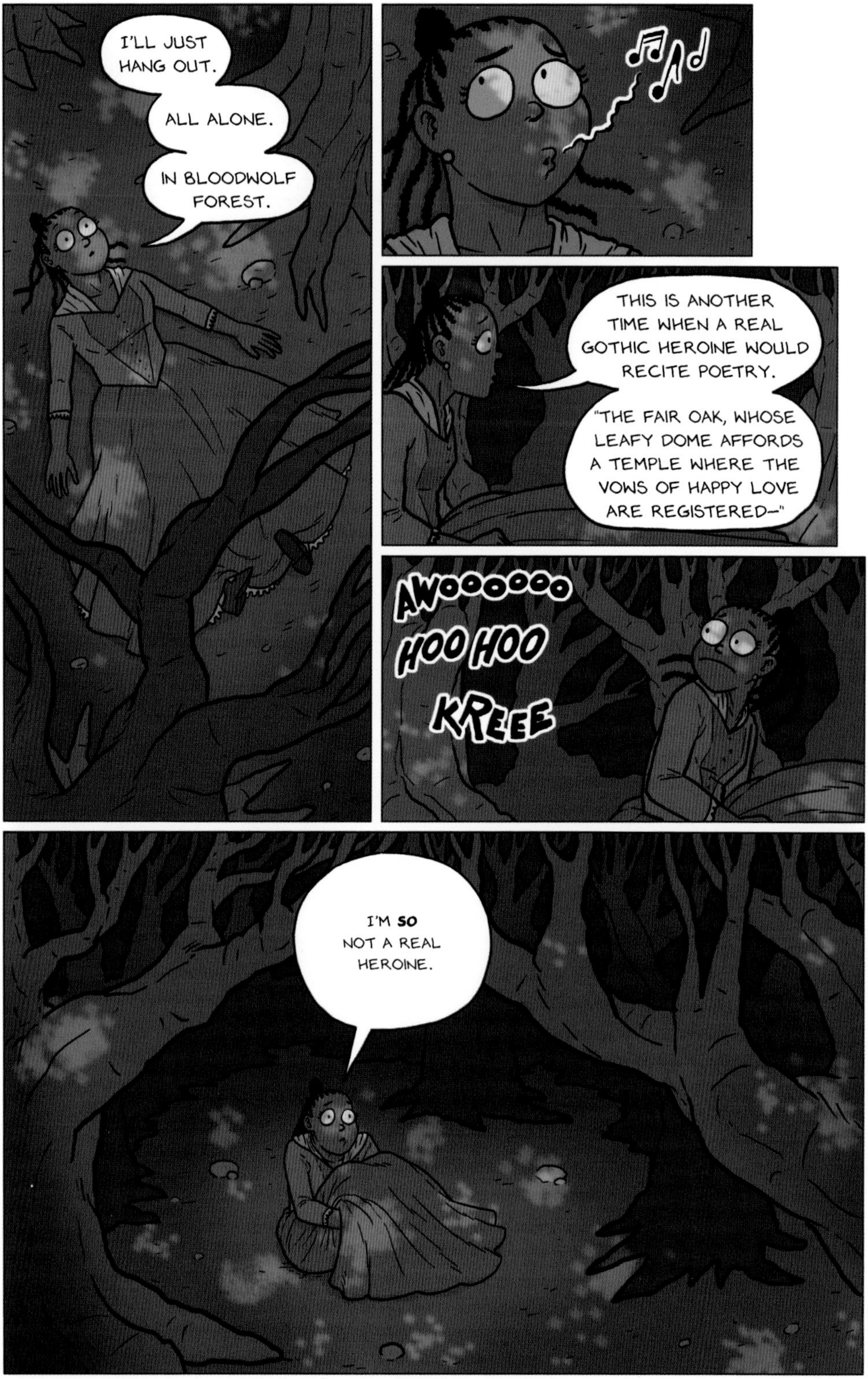
I'LL JUST HANG OUT.
ALL ALONE.
IN BLOODWOLF FOREST.
THIS IS ANOTHER TIME WHEN A REAL GOTHIC HEROINE WOULD RECITE POETRY.
"THE FAIR OAK, WHOSE LEAFY DOME AFFORDS A TEMPLE WHERE THE VOWS OF HAPPY LOVE ARE REGISTERED—"
AWOOOOOO
HOO HOO
KREEE
I'M **SO** NOT A REAL HEROINE.

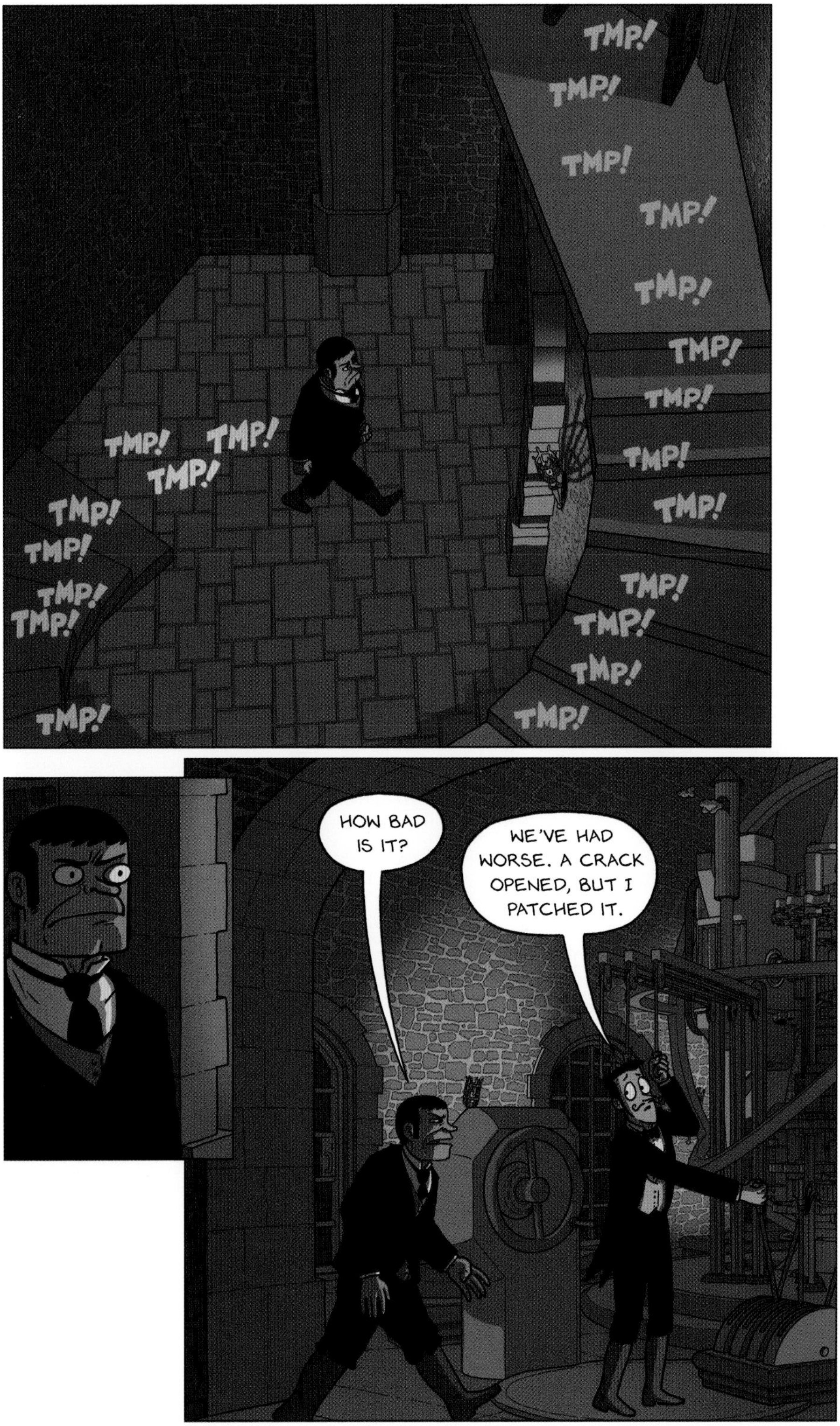
TMP!
TMP!
TMP!
TMP!
TMP!
TMP!
TMP!
TMP!
TMP!
TMP!
TMP!
TMP!
TMP!
TMP!
TMP!
TMP!
TMP!
TMP!
TMP!
TMP!
TMP!
HOW BAD IS IT?
WE'VE HAD WORSE. A CRACK OPENED, BUT I PATCHED IT.

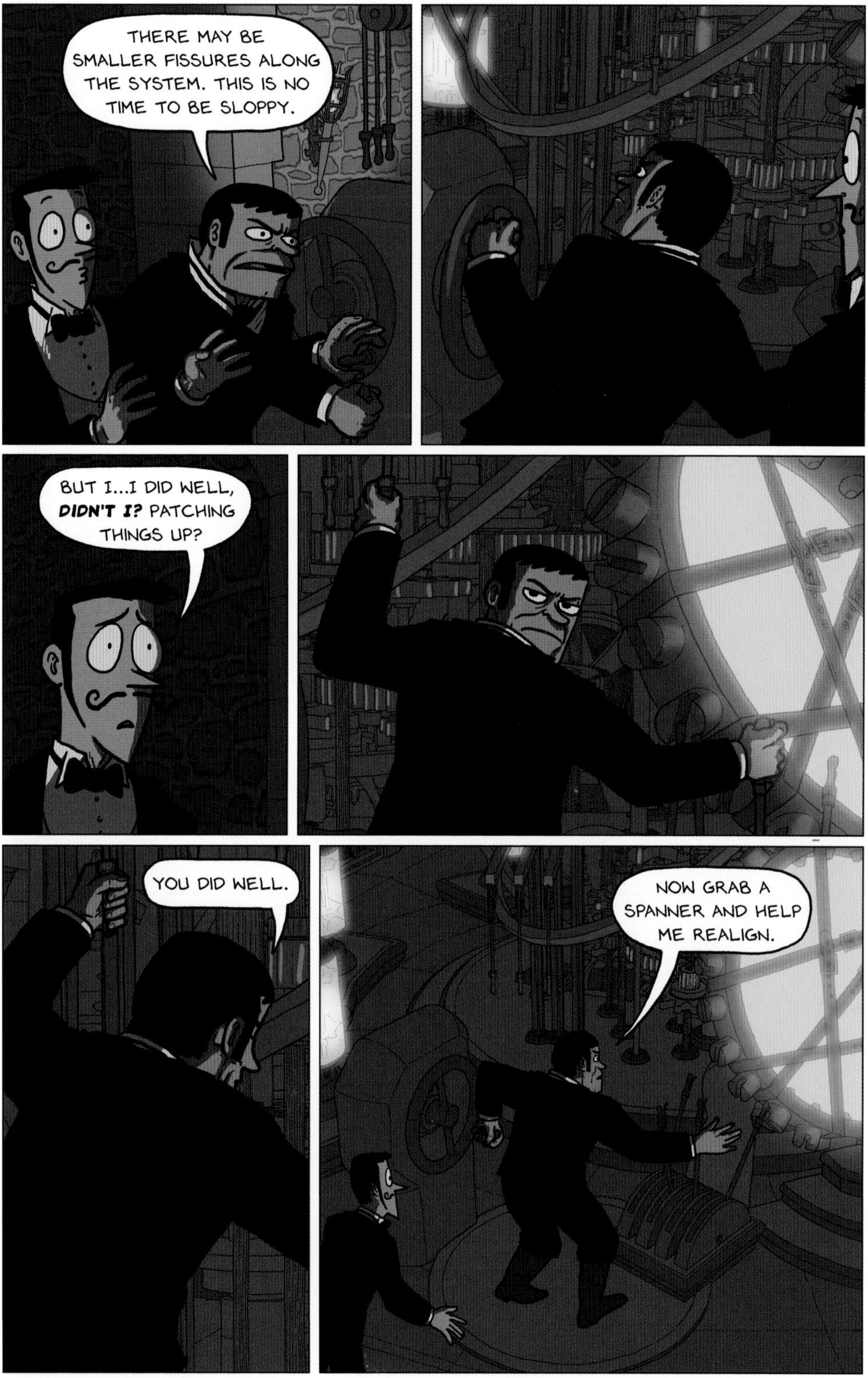
THERE MAY BE SMALLER FISSURES ALONG THE SYSTEM. THIS IS NO TIME TO BE SLOPPY.
BUT I...I DID WELL, **DIDN'T I?** PATCHING THINGS UP?
YOU DID WELL.
NOW GRAB A SPANNER AND HELP ME REALIGN.

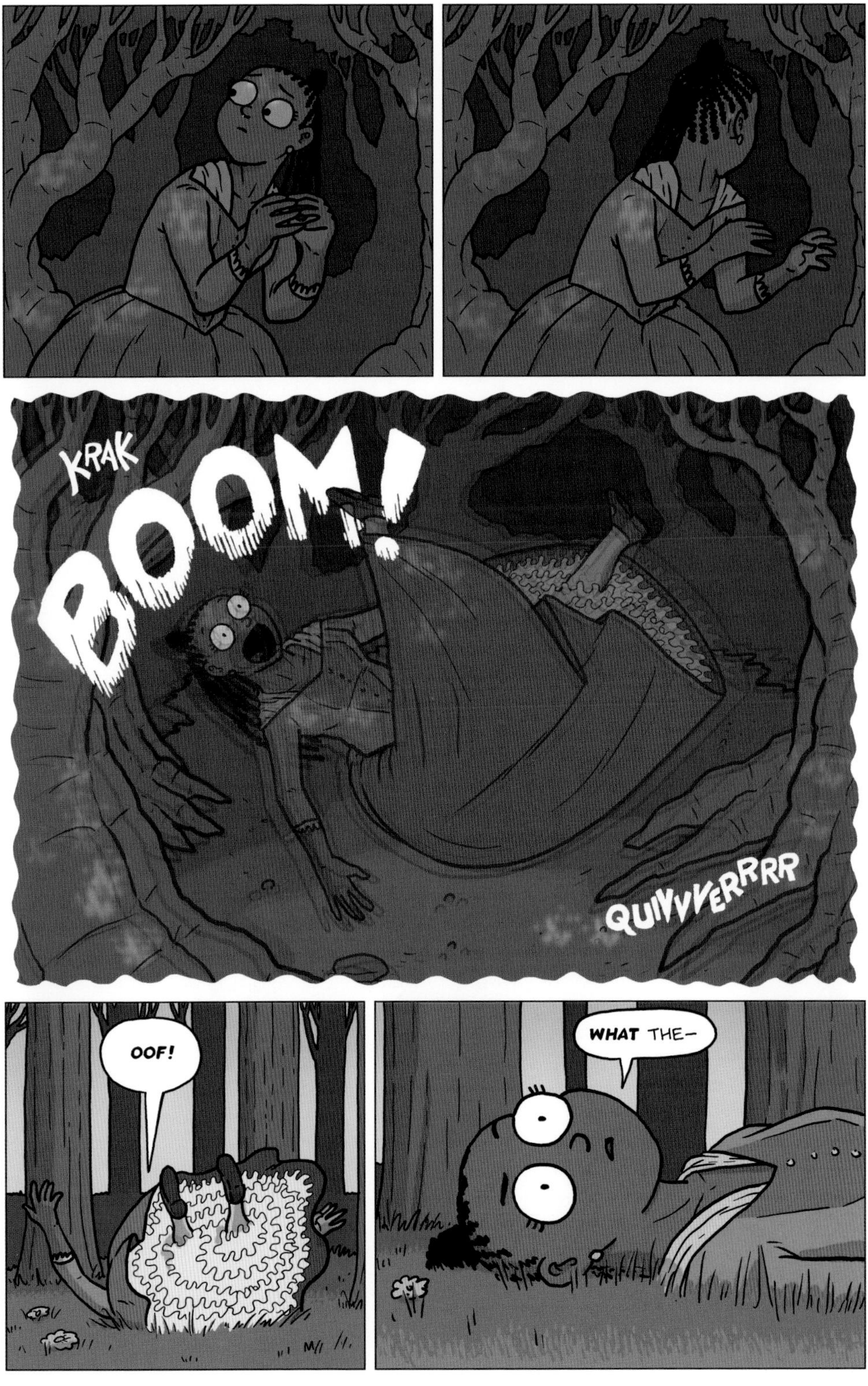
KRAK
BOOM!
QUIVVVERRRR
OOF!
WHAT THE-

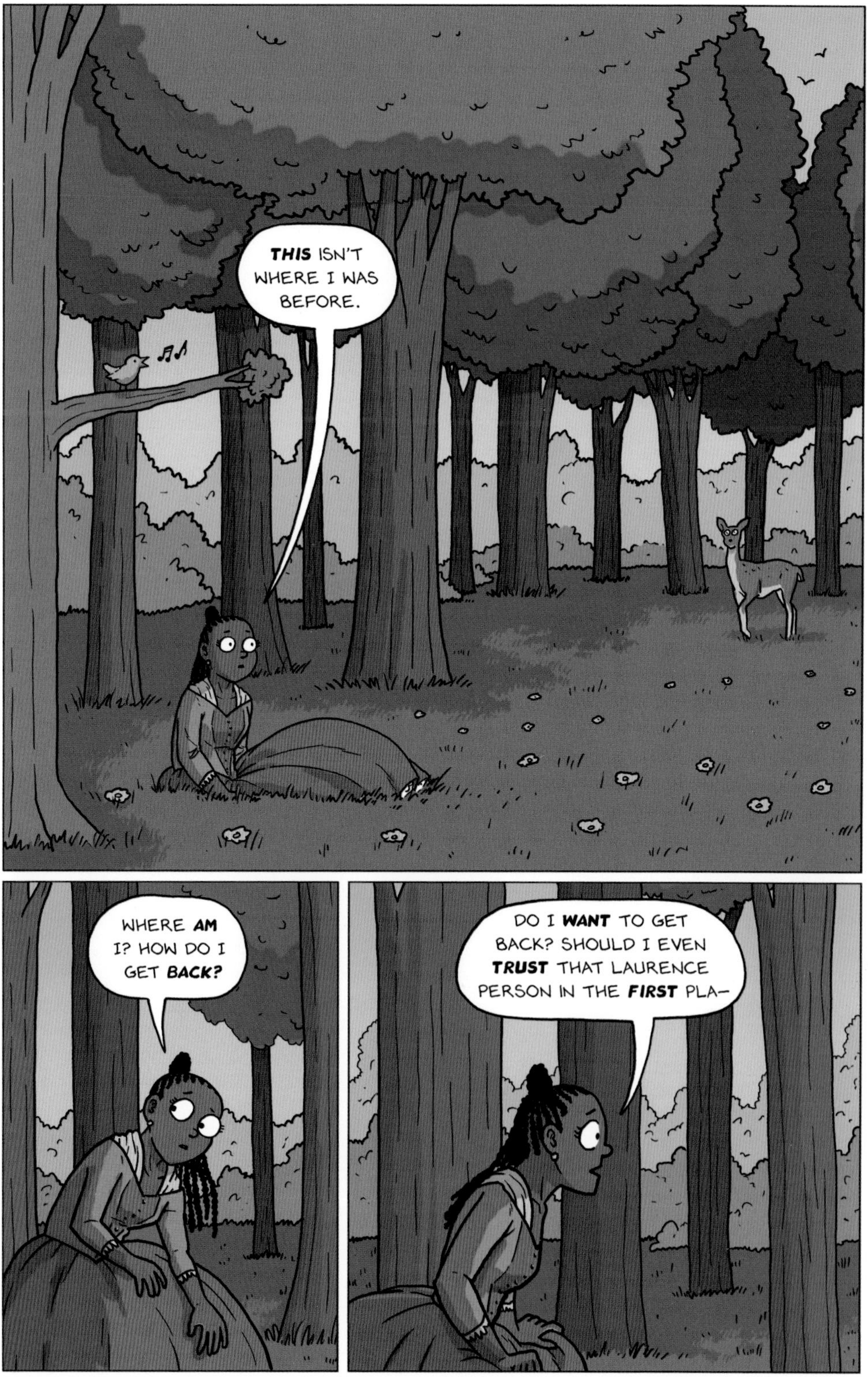
THIS ISN'T WHERE I WAS BEFORE.
WHERE **AM** I? HOW DO I GET **BACK?**
DO I **WANT** TO GET BACK? SHOULD I EVEN **TRUST** THAT LAURENCE PERSON IN THE **FIRST** PLA—

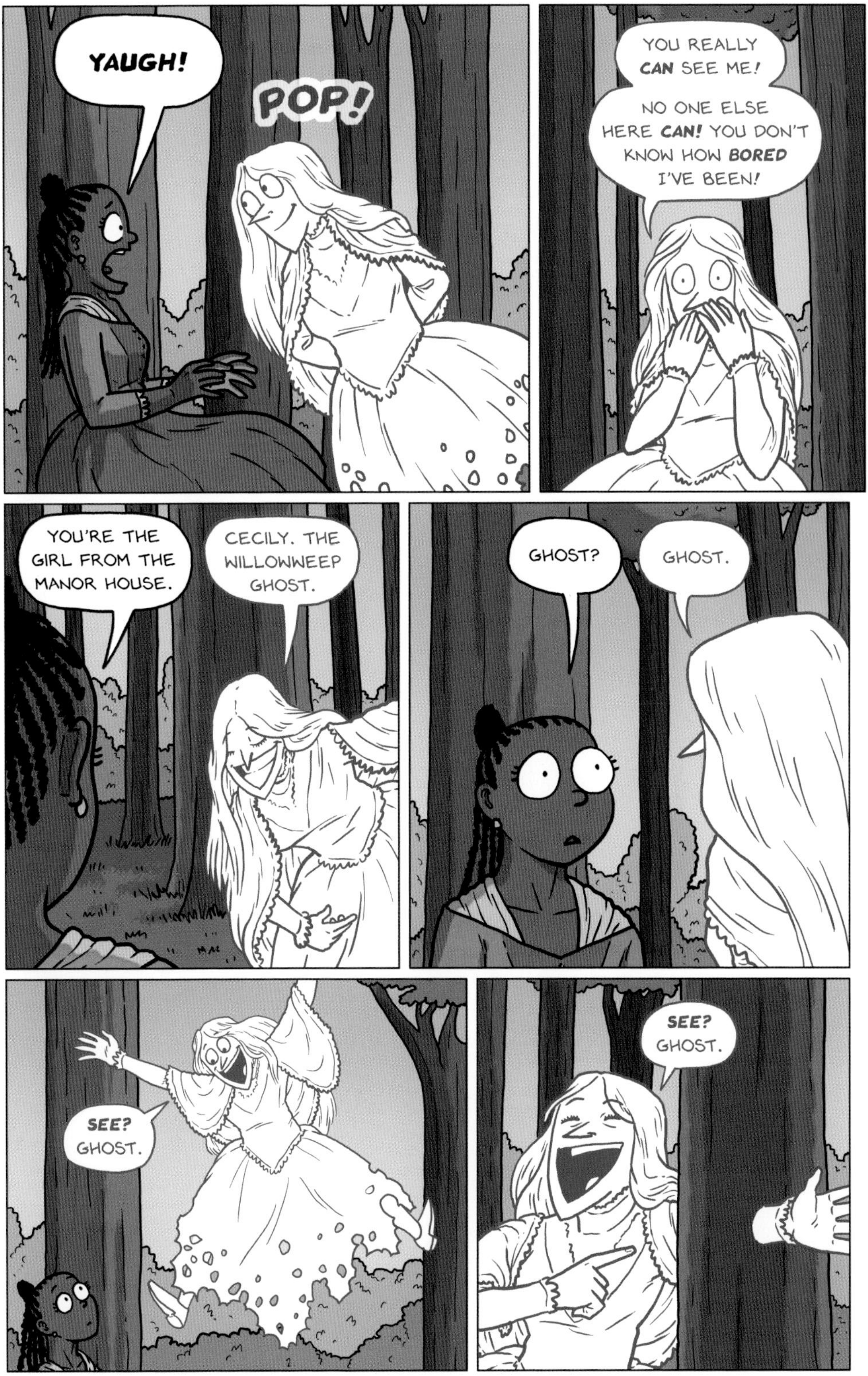
YAUGH!
POP!
YOU REALLY CAN SEE ME!
NO ONE ELSE HERE CAN! YOU DON'T KNOW HOW BORED I'VE BEEN!
YOU'RE THE GIRL FROM THE MANOR HOUSE.
CECILY. THE WILLOWWEEP GHOST.
GHOST?
GHOST.
SEE? GHOST.
SEE? GHOST.

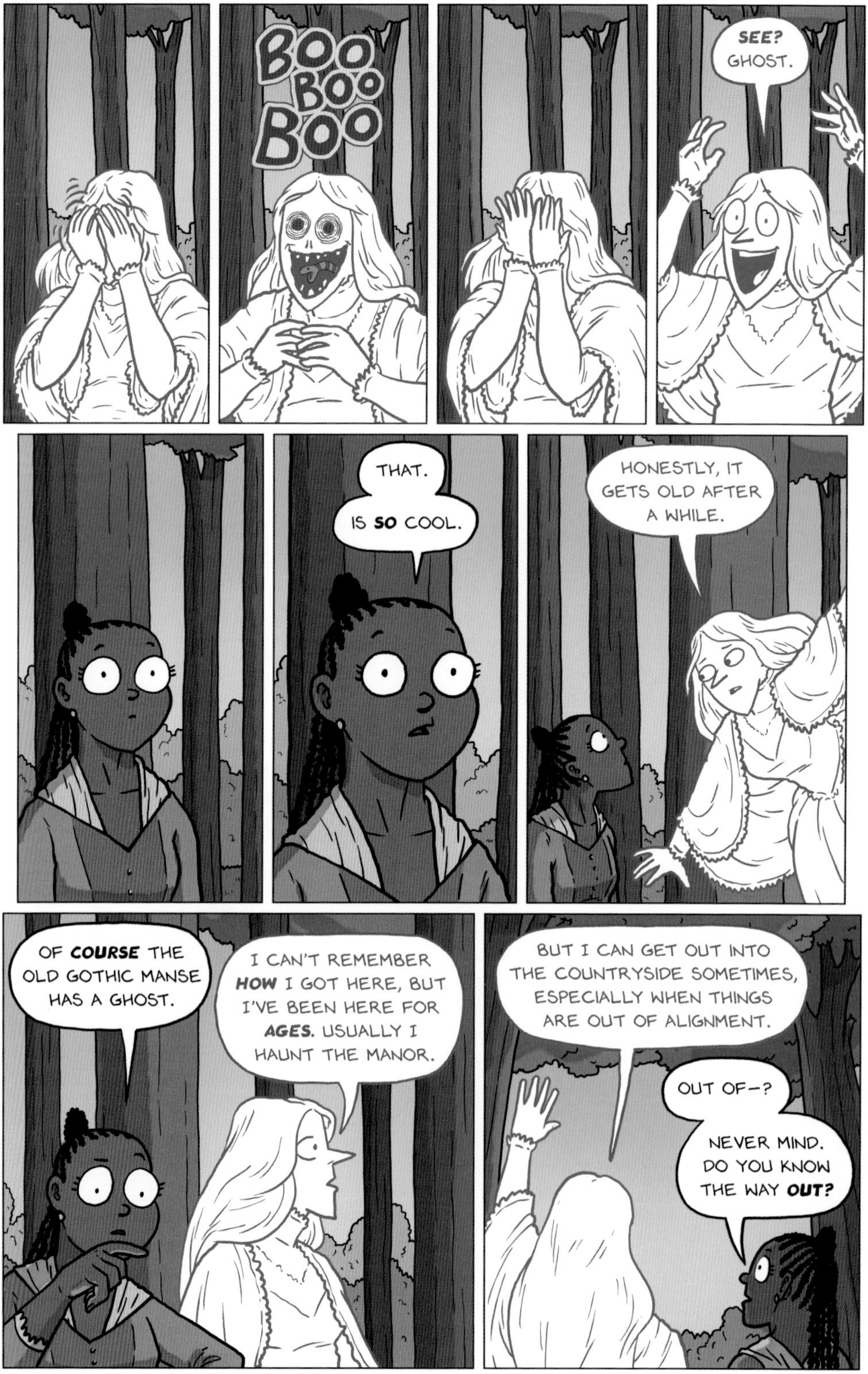
BOO BOO BOO
SEE? GHOST.
THAT.
IS SO COOL.
HONESTLY, IT GETS OLD AFTER A WHILE.
OF COURSE THE OLD GOTHIC MANSE HAS A GHOST.
I CAN'T REMEMBER HOW I GOT HERE, BUT I'VE BEEN HERE FOR AGES. USUALLY I HAUNT THE MANOR.
BUT I CAN GET OUT INTO THE COUNTRYSIDE SOMETIMES, ESPECIALLY WHEN THINGS ARE OUT OF ALIGNMENT.
OUT OF—?
NEVER MIND. DO YOU KNOW THE WAY OUT?

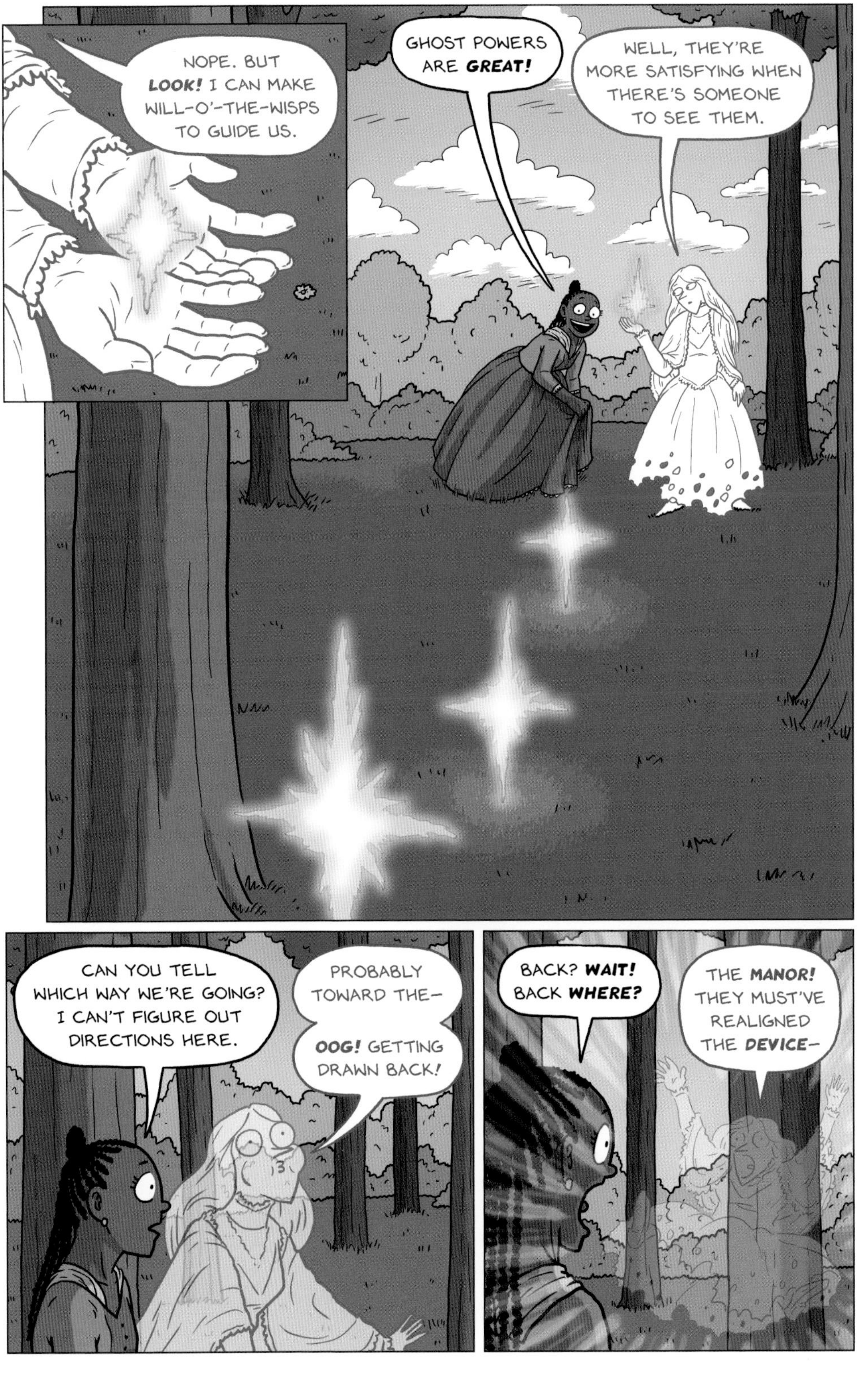
NOPE. BUT **LOOK!** I CAN MAKE WILL-O'-THE-WISPS TO GUIDE US.
GHOST POWERS ARE **GREAT!**
WELL, THEY'RE MORE SATISFYING WHEN THERE'S SOMEONE TO SEE THEM.
CAN YOU TELL WHICH WAY WE'RE GOING? I CAN'T FIGURE OUT DIRECTIONS HERE.
PROBABLY TOWARD THE—
OOG! GETTING DRAWN BACK!
BACK? **WAIT!** BACK **WHERE?**
THE **MANOR!** THEY MUST'VE REALIGNED THE **DEVICE**—

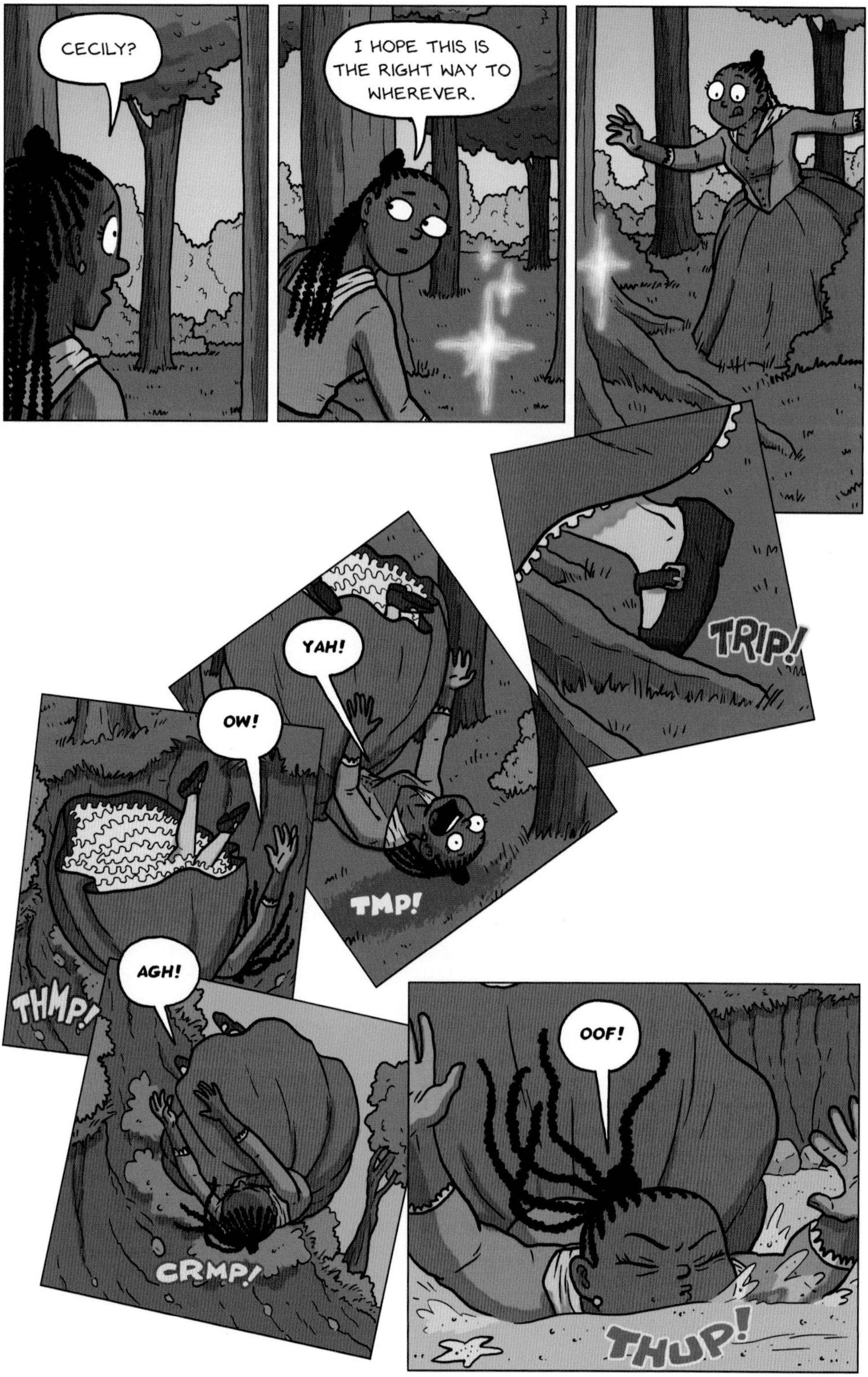
CECILY?
I HOPE THIS IS THE RIGHT WAY TO WHEREVER.
TRIP!
YAH!
TMP!
OW!
THMP!
AGH!
CRMP!
OOF!
THUP!

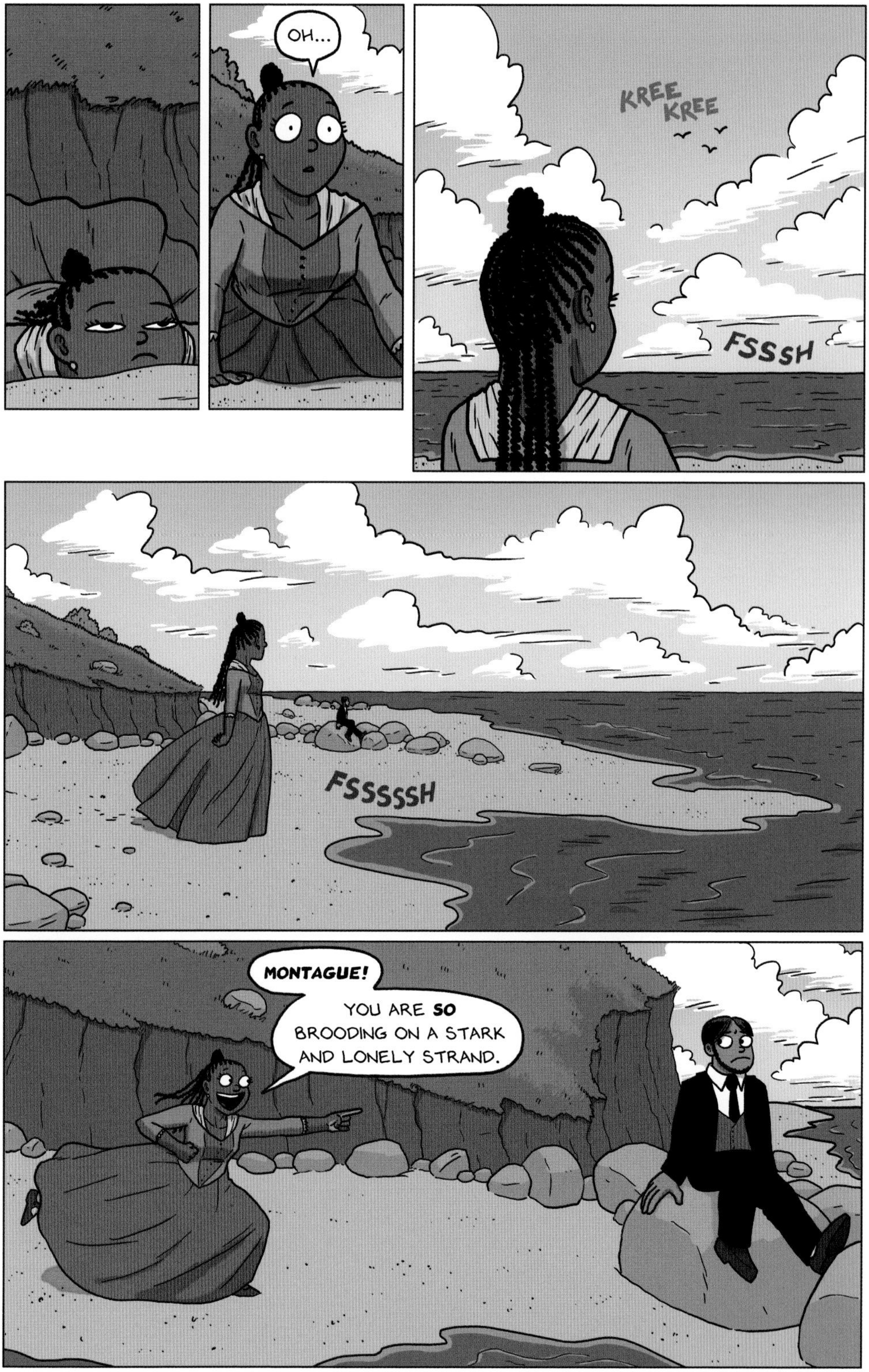
OH...
KREE KREE
FSSSH
FSSSSSH
MONTAGUE!
YOU ARE **SO** BROODING ON A STARK AND LONELY STRAND.

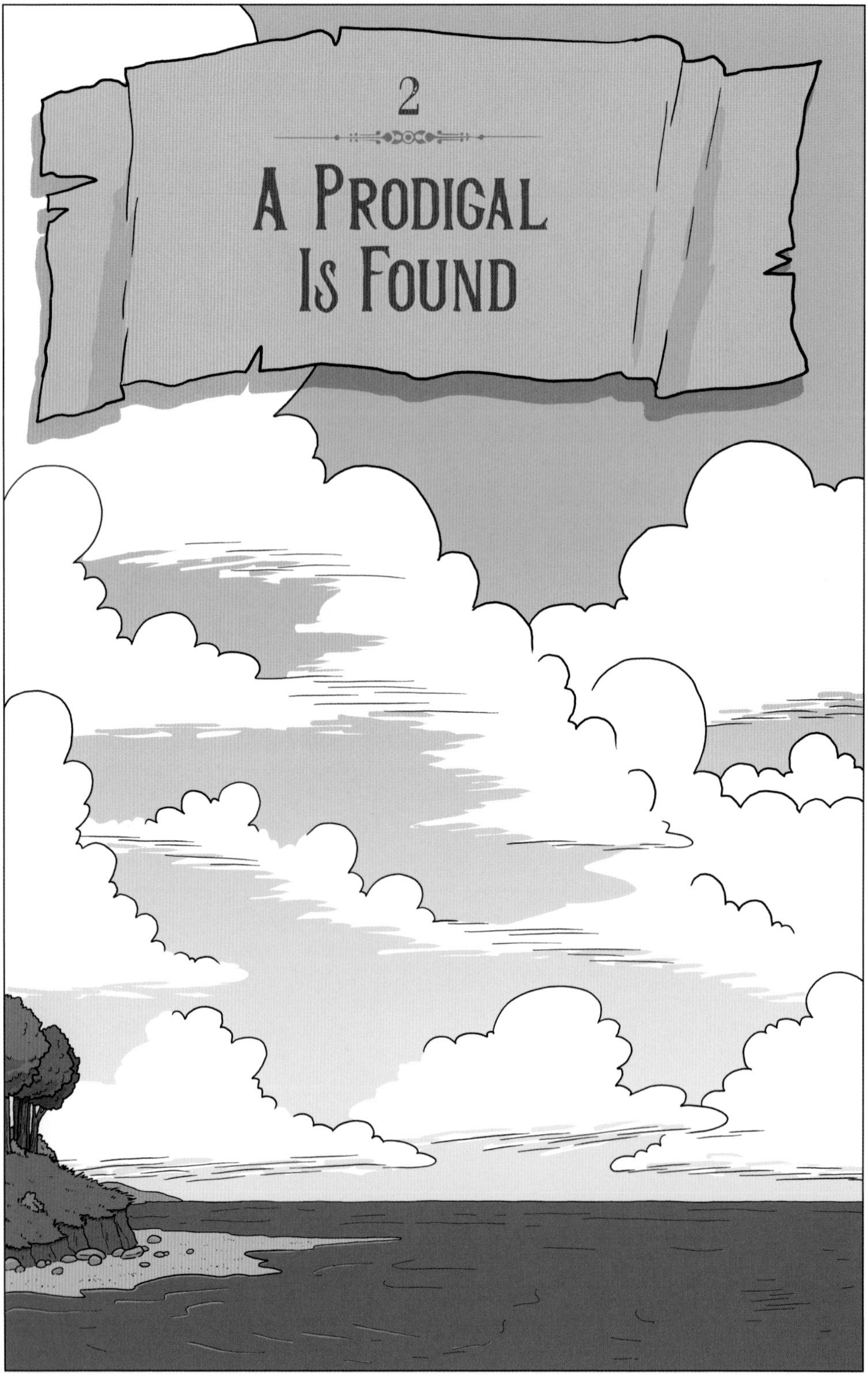
2
A Prodigal Is Found

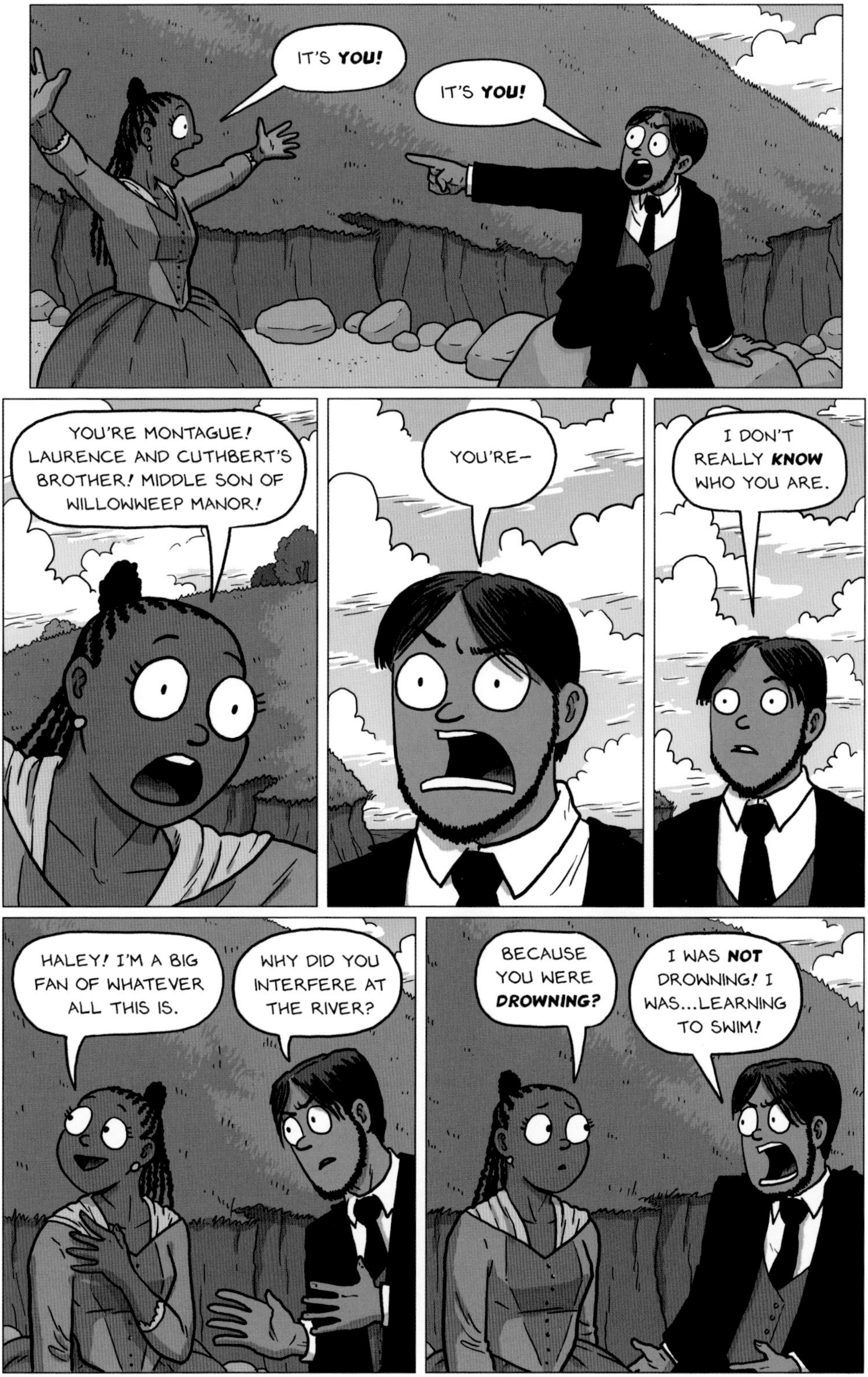
IT'S **YOU!**
IT'S **YOU!**
YOU'RE MONTAGUE! LAURENCE AND CUTHBERT'S BROTHER! MIDDLE SON OF WILLOWWEEP MANOR!
YOU'RE-
I DON'T REALLY **KNOW** WHO YOU ARE.
HALEY! I'M A BIG FAN OF WHATEVER ALL THIS IS.
WHY DID YOU INTERFERE AT THE RIVER?
BECAUSE YOU WERE **DROWNING?**
I WAS **NOT** DROWNING! I WAS...LEARNING TO SWIM!

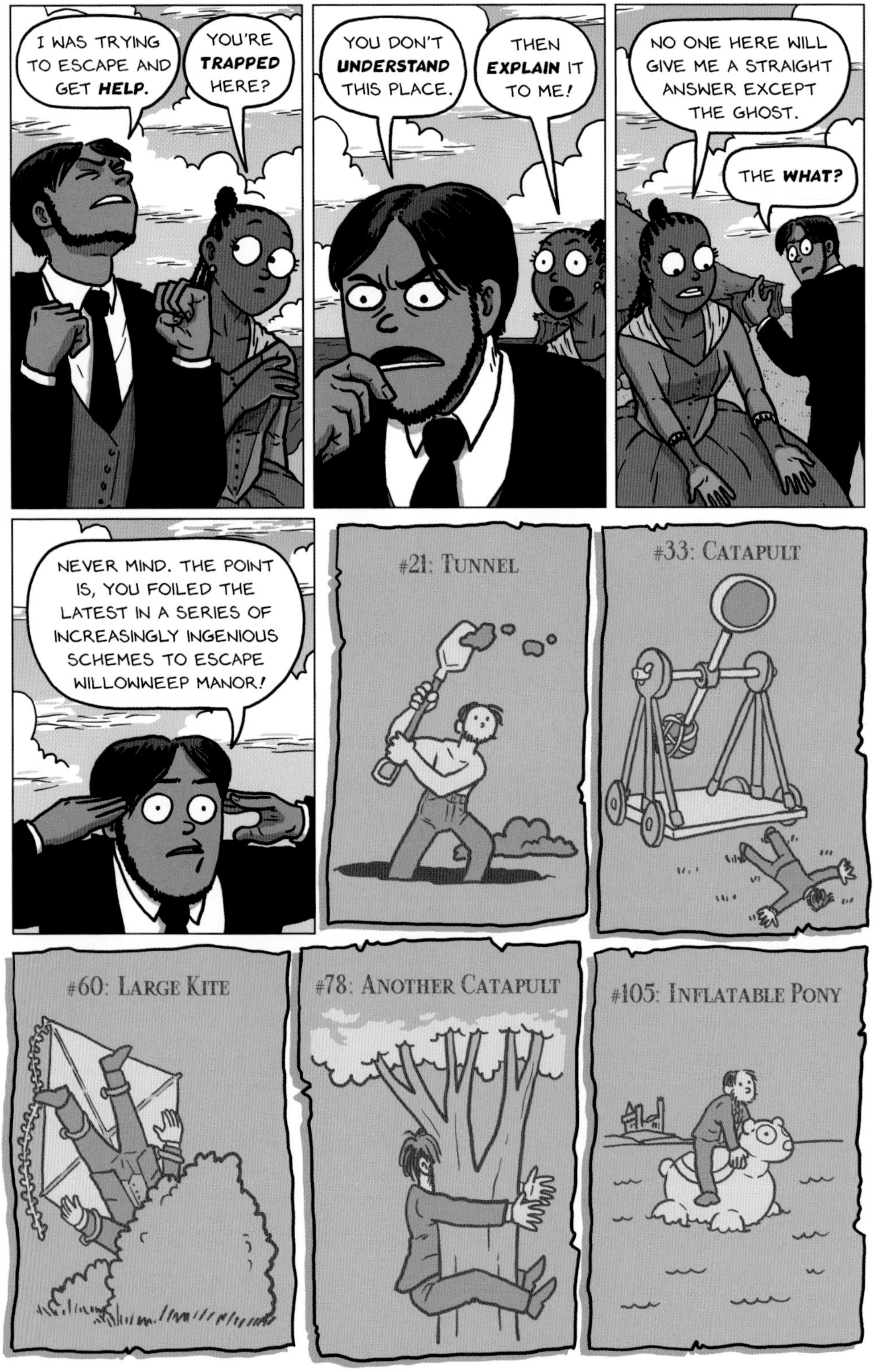

I WAS TRYING TO ESCAPE AND GET **HELP**.
YOU'RE **TRAPPED** HERE?
YOU DON'T **UNDERSTAND** THIS PLACE.
THEN **EXPLAIN** IT TO ME!
NO ONE HERE WILL GIVE ME A STRAIGHT ANSWER EXCEPT THE GHOST.
THE **WHAT?**
NEVER MIND. THE POINT IS, YOU FOILED THE LATEST IN A SERIES OF INCREASINGLY INGENIOUS SCHEMES TO ESCAPE WILLOWWEEP MANOR!
#21: TUNNEL
#33: CATAPULT
#60: LARGE KITE
#78: ANOTHER CATAPULT
#105: INFLATABLE PONY

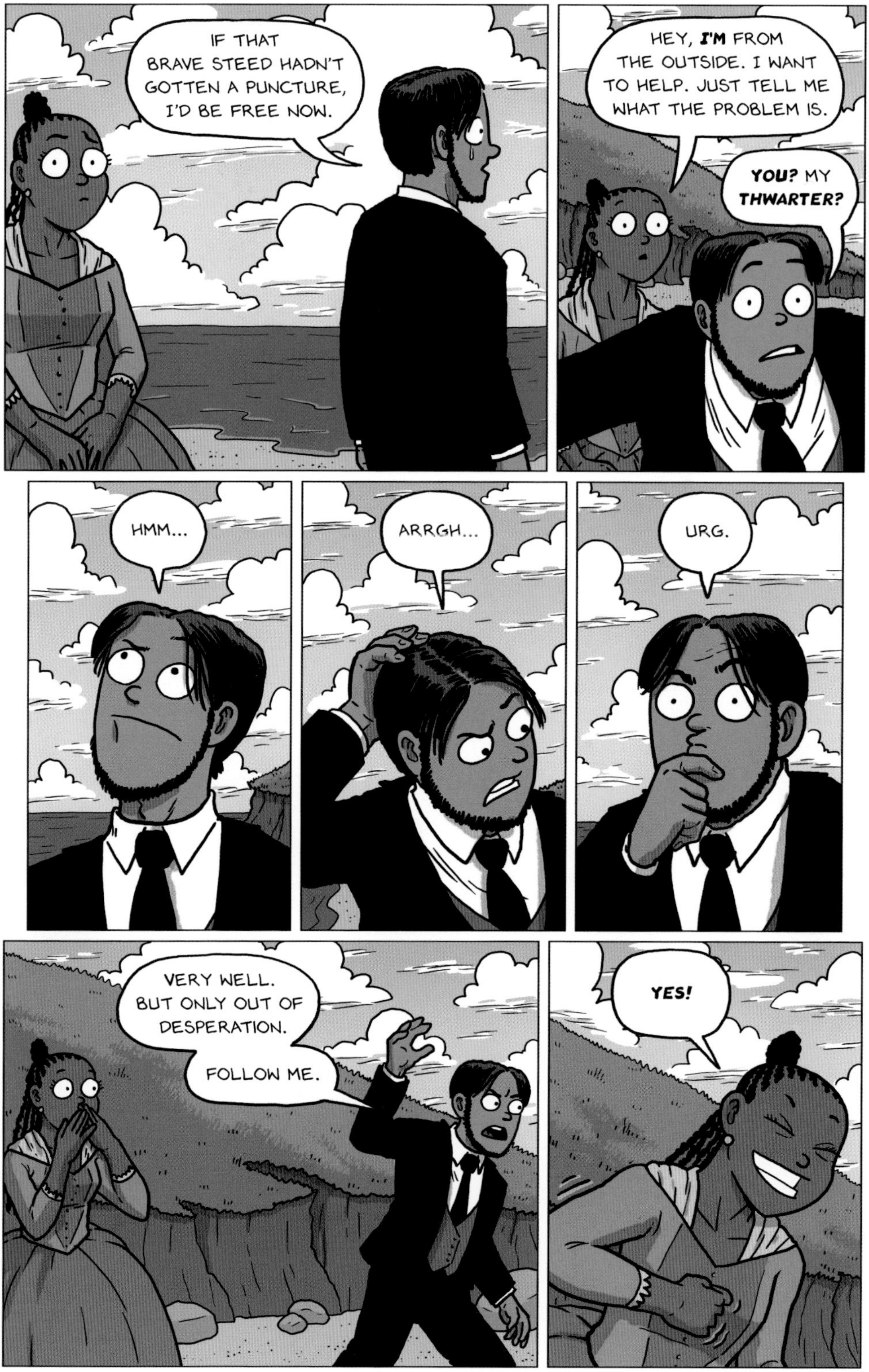
IF THAT BRAVE STEED HADN'T GOTTEN A PUNCTURE, I'D BE FREE NOW.
HEY, I'M FROM THE OUTSIDE. I WANT TO HELP. JUST TELL ME WHAT THE PROBLEM IS.
YOU? MY THWARTER?
HMM...
ARRGH...
URG.
VERY WELL. BUT ONLY OUT OF DESPERATION.
FOLLOW ME.
YES!

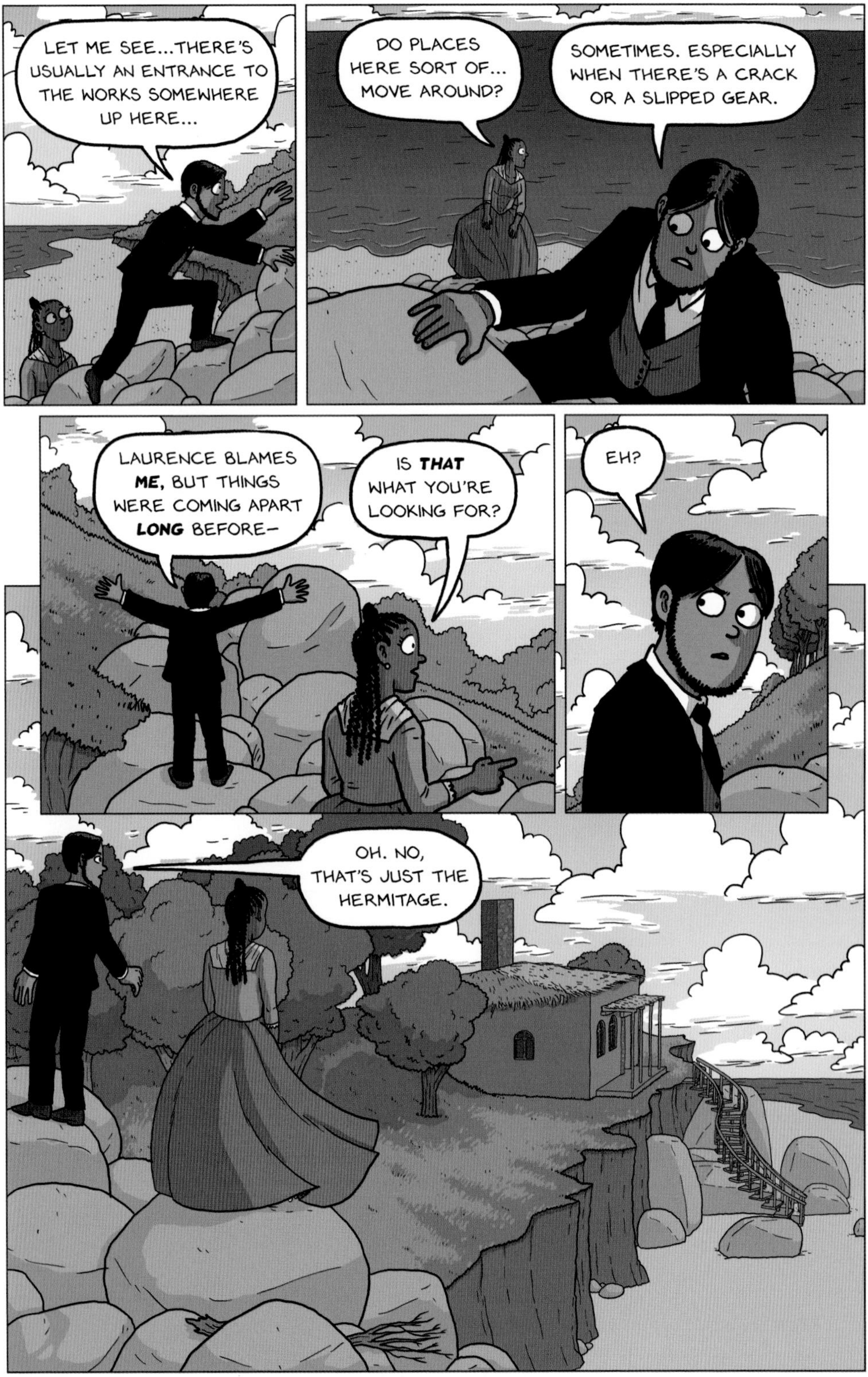
LET ME SEE...THERE'S USUALLY AN ENTRANCE TO THE WORKS SOMEWHERE UP HERE...
DO PLACES HERE SORT OF... MOVE AROUND?
SOMETIMES. ESPECIALLY WHEN THERE'S A CRACK OR A SLIPPED GEAR.
LAURENCE BLAMES **ME,** BUT THINGS WERE COMING APART **LONG** BEFORE—
IS **THAT** WHAT YOU'RE LOOKING FOR?
EH?
OH. NO, THAT'S JUST THE HERMITAGE.

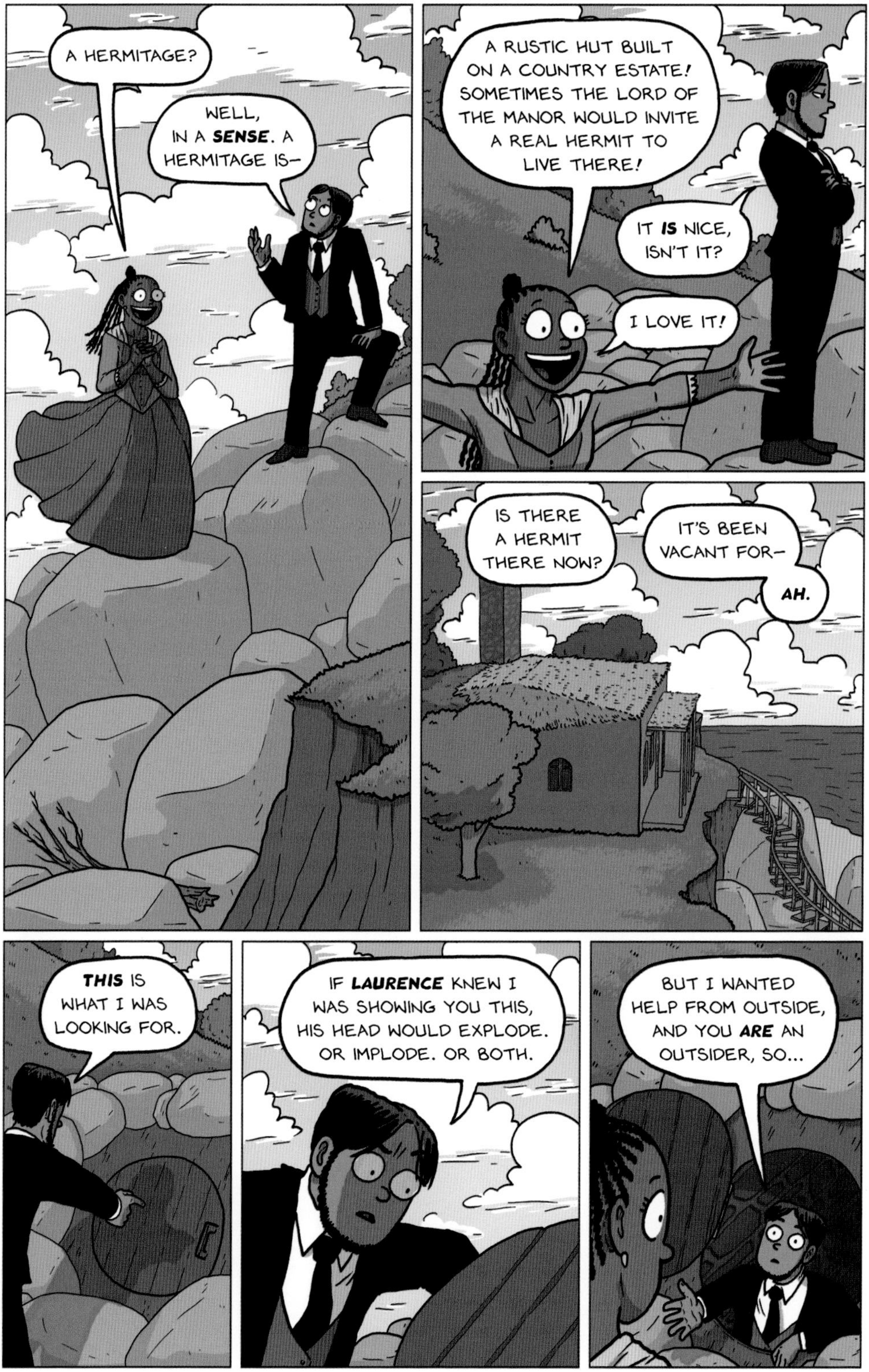
A HERMITAGE?
WELL, IN A SENSE. A HERMITAGE IS–
A RUSTIC HUT BUILT ON A COUNTRY ESTATE! SOMETIMES THE LORD OF THE MANOR WOULD INVITE A REAL HERMIT TO LIVE THERE!
IT IS NICE, ISN'T IT?
I LOVE IT!
IS THERE A HERMIT THERE NOW?
IT'S BEEN VACANT FOR–
AH.
THIS IS WHAT I WAS LOOKING FOR.
IF LAURENCE KNEW I WAS SHOWING YOU THIS, HIS HEAD WOULD EXPLODE. OR IMPLODE. OR BOTH.
BUT I WANTED HELP FROM OUTSIDE, AND YOU ARE AN OUTSIDER, SO...

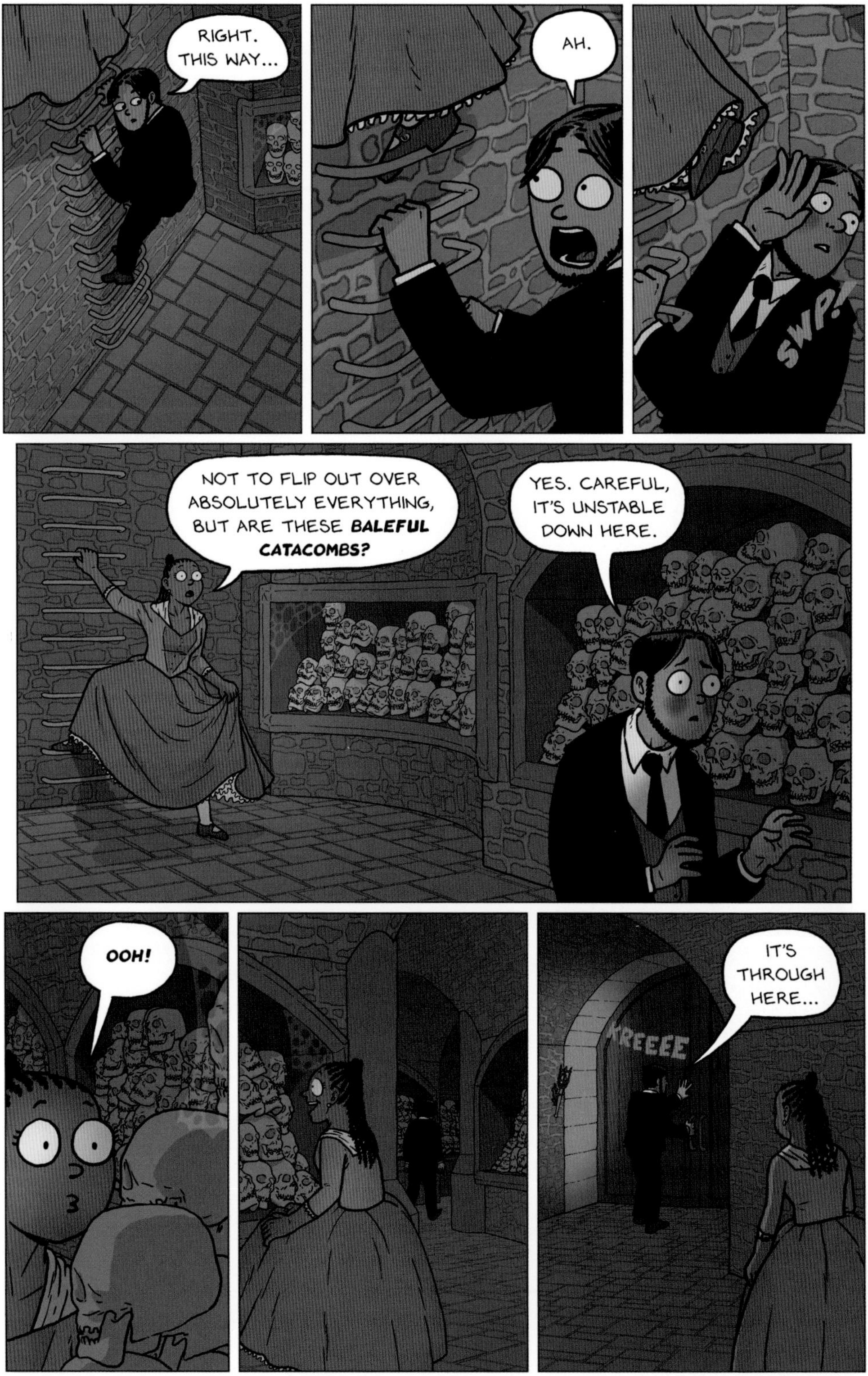
RIGHT. THIS WAY...
AH.
SWP!
NOT TO FLIP OUT OVER ABSOLUTELY EVERYTHING, BUT ARE THESE **BALEFUL CATACOMBS?**
YES. CAREFUL, IT'S UNSTABLE DOWN HERE.
OOH!
KREEEE
IT'S THROUGH HERE...

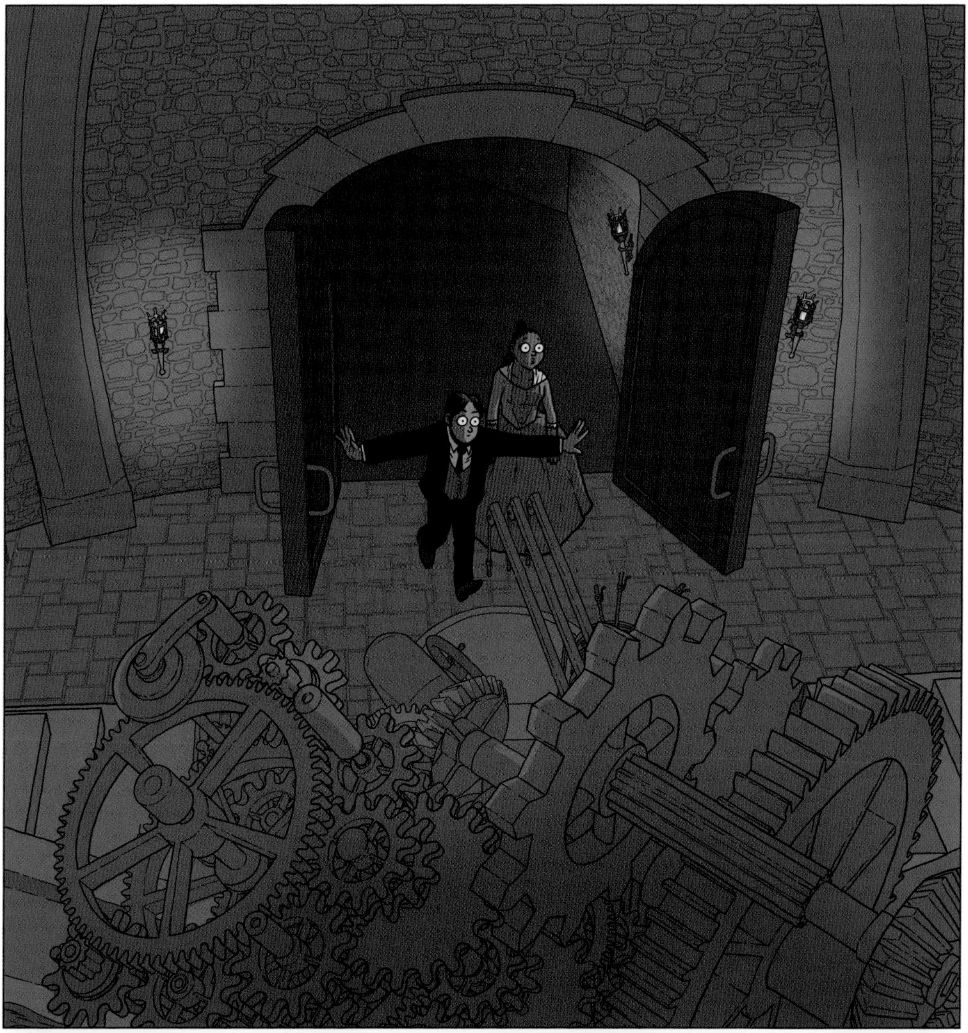

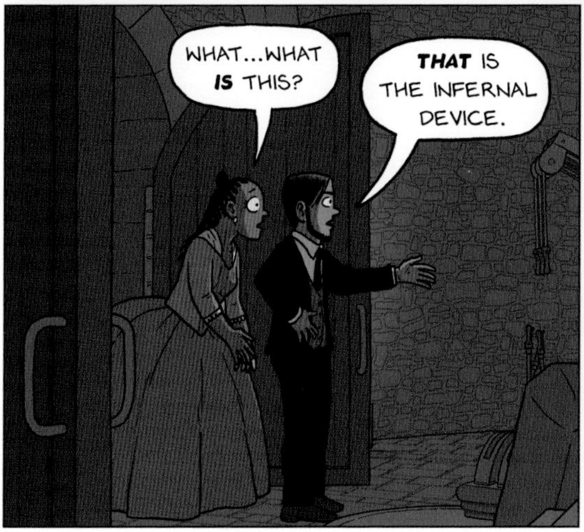
WHAT...WHAT **IS** THIS?
THAT IS THE INFERNAL DEVICE.

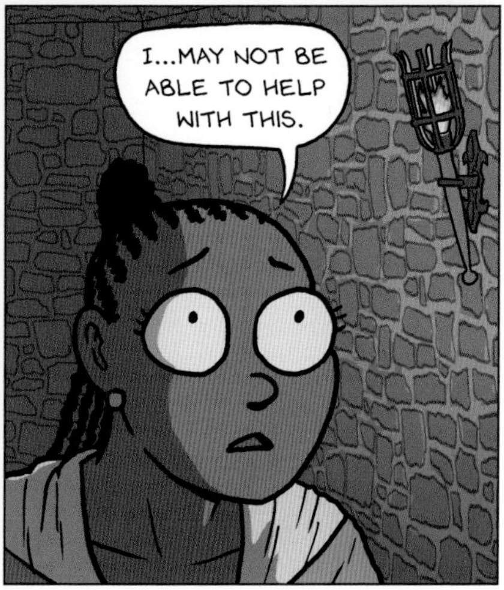
I...MAY NOT BE ABLE TO HELP WITH THIS.

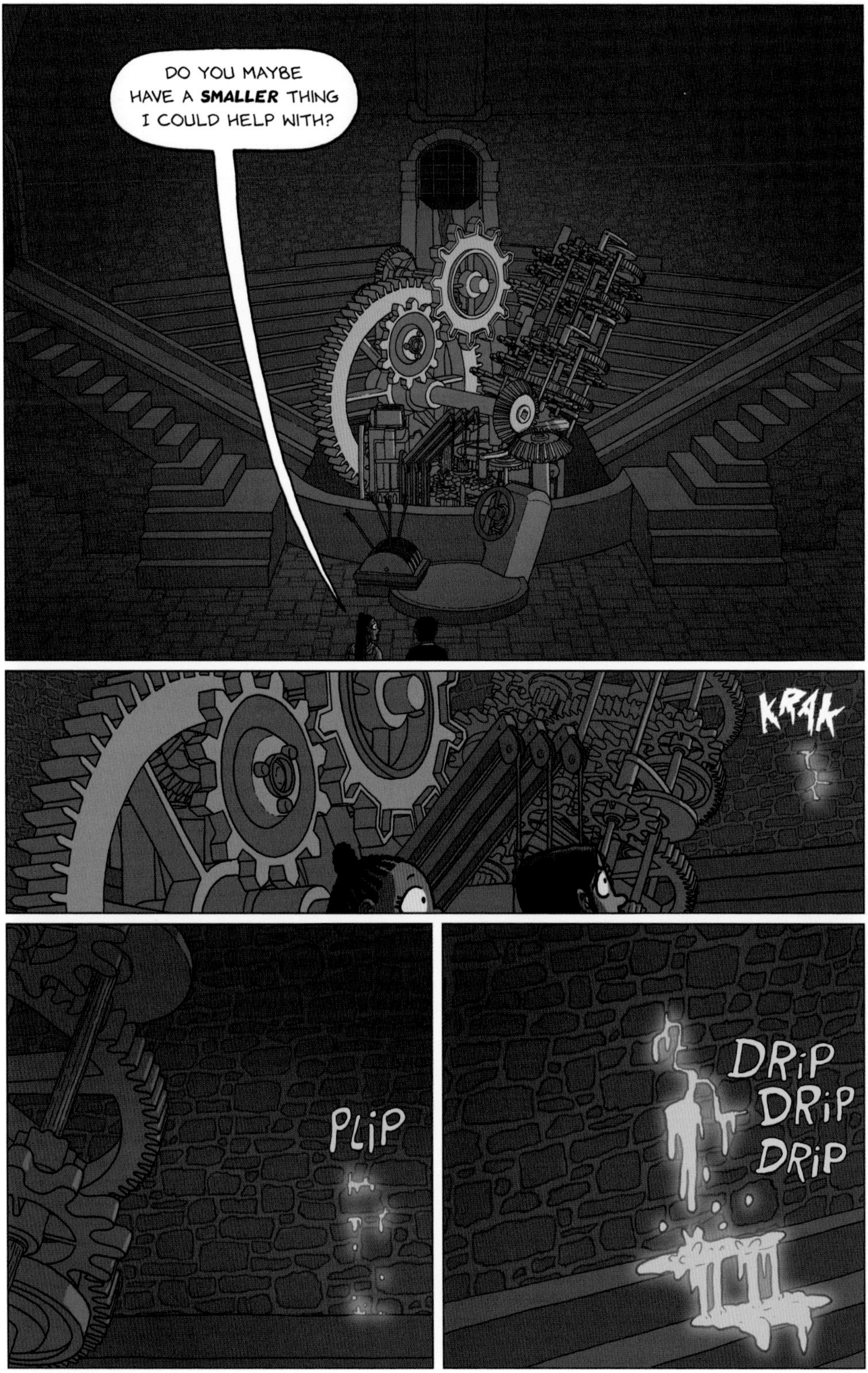
DO YOU MAYBE HAVE A **SMALLER** THING I COULD HELP WITH?
KRAK
PLIP
DRIP DRIP DRIP

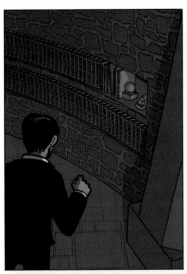

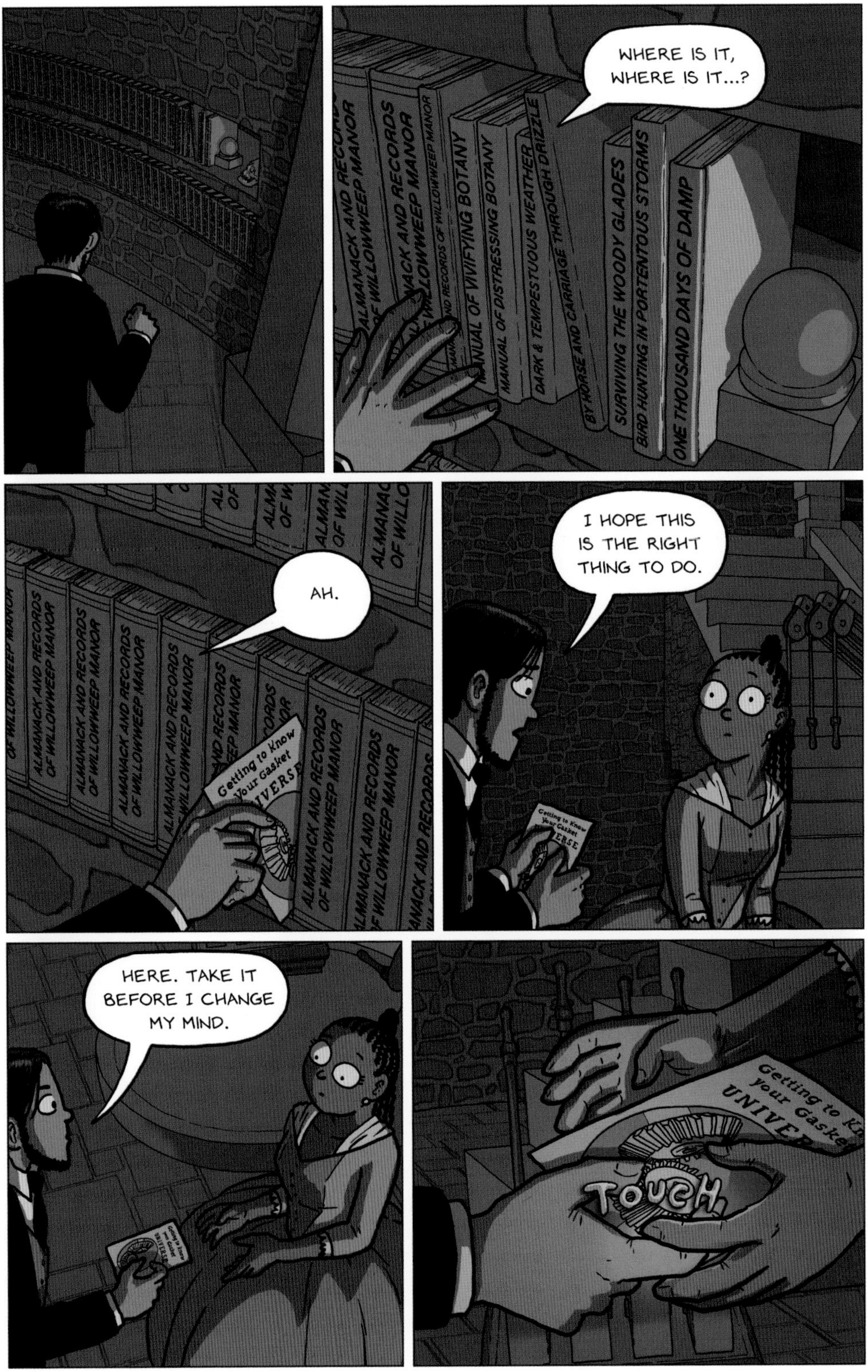
WHERE IS IT, WHERE IS IT...?
ALMANACK AND RECORDS OF WILLOWWEEP MANOR
MANUAL OF VIVIFYING BOTANY
MANUAL OF DISTRESSING BOTANY
DARK & TEMPESTUOUS WEATHER
BY HORSE AND CARRIAGE THROUGH DRIZZLE
SURVIVING THE WOODY GLADES
BIRD HUNTING IN PORTENTOUS STORMS
ONE THOUSAND DAYS OF DAMP
AH.
ALMANACK AND RECORDS OF WILLOWWEEP MANOR
Getting to Know Your Gasket
I HOPE THIS IS THE RIGHT THING TO DO.
HERE. TAKE IT BEFORE I CHANGE MY MIND.
TOUCH

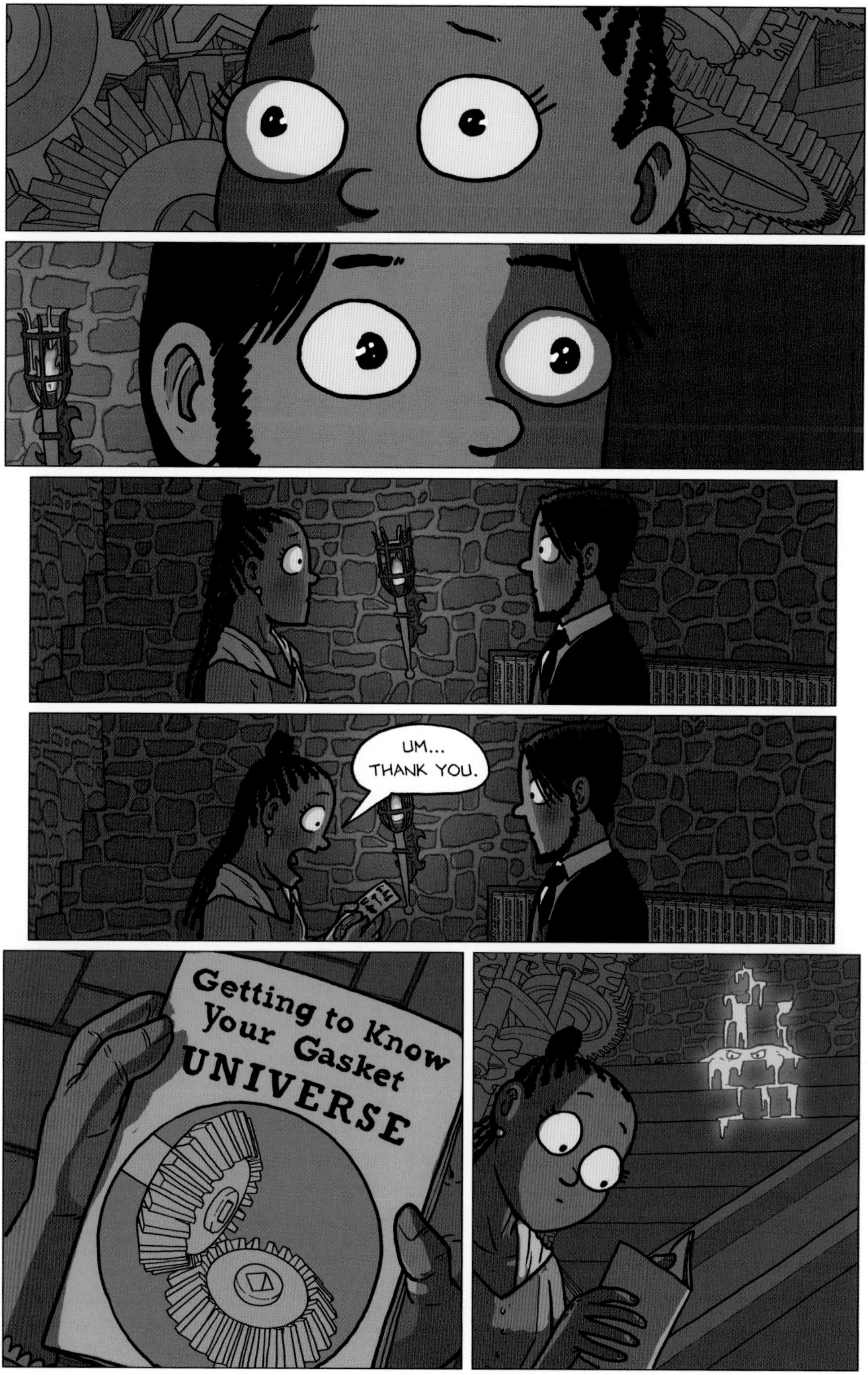
UM...
THANK YOU.
Getting to Know Your Gasket UNIVERSE

3

An Unwelcome Revelation

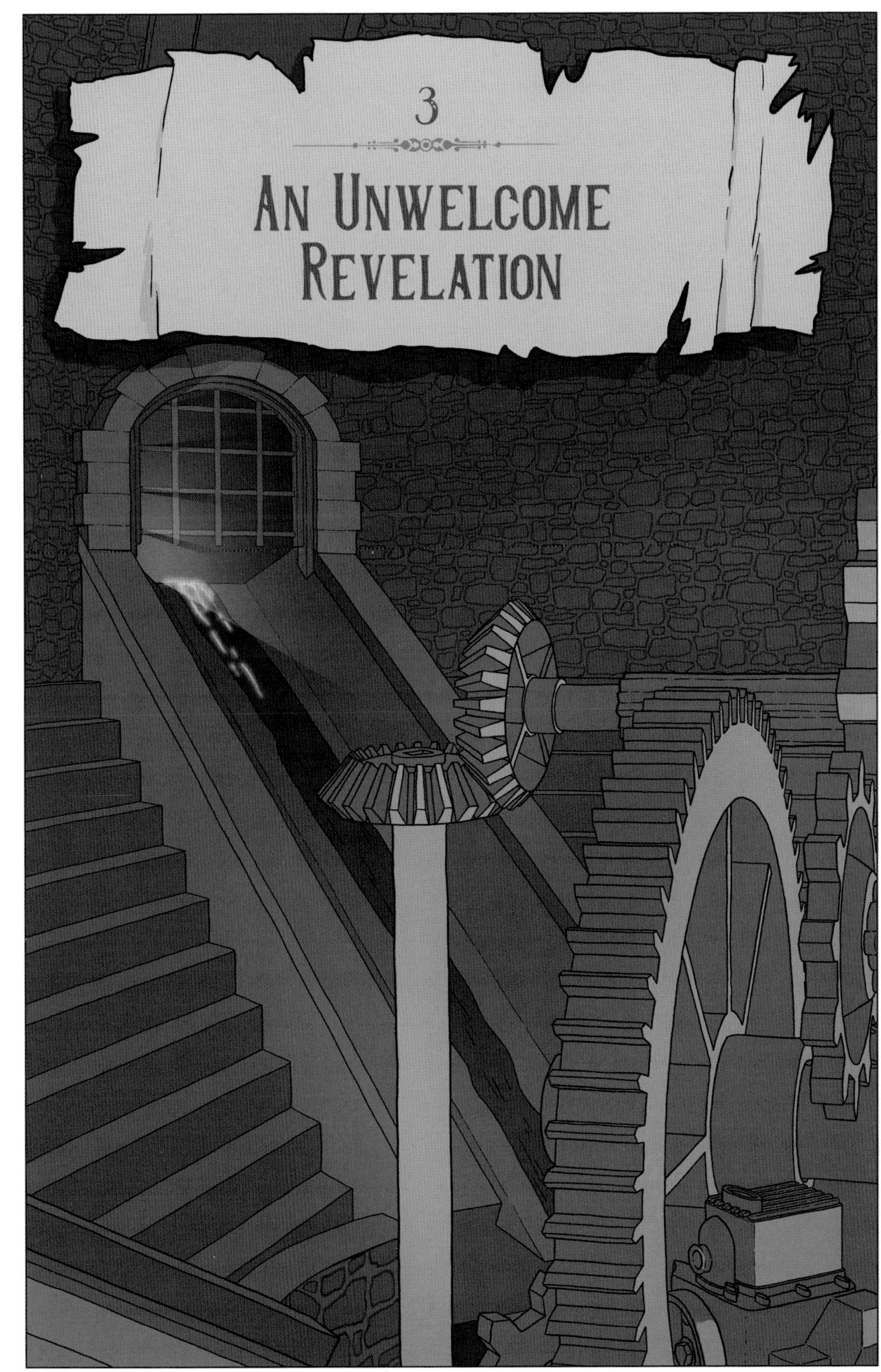

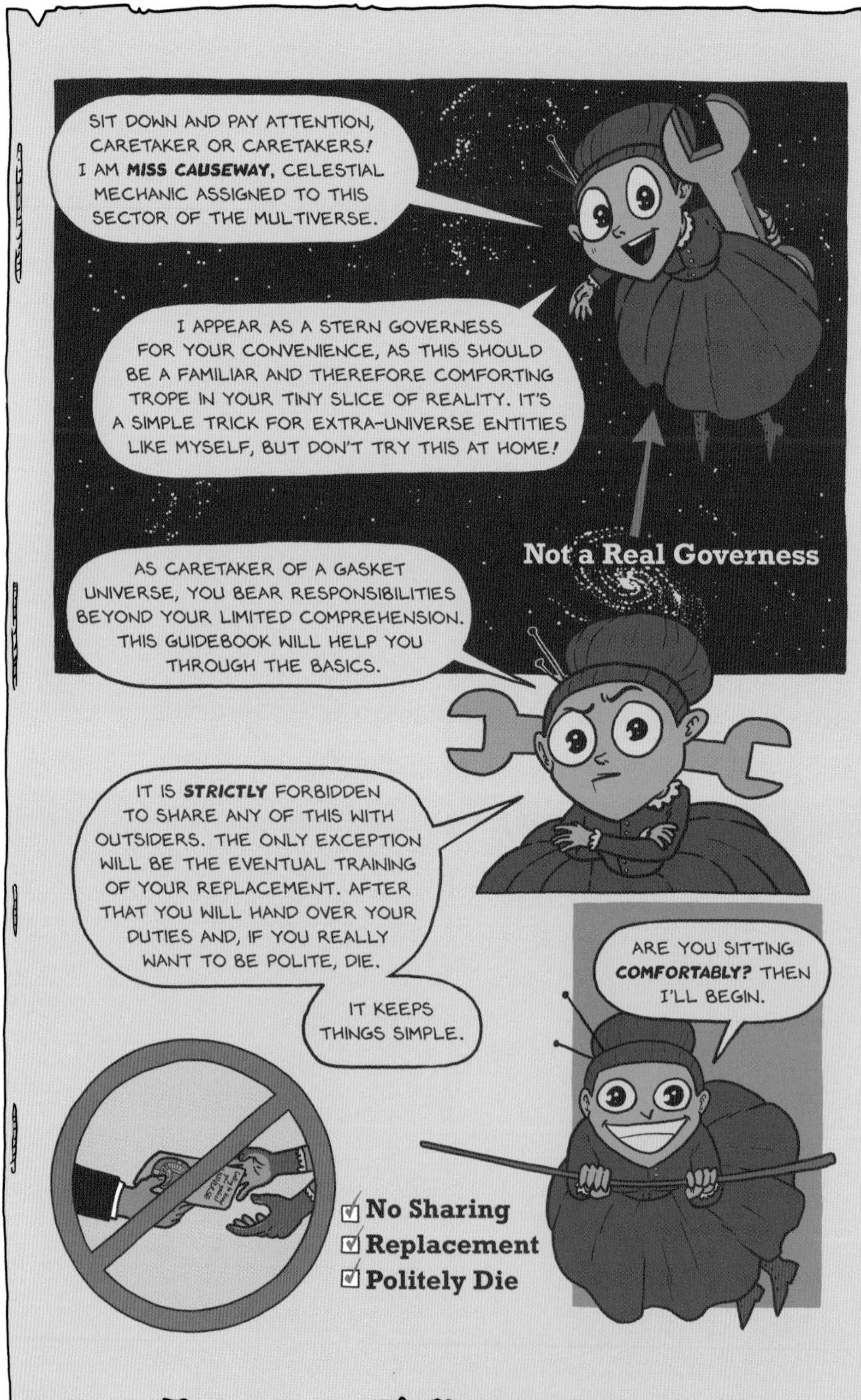
SIT DOWN AND PAY ATTENTION, CARETAKER OR CARETAKERS! I AM **MISS CAUSEWAY**, CELESTIAL MECHANIC ASSIGNED TO THIS SECTOR OF THE MULTIVERSE.
I APPEAR AS A STERN GOVERNESS FOR YOUR CONVENIENCE, AS THIS SHOULD BE A FAMILIAR AND THEREFORE COMFORTING TROPE IN YOUR TINY SLICE OF REALITY. IT'S A SIMPLE TRICK FOR EXTRA-UNIVERSE ENTITIES LIKE MYSELF, BUT DON'T TRY THIS AT HOME!
Not a Real Governess
AS CARETAKER OF A GASKET UNIVERSE, YOU BEAR RESPONSIBILITIES BEYOND YOUR LIMITED COMPREHENSION. THIS GUIDEBOOK WILL HELP YOU THROUGH THE BASICS.
IT IS **STRICTLY** FORBIDDEN TO SHARE ANY OF THIS WITH OUTSIDERS. THE ONLY EXCEPTION WILL BE THE EVENTUAL TRAINING OF YOUR REPLACEMENT. AFTER THAT YOU WILL HAND OVER YOUR DUTIES AND, IF YOU REALLY WANT TO BE POLITE, DIE.
IT KEEPS THINGS SIMPLE.
ARE YOU SITTING **COMFORTABLY?** THEN I'LL BEGIN.
No Sharing
Replacement
Politely Die

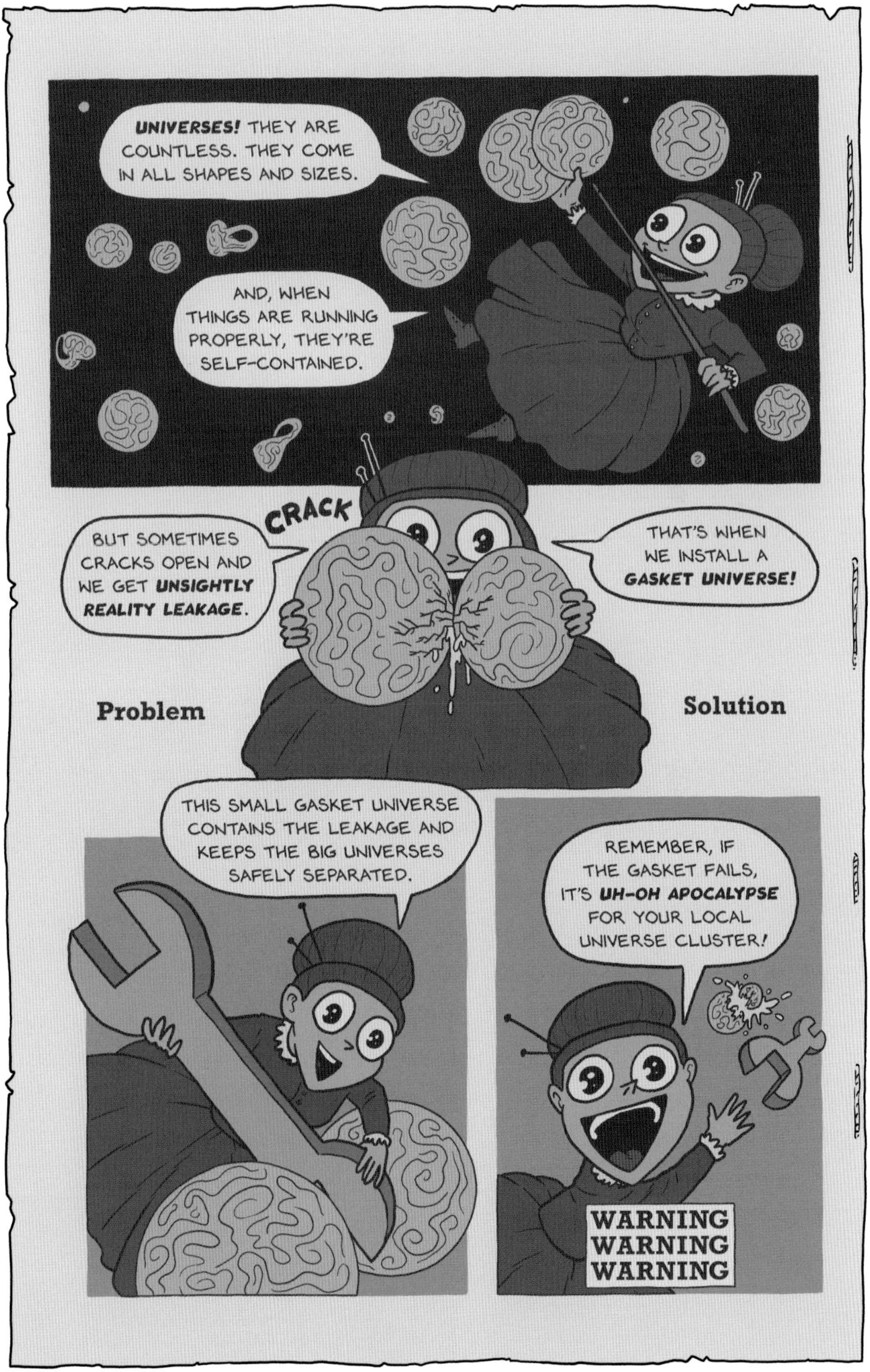
UNIVERSES! THEY ARE COUNTLESS. THEY COME IN ALL SHAPES AND SIZES.
AND, WHEN THINGS ARE RUNNING PROPERLY, THEY'RE SELF-CONTAINED.
CRACK
BUT SOMETIMES CRACKS OPEN AND WE GET UNSIGHTLY REALITY LEAKAGE.
THAT'S WHEN WE INSTALL A GASKET UNIVERSE!
Problem
Solution
THIS SMALL GASKET UNIVERSE CONTAINS THE LEAKAGE AND KEEPS THE BIG UNIVERSES SAFELY SEPARATED.
REMEMBER, IF THE GASKET FAILS, IT'S UH-OH APOCALYPSE FOR YOUR LOCAL UNIVERSE CLUSTER!
WARNING
WARNING
WARNING

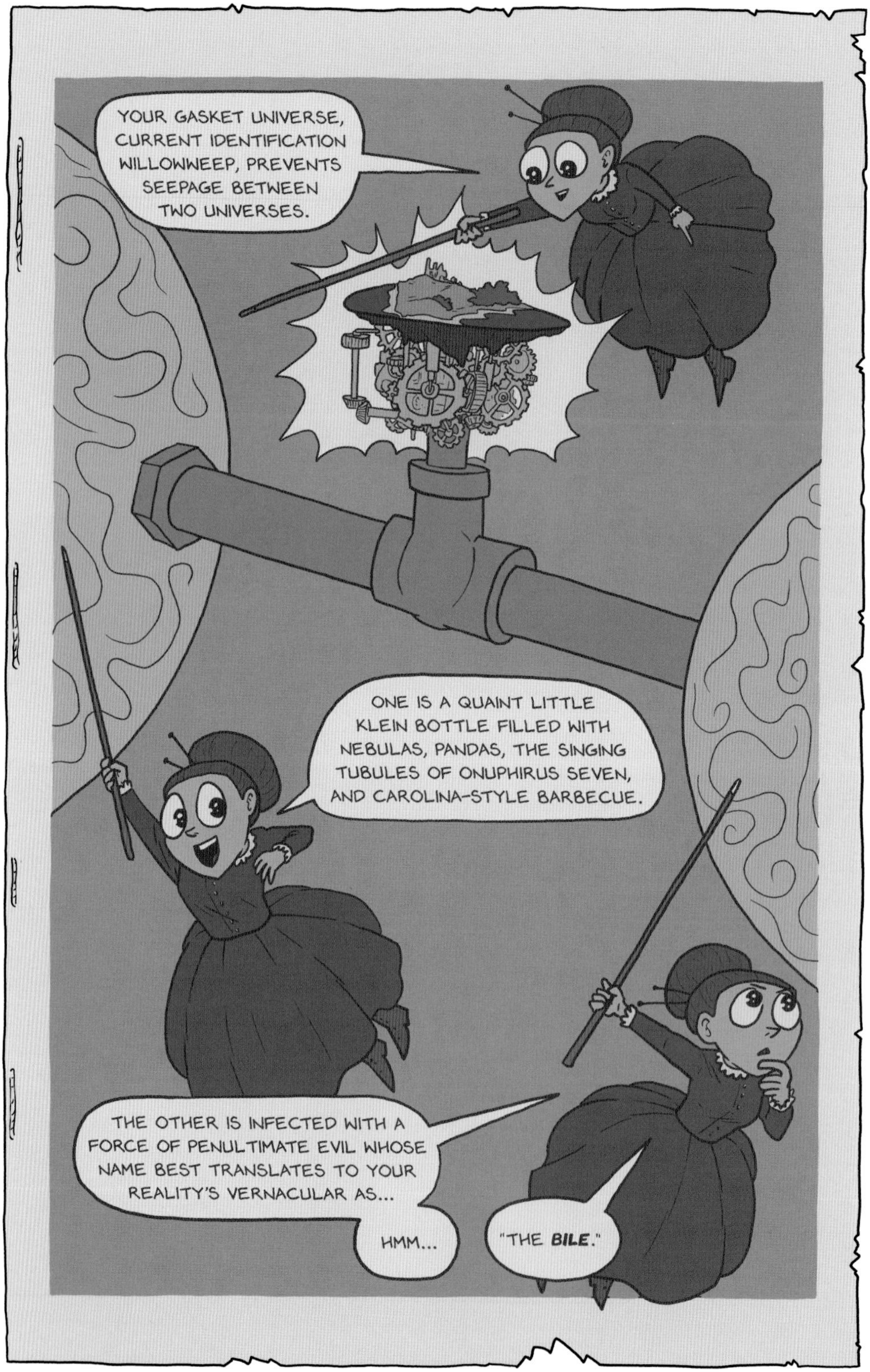
YOUR GASKET UNIVERSE, CURRENT IDENTIFICATION WILLOWWEEP, PREVENTS SEEPAGE BETWEEN TWO UNIVERSES.
ONE IS A QUAINT LITTLE KLEIN BOTTLE FILLED WITH NEBULAS, PANDAS, THE SINGING TUBULES OF ONUPHIRUS SEVEN, AND CAROLINA-STYLE BARBECUE.
THE OTHER IS INFECTED WITH A FORCE OF PENULTIMATE EVIL WHOSE NAME BEST TRANSLATES TO YOUR REALITY'S VERNACULAR AS...
HMM...
"THE BILE."

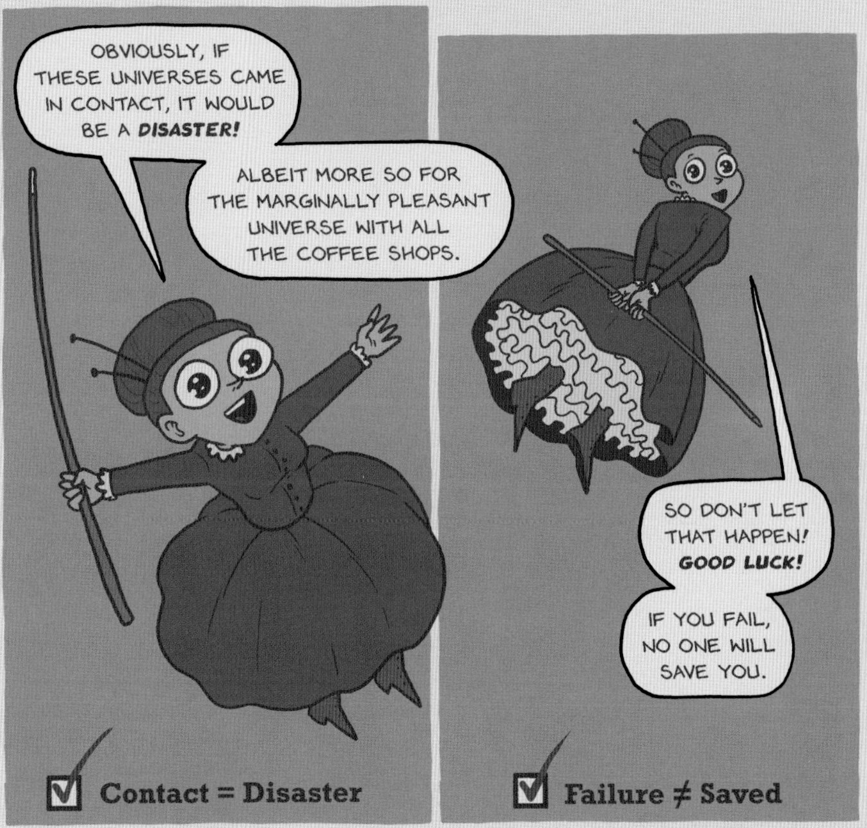
OBVIOUSLY, IF THESE UNIVERSES CAME IN CONTACT, IT WOULD BE A DISASTER!
ALBEIT MORE SO FOR THE MARGINALLY PLEASANT UNIVERSE WITH ALL THE COFFEE SHOPS.
Contact = Disaster
SO DON'T LET THAT HAPPEN! GOOD LUCK!
IF YOU FAIL, NO ONE WILL SAVE YOU.
Failure ≠ Saved

THIS HAS BEEN A MESSAGE FROM

ALL CREATION ITSELF

WE RUN THINGS.
YOU'RE WELCOME.

COMPLAINTS? Call your mom. Maybe she'll make you some nice soup.

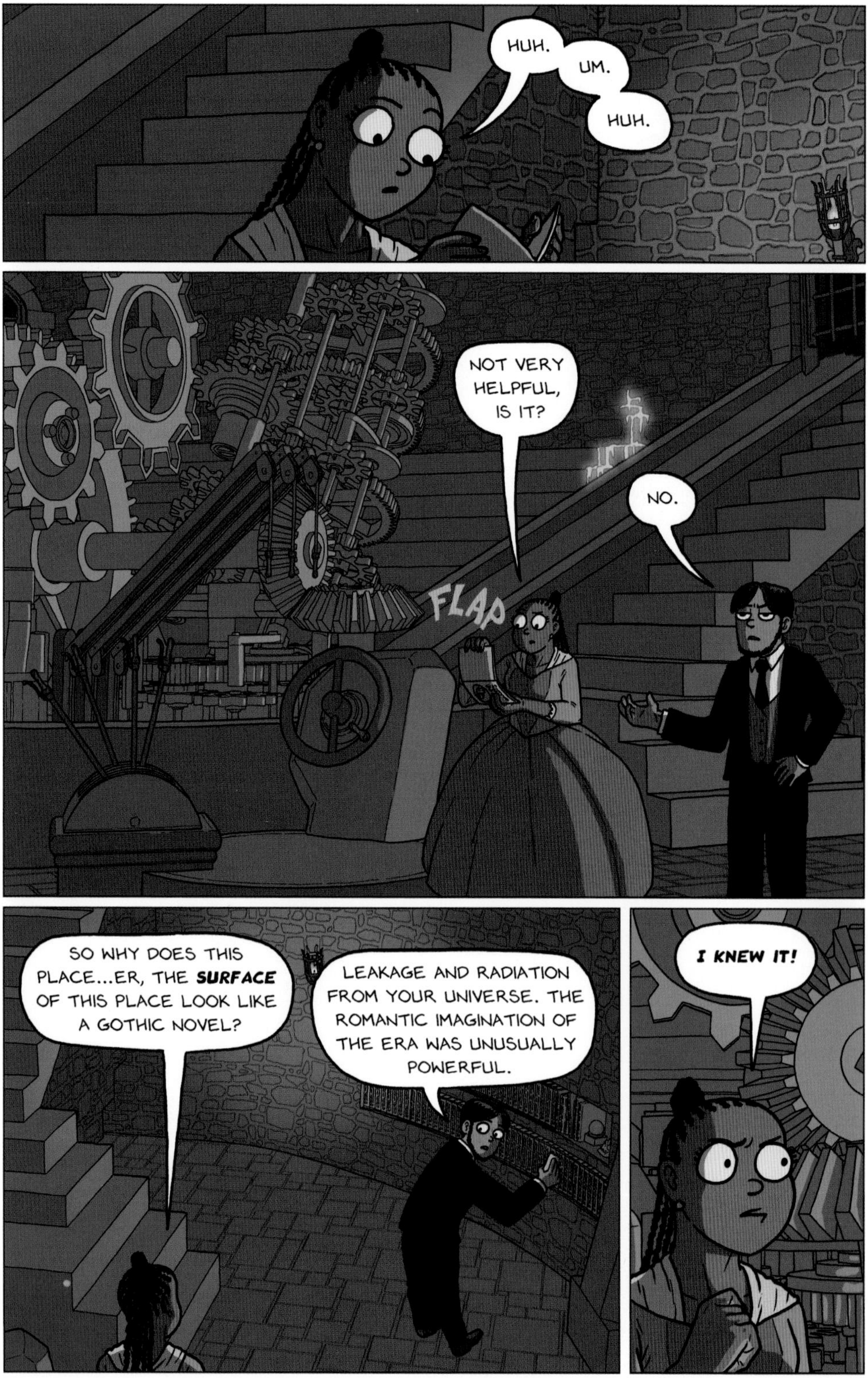
HUH.
UM.
HUH.
NOT VERY HELPFUL, IS IT?
NO.
FLAP
SO WHY DOES THIS PLACE...ER, THE **SURFACE** OF THIS PLACE LOOK LIKE A GOTHIC NOVEL?
LEAKAGE AND RADIATION FROM YOUR UNIVERSE. THE ROMANTIC IMAGINATION OF THE ERA WAS UNUSUALLY POWERFUL.
I KNEW IT!

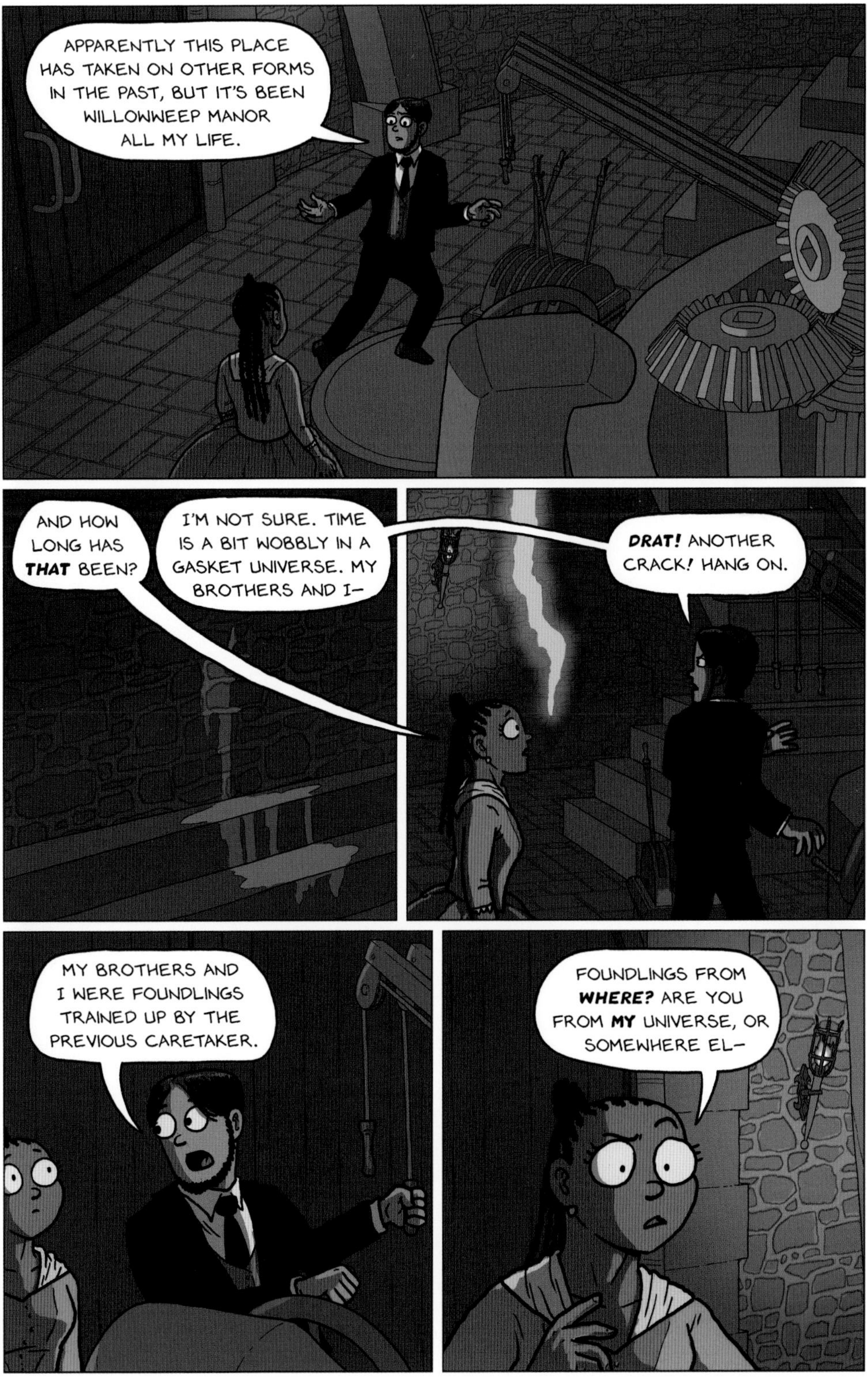
APPARENTLY THIS PLACE HAS TAKEN ON OTHER FORMS IN THE PAST, BUT IT'S BEEN WILLOWWEEP MANOR ALL MY LIFE.
AND HOW LONG HAS **THAT** BEEN?
I'M NOT SURE. TIME IS A BIT WOBBLY IN A GASKET UNIVERSE. MY BROTHERS AND I—
DRAT! ANOTHER CRACK! HANG ON.
MY BROTHERS AND I WERE FOUNDLINGS TRAINED UP BY THE PREVIOUS CARETAKER.
FOUNDLINGS FROM **WHERE?** ARE YOU FROM **MY** UNIVERSE, OR SOMEWHERE EL—

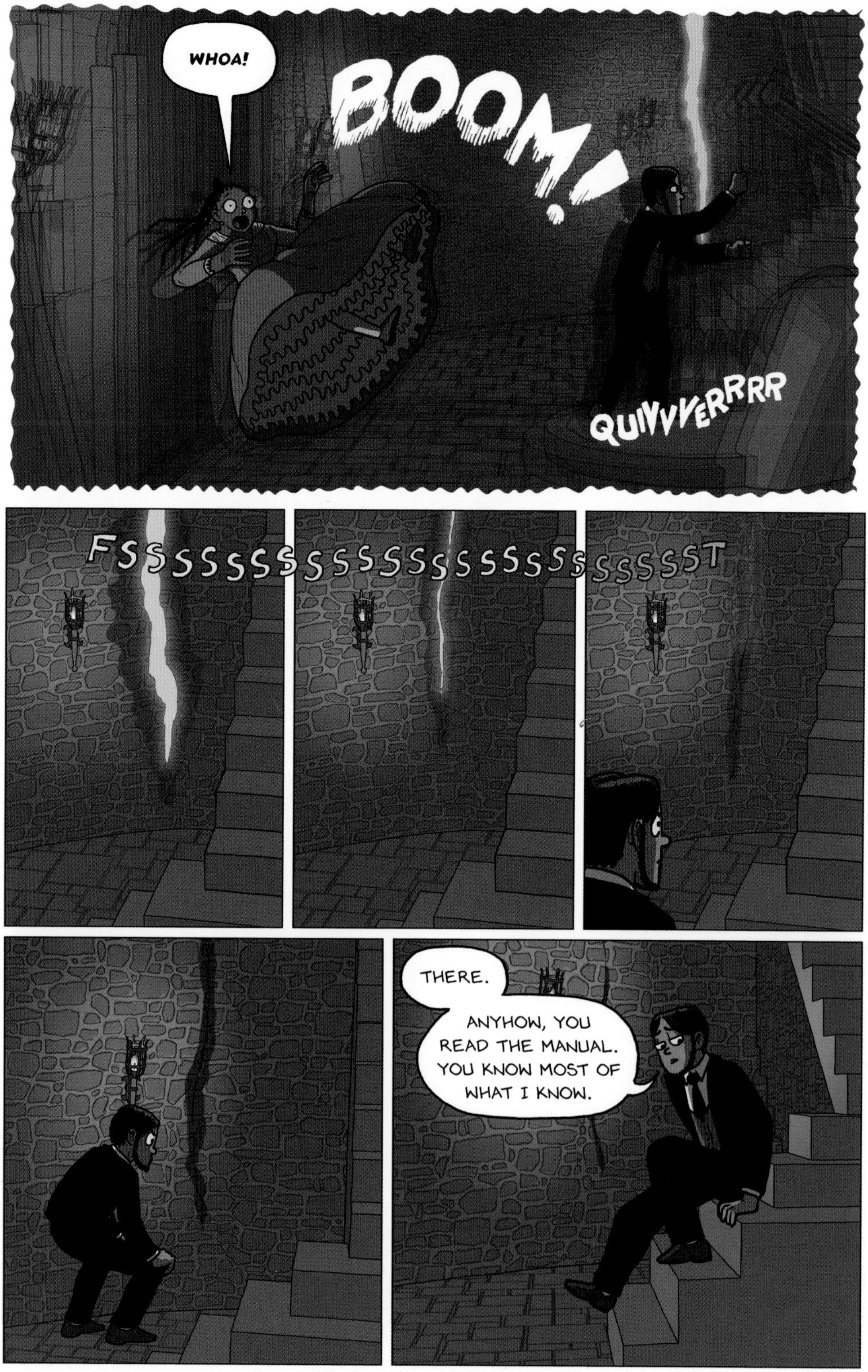
WHOA!
BOOM!
QUIVVVERRRR
FSSSSSSSSSSSSSSSSSSSSSSSSST
THERE.
ANYHOW, YOU READ THE MANUAL. YOU KNOW MOST OF WHAT I KNOW.

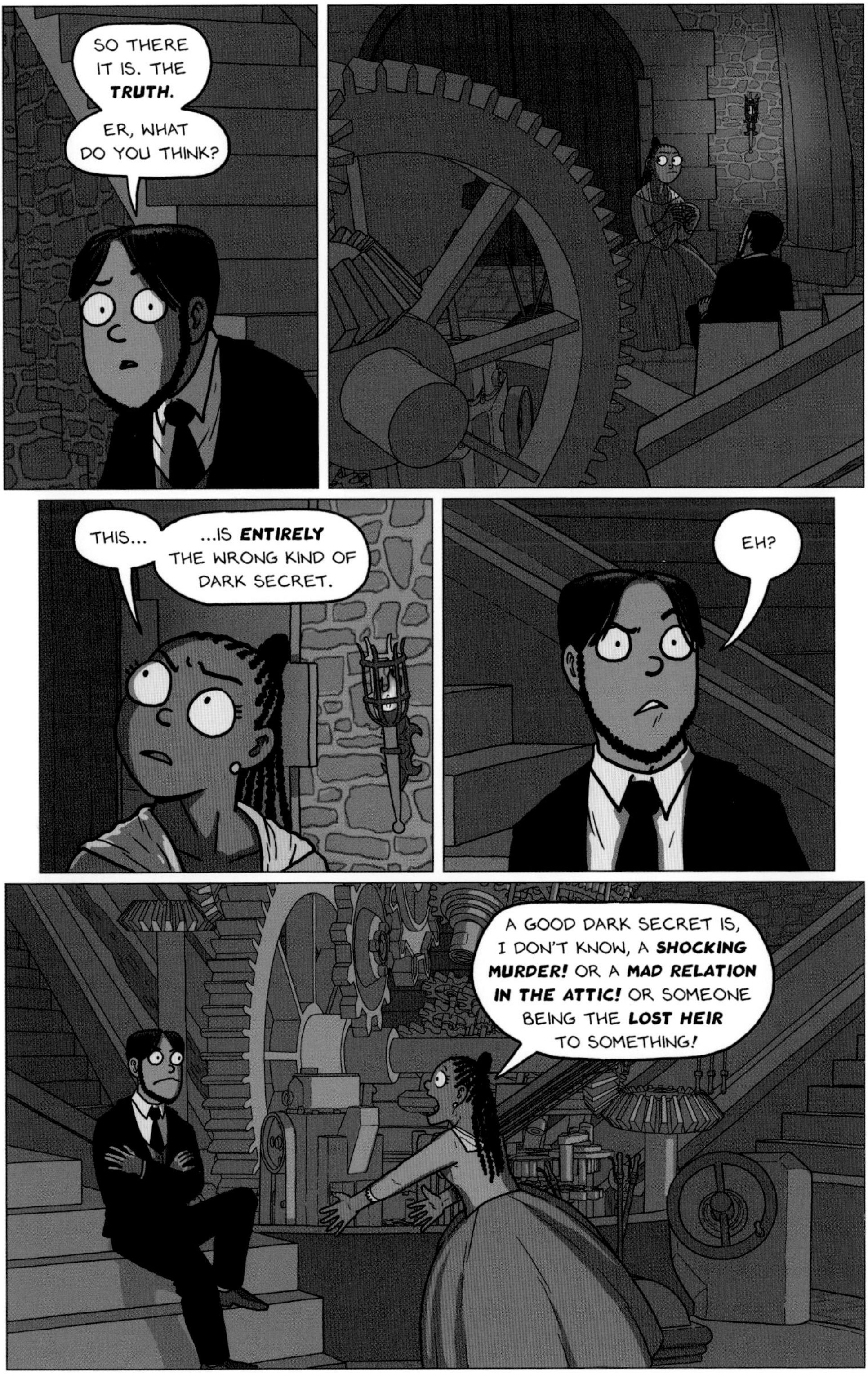
SO THERE IT IS. THE **TRUTH**.
ER, WHAT DO YOU THINK?
THIS...
...IS **ENTIRELY** THE WRONG KIND OF DARK SECRET.
EH?
A GOOD DARK SECRET IS, I DON'T KNOW, A **SHOCKING MURDER!** OR A **MAD RELATION IN THE ATTIC!** OR SOMEONE BEING THE **LOST HEIR** TO SOMETHING!

THIS IS...

WAVE WAVE WAVE WAVE WAVE WAVE

...COMPLICATED!

I CAN'T DEAL WITH *THIS!*

WELL, *EXCUSE* US FOR EXISTING ON OUR OWN LEVEL OF REALITY AND NOT IN YOUR *PERSONAL FANTASY WORLD!*

ARGH...I *KNEW* THIS WOULD BE HARD TO EXPLAIN TO OUTSIDERS. I'D HOPED TO CONTACT SOMEONE *USEFUL.*

LIKE A GOOD DUKE OR A FRIAR OR A NATURAL SCIENTIST—

I...I NEED FRESH AIR.

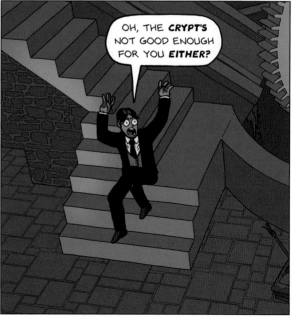

OH, THE *CRYPT'S* NOT GOOD ENOUGH FOR YOU *EITHER?*

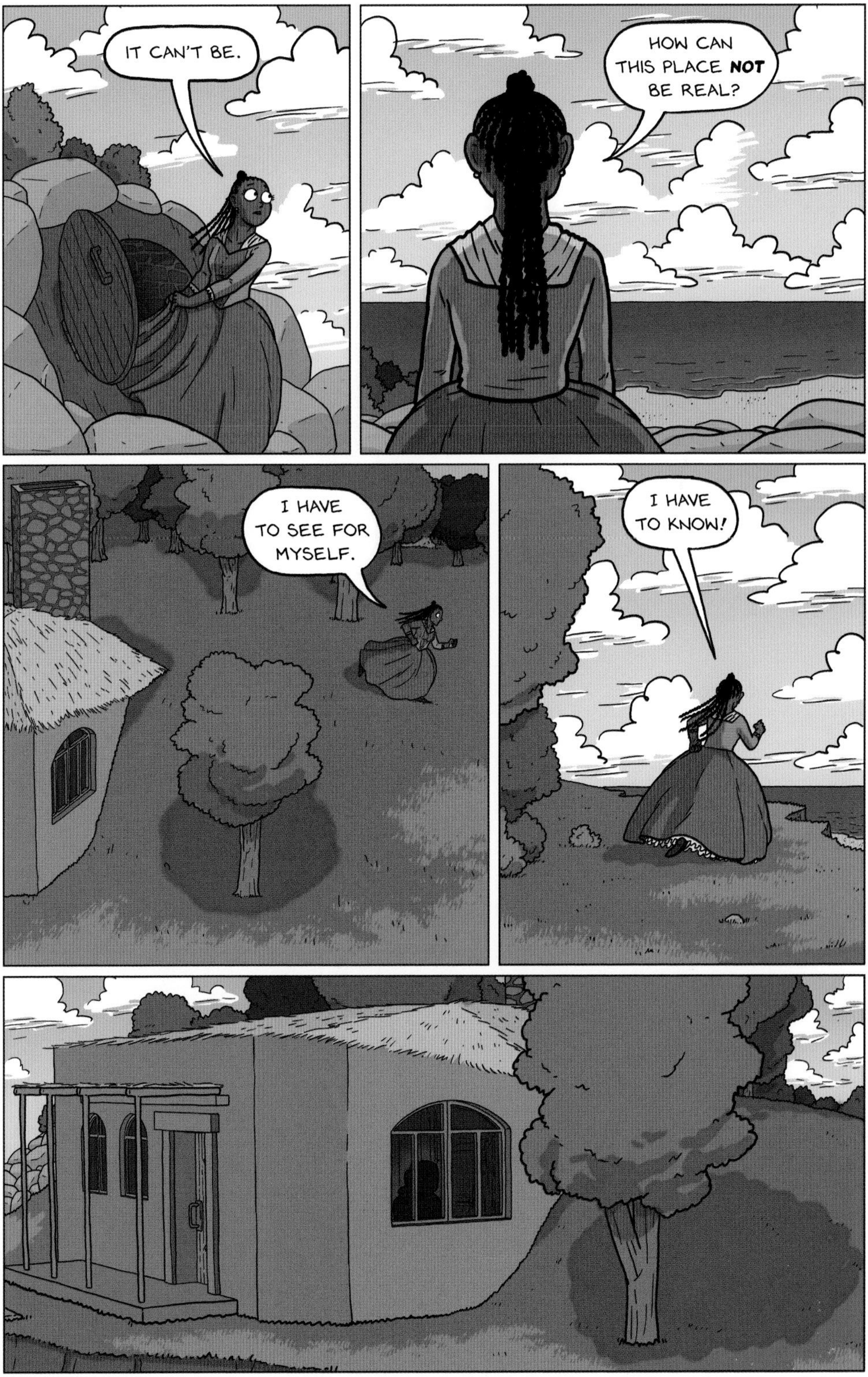
IT CAN'T BE.
HOW CAN THIS PLACE **NOT** BE REAL?
I HAVE TO SEE FOR MYSELF.
I HAVE TO KNOW!

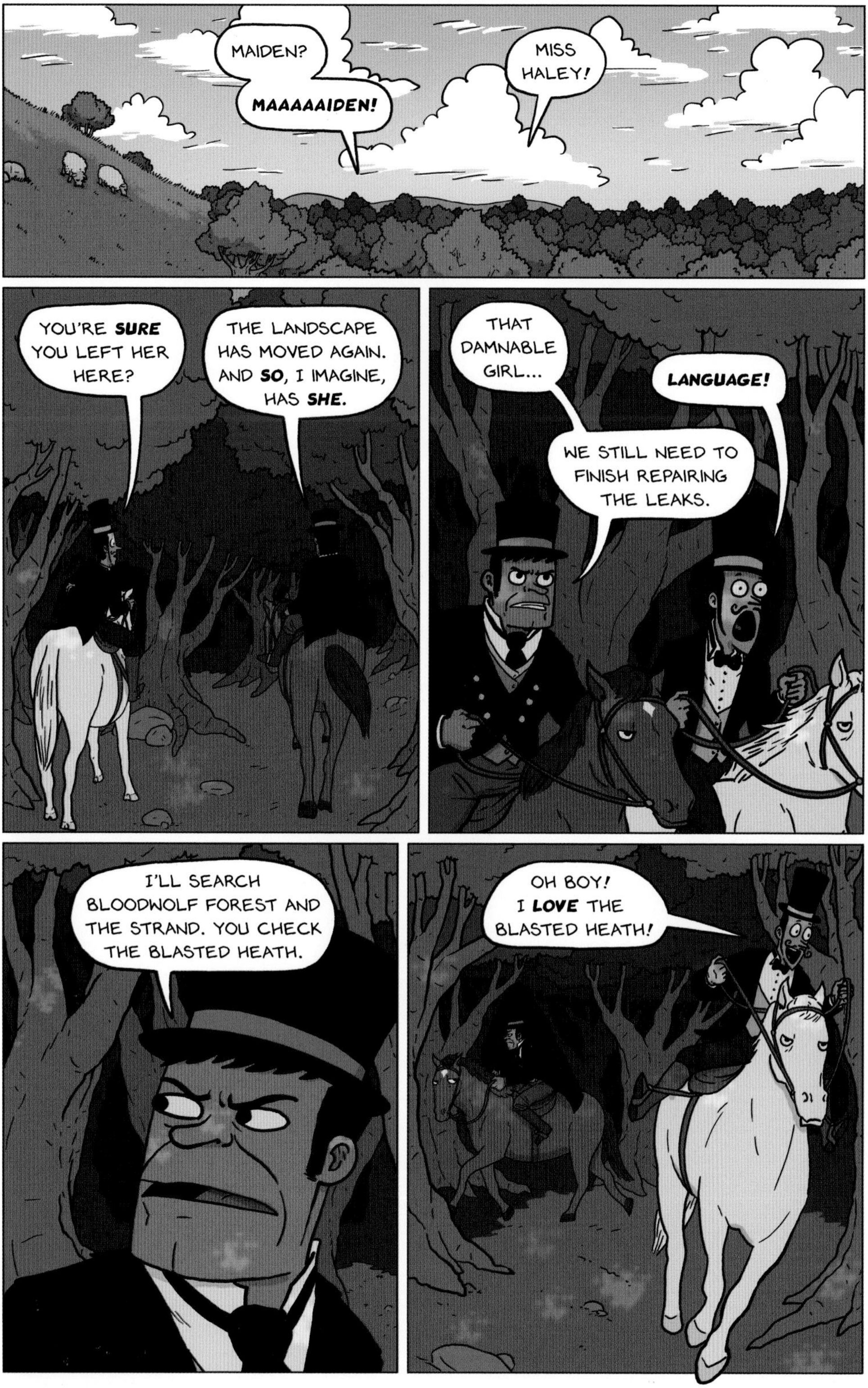
MAIDEN?
MAAAAAIDEN!
MISS HALEY!
YOU'RE SURE YOU LEFT HER HERE?
THE LANDSCAPE HAS MOVED AGAIN. AND SO, I IMAGINE, HAS SHE.
THAT DAMNABLE GIRL...
LANGUAGE!
WE STILL NEED TO FINISH REPAIRING THE LEAKS.
I'LL SEARCH BLOODWOLF FOREST AND THE STRAND. YOU CHECK THE BLASTED HEATH.
OH BOY! I LOVE THE BLASTED HEATH!

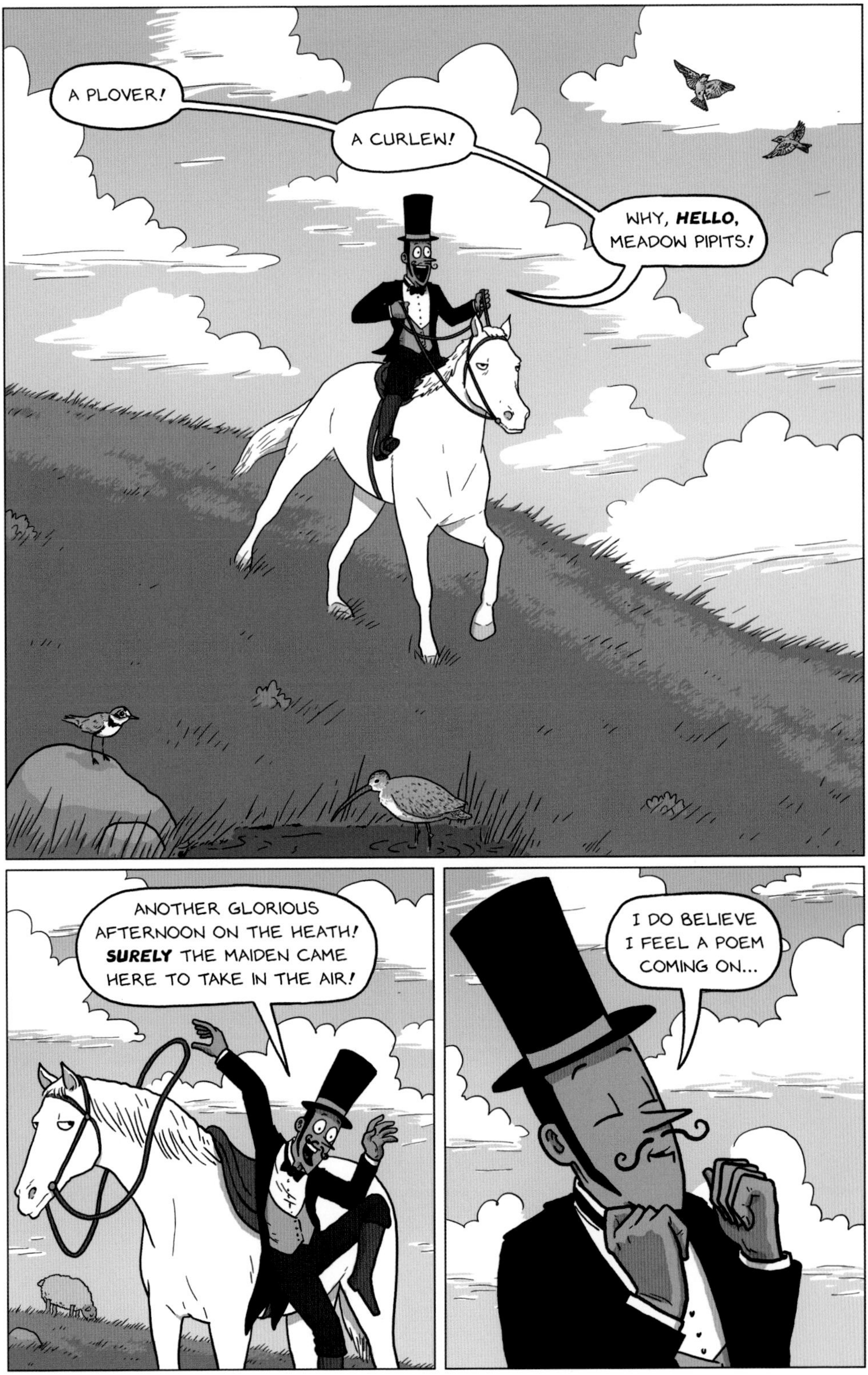
A PLOVER!
A CURLEW!
WHY, **HELLO,** MEADOW PIPITS!
ANOTHER GLORIOUS AFTERNOON ON THE HEATH! **SURELY** THE MAIDEN CAME HERE TO TAKE IN THE AIR!
I DO BELIEVE I FEEL A POEM COMING ON...

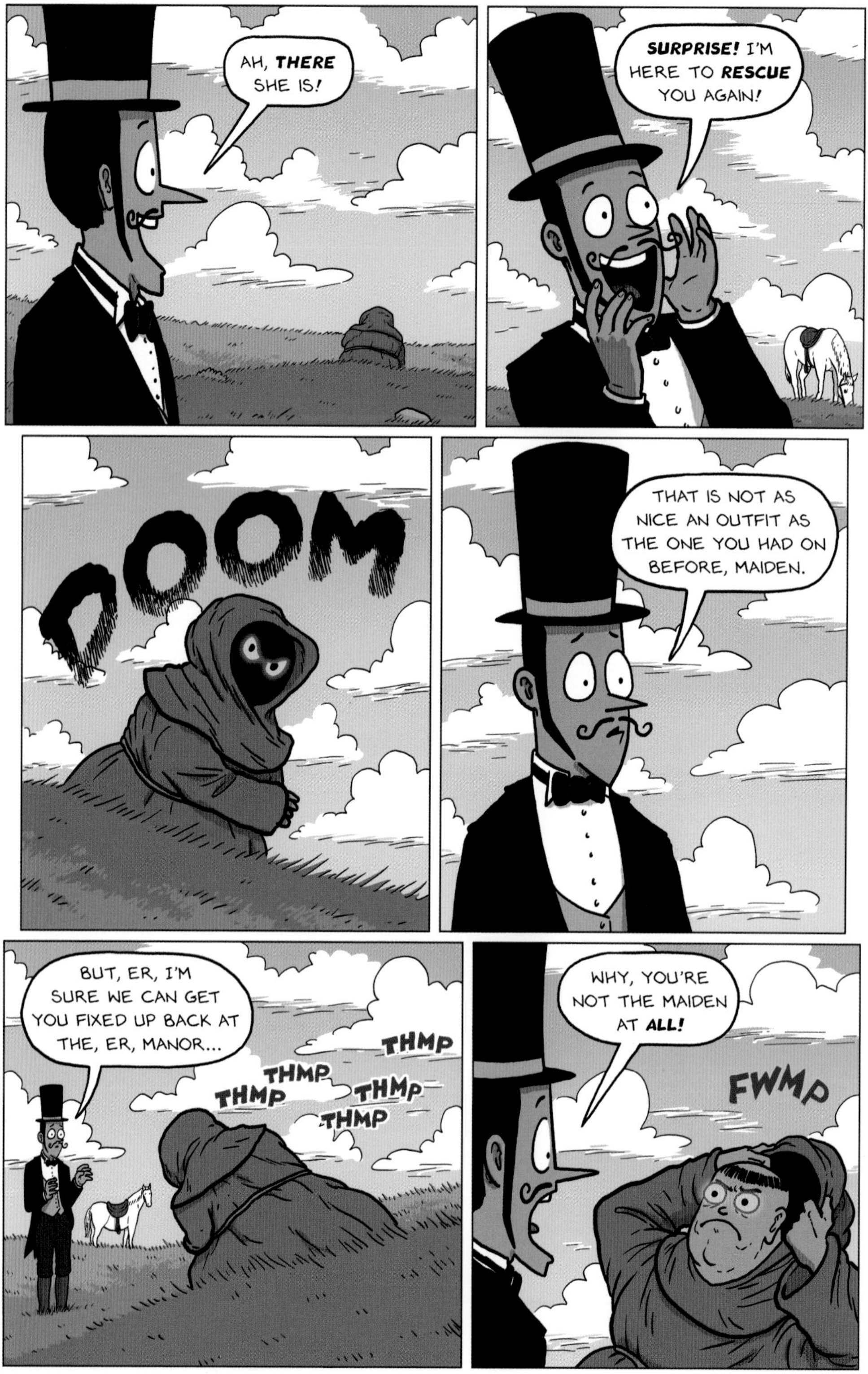
AH, **THERE** SHE IS!
SURPRISE! I'M HERE TO **RESCUE** YOU AGAIN!
DOOM
THAT IS NOT AS NICE AN OUTFIT AS THE ONE YOU HAD ON BEFORE, MAIDEN.
BUT, ER, I'M SURE WE CAN GET YOU FIXED UP BACK AT THE, ER, MANOR...
THMP
THMP
THMP
THMP
THMP
WHY, YOU'RE NOT THE MAIDEN AT **ALL!**
FWMP

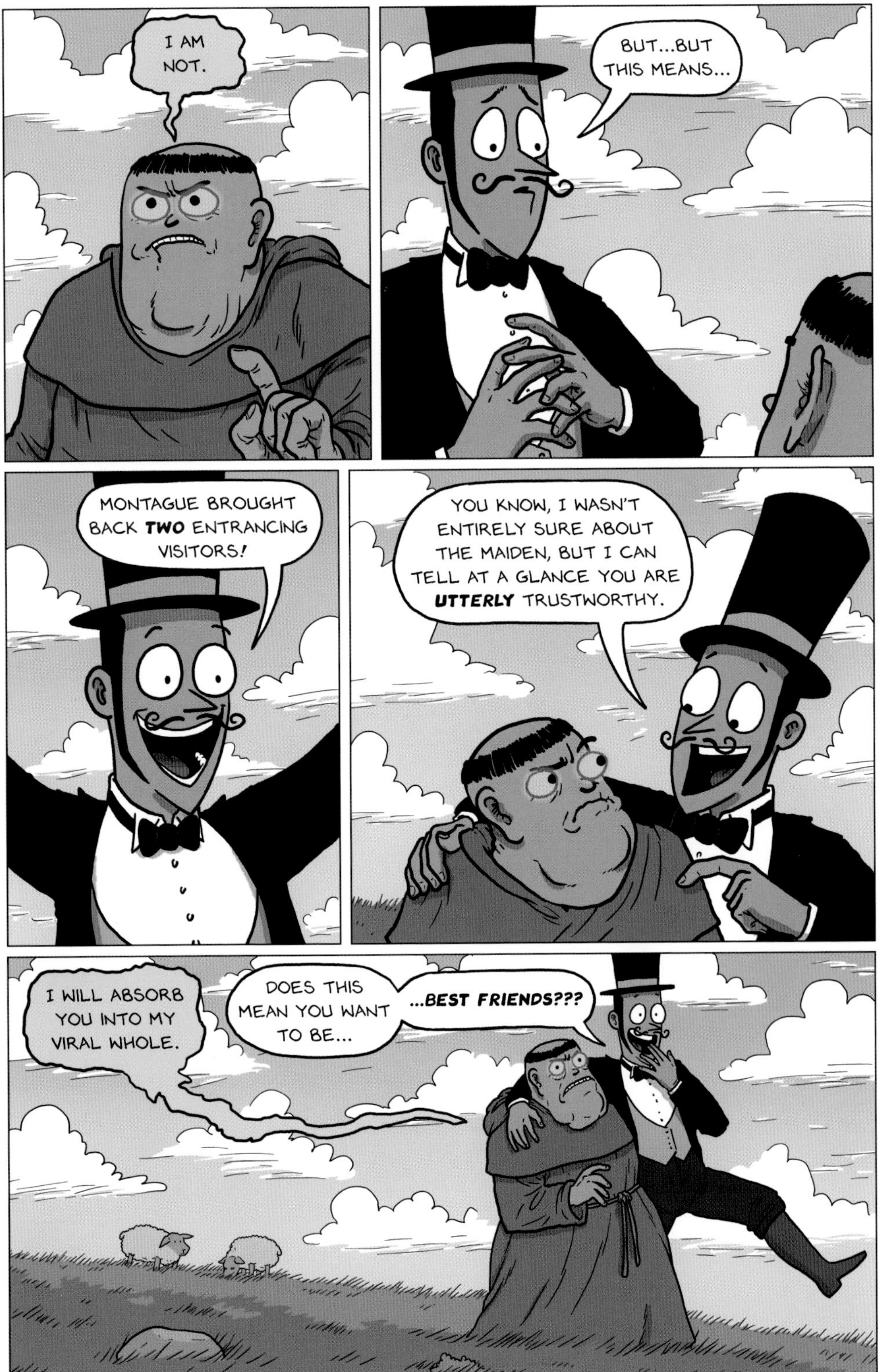
I AM NOT.
BUT...BUT THIS MEANS...
MONTAGUE BROUGHT BACK **TWO** ENTRANCING VISITORS!
YOU KNOW, I WASN'T ENTIRELY SURE ABOUT THE MAIDEN, BUT I CAN TELL AT A GLANCE YOU ARE **UTTERLY** TRUSTWORTHY.
I WILL ABSORB YOU INTO MY VIRAL WHOLE.
DOES THIS MEAN YOU WANT TO BE...
...BEST FRIENDS???

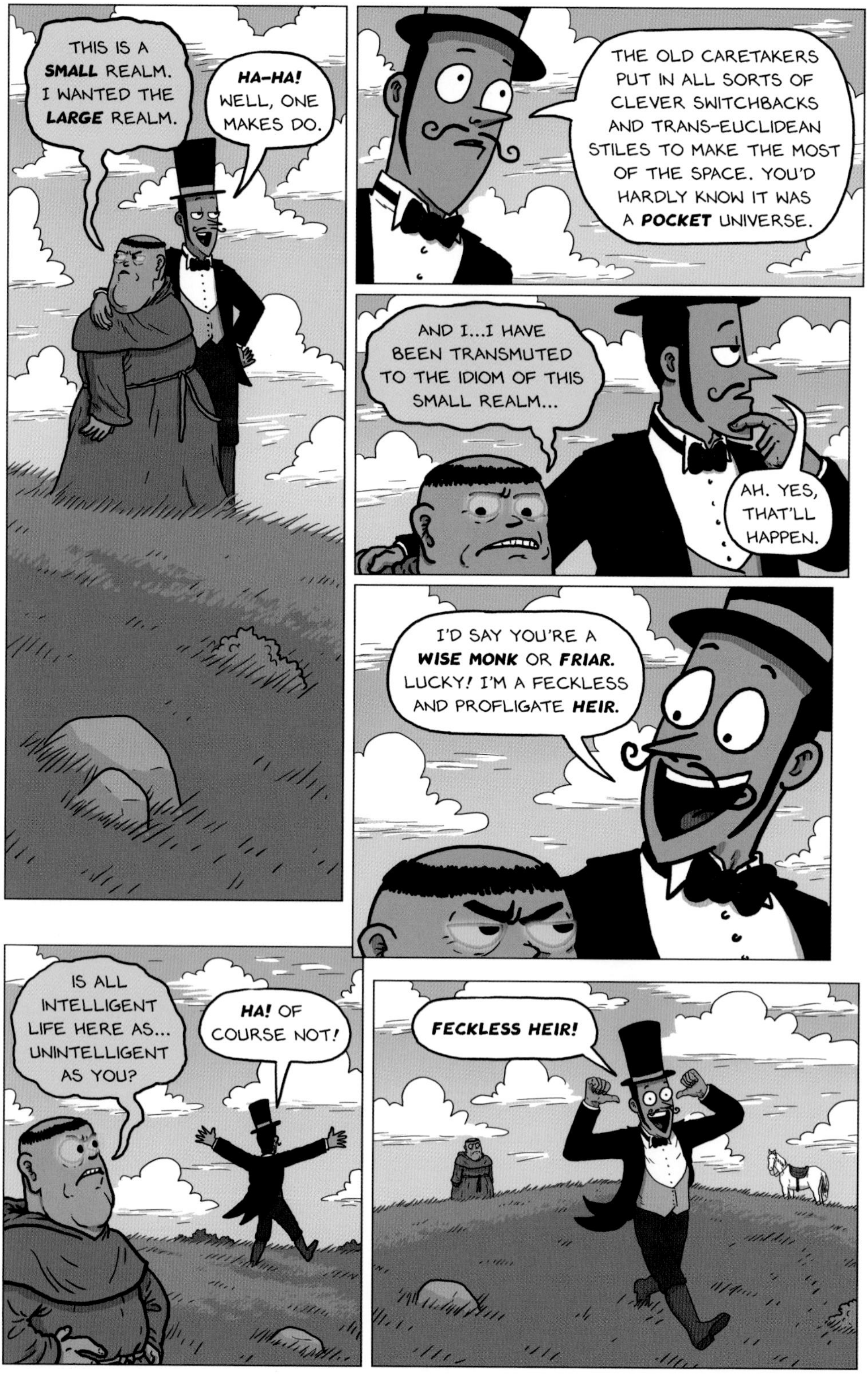

THIS IS A SMALL REALM. I WANTED THE LARGE REALM.
HA-HA! WELL, ONE MAKES DO.
THE OLD CARETAKERS PUT IN ALL SORTS OF CLEVER SWITCHBACKS AND TRANS-EUCLIDEAN STILES TO MAKE THE MOST OF THE SPACE. YOU'D HARDLY KNOW IT WAS A POCKET UNIVERSE.
AND I...I HAVE BEEN TRANSMUTED TO THE IDIOM OF THIS SMALL REALM...
AH. YES, THAT'LL HAPPEN.
I'D SAY YOU'RE A WISE MONK OR FRIAR. LUCKY! I'M A FECKLESS AND PROFLIGATE HEIR.
IS ALL INTELLIGENT LIFE HERE AS... UNINTELLIGENT AS YOU?
HA! OF COURSE NOT!
FECKLESS HEIR!

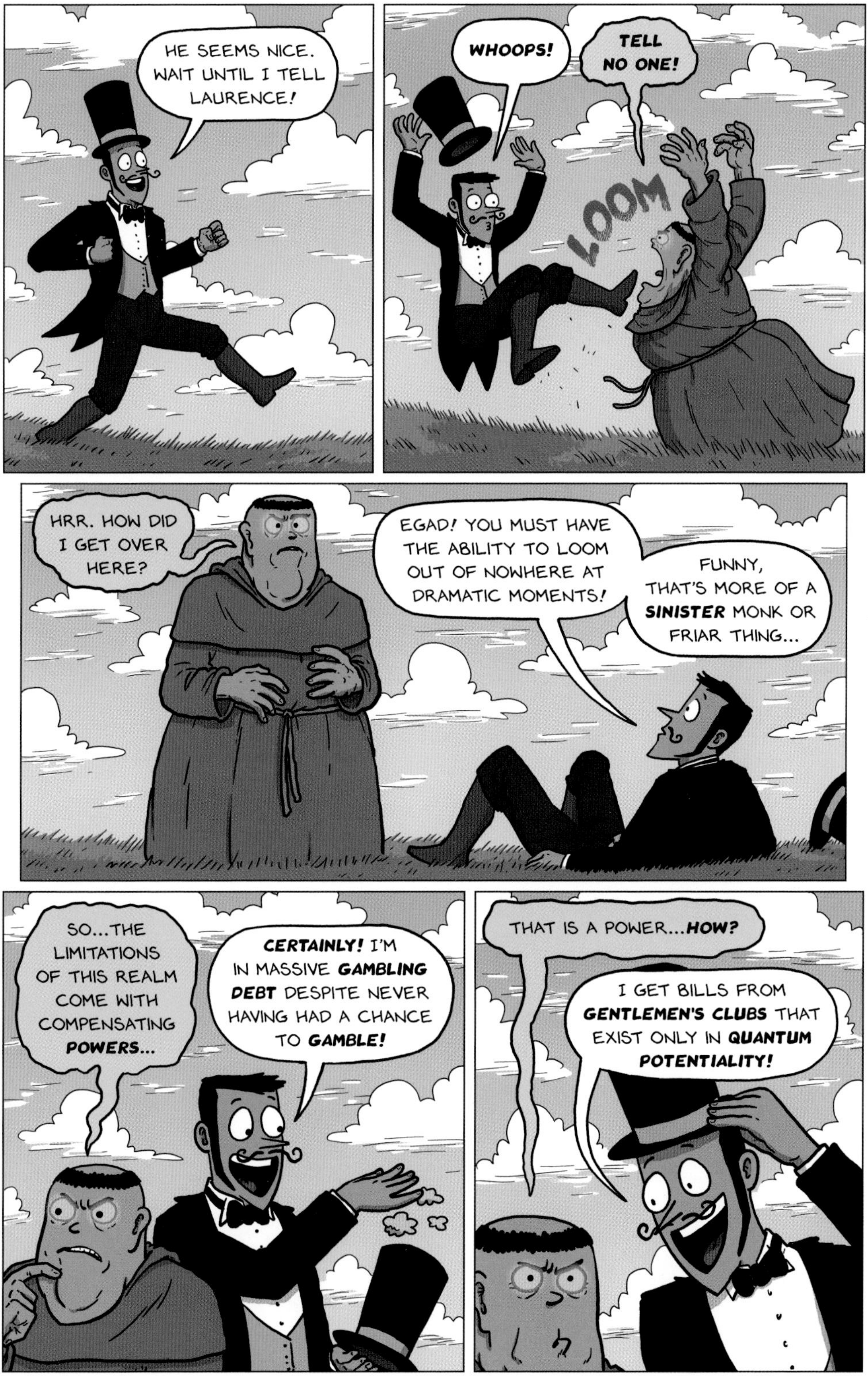
HE SEEMS NICE. WAIT UNTIL I TELL LAURENCE!
WHOOPS!
TELL NO ONE!
LOOM
HRR. HOW DID I GET OVER HERE?
EGAD! YOU MUST HAVE THE ABILITY TO LOOM OUT OF NOWHERE AT DRAMATIC MOMENTS!
FUNNY, THAT'S MORE OF A **SINISTER** MONK OR FRIAR THING...
SO...THE LIMITATIONS OF THIS REALM COME WITH COMPENSATING **POWERS...**
CERTAINLY! I'M IN MASSIVE **GAMBLING DEBT** DESPITE NEVER HAVING HAD A CHANCE TO **GAMBLE!**
THAT IS A POWER...**HOW?**
I GET BILLS FROM **GENTLEMEN'S CLUBS** THAT EXIST ONLY IN **QUANTUM POTENTIALITY!**

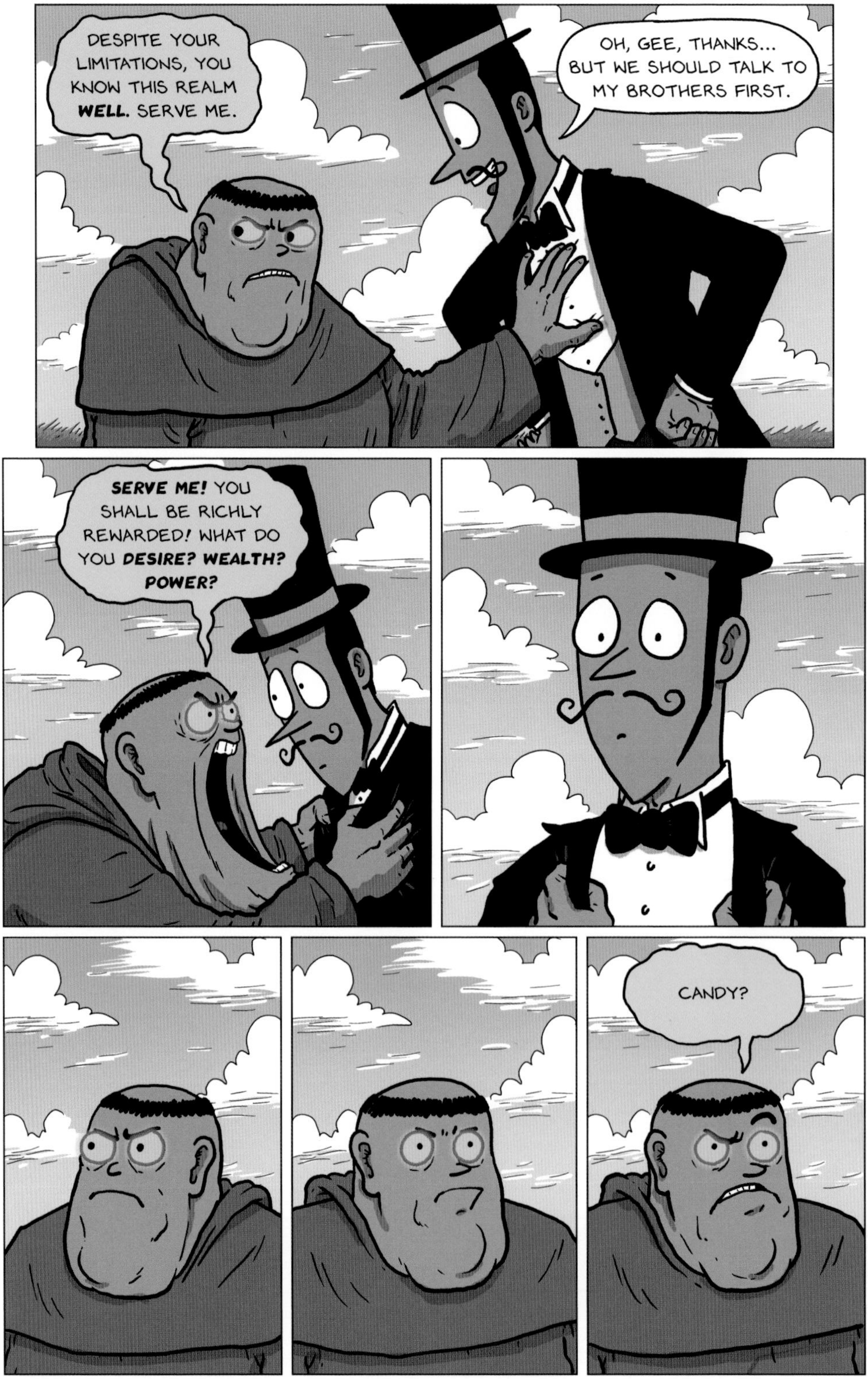
DESPITE YOUR LIMITATIONS, YOU KNOW THIS REALM **WELL.** SERVE ME.
OH, GEE, THANKS... BUT WE SHOULD TALK TO MY BROTHERS FIRST.
SERVE ME! YOU SHALL BE RICHLY REWARDED! WHAT DO YOU **DESIRE? WEALTH? POWER?**
CANDY?

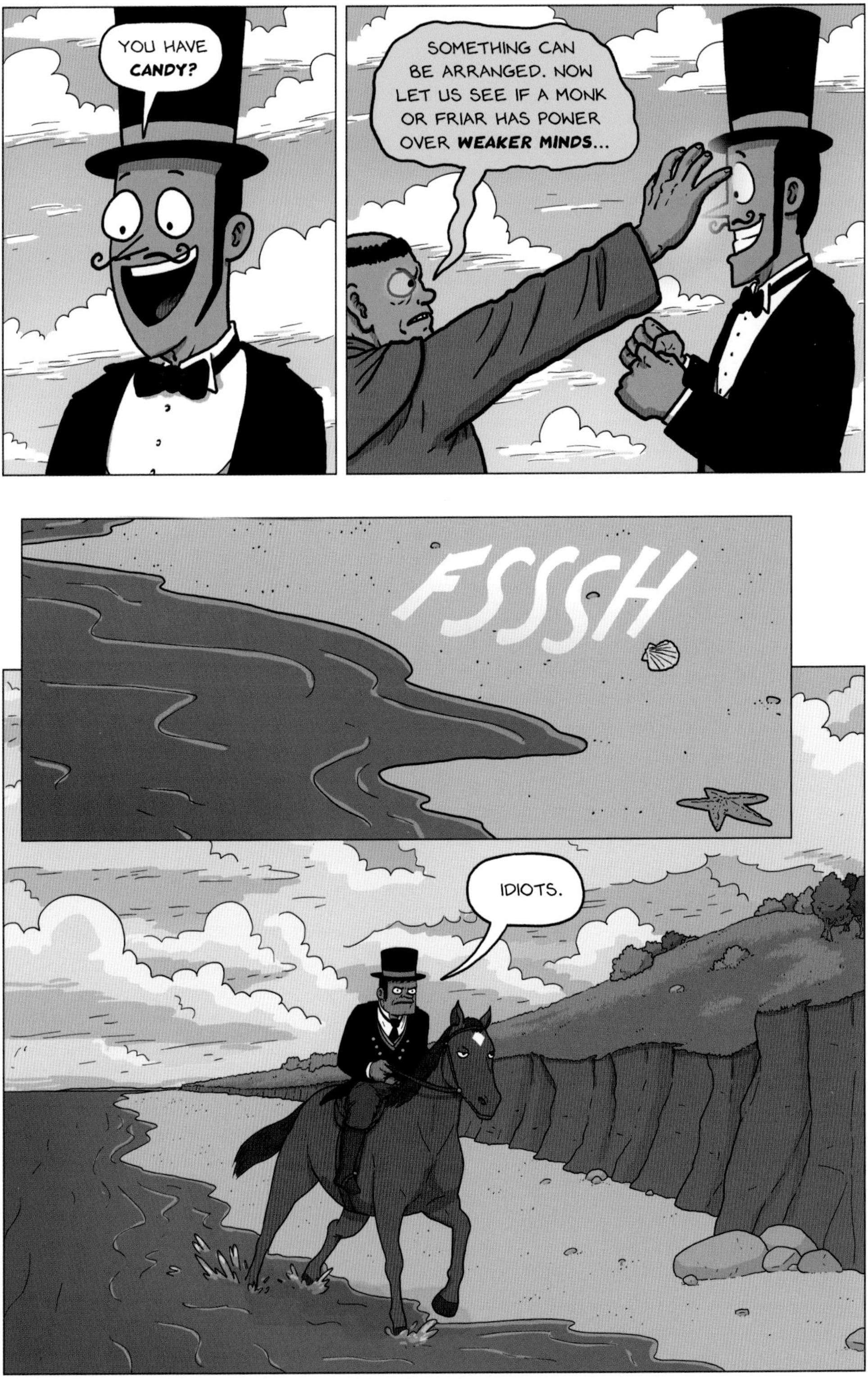
YOU HAVE **CANDY?**
SOMETHING CAN BE ARRANGED. NOW LET US SEE IF A MONK OR FRIAR HAS POWER OVER **WEAKER MINDS...**
FSSSH
IDIOTS.

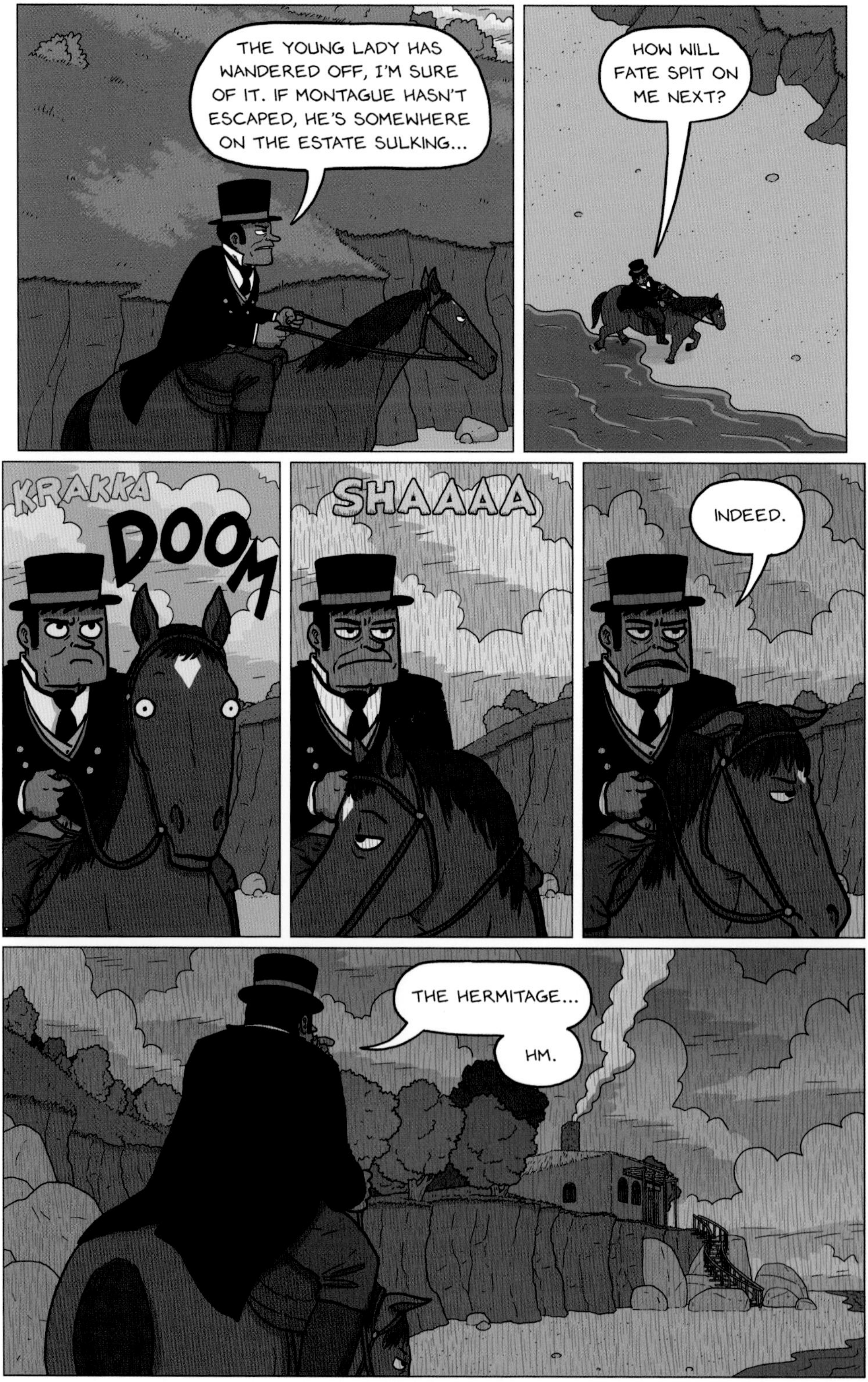
THE YOUNG LADY HAS WANDERED OFF, I'M SURE OF IT. IF MONTAGUE HASN'T ESCAPED, HE'S SOMEWHERE ON THE ESTATE SULKING...
HOW WILL FATE SPIT ON ME NEXT?
KRAKKA
DOOM
SHAAAA
INDEED.
THE HERMITAGE...
HM.

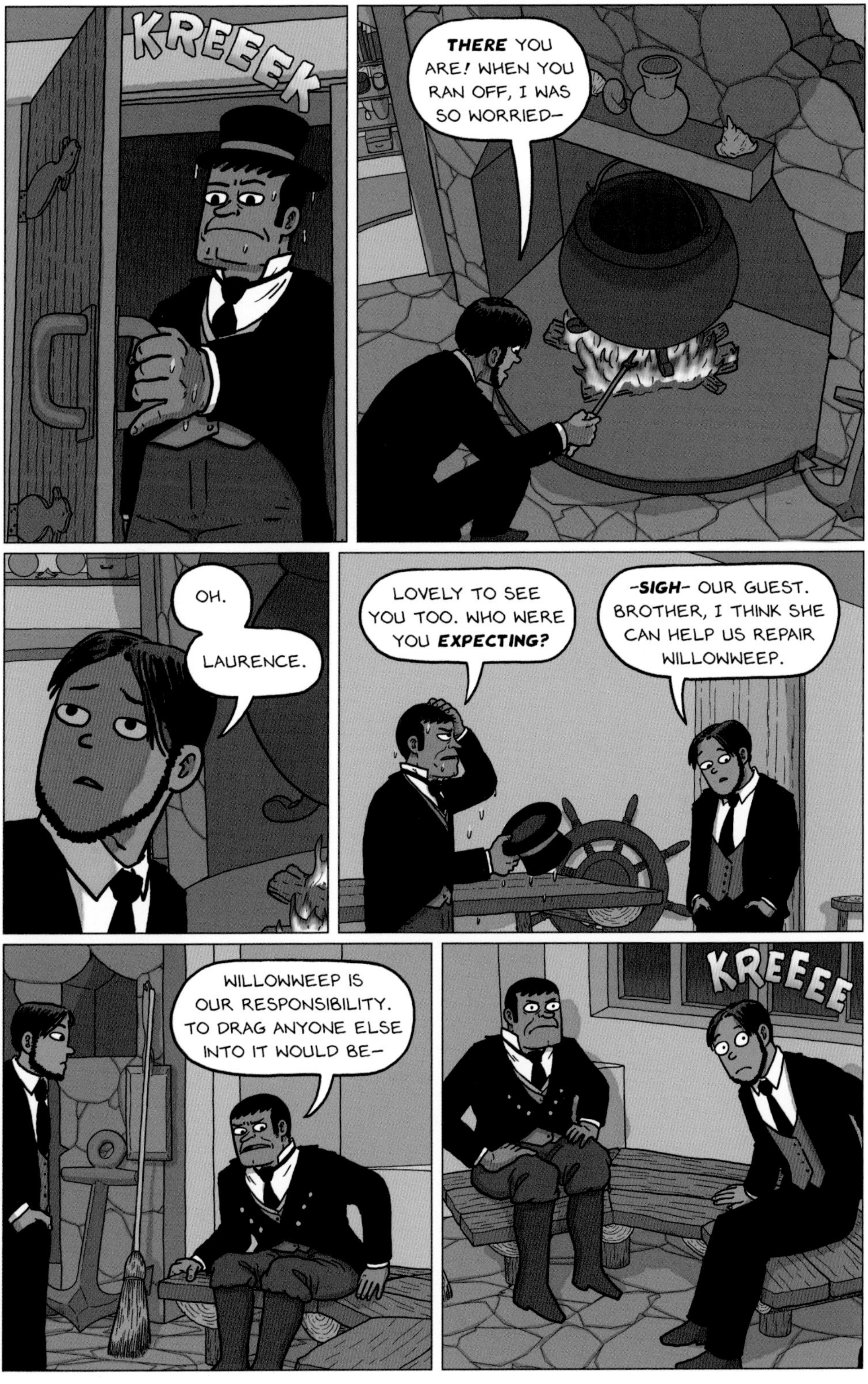

KREEEK
THERE YOU ARE! WHEN YOU RAN OFF, I WAS SO WORRIED—
OH.
LAURENCE.
LOVELY TO SEE YOU TOO. WHO WERE YOU EXPECTING?
-SIGH- OUR GUEST. BROTHER, I THINK SHE CAN HELP US REPAIR WILLOWWEEP.
WILLOWWEEP IS OUR RESPONSIBILITY. TO DRAG ANYONE ELSE INTO IT WOULD BE—
KREEEE

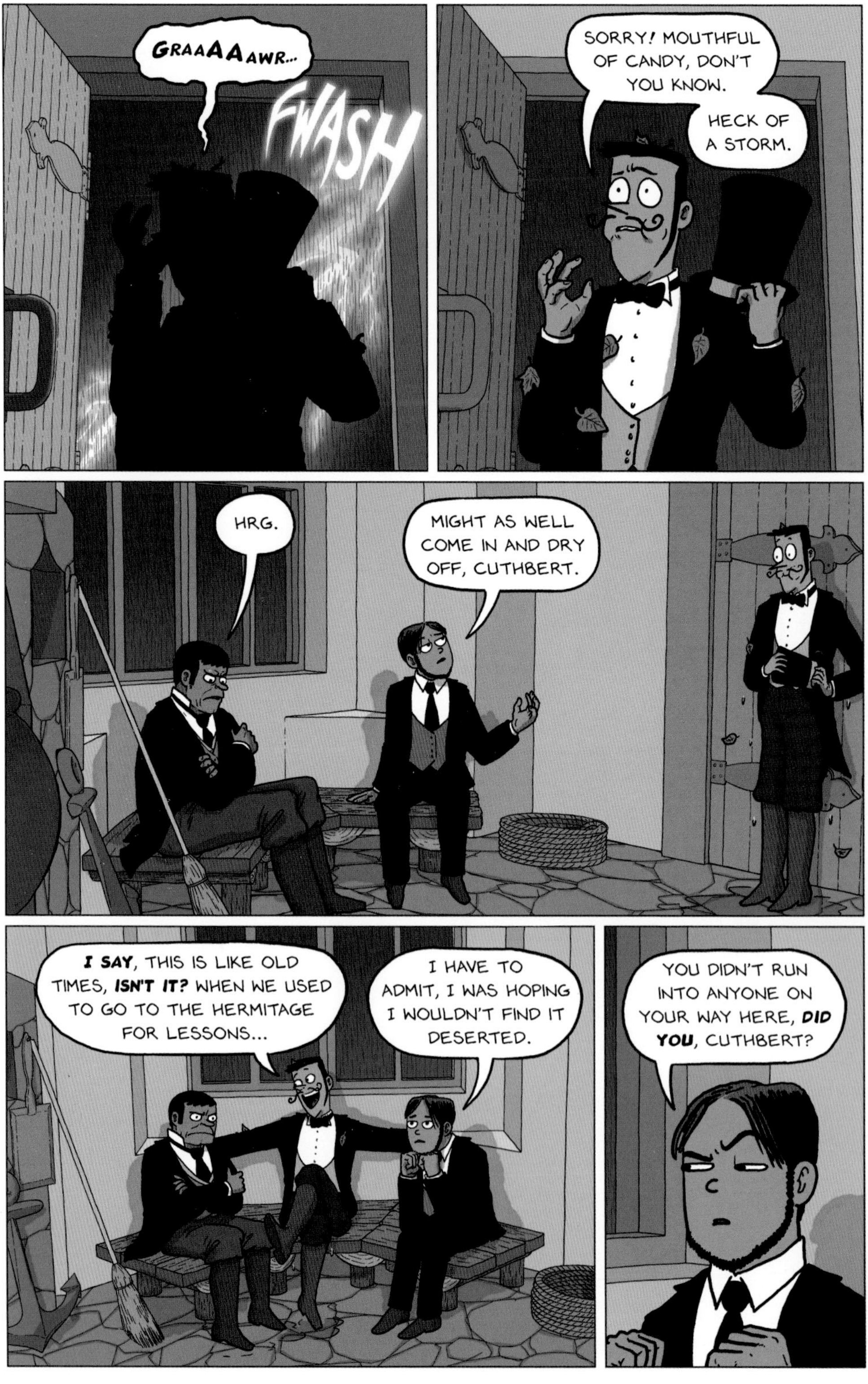
GRAAAAAWR...
FWASH
SORRY! MOUTHFUL OF CANDY, DON'T YOU KNOW.
HECK OF A STORM.
HRG.
MIGHT AS WELL COME IN AND DRY OFF, CUTHBERT.
I SAY, THIS IS LIKE OLD TIMES, ISN'T IT? WHEN WE USED TO GO TO THE HERMITAGE FOR LESSONS...
I HAVE TO ADMIT, I WAS HOPING I WOULDN'T FIND IT DESERTED.
YOU DIDN'T RUN INTO ANYONE ON YOUR WAY HERE, DID YOU, CUTHBERT?

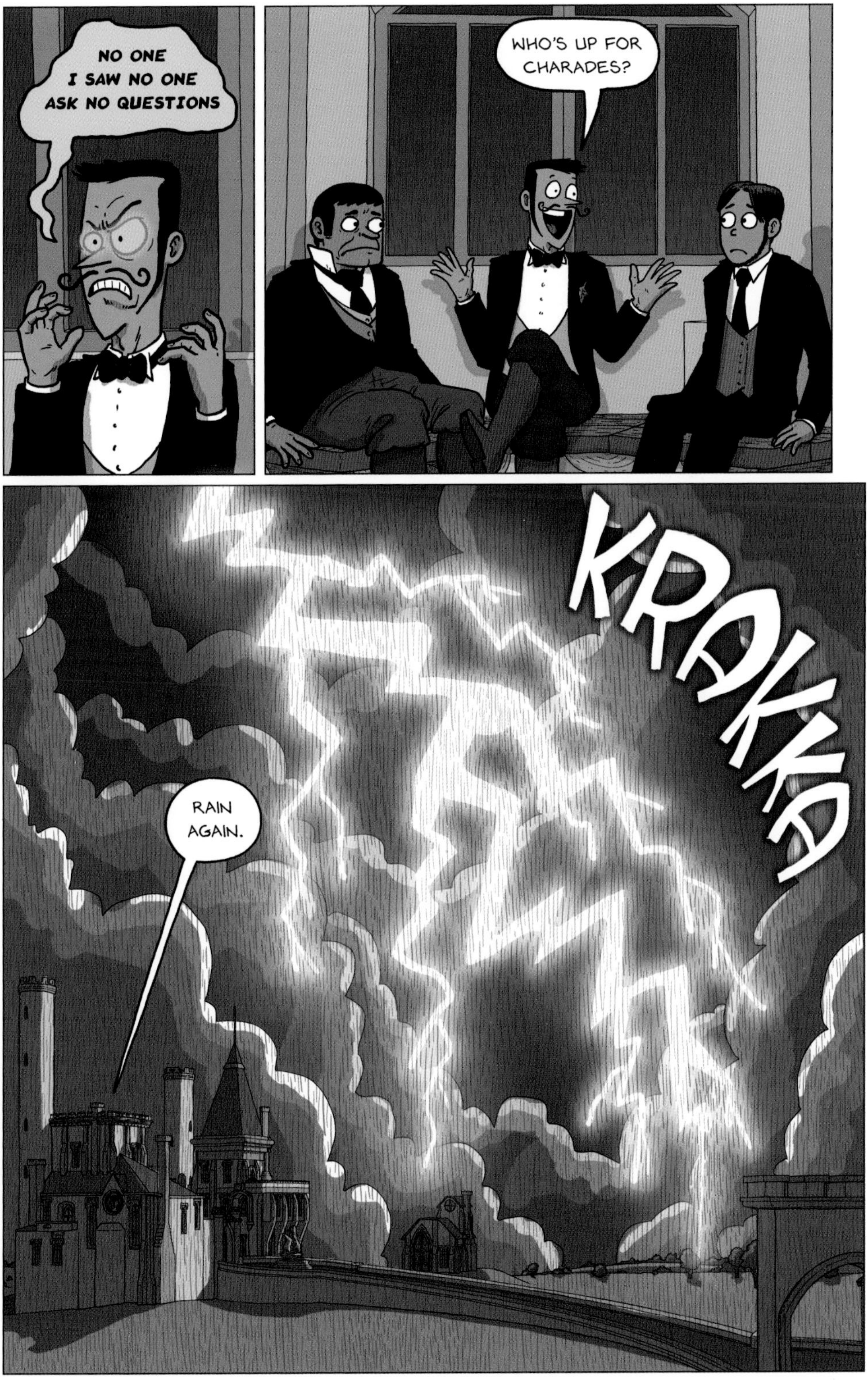
NO ONE
I SAW NO ONE
ASK NO QUESTIONS
WHO'S UP FOR CHARADES?
KRAKKA
RAIN AGAIN.

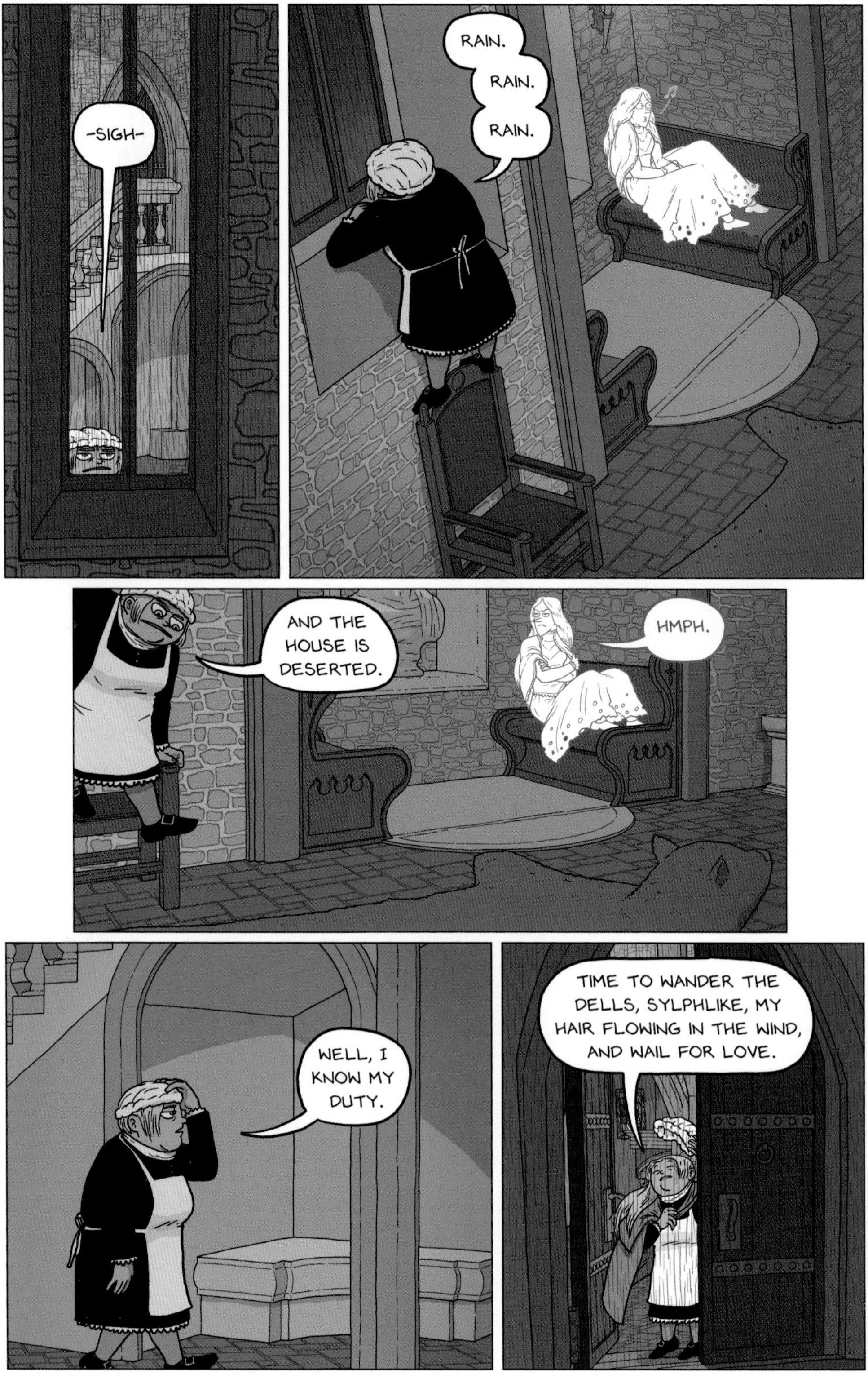
-SIGH-
RAIN.
RAIN.
RAIN.
AND THE HOUSE IS DESERTED.
HMPH.
WELL, I KNOW MY DUTY.
TIME TO WANDER THE DELLS, SYLPHLIKE, MY HAIR FLOWING IN THE WIND, AND WAIL FOR LOVE.

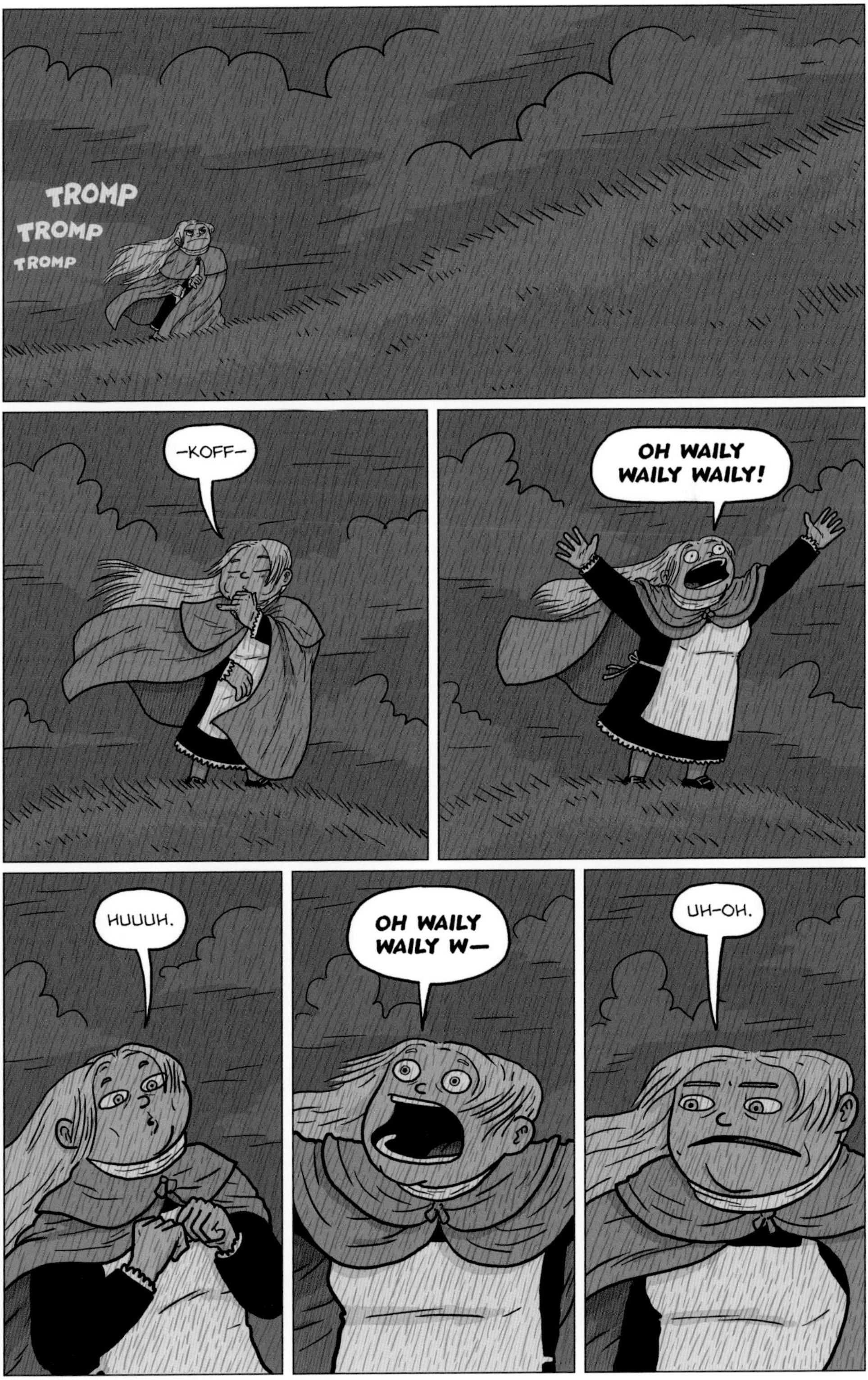
TROMP
TROMP
TROMP
-KOFF-
OH WAILY WAILY WAILY!
HUUUH.
OH WAILY WAILY W—
UH-OH.

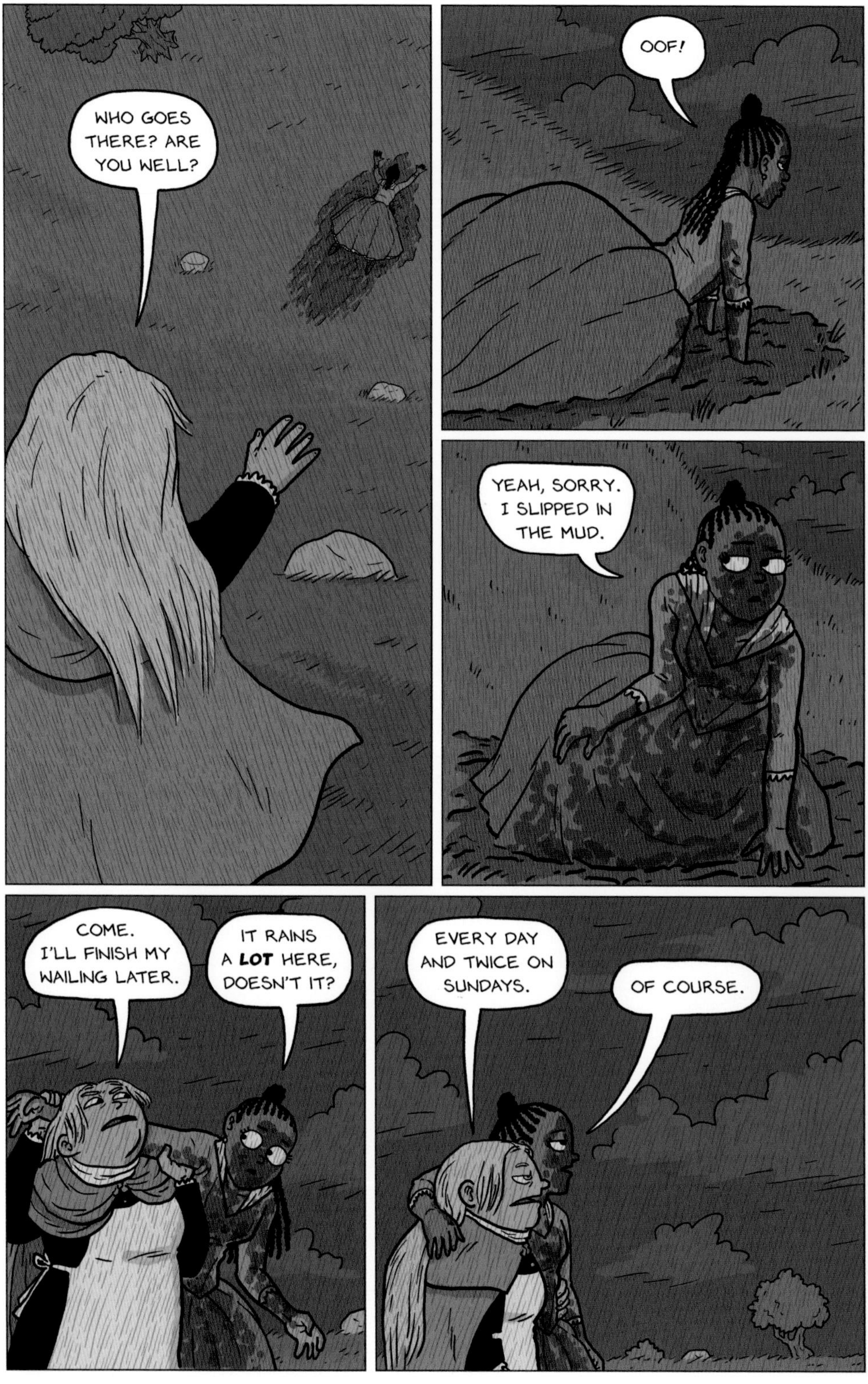
WHO GOES THERE? ARE YOU WELL?
OOF!
YEAH, SORRY. I SLIPPED IN THE MUD.
COME. I'LL FINISH MY WAILING LATER.
IT RAINS A **LOT** HERE, DOESN'T IT?
EVERY DAY AND TWICE ON SUNDAYS.
OF COURSE.

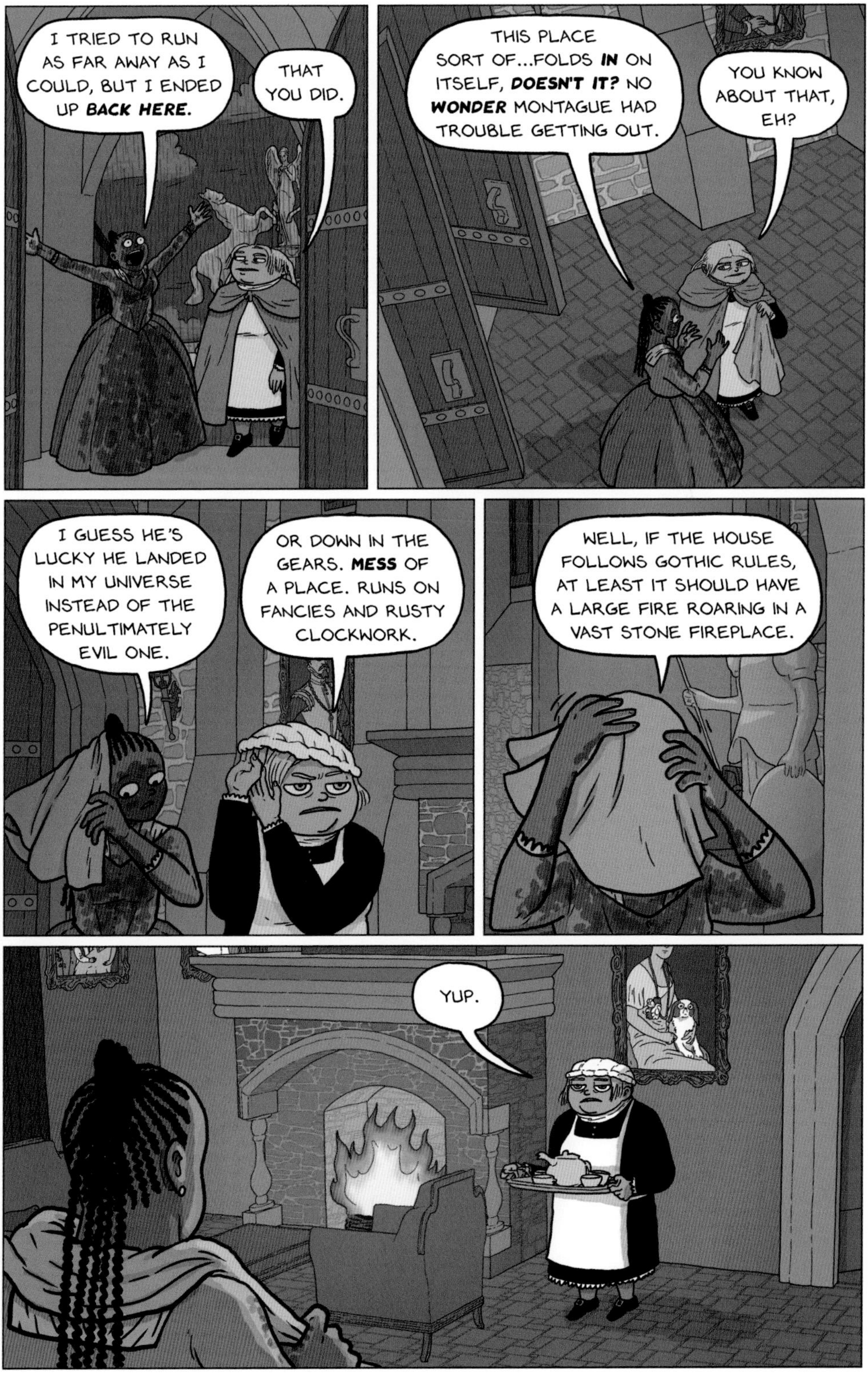
I TRIED TO RUN AS FAR AWAY AS I COULD, BUT I ENDED UP **BACK HERE**.
THAT YOU DID.
THIS PLACE SORT OF...FOLDS **IN** ON ITSELF, **DOESN'T IT?** NO **WONDER** MONTAGUE HAD TROUBLE GETTING OUT.
YOU KNOW ABOUT THAT, EH?
I GUESS HE'S LUCKY HE LANDED IN MY UNIVERSE INSTEAD OF THE PENULTIMATELY EVIL ONE.
OR DOWN IN THE GEARS. **MESS** OF A PLACE. RUNS ON FANCIES AND RUSTY CLOCKWORK.
WELL, IF THE HOUSE FOLLOWS GOTHIC RULES, AT LEAST IT SHOULD HAVE A LARGE FIRE ROARING IN A VAST STONE FIREPLACE.
YUP.

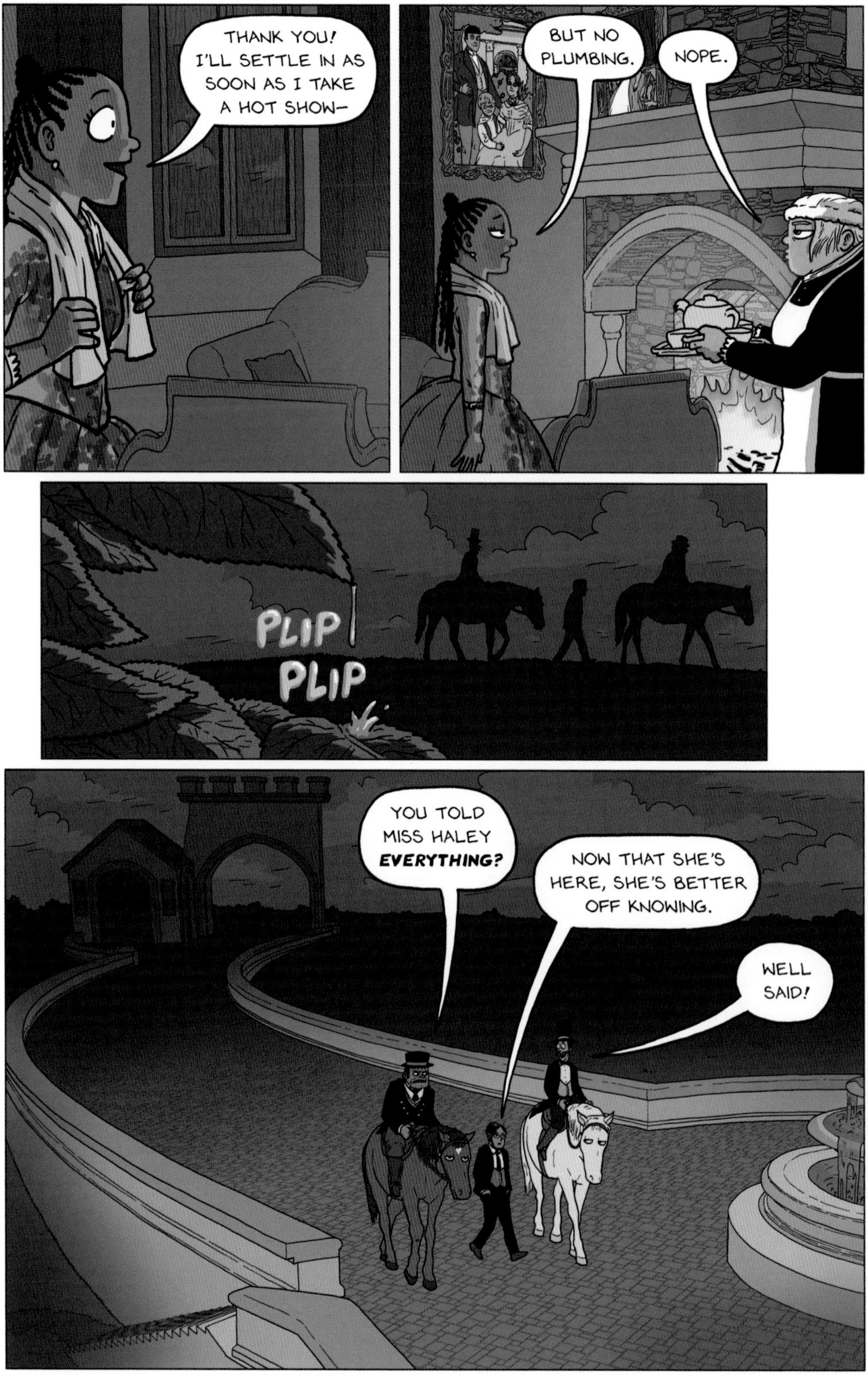
THANK YOU! I'LL SETTLE IN AS SOON AS I TAKE A HOT SHOW—
BUT NO PLUMBING.
NOPE.
PLIP
PLIP
YOU TOLD MISS HALEY *EVERYTHING?*
NOW THAT SHE'S HERE, SHE'S BETTER OFF KNOWING.
WELL SAID!

HRRMF...I WANTED TO OPEN A RIFT TO SEND HER BACK. BUT THE DEVICE IS TOO UNSTABLE RIGHT NOW.

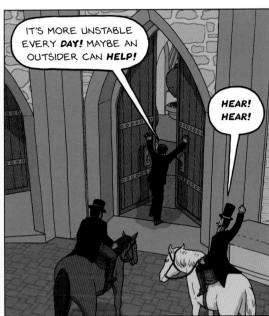

IT'S MORE UNSTABLE EVERY *DAY!* MAYBE AN OUTSIDER CAN *HELP!*

HEAR! HEAR!

SHE MAY HAVE VALUABLE KNOWLEDGE FROM HER WORLD!

OR *CANDY!*

I SEE I'M OUTVOTED.

WHO ELSE COULD GO FOR MORE CANDY RIGHT NOW?

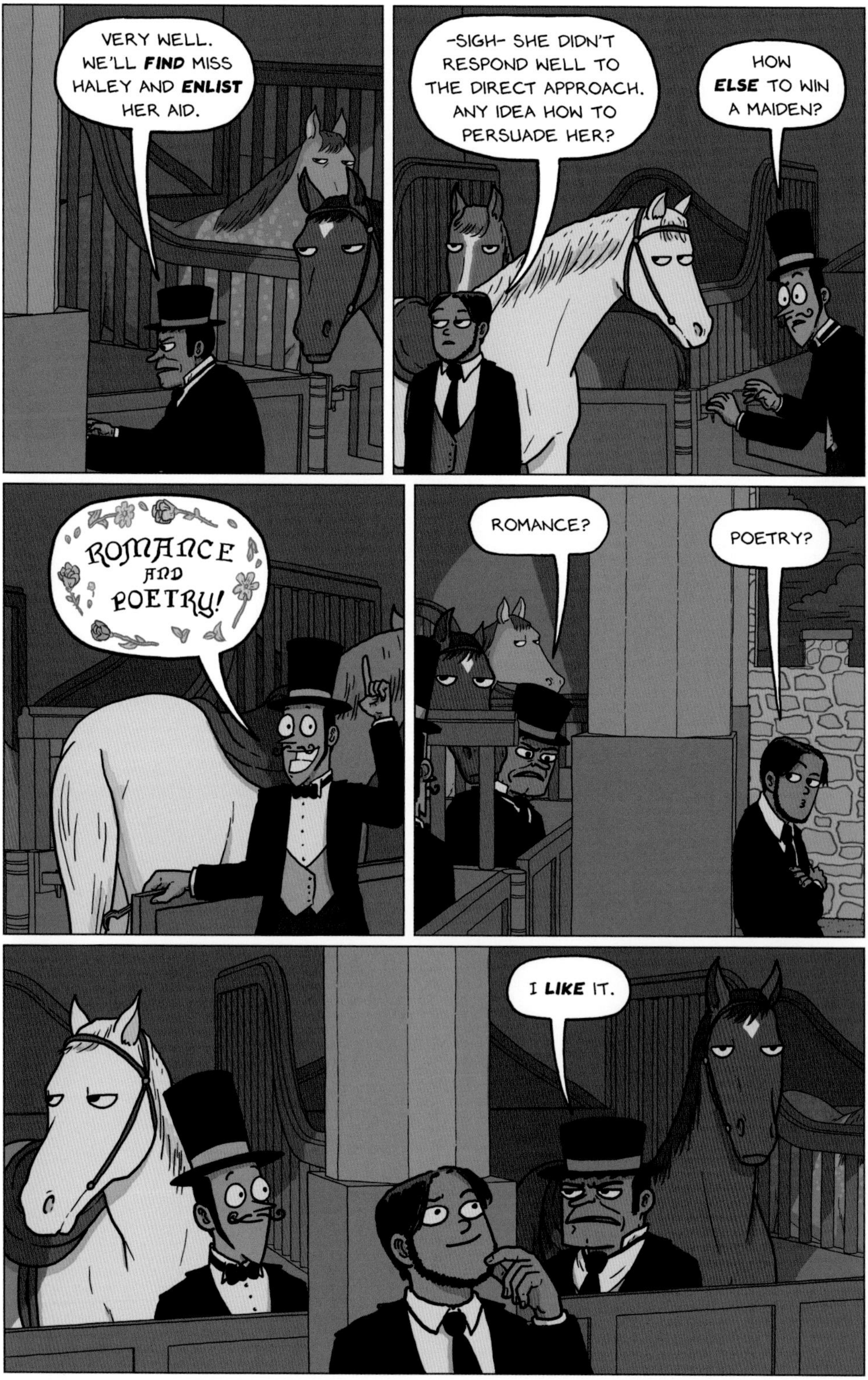
VERY WELL. WE'LL **FIND** MISS HALEY AND **ENLIST** HER AID.
-SIGH- SHE DIDN'T RESPOND WELL TO THE DIRECT APPROACH. ANY IDEA HOW TO PERSUADE HER?
HOW **ELSE** TO WIN A MAIDEN?
ROMANCE AND POETRY!
ROMANCE?
POETRY?
I **LIKE** IT.

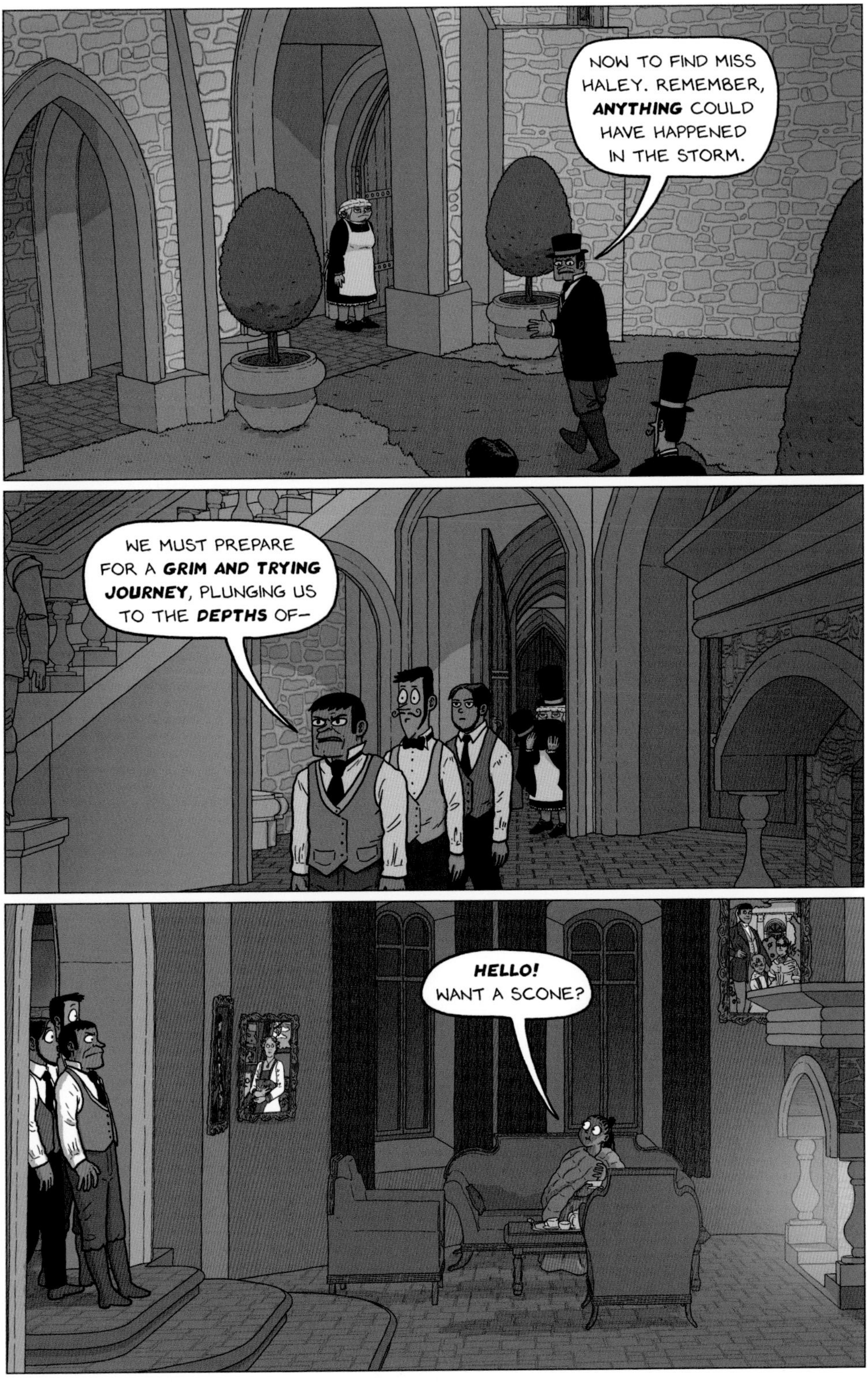
NOW TO FIND MISS HALEY. REMEMBER, **ANYTHING** COULD HAVE HAPPENED IN THE STORM.
WE MUST PREPARE FOR A **GRIM AND TRYING JOURNEY**, PLUNGING US TO THE **DEPTHS** OF–
HELLO! WANT A SCONE?

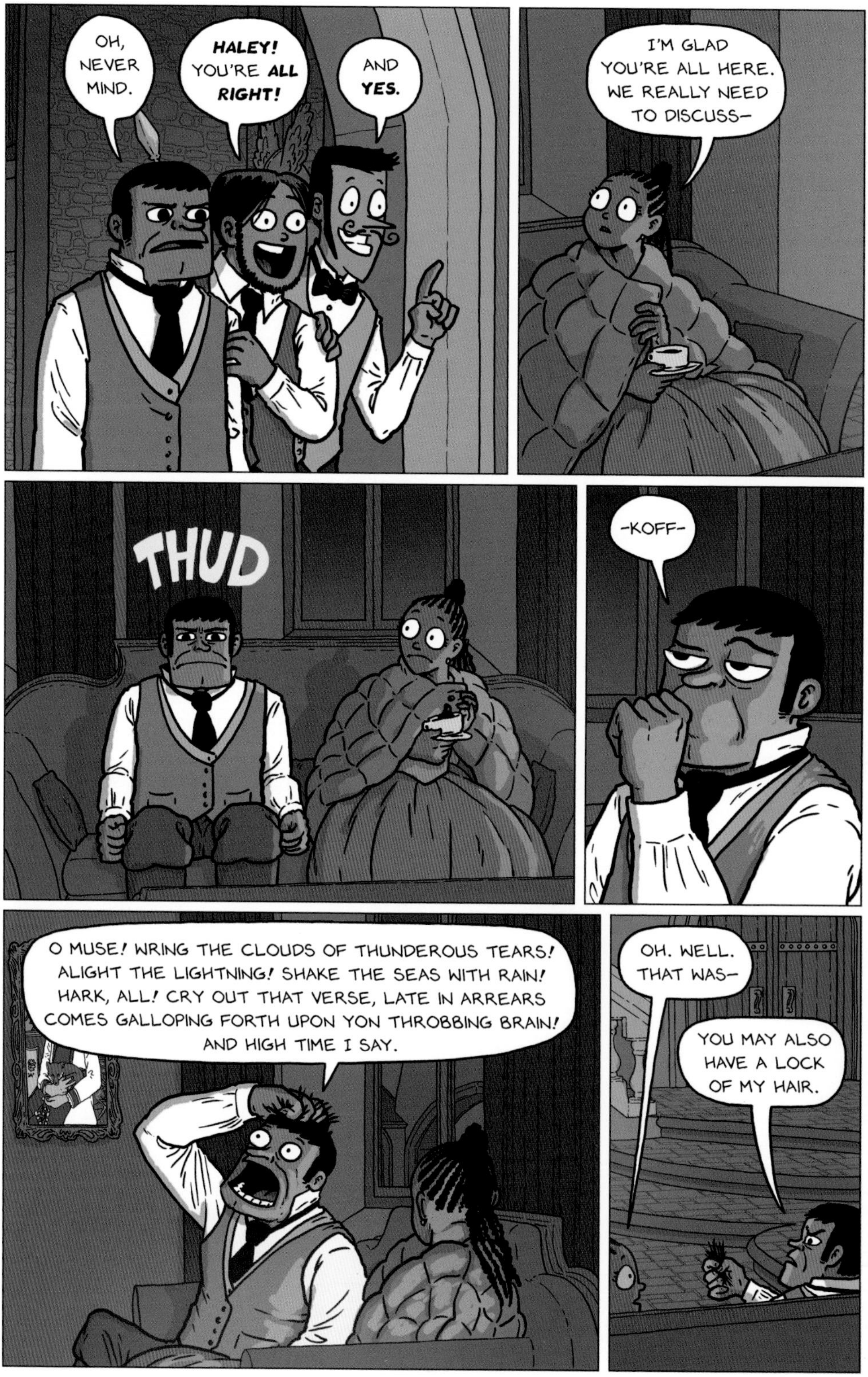
OH, NEVER MIND.
HALEY! YOU'RE ALL RIGHT!
AND YES.
I'M GLAD YOU'RE ALL HERE. WE REALLY NEED TO DISCUSS–
THUD
-KOFF-
O MUSE! WRING THE CLOUDS OF THUNDEROUS TEARS! ALIGHT THE LIGHTNING! SHAKE THE SEAS WITH RAIN! HARK, ALL! CRY OUT THAT VERSE, LATE IN ARREARS COMES GALLOPING FORTH UPON YON THROBBING BRAIN! AND HIGH TIME I SAY.
OH. WELL. THAT WAS–
YOU MAY ALSO HAVE A LOCK OF MY HAIR.

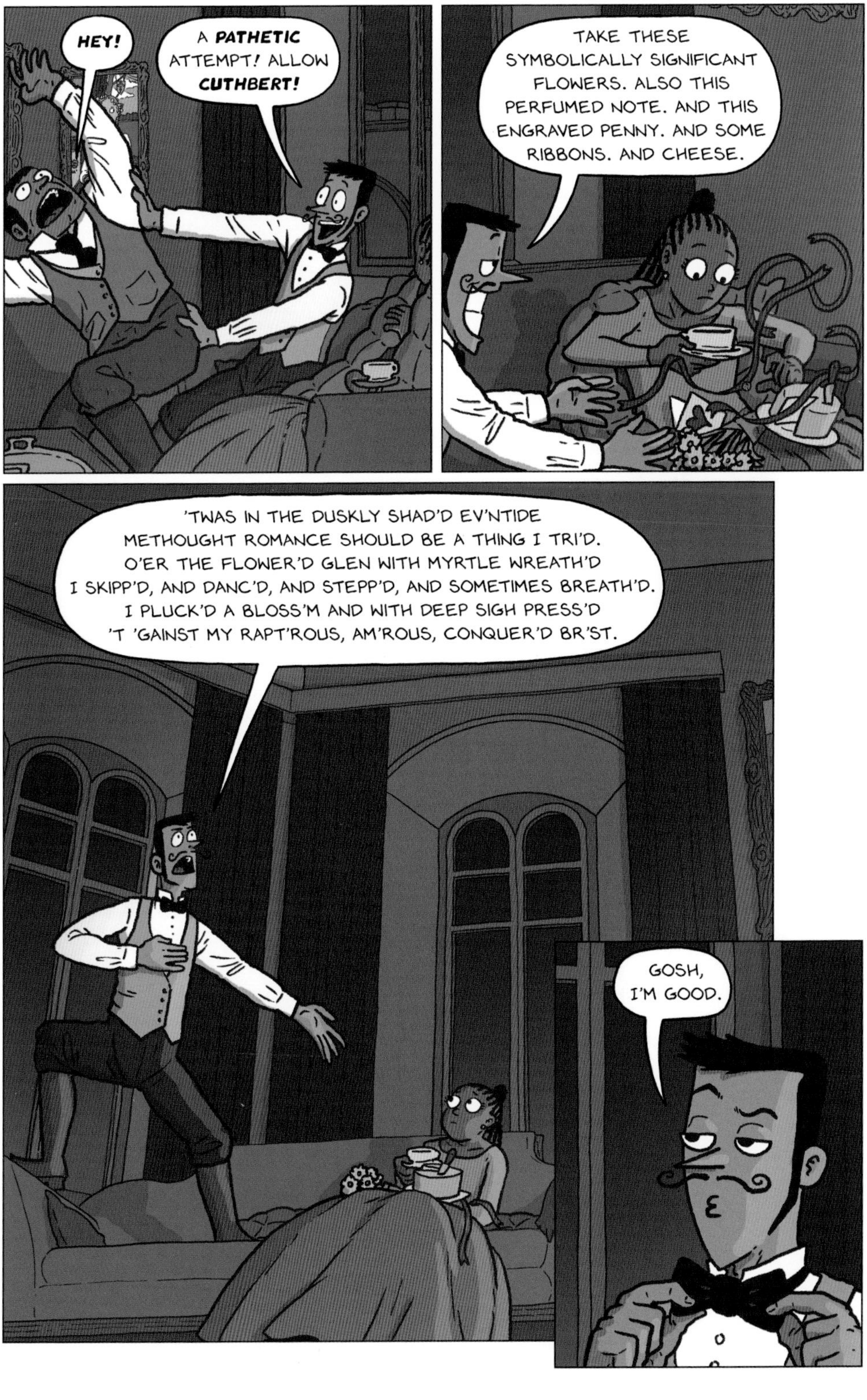
HEY!
A **PATHETIC** ATTEMPT! ALLOW **CUTHBERT!**
TAKE THESE SYMBOLICALLY SIGNIFICANT FLOWERS. ALSO THIS PERFUMED NOTE. AND THIS ENGRAVED PENNY. AND SOME RIBBONS. AND CHEESE.
'TWAS IN THE DUSKLY SHAD'D EV'NTIDE METHOUGHT ROMANCE SHOULD BE A THING I TRI'D. O'ER THE FLOWER'D GLEN WITH MYRTLE WREATH'D I SKIPP'D, AND DANC'D, AND STEPP'D, AND SOMETIMES BREATH'D. I PLUCK'D A BLOSS'M AND WITH DEEP SIGH PRESS'D 'T 'GAINST MY RAPT'ROUS, AM'ROUS, CONQUER'D BR'ST.
GOSH, I'M GOOD.

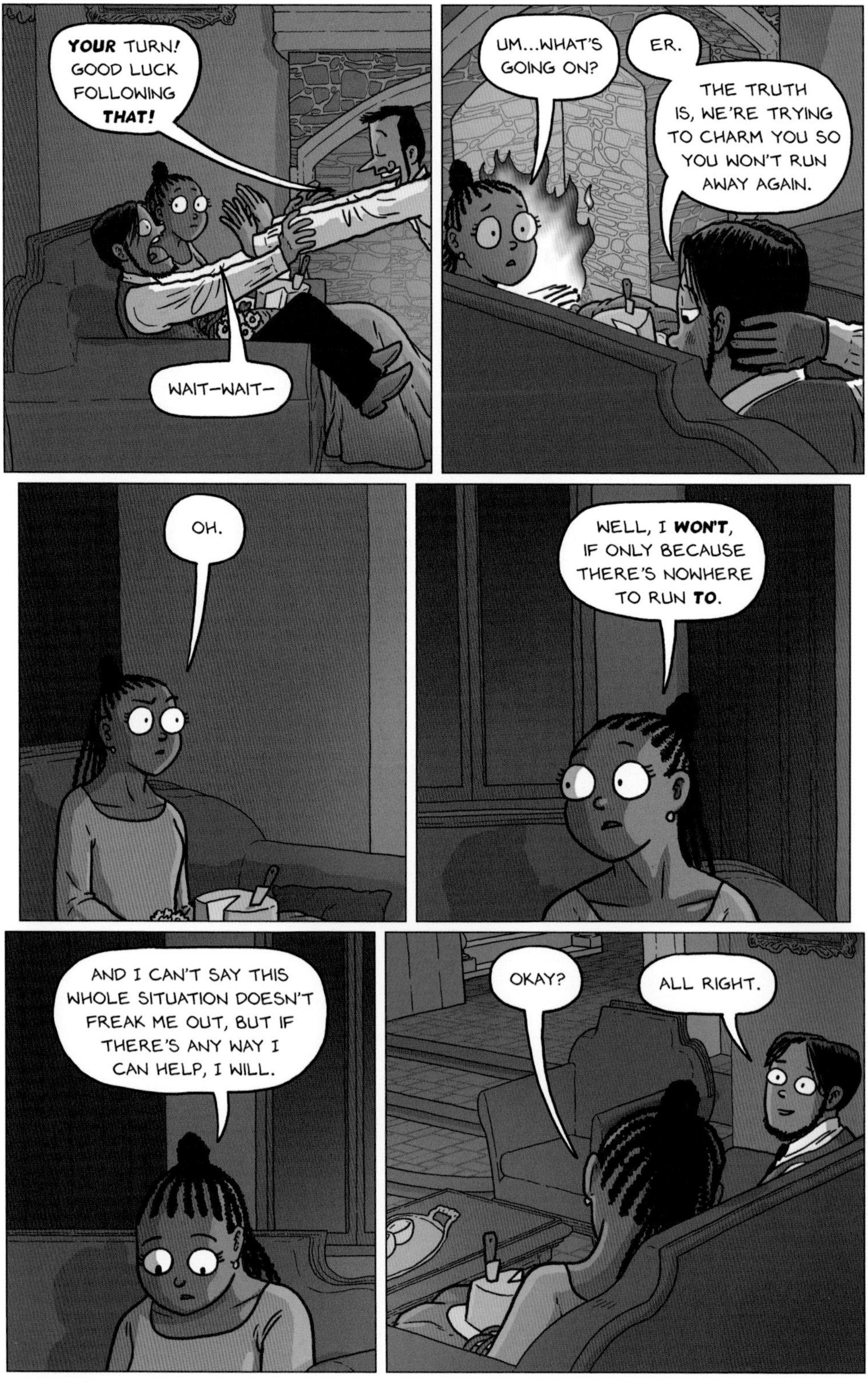
YOUR TURN! GOOD LUCK FOLLOWING THAT!
WAIT—WAIT—
UM...WHAT'S GOING ON?
ER.
THE TRUTH IS, WE'RE TRYING TO CHARM YOU SO YOU WON'T RUN AWAY AGAIN.
OH.
WELL, I WON'T, IF ONLY BECAUSE THERE'S NOWHERE TO RUN TO.
AND I CAN'T SAY THIS WHOLE SITUATION DOESN'T FREAK ME OUT, BUT IF THERE'S ANY WAY I CAN HELP, I WILL.
OKAY?
ALL RIGHT.

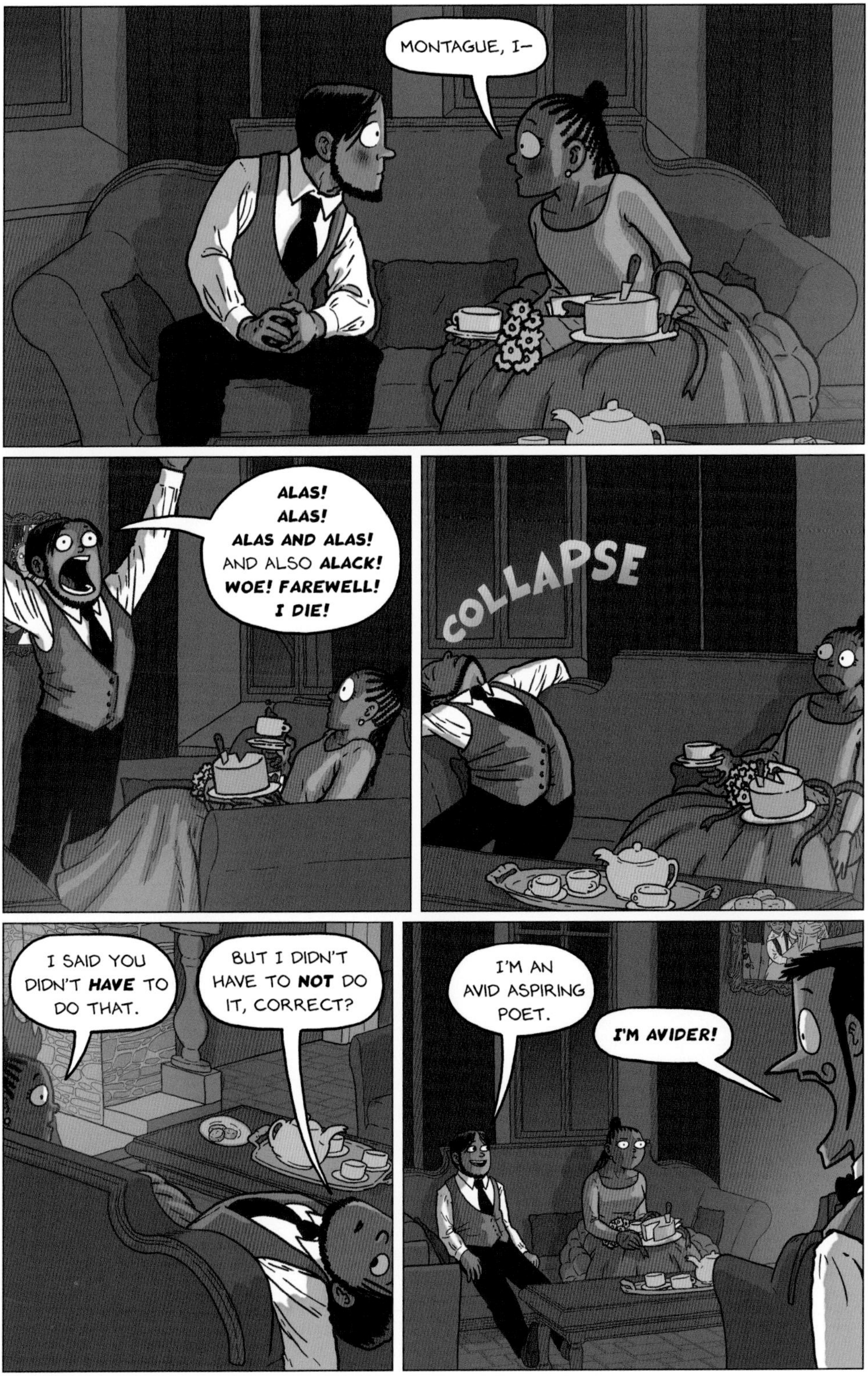
MONTAGUE, I—
ALAS! ALAS! ALAS AND ALAS! AND ALSO ALACK! WOE! FAREWELL! I DIE!
COLLAPSE
I SAID YOU DIDN'T HAVE TO DO THAT.
BUT I DIDN'T HAVE TO NOT DO IT, CORRECT?
I'M AN AVID ASPIRING POET.
I'M AVIDER!

4

The Bile Spreads

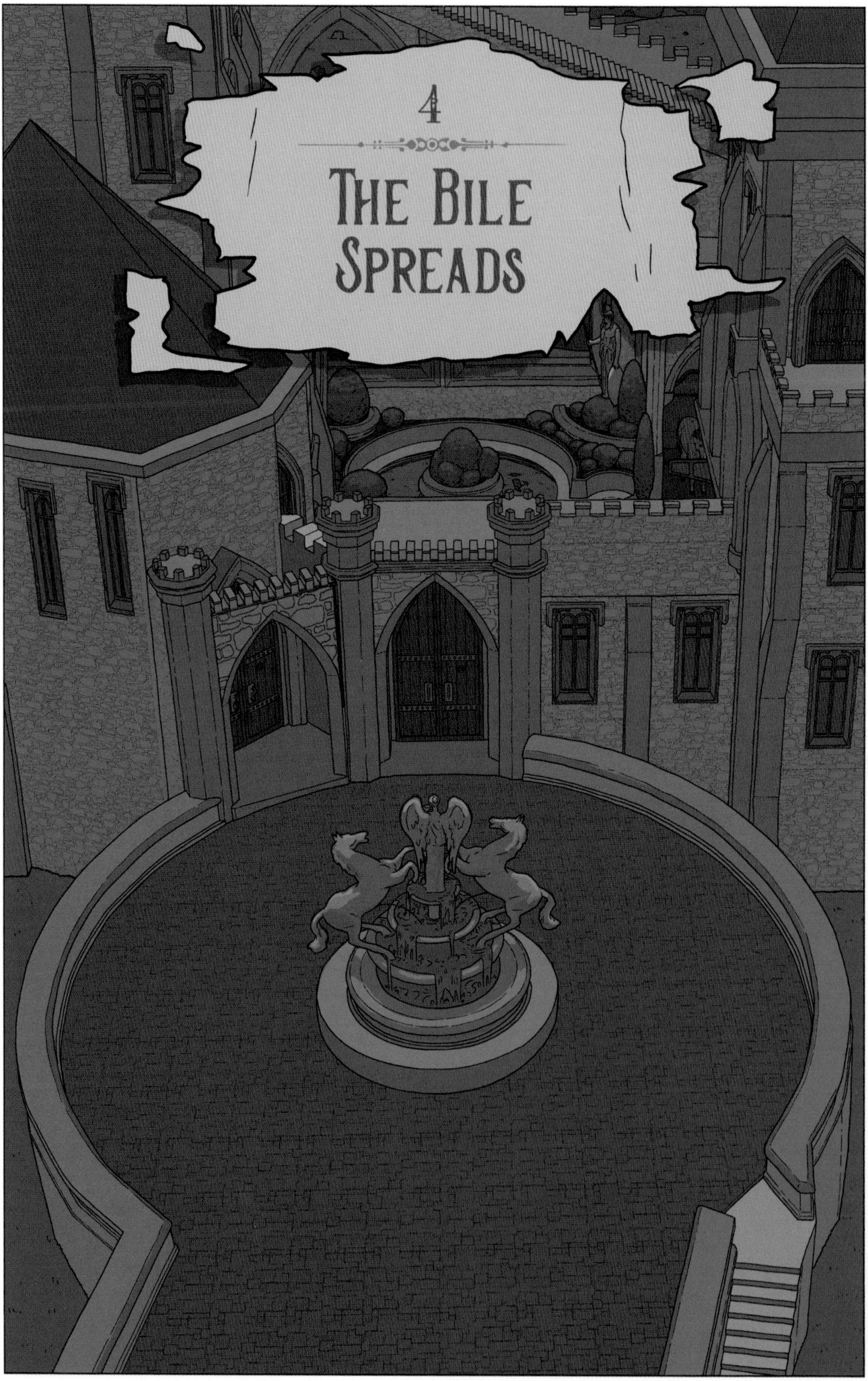

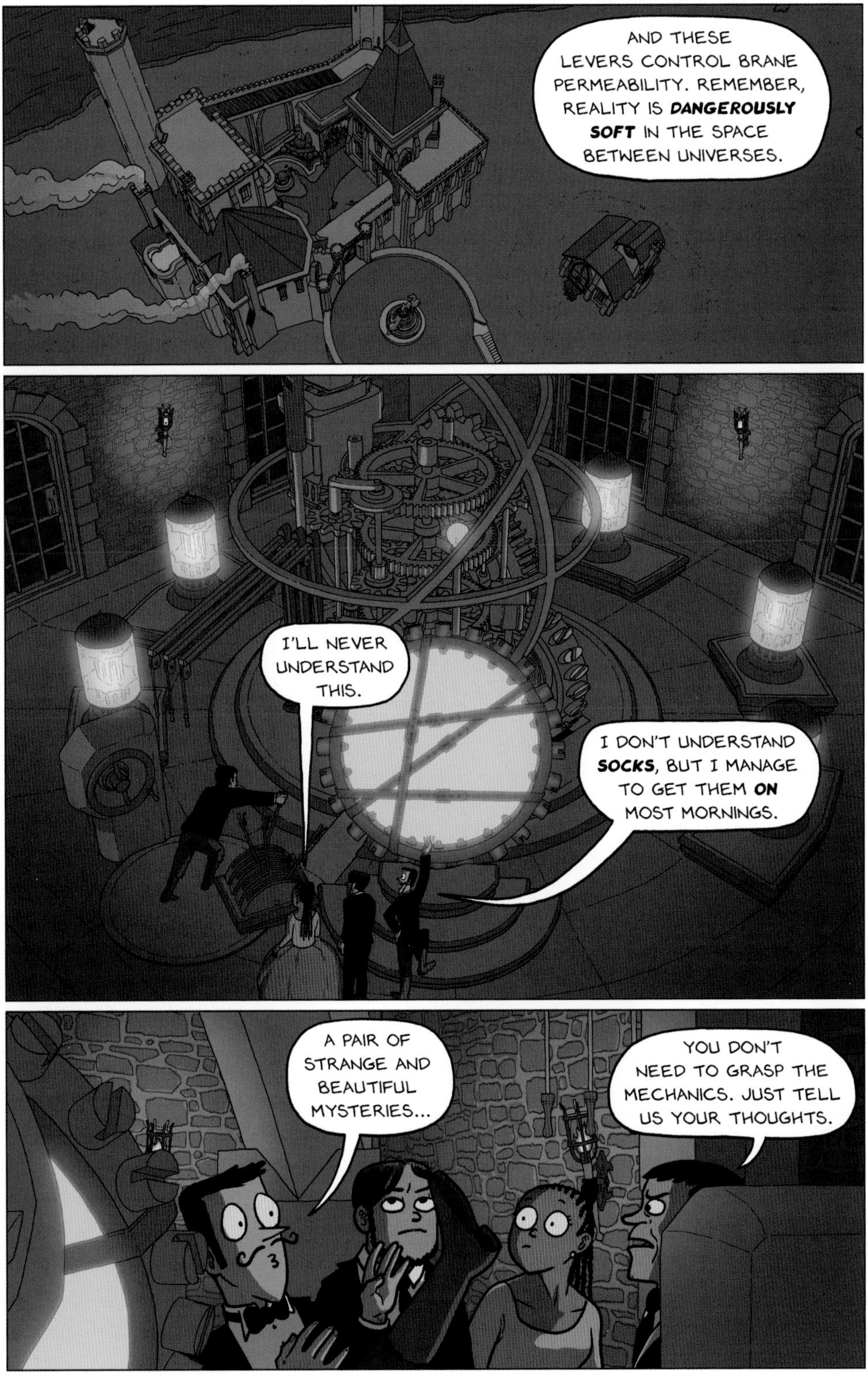
AND THESE LEVERS CONTROL BRANE PERMEABILITY. REMEMBER, REALITY IS **DANGEROUSLY SOFT** IN THE SPACE BETWEEN UNIVERSES.
I'LL NEVER UNDERSTAND THIS.
I DON'T UNDERSTAND **SOCKS**, BUT I MANAGE TO GET THEM **ON** MOST MORNINGS.
A PAIR OF STRANGE AND BEAUTIFUL MYSTERIES...
YOU DON'T NEED TO GRASP THE MECHANICS. JUST TELL US YOUR THOUGHTS.

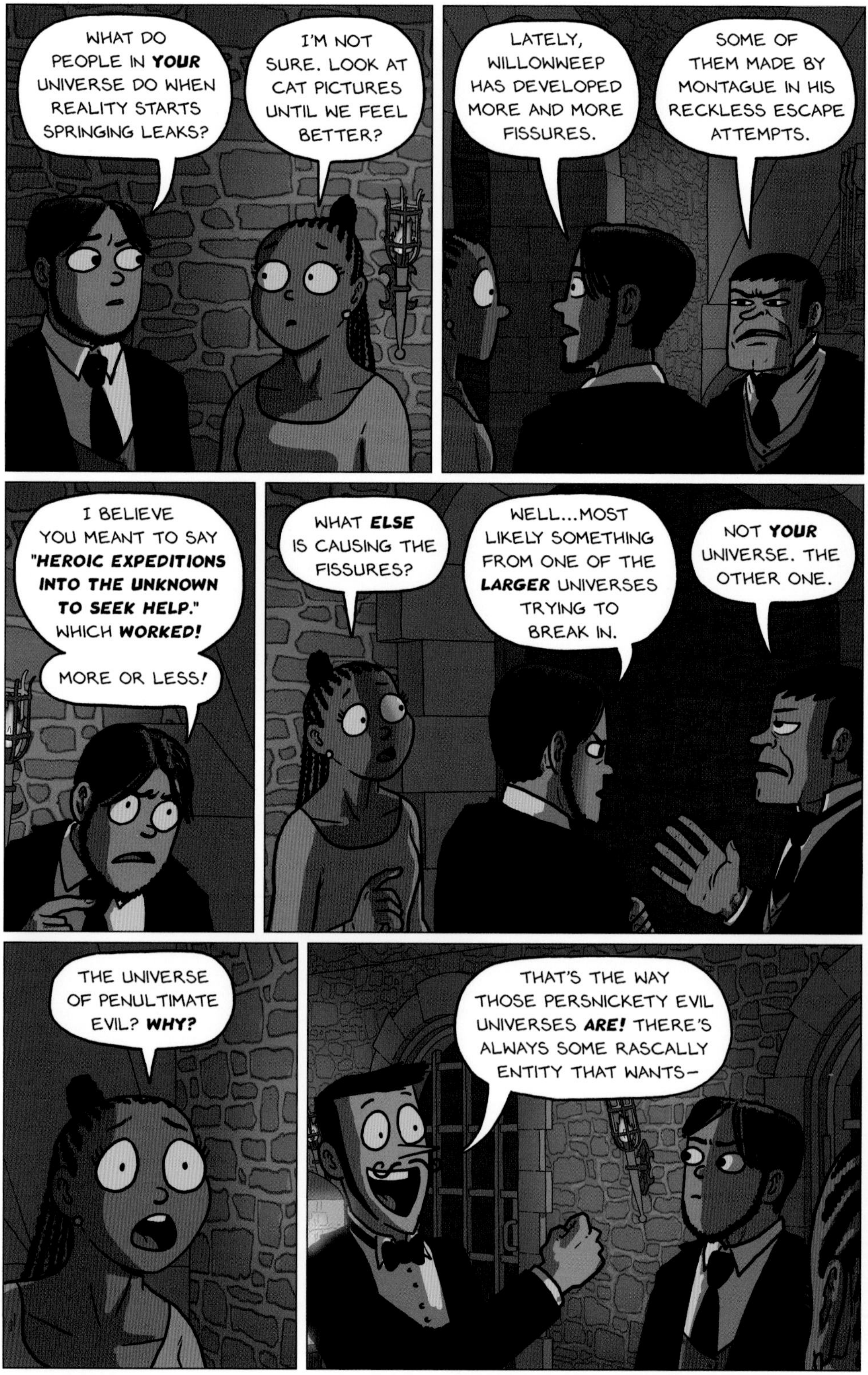

WHAT DO PEOPLE IN **YOUR** UNIVERSE DO WHEN REALITY STARTS SPRINGING LEAKS?
I'M NOT SURE. LOOK AT CAT PICTURES UNTIL WE FEEL BETTER?
LATELY, WILLOWWEEP HAS DEVELOPED MORE AND MORE FISSURES.
SOME OF THEM MADE BY MONTAGUE IN HIS RECKLESS ESCAPE ATTEMPTS.
I BELIEVE YOU MEANT TO SAY "**HEROIC EXPEDITIONS INTO THE UNKNOWN TO SEEK HELP**." WHICH **WORKED!**
MORE OR LESS!
WHAT **ELSE** IS CAUSING THE FISSURES?
WELL...MOST LIKELY SOMETHING FROM ONE OF THE **LARGER** UNIVERSES TRYING TO BREAK IN.
NOT **YOUR** UNIVERSE. THE OTHER ONE.
THE UNIVERSE OF PENULTIMATE EVIL? **WHY?**
THAT'S THE WAY THOSE PERSNICKETY EVIL UNIVERSES **ARE!** THERE'S ALWAYS SOME RASCALLY ENTITY THAT WANTS—

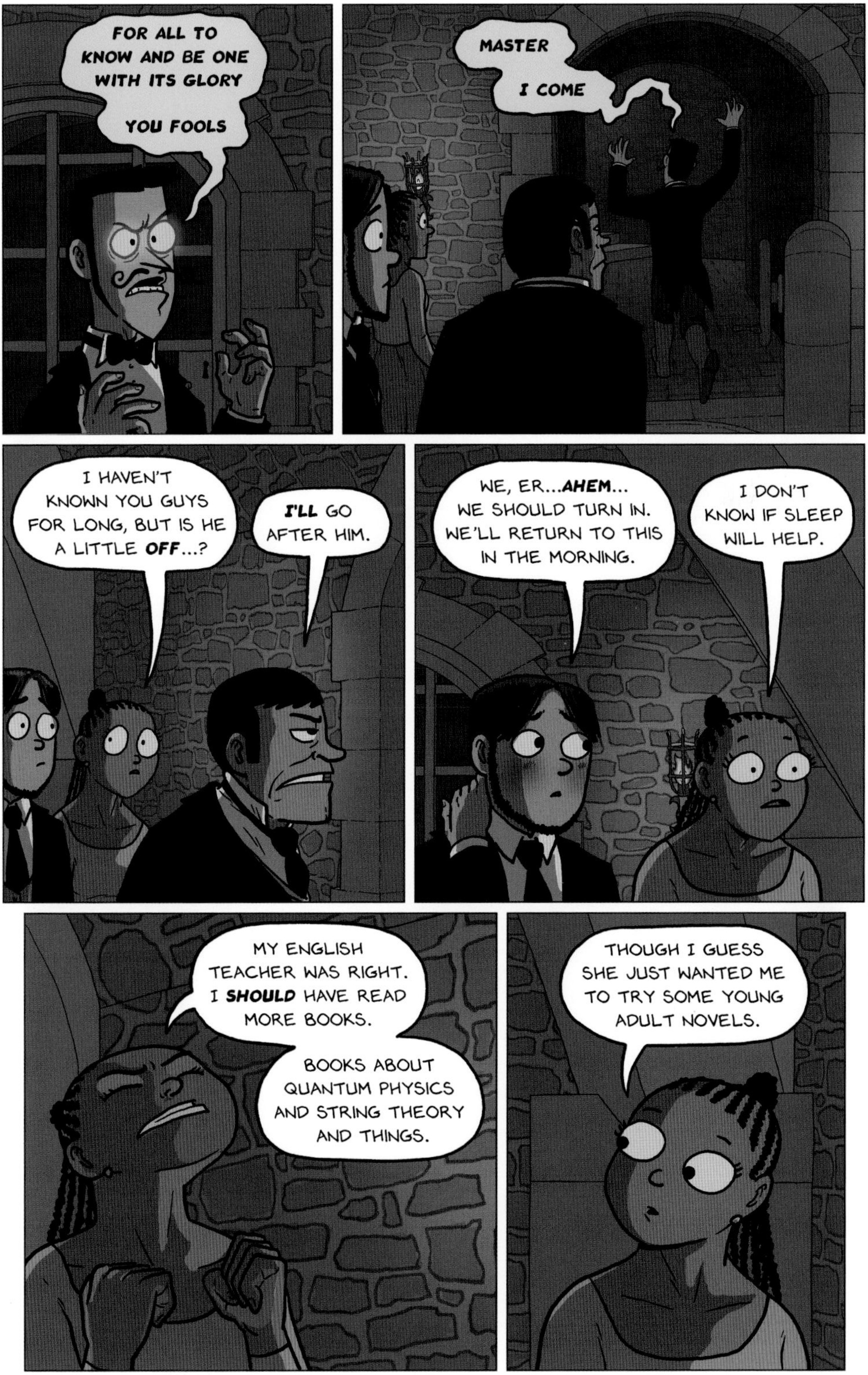
FOR ALL TO KNOW AND BE ONE WITH ITS GLORY
YOU FOOLS
MASTER
I COME
I HAVEN'T KNOWN YOU GUYS FOR LONG, BUT IS HE A LITTLE **OFF**...?
I'LL GO AFTER HIM.
WE, ER...**AHEM**... WE SHOULD TURN IN. WE'LL RETURN TO THIS IN THE MORNING.
I DON'T KNOW IF SLEEP WILL HELP.
MY ENGLISH TEACHER WAS RIGHT. I **SHOULD** HAVE READ MORE BOOKS.
BOOKS ABOUT QUANTUM PHYSICS AND STRING THEORY AND THINGS.
THOUGH I GUESS SHE JUST WANTED ME TO TRY SOME YOUNG ADULT NOVELS.

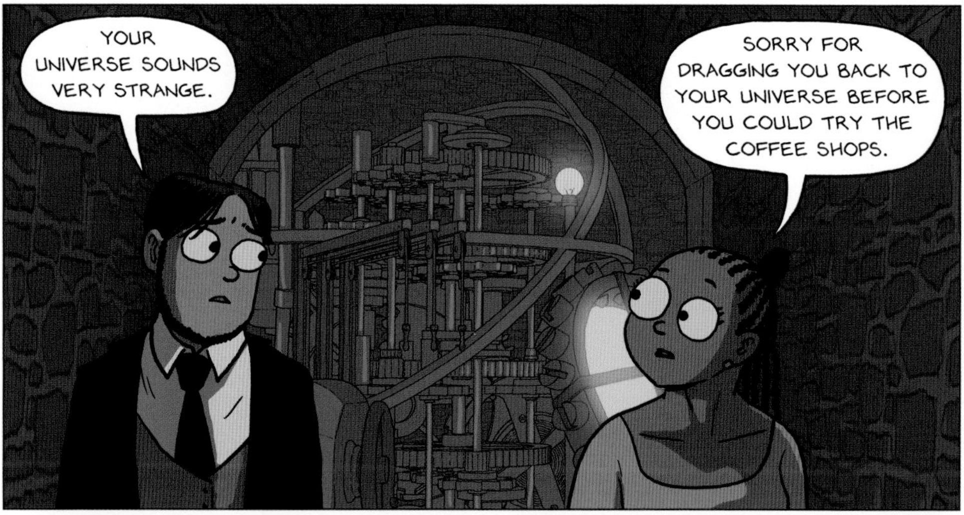
YOUR UNIVERSE SOUNDS VERY STRANGE.
SORRY FOR DRAGGING YOU BACK TO YOUR UNIVERSE BEFORE YOU COULD TRY THE COFFEE SHOPS.

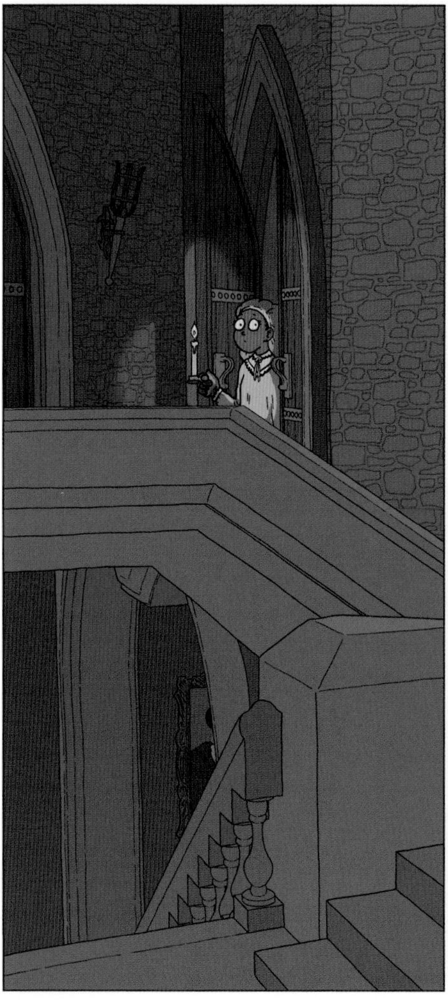

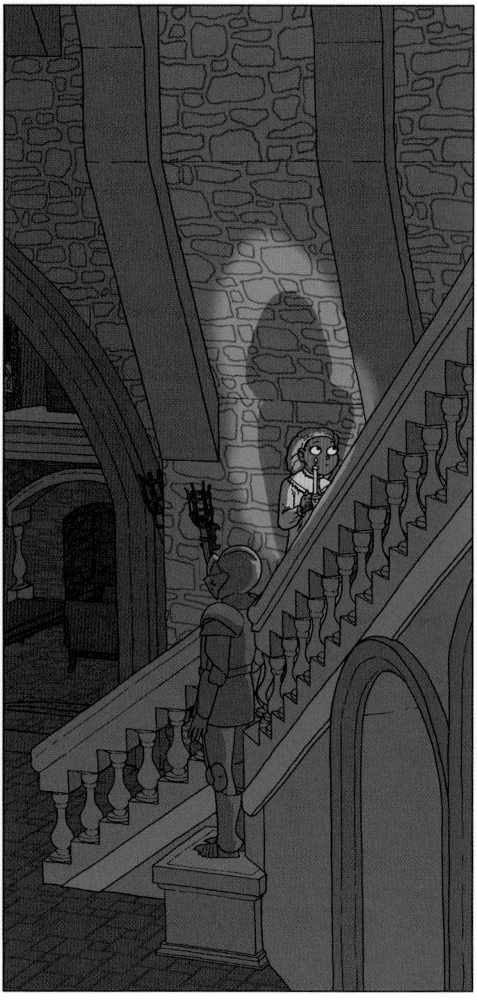

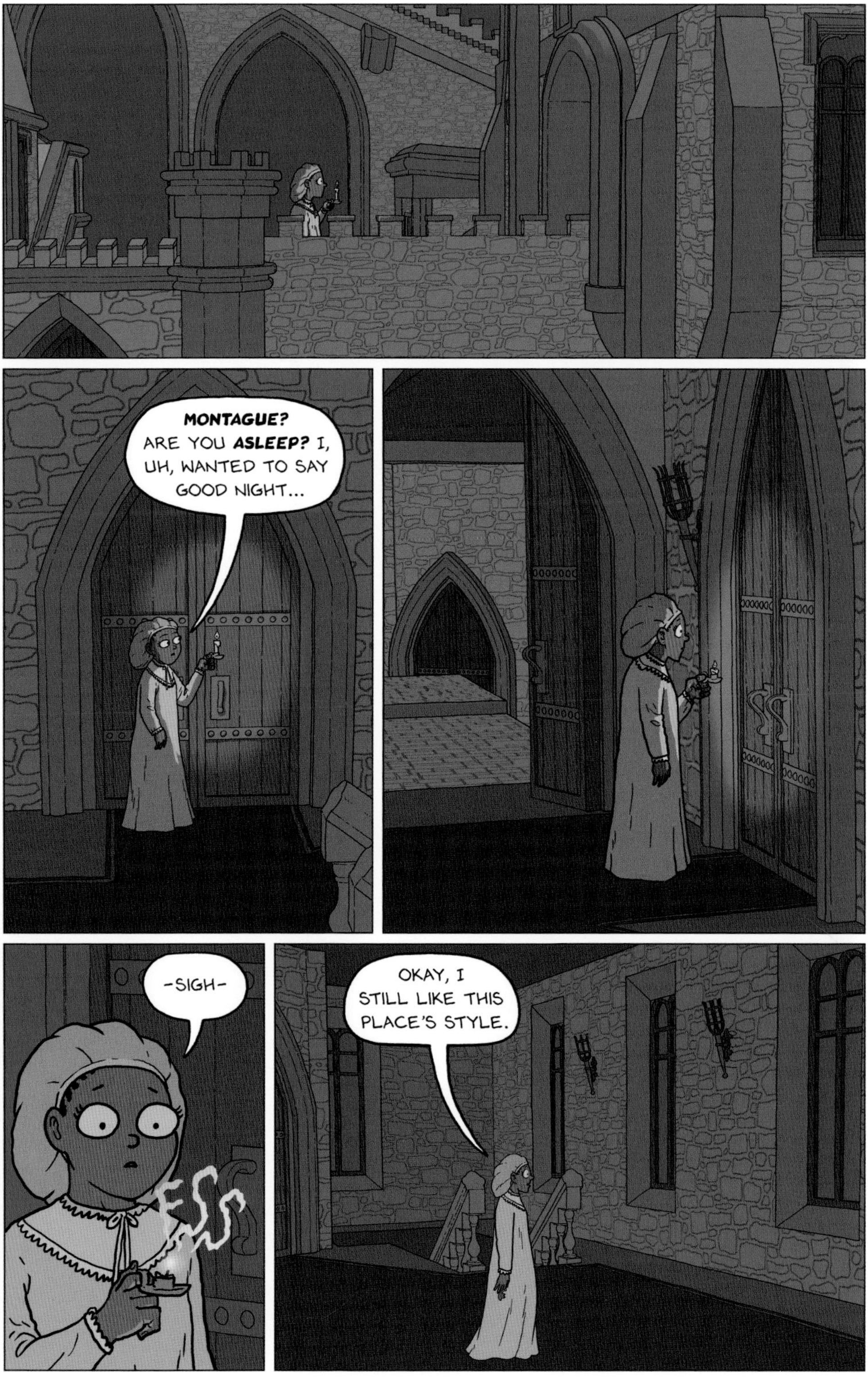
MONTAGUE? ARE YOU ASLEEP? I, UH, WANTED TO SAY GOOD NIGHT...
-SIGH-
OKAY, I STILL LIKE THIS PLACE'S STYLE.

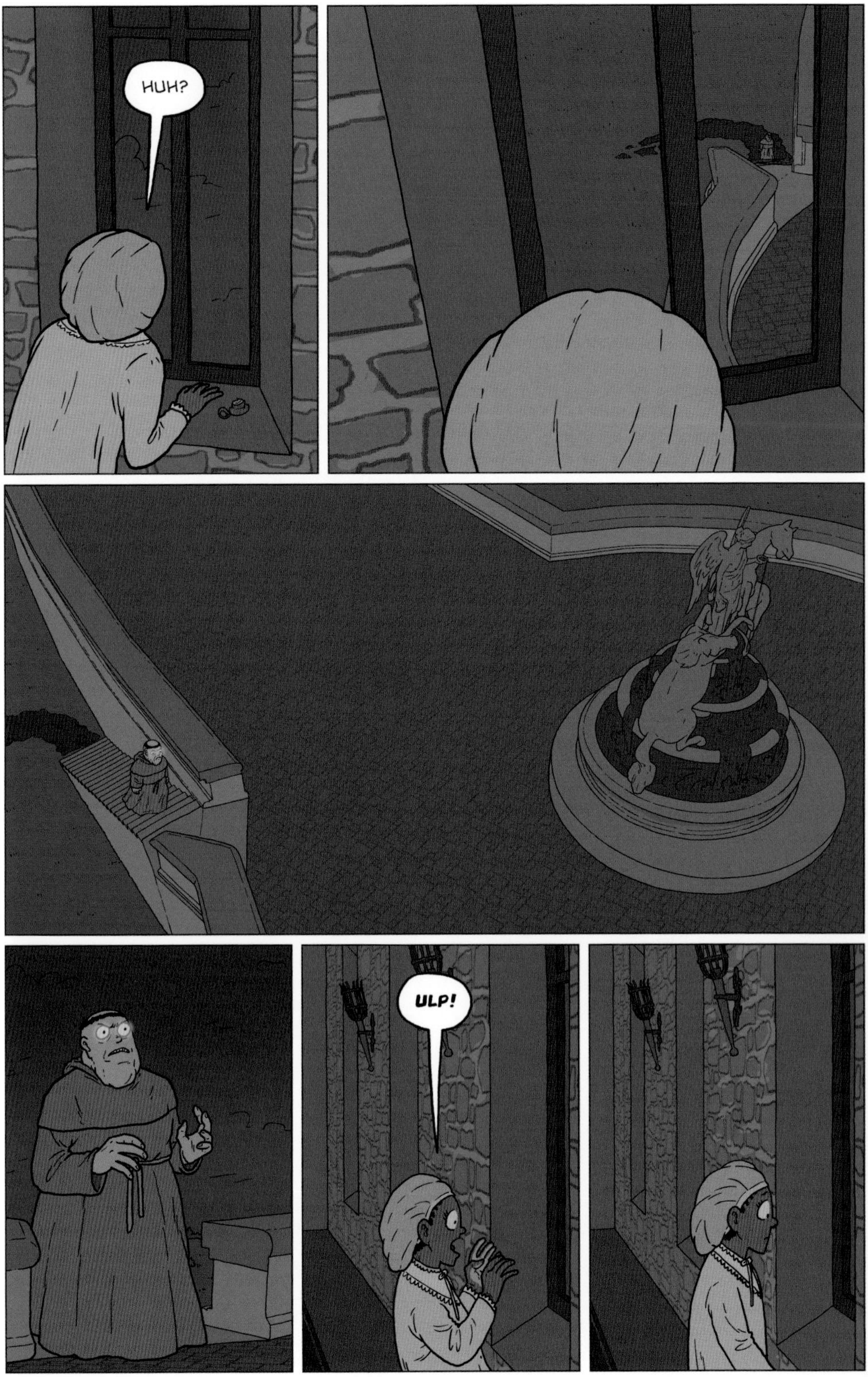
HUH?
ULP!

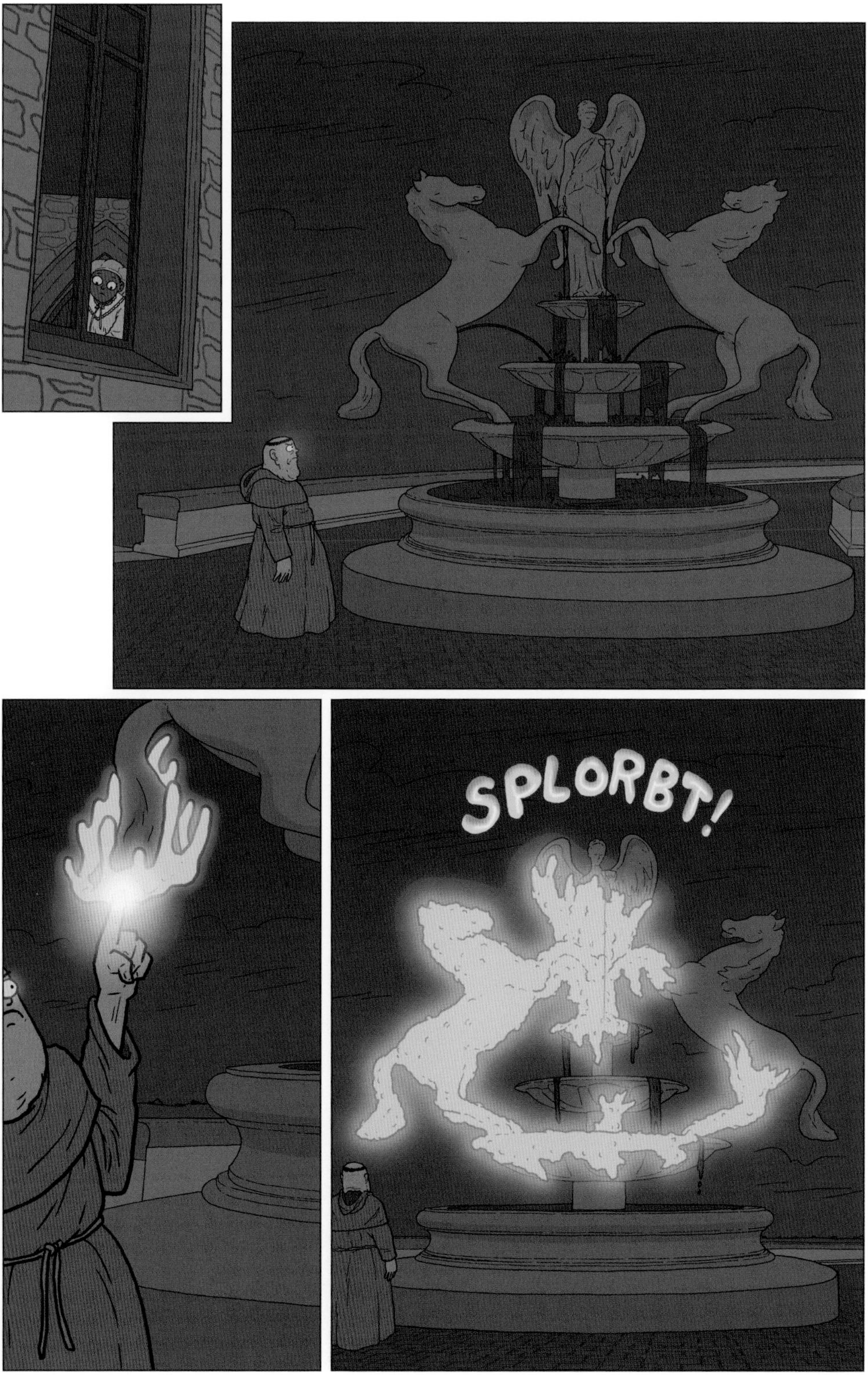
SPLORBT!

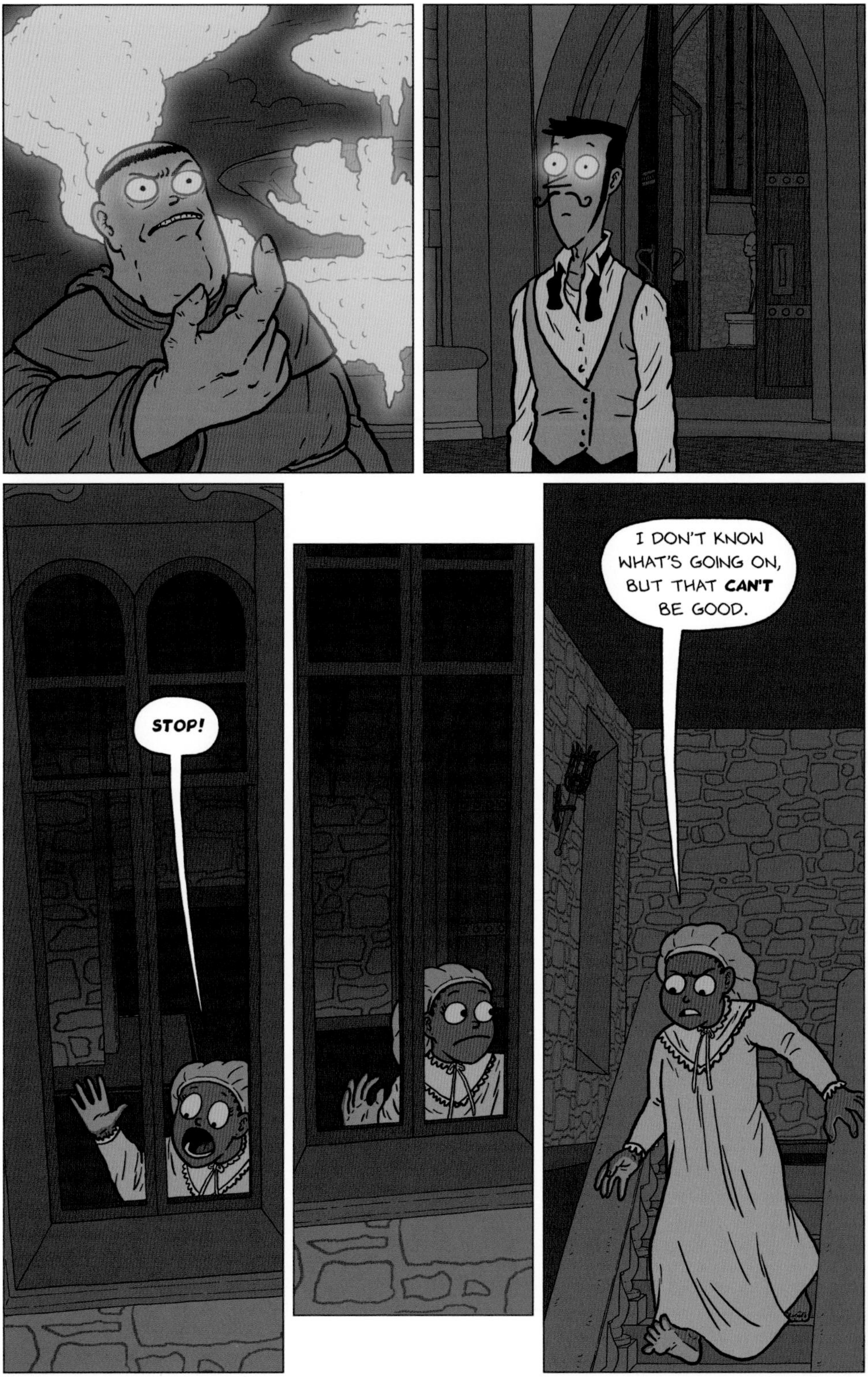
STOP!
I DON'T KNOW WHAT'S GOING ON, BUT THAT **CAN'T** BE GOOD.

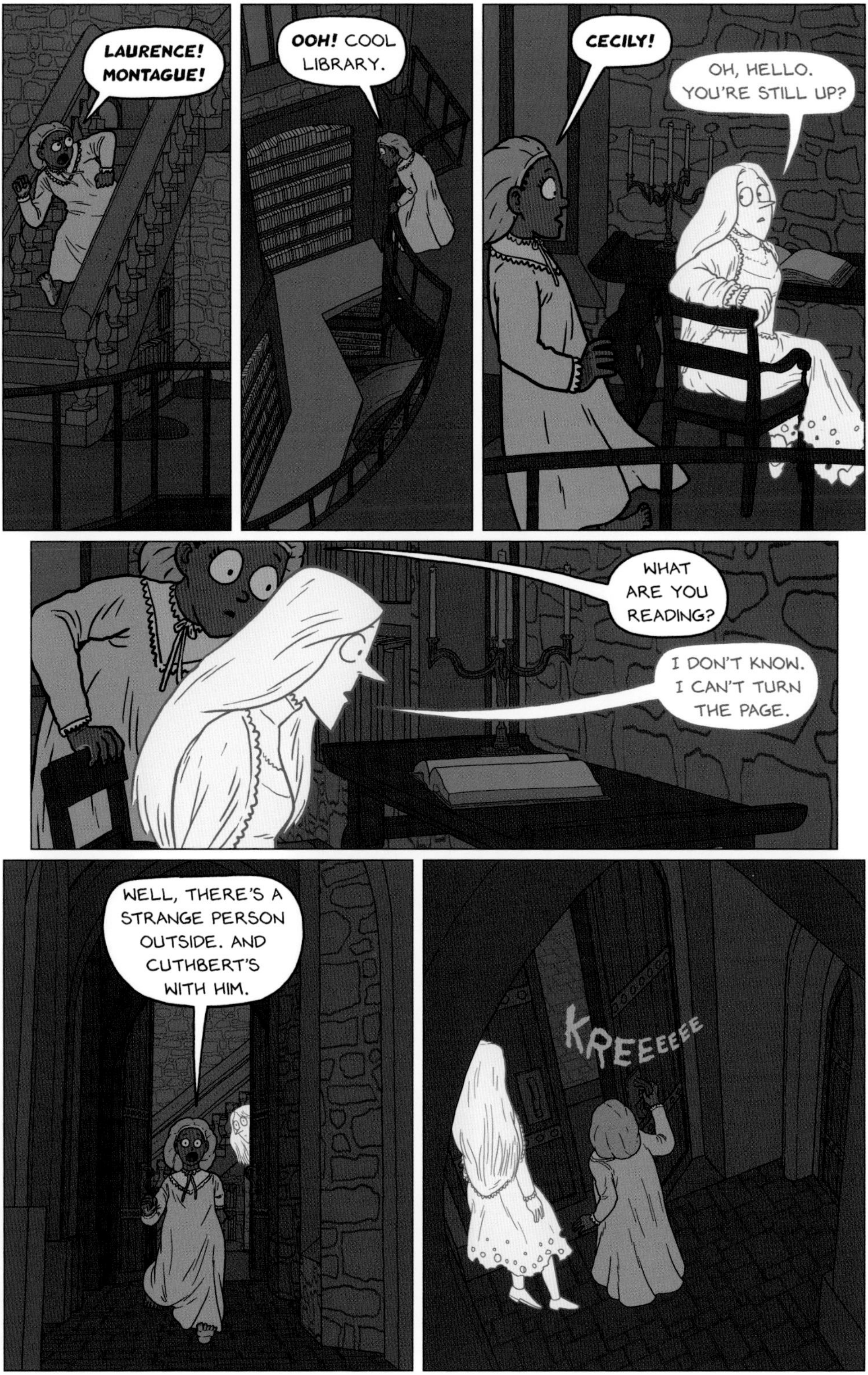
LAURENCE! MONTAGUE!
OOH! COOL LIBRARY.
CECILY!
OH, HELLO. YOU'RE STILL UP?
WHAT ARE YOU READING?
I DON'T KNOW. I CAN'T TURN THE PAGE.
WELL, THERE'S A STRANGE PERSON OUTSIDE. AND CUTHBERT'S WITH HIM.
KREEEEEE

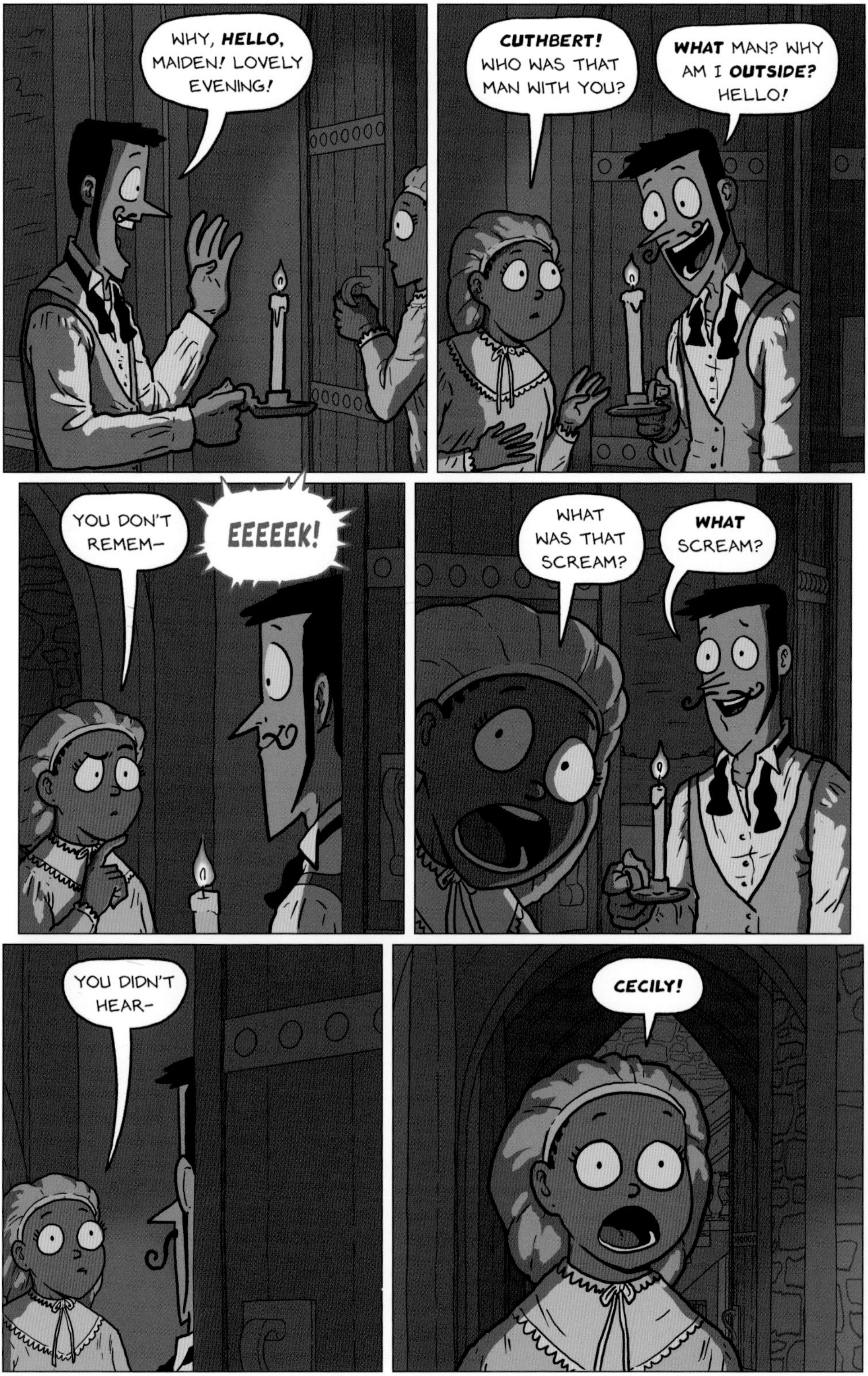
WHY, **HELLO,** MAIDEN! LOVELY EVENING!
CUTHBERT! WHO WAS THAT MAN WITH YOU?
WHAT MAN? WHY AM I **OUTSIDE?** HELLO!
YOU DON'T REMEM-
EEEEEK!
WHAT WAS THAT SCREAM?
WHAT SCREAM?
YOU DIDN'T HEAR-
CECILY!

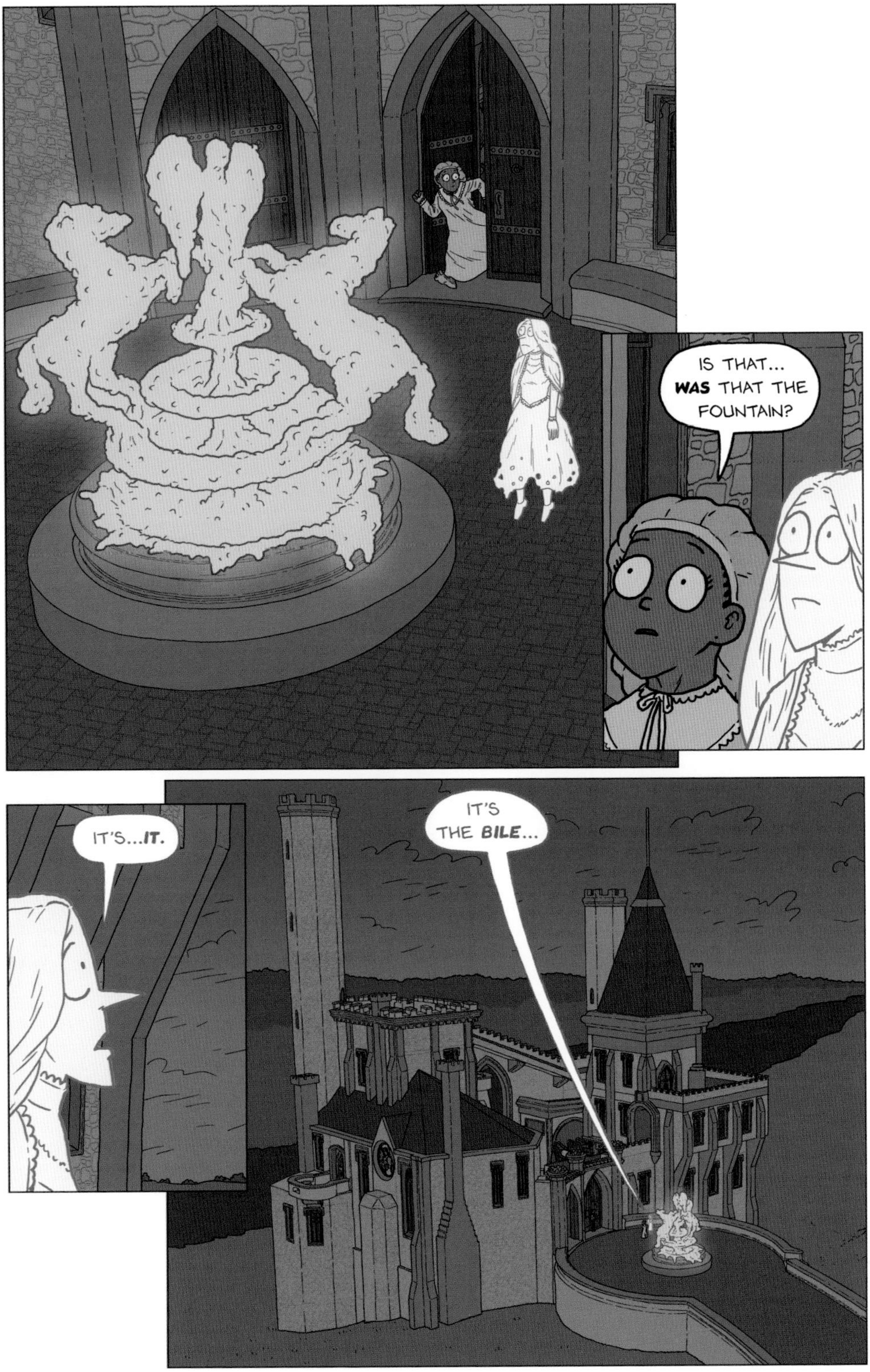
IS THAT... **WAS** THAT THE FOUNTAIN?
IT'S...**IT.**
IT'S THE **BILE**...

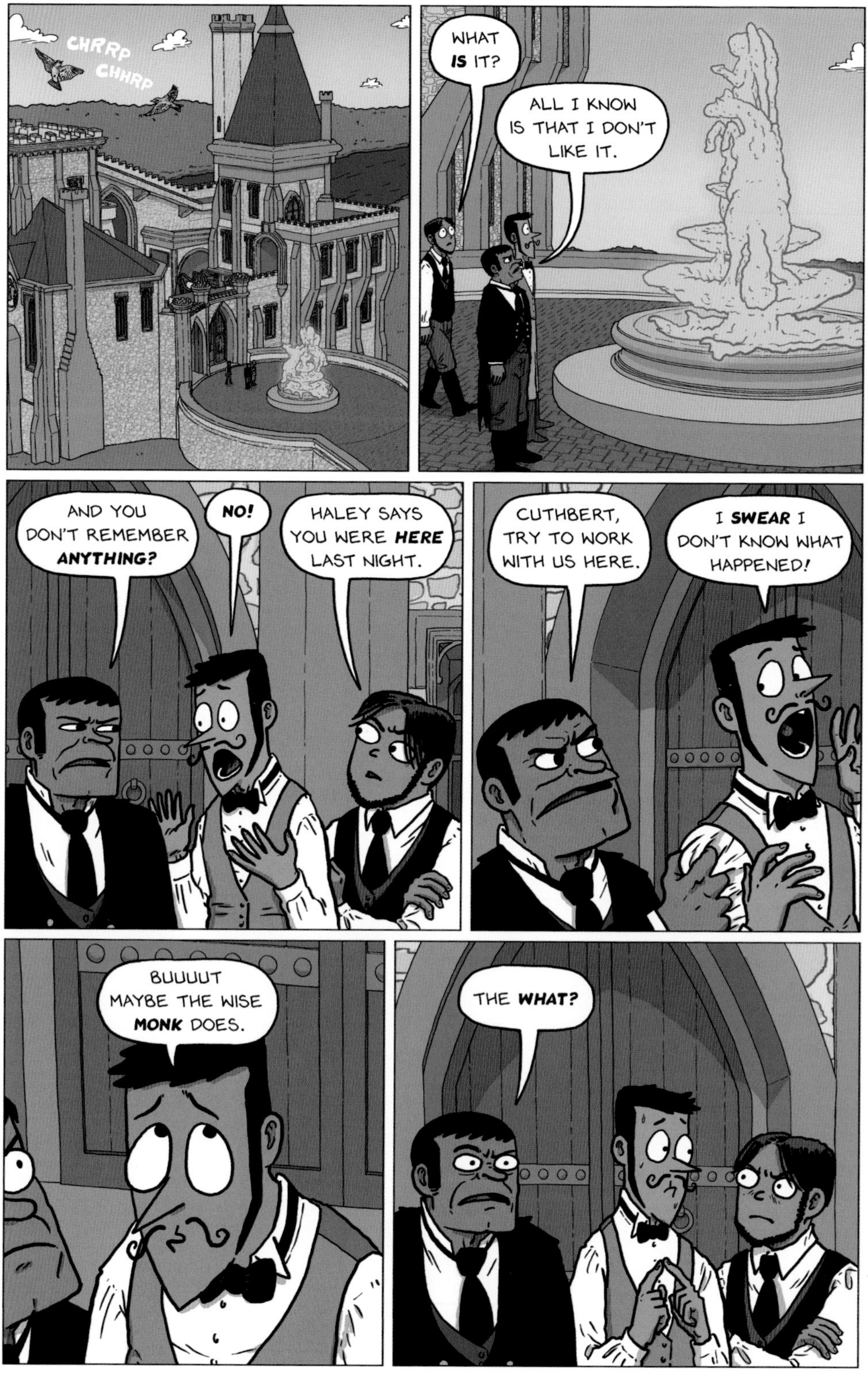
CHRRP
CHHRP
WHAT IS IT?
ALL I KNOW IS THAT I DON'T LIKE IT.
AND YOU DON'T REMEMBER ANYTHING?
NO!
HALEY SAYS YOU WERE HERE LAST NIGHT.
CUTHBERT, TRY TO WORK WITH US HERE.
I SWEAR I DON'T KNOW WHAT HAPPENED!
BUUUUT MAYBE THE WISE MONK DOES.
THE WHAT?

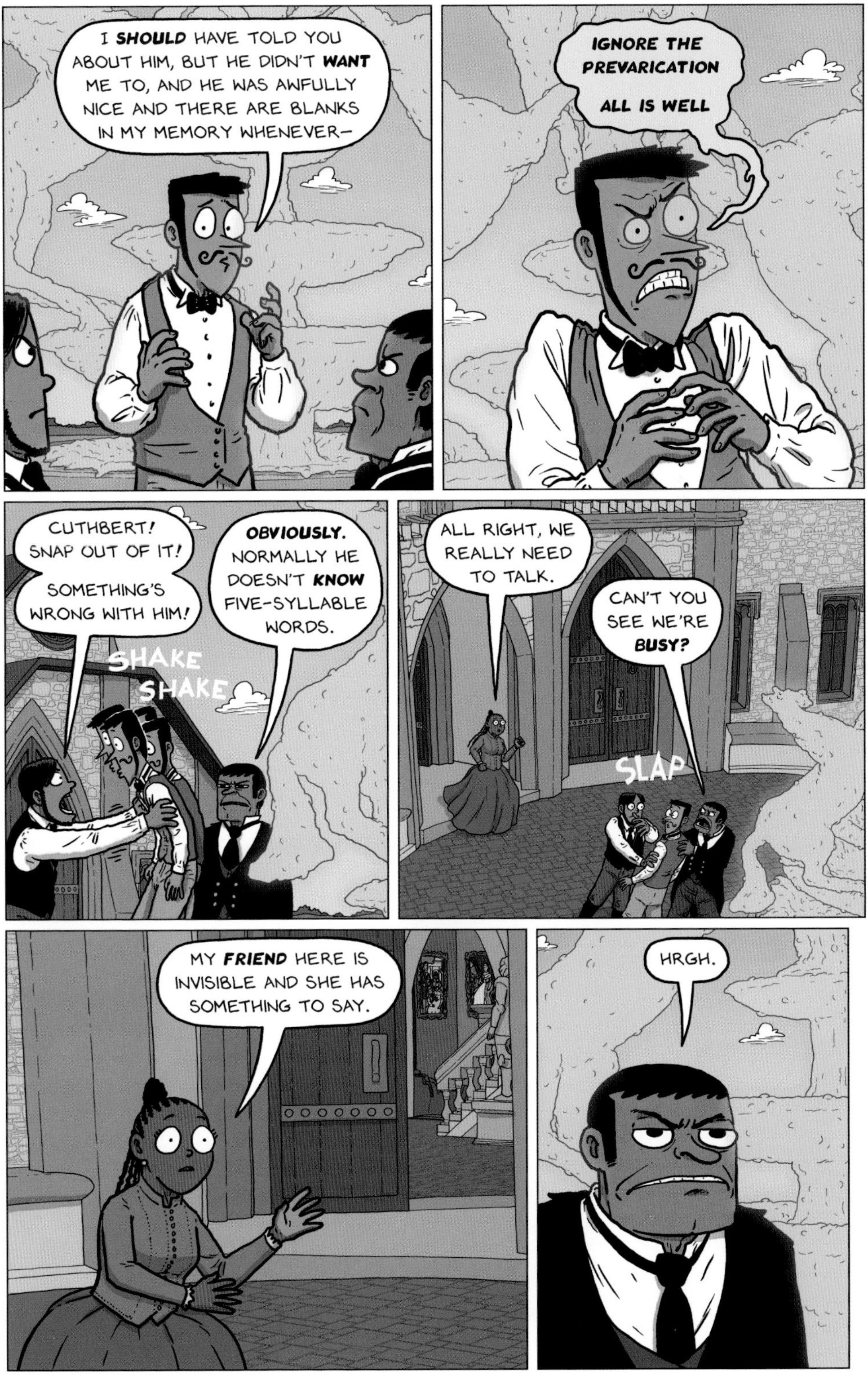
I SHOULD HAVE TOLD YOU ABOUT HIM, BUT HE DIDN'T WANT ME TO, AND HE WAS AWFULLY NICE AND THERE ARE BLANKS IN MY MEMORY WHENEVER–
IGNORE THE PREVARICATION
ALL IS WELL
CUTHBERT! SNAP OUT OF IT!
SOMETHING'S WRONG WITH HIM!
SHAKE
SHAKE
OBVIOUSLY. NORMALLY HE DOESN'T KNOW FIVE-SYLLABLE WORDS.
ALL RIGHT, WE REALLY NEED TO TALK.
CAN'T YOU SEE WE'RE BUSY?
SLAP
MY FRIEND HERE IS INVISIBLE AND SHE HAS SOMETHING TO SAY.
HRGH.

THE STORY OF CECILY THE WILLOWWEEP GHOST

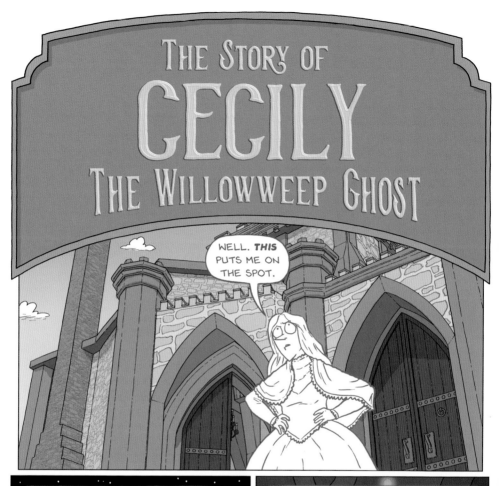

WELL. **THIS** PUTS ME ON THE SPOT.

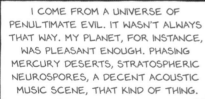

I COME FROM A UNIVERSE OF PENULTIMATE EVIL. IT WASN'T ALWAYS THAT WAY. MY PLANET, FOR INSTANCE, WAS PLEASANT ENOUGH. PHASING MERCURY DESERTS, STRATOSPHERIC NEUROSPORES, A DECENT ACOUSTIC MUSIC SCENE, THAT KIND OF THING.

THEN THE BILE SPREAD.

A TEAM OF SCIENTISTS DISCOVERED THE BILE APPROACHING OUR WORLD. WE DIDN'T CALL IT **THAT**, OF COURSE. WE HAD OUR **OWN** NAMES FOR ALL-DEVOURING SAPIENT MIASMA.

THAT ABSOLUTE ⊐⅃ᵹ⅃ᖴ⅃ᕼᗷᏩᎽ⅁.

LANGUAGE.

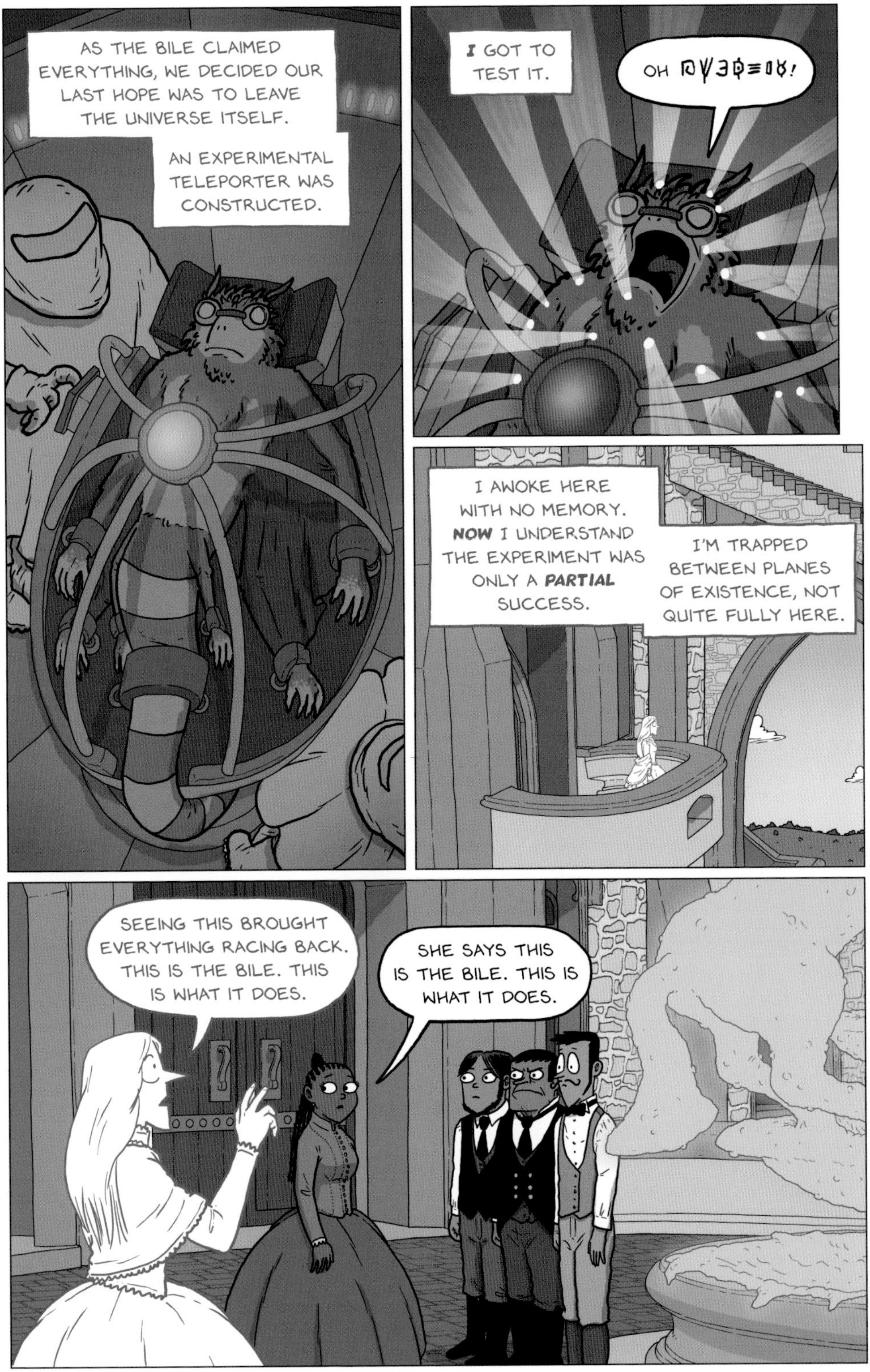
AS THE BILE CLAIMED EVERYTHING, WE DECIDED OUR LAST HOPE WAS TO LEAVE THE UNIVERSE ITSELF.
AN EXPERIMENTAL TELEPORTER WAS CONSTRUCTED.
I GOT TO TEST IT.
OH
I AWOKE HERE WITH NO MEMORY. **NOW** I UNDERSTAND THE EXPERIMENT WAS ONLY A **PARTIAL** SUCCESS.
I'M TRAPPED BETWEEN PLANES OF EXISTENCE, NOT QUITE FULLY HERE.
SEEING THIS BROUGHT EVERYTHING RACING BACK. THIS IS THE BILE. THIS IS WHAT IT DOES.
SHE SAYS THIS IS THE BILE. THIS IS WHAT IT DOES.

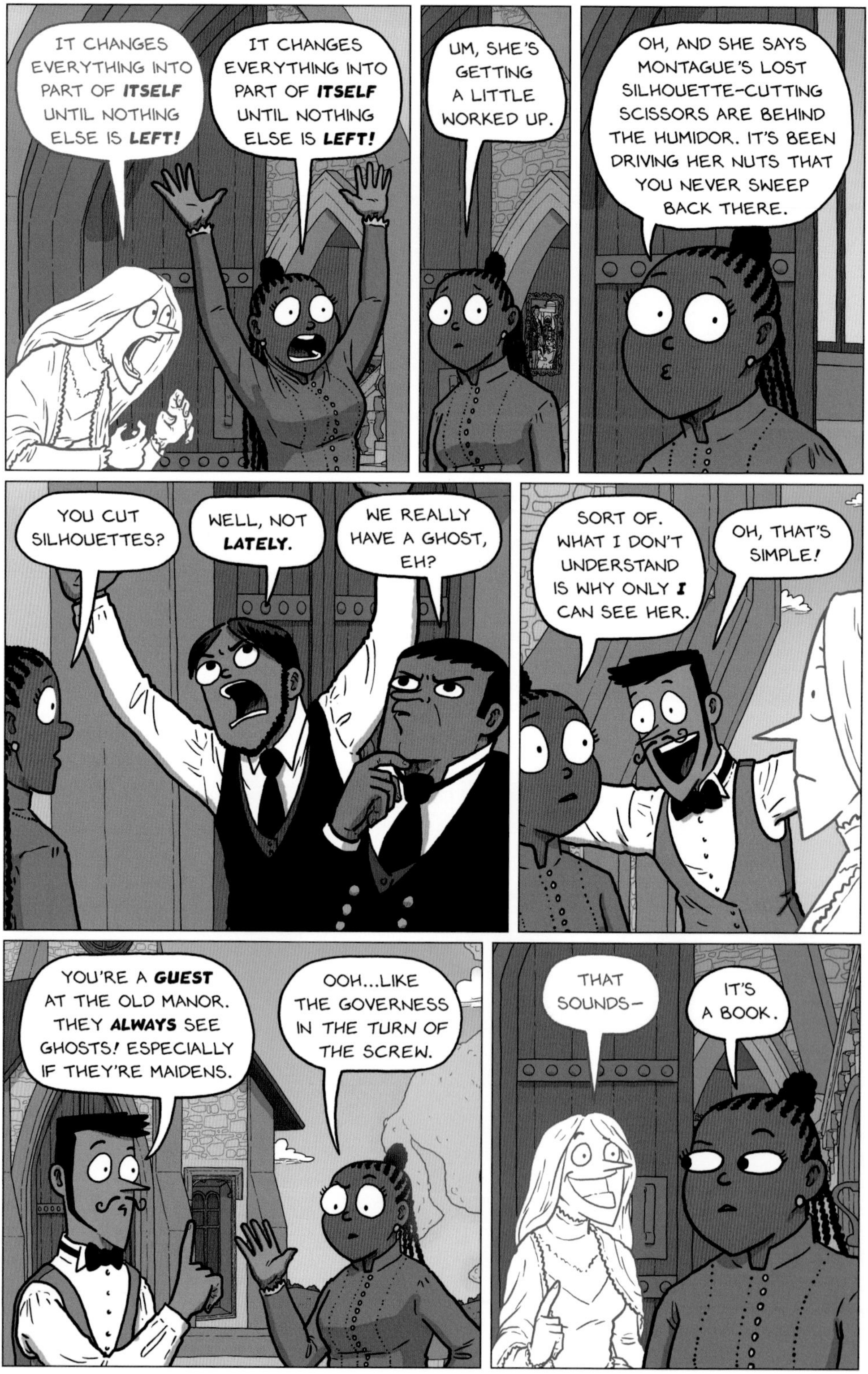

IT CHANGES EVERYTHING INTO PART OF ITSELF UNTIL NOTHING ELSE IS LEFT!
IT CHANGES EVERYTHING INTO PART OF ITSELF UNTIL NOTHING ELSE IS LEFT!
UM, SHE'S GETTING A LITTLE WORKED UP.
OH, AND SHE SAYS MONTAGUE'S LOST SILHOUETTE-CUTTING SCISSORS ARE BEHIND THE HUMIDOR. IT'S BEEN DRIVING HER NUTS THAT YOU NEVER SWEEP BACK THERE.
YOU CUT SILHOUETTES?
WELL, NOT LATELY.
WE REALLY HAVE A GHOST, EH?
SORT OF. WHAT I DON'T UNDERSTAND IS WHY ONLY I CAN SEE HER.
OH, THAT'S SIMPLE!
YOU'RE A GUEST AT THE OLD MANOR. THEY ALWAYS SEE GHOSTS! ESPECIALLY IF THEY'RE MAIDENS.
OOH...LIKE THE GOVERNESS IN THE TURN OF THE SCREW.
THAT SOUNDS—
IT'S A BOOK.

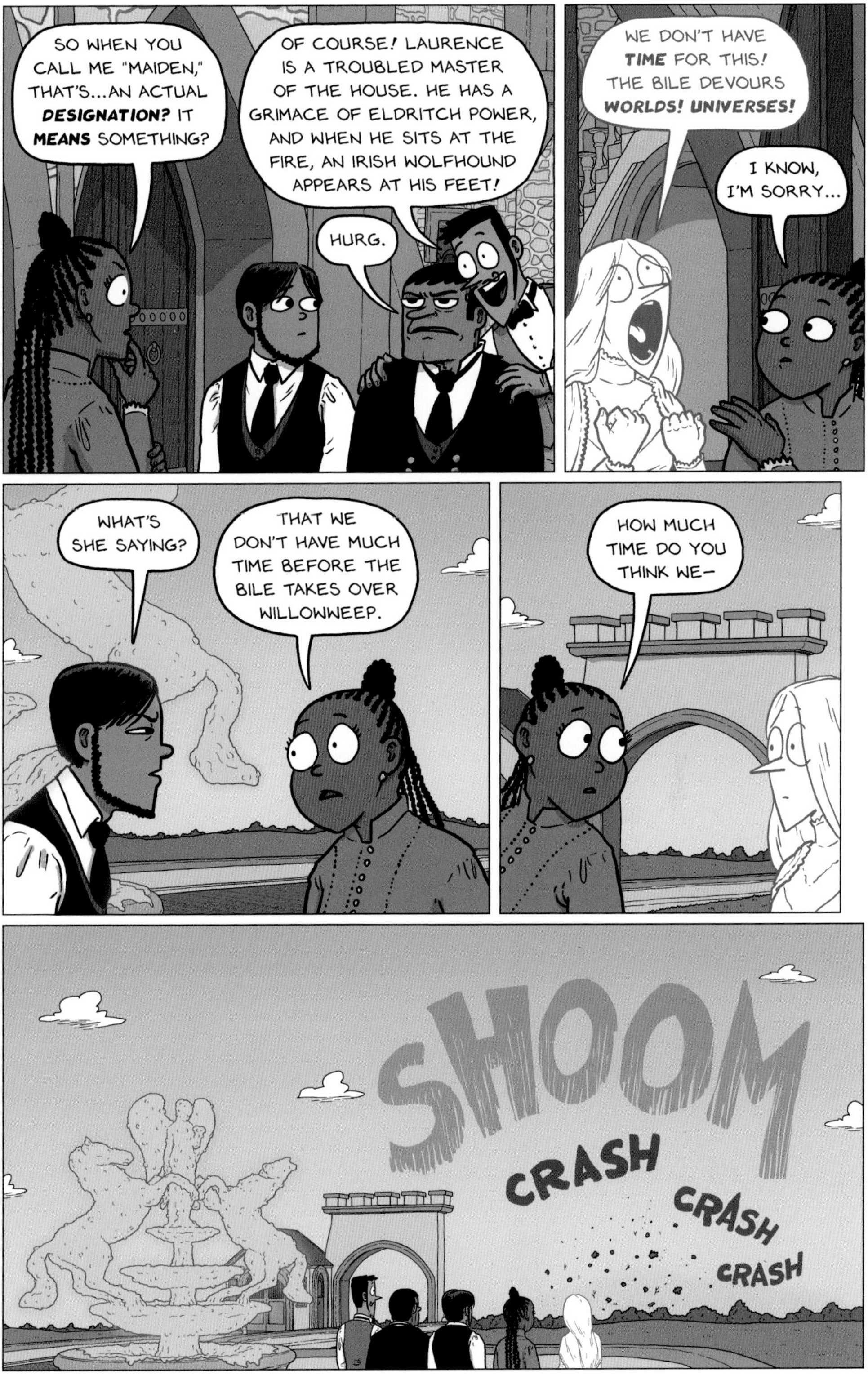
SO WHEN YOU CALL ME "MAIDEN," THAT'S...AN ACTUAL **DESIGNATION?** IT **MEANS** SOMETHING?
OF COURSE! LAURENCE IS A TROUBLED MASTER OF THE HOUSE. HE HAS A GRIMACE OF ELDRITCH POWER, AND WHEN HE SITS AT THE FIRE, AN IRISH WOLFHOUND APPEARS AT HIS FEET!
HURG.
WE DON'T HAVE **TIME** FOR THIS! THE BILE DEVOURS **WORLDS! UNIVERSES!**
I KNOW, I'M SORRY...
WHAT'S SHE SAYING?
THAT WE DON'T HAVE MUCH TIME BEFORE THE BILE TAKES OVER WILLOWWEEP.
HOW MUCH TIME DO YOU THINK WE—
SHOOM
CRASH
CRASH
CRASH

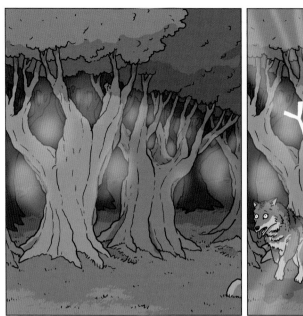

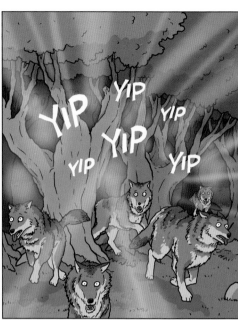

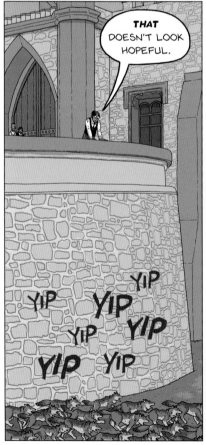

YIP
YIP
YIP
YIP
YIP
YIP
THAT DOESN'T LOOK HOPEFUL.
YIP
YIP
YIP
YIP
YIP
YIP
YIP
VERY WELL. I AM THE MASTER OF THE HOUSE, AND I'LL REMAIN SUCH AS LONG AS THE HOUSE STANDS.
FOLLOW ME.
CUTHBERT! YOU HAVE BEHAVED ABOMINABLY, EVEN IF IT WAS DUE MORE TO A MALLEABLE MIND THAN ILL INTENT.
I KNOW.

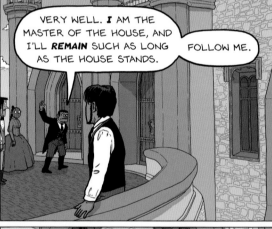

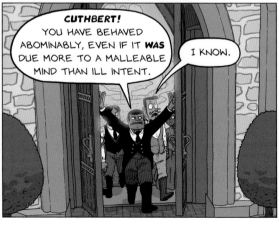

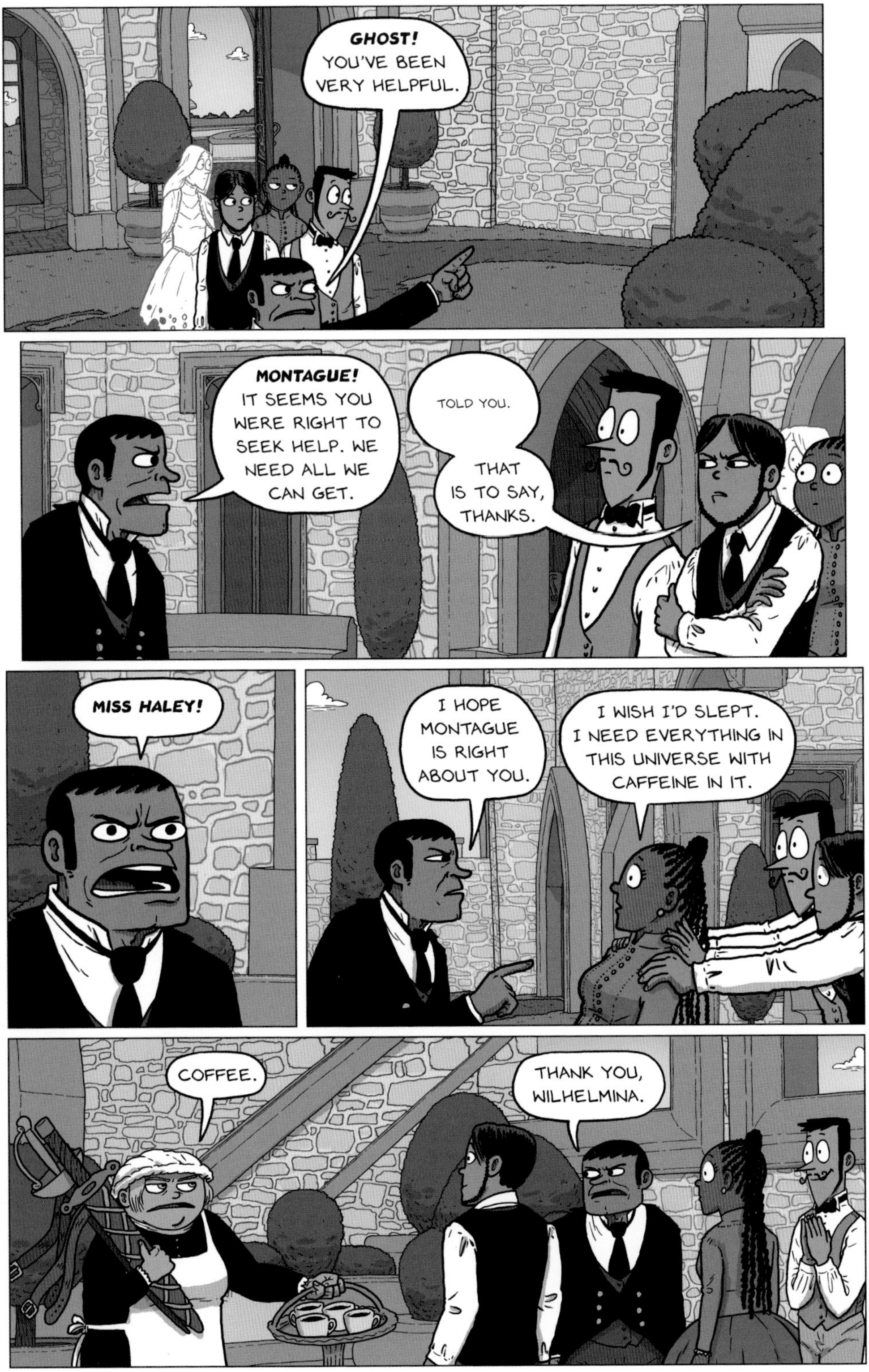
GHOST! YOU'VE BEEN VERY HELPFUL.
MONTAGUE! IT SEEMS YOU WERE RIGHT TO SEEK HELP. WE NEED ALL WE CAN GET.
TOLD YOU.
THAT IS TO SAY, THANKS.
MISS HALEY!
I HOPE MONTAGUE IS RIGHT ABOUT YOU.
I WISH I'D SLEPT. I NEED EVERYTHING IN THIS UNIVERSE WITH CAFFEINE IN IT.
COFFEE.
THANK YOU, WILHELMINA.

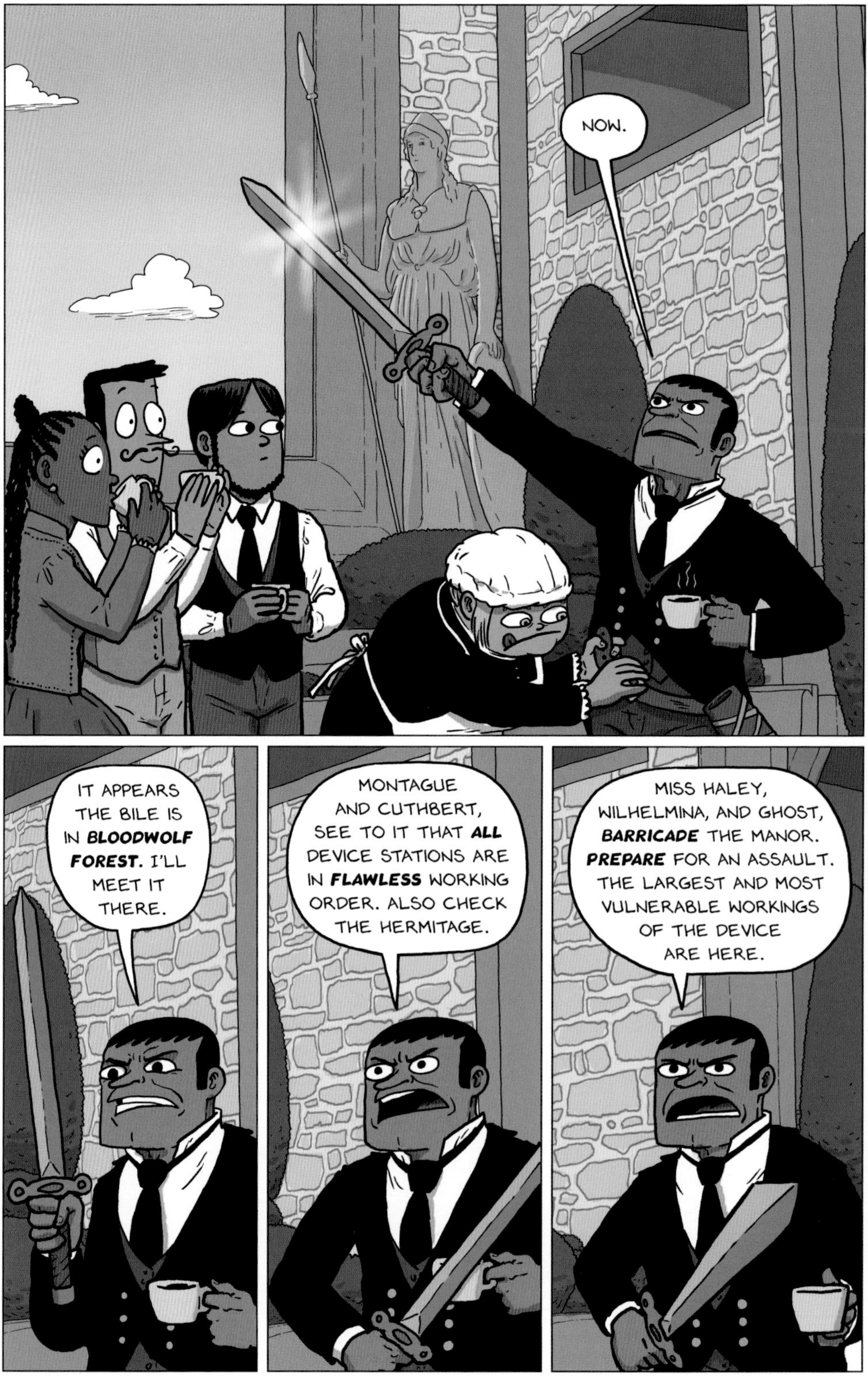
NOW.
IT APPEARS THE BILE IS IN **BLOODWOLF FOREST.** I'LL MEET IT THERE.
MONTAGUE AND CUTHBERT, SEE TO IT THAT **ALL** DEVICE STATIONS ARE IN **FLAWLESS** WORKING ORDER. ALSO CHECK THE HERMITAGE.
MISS HALEY, WILHELMINA, AND GHOST, **BARRICADE** THE MANOR. **PREPARE** FOR AN ASSAULT. THE LARGEST AND MOST VULNERABLE WORKINGS OF THE DEVICE ARE HERE.

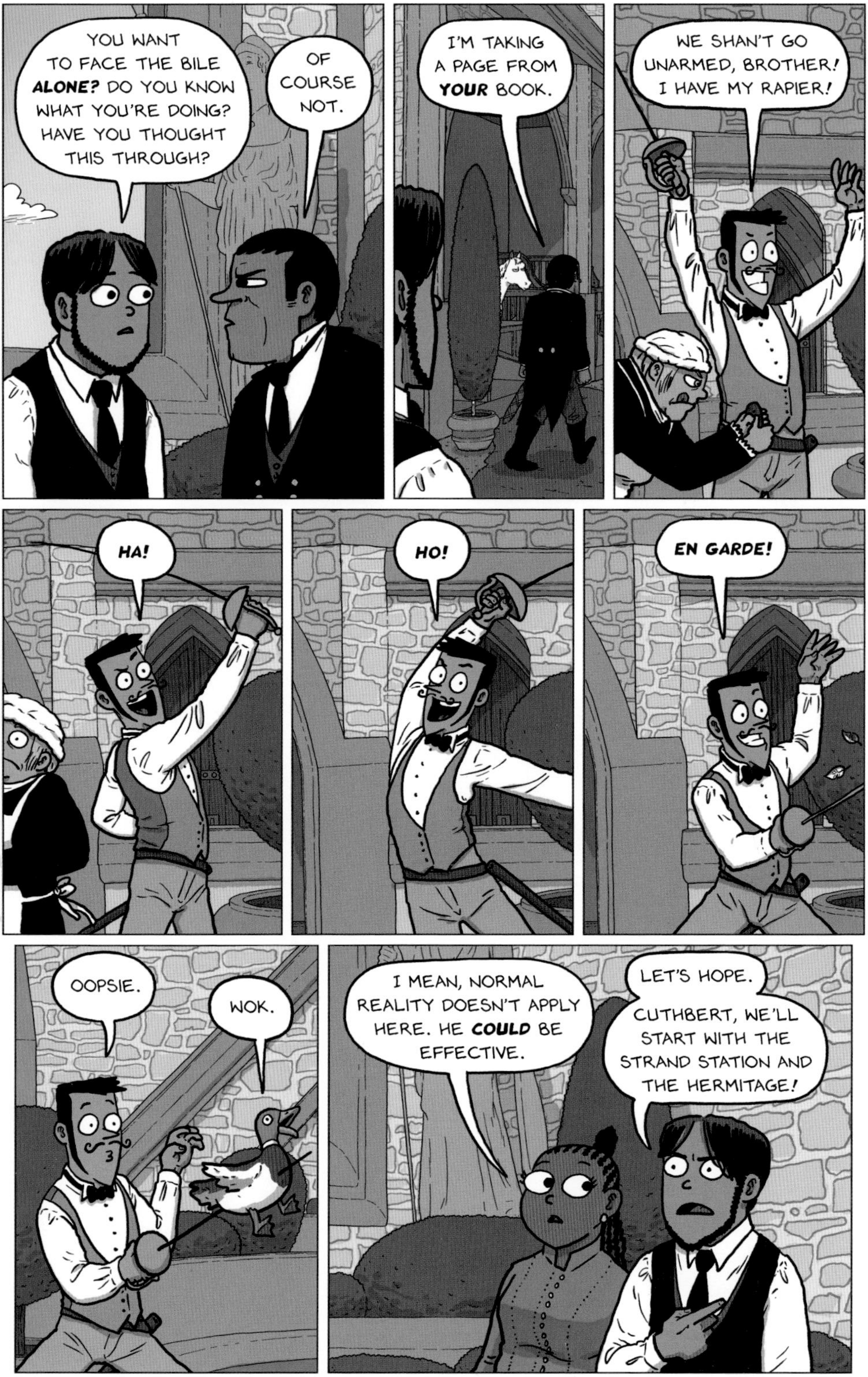
YOU WANT TO FACE THE BILE **ALONE?** DO YOU KNOW WHAT YOU'RE DOING? HAVE YOU THOUGHT THIS THROUGH?
OF COURSE NOT.
I'M TAKING A PAGE FROM **YOUR** BOOK.
WE SHAN'T GO UNARMED, BROTHER! I HAVE MY RAPIER!
HA!
HO!
EN GARDE!
OOPSIE.
WOK.
I MEAN, NORMAL REALITY DOESN'T APPLY HERE. HE **COULD** BE EFFECTIVE.
LET'S HOPE.
CUTHBERT, WE'LL START WITH THE STRAND STATION AND THE HERMITAGE!

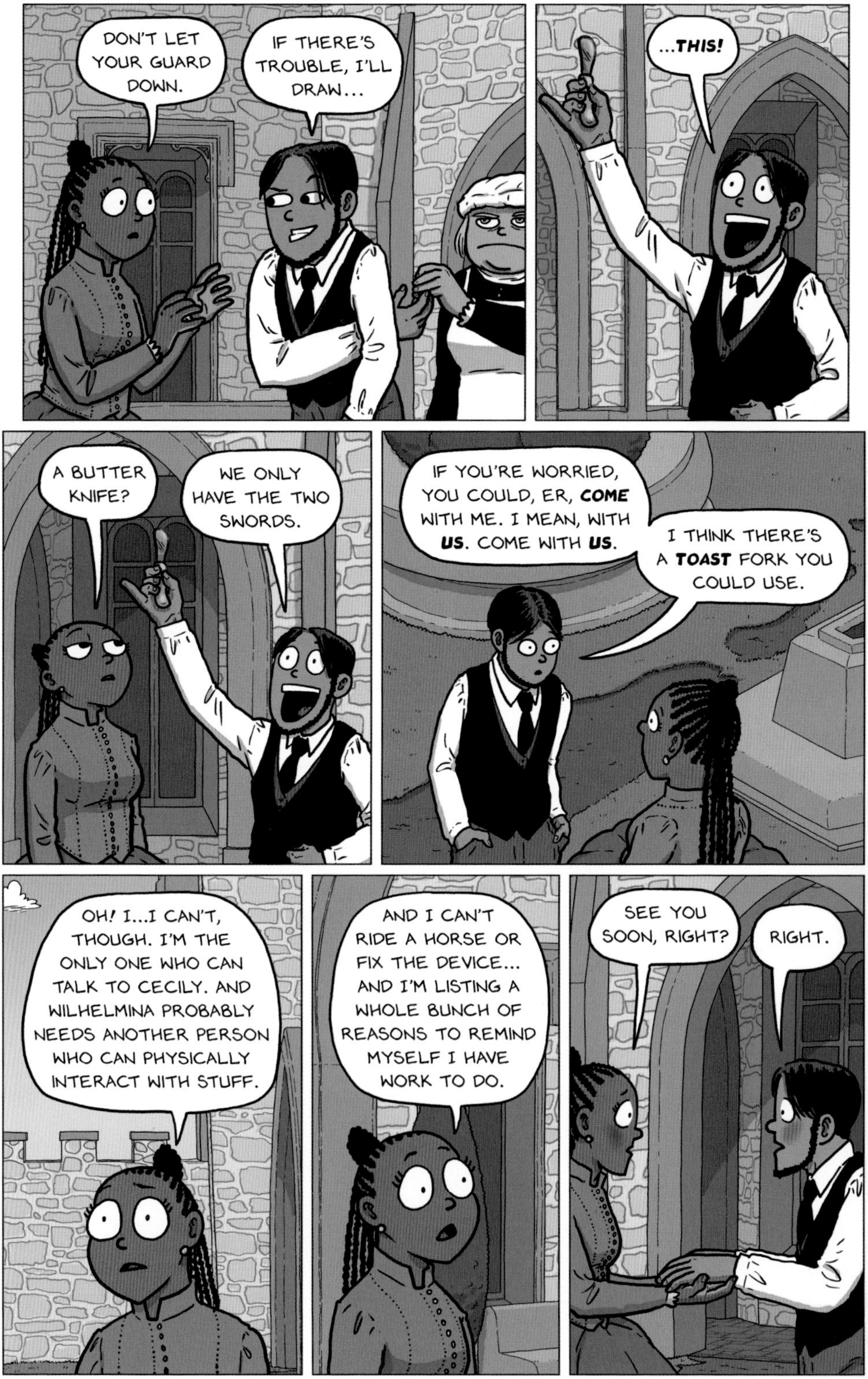
DON'T LET YOUR GUARD DOWN.
IF THERE'S TROUBLE, I'LL DRAW...
...**THIS!**
A BUTTER KNIFE?
WE ONLY HAVE THE TWO SWORDS.
IF YOU'RE WORRIED, YOU COULD, ER, **COME** WITH ME. I MEAN, WITH **US**. COME WITH **US**.
I THINK THERE'S A **TOAST** FORK YOU COULD USE.
OH! I...I CAN'T, THOUGH. I'M THE ONLY ONE WHO CAN TALK TO CECILY. AND WILHELMINA PROBABLY NEEDS ANOTHER PERSON WHO CAN PHYSICALLY INTERACT WITH STUFF.
AND I CAN'T RIDE A HORSE OR FIX THE DEVICE... AND I'M LISTING A WHOLE BUNCH OF REASONS TO REMIND MYSELF I HAVE WORK TO DO.
SEE YOU SOON, RIGHT?
RIGHT.

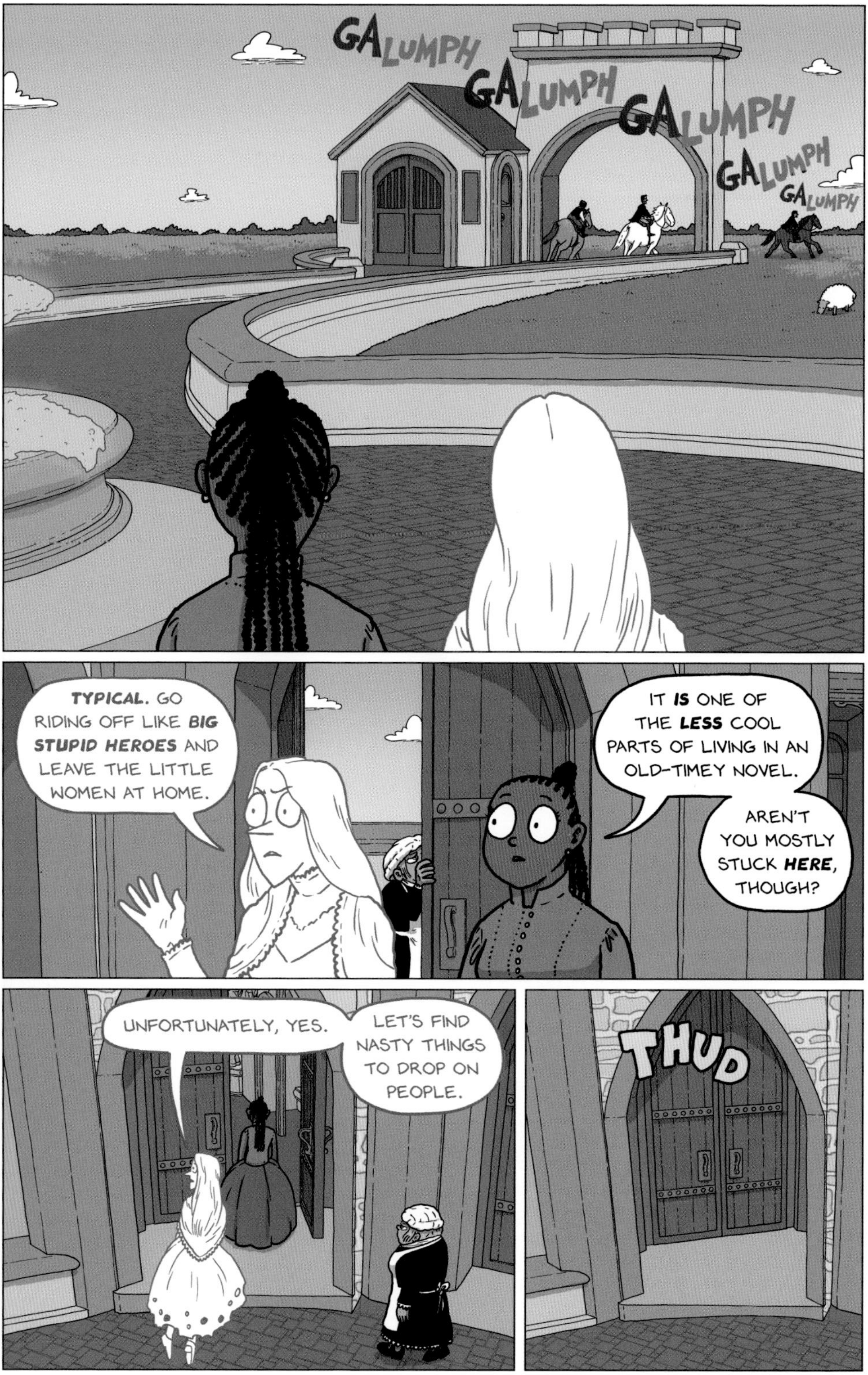
GALUMPH
GALUMPH
GALUMPH
GALUMPH
GALUMPH
TYPICAL. GO RIDING OFF LIKE BIG STUPID HEROES AND LEAVE THE LITTLE WOMEN AT HOME.
IT IS ONE OF THE LESS COOL PARTS OF LIVING IN AN OLD-TIMEY NOVEL.
AREN'T YOU MOSTLY STUCK HERE, THOUGH?
UNFORTUNATELY, YES.
LET'S FIND NASTY THINGS TO DROP ON PEOPLE.
THUD

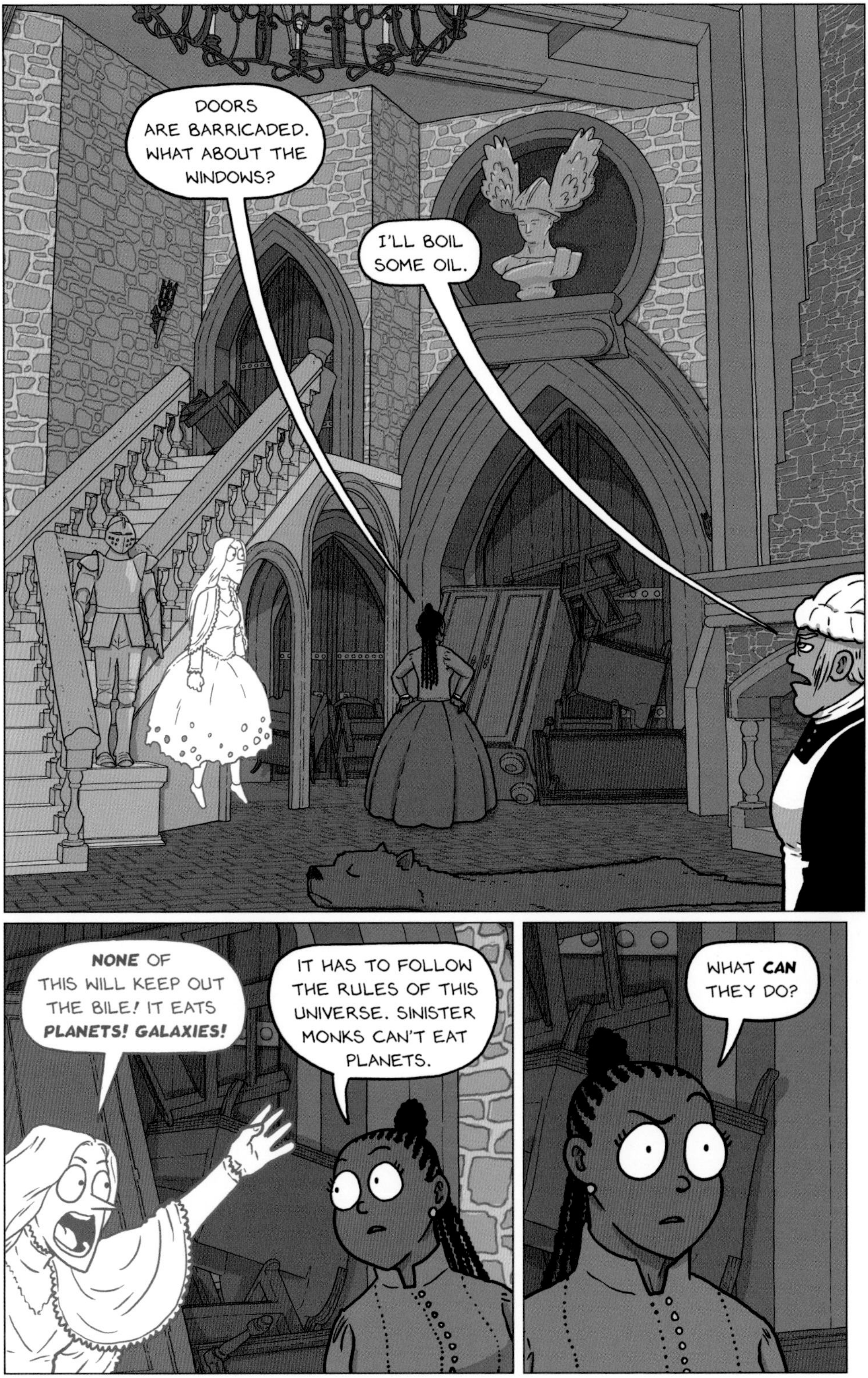
DOORS ARE BARRICADED. WHAT ABOUT THE WINDOWS?
I'LL BOIL SOME OIL.
NONE OF THIS WILL KEEP OUT THE BILE! IT EATS ***PLANETS! GALAXIES!***
IT HAS TO FOLLOW THE RULES OF THIS UNIVERSE. SINISTER MONKS CAN'T EAT PLANETS.
WHAT **CAN** THEY DO?

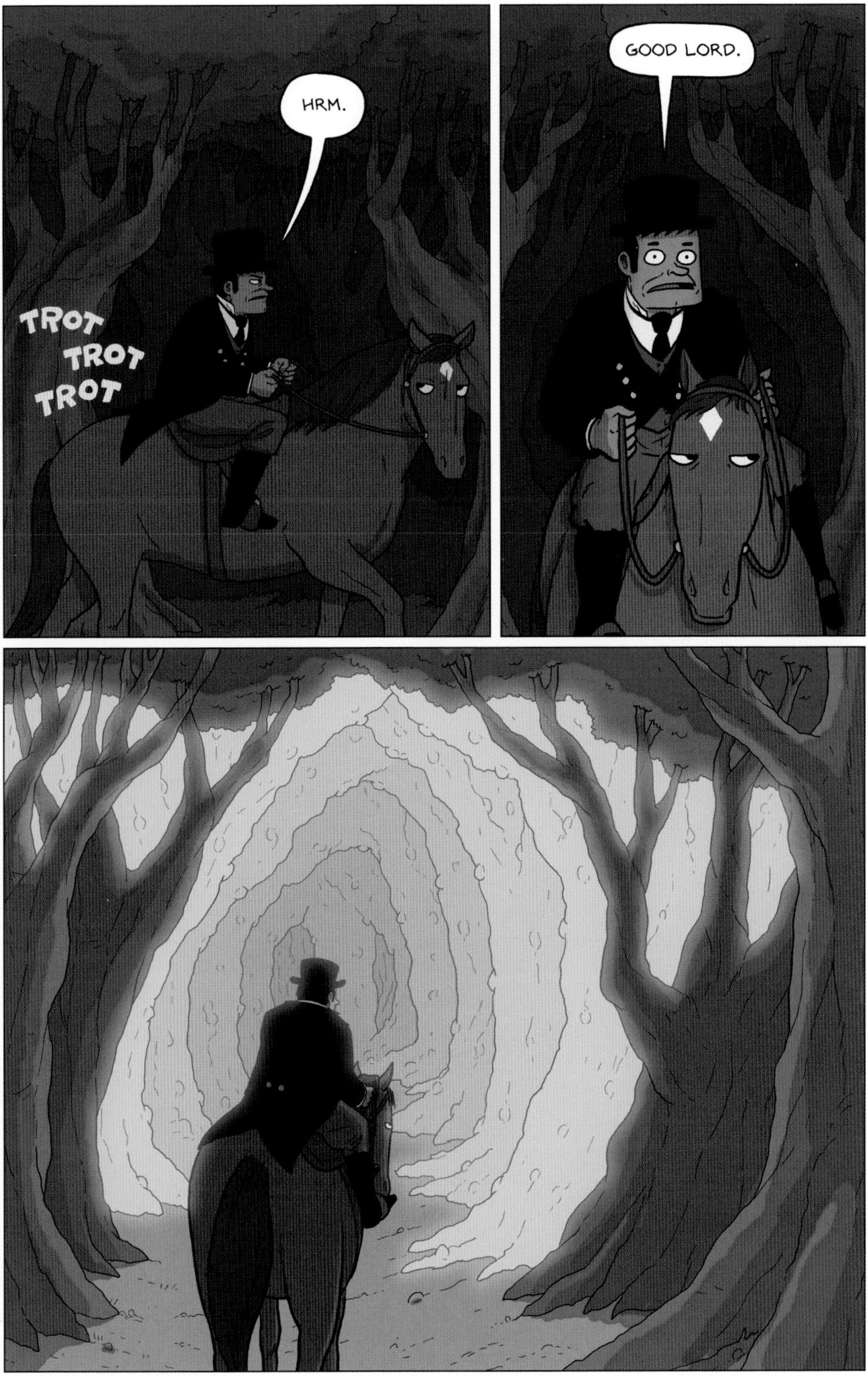
HRM.
TROT
TROT
TROT
GOOD LORD.

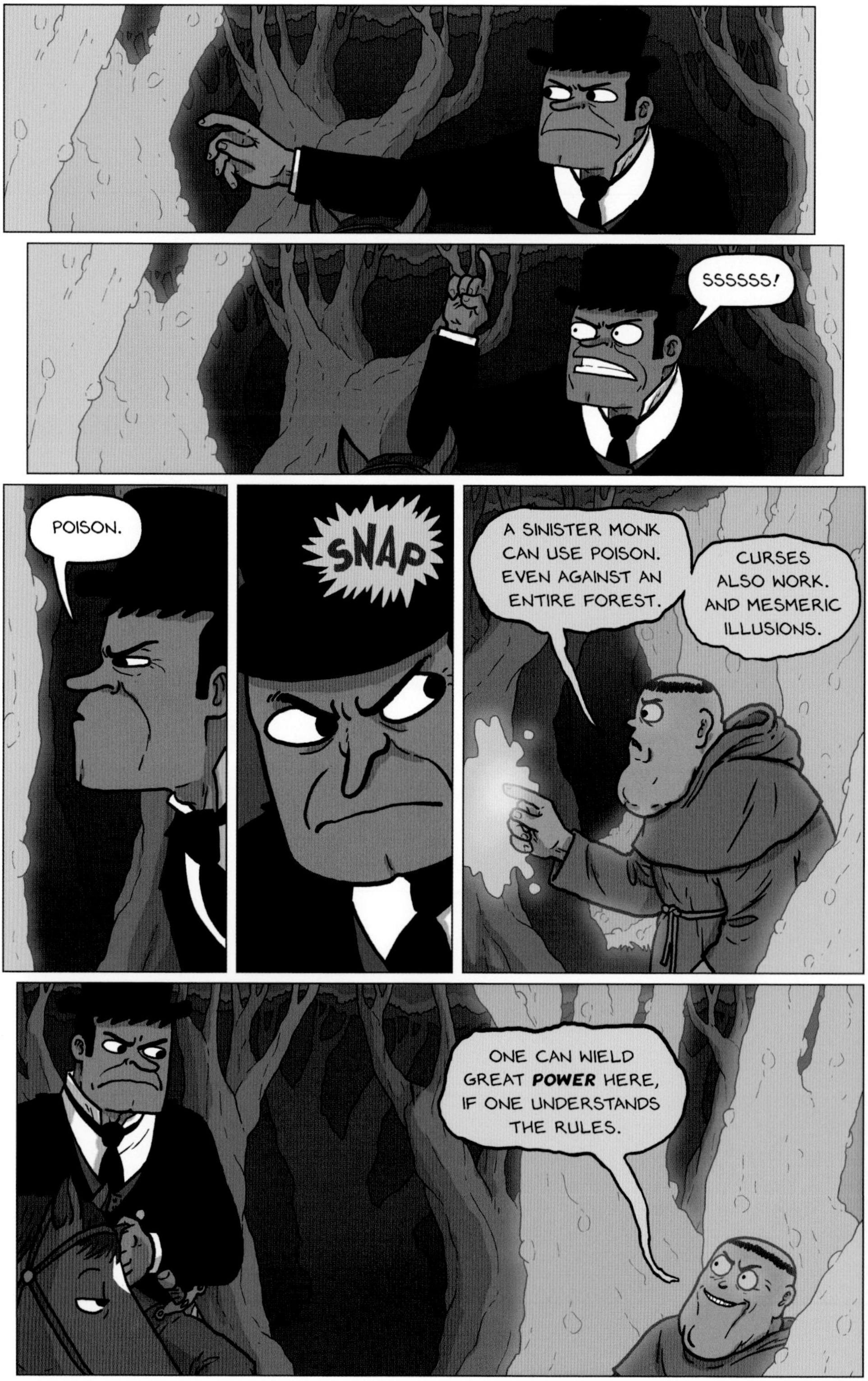
SSSSSS!
POISON.
SNAP
A SINISTER MONK CAN USE POISON. EVEN AGAINST AN ENTIRE FOREST.
CURSES ALSO WORK. AND MESMERIC ILLUSIONS.
ONE CAN WIELD GREAT **POWER** HERE, IF ONE UNDERSTANDS THE RULES.

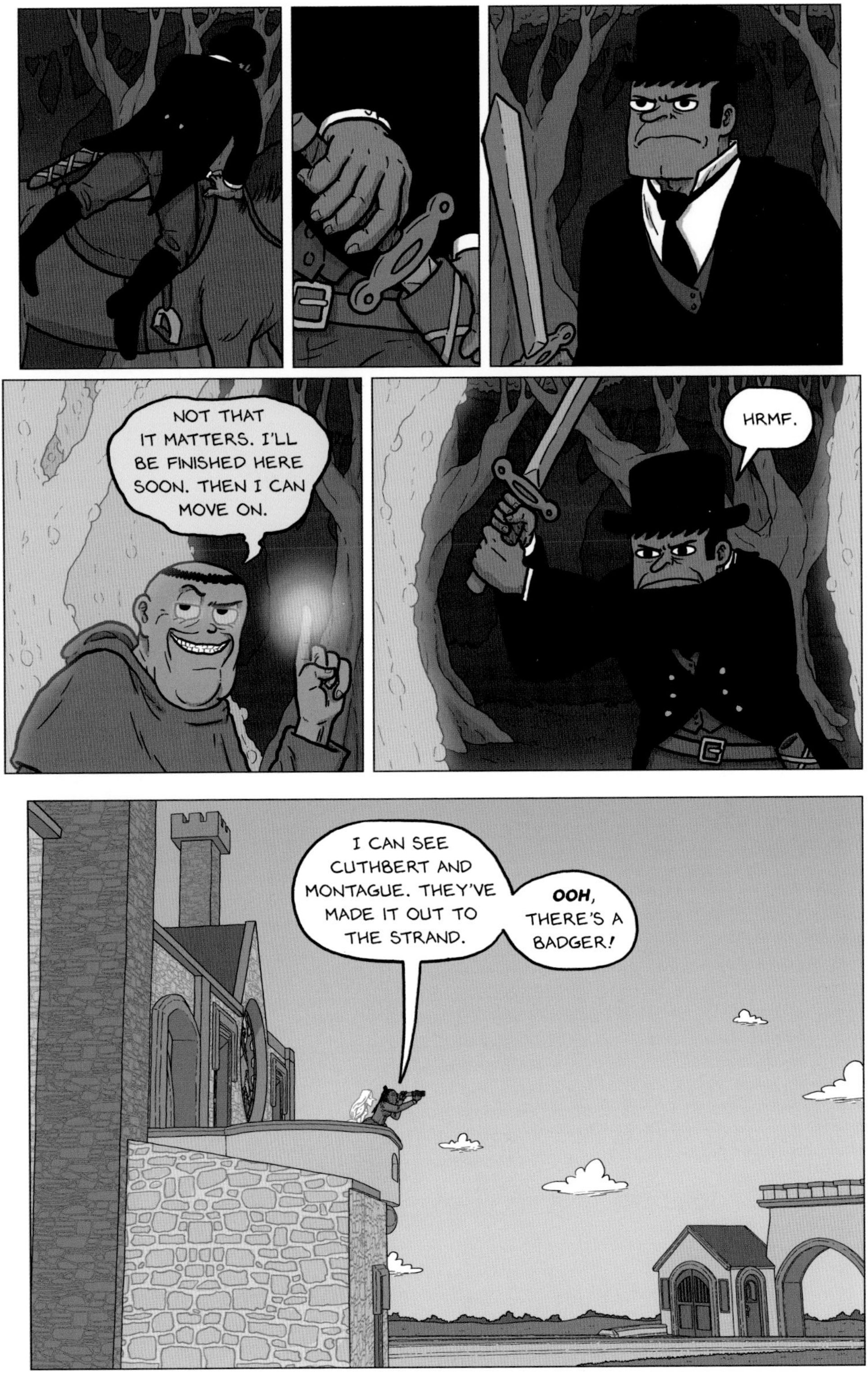
NOT THAT IT MATTERS. I'LL BE FINISHED HERE SOON. THEN I CAN MOVE ON.
HRMF.
I CAN SEE CUTHBERT AND MONTAGUE. THEY'VE MADE IT OUT TO THE STRAND.
OOH, THERE'S A BADGER!

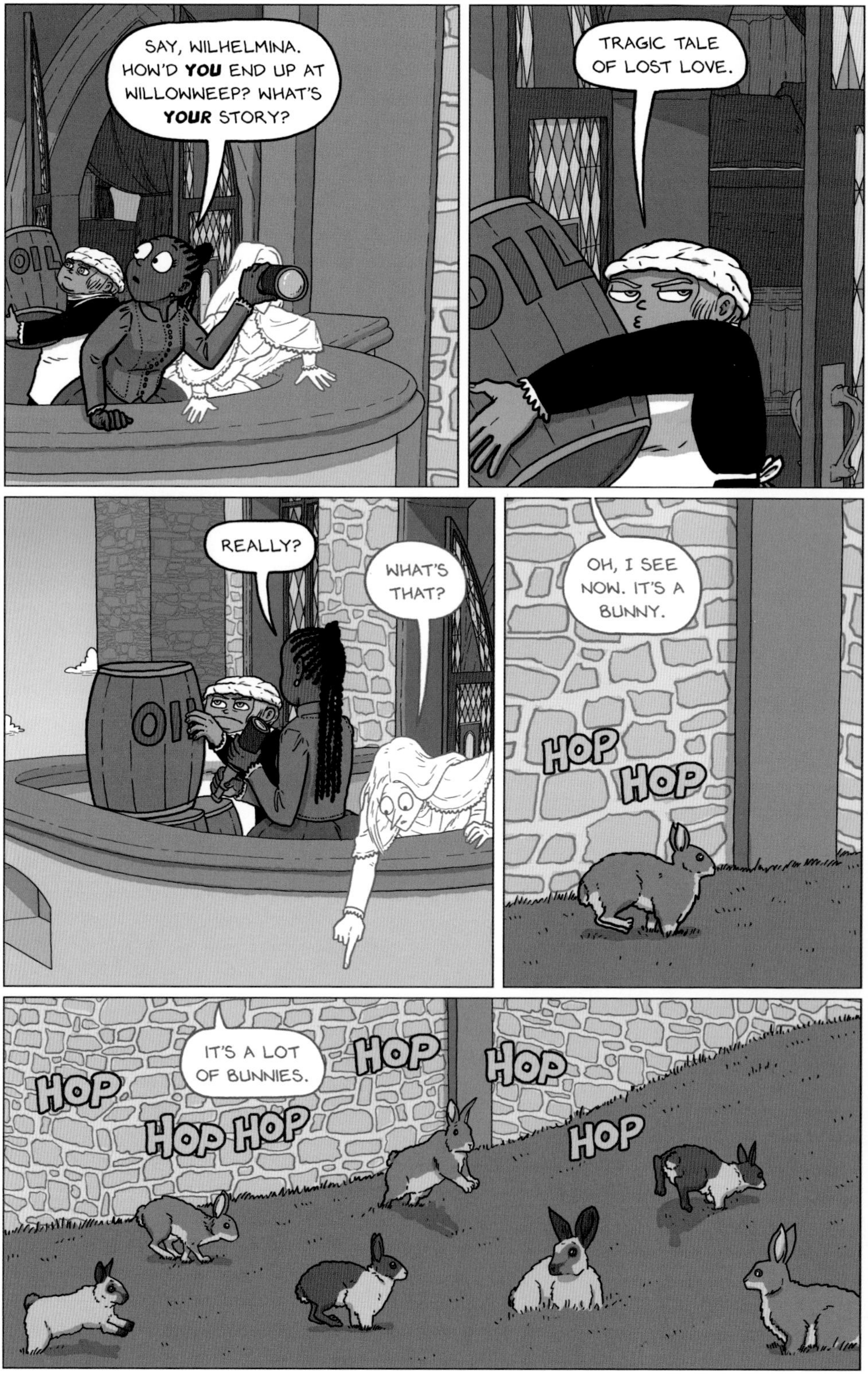
SAY, WILHELMINA. HOW'D **YOU** END UP AT WILLOWWEEP? WHAT'S **YOUR** STORY?
OIL
TRAGIC TALE OF LOST LOVE.
OIL
REALLY?
WHAT'S THAT?
OIL
OH, I SEE NOW. IT'S A BUNNY.
HOP
HOP
IT'S A LOT OF BUNNIES.
HOP
HOP
HOP
HOP HOP
HOP

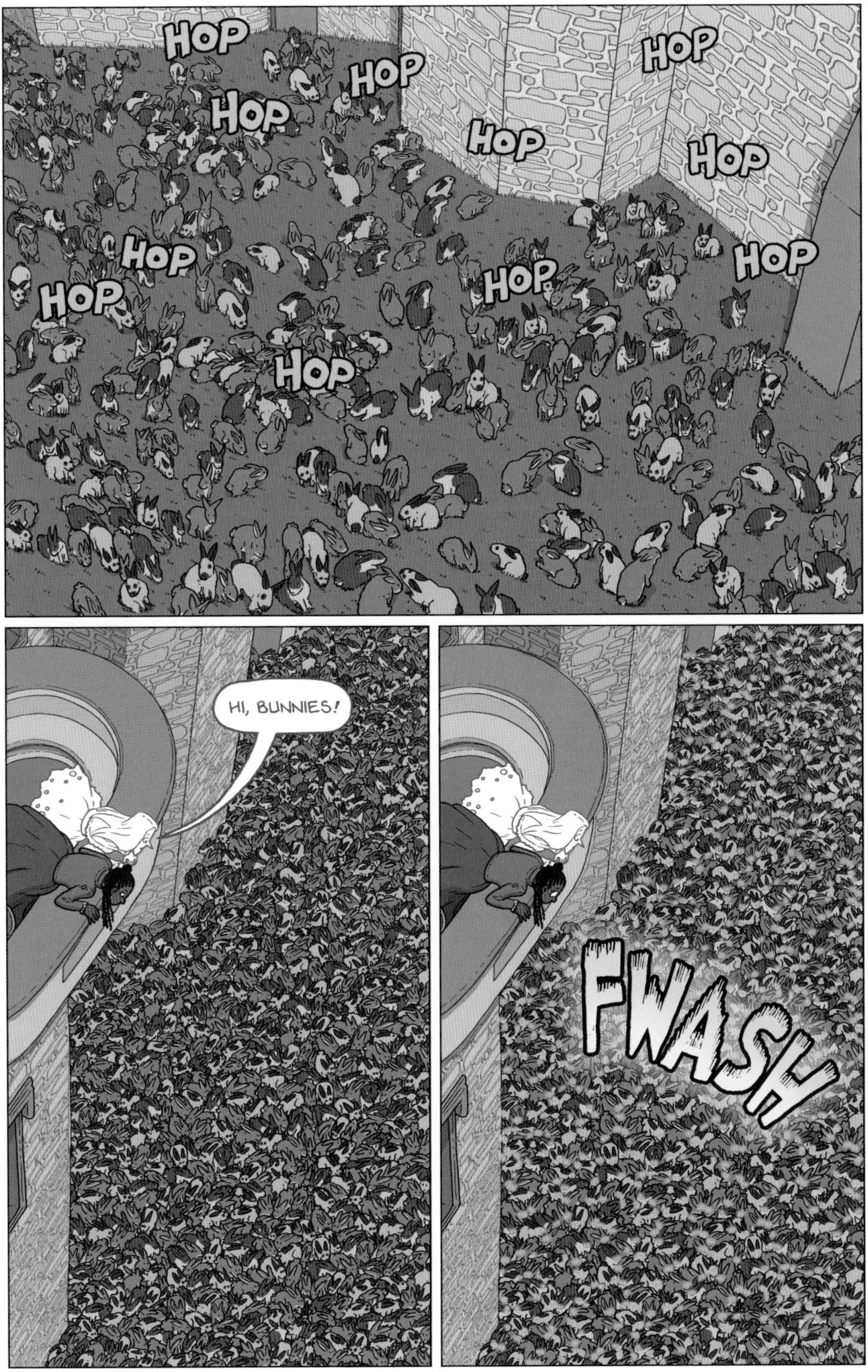
HOP
HOP
HOP
HOP
HOP
HOP
HOP
HOP
HOP
HOP
HOP
HI, BUNNIES!
FWASH

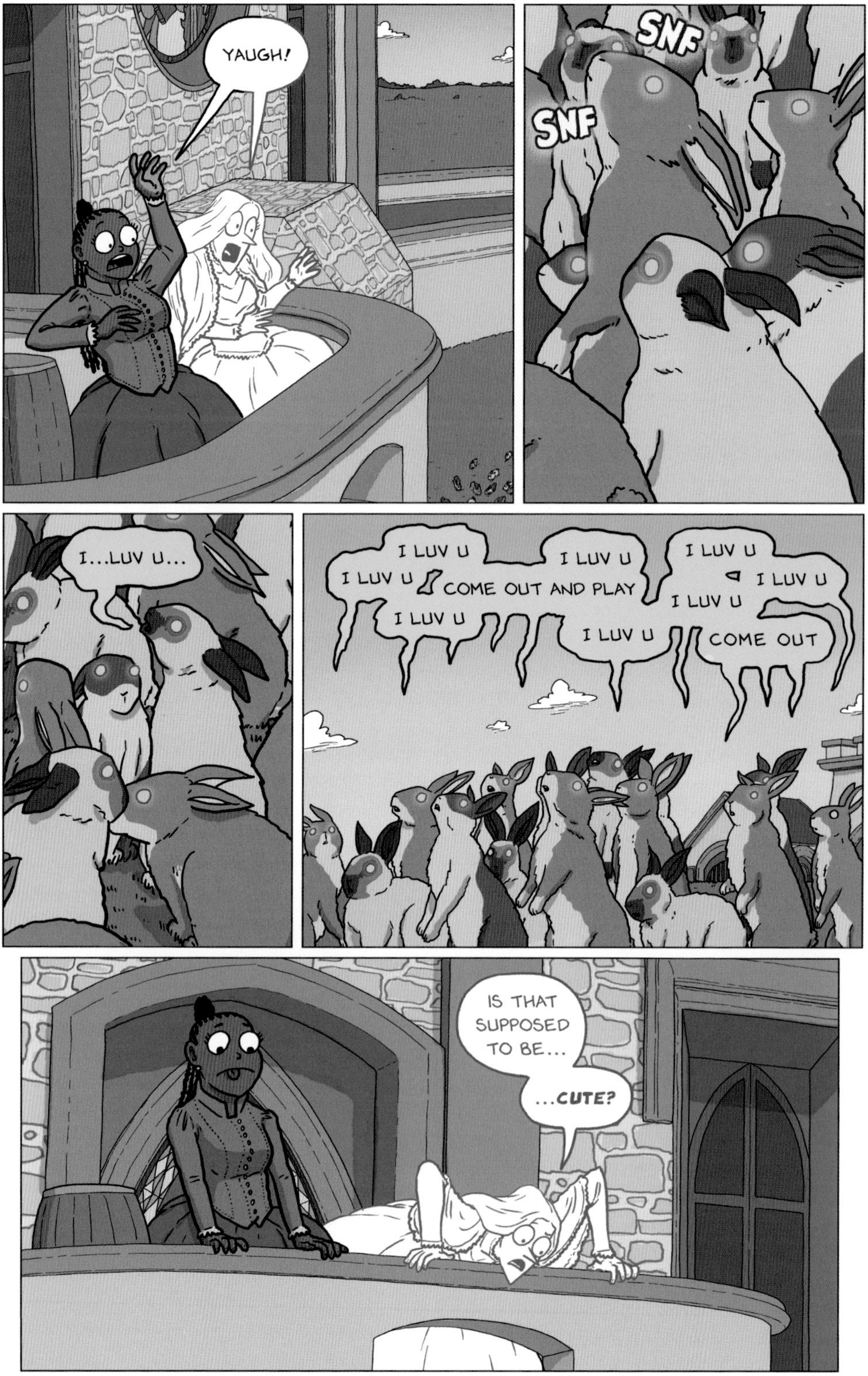
YAUGH!
SNF
SNF
I...LUV U...
I LUV U
I LUV U
I LUV U
I LUV U
COME OUT AND PLAY
I LUV U
I LUV U
I LUV U
I LUV U
COME OUT
IS THAT SUPPOSED TO BE...
...CUTE?

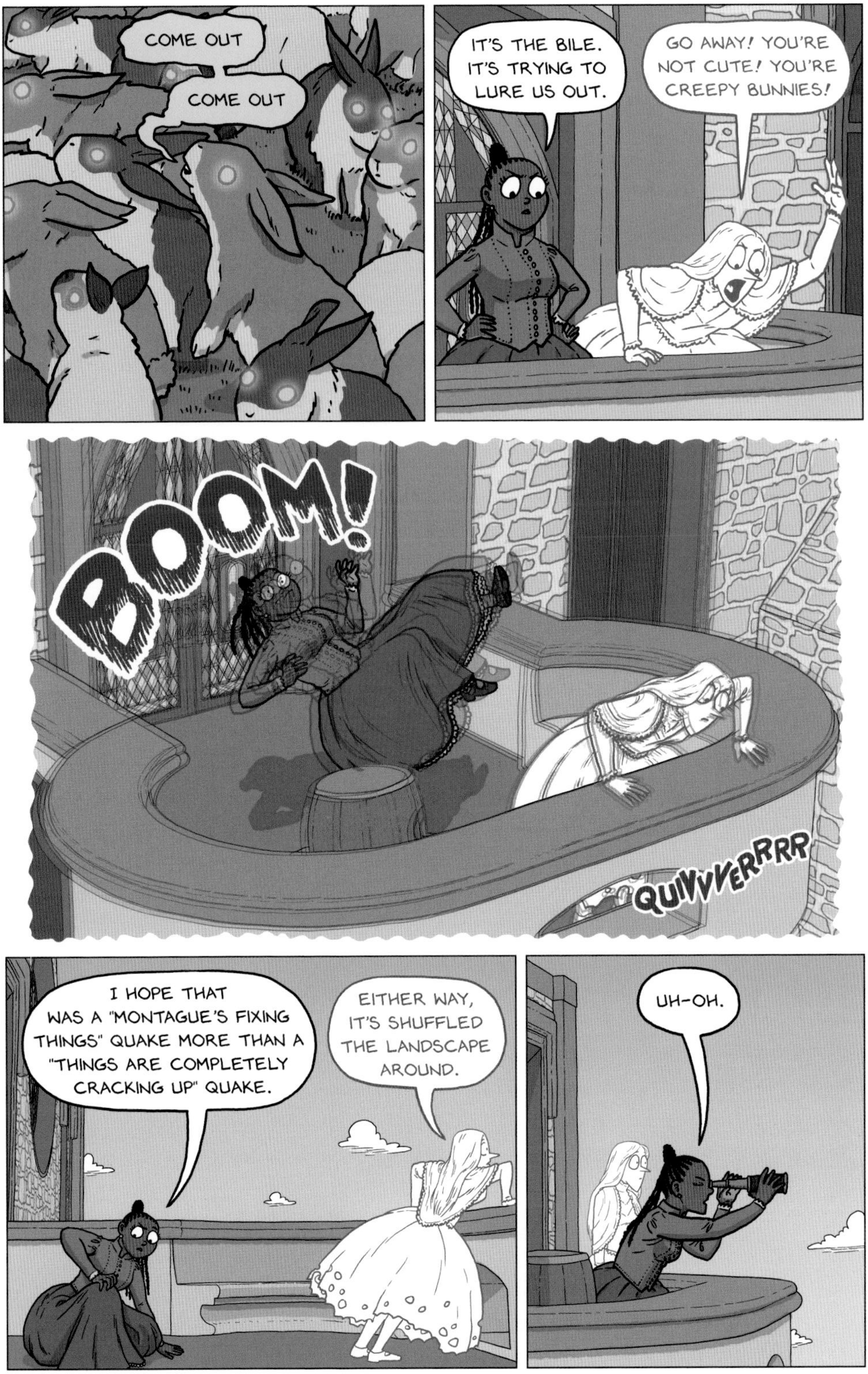
COME OUT
COME OUT
IT'S THE BILE. IT'S TRYING TO LURE US OUT.
GO AWAY! YOU'RE NOT CUTE! YOU'RE CREEPY BUNNIES!
BOOM!
QUIVVVERRRR
I HOPE THAT WAS A "MONTAGUE'S FIXING THINGS" QUAKE MORE THAN A "THINGS ARE COMPLETELY CRACKING UP" QUAKE.
EITHER WAY, IT'S SHUFFLED THE LANDSCAPE AROUND.
UH-OH.

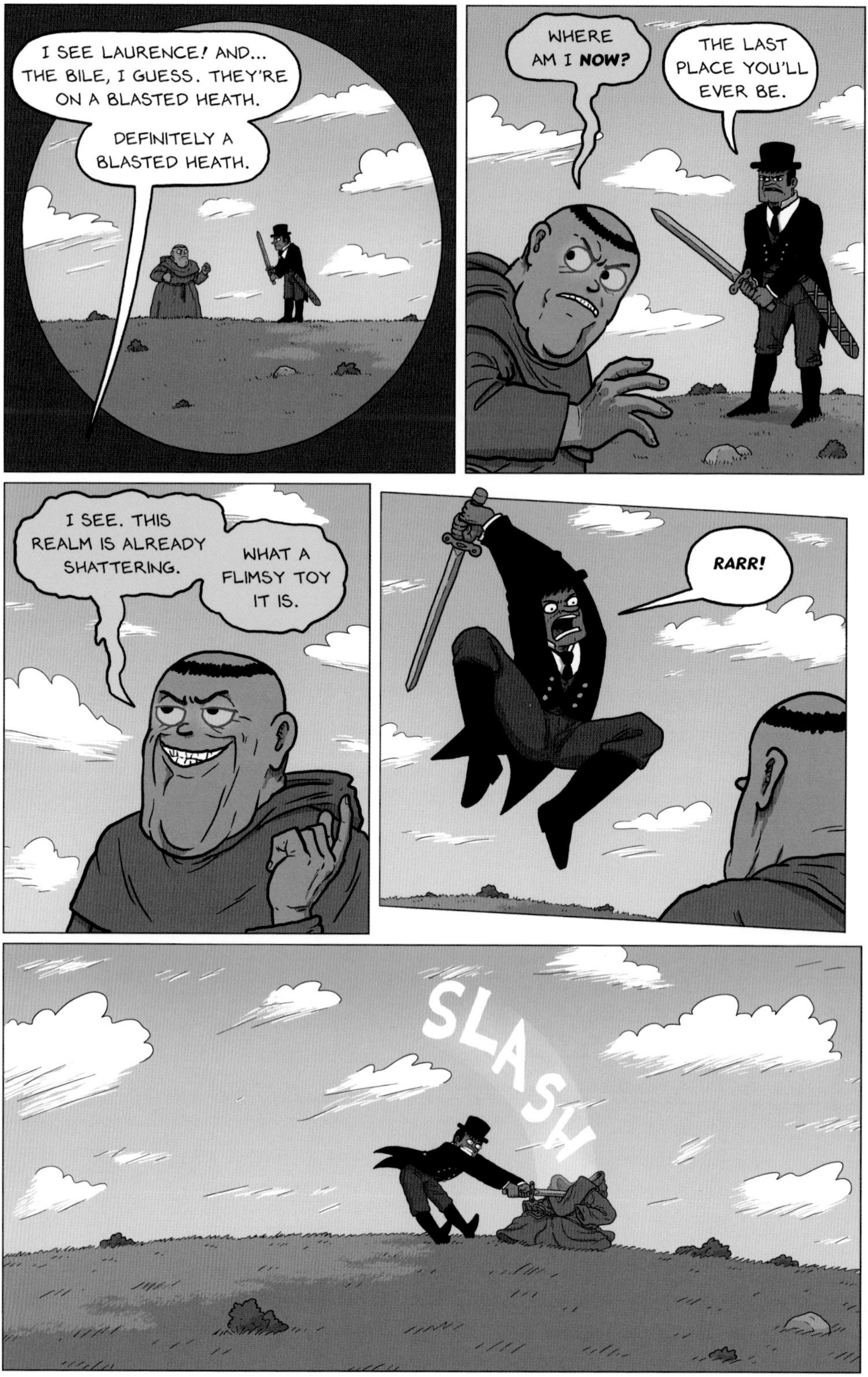
I SEE LAURENCE! AND... THE BILE, I GUESS. THEY'RE ON A BLASTED HEATH.
DEFINITELY A BLASTED HEATH.
WHERE AM I **NOW?**
THE LAST PLACE YOU'LL EVER BE.
I SEE. THIS REALM IS ALREADY SHATTERING.
WHAT A FLIMSY TOY IT IS.
RARR!
SLASH

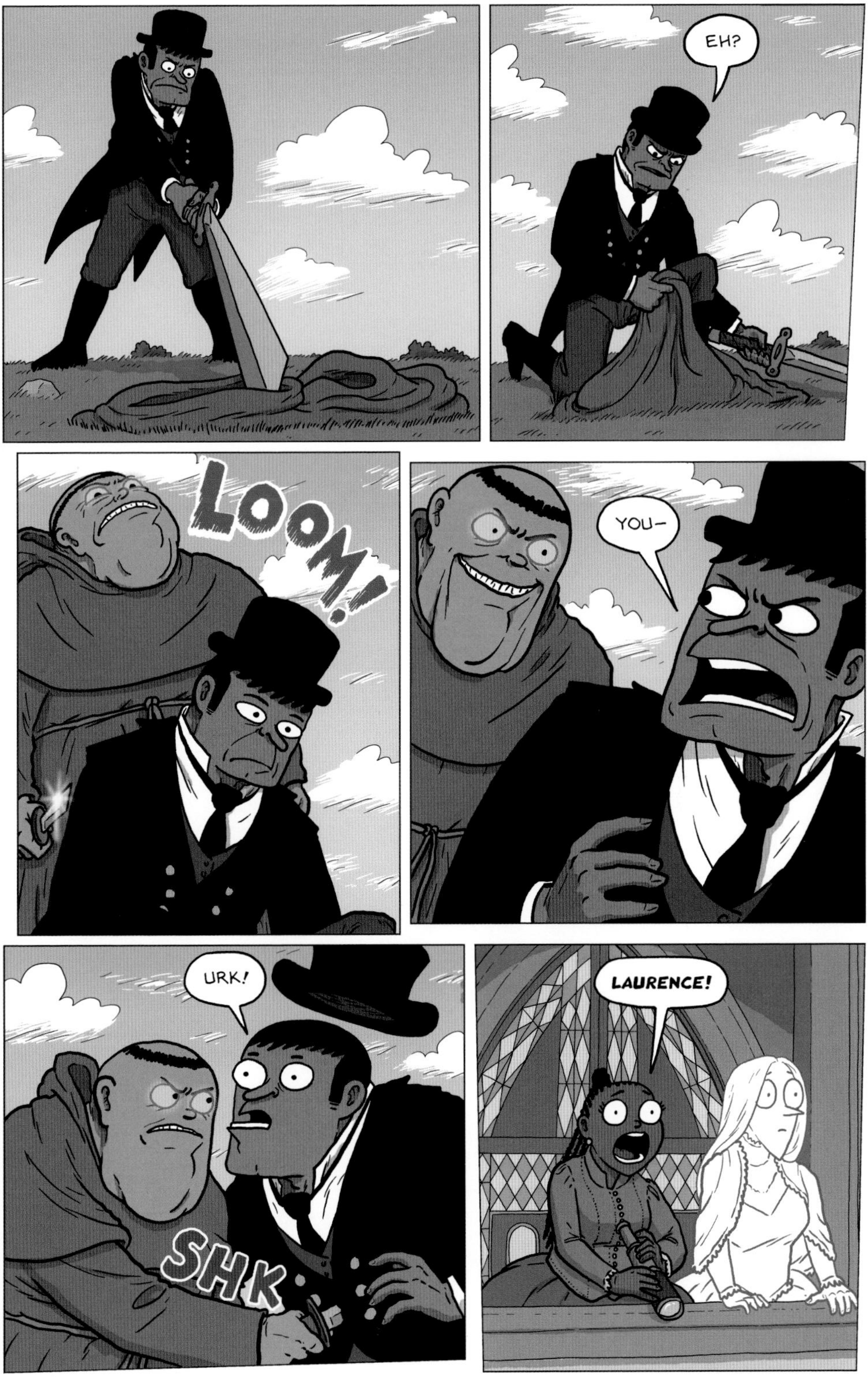
EH?
LOOM!
YOU—
URK!
SHK
LAURENCE!

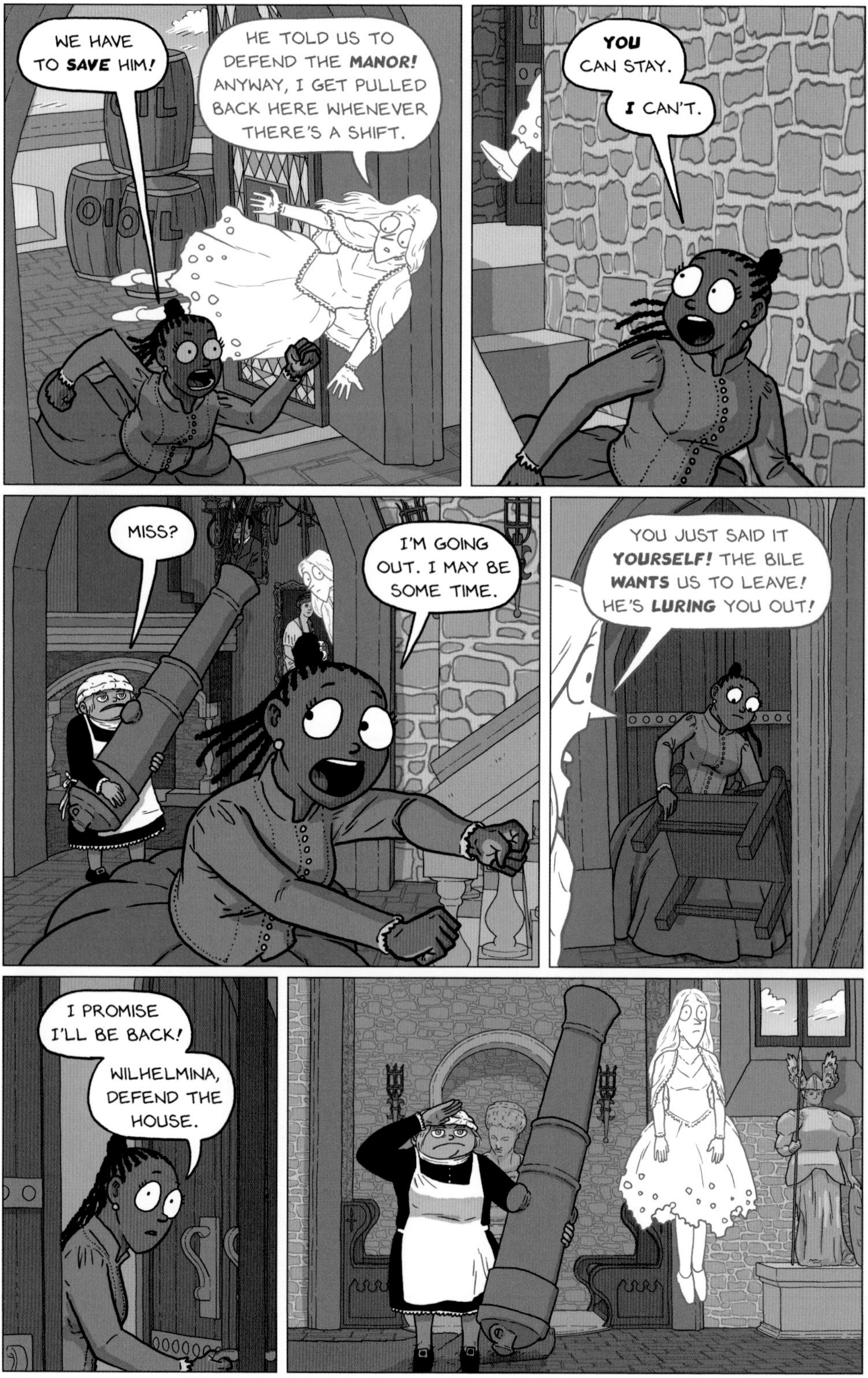
WE HAVE TO SAVE HIM!
HE TOLD US TO DEFEND THE MANOR! ANYWAY, I GET PULLED BACK HERE WHENEVER THERE'S A SHIFT.
YOU CAN STAY.
I CAN'T.
MISS?
I'M GOING OUT. I MAY BE SOME TIME.
YOU JUST SAID IT YOURSELF! THE BILE WANTS US TO LEAVE! HE'S LURING YOU OUT!
I PROMISE I'LL BE BACK!
WILHELMINA, DEFEND THE HOUSE.

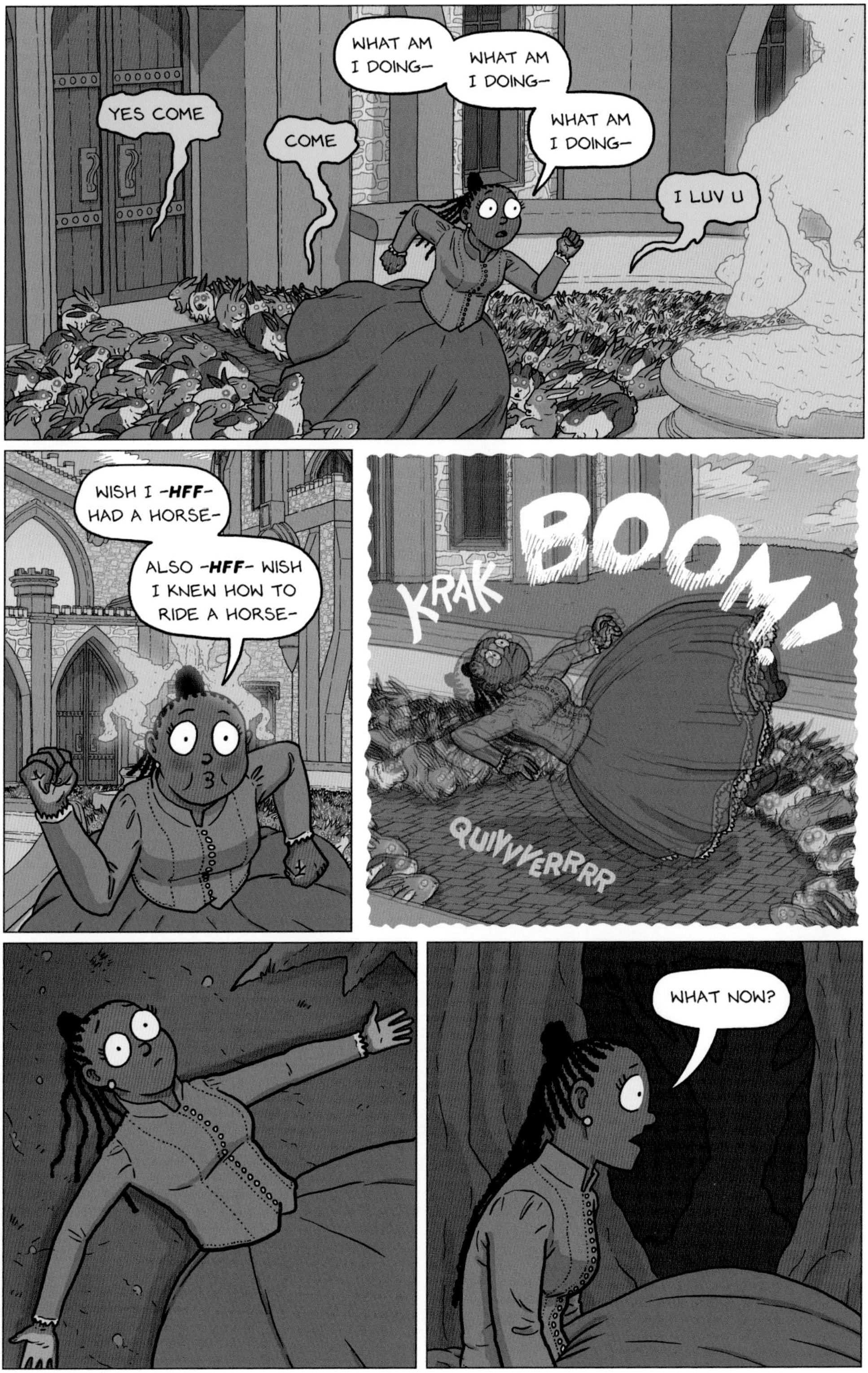
YES COME
COME
WHAT AM I DOING—
WHAT AM I DOING—
WHAT AM I DOING—
I LUV U
WISH I -HFF- HAD A HORSE-
ALSO -HFF- WISH I KNEW HOW TO RIDE A HORSE-
KRAK
BOOM!
QUIVVVERRRR
WHAT NOW?

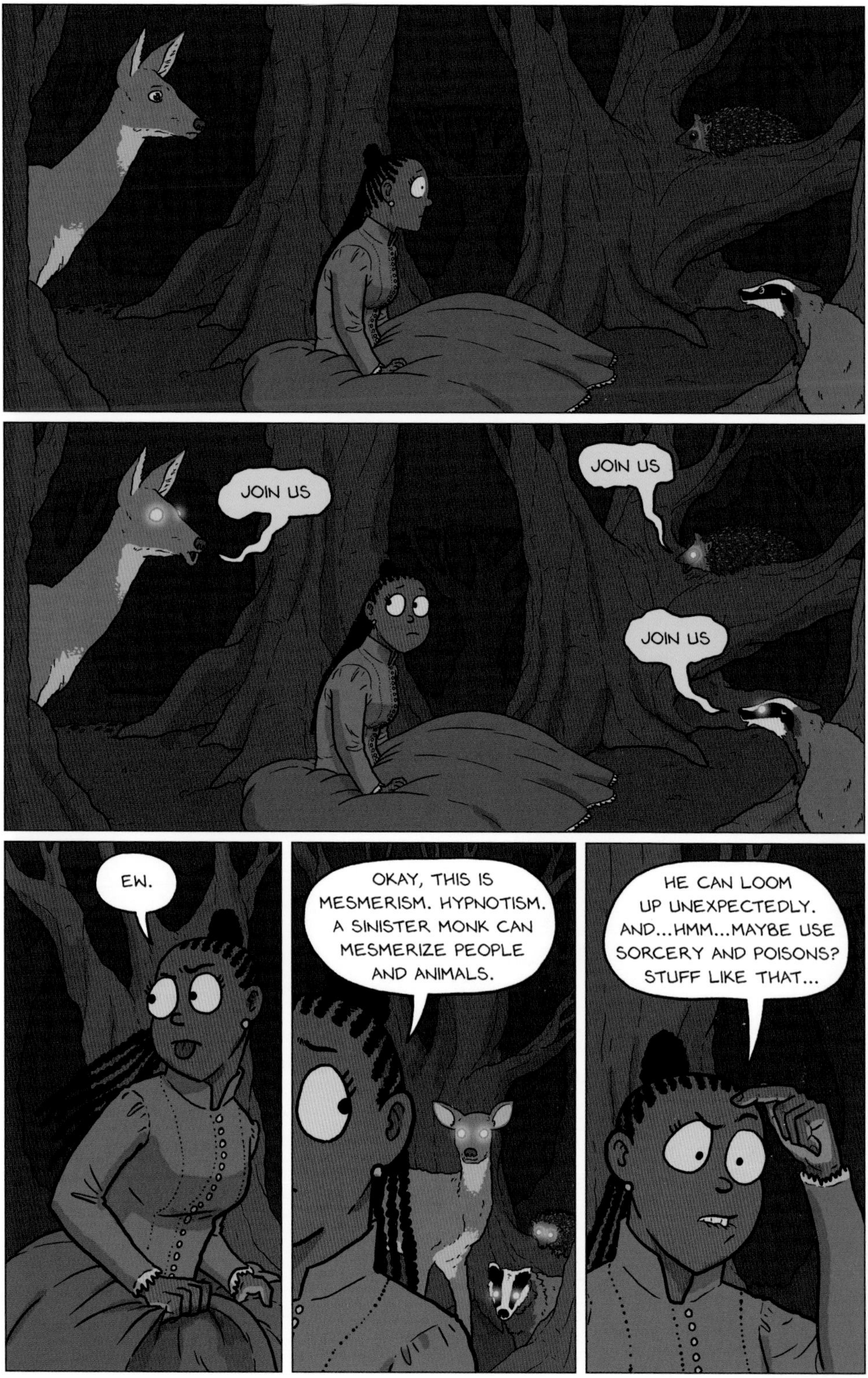
JOIN US
JOIN US
JOIN US
EW.
OKAY, THIS IS MESMERISM. HYPNOTISM. A SINISTER MONK CAN MESMERIZE PEOPLE AND ANIMALS.
HE CAN LOOM UP UNEXPECTEDLY. AND...HMM...MAYBE USE SORCERY AND POISONS? STUFF LIKE THAT...

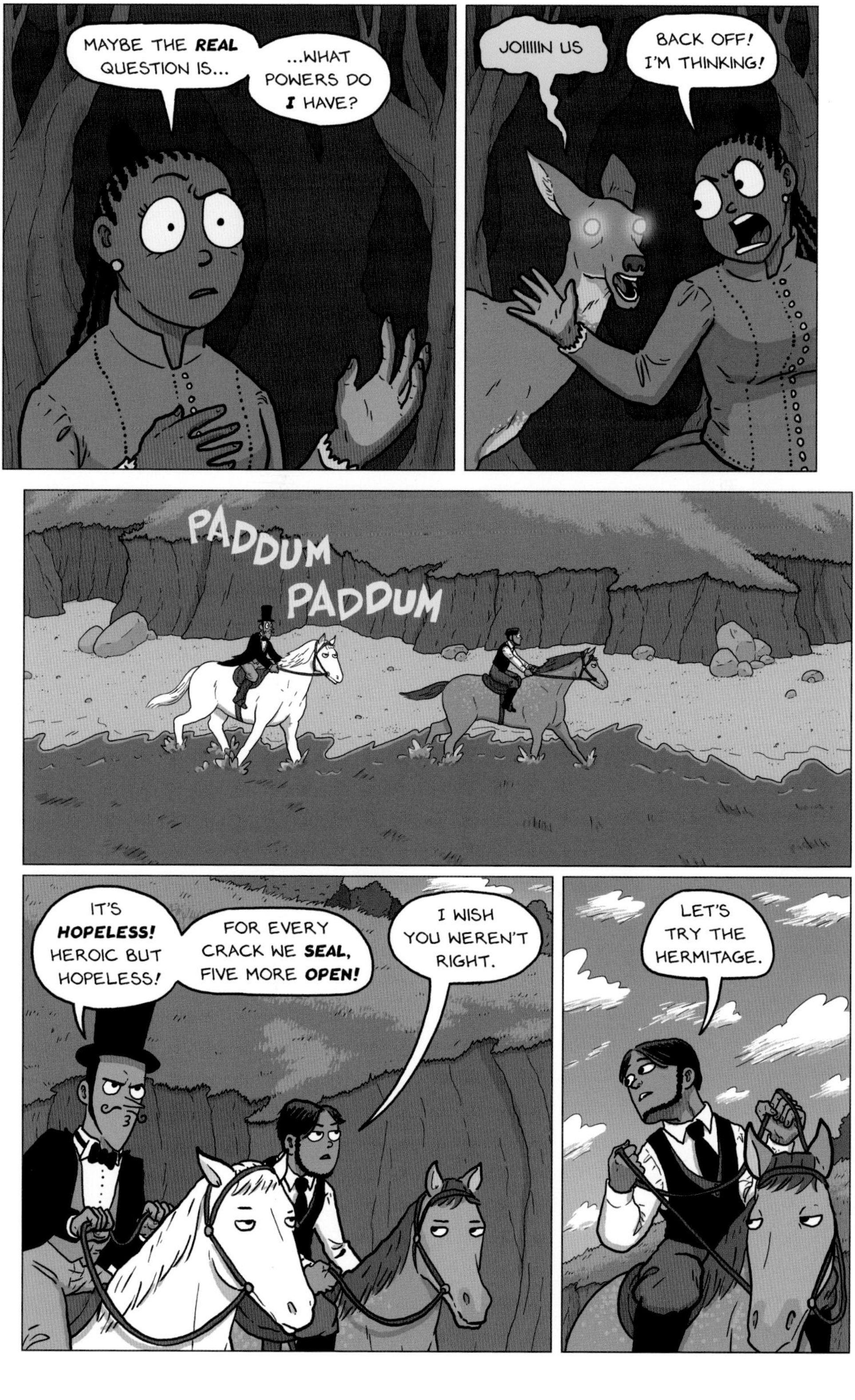
MAYBE THE **REAL** QUESTION IS...
...WHAT POWERS DO **I** HAVE?
JOIIIIIN US
BACK OFF! I'M THINKING!
PADDUM
PADDUM
IT'S **HOPELESS!** HEROIC BUT HOPELESS!
FOR EVERY CRACK WE **SEAL**, FIVE MORE **OPEN!**
I WISH YOU WEREN'T RIGHT.
LET'S TRY THE HERMITAGE.

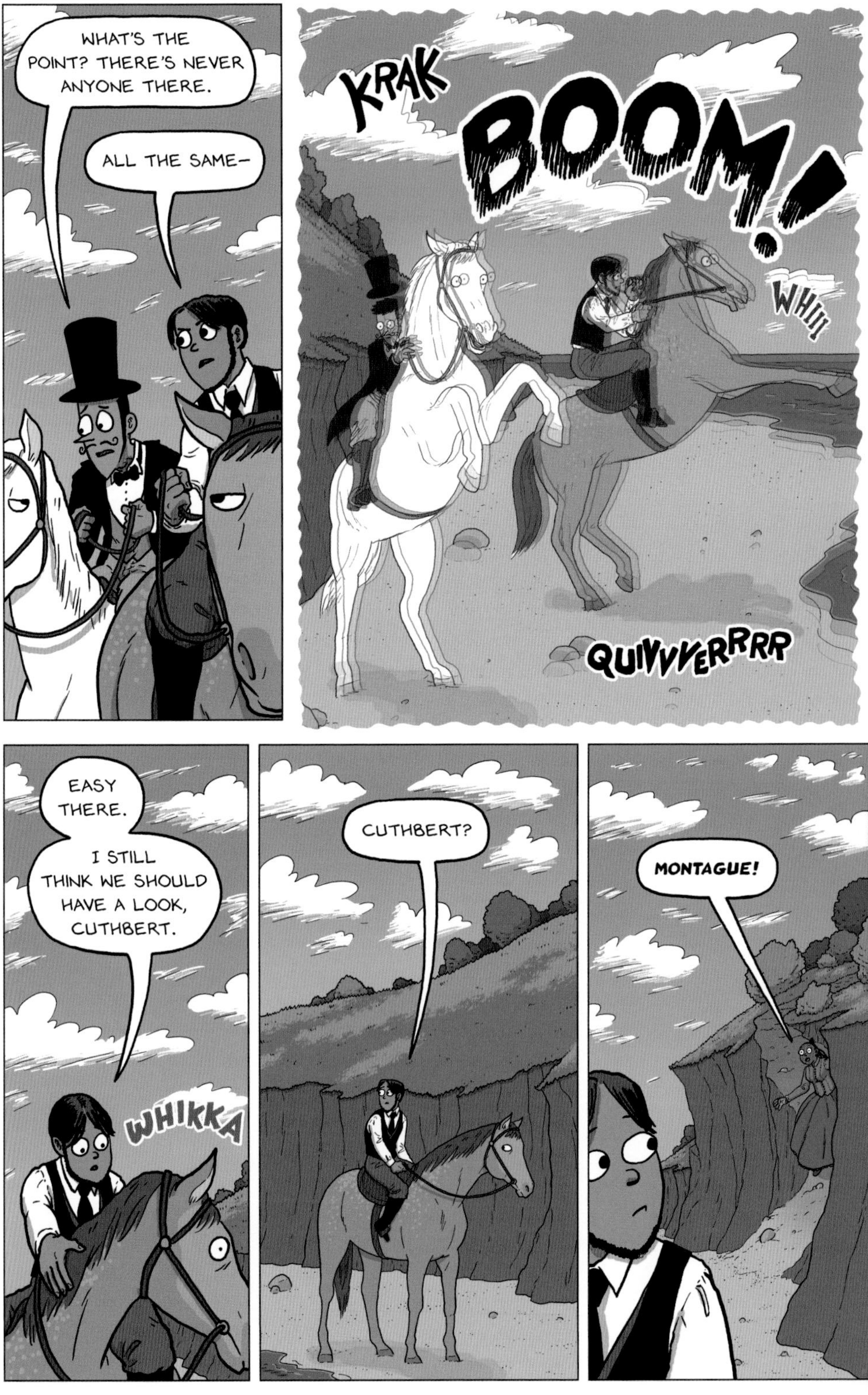
WHAT'S THE POINT? THERE'S NEVER ANYONE THERE.
ALL THE SAME—
KRAK
BOOM!
WHII
QUIVVVERRRR
EASY THERE.
I STILL THINK WE SHOULD HAVE A LOOK, CUTHBERT.
WHIKKA
CUTHBERT?
MONTAGUE!

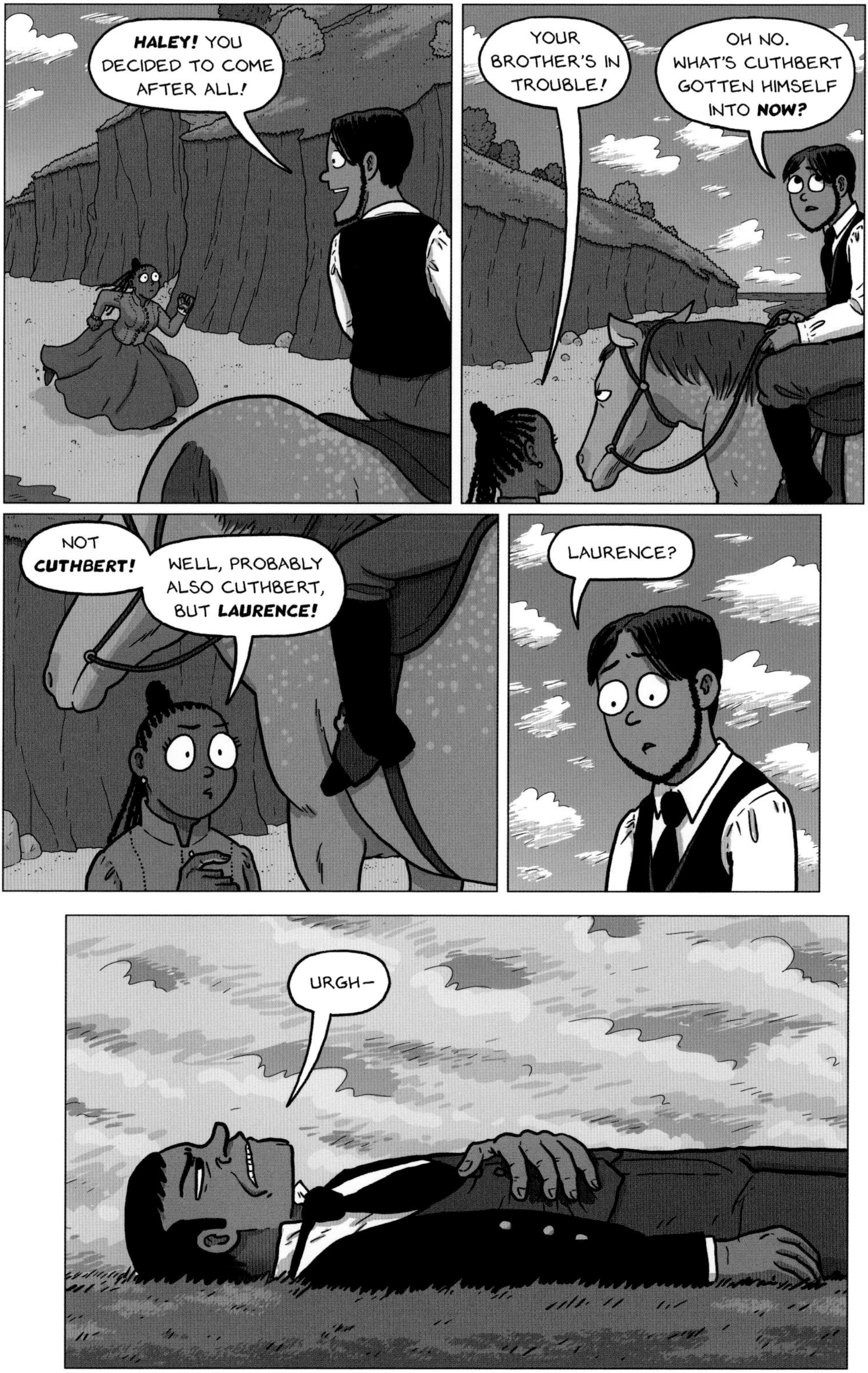
HALEY! YOU DECIDED TO COME AFTER ALL!
YOUR BROTHER'S IN TROUBLE!
OH NO. WHAT'S CUTHBERT GOTTEN HIMSELF INTO NOW?
NOT CUTHBERT!
WELL, PROBABLY ALSO CUTHBERT, BUT LAURENCE!
LAURENCE?
URGH—

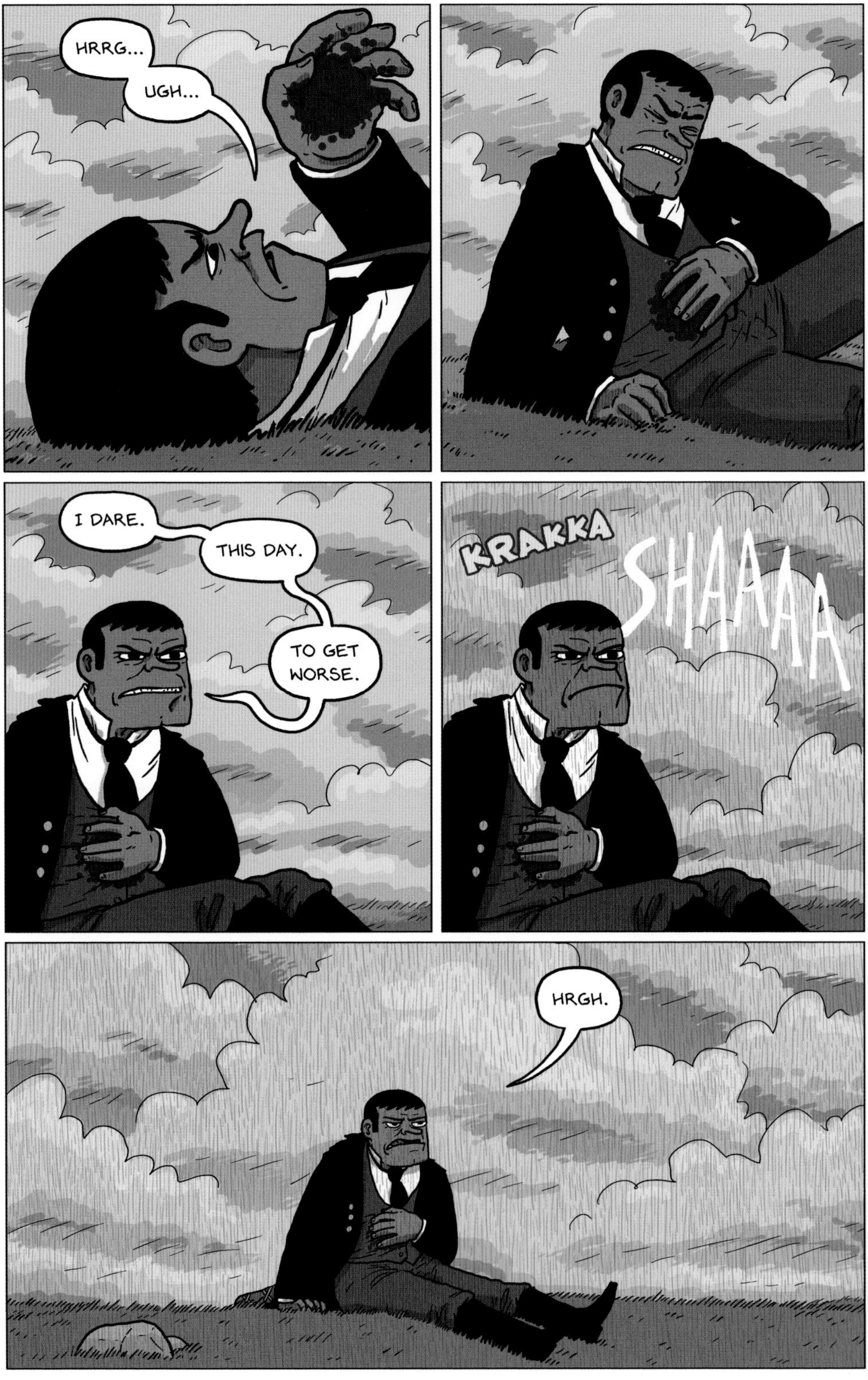
HRRG...
UGH...
I DARE.
THIS DAY.
TO GET WORSE.
KRAKKA
SHAAAAA
HRGH.

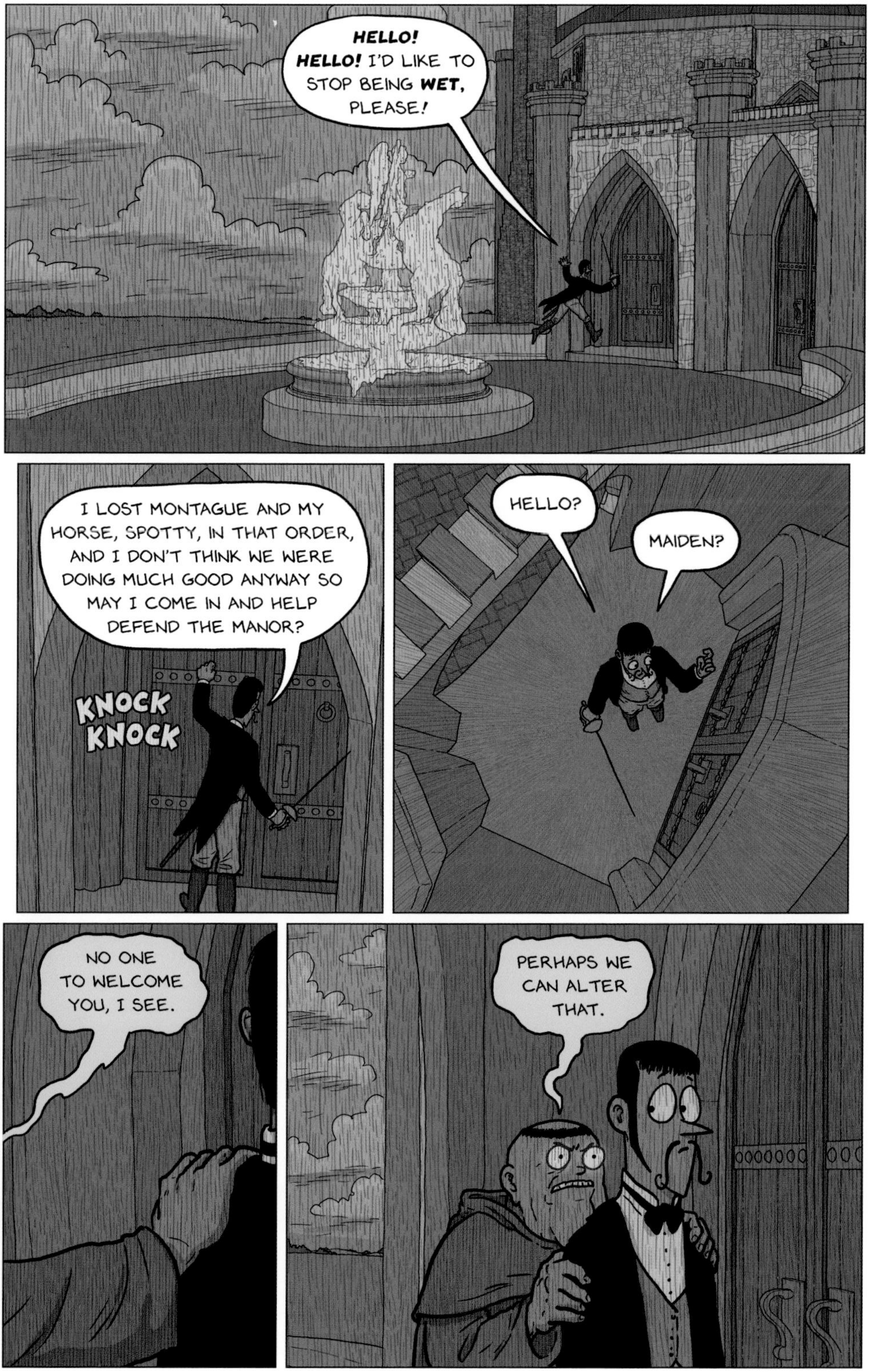
HELLO! HELLO! I'D LIKE TO STOP BEING WET, PLEASE!
I LOST MONTAGUE AND MY HORSE, SPOTTY, IN THAT ORDER, AND I DON'T THINK WE WERE DOING MUCH GOOD ANYWAY SO MAY I COME IN AND HELP DEFEND THE MANOR?
KNOCK KNOCK
HELLO?
MAIDEN?
NO ONE TO WELCOME YOU, I SEE.
PERHAPS WE CAN ALTER THAT.

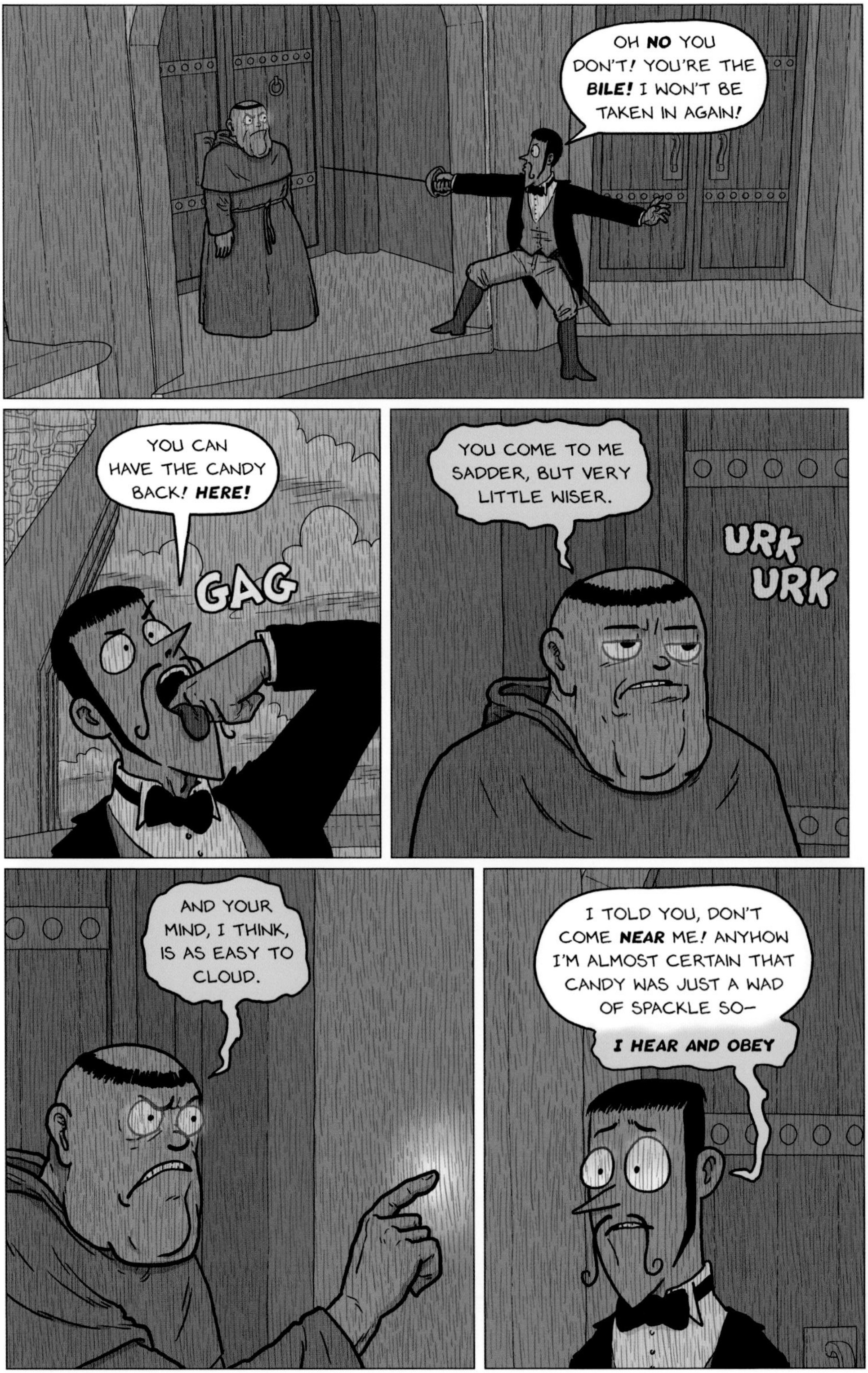
OH **NO** YOU DON'T! YOU'RE THE **BILE!** I WON'T BE TAKEN IN AGAIN!
YOU CAN HAVE THE CANDY BACK! **HERE!**
GAG
YOU COME TO ME SADDER, BUT VERY LITTLE WISER.
URK URK
AND YOUR MIND, I THINK, IS AS EASY TO CLOUD.
I TOLD YOU, DON'T COME **NEAR** ME! ANYHOW I'M ALMOST CERTAIN THAT CANDY WAS JUST A WAD OF SPACKLE SO–
I HEAR AND OBEY

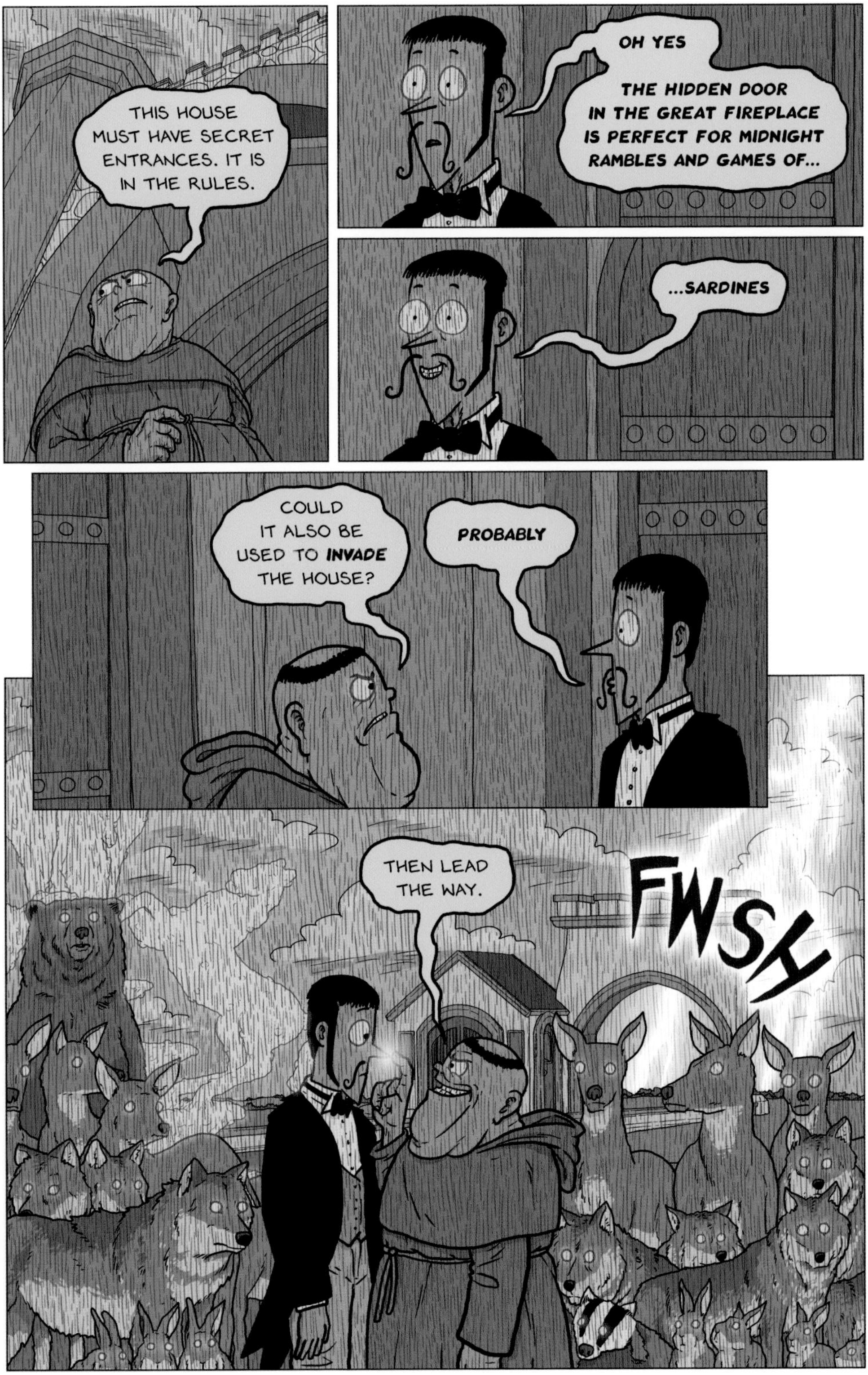
THIS HOUSE MUST HAVE SECRET ENTRANCES. IT IS IN THE RULES.
OH YES
THE HIDDEN DOOR IN THE GREAT FIREPLACE IS PERFECT FOR MIDNIGHT RAMBLES AND GAMES OF...
...SARDINES
COULD IT ALSO BE USED TO INVADE THE HOUSE?
PROBABLY
THEN LEAD THE WAY.
FWSH

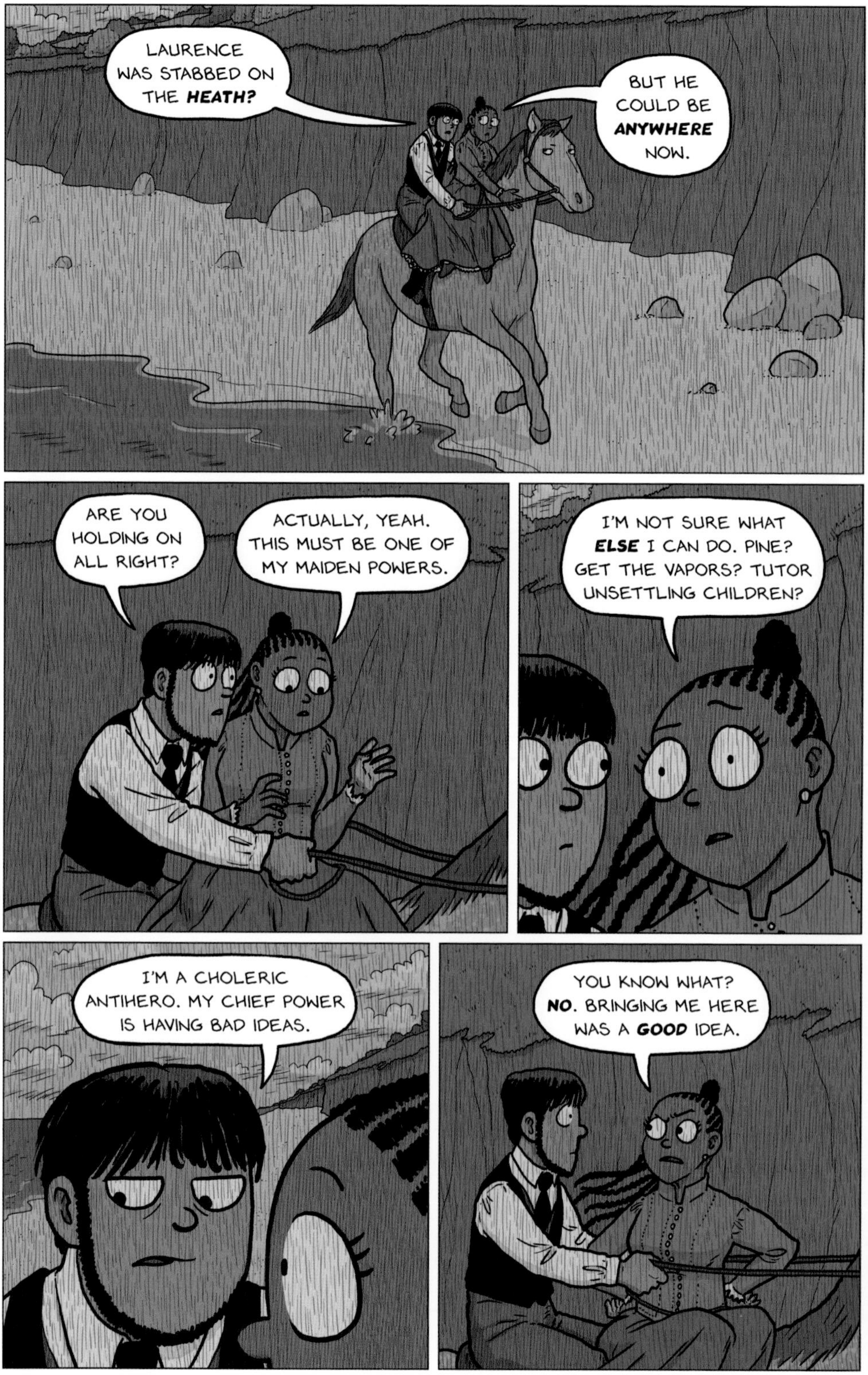
LAURENCE WAS STABBED ON THE **HEATH?**
BUT HE COULD BE **ANYWHERE** NOW.
ARE YOU HOLDING ON ALL RIGHT?
ACTUALLY, YEAH. THIS MUST BE ONE OF MY MAIDEN POWERS.
I'M NOT SURE WHAT **ELSE** I CAN DO. PINE? GET THE VAPORS? TUTOR UNSETTLING CHILDREN?
I'M A CHOLERIC ANTIHERO. MY CHIEF POWER IS HAVING BAD IDEAS.
YOU KNOW WHAT? **NO**. BRINGING ME HERE WAS A **GOOD** IDEA.

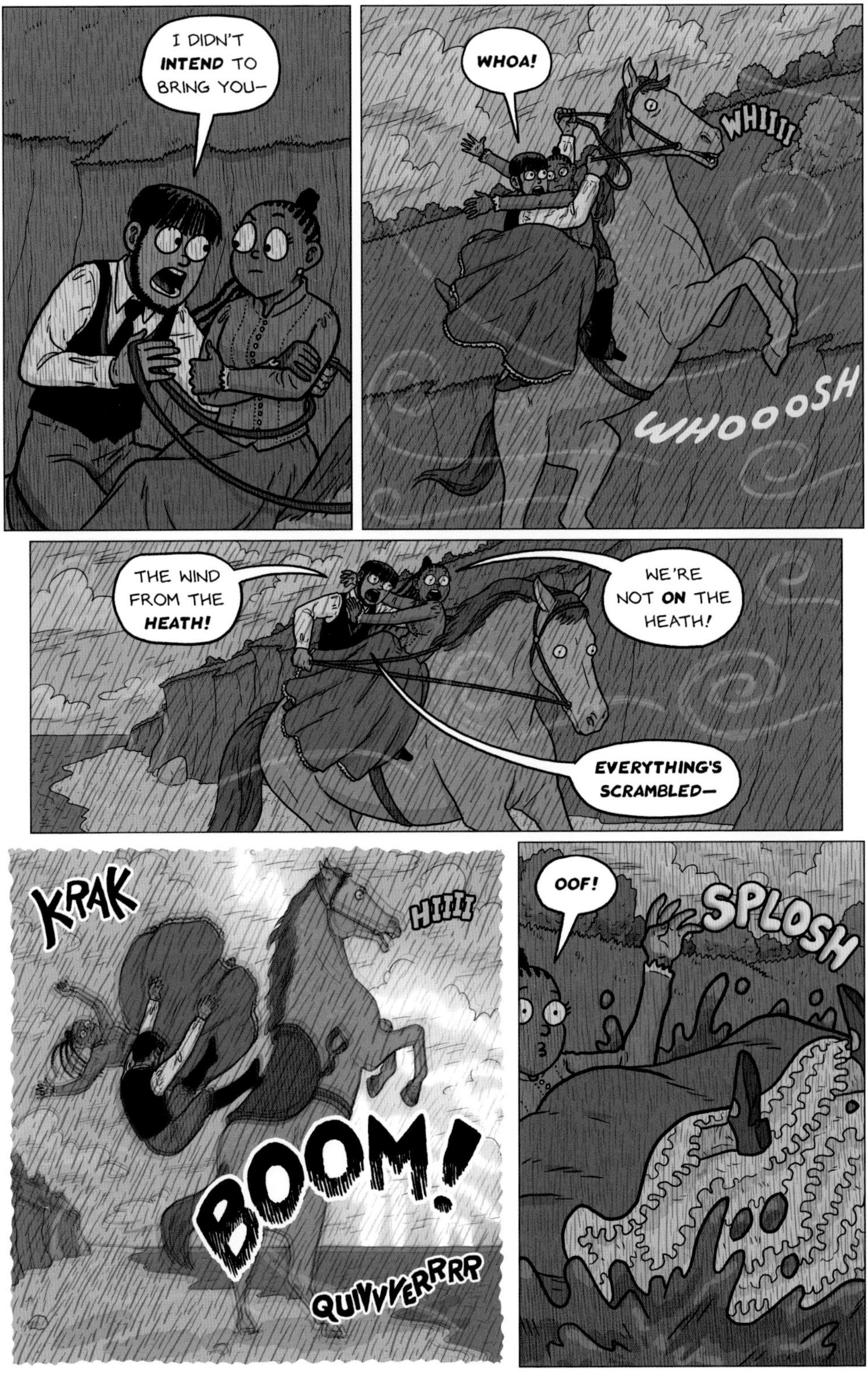
I DIDN'T INTEND TO BRING YOU—
WHOA!
WHIIII
WHOOOOSH
THE WIND FROM THE HEATH!
WE'RE NOT ON THE HEATH!
EVERYTHING'S SCRAMBLED—
KRAK
HIIII
BOOM!
QUIVVVERRRR
OOF!
SPLOSH

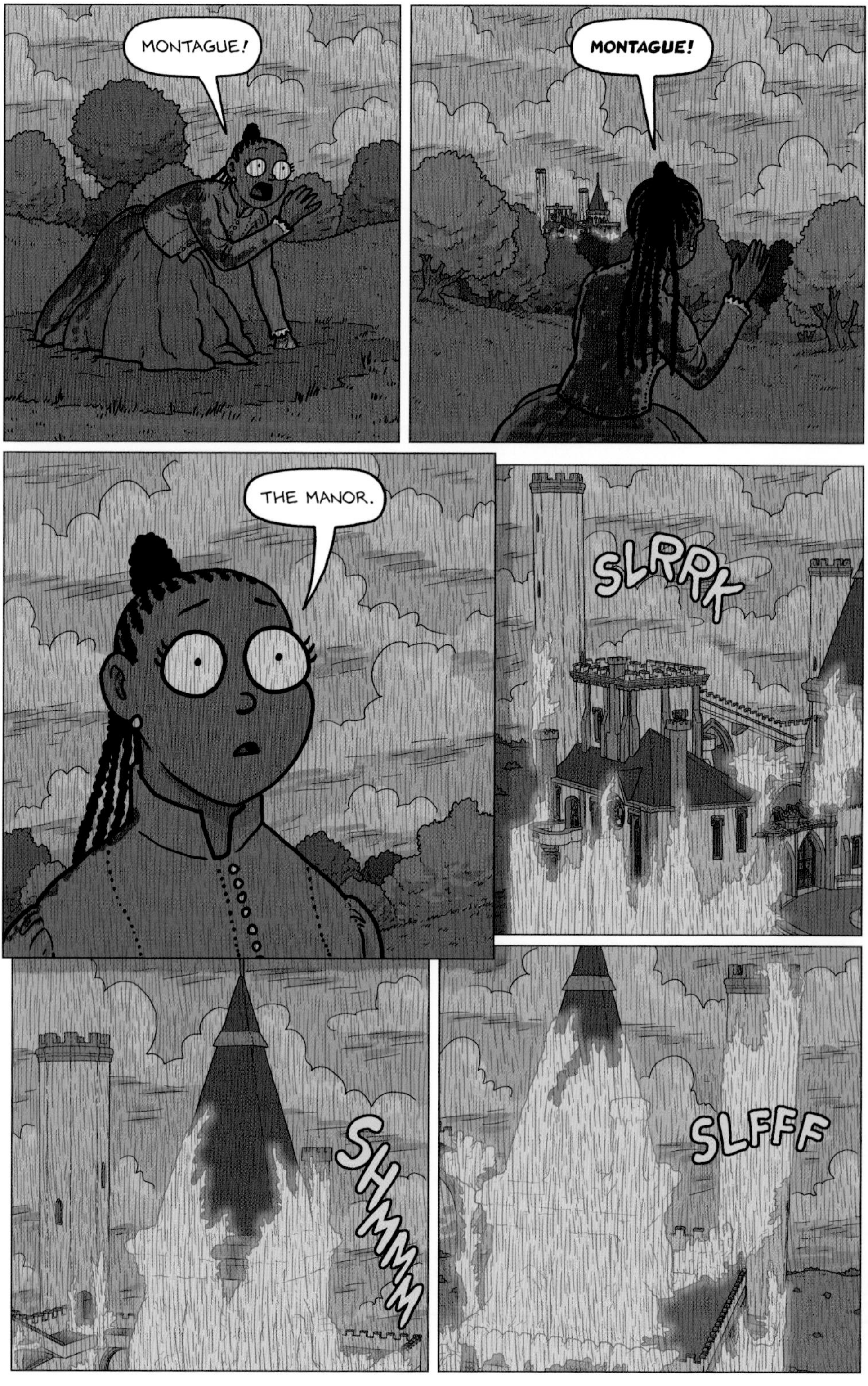
MONTAGUE!
MONTAGUE!
THE MANOR.
SLRRK
SHMMM
SLFFF

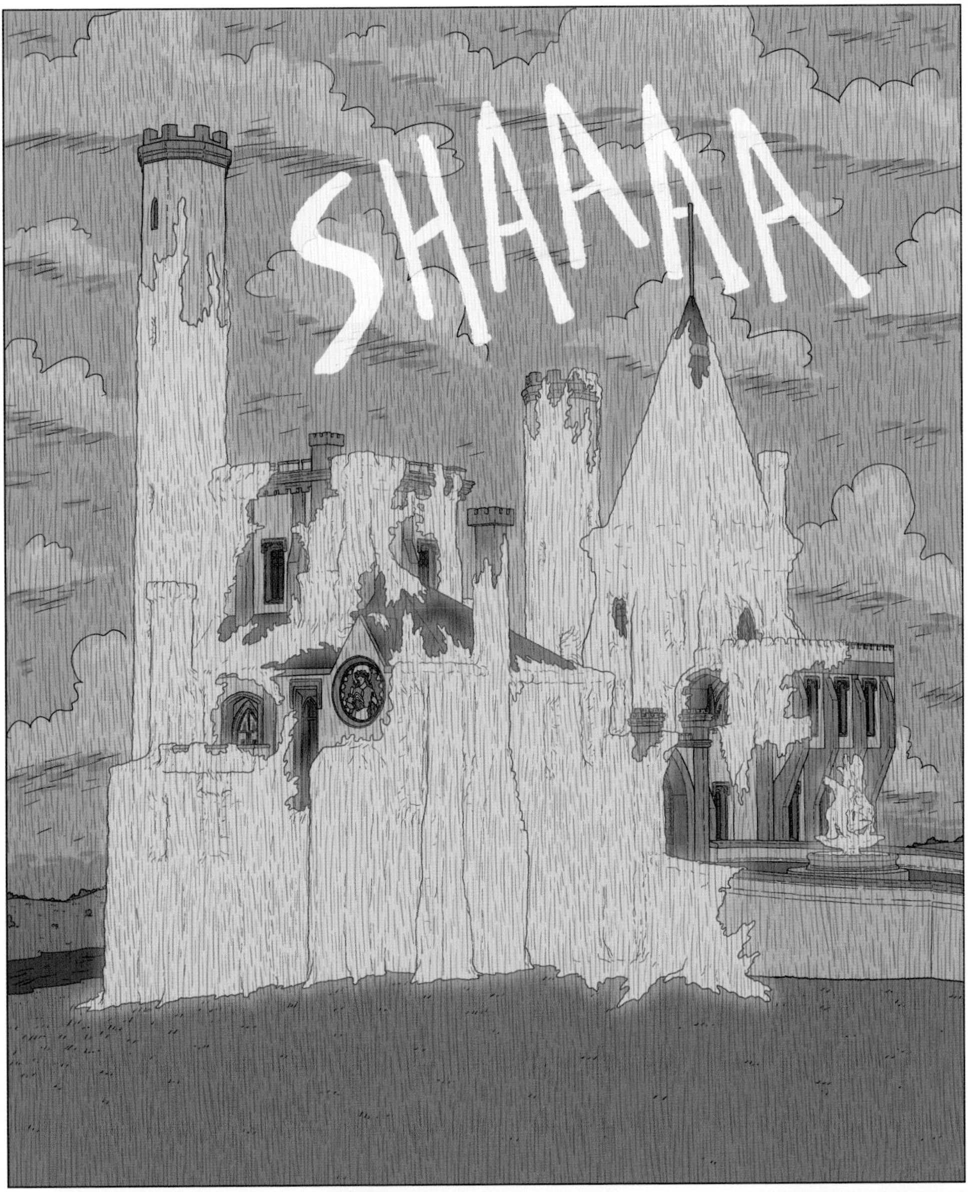
SHAAAA

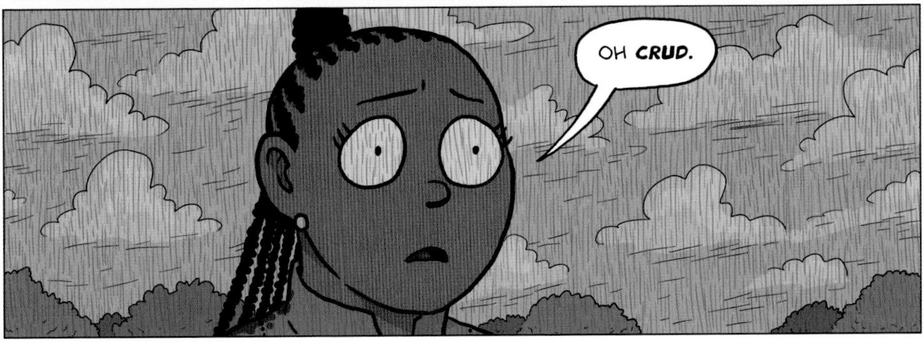
OH CRUD.

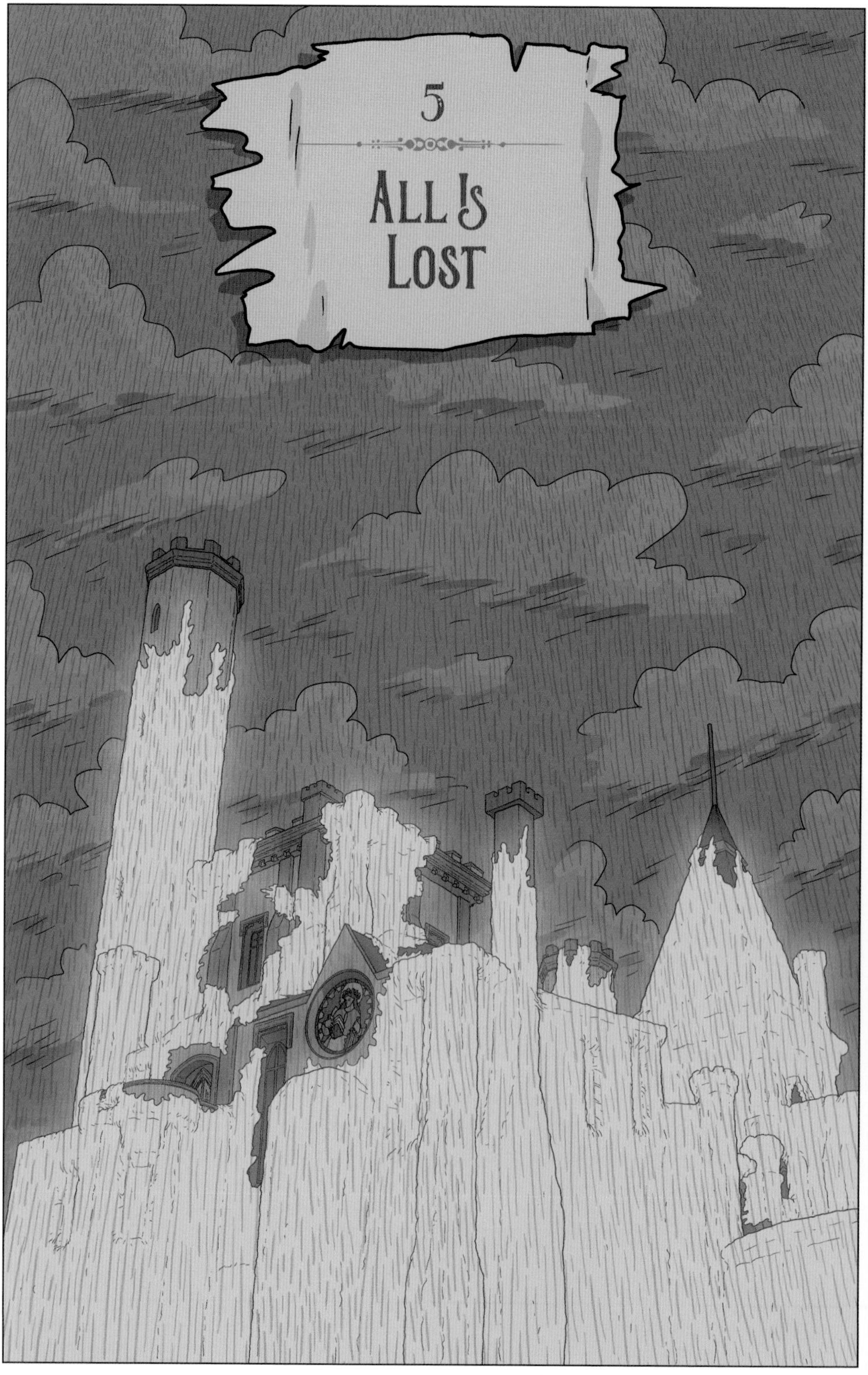
5
All Is Lost

SLUK SLUK

SLUK SLUK

I'LL GET BACK TO THE MANOR AND *FIGHT*. I'LL FIND **MONTAGUE**. OR **LAURENCE**. OR **ANYONE**.

SPLOSH

I WILL BE A USELESS SOGGY **RAG**.

ALSO, I NEVER WANT TO READ ANOTHER FRIGGIN' GOTHIC ROMANCE **AGAIN**.

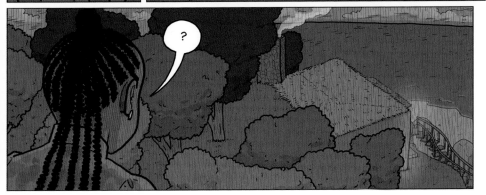

?

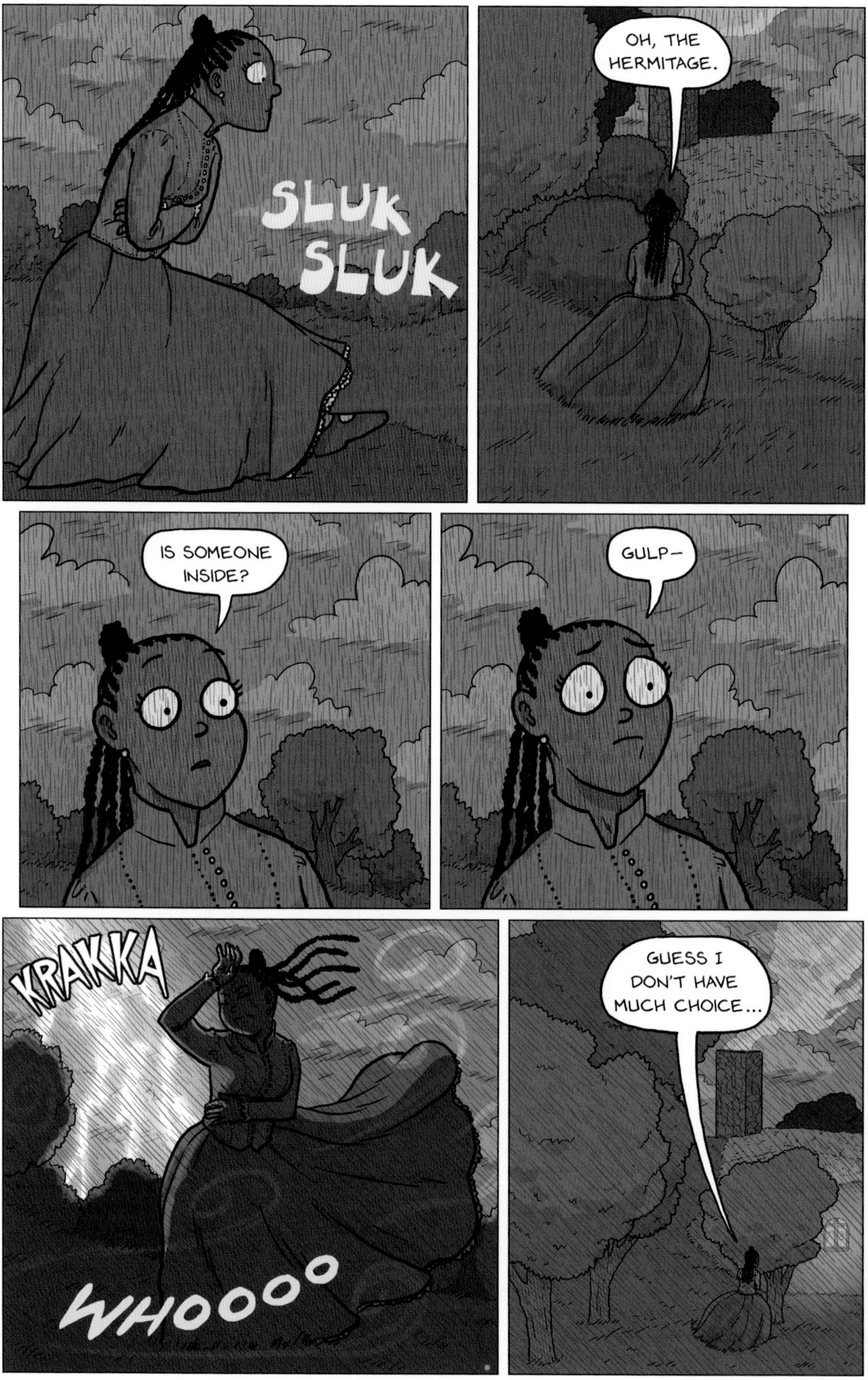
SLUK
SLUK
OH, THE HERMITAGE.
IS SOMEONE INSIDE?
GULP—
KRAKKA
WHOOOO
GUESS I DON'T HAVE MUCH CHOICE...

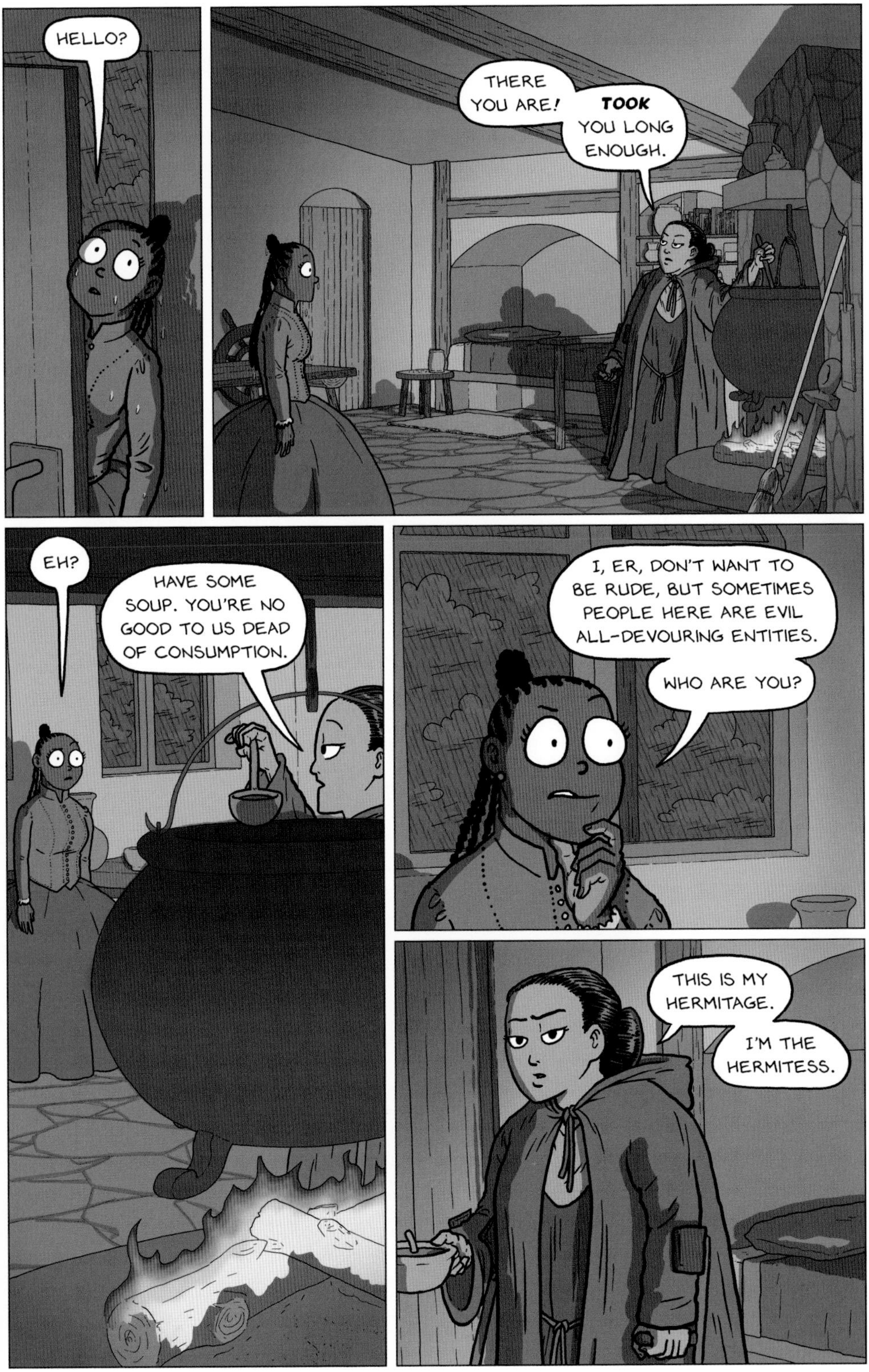
HELLO?
THERE YOU ARE!
TOOK YOU LONG ENOUGH.
EH?
HAVE SOME SOUP. YOU'RE NO GOOD TO US DEAD OF CONSUMPTION.
I, ER, DON'T WANT TO BE RUDE, BUT SOMETIMES PEOPLE HERE ARE EVIL ALL-DEVOURING ENTITIES.
WHO ARE YOU?
THIS IS MY HERMITAGE.
I'M THE HERMITESS.

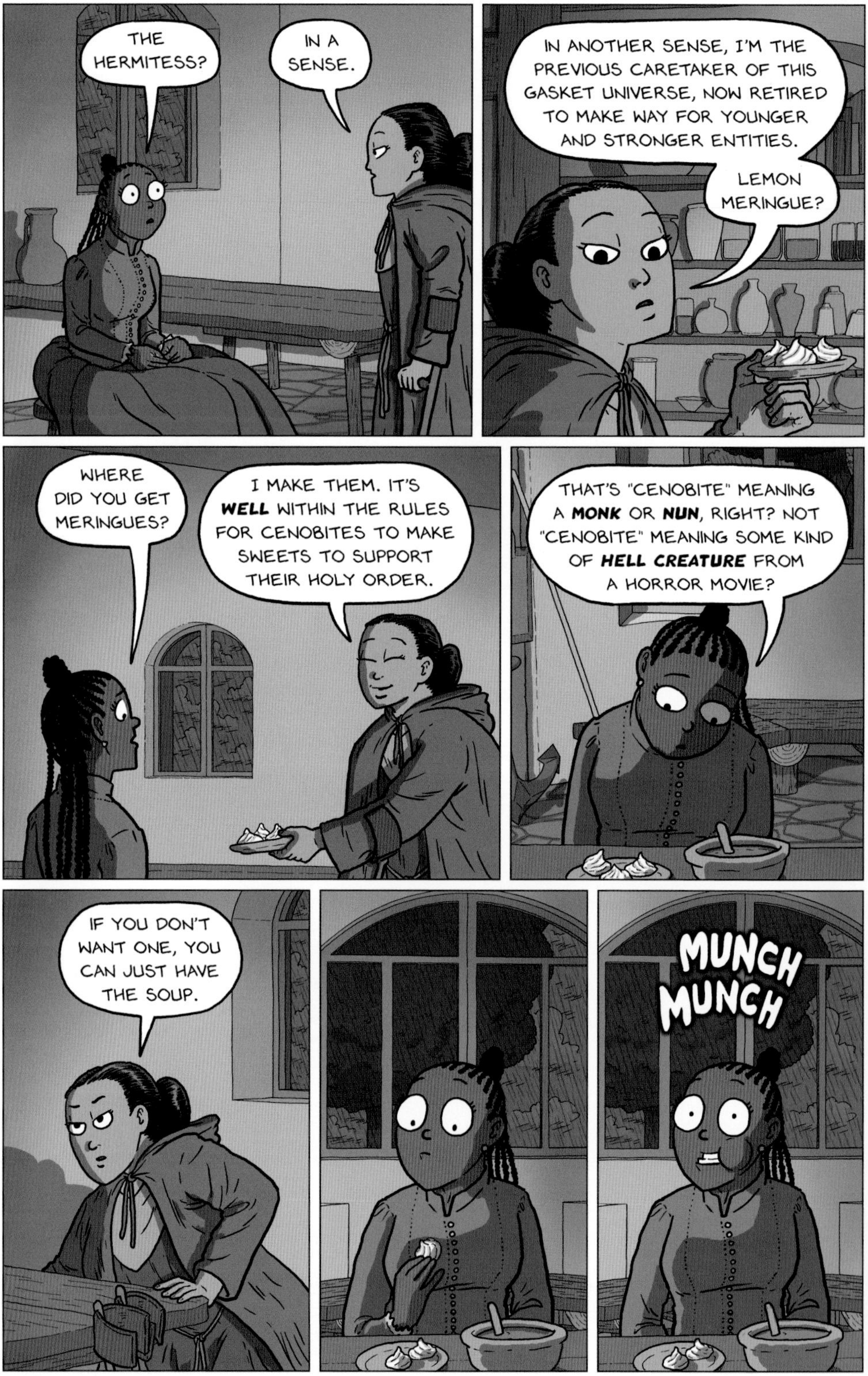
THE HERMITESS?
IN A SENSE.
IN ANOTHER SENSE, I'M THE PREVIOUS CARETAKER OF THIS GASKET UNIVERSE, NOW RETIRED TO MAKE WAY FOR YOUNGER AND STRONGER ENTITIES.
LEMON MERINGUE?
WHERE DID YOU GET MERINGUES?
I MAKE THEM. IT'S WELL WITHIN THE RULES FOR CENOBITES TO MAKE SWEETS TO SUPPORT THEIR HOLY ORDER.
THAT'S "CENOBITE" MEANING A MONK OR NUN, RIGHT? NOT "CENOBITE" MEANING SOME KIND OF HELL CREATURE FROM A HORROR MOVIE?
IF YOU DON'T WANT ONE, YOU CAN JUST HAVE THE SOUP.
MUNCH MUNCH

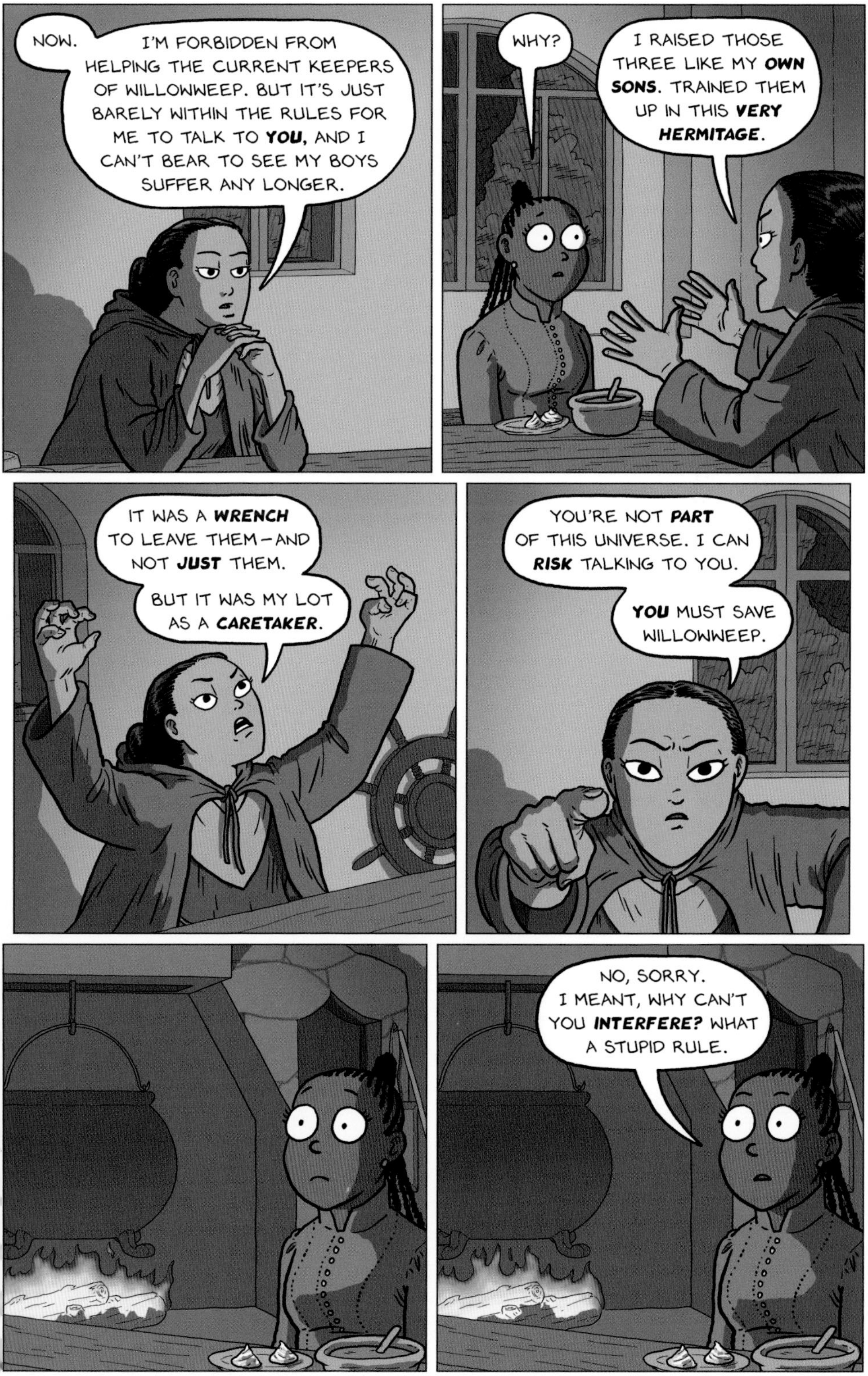
NOW.
I'M FORBIDDEN FROM HELPING THE CURRENT KEEPERS OF WILLOWWEEP. BUT IT'S JUST BARELY WITHIN THE RULES FOR ME TO TALK TO **YOU,** AND I CAN'T BEAR TO SEE MY BOYS SUFFER ANY LONGER.
WHY?
I RAISED THOSE THREE LIKE MY **OWN SONS**. TRAINED THEM UP IN THIS **VERY HERMITAGE**.
IT WAS A **WRENCH** TO LEAVE THEM—AND NOT **JUST** THEM.
BUT IT WAS MY LOT AS A **CARETAKER**.
YOU'RE NOT **PART** OF THIS UNIVERSE. I CAN **RISK** TALKING TO YOU.
YOU MUST SAVE WILLOWWEEP.
NO, SORRY. I MEANT, WHY CAN'T YOU **INTERFERE?** WHAT A STUPID RULE.

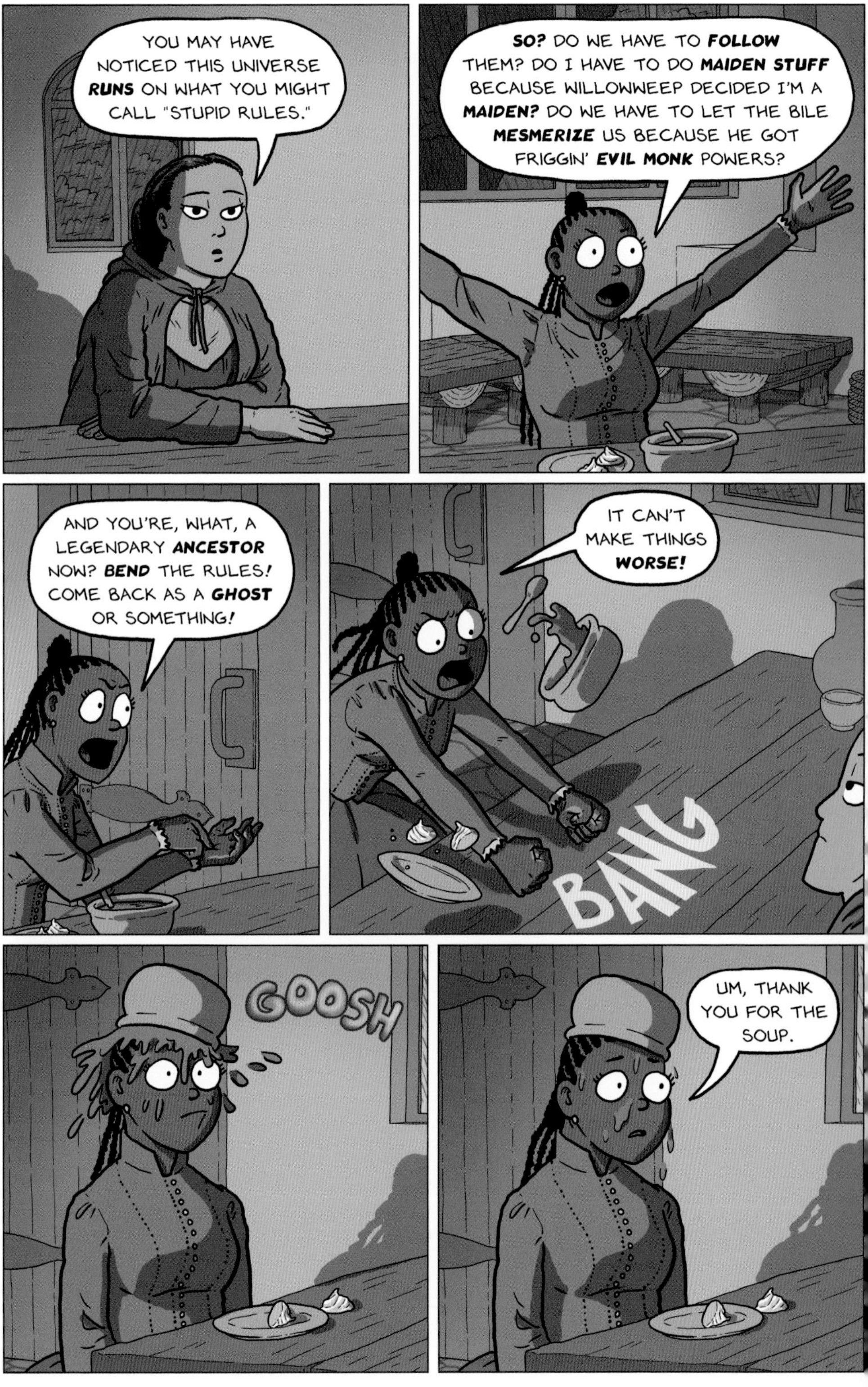
YOU MAY HAVE NOTICED THIS UNIVERSE **RUNS** ON WHAT YOU MIGHT CALL "STUPID RULES."
SO? DO WE HAVE TO **FOLLOW** THEM? DO I HAVE TO DO **MAIDEN STUFF** BECAUSE WILLOWWEEP DECIDED I'M A **MAIDEN?** DO WE HAVE TO LET THE BILE **MESMERIZE** US BECAUSE HE GOT FRIGGIN' **EVIL MONK** POWERS?
AND YOU'RE, WHAT, A LEGENDARY **ANCESTOR** NOW? **BEND** THE RULES! COME BACK AS A **GHOST** OR SOMETHING!
IT CAN'T MAKE THINGS **WORSE!**
BANG
GOOSH
UM, THANK YOU FOR THE SOUP.

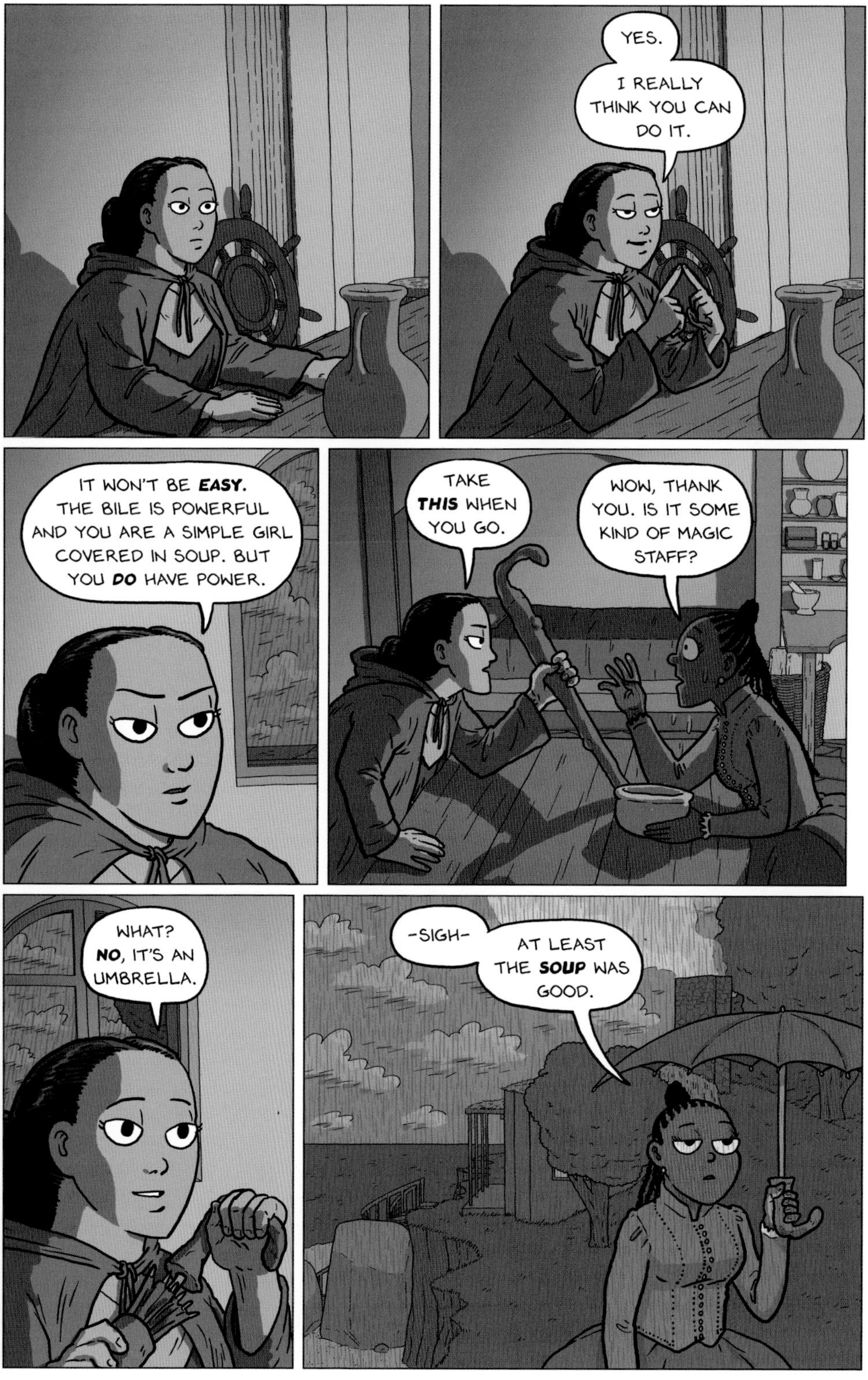
YES.
I REALLY THINK YOU CAN DO IT.
IT WON'T BE EASY. THE BILE IS POWERFUL AND YOU ARE A SIMPLE GIRL COVERED IN SOUP. BUT YOU DO HAVE POWER.
TAKE THIS WHEN YOU GO.
WOW, THANK YOU. IS IT SOME KIND OF MAGIC STAFF?
WHAT? NO, IT'S AN UMBRELLA.
-SIGH-
AT LEAST THE SOUP WAS GOOD.

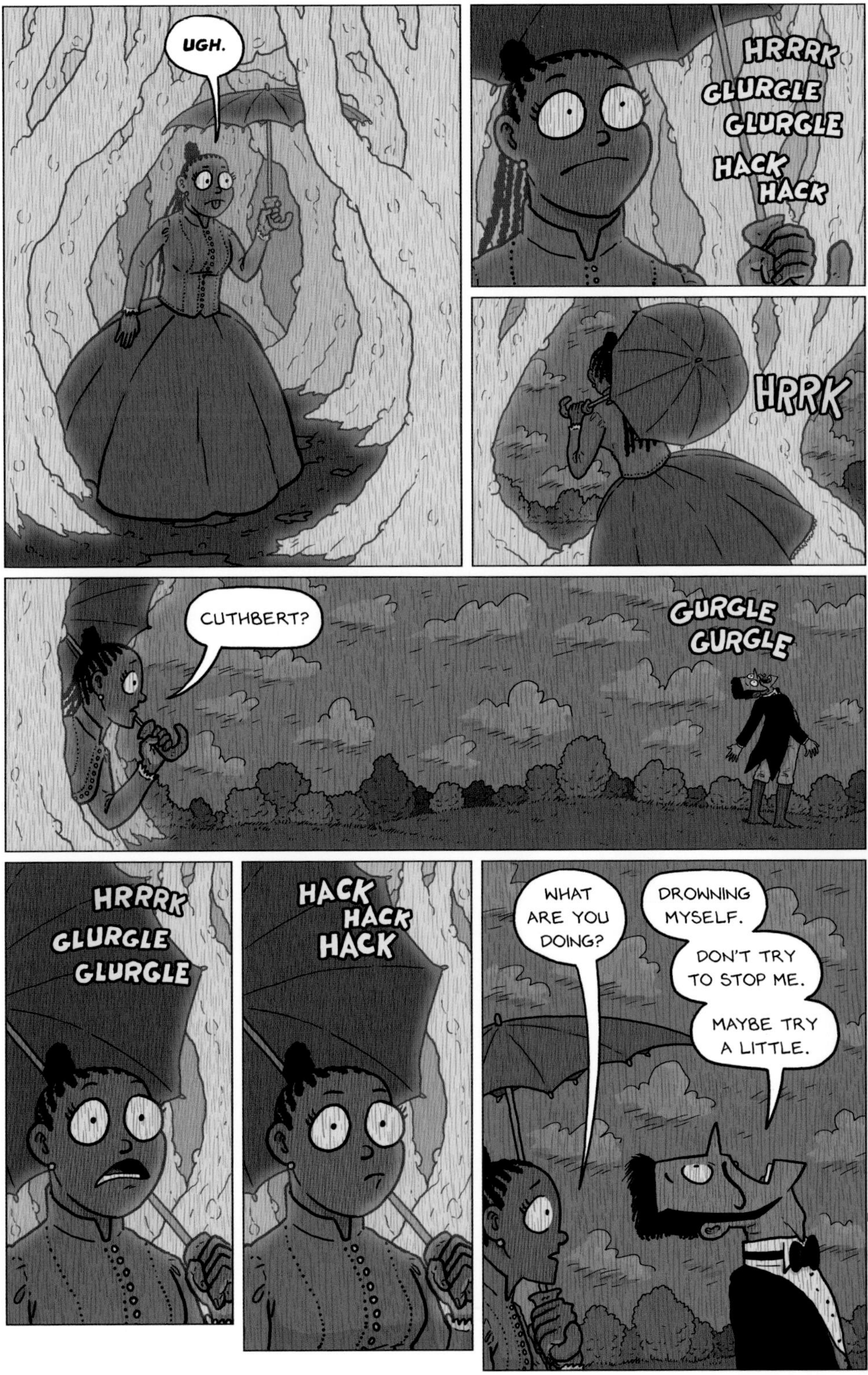
UGH.
HRRRK
GLURGLE
GLURGLE
HACK
HACK
HRRK
CUTHBERT?
GURGLE
GURGLE
HRRRK
GLURGLE
GLURGLE
HACK
HACK
HACK
WHAT ARE YOU DOING?
DROWNING MYSELF.
DON'T TRY TO STOP ME.
MAYBE TRY A LITTLE.

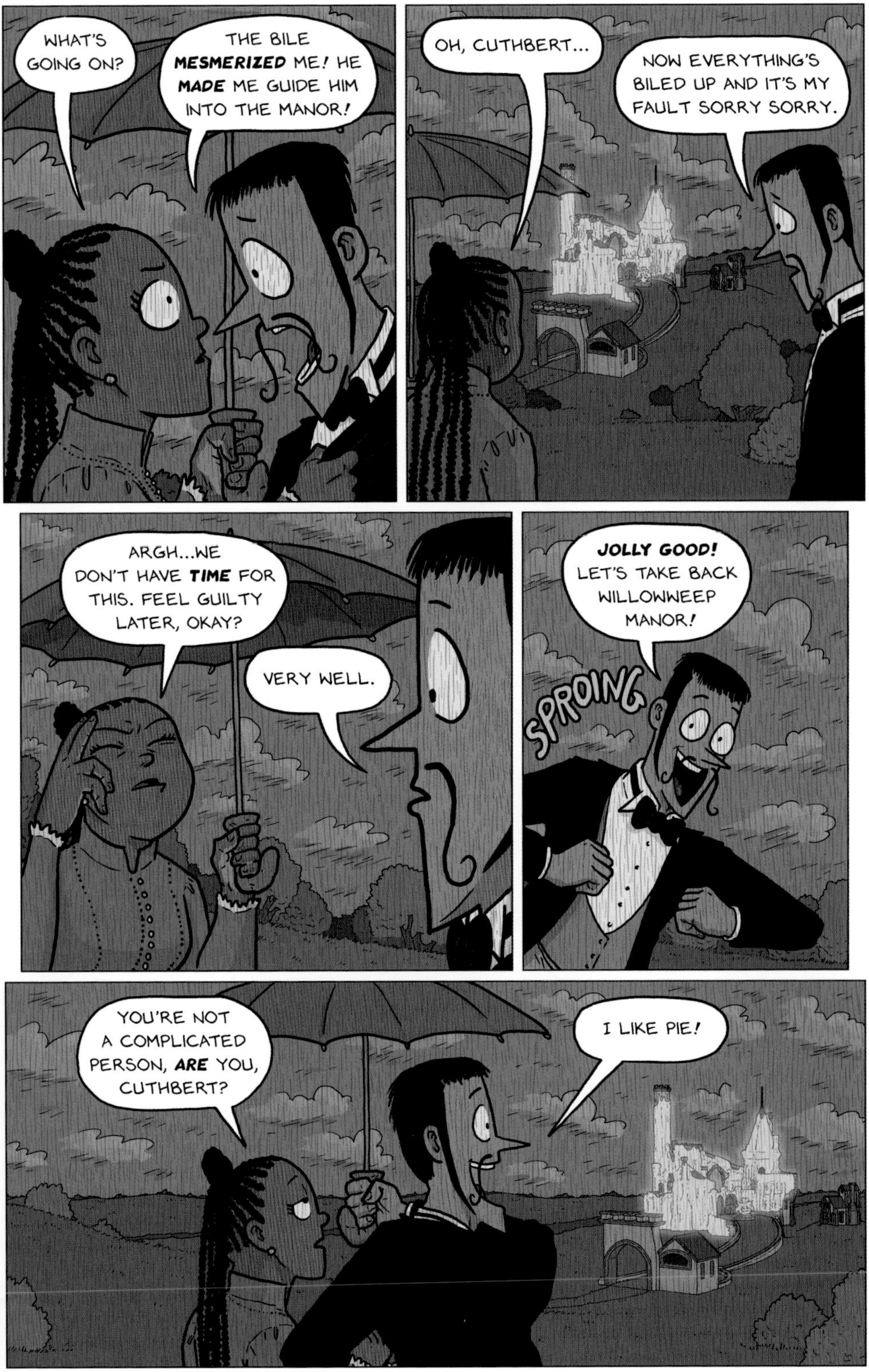
WHAT'S GOING ON?
THE BILE MESMERIZED ME! HE MADE ME GUIDE HIM INTO THE MANOR!
OH, CUTHBERT...
NOW EVERYTHING'S BILED UP AND IT'S MY FAULT SORRY SORRY.
ARGH...WE DON'T HAVE TIME FOR THIS. FEEL GUILTY LATER, OKAY?
VERY WELL.
JOLLY GOOD! LET'S TAKE BACK WILLOWWEEP MANOR!
SPROING
YOU'RE NOT A COMPLICATED PERSON, ARE YOU, CUTHBERT?
I LIKE PIE!

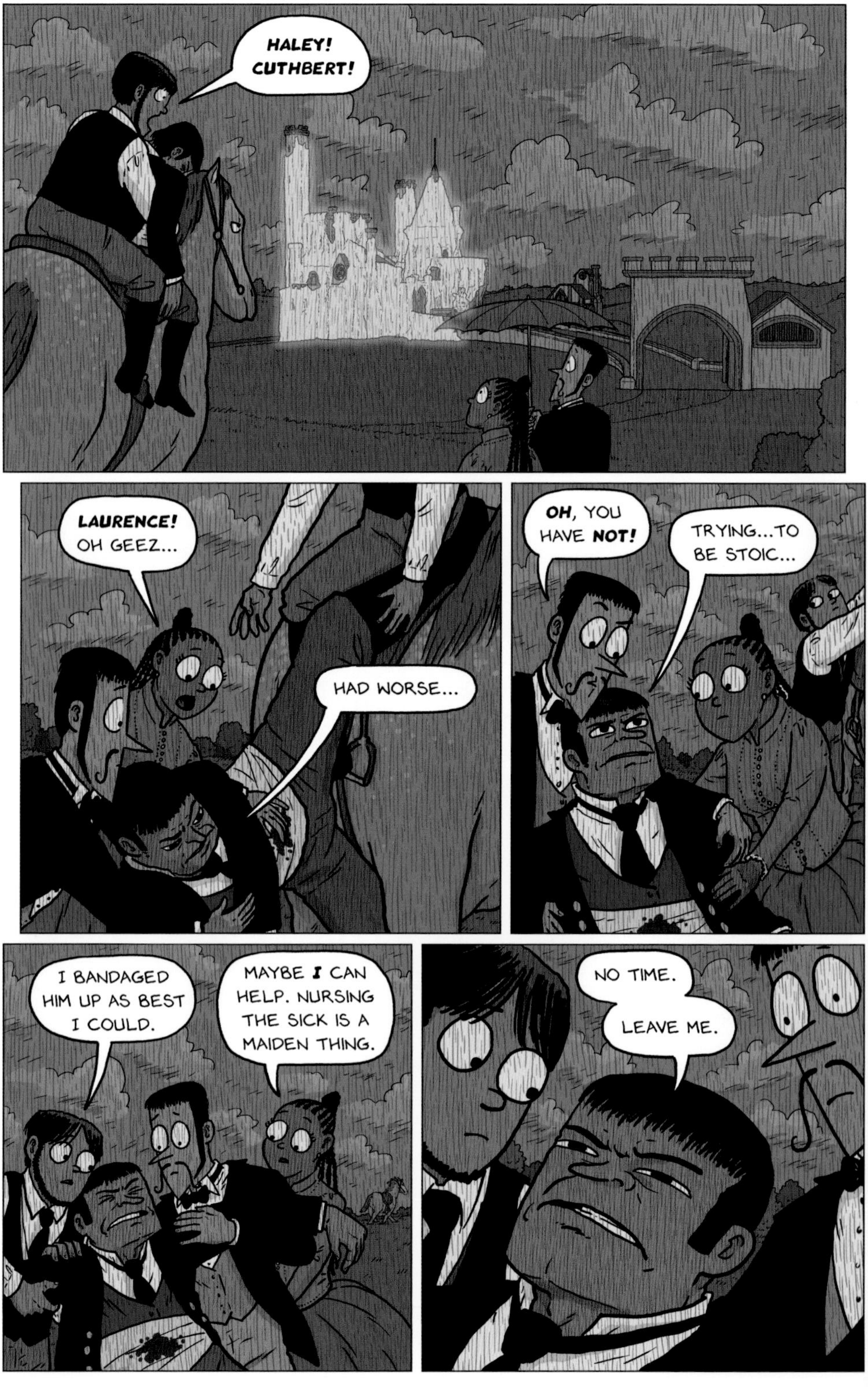
HALEY! CUTHBERT!
LAURENCE! OH GEEZ...
HAD WORSE...
OH, YOU HAVE NOT!
TRYING...TO BE STOIC...
I BANDAGED HIM UP AS BEST I COULD.
MAYBE I CAN HELP. NURSING THE SICK IS A MAIDEN THING.
NO TIME.
LEAVE ME.

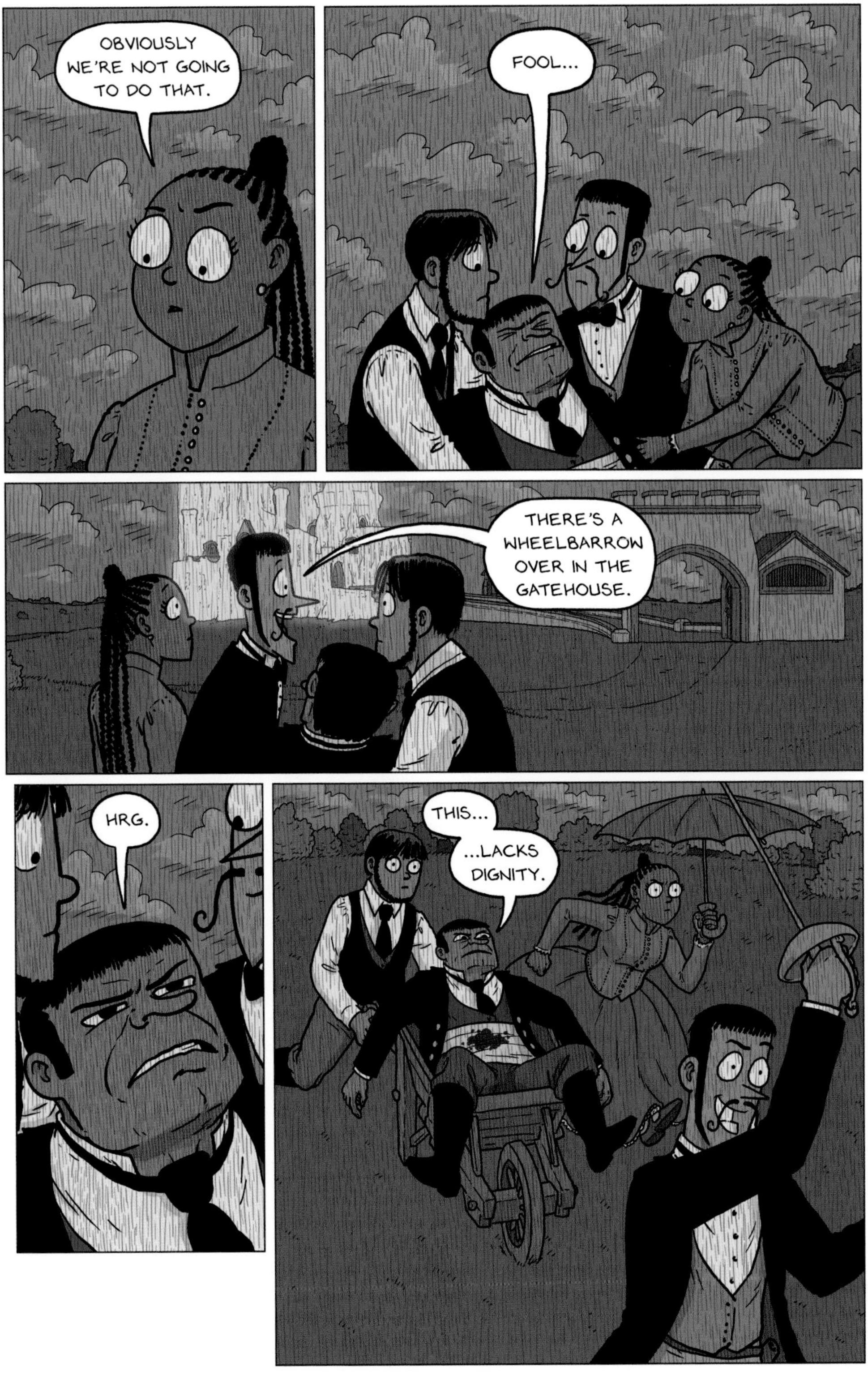
OBVIOUSLY WE'RE NOT GOING TO DO THAT.
FOOL...
THERE'S A WHEELBARROW OVER IN THE GATEHOUSE.
HRG.
THIS...
...LACKS DIGNITY.

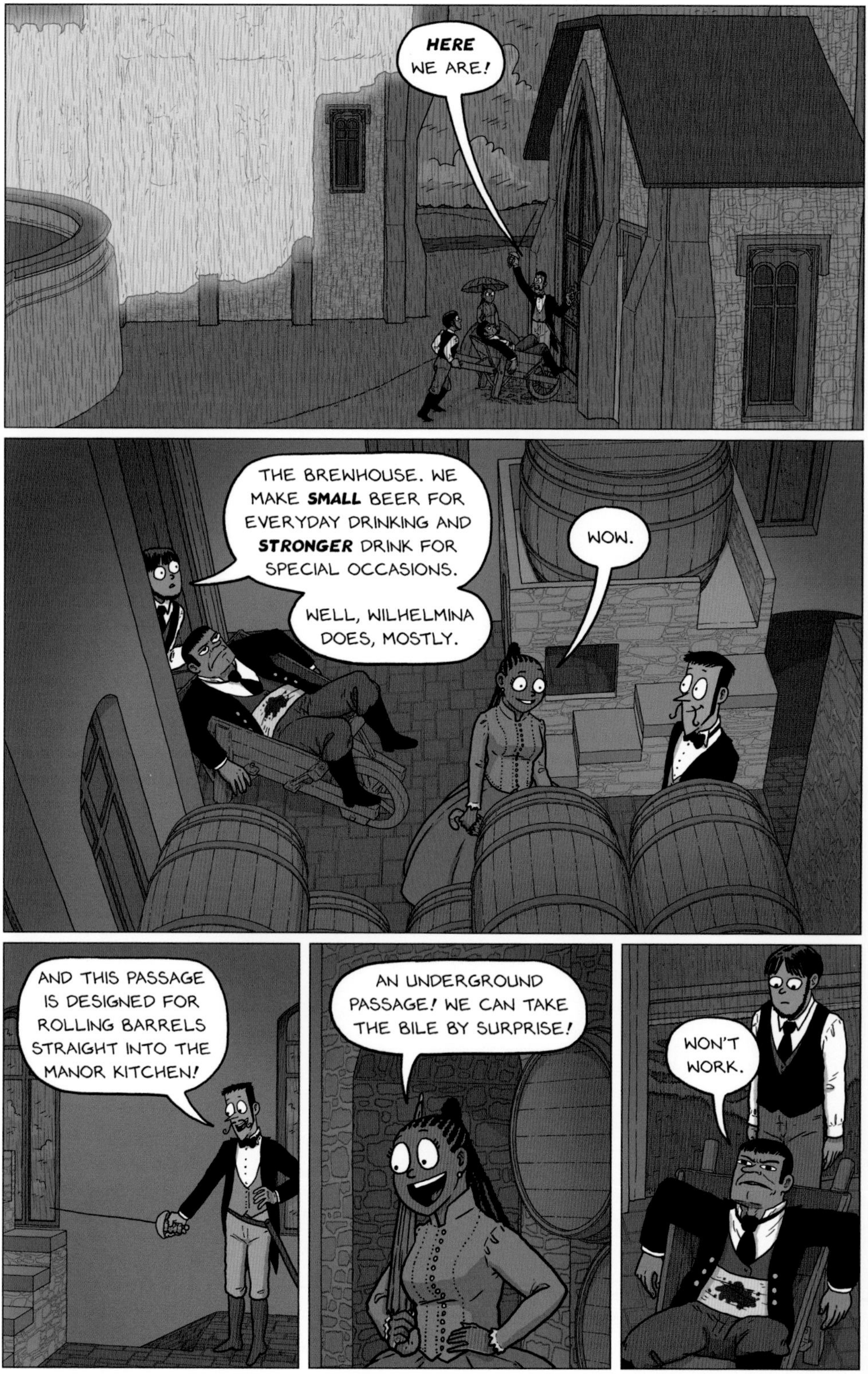
HERE WE ARE!
THE BREWHOUSE. WE MAKE SMALL BEER FOR EVERYDAY DRINKING AND STRONGER DRINK FOR SPECIAL OCCASIONS.
WELL, WILHELMINA DOES, MOSTLY.
WOW.
AND THIS PASSAGE IS DESIGNED FOR ROLLING BARRELS STRAIGHT INTO THE MANOR KITCHEN!
AN UNDERGROUND PASSAGE! WE CAN TAKE THE BILE BY SURPRISE!
WON'T WORK.

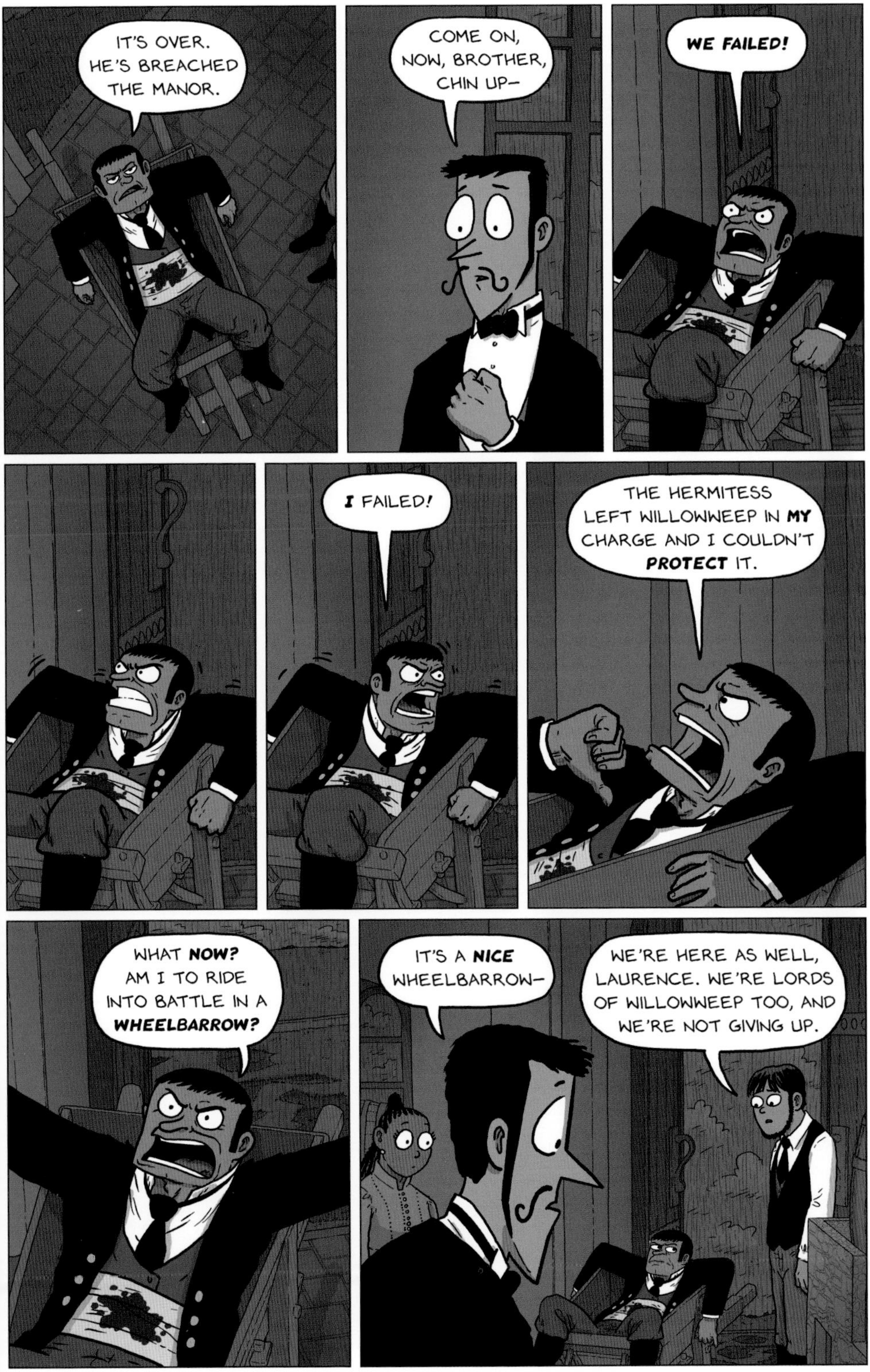
IT'S OVER. HE'S BREACHED THE MANOR.
COME ON, NOW, BROTHER, CHIN UP–
WE FAILED!
I FAILED!
THE HERMITESS LEFT WILLOWWEEP IN **MY** CHARGE AND I COULDN'T **PROTECT** IT.
WHAT **NOW?** AM I TO RIDE INTO BATTLE IN A **WHEELBARROW?**
IT'S A **NICE** WHEELBARROW–
WE'RE HERE AS WELL, LAURENCE. WE'RE LORDS OF WILLOWWEEP TOO, AND WE'RE NOT GIVING UP.

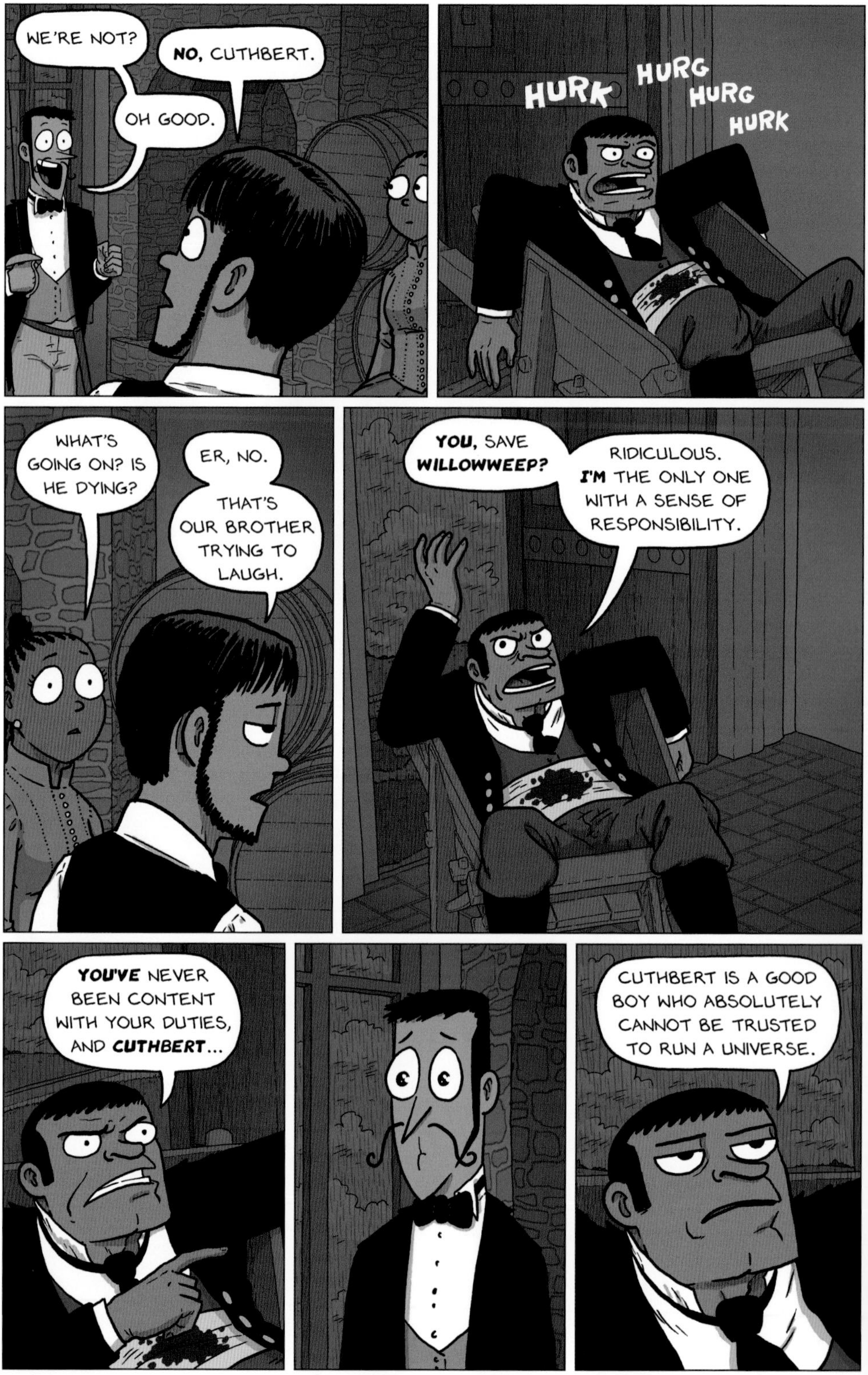
WE'RE NOT?
NO, CUTHBERT.
OH GOOD.
HURK
HURG
HURG
HURK
WHAT'S GOING ON? IS HE DYING?
ER, NO.
THAT'S OUR BROTHER TRYING TO LAUGH.
YOU, SAVE WILLOWWEEP?
RIDICULOUS. I'M THE ONLY ONE WITH A SENSE OF RESPONSIBILITY.
YOU'VE NEVER BEEN CONTENT WITH YOUR DUTIES, AND CUTHBERT...
CUTHBERT IS A GOOD BOY WHO ABSOLUTELY CANNOT BE TRUSTED TO RUN A UNIVERSE.

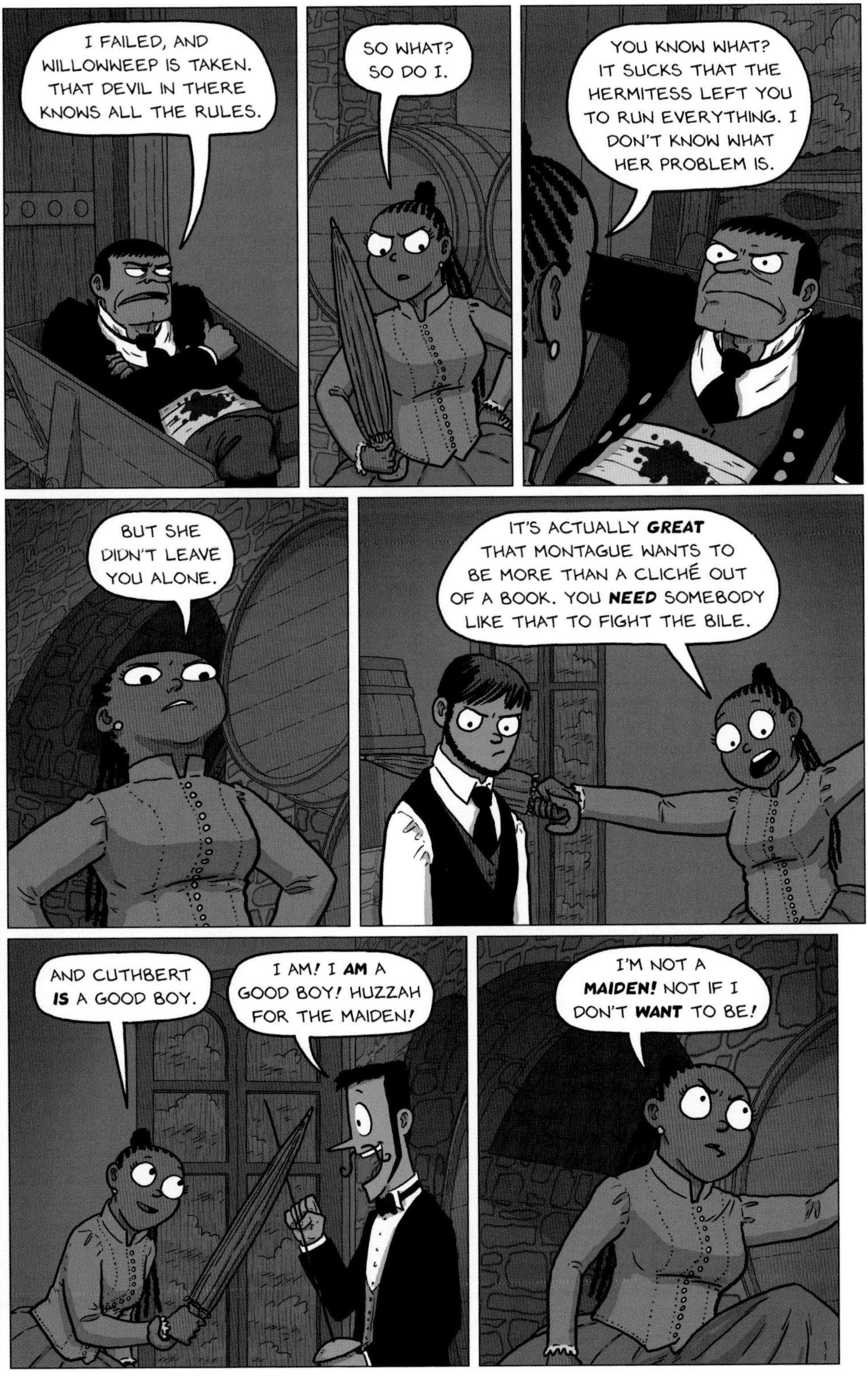
I FAILED, AND WILLOWWEEP IS TAKEN. THAT DEVIL IN THERE KNOWS ALL THE RULES.
SO WHAT? SO DO I.
YOU KNOW WHAT? IT SUCKS THAT THE HERMITESS LEFT YOU TO RUN EVERYTHING. I DON'T KNOW WHAT HER PROBLEM IS.
BUT SHE DIDN'T LEAVE YOU ALONE.
IT'S ACTUALLY **GREAT** THAT MONTAGUE WANTS TO BE MORE THAN A CLICHÉ OUT OF A BOOK. YOU **NEED** SOMEBODY LIKE THAT TO FIGHT THE BILE.
AND CUTHBERT **IS** A GOOD BOY.
I AM! I **AM** A GOOD BOY! HUZZAH FOR THE MAIDEN!
I'M NOT A **MAIDEN!** NOT IF I DON'T **WANT** TO BE!

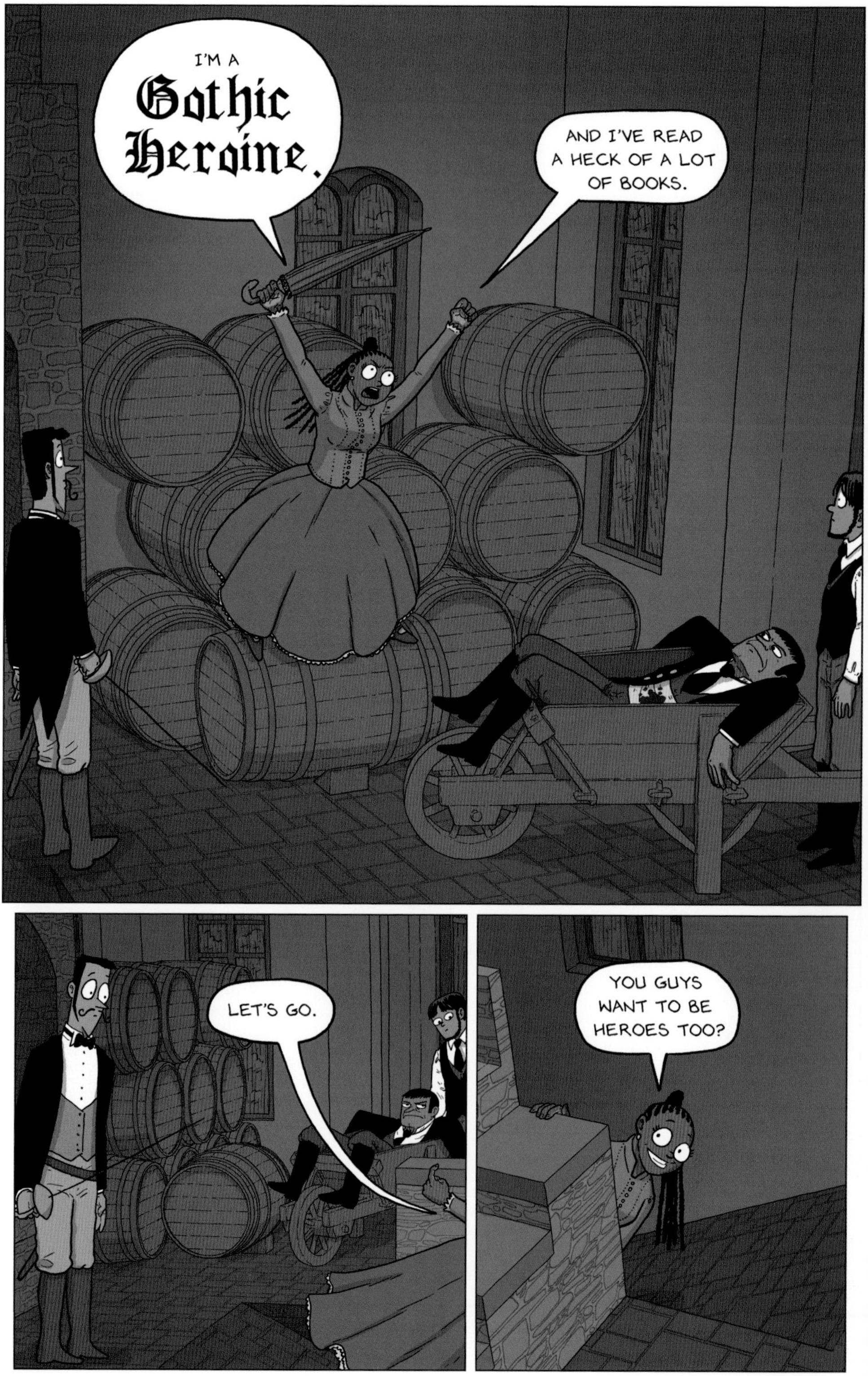
I'M A
Gothic
Heroine.
AND I'VE READ A HECK OF A LOT OF BOOKS.
LET'S GO.
YOU GUYS WANT TO BE HEROES TOO?

6

A Desperate Stand

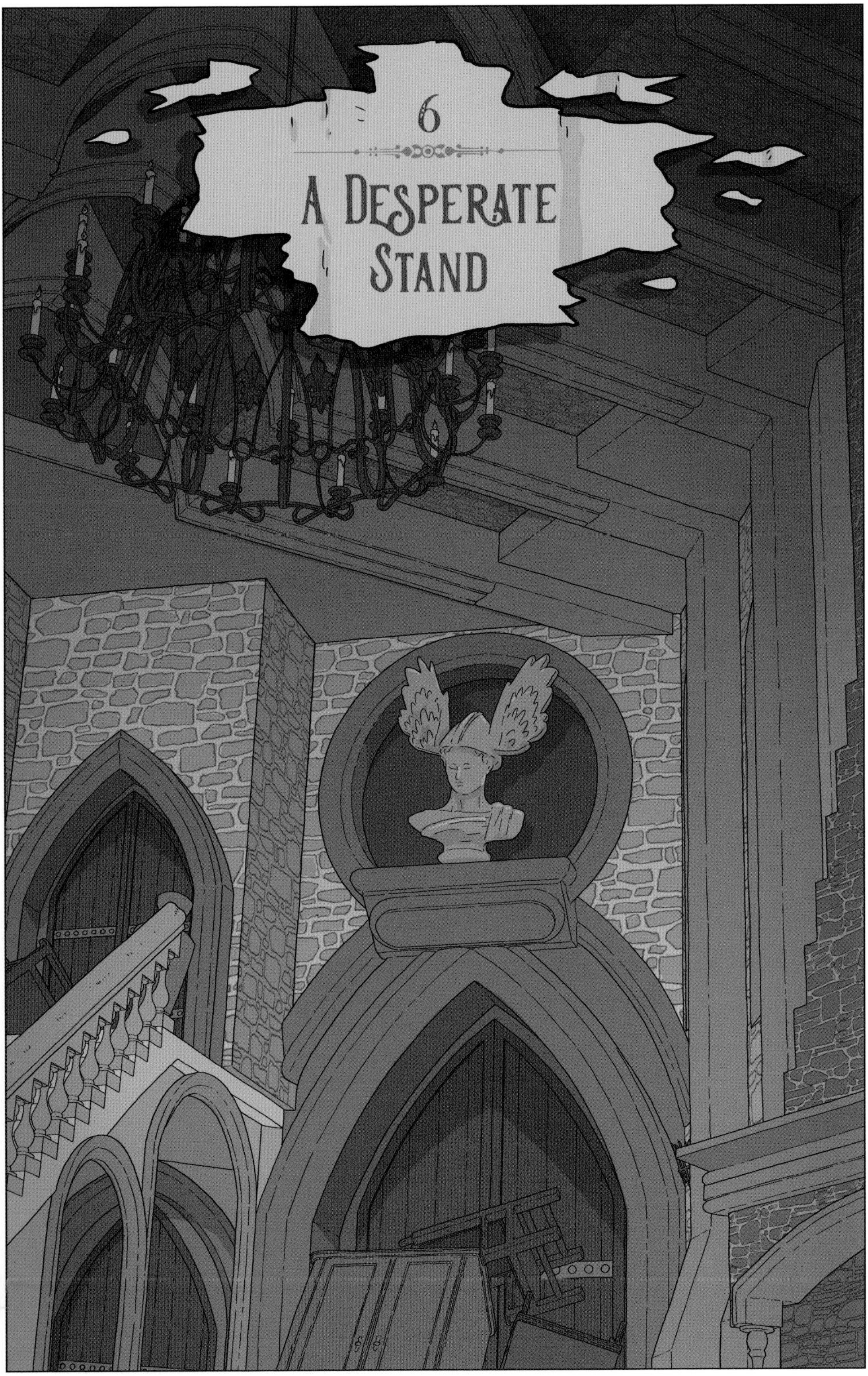

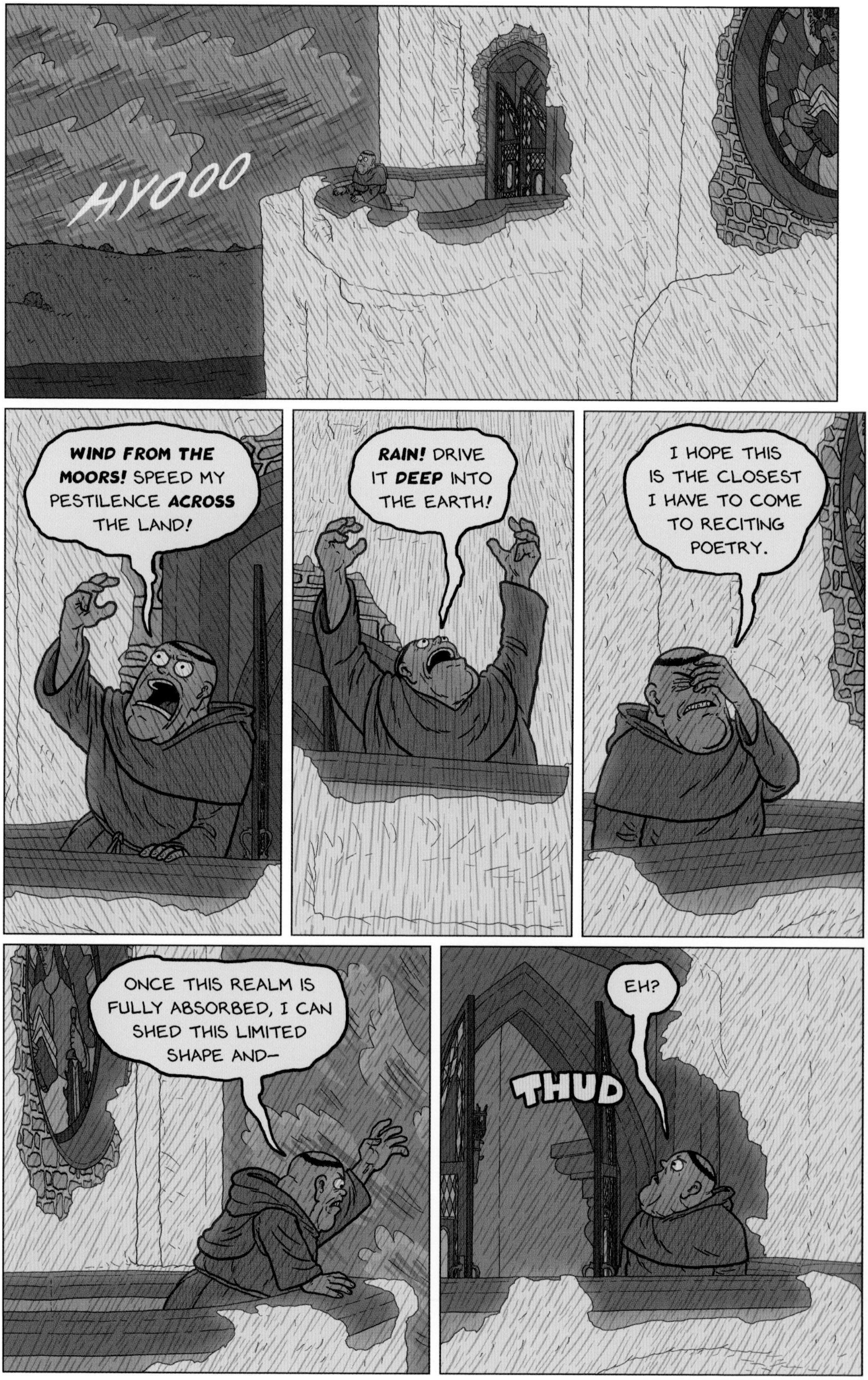
HYOOO
WIND FROM THE MOORS! SPEED MY PESTILENCE ACROSS THE LAND!
RAIN! DRIVE IT DEEP INTO THE EARTH!
I HOPE THIS IS THE CLOSEST I HAVE TO COME TO RECITING POETRY.
ONCE THIS REALM IS FULLY ABSORBED, I CAN SHED THIS LIMITED SHAPE AND—
THUD
EH?

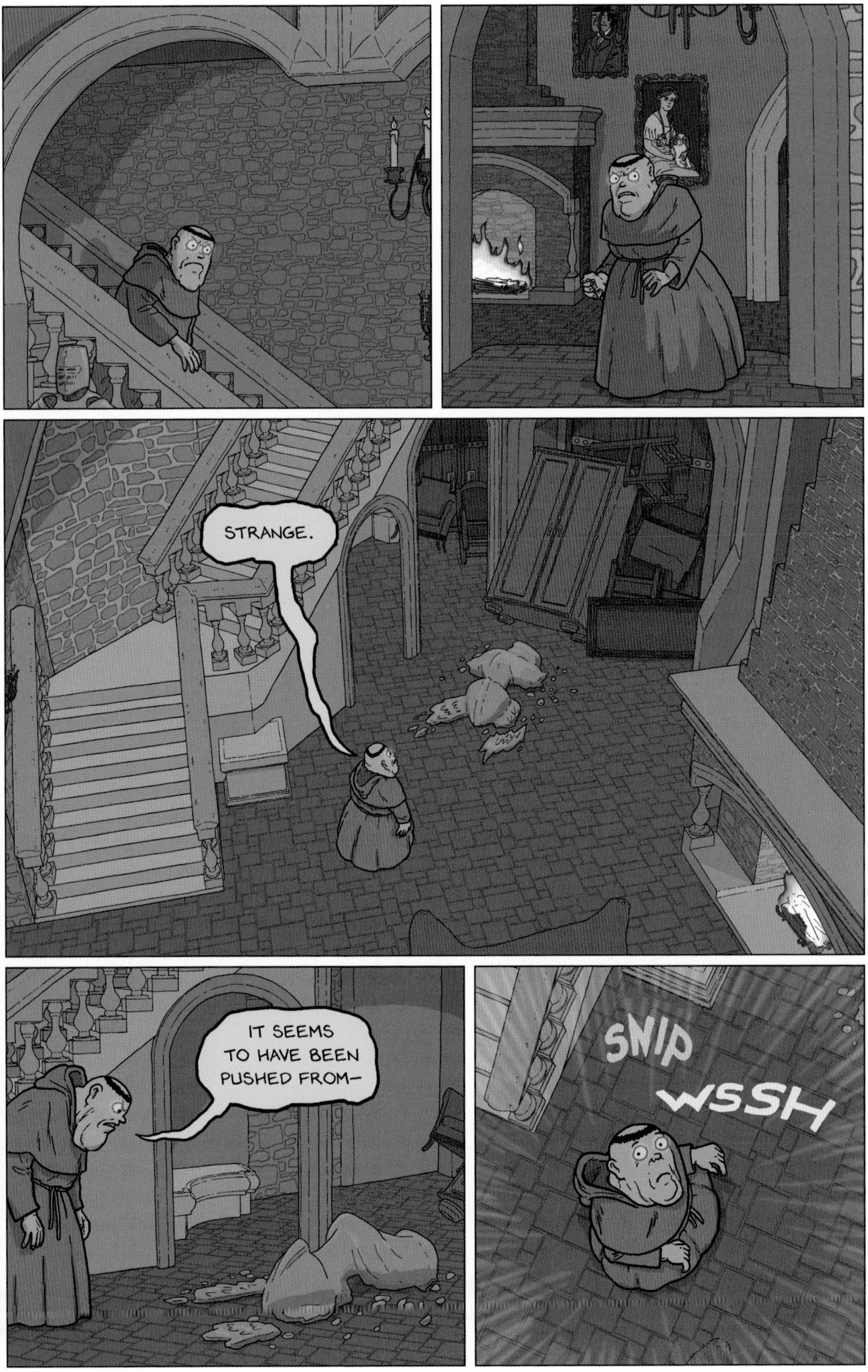
STRANGE.
IT SEEMS TO HAVE BEEN PUSHED FROM—
SNIP
WSSH

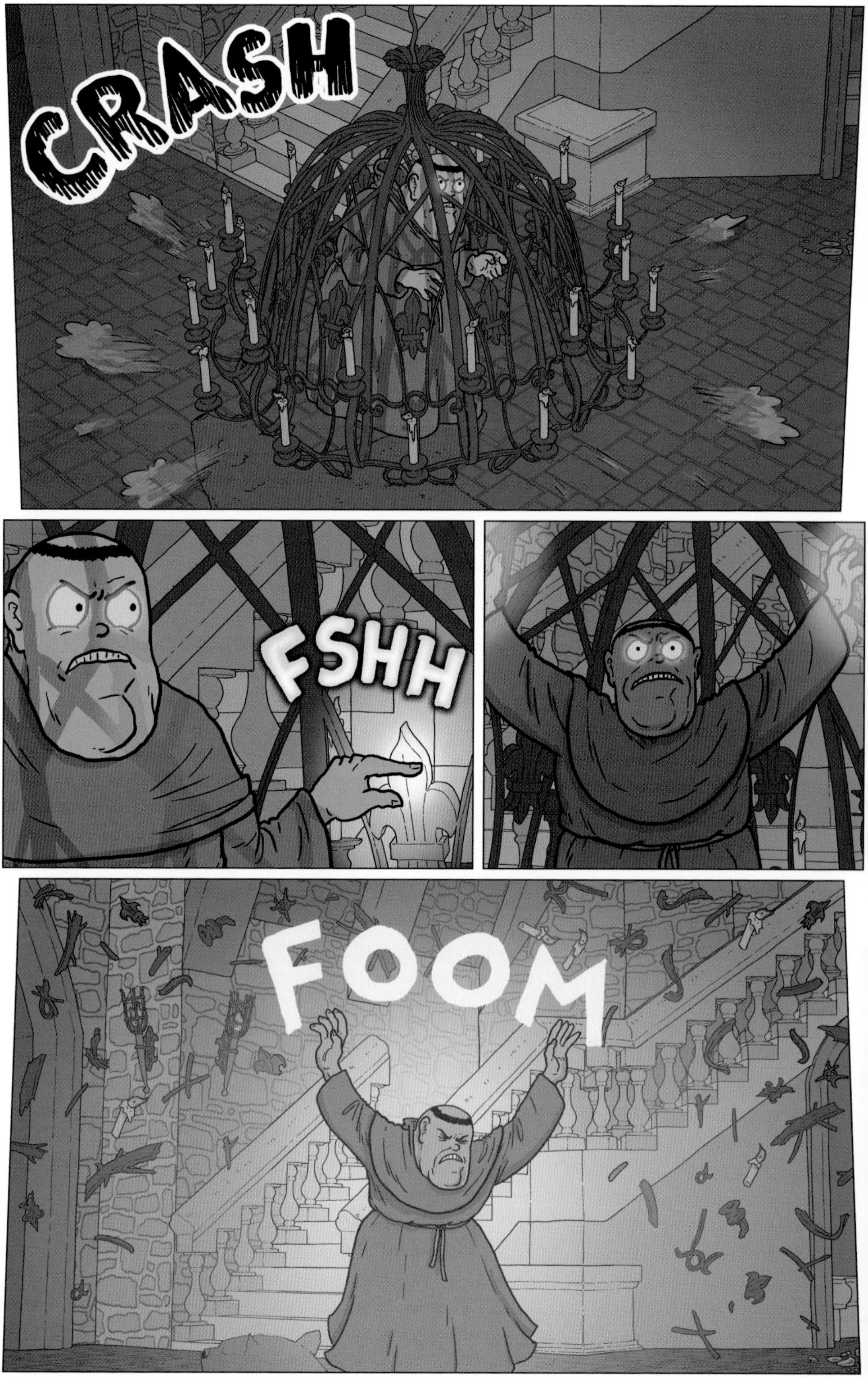
CRASH
FSHH
FOOM

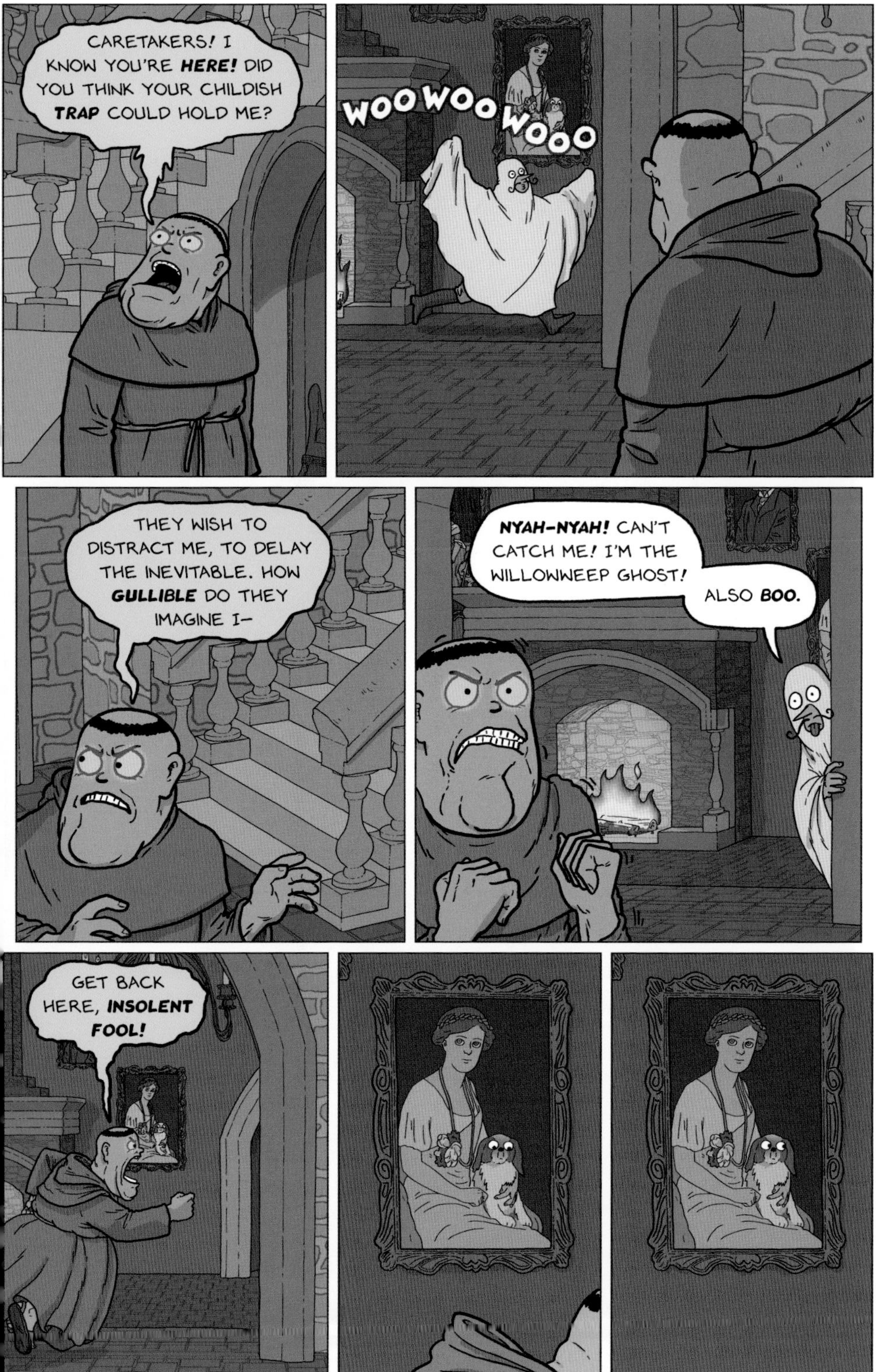
CARETAKERS! I KNOW YOU'RE **HERE!** DID YOU THINK YOUR CHILDISH **TRAP** COULD HOLD ME?
WOOWOOWOOO
THEY WISH TO DISTRACT ME, TO DELAY THE INEVITABLE. HOW **GULLIBLE** DO THEY IMAGINE I—
NYAH-NYAH! CAN'T CATCH ME! I'M THE WILLOWWEEP GHOST!
ALSO **BOO.**
GET BACK HERE, **INSOLENT FOOL!**

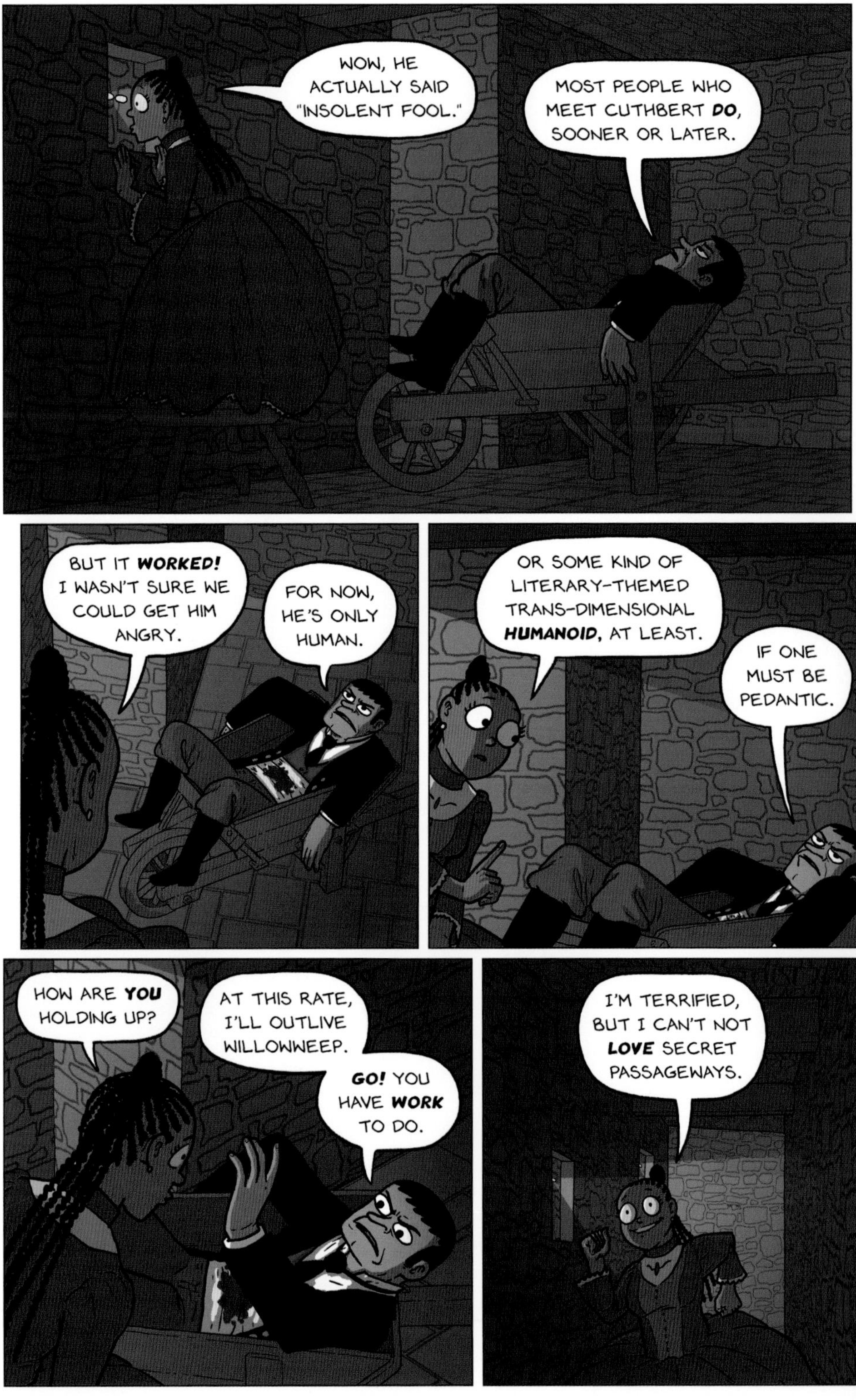
WOW, HE ACTUALLY SAID "INSOLENT FOOL."
MOST PEOPLE WHO MEET CUTHBERT **DO**, SOONER OR LATER.
BUT IT **WORKED!** I WASN'T SURE WE COULD GET HIM ANGRY.
FOR NOW, HE'S ONLY HUMAN.
OR SOME KIND OF LITERARY-THEMED TRANS-DIMENSIONAL **HUMANOID**, AT LEAST.
IF ONE MUST BE PEDANTIC.
HOW ARE **YOU** HOLDING UP?
AT THIS RATE, I'LL OUTLIVE WILLOWWEEP.
GO! YOU HAVE **WORK** TO DO.
I'M TERRIFIED, BUT I CAN'T NOT **LOVE** SECRET PASSAGEWAYS.

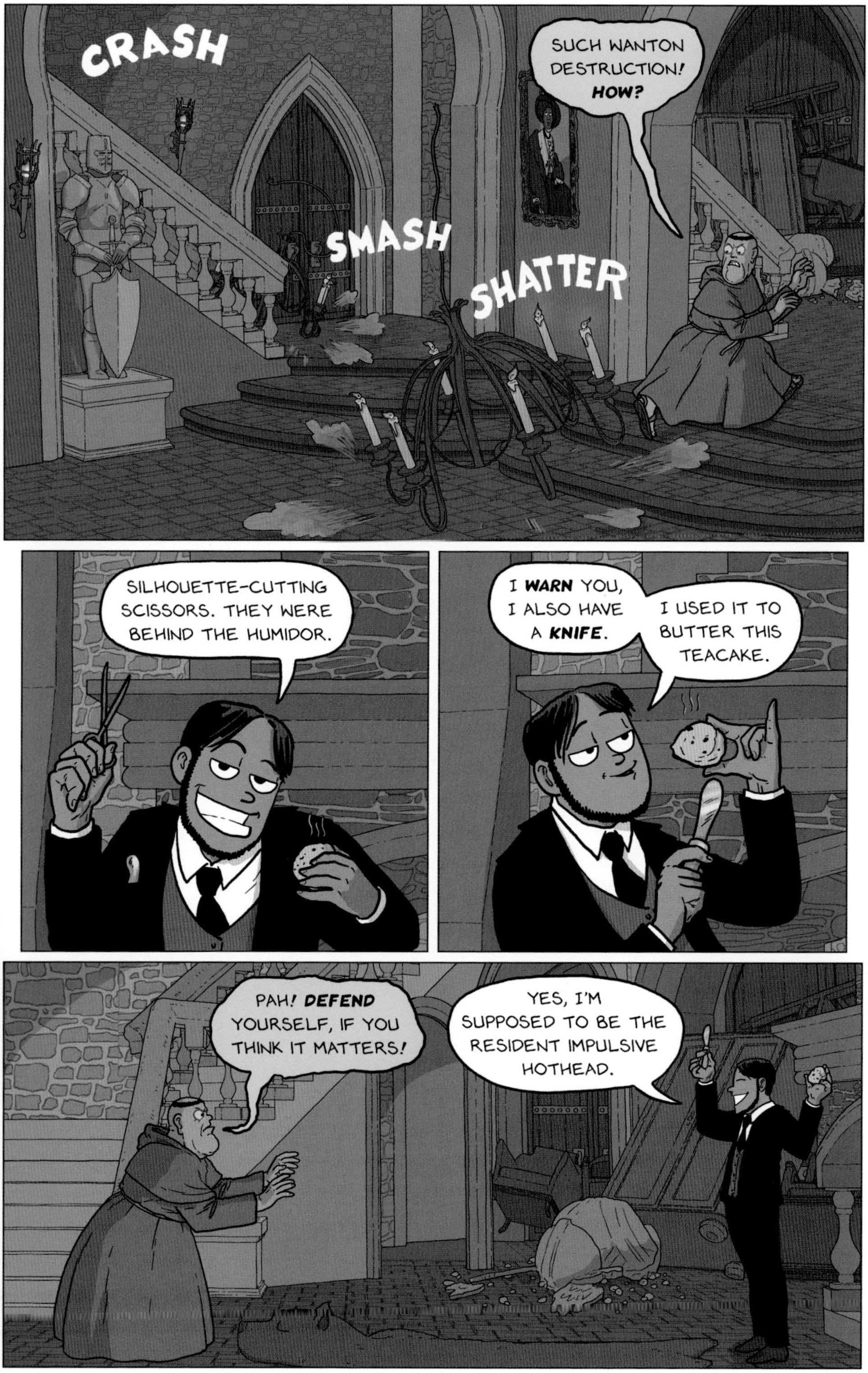
CRASH
SUCH WANTON DESTRUCTION! HOW?
SMASH
SHATTER
SILHOUETTE-CUTTING SCISSORS. THEY WERE BEHIND THE HUMIDOR.
I WARN YOU, I ALSO HAVE A KNIFE.
I USED IT TO BUTTER THIS TEACAKE.
PAH! DEFEND YOURSELF, IF YOU THINK IT MATTERS!
YES, I'M SUPPOSED TO BE THE RESIDENT IMPULSIVE HOTHEAD.

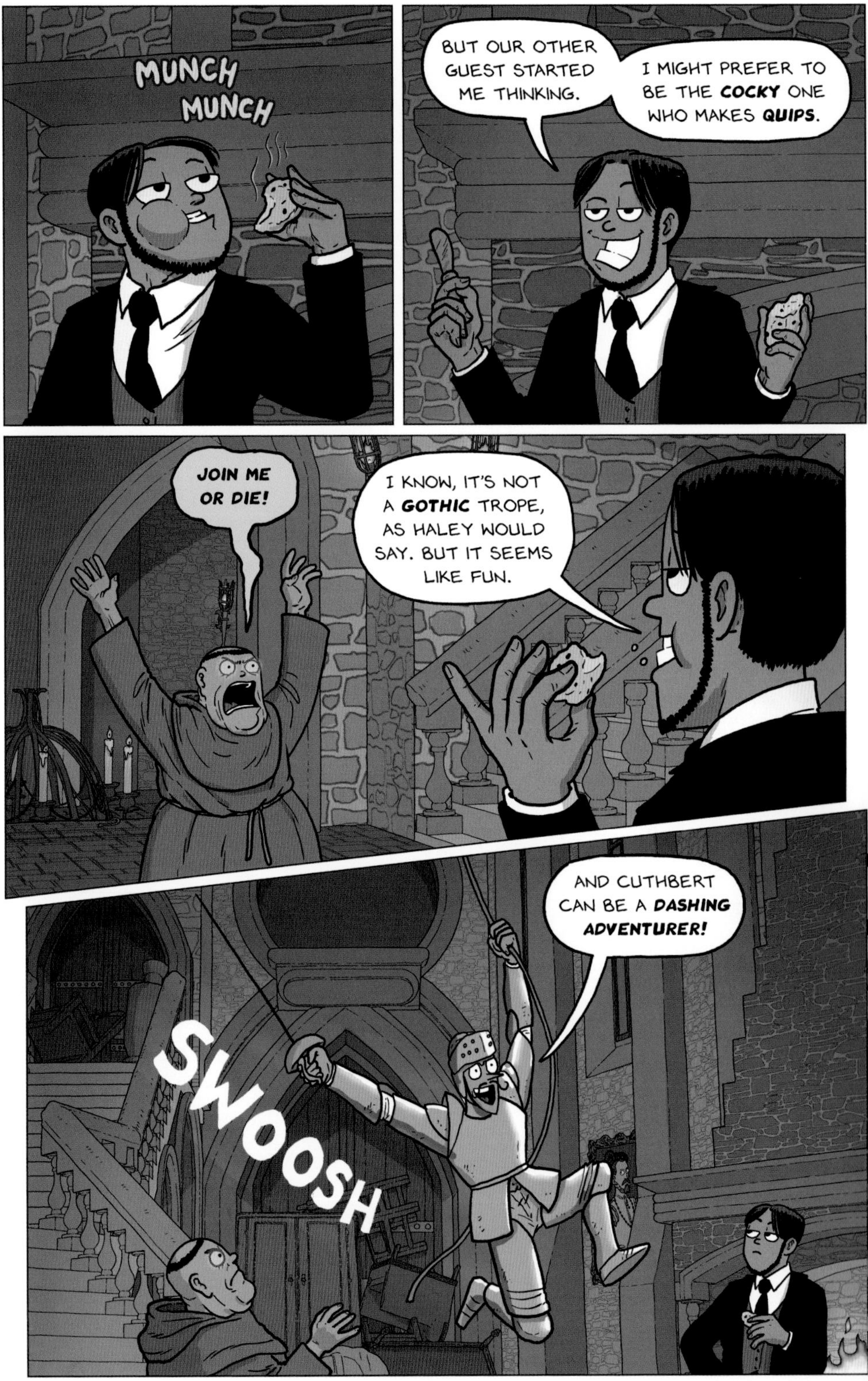
MUNCH
MUNCH
BUT OUR OTHER GUEST STARTED ME THINKING.
I MIGHT PREFER TO BE THE **COCKY** ONE WHO MAKES **QUIPS**.
JOIN ME OR DIE!
I KNOW, IT'S NOT A **GOTHIC** TROPE, AS HALEY WOULD SAY. BUT IT SEEMS LIKE FUN.
AND CUTHBERT CAN BE A **DASHING ADVENTURER!**
SWOOSH

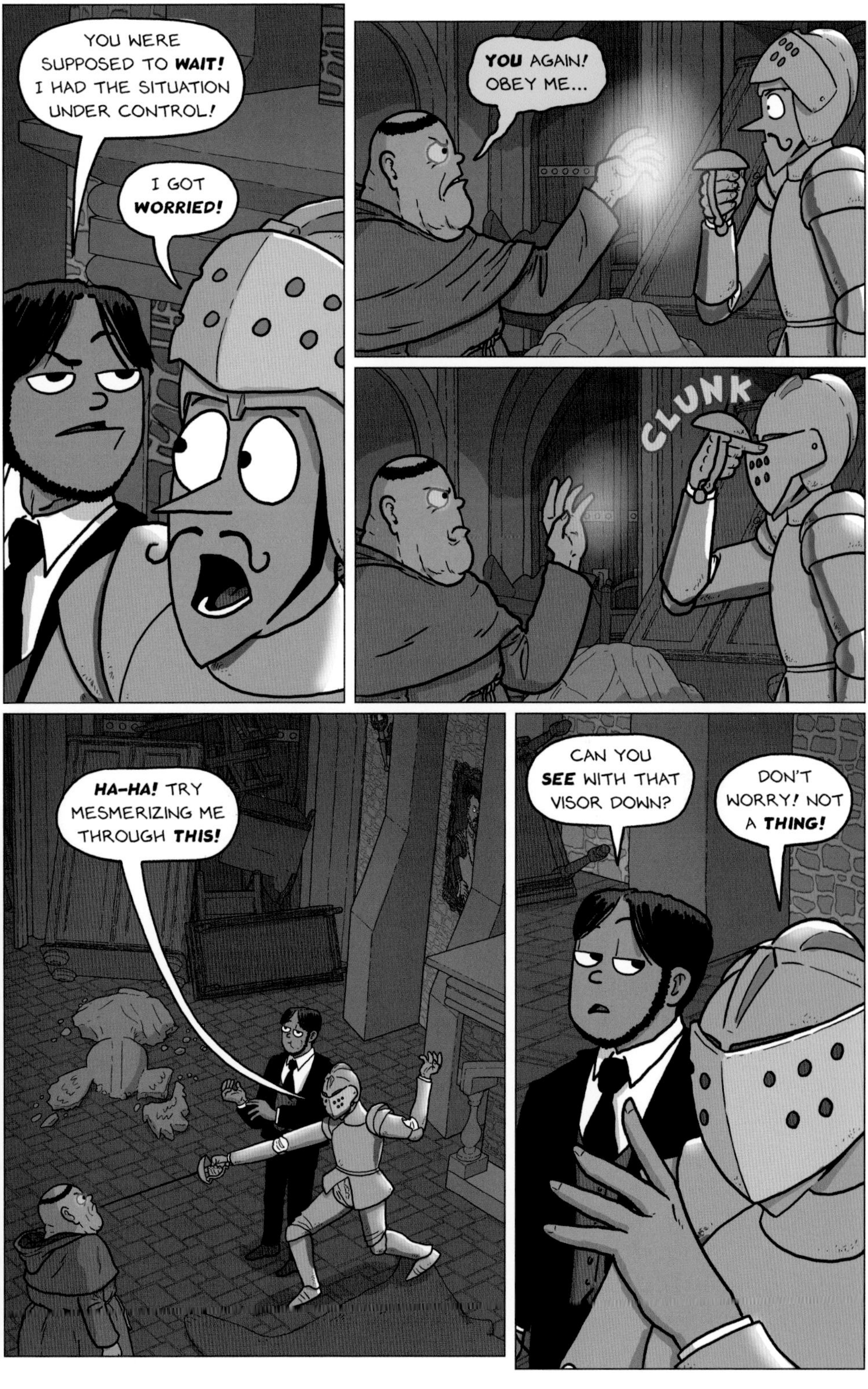
YOU WERE SUPPOSED TO **WAIT!** I HAD THE SITUATION UNDER CONTROL!
I GOT **WORRIED!**
YOU AGAIN! OBEY ME...
CLUNK
HA-HA! TRY MESMERIZING ME THROUGH **THIS!**
CAN YOU **SEE** WITH THAT VISOR DOWN?
DON'T WORRY! NOT A **THING!**

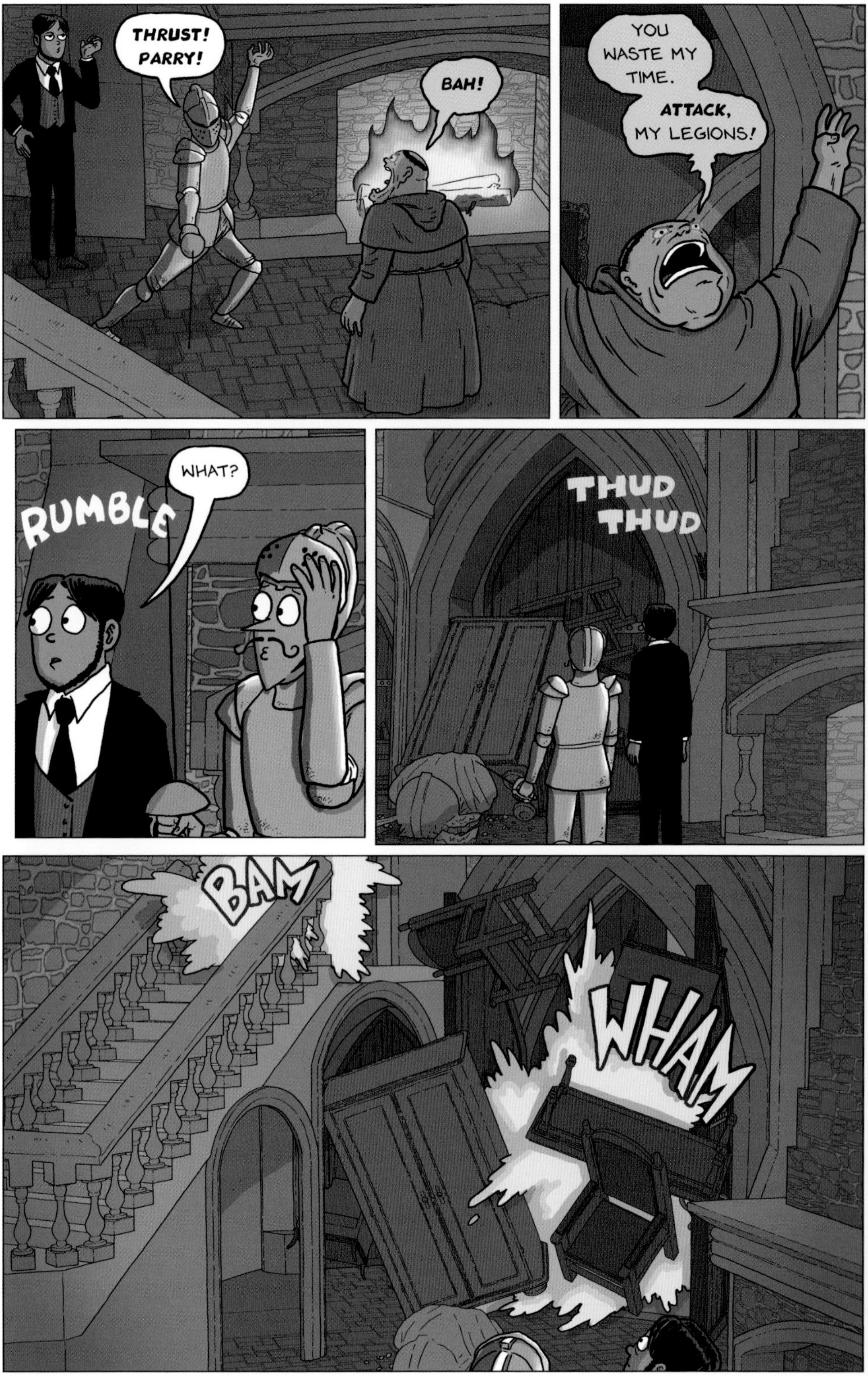
THRUST!
PARRY!
BAH!
YOU WASTE MY TIME.
ATTACK, MY LEGIONS!
RUMBLE
WHAT?
THUD
THUD
BAM
WHAM

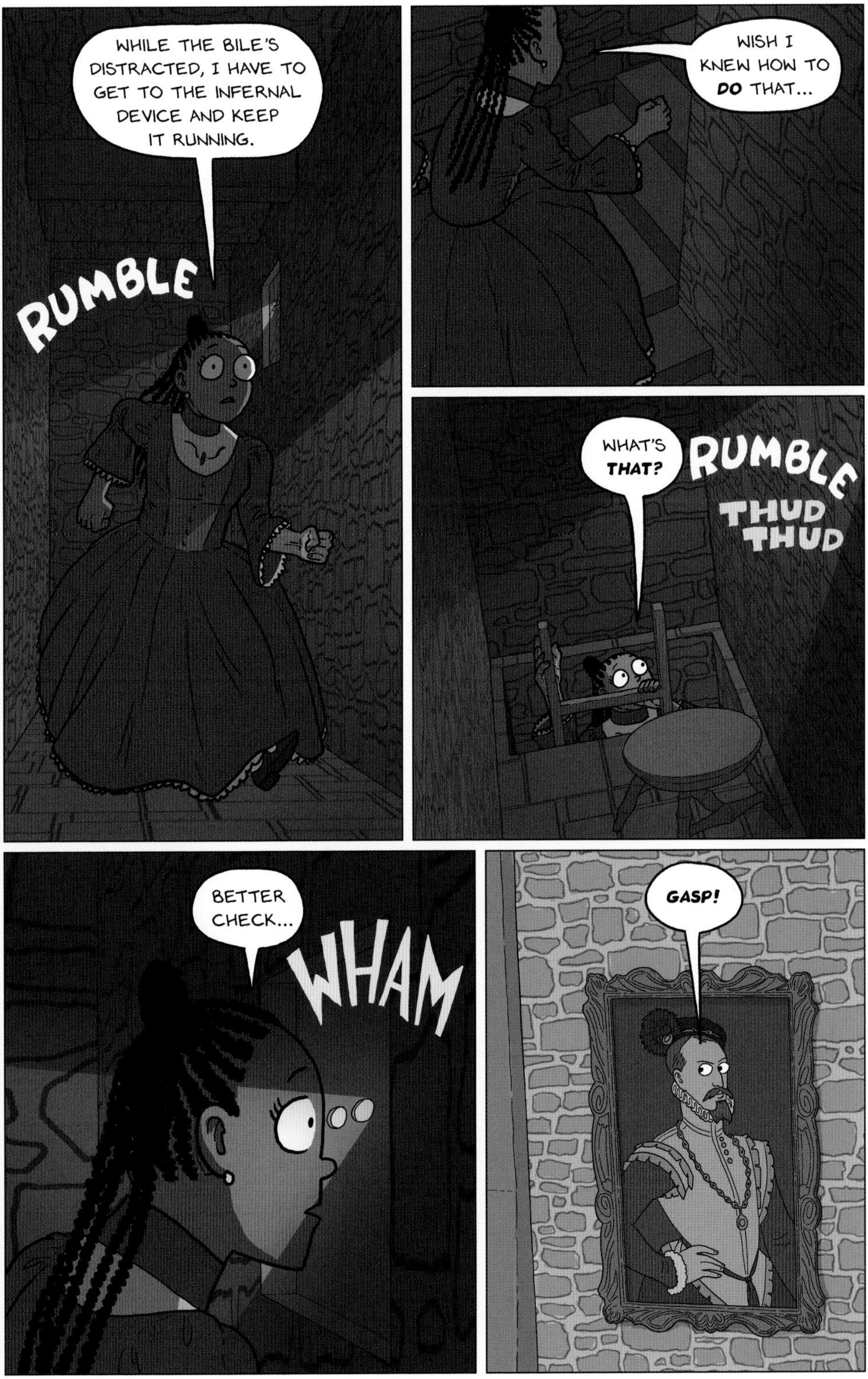
WHILE THE BILE'S DISTRACTED, I HAVE TO GET TO THE INFERNAL DEVICE AND KEEP IT RUNNING.
RUMBLE
WISH I KNEW HOW TO **DO** THAT...
WHAT'S **THAT?**
RUMBLE
THUD THUD
BETTER CHECK...
WHAM
GASP!

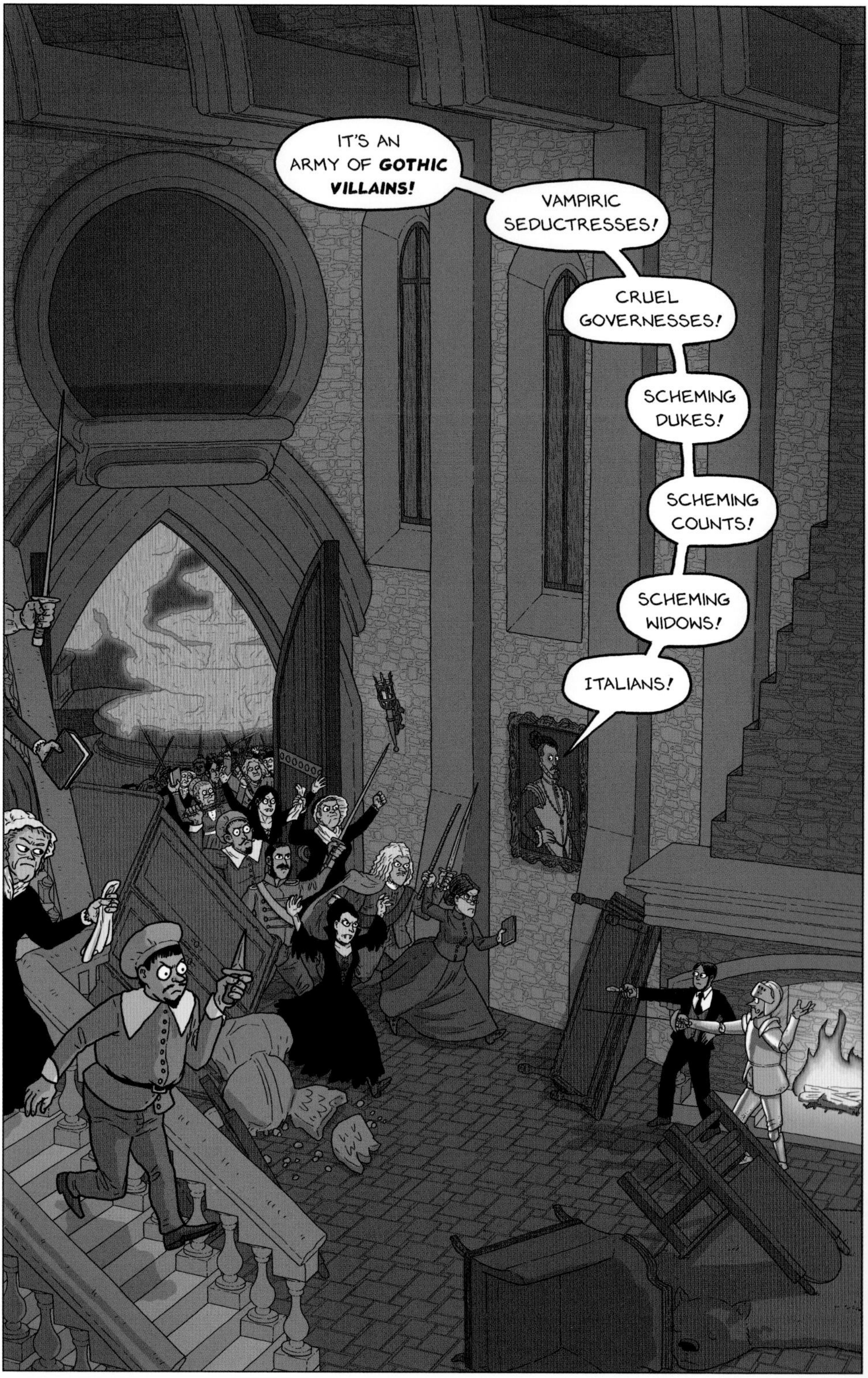
IT'S AN ARMY OF **GOTHIC VILLAINS!**
VAMPIRIC SEDUCTRESSES!
CRUEL GOVERNESSES!
SCHEMING DUKES!
SCHEMING COUNTS!
SCHEMING WIDOWS!
ITALIANS!

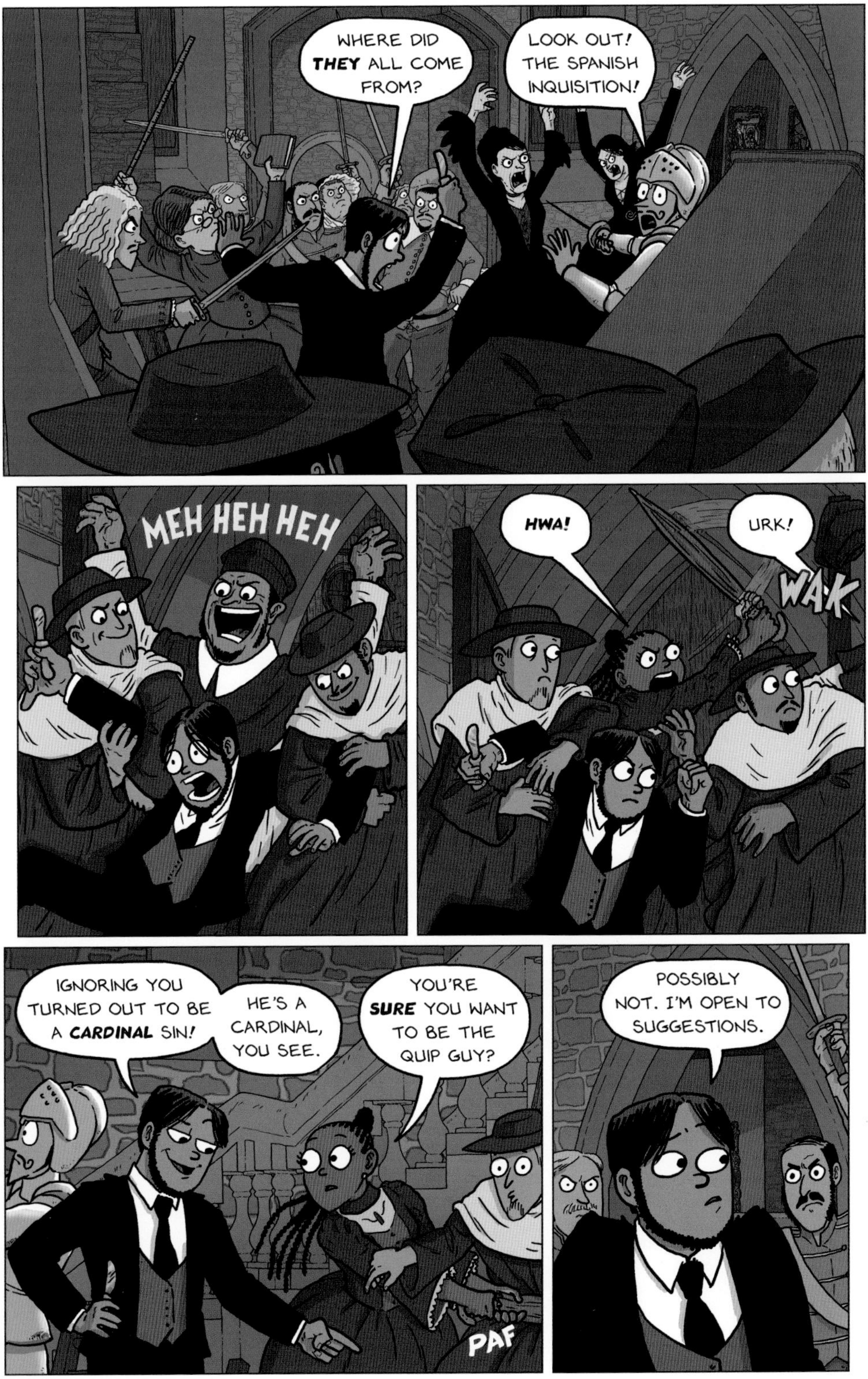
WHERE DID THEY ALL COME FROM?
LOOK OUT! THE SPANISH INQUISITION!
MEH HEH HEH
HWA!
URK!
WAK
IGNORING YOU TURNED OUT TO BE A CARDINAL SIN!
HE'S A CARDINAL, YOU SEE.
YOU'RE SURE YOU WANT TO BE THE QUIP GUY?
PAF
POSSIBLY NOT. I'M OPEN TO SUGGESTIONS.

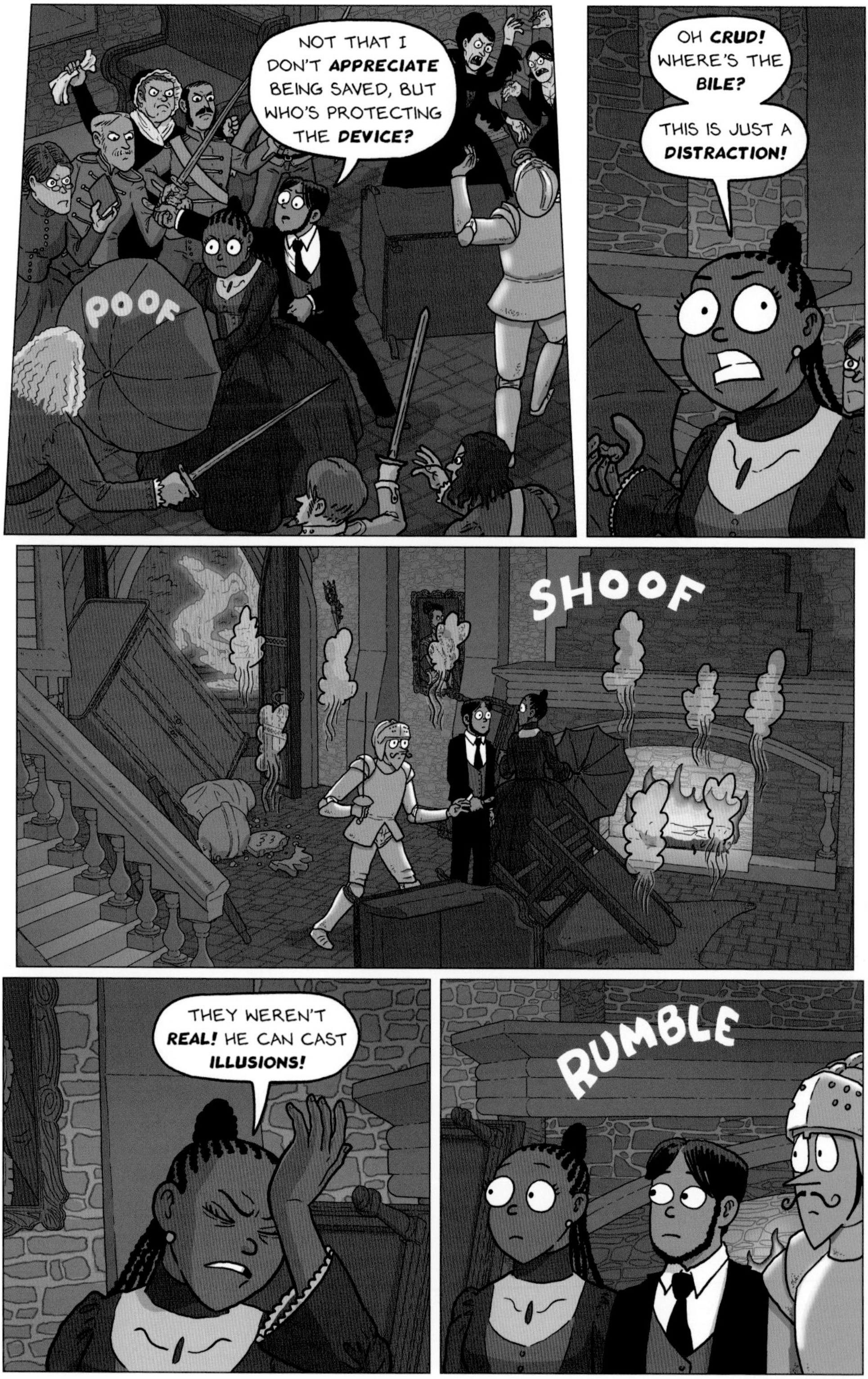
NOT THAT I DON'T **APPRECIATE** BEING SAVED, BUT WHO'S PROTECTING THE **DEVICE?**
POOF
OH **CRUD!** WHERE'S THE **BILE?**
THIS IS JUST A **DISTRACTION!**
SHOOF
THEY WEREN'T **REAL!** HE CAN CAST **ILLUSIONS!**
RUMBLE

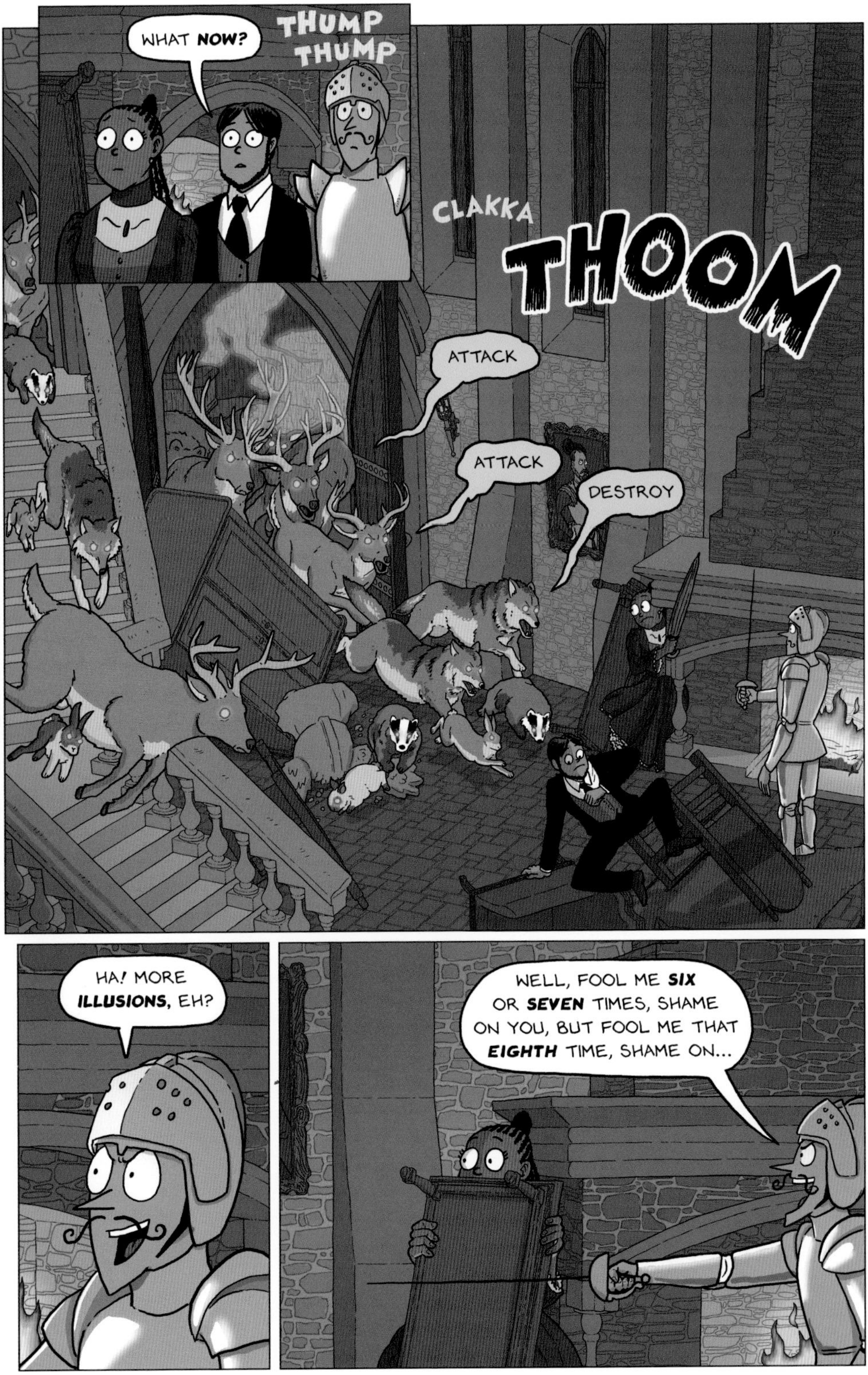
WHAT NOW?
THUMP THUMP
CLAKKA
THOOM
ATTACK
ATTACK
DESTROY
HA! MORE ILLUSIONS, EH?
WELL, FOOL ME SIX OR SEVEN TIMES, SHAME ON YOU, BUT FOOL ME THAT EIGHTH TIME, SHAME ON...

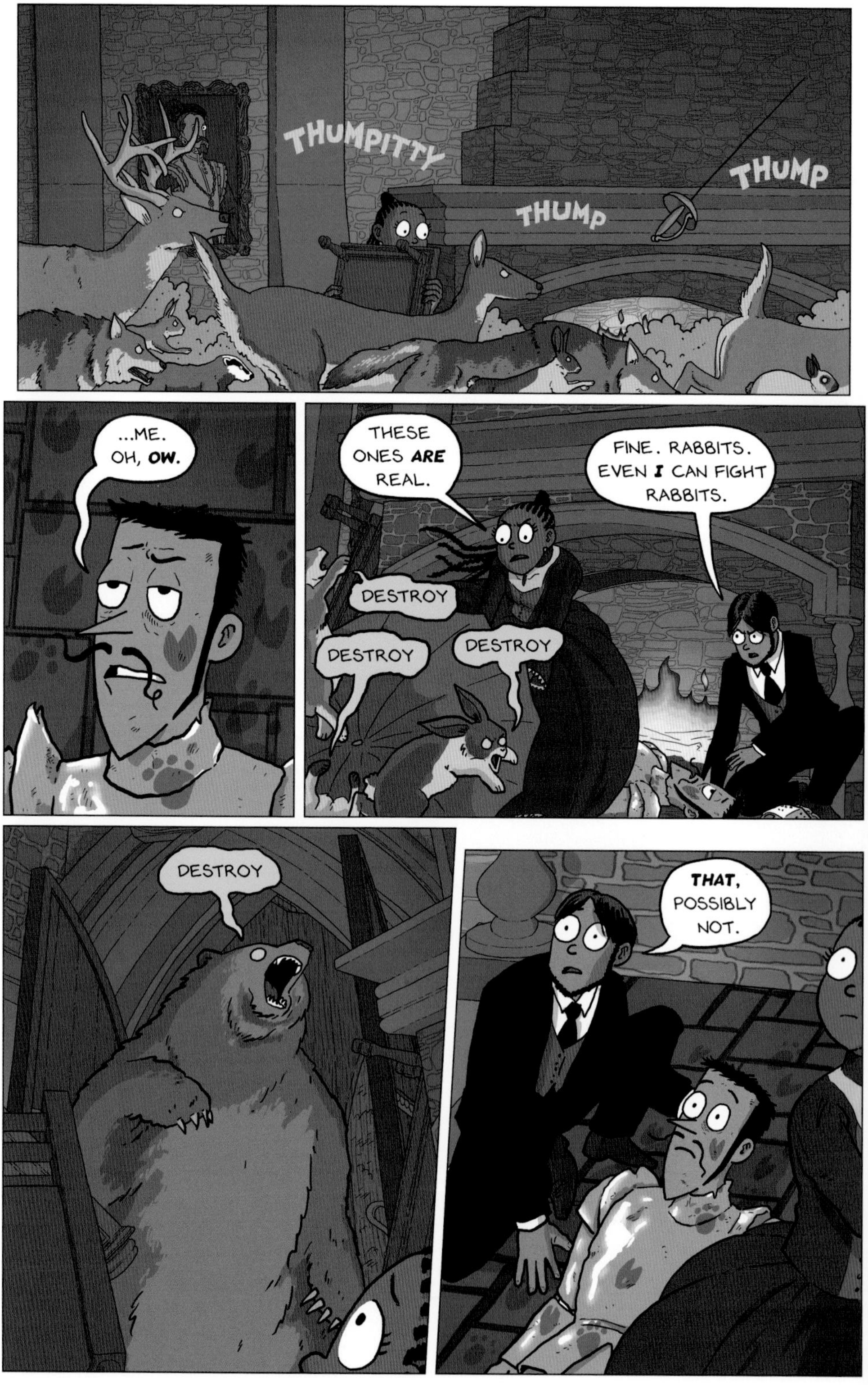
THUMPITTY
THUMP
THUMP
...ME.
OH, OW.
THESE ONES ARE REAL.
DESTROY
DESTROY
DESTROY
FINE. RABBITS. EVEN I CAN FIGHT RABBITS.
DESTROY
THAT, POSSIBLY NOT.

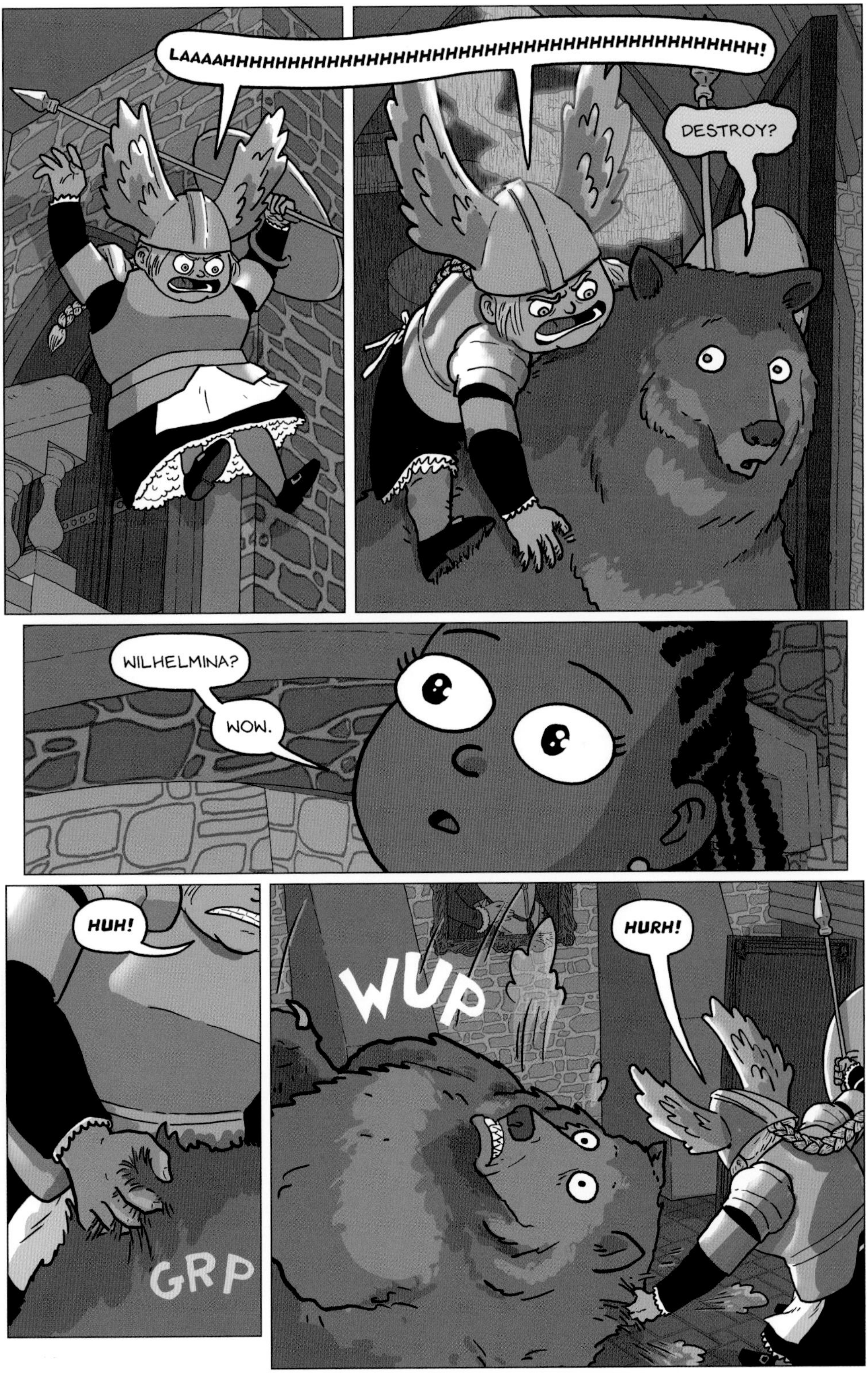
LAAAAHHHHHHHHHHHHHHHHHHHHHHHHHHHHHHHHHHHHHHHHHHHHH!
DESTROY?
WILHELMINA?
WOW.
HUH!
GRP
WUP
HURH!

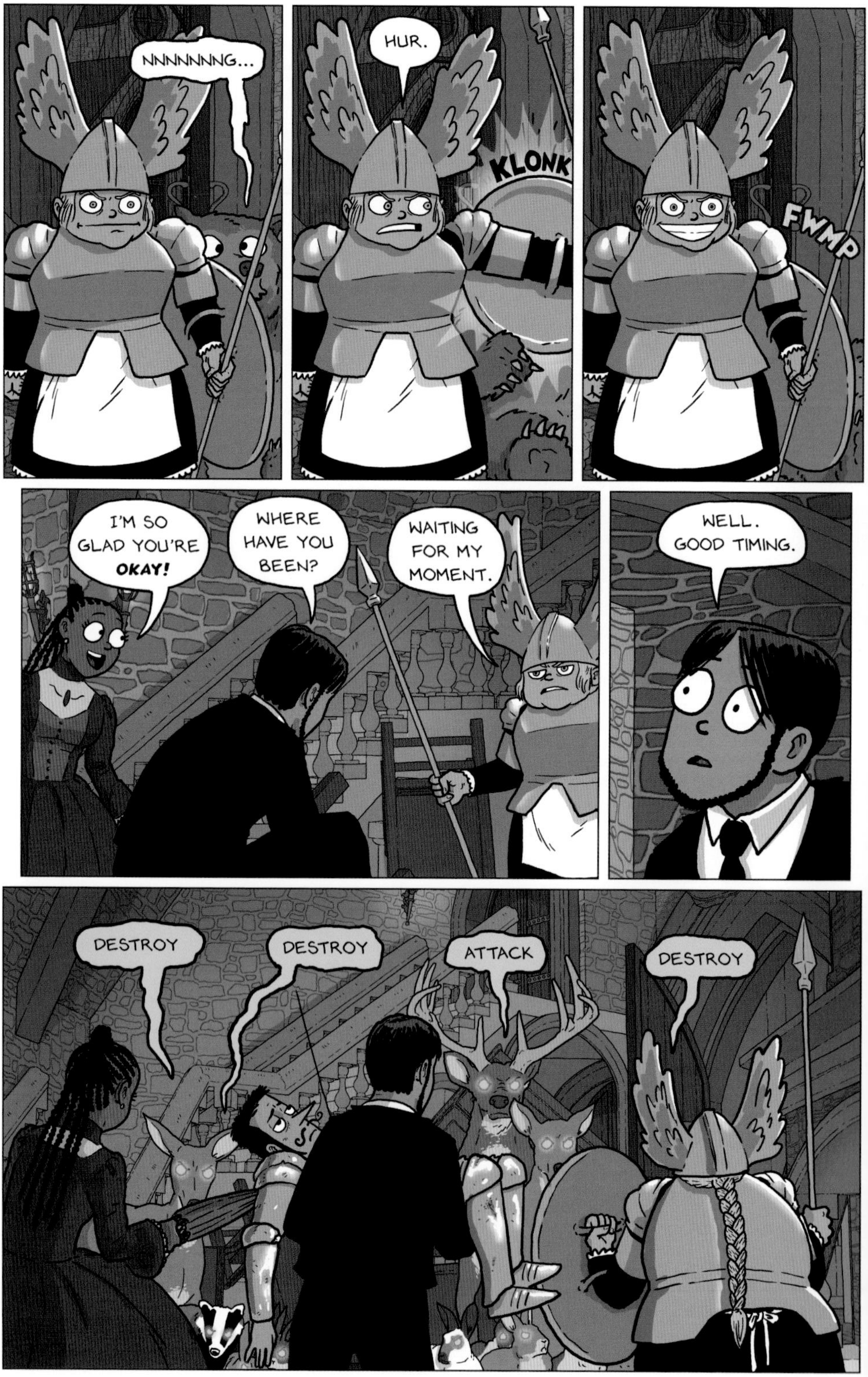

NNNNNNNG...
HUR.
KLONK
FWMP
I'M SO GLAD YOU'RE OKAY!
WHERE HAVE YOU BEEN?
WAITING FOR MY MOMENT.
WELL. GOOD TIMING.
DESTROY
DESTROY
ATTACK
DESTROY

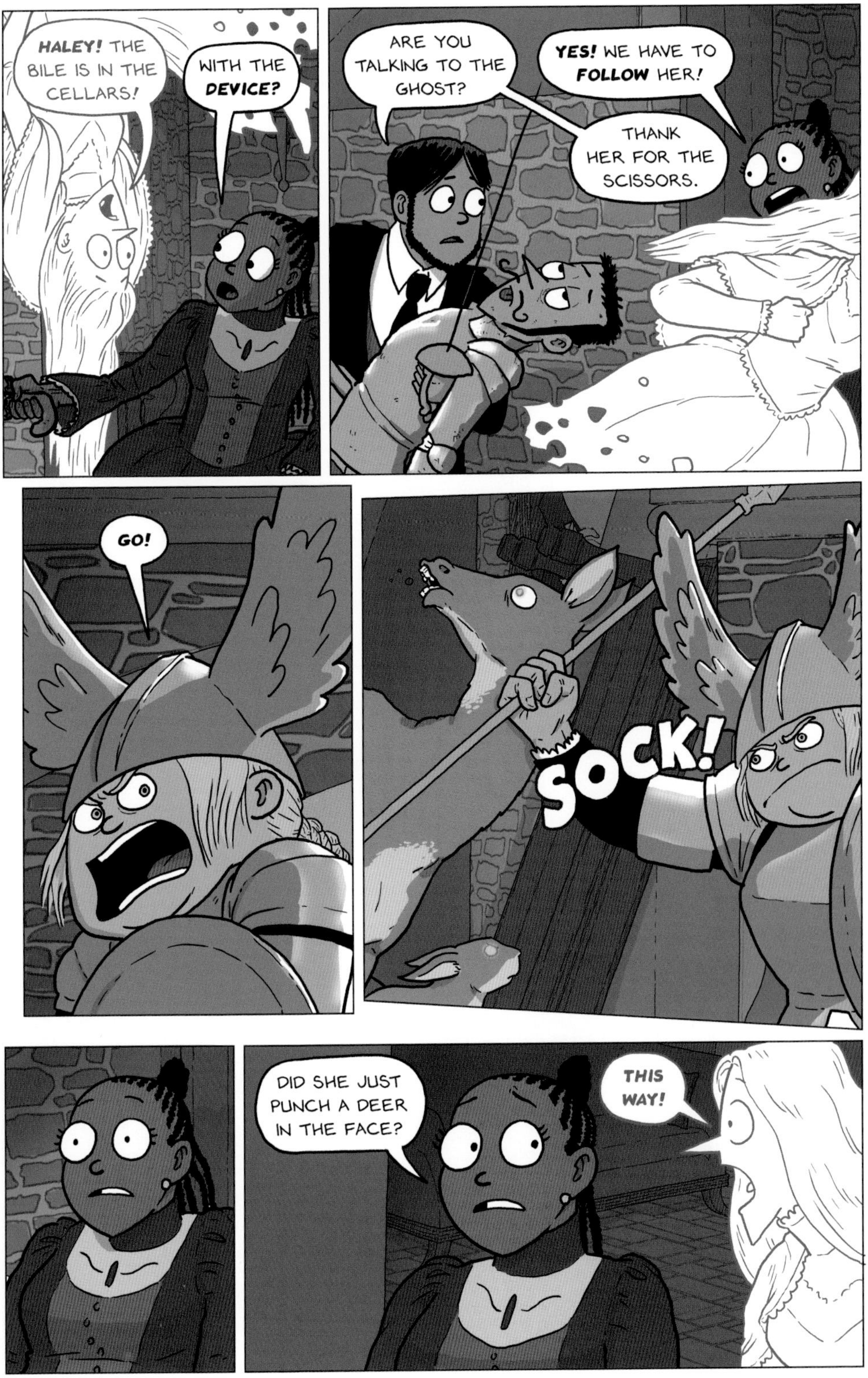
HALEY! THE BILE IS IN THE CELLARS!
WITH THE **DEVICE?**
ARE YOU TALKING TO THE GHOST?
YES! WE HAVE TO **FOLLOW** HER!
THANK HER FOR THE SCISSORS.
GO!
SOCK!
DID SHE JUST PUNCH A DEER IN THE FACE?
THIS WAY!

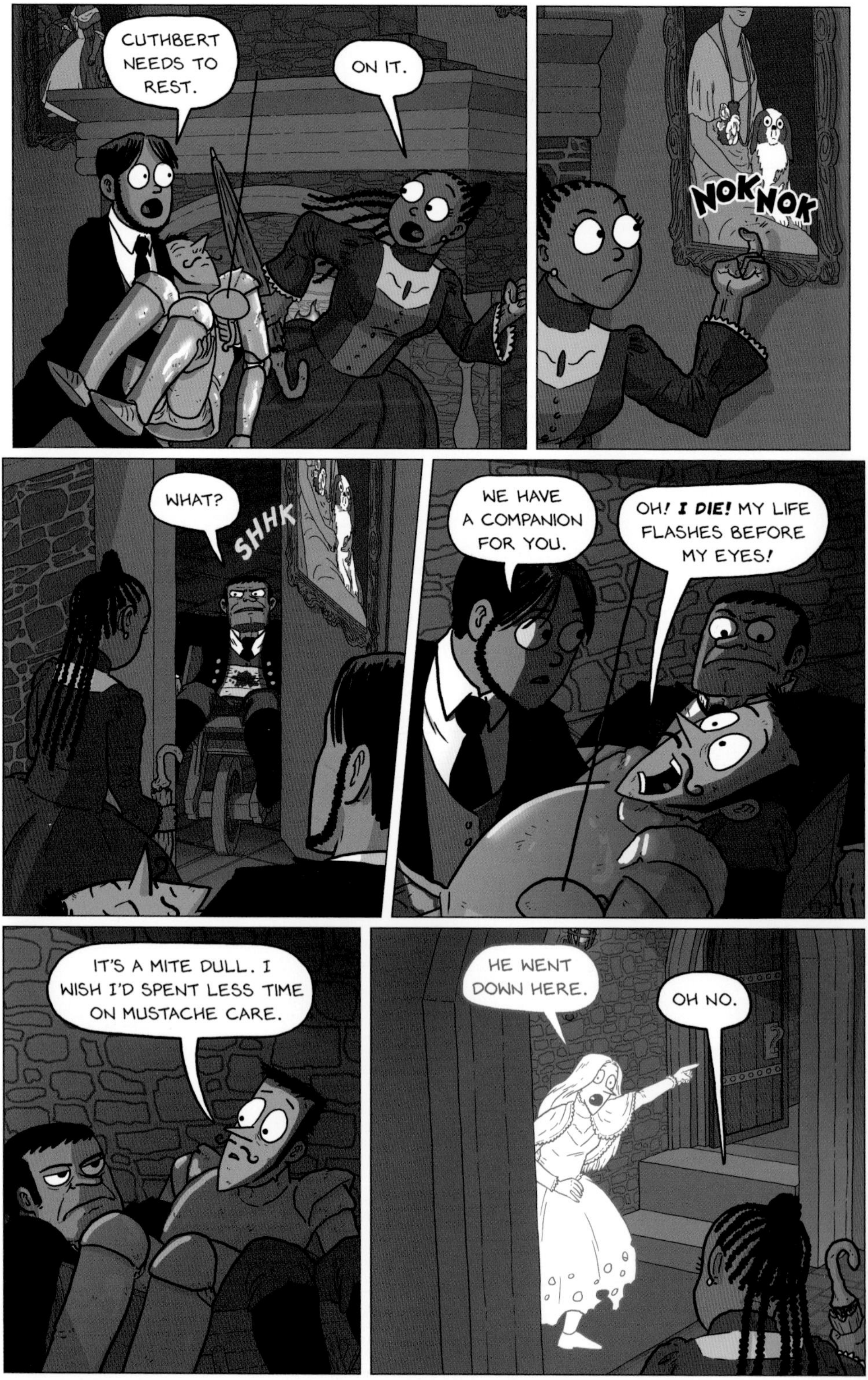
CUTHBERT NEEDS TO REST.
ON IT.
NOKNOK
WHAT?
SHHK
WE HAVE A COMPANION FOR YOU.
OH! I DIE! MY LIFE FLASHES BEFORE MY EYES!
IT'S A MITE DULL. I WISH I'D SPENT LESS TIME ON MUSTACHE CARE.
HE WENT DOWN HERE.
OH NO.

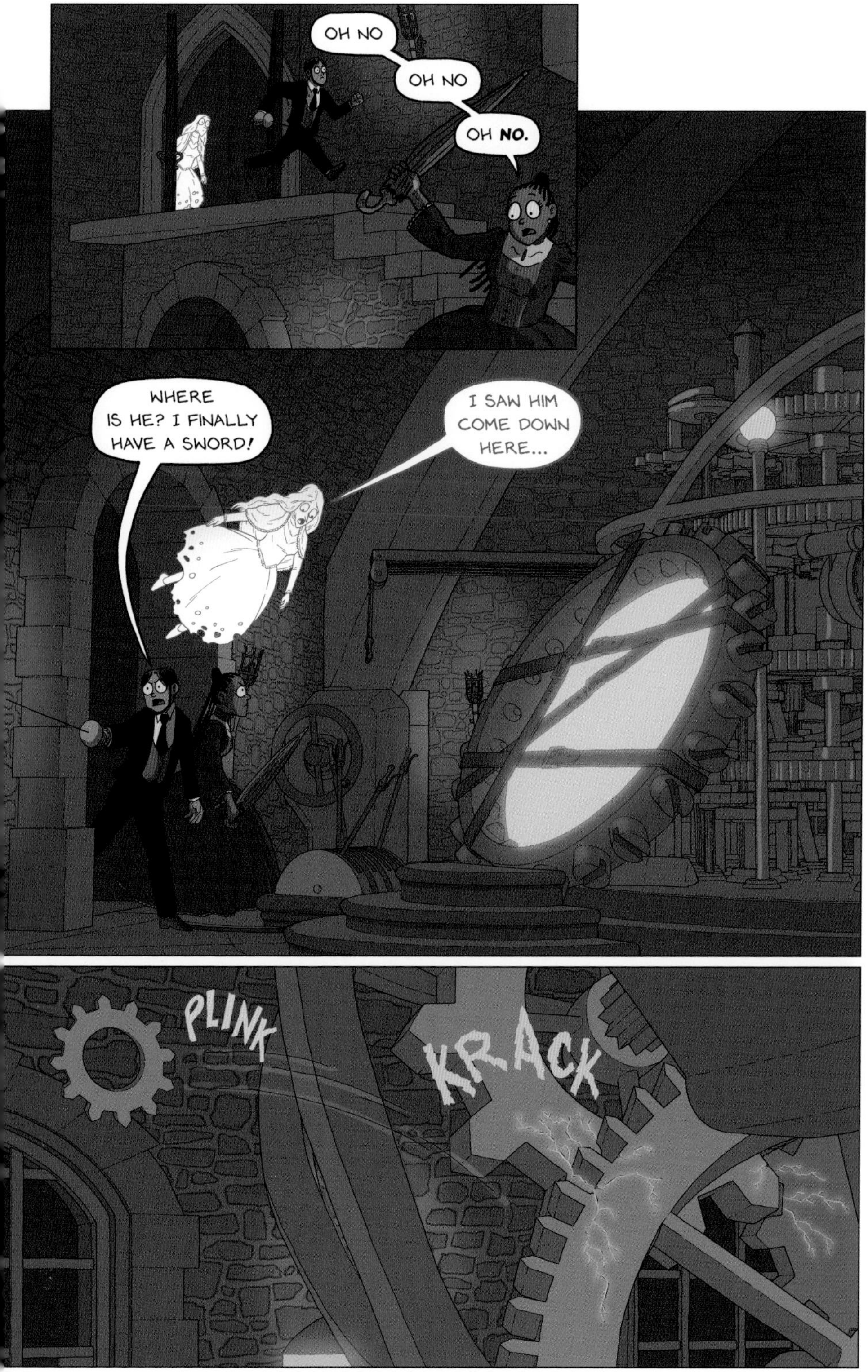
OH NO
OH NO
OH NO.
WHERE IS HE? I FINALLY HAVE A SWORD!
I SAW HIM COME DOWN HERE...
PLINK
KRACK

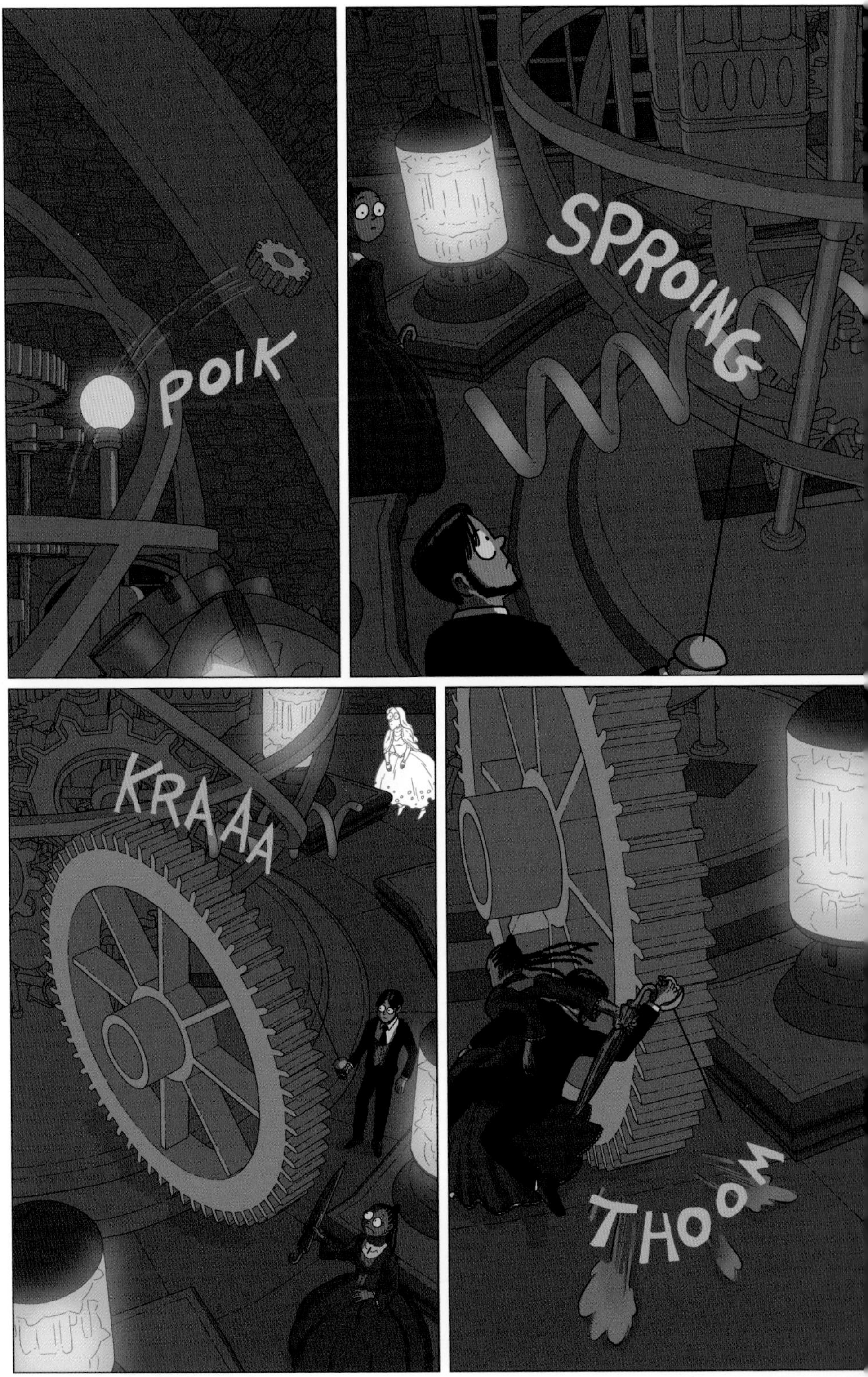
POIK
SPROING
KRAAA
THOOM

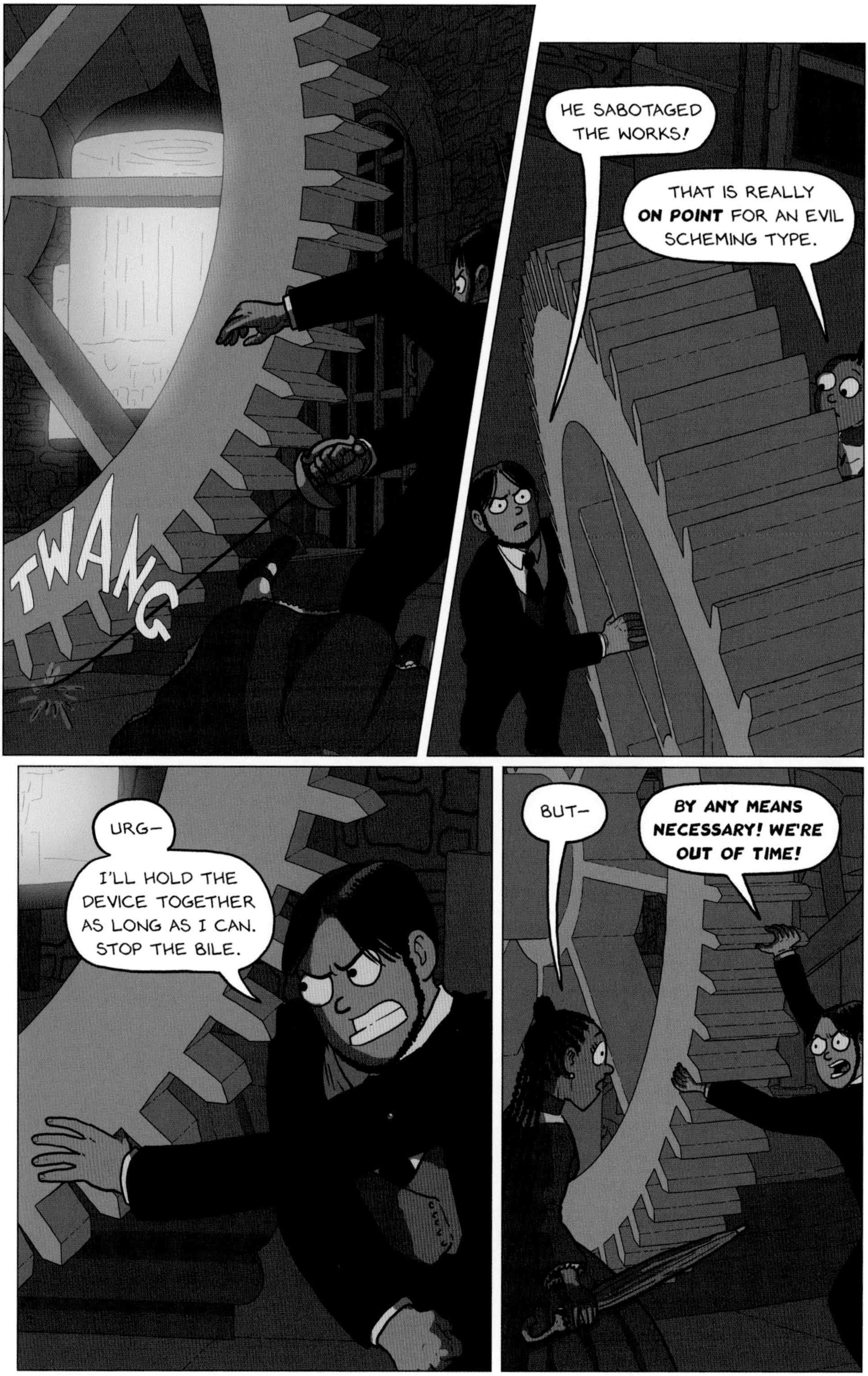
TWANG
HE SABOTAGED THE WORKS!
THAT IS REALLY ON POINT FOR AN EVIL SCHEMING TYPE.
URG—
I'LL HOLD THE DEVICE TOGETHER AS LONG AS I CAN. STOP THE BILE.
BUT—
BY ANY MEANS NECESSARY! WE'RE OUT OF TIME!

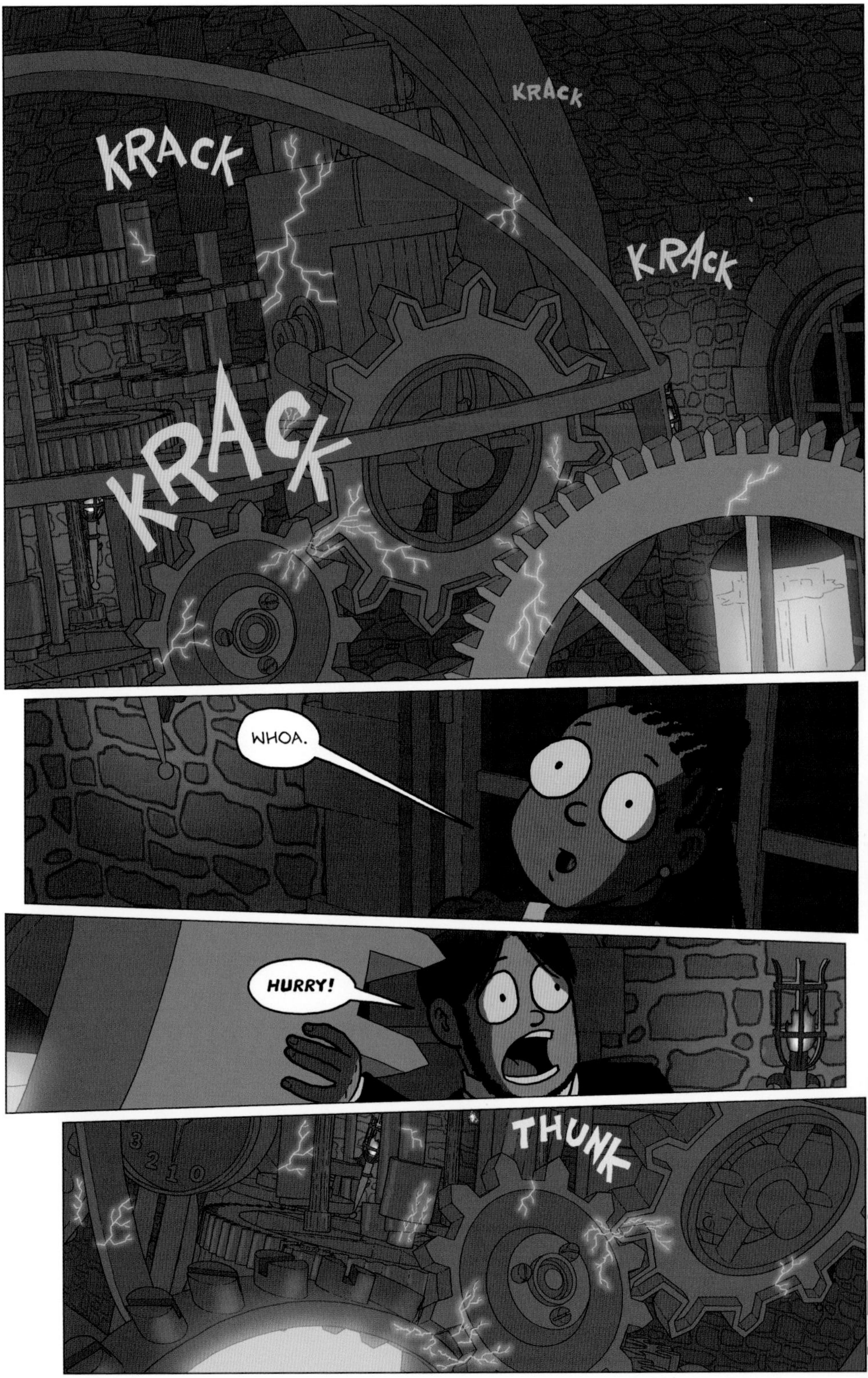
KRACK
KRACK
KRACK
KRACK
WHOA.
HURRY!
THUNK

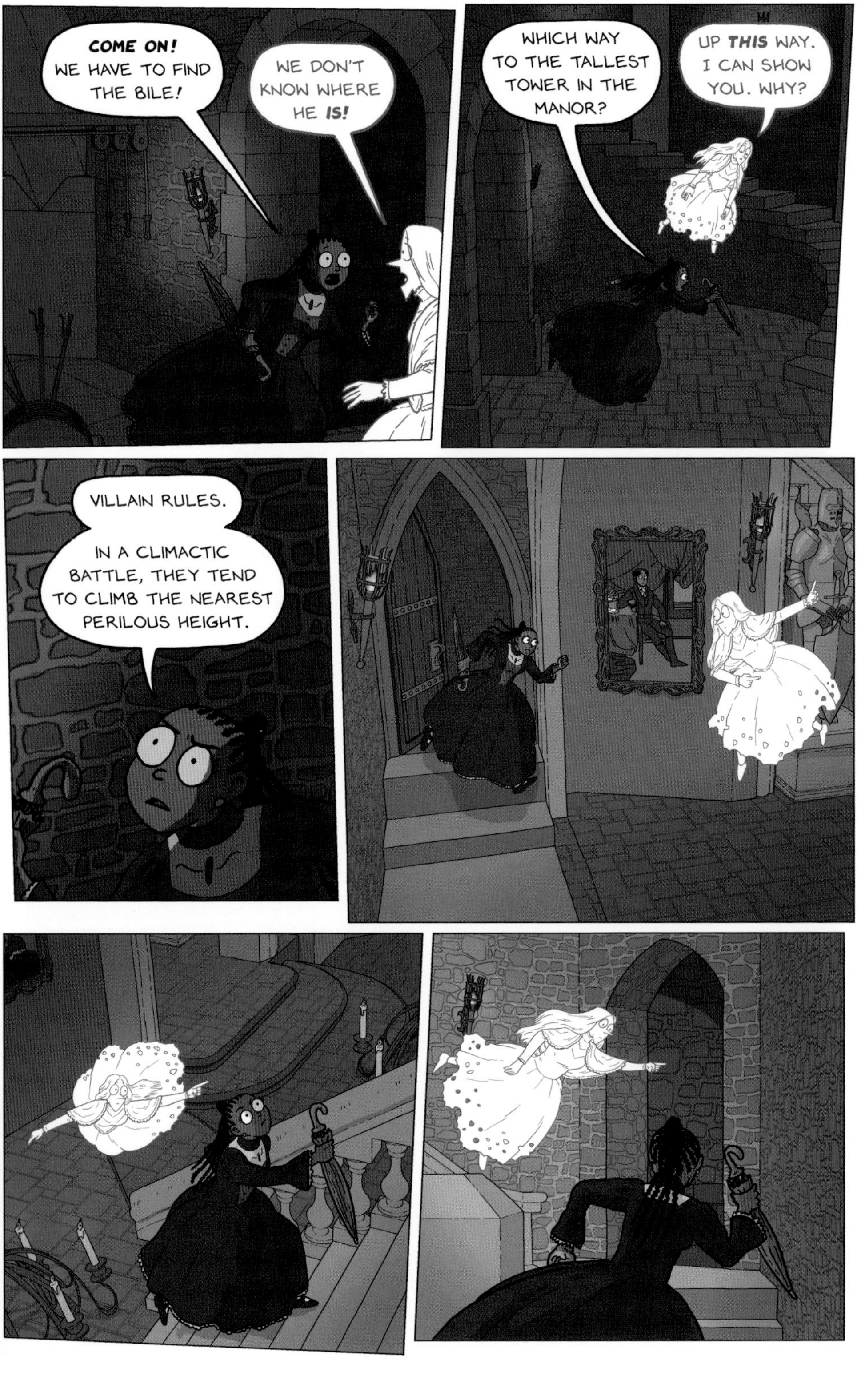
COME ON! WE HAVE TO FIND THE BILE!
WE DON'T KNOW WHERE HE IS!
WHICH WAY TO THE TALLEST TOWER IN THE MANOR?
UP THIS WAY. I CAN SHOW YOU. WHY?
VILLAIN RULES.
IN A CLIMACTIC BATTLE, THEY TEND TO CLIMB THE NEAREST PERILOUS HEIGHT.

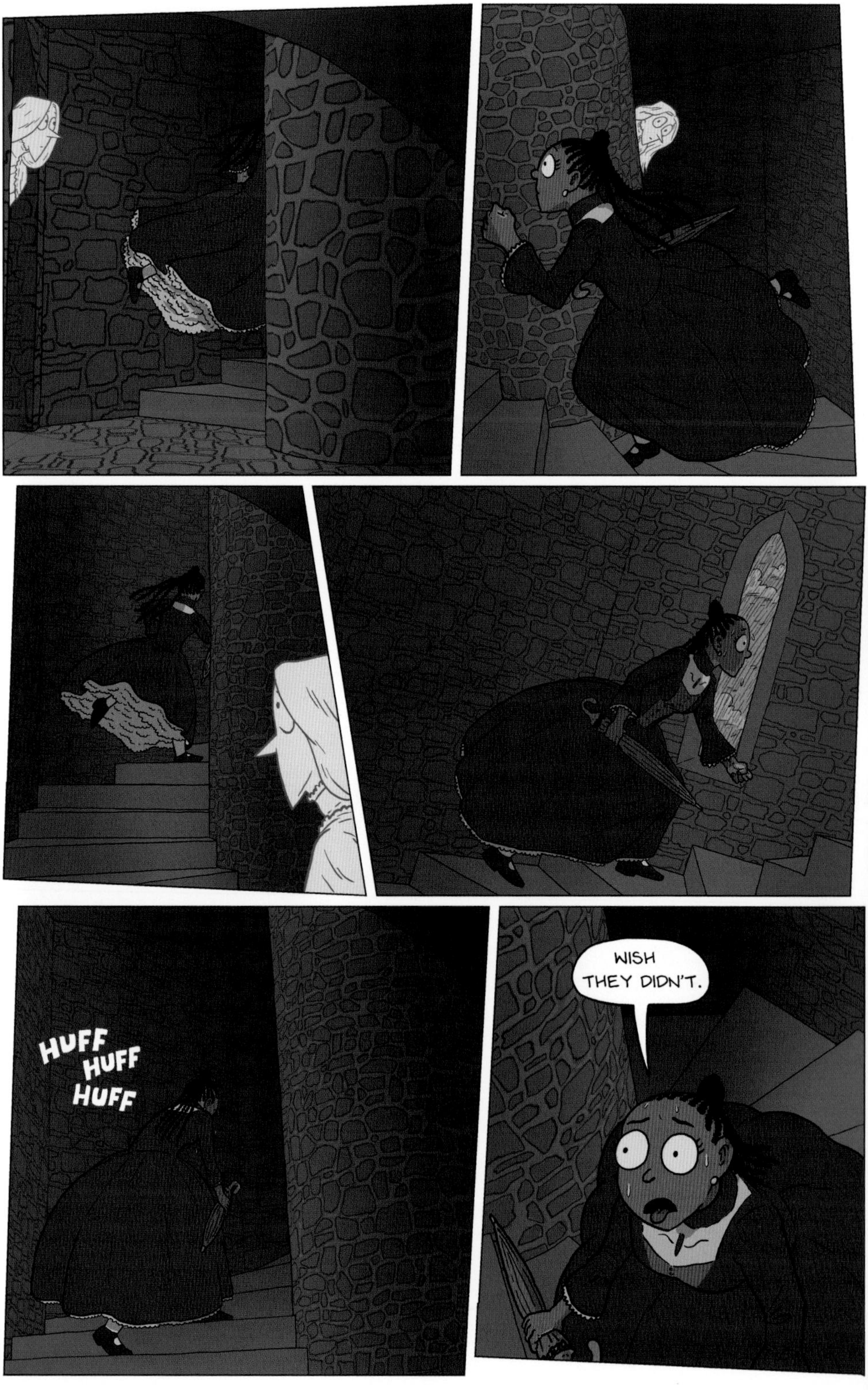
HUFF
HUFF
HUFF
WISH
THEY DIDN'T.

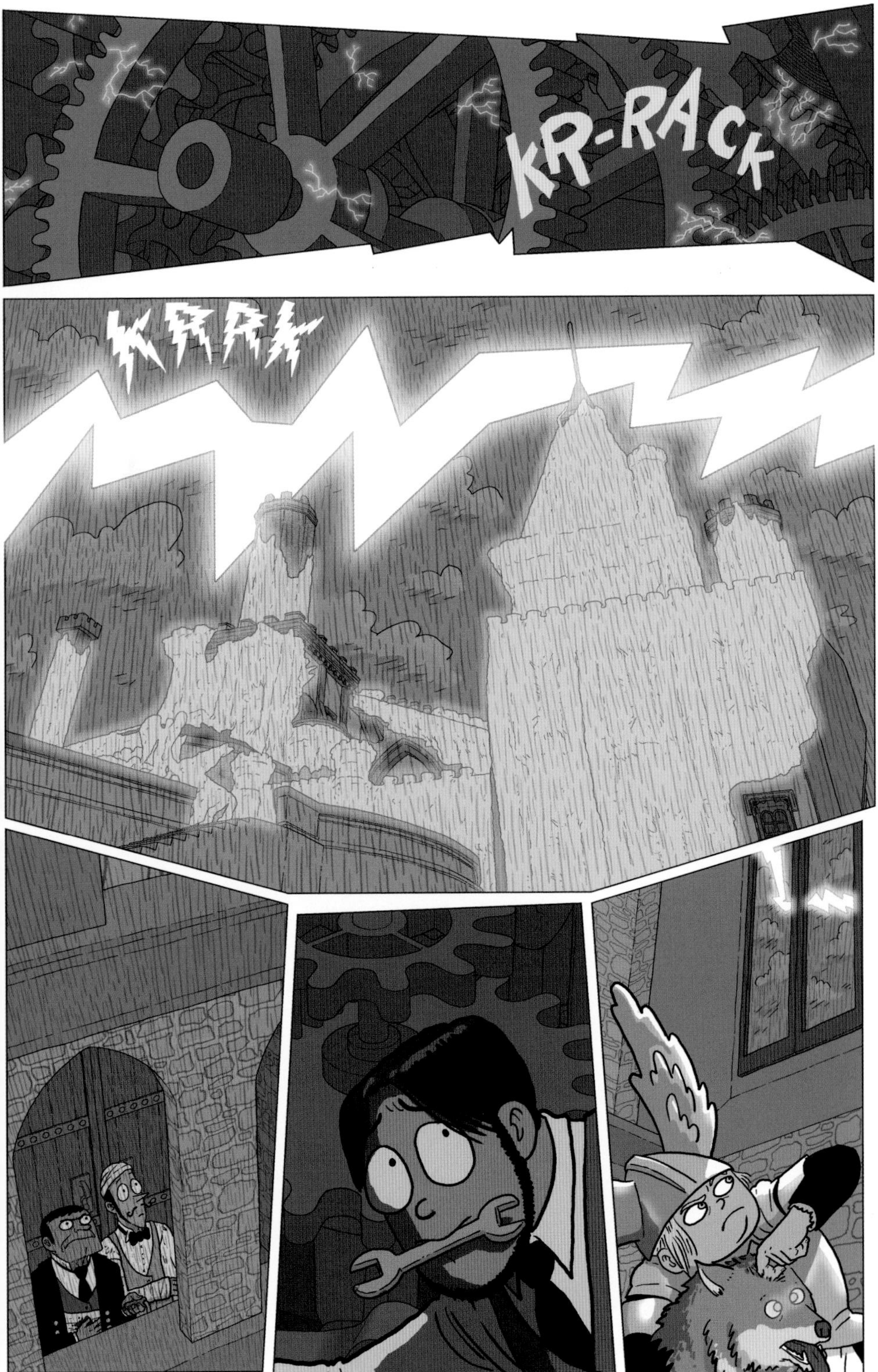
KR-RACK
KRRK

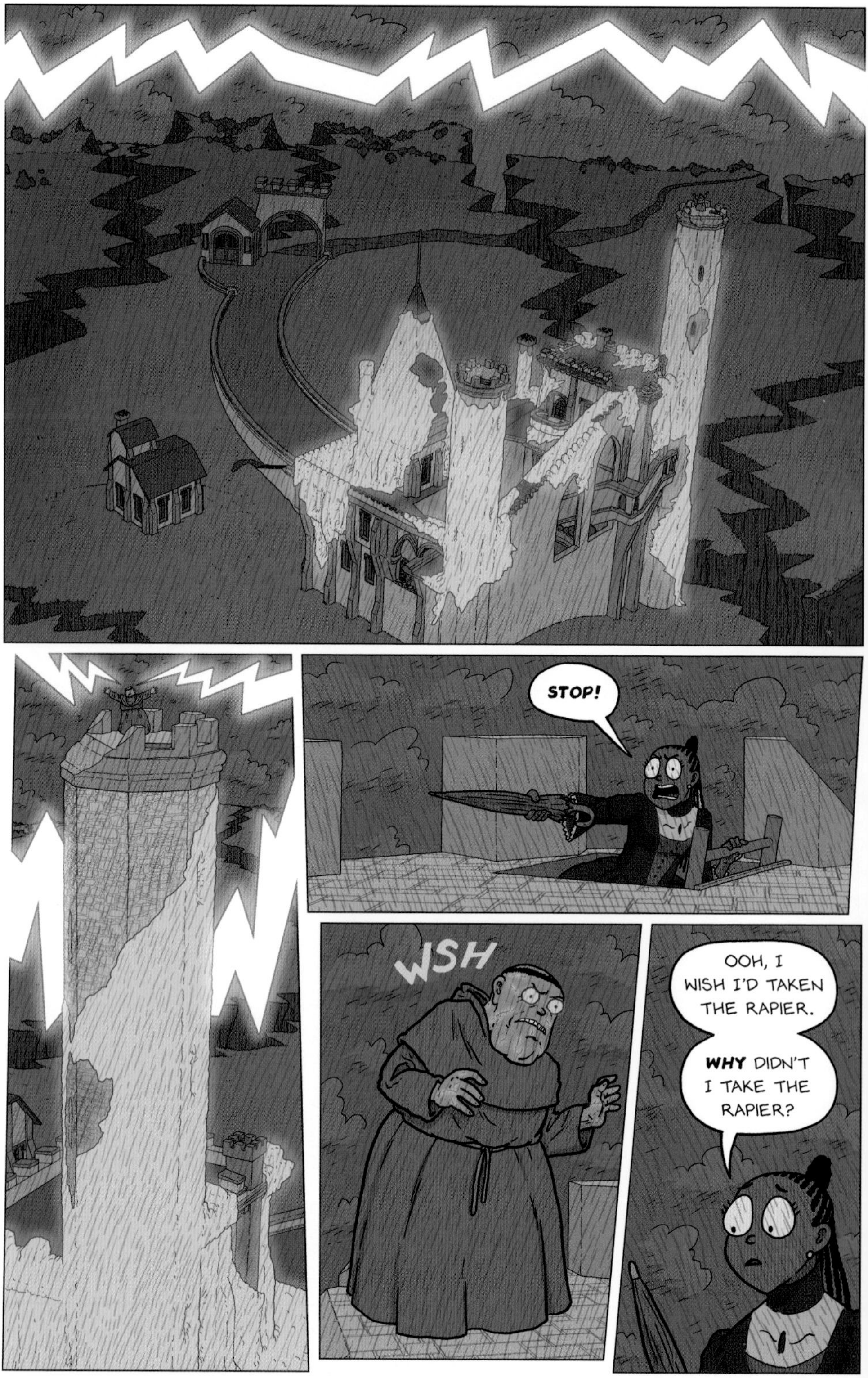
STOP!
WSH
OOH, I WISH I'D TAKEN THE RAPIER.
WHY DIDN'T I TAKE THE RAPIER?

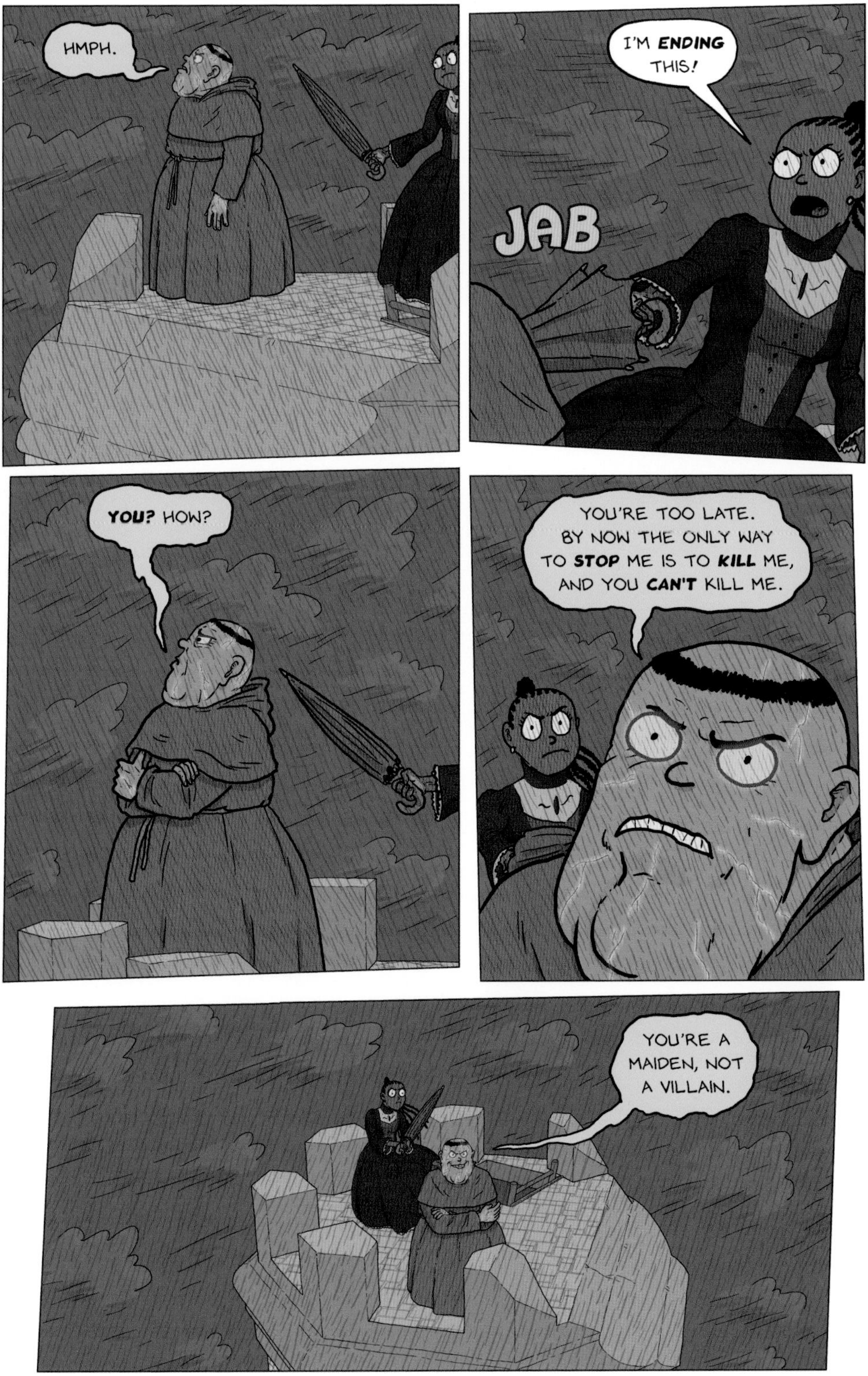
HMPH.
I'M ENDING THIS!
JAB
YOU? HOW?
YOU'RE TOO LATE. BY NOW THE ONLY WAY TO STOP ME IS TO KILL ME, AND YOU CAN'T KILL ME.
YOU'RE A MAIDEN, NOT A VILLAIN.

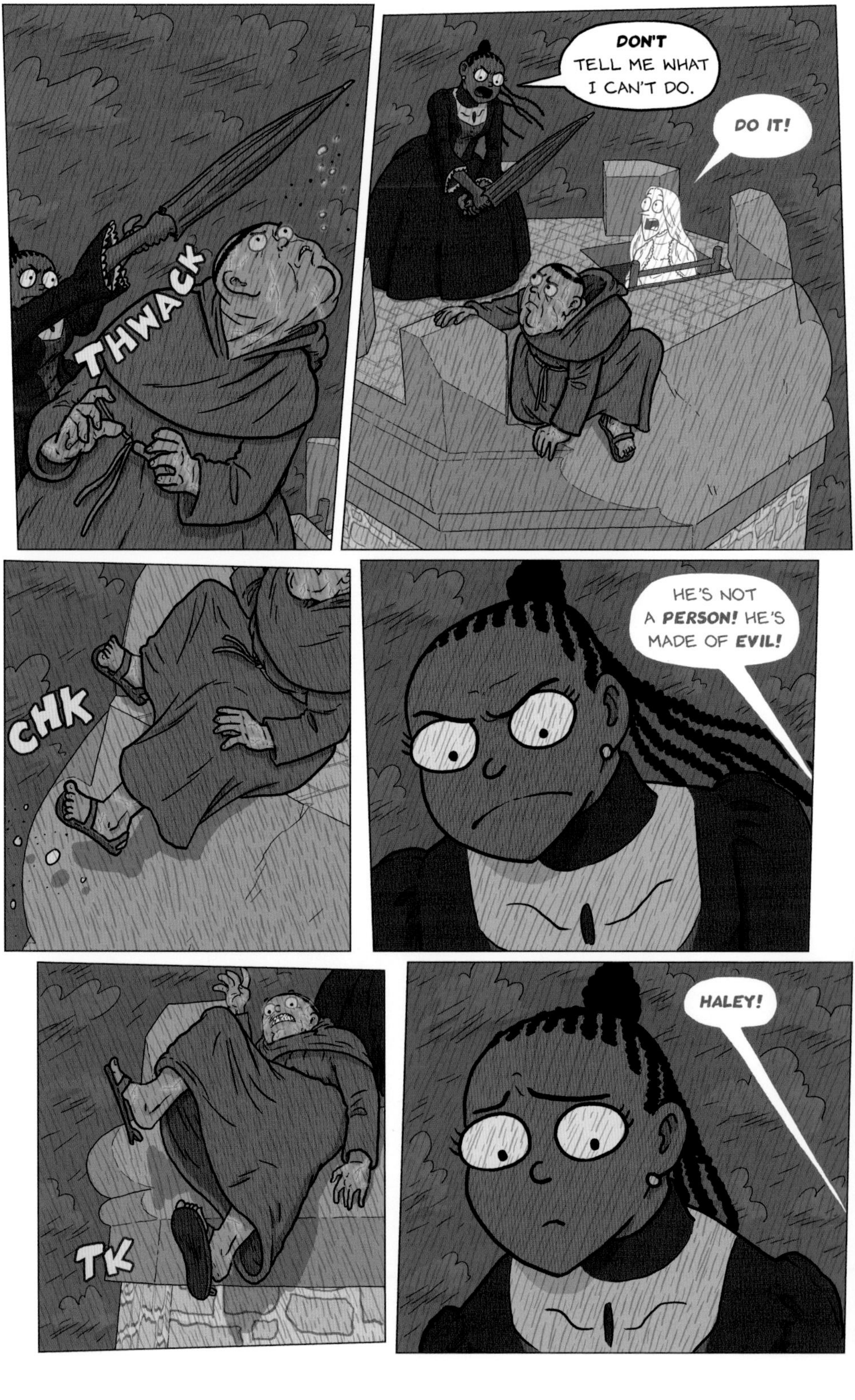
THWACK
DON'T TELL ME WHAT I CAN'T DO.
DO IT!
CHK
HE'S NOT A PERSON! HE'S MADE OF EVIL!
TK
HALEY!

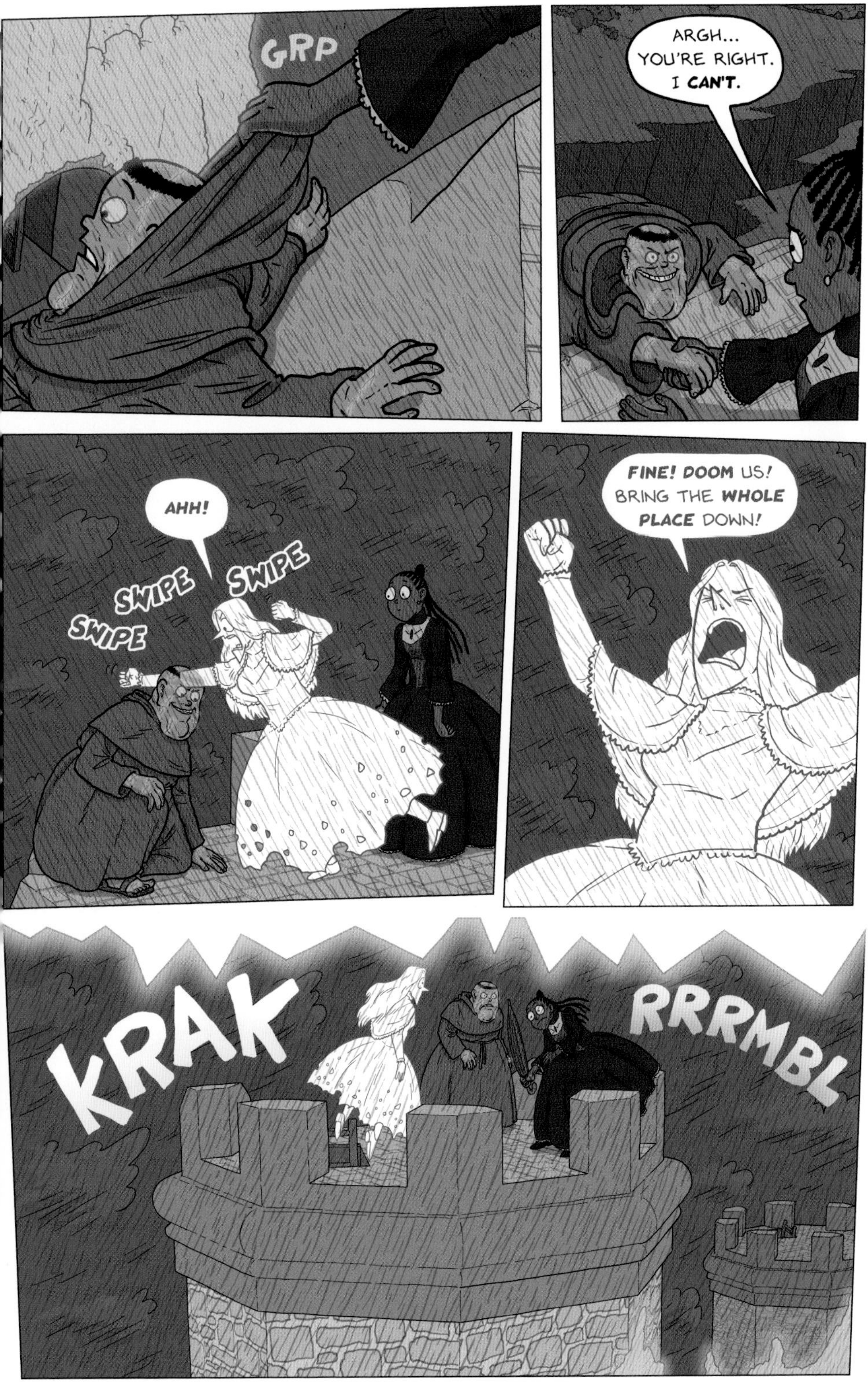
GRP
ARGH...
YOU'RE RIGHT.
I **CAN'T.**
AHH!
SWIPE
SWIPE
SWIPE
FINE! DOOM US!
BRING THE **WHOLE**
PLACE DOWN!
KRAK
RRRMBL

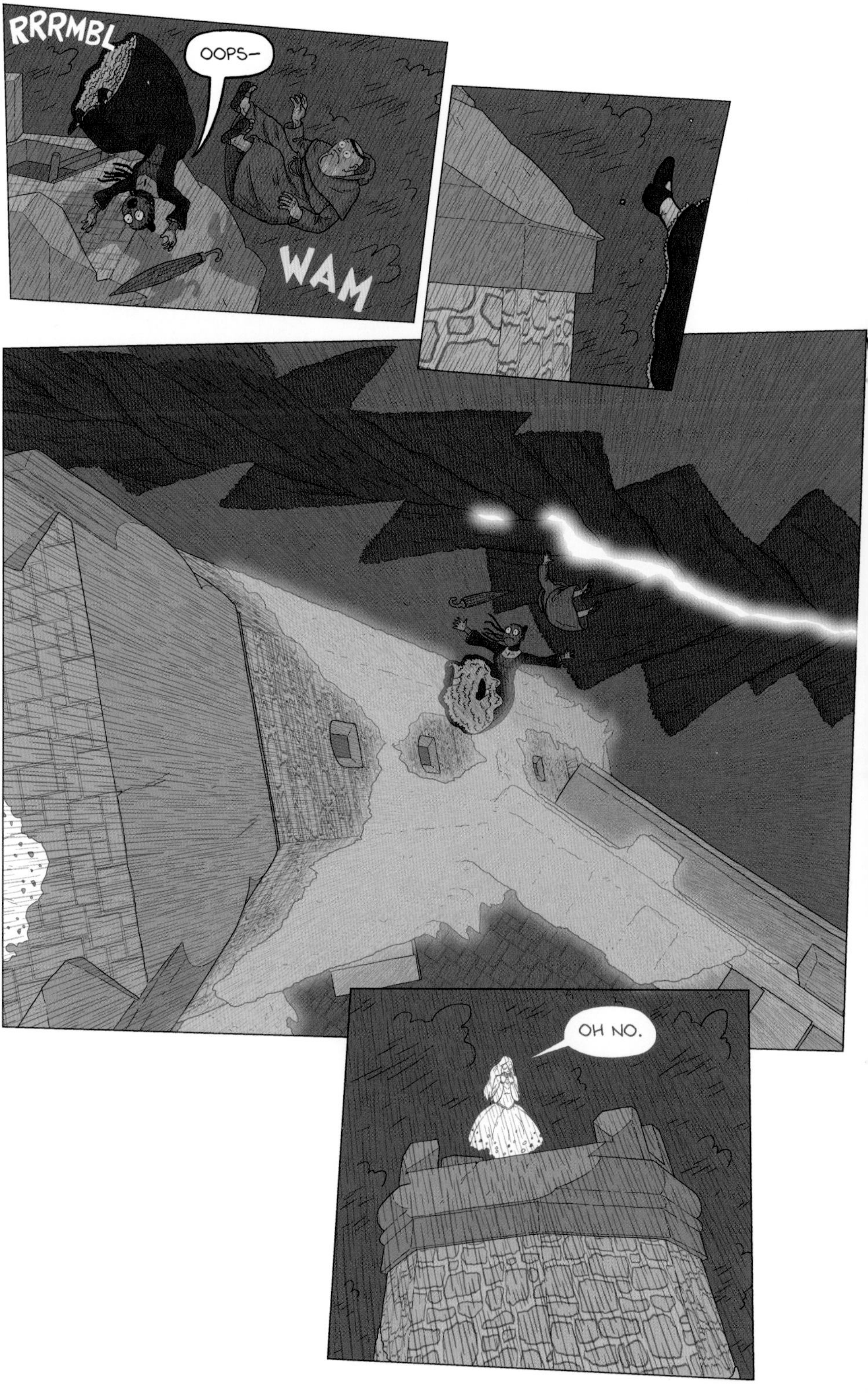
RRRMBL
OOPS—
WAM
OH NO.

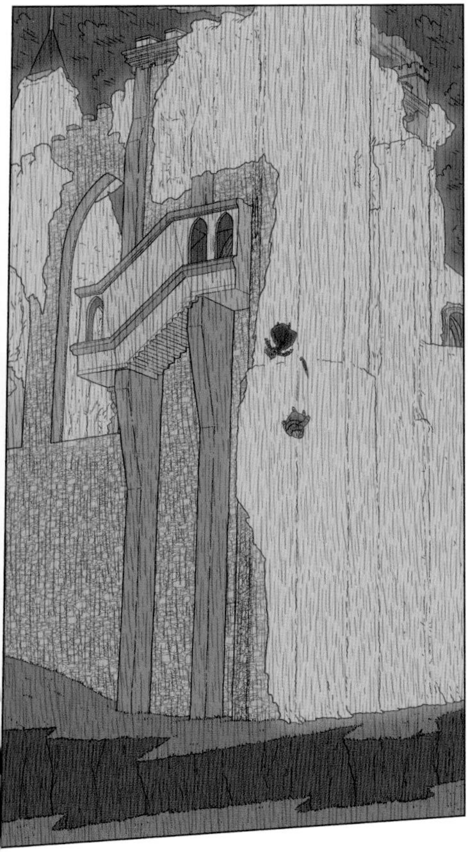
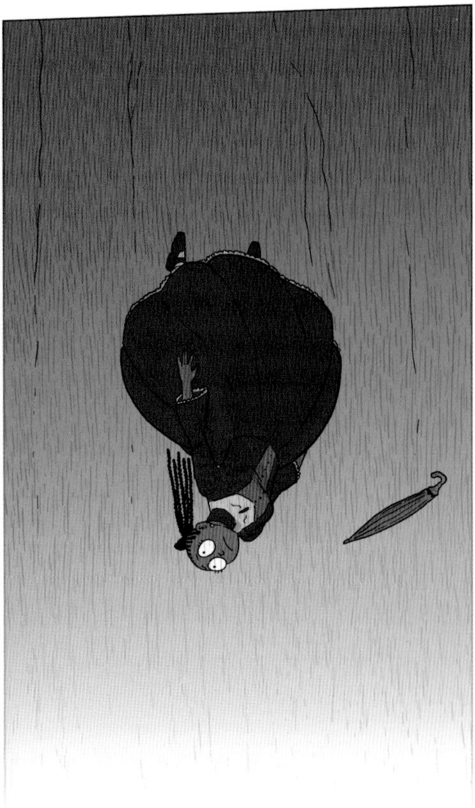
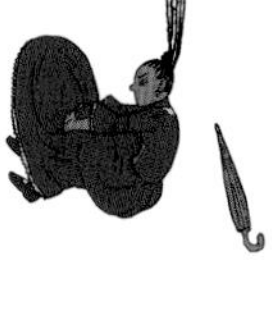

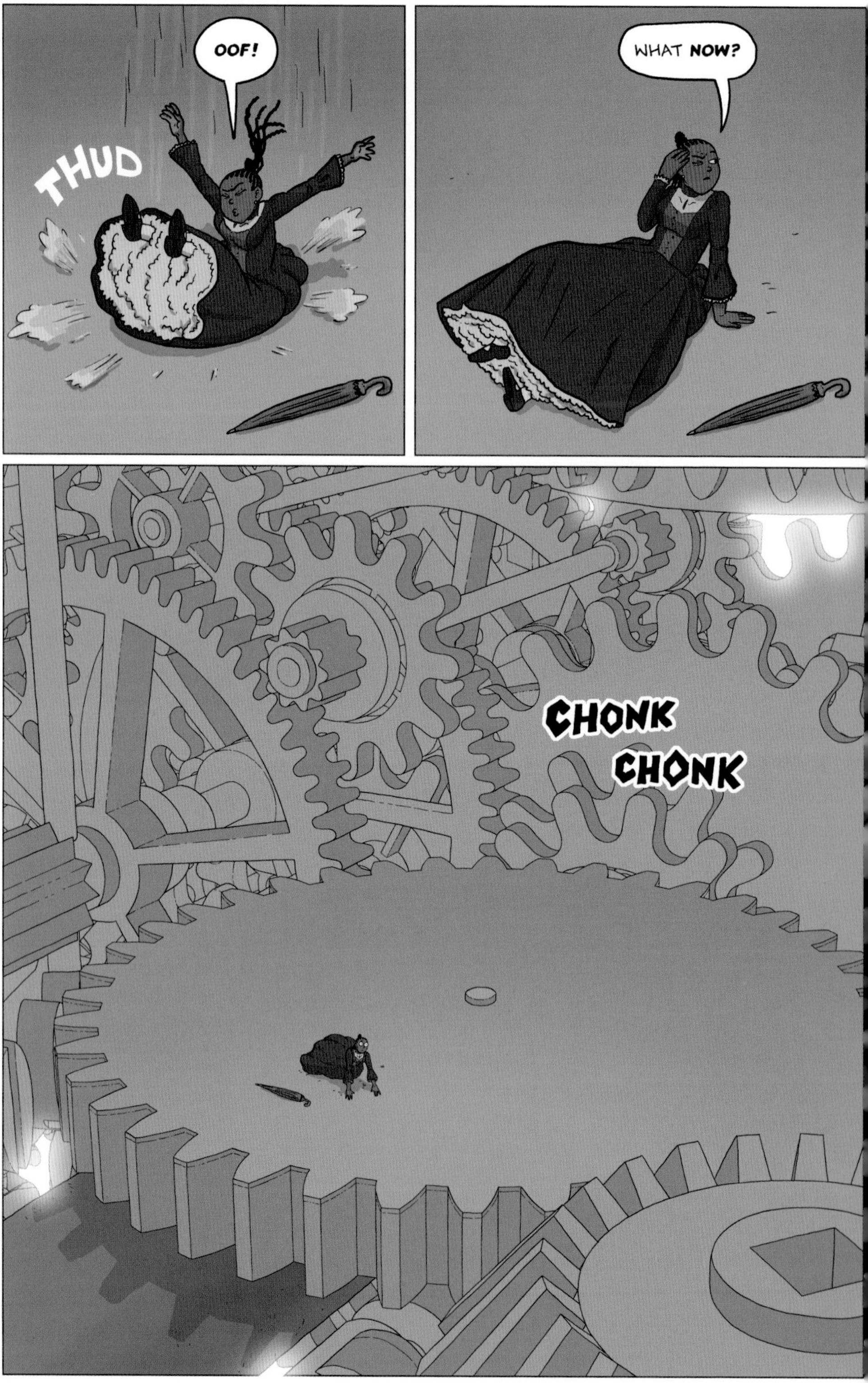
OOF!
THUD
WHAT NOW?
CHONK
CHONK

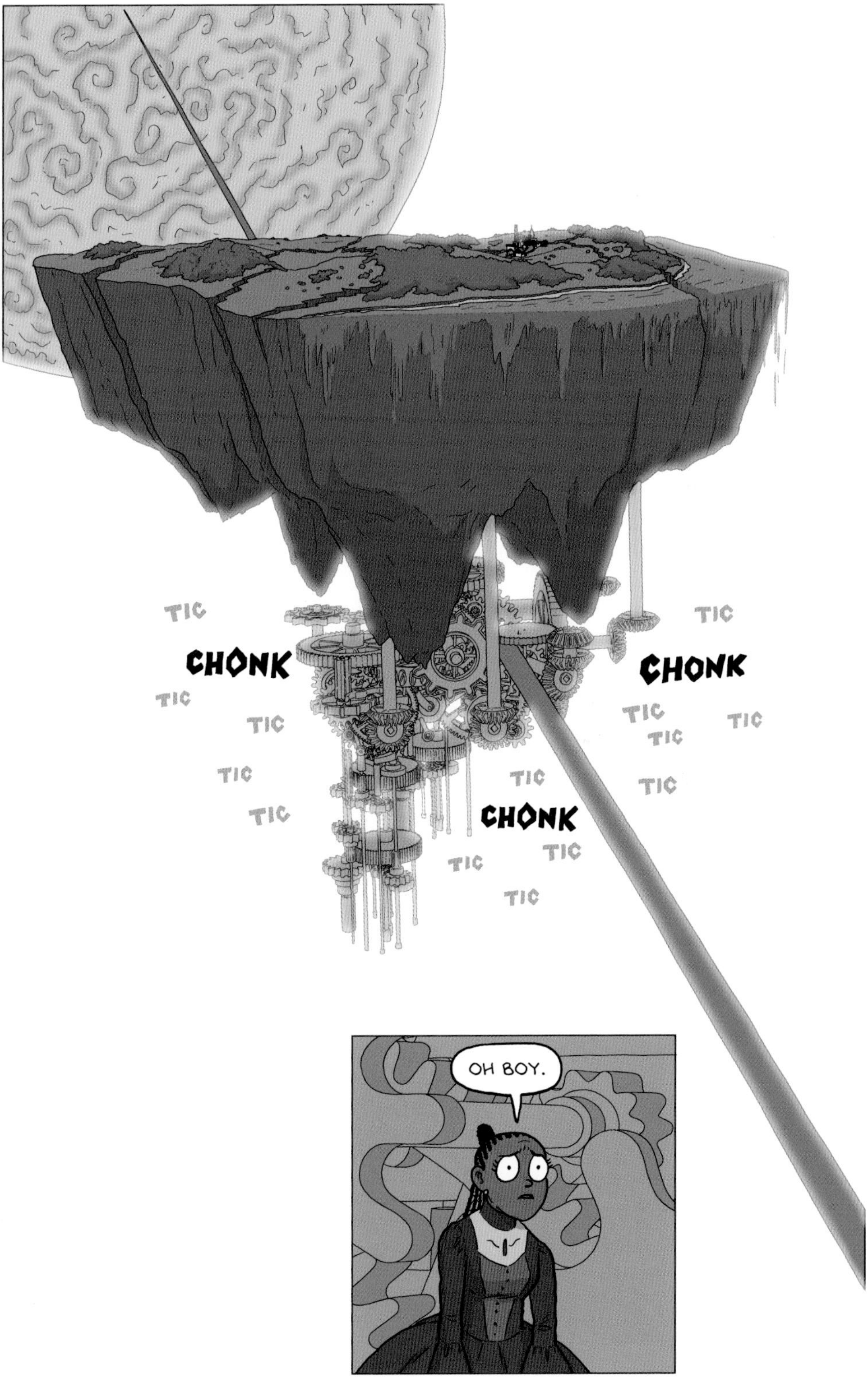
TIC
CHONK
TIC
TIC
TIC
TIC
TIC
CHONK
TIC
TIC
TIC
TIC
TIC
CHONK
TIC
TIC
TIC
OH BOY.

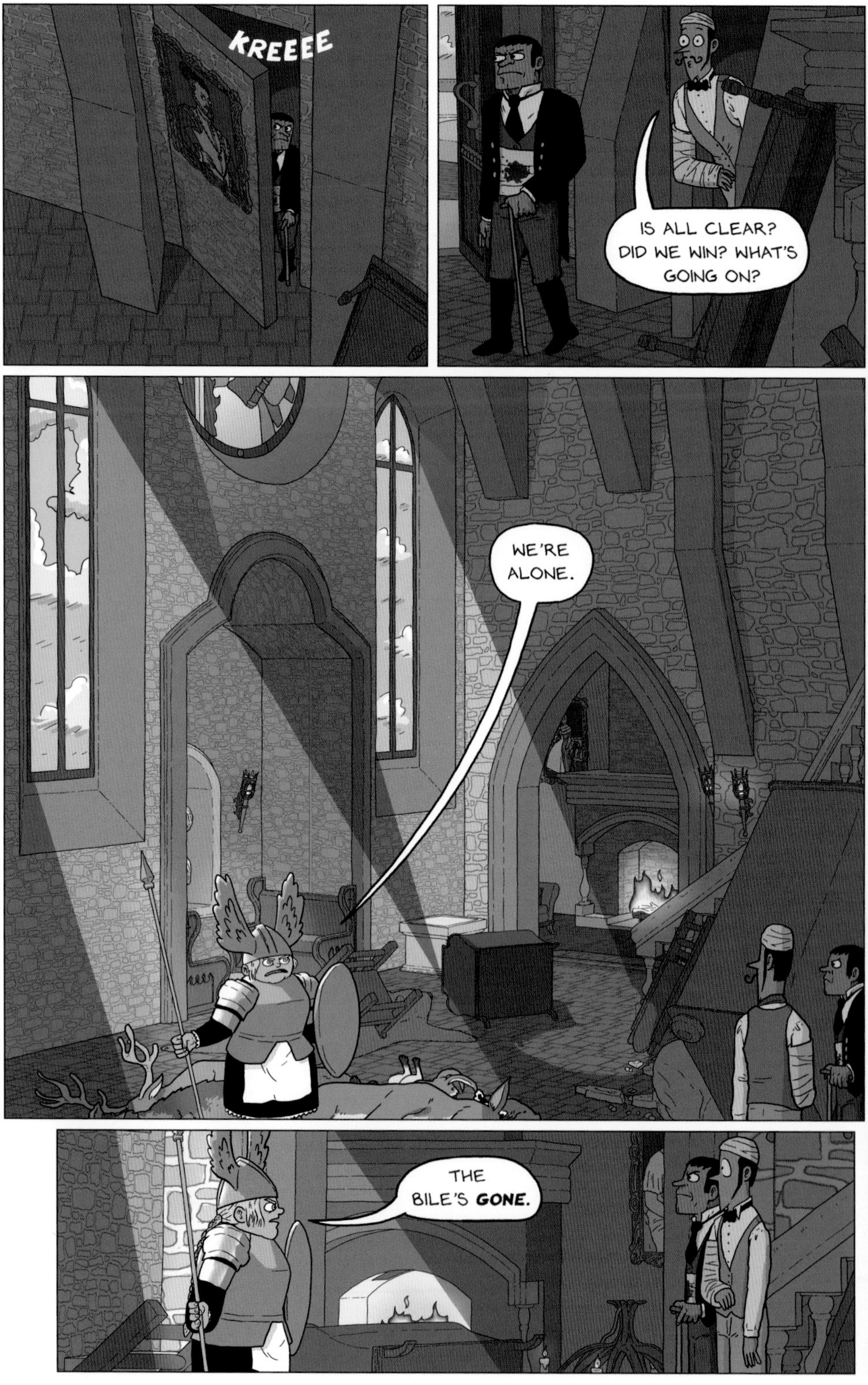
KREEEE
IS ALL CLEAR? DID WE WIN? WHAT'S GOING ON?
WE'RE ALONE.
THE BILE'S **GONE.**

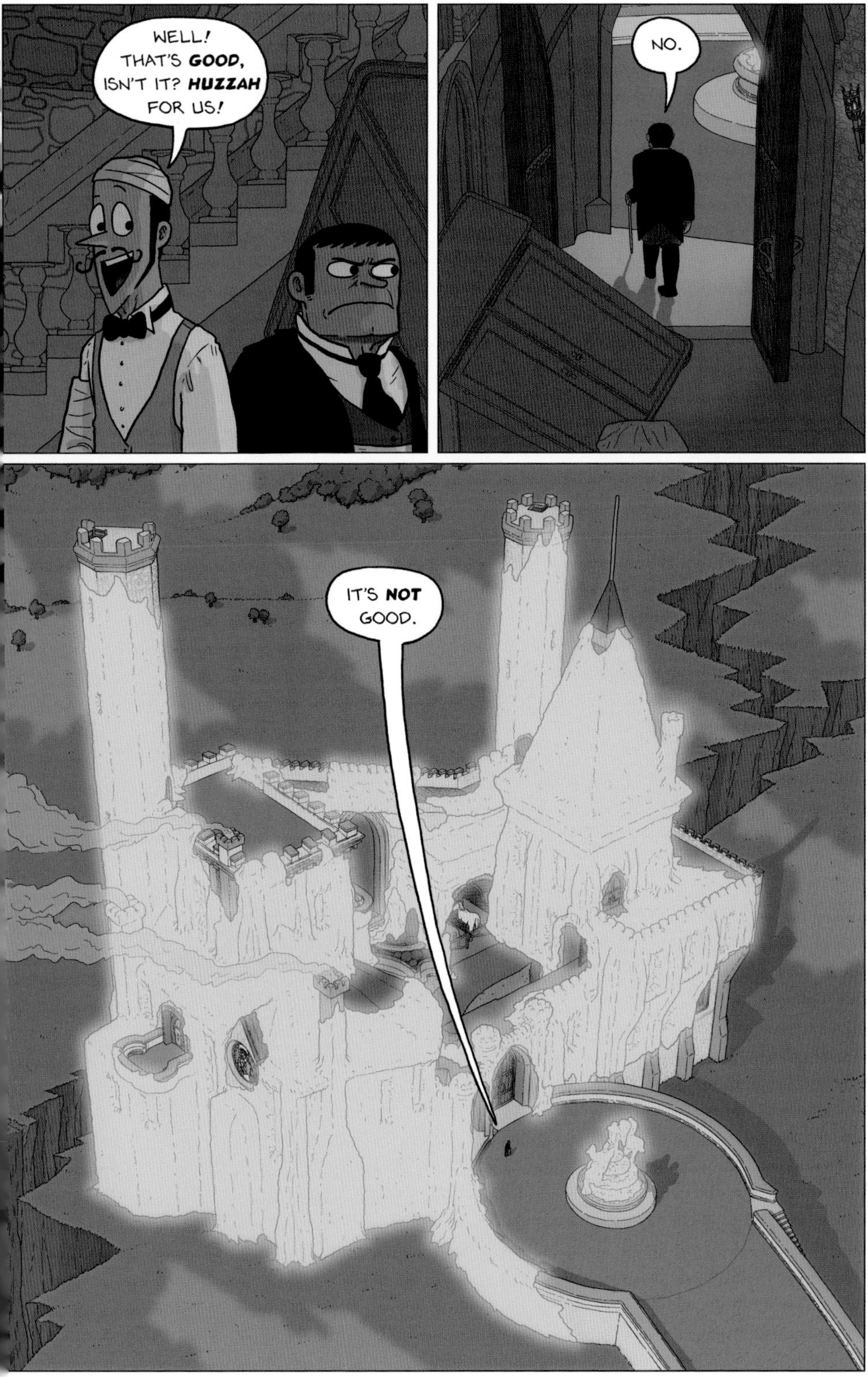
WELL! THAT'S **GOOD,** ISN'T IT? **HUZZAH** FOR US!
NO.
IT'S **NOT** GOOD.

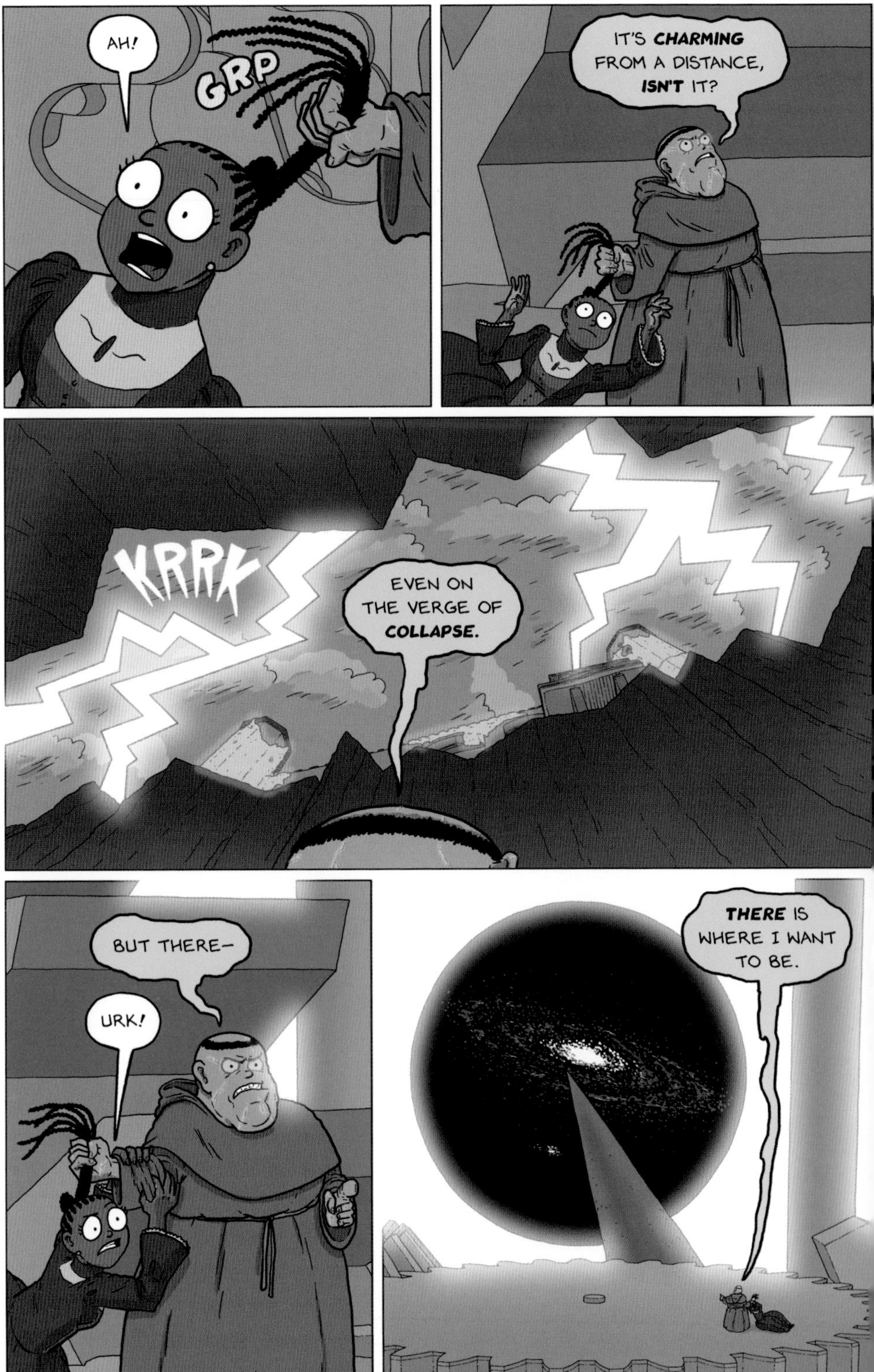
AH!
GRP
IT'S **CHARMING** FROM A DISTANCE, **ISN'T** IT?
KRRK
EVEN ON THE VERGE OF **COLLAPSE.**
BUT THERE—
URK!
THERE IS WHERE I WANT TO BE.

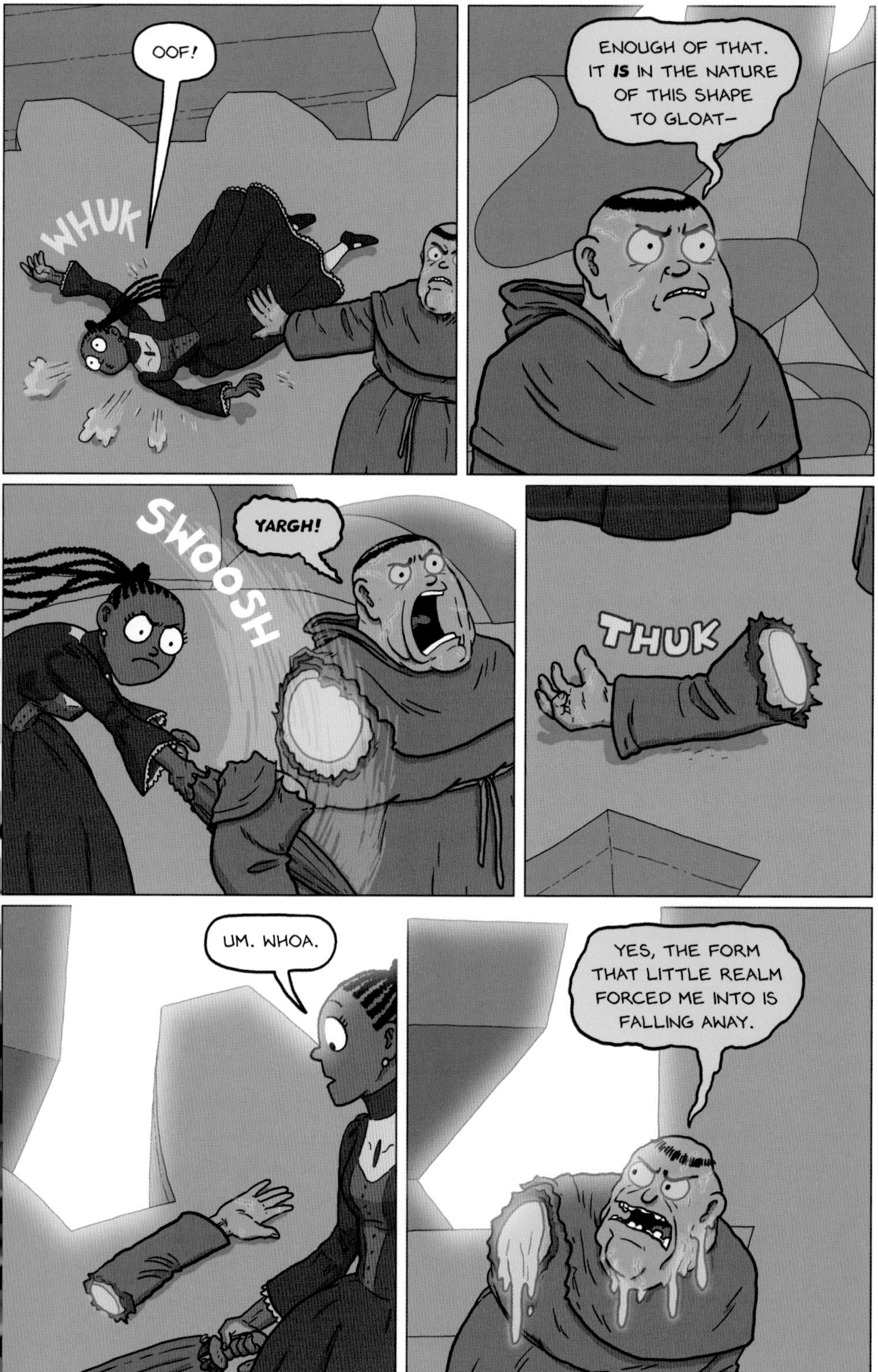
OOF!
WHUK
ENOUGH OF THAT. IT **IS** IN THE NATURE OF THIS SHAPE TO GLOAT—
SWOOSH
YARGH!
THUK
UM. WHOA.
YES, THE FORM THAT LITTLE REALM FORCED ME INTO IS FALLING AWAY.

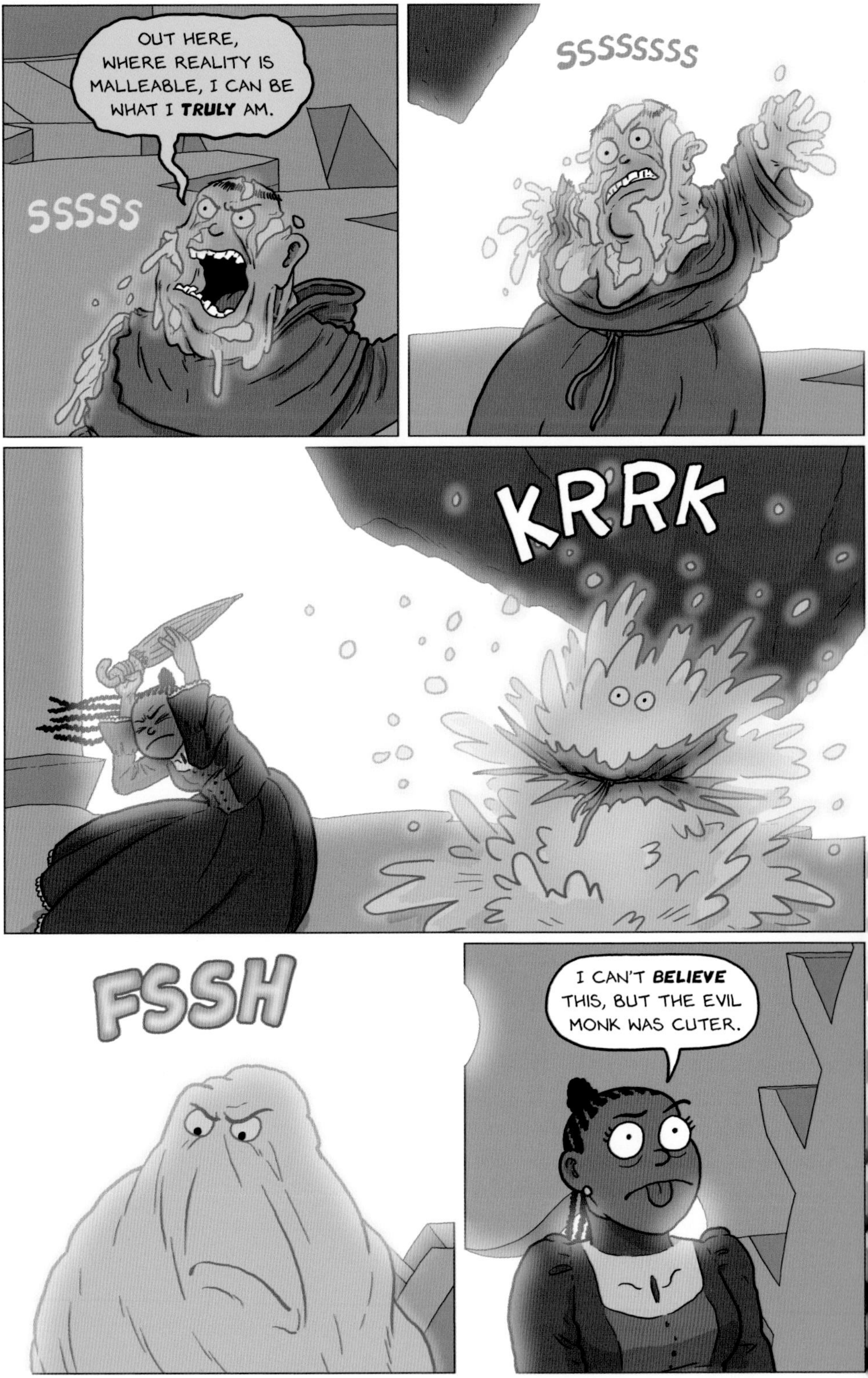
OUT HERE, WHERE REALITY IS MALLEABLE, I CAN BE WHAT I **TRULY** AM.
SSSSS
SSSSSSSS
KRRK
FSSH
I CAN'T **BELIEVE** THIS, BUT THE EVIL MONK WAS CUTER.

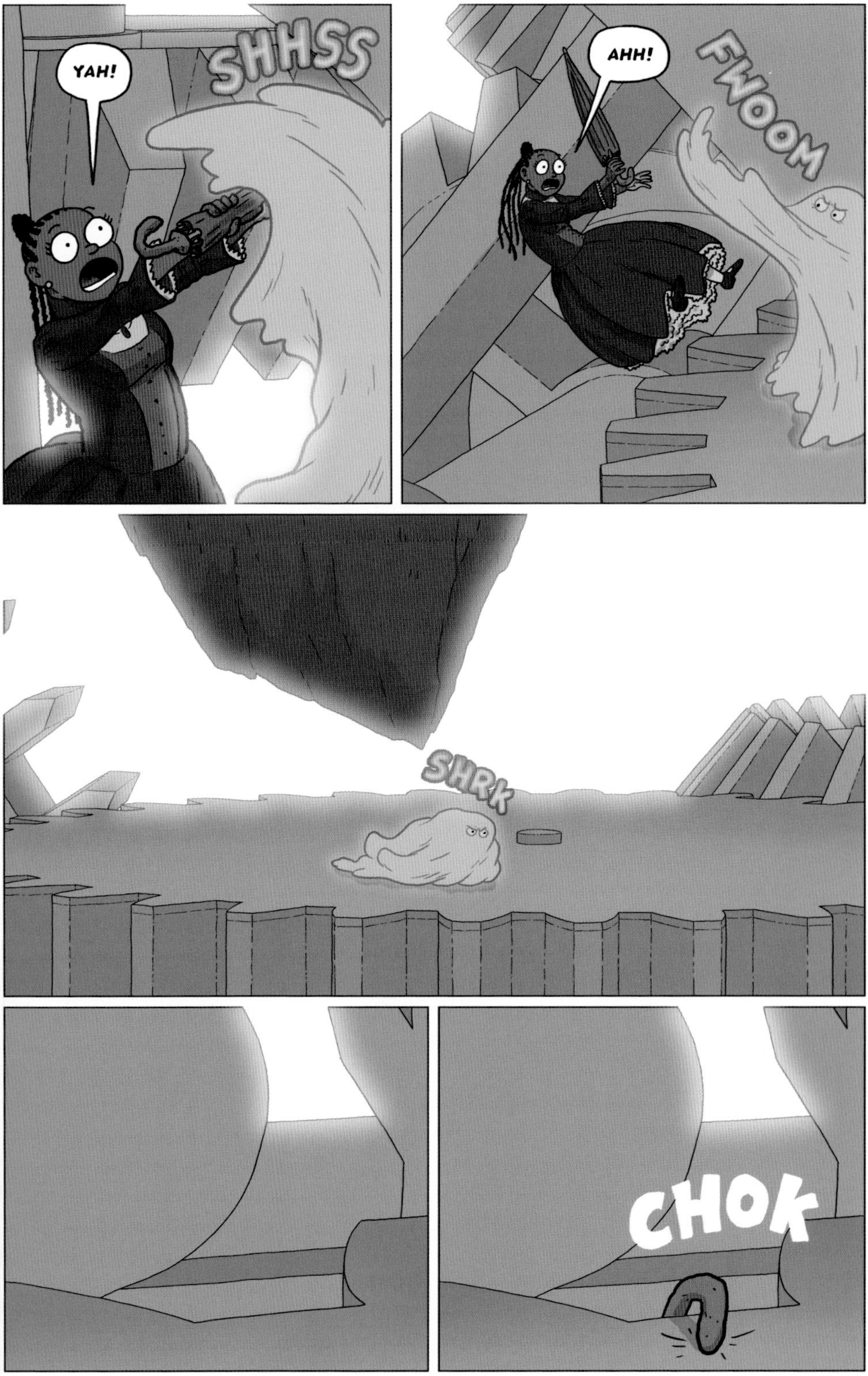
YAH!
SHHSS
AHH!
FWOOM
SHRK
CHOK

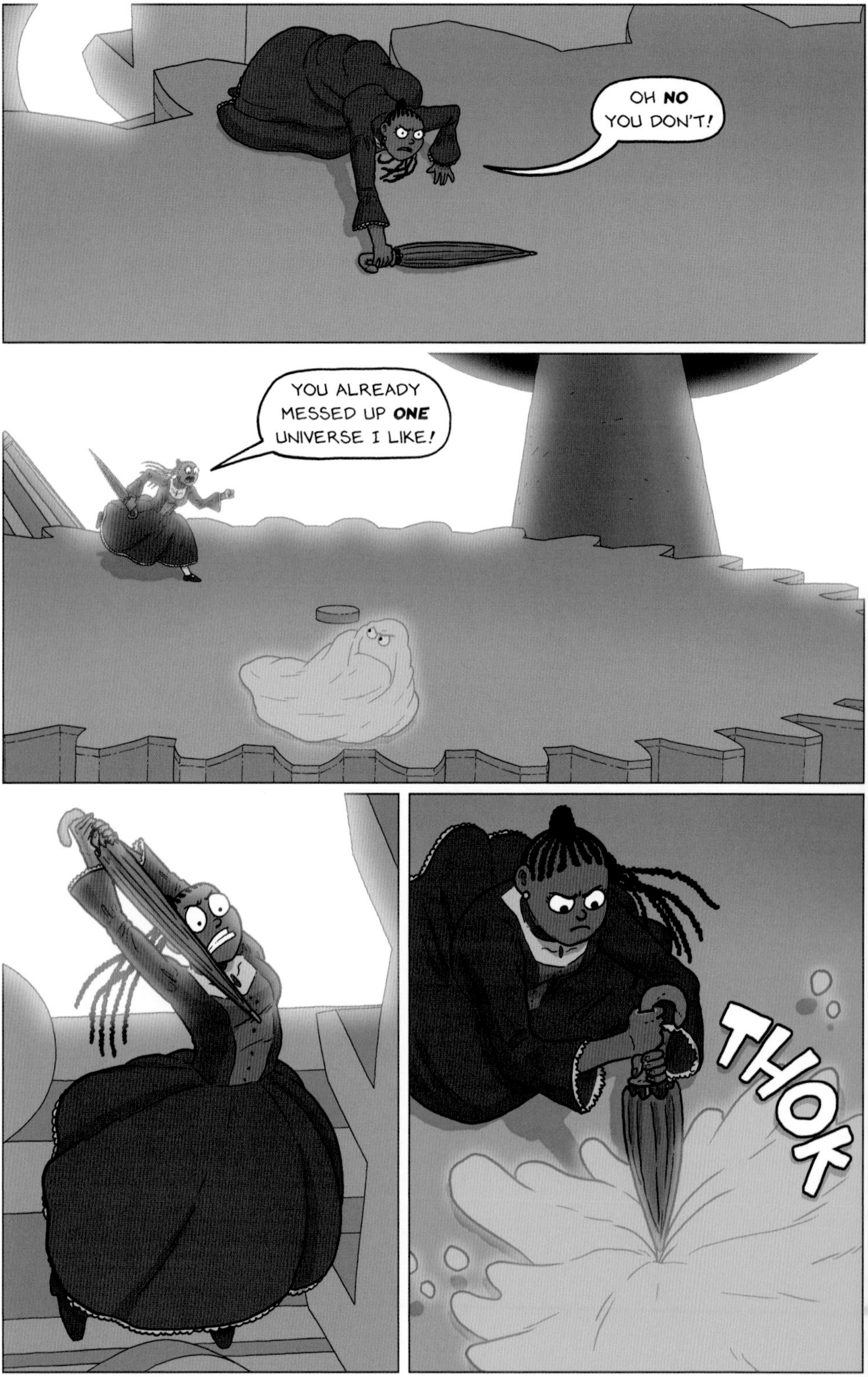
OH NO YOU DON'T!
YOU ALREADY MESSED UP ONE UNIVERSE I LIKE!
THOK

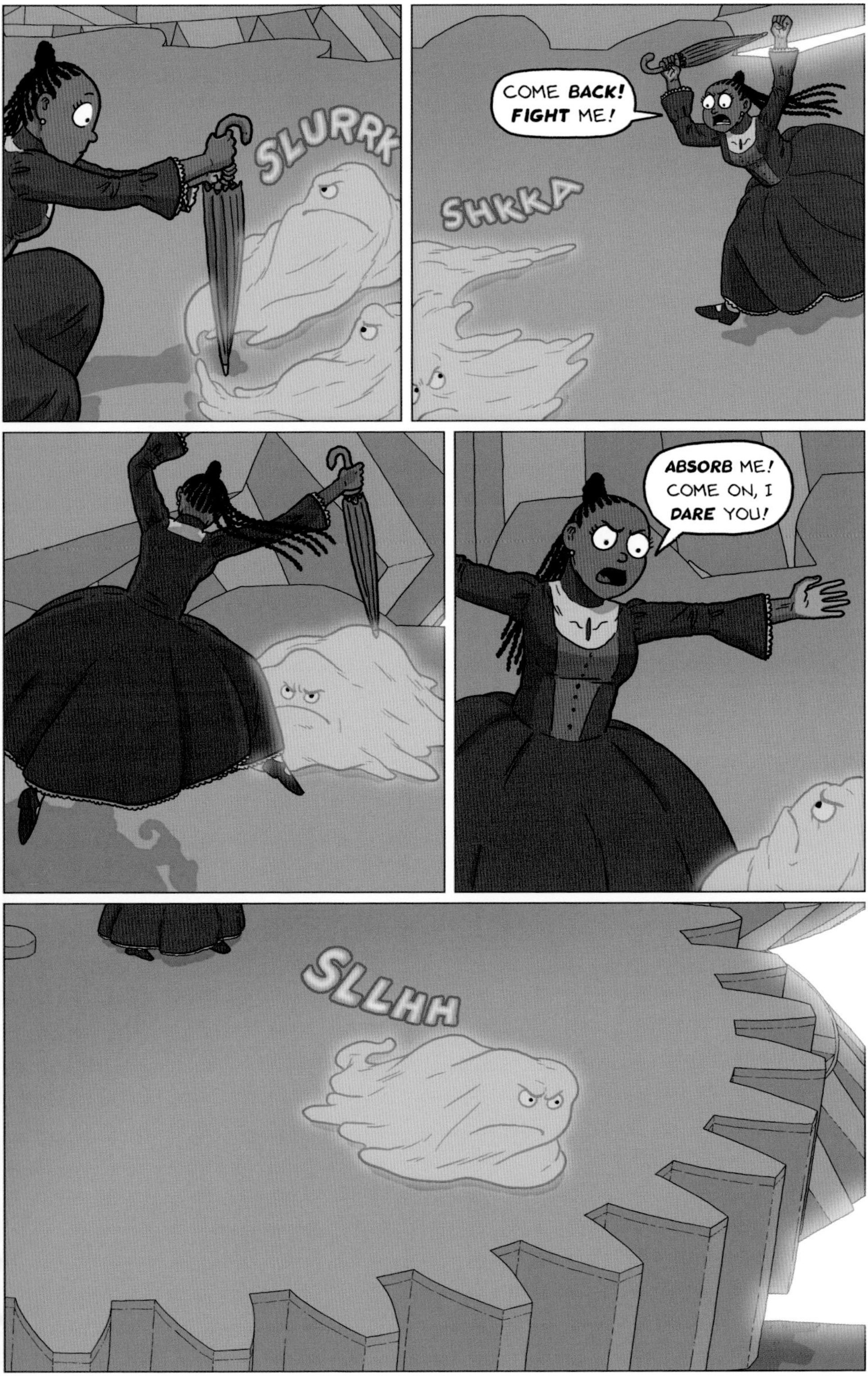
SLURRK
COME BACK! FIGHT ME!
SHKKA
ABSORB ME! COME ON, I DARE YOU!
SLLHH

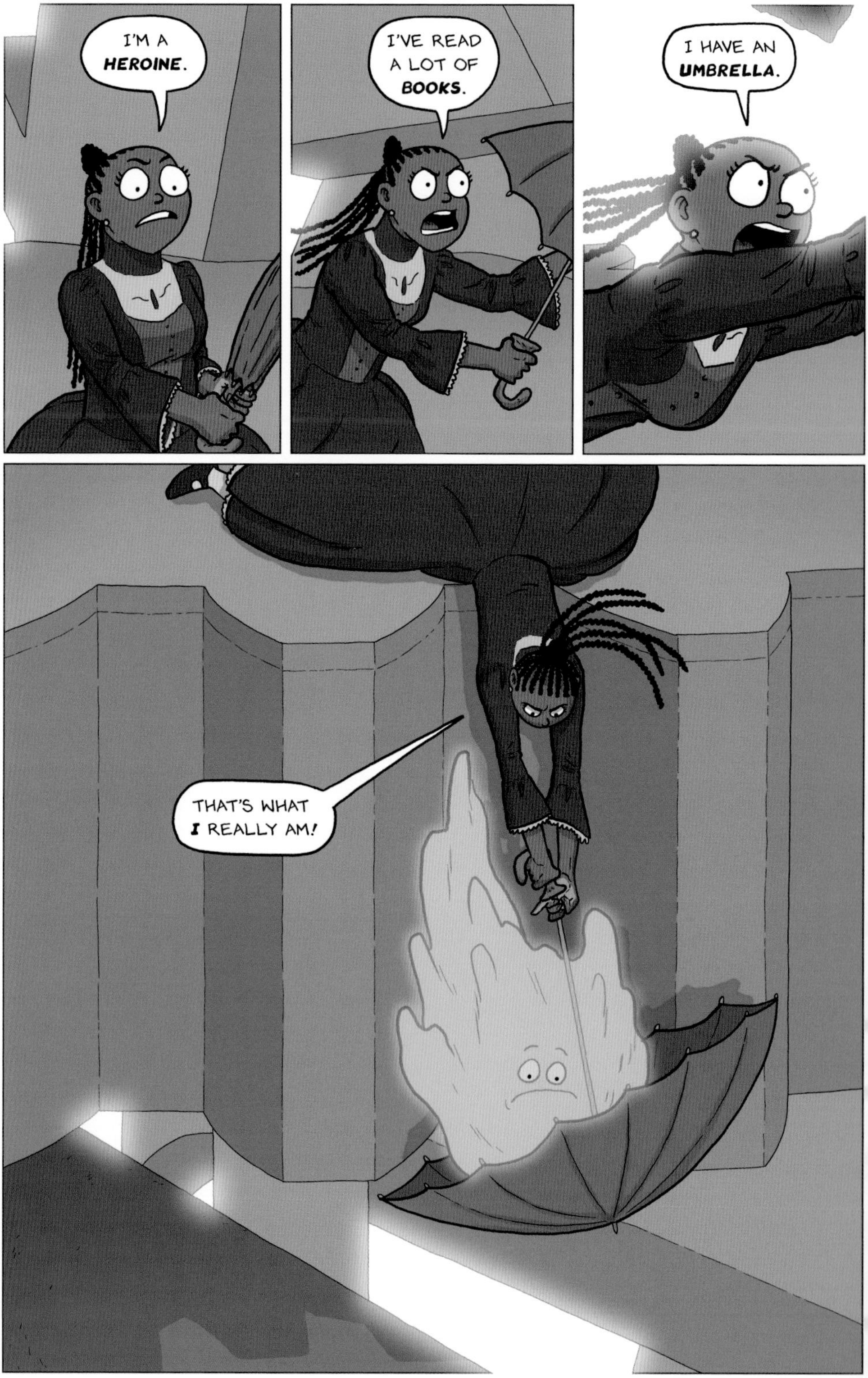
I'M A **HEROINE**.
I'VE READ A LOT OF **BOOKS**.
I HAVE AN **UMBRELLA**.
THAT'S WHAT *I* REALLY AM!

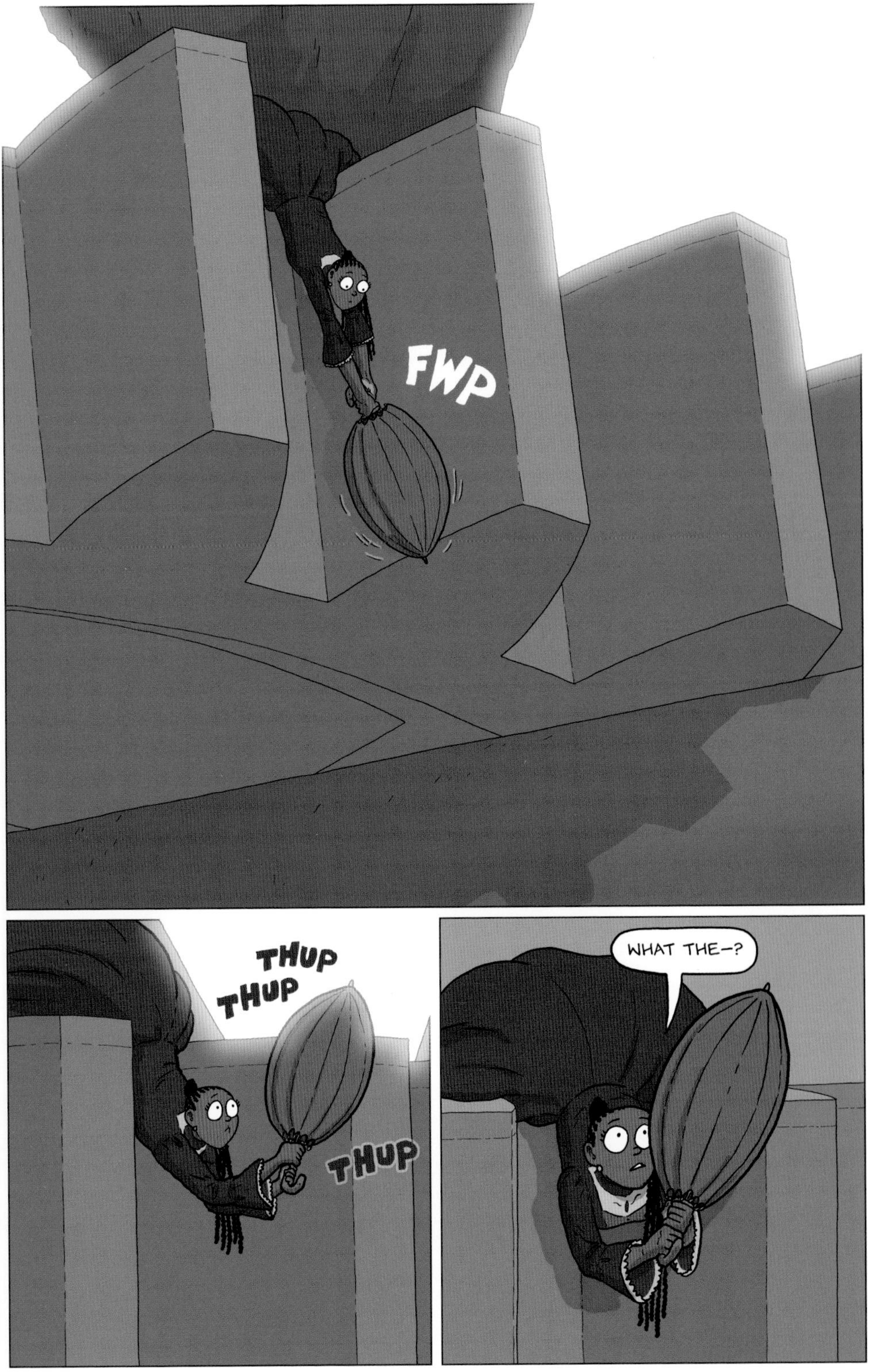
FWP
THUP
THUP
THUP
WHAT THE—?

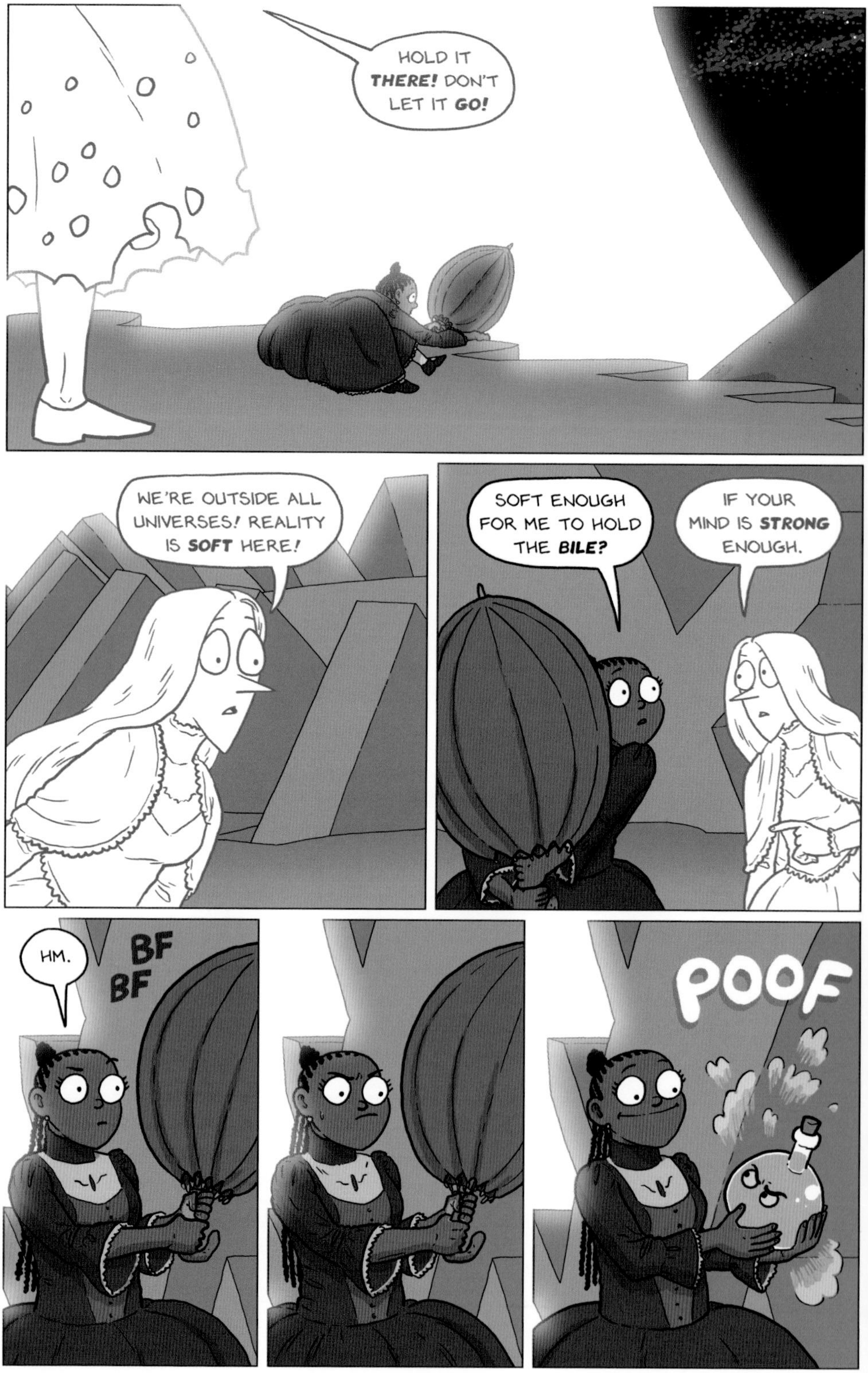
HOLD IT **THERE!** DON'T LET IT **GO!**
WE'RE OUTSIDE ALL UNIVERSES! REALITY IS **SOFT** HERE!
SOFT ENOUGH FOR ME TO HOLD THE **BILE?**
IF YOUR MIND IS **STRONG** ENOUGH.
HM.
BF BF
POOF

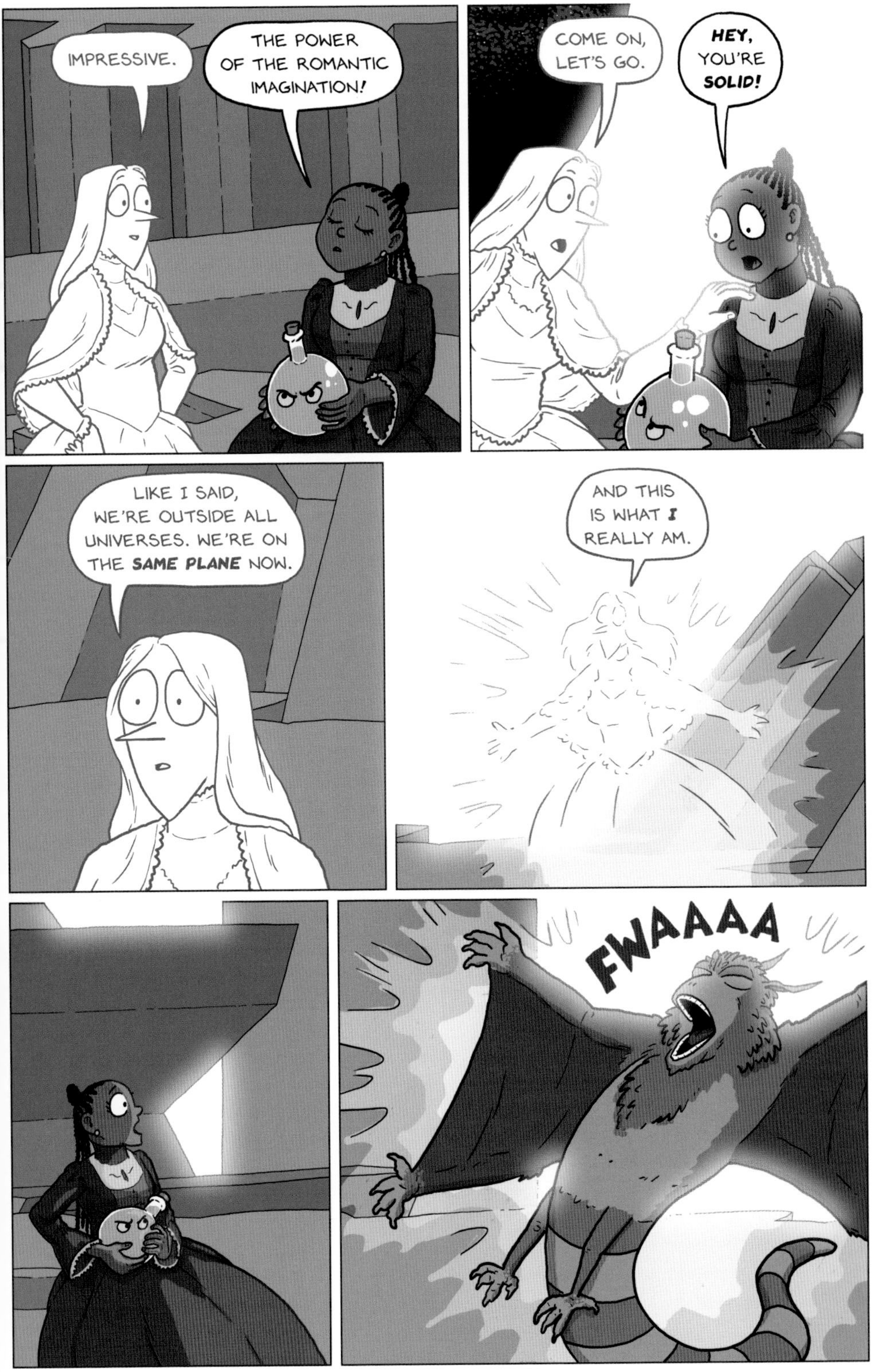
IMPRESSIVE.
THE POWER OF THE ROMANTIC IMAGINATION!
COME ON, LET'S GO.
HEY, YOU'RE SOLID!
LIKE I SAID, WE'RE OUTSIDE ALL UNIVERSES. WE'RE ON THE SAME PLANE NOW.
AND THIS IS WHAT I REALLY AM.
FWAAAA

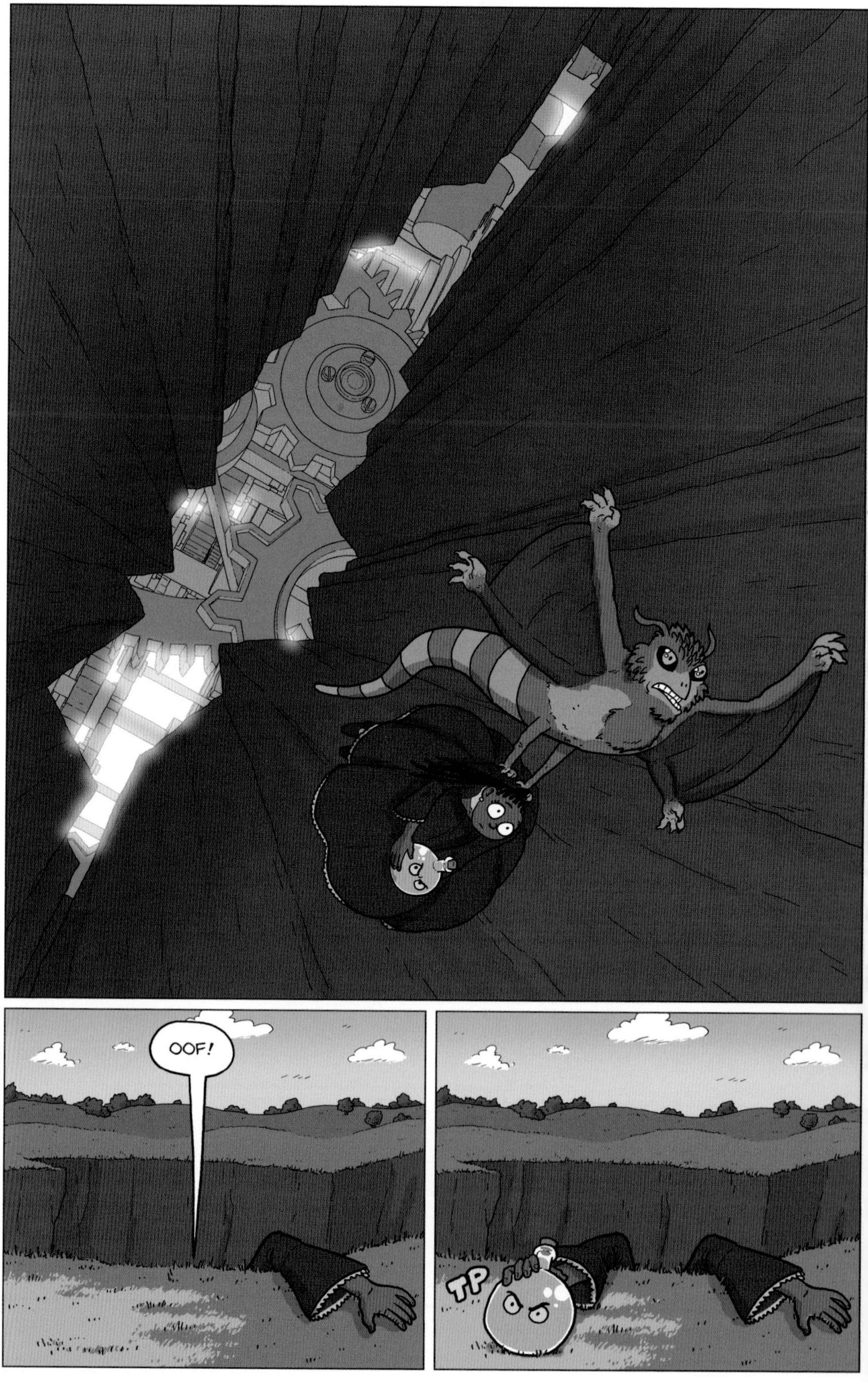
OOF!
TP

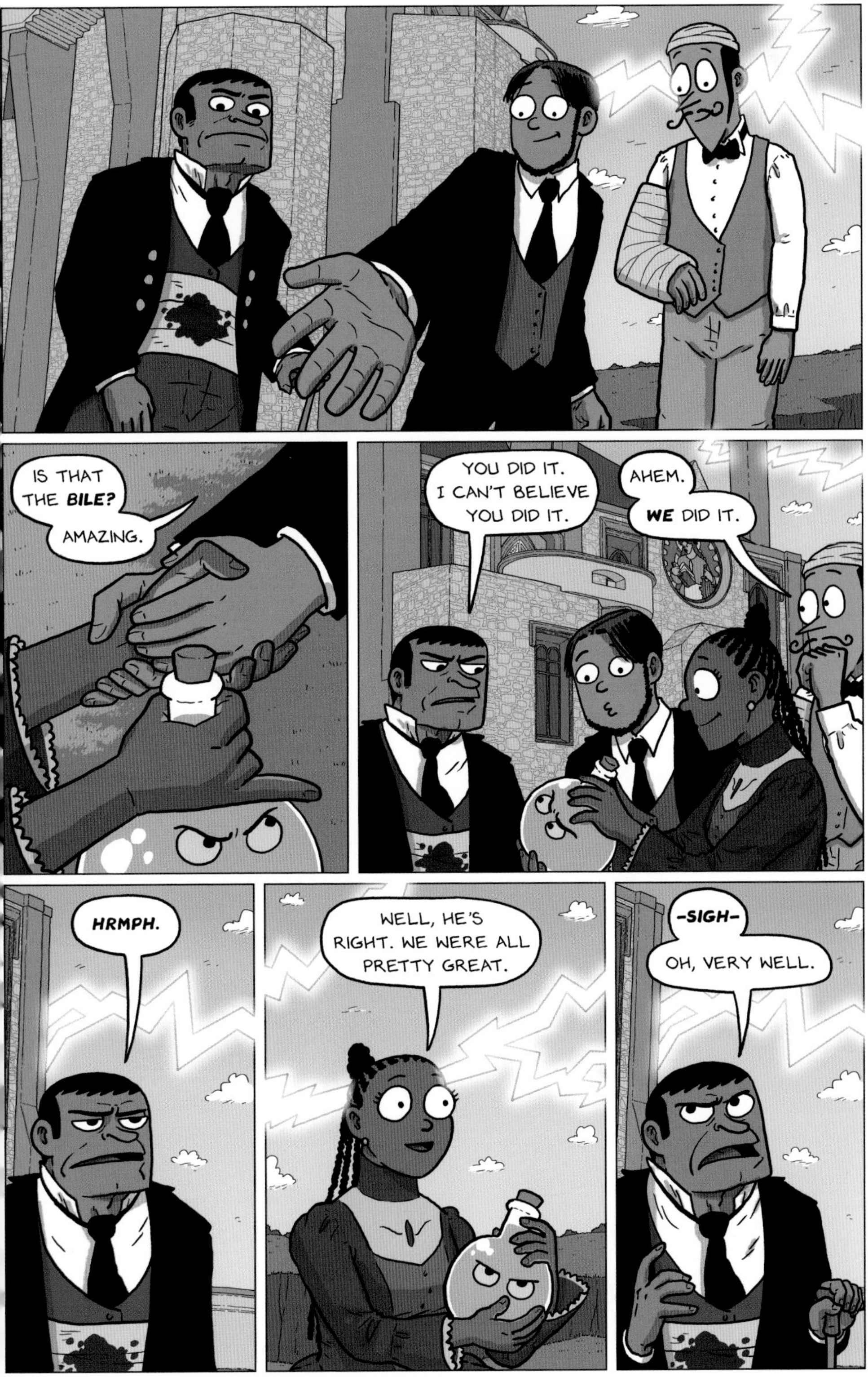
IS THAT THE **BILE?** AMAZING.
YOU DID IT. I CAN'T BELIEVE YOU DID IT.
AHEM. **WE** DID IT.
HRMPH.
WELL, HE'S RIGHT. WE WERE ALL PRETTY GREAT.
-SIGH- OH, VERY WELL.

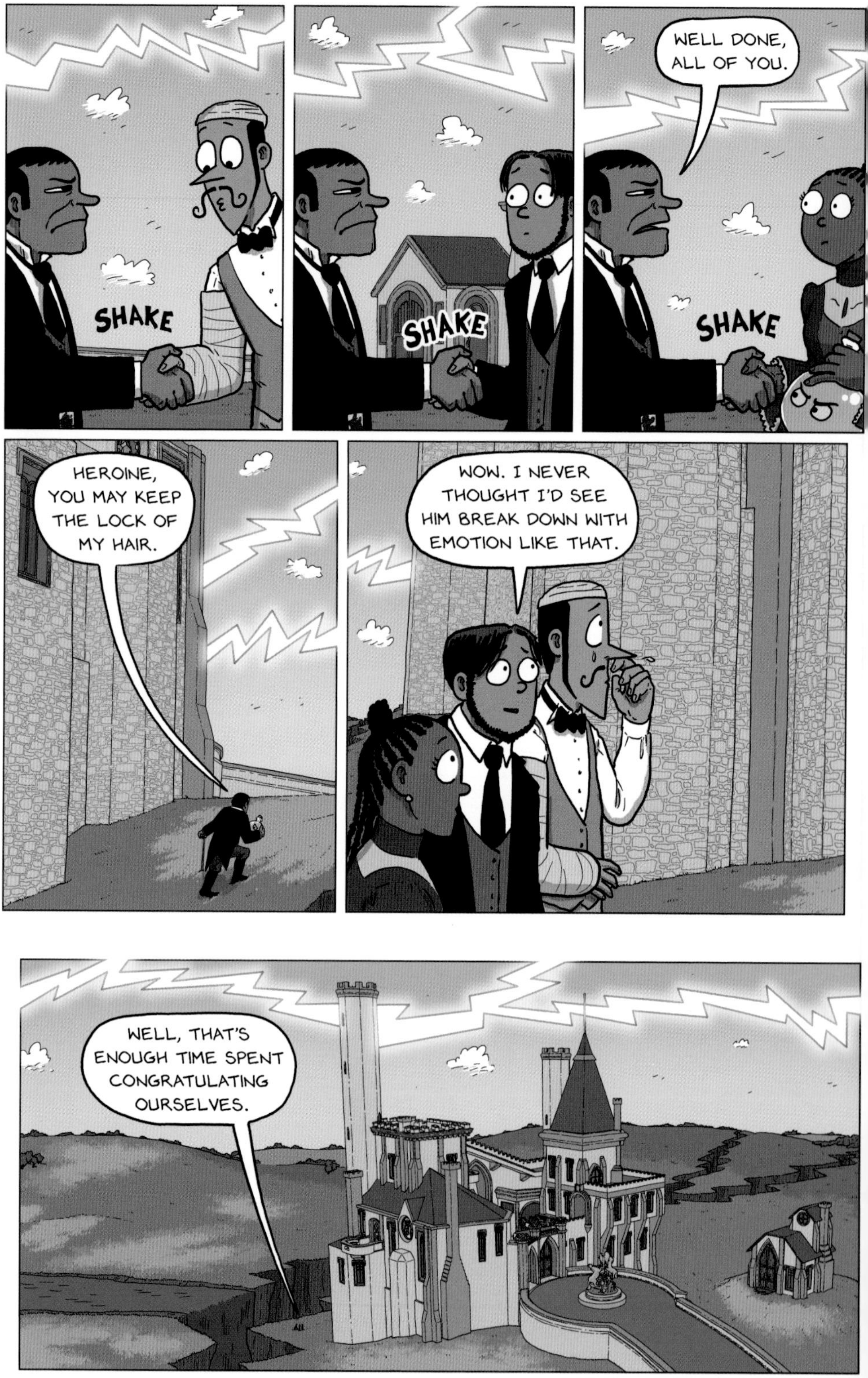
SHAKE
SHAKE
WELL DONE, ALL OF YOU.
SHAKE
HEROINE, YOU MAY KEEP THE LOCK OF MY HAIR.
WOW. I NEVER THOUGHT I'D SEE HIM BREAK DOWN WITH EMOTION LIKE THAT.
WELL, THAT'S ENOUGH TIME SPENT CONGRATULATING OURSELVES.

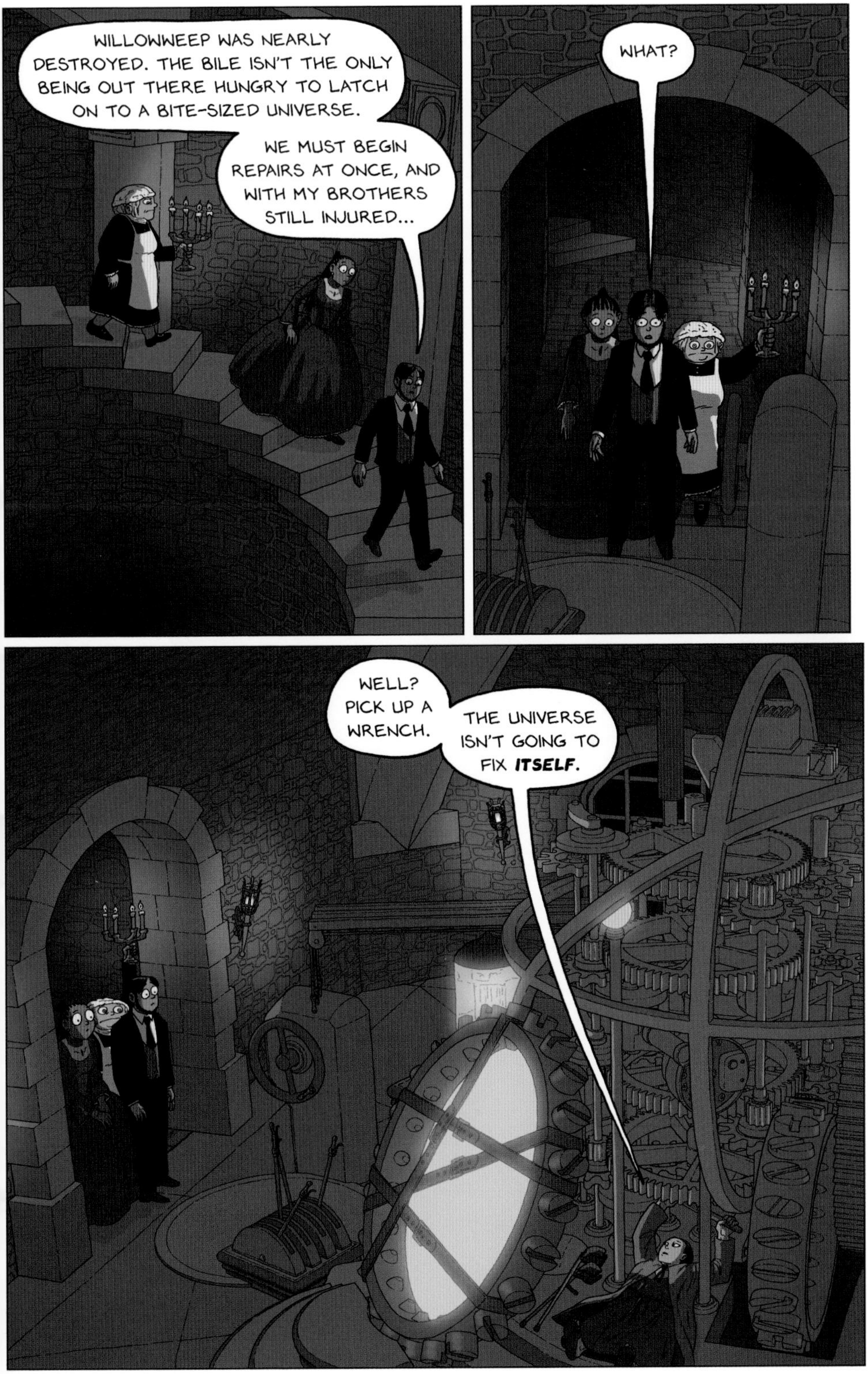
WILLOWWEEP WAS NEARLY DESTROYED. THE BILE ISN'T THE ONLY BEING OUT THERE HUNGRY TO LATCH ON TO A BITE-SIZED UNIVERSE.
WE MUST BEGIN REPAIRS AT ONCE, AND WITH MY BROTHERS STILL INJURED...
WHAT?
WELL? PICK UP A WRENCH.
THE UNIVERSE ISN'T GOING TO FIX **ITSELF**.

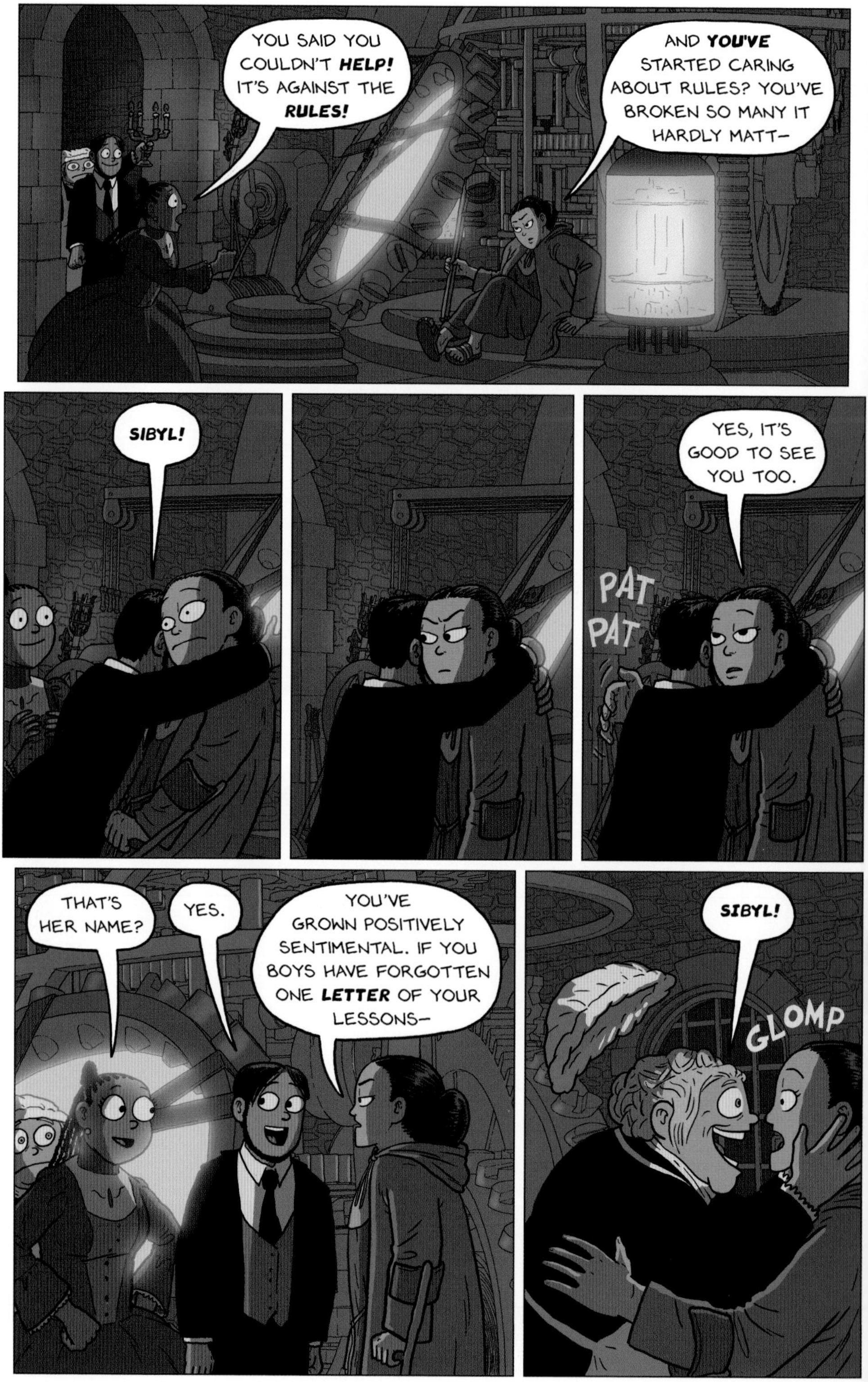
YOU SAID YOU COULDN'T HELP! IT'S AGAINST THE RULES!
AND YOU'VE STARTED CARING ABOUT RULES? YOU'VE BROKEN SO MANY IT HARDLY MATT—
SIBYL!
YES, IT'S GOOD TO SEE YOU TOO.
PAT PAT
THAT'S HER NAME?
YES.
YOU'VE GROWN POSITIVELY SENTIMENTAL. IF YOU BOYS HAVE FORGOTTEN ONE LETTER OF YOUR LESSONS—
SIBYL!
GLOMP

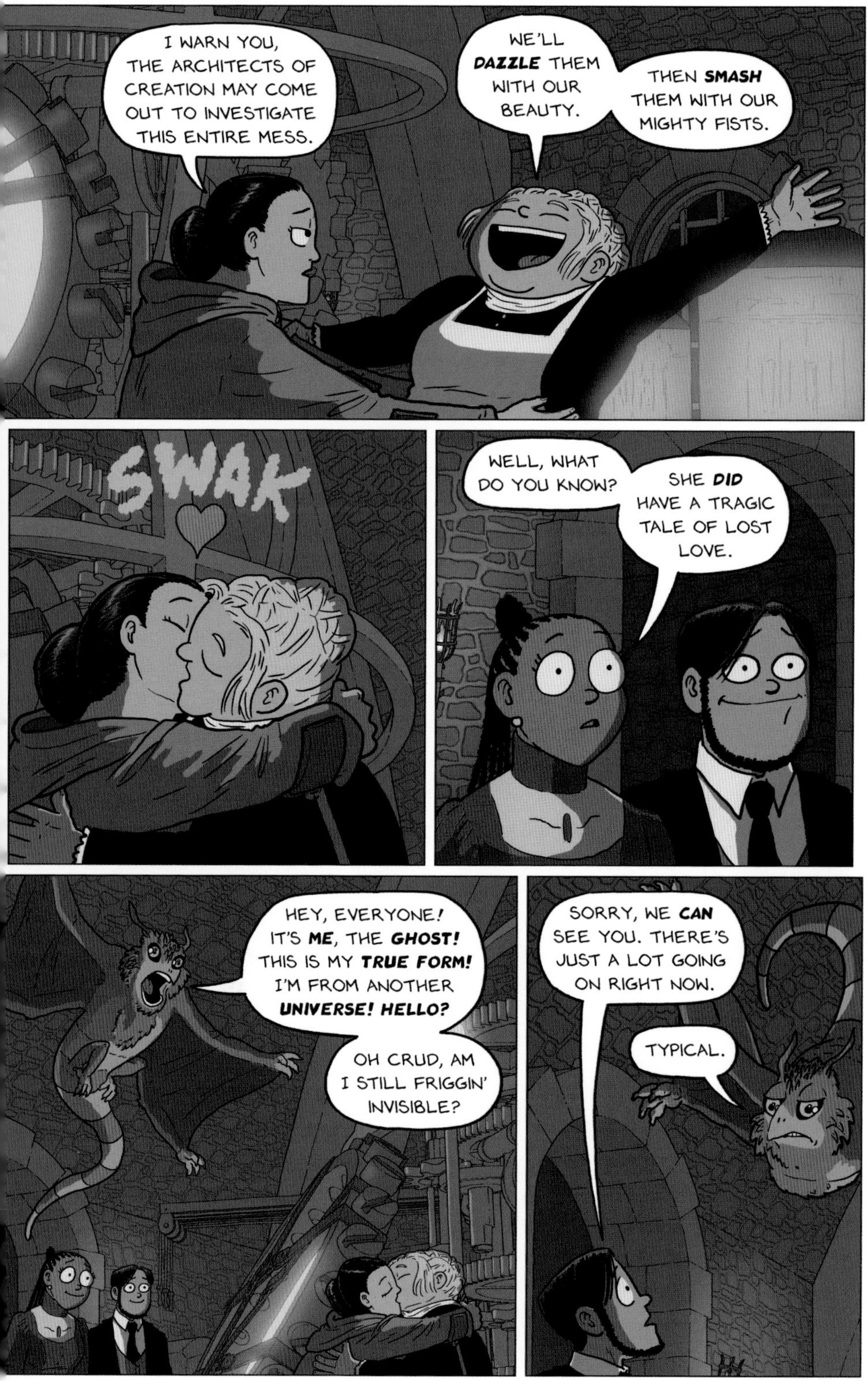

I WARN YOU, THE ARCHITECTS OF CREATION MAY COME OUT TO INVESTIGATE THIS ENTIRE MESS.
WE'LL **DAZZLE** THEM WITH OUR BEAUTY.
THEN **SMASH** THEM WITH OUR MIGHTY FISTS.
SWAK
WELL, WHAT DO YOU KNOW?
SHE **DID** HAVE A TRAGIC TALE OF LOST LOVE.
HEY, EVERYONE! IT'S **ME**, THE **GHOST!** THIS IS MY **TRUE FORM!** I'M FROM ANOTHER **UNIVERSE! HELLO?**
OH CRUD, AM I STILL FRIGGIN' INVISIBLE?
SORRY, WE **CAN** SEE YOU. THERE'S JUST A LOT GOING ON RIGHT NOW.
TYPICAL.

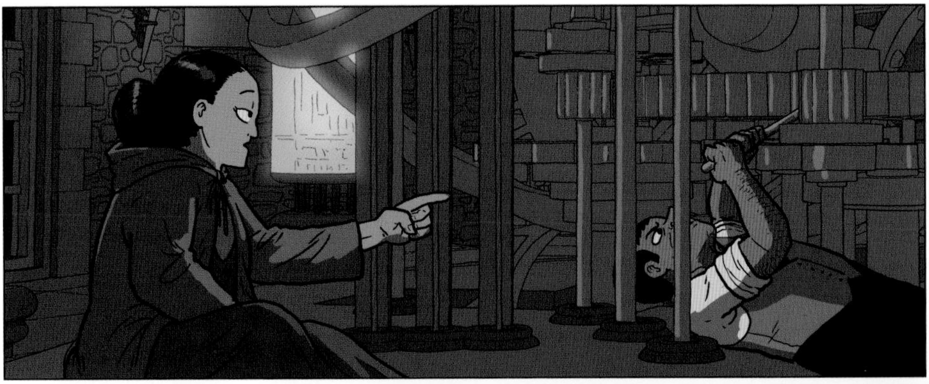

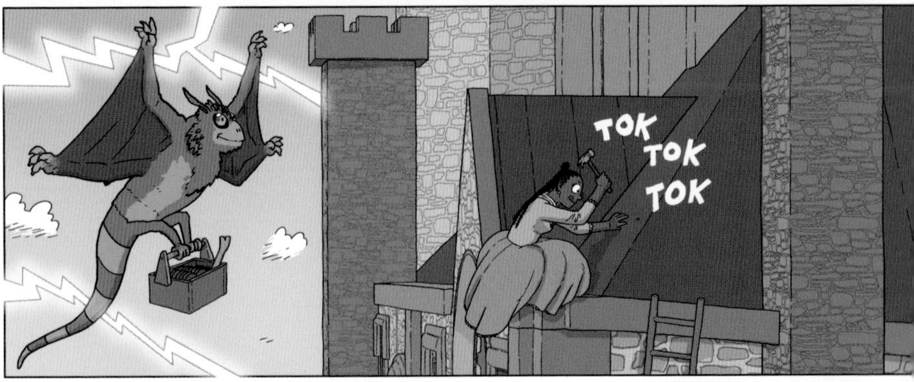
TOK
TOK
TOK

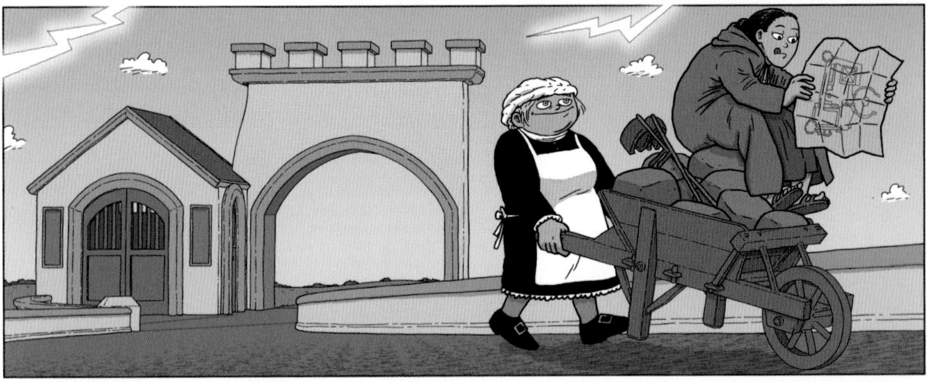

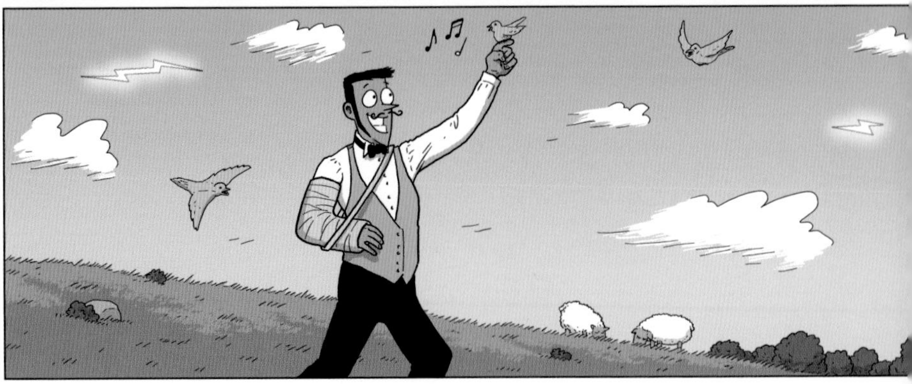

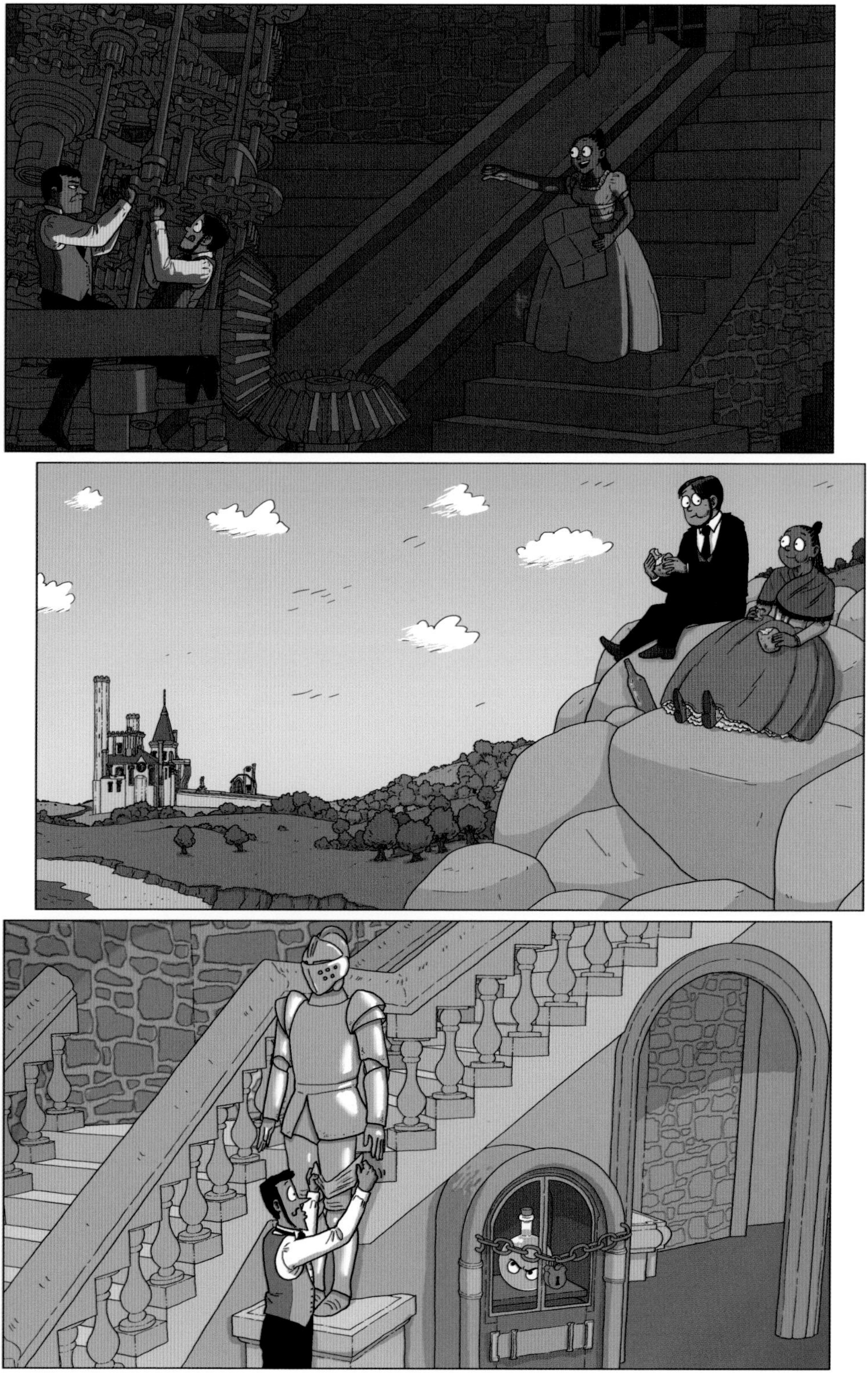

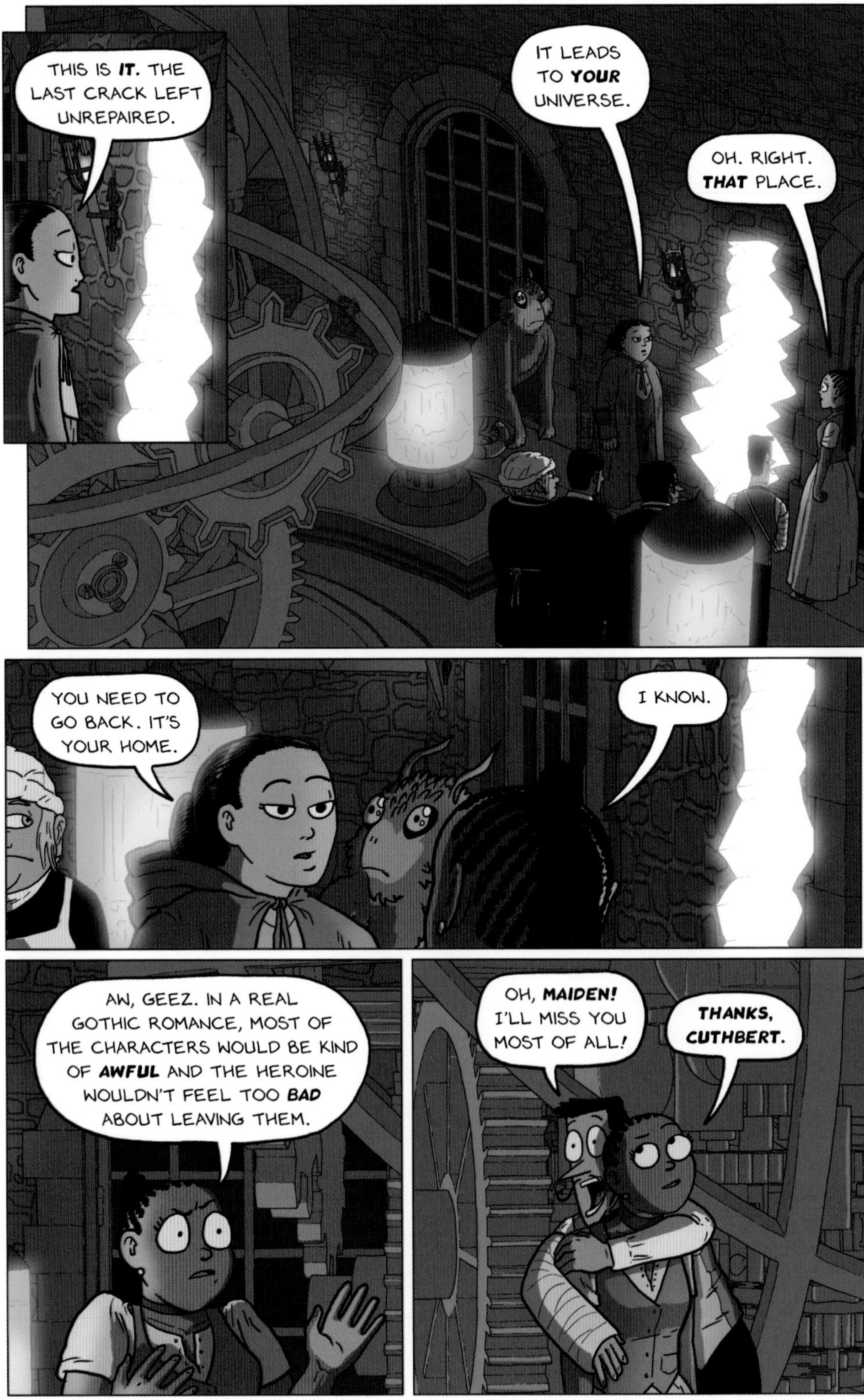
THIS IS **IT.** THE LAST CRACK LEFT UNREPAIRED.
IT LEADS TO **YOUR** UNIVERSE.
OH. RIGHT. **THAT** PLACE.
YOU NEED TO GO BACK. IT'S YOUR HOME.
I KNOW.
AW, GEEZ. IN A REAL GOTHIC ROMANCE, MOST OF THE CHARACTERS WOULD BE KIND OF **AWFUL** AND THE HEROINE WOULDN'T FEEL TOO **BAD** ABOUT LEAVING THEM.
OH, **MAIDEN!** I'LL MISS YOU MOST OF ALL!
THANKS, CUTHBERT.

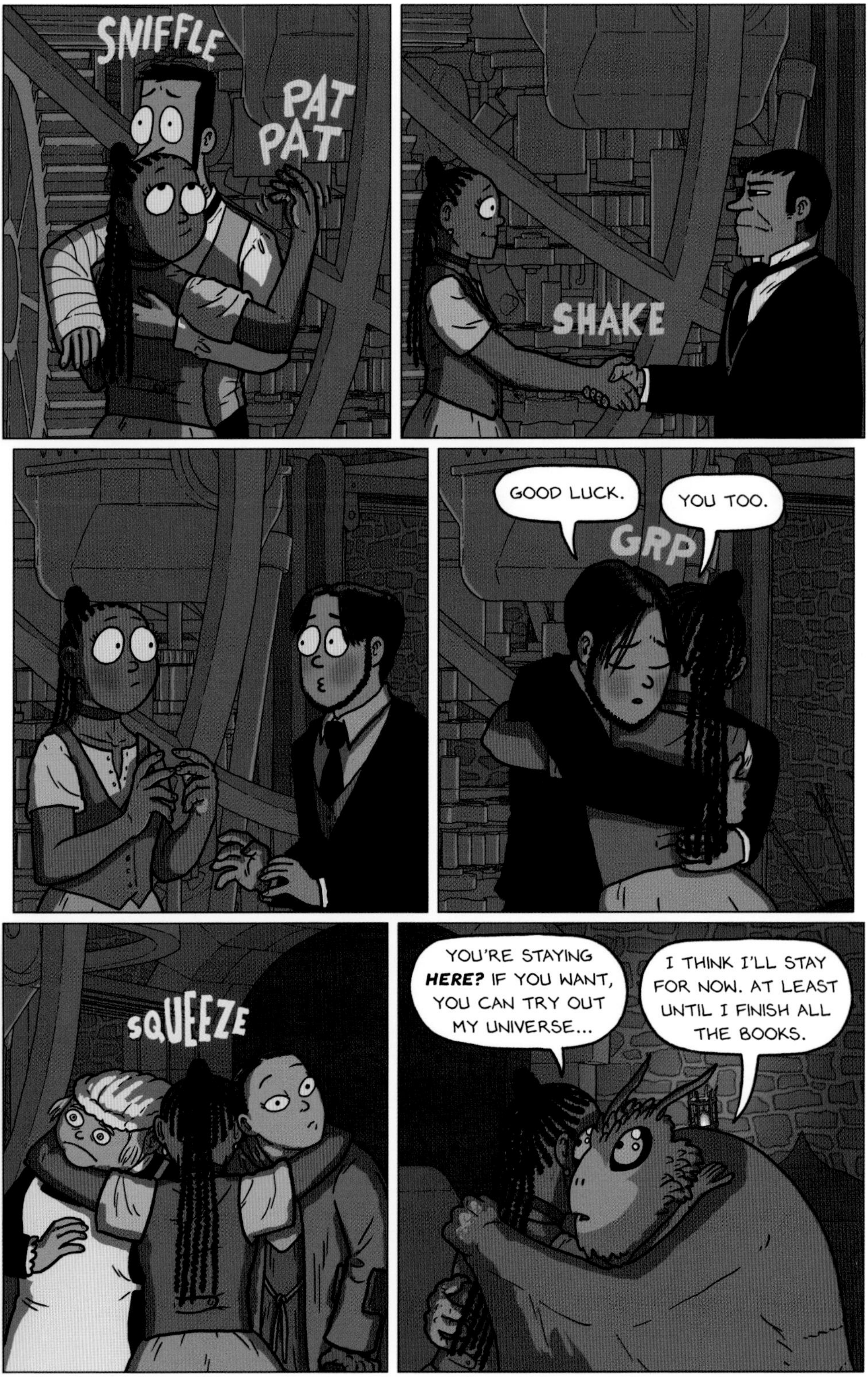

SNIFFLE
PAT PAT
SHAKE
GOOD LUCK.
YOU TOO.
GRP
SQUEEZE
YOU'RE STAYING **HERE?** IF YOU WANT, YOU CAN TRY OUT MY UNIVERSE...
I THINK I'LL STAY FOR NOW. AT LEAST UNTIL I FINISH ALL THE BOOKS.

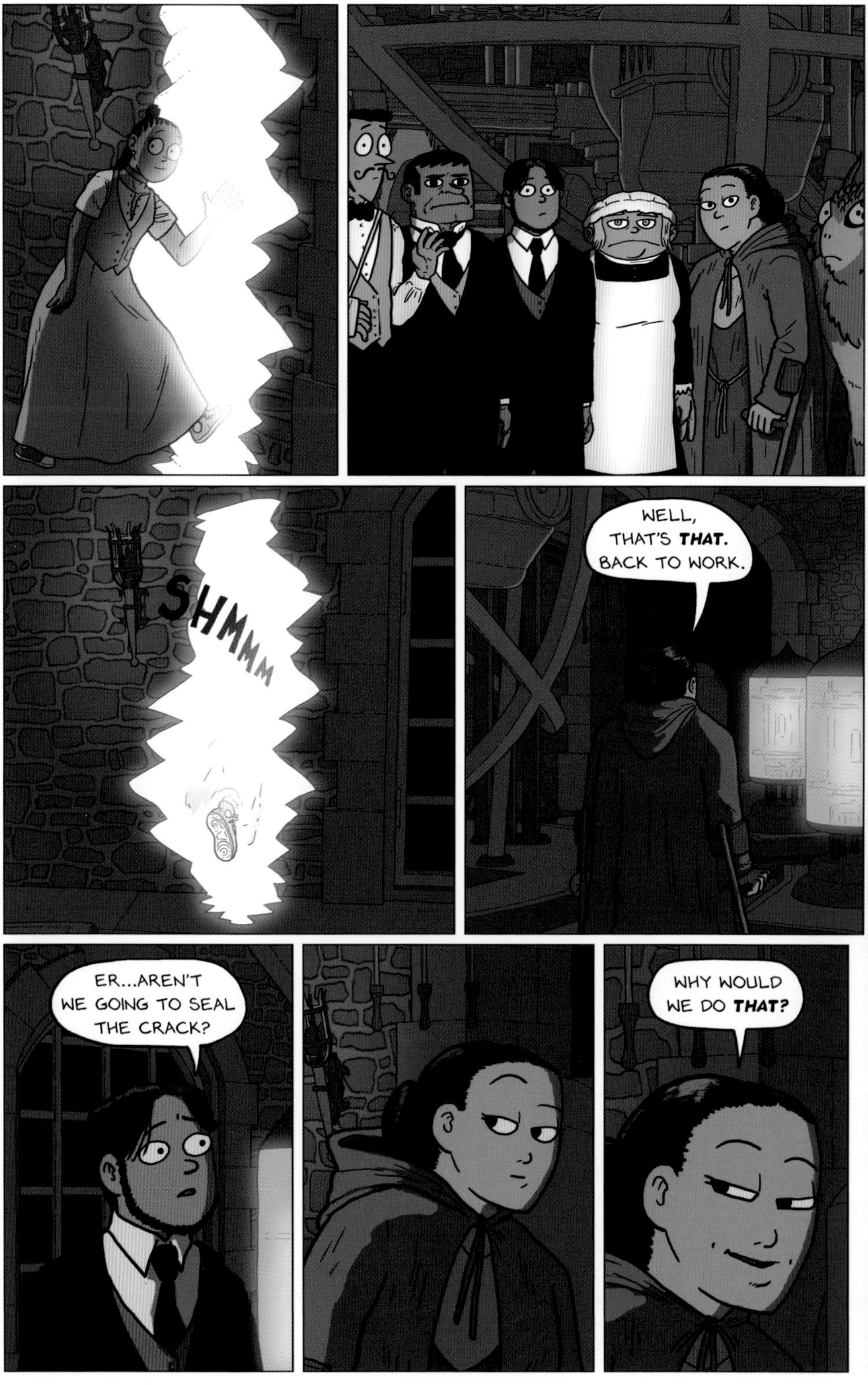
SHMMM
WELL, THAT'S **THAT.** BACK TO WORK.
ER...AREN'T WE GOING TO SEAL THE CRACK?
WHY WOULD WE DO **THAT?**

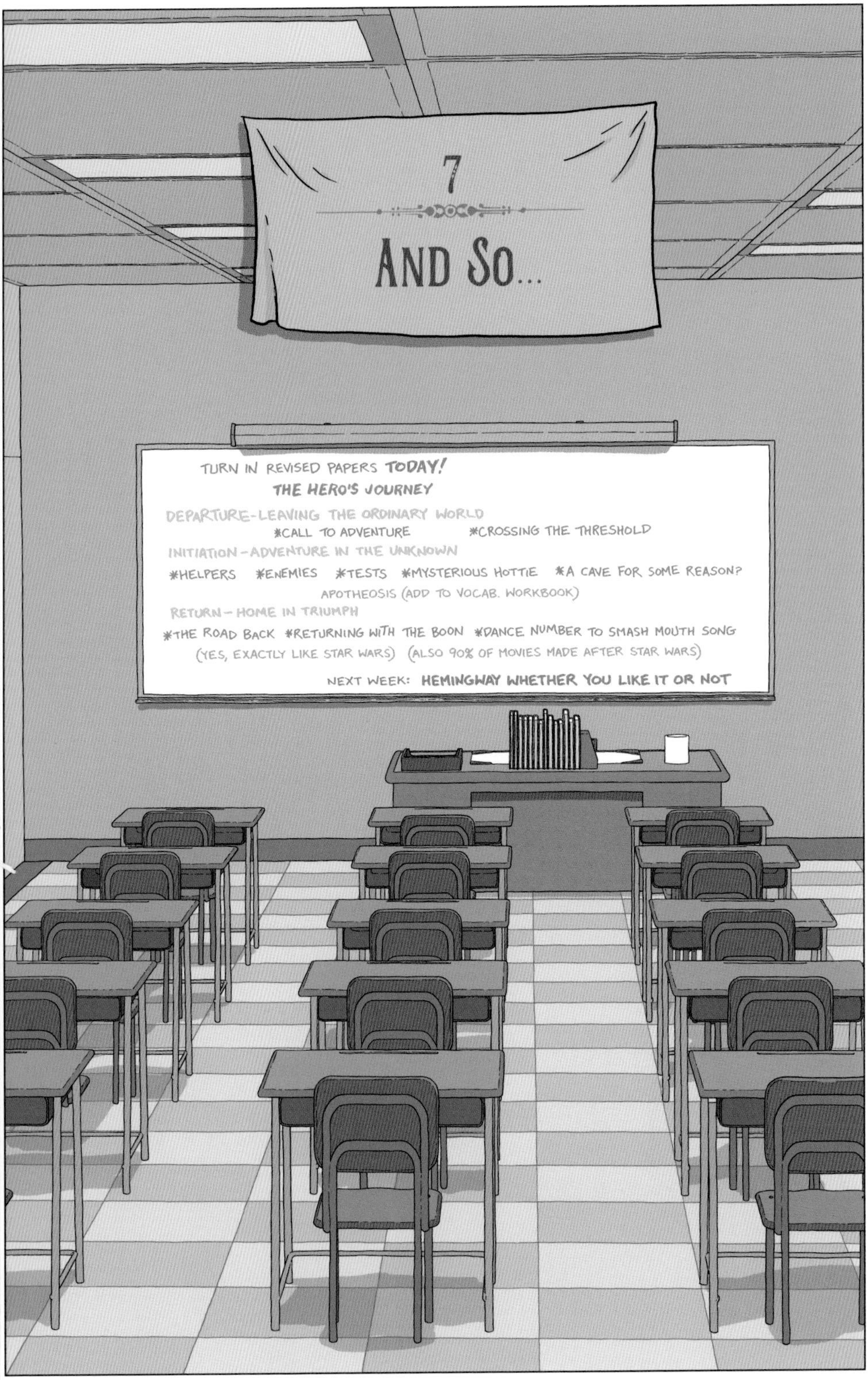
7
AND SO...
TURN IN REVISED PAPERS TODAY!
THE HERO'S JOURNEY
DEPARTURE-LEAVING THE ORDINARY WORLD
*CALL TO ADVENTURE *CROSSING THE THRESHOLD
INITIATION-ADVENTURE IN THE UNKNOWN
*HELPERS *ENEMIES *TESTS *MYSTERIOUS HOTTIE *A CAVE FOR SOME REASON?
APOTHEOSIS (ADD TO VOCAB. WORKBOOK)
RETURN-HOME IN TRIUMPH
*THE ROAD BACK *RETURNING WITH THE BOON *DANCE NUMBER TO SMASH MOUTH SONG
(YES, EXACTLY LIKE STAR WARS) (ALSO 90% OF MOVIES MADE AFTER STAR WARS)
NEXT WEEK: HEMINGWAY WHETHER YOU LIKE IT OR NOT

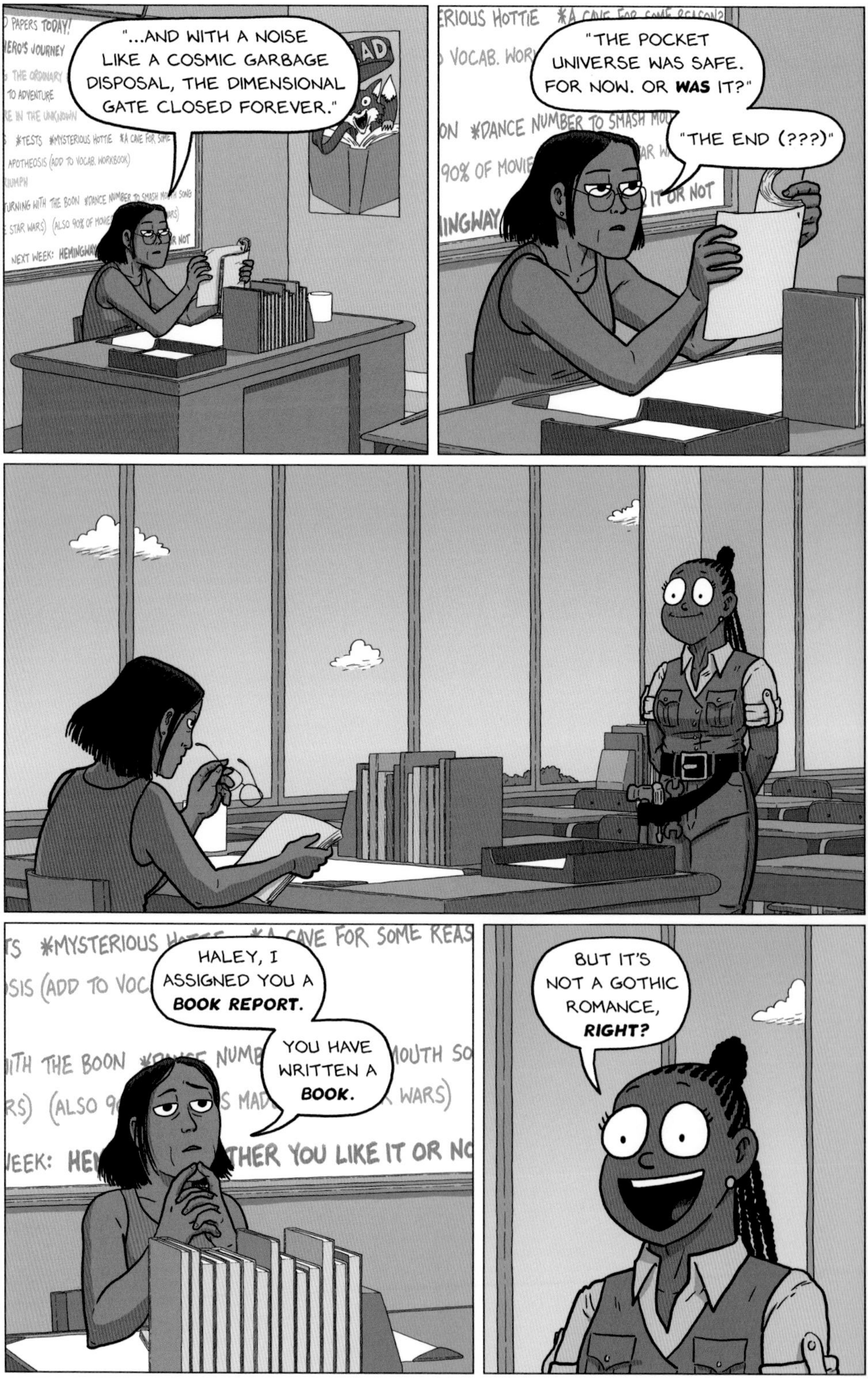
"...AND WITH A NOISE LIKE A COSMIC GARBAGE DISPOSAL, THE DIMENSIONAL GATE CLOSED FOREVER."
"THE POCKET UNIVERSE WAS SAFE. FOR NOW. OR **WAS** IT?"
"THE END (???)"
HALEY, I ASSIGNED YOU A ***BOOK REPORT.***
YOU HAVE WRITTEN A ***BOOK.***
BUT IT'S NOT A GOTHIC ROMANCE, ***RIGHT?***

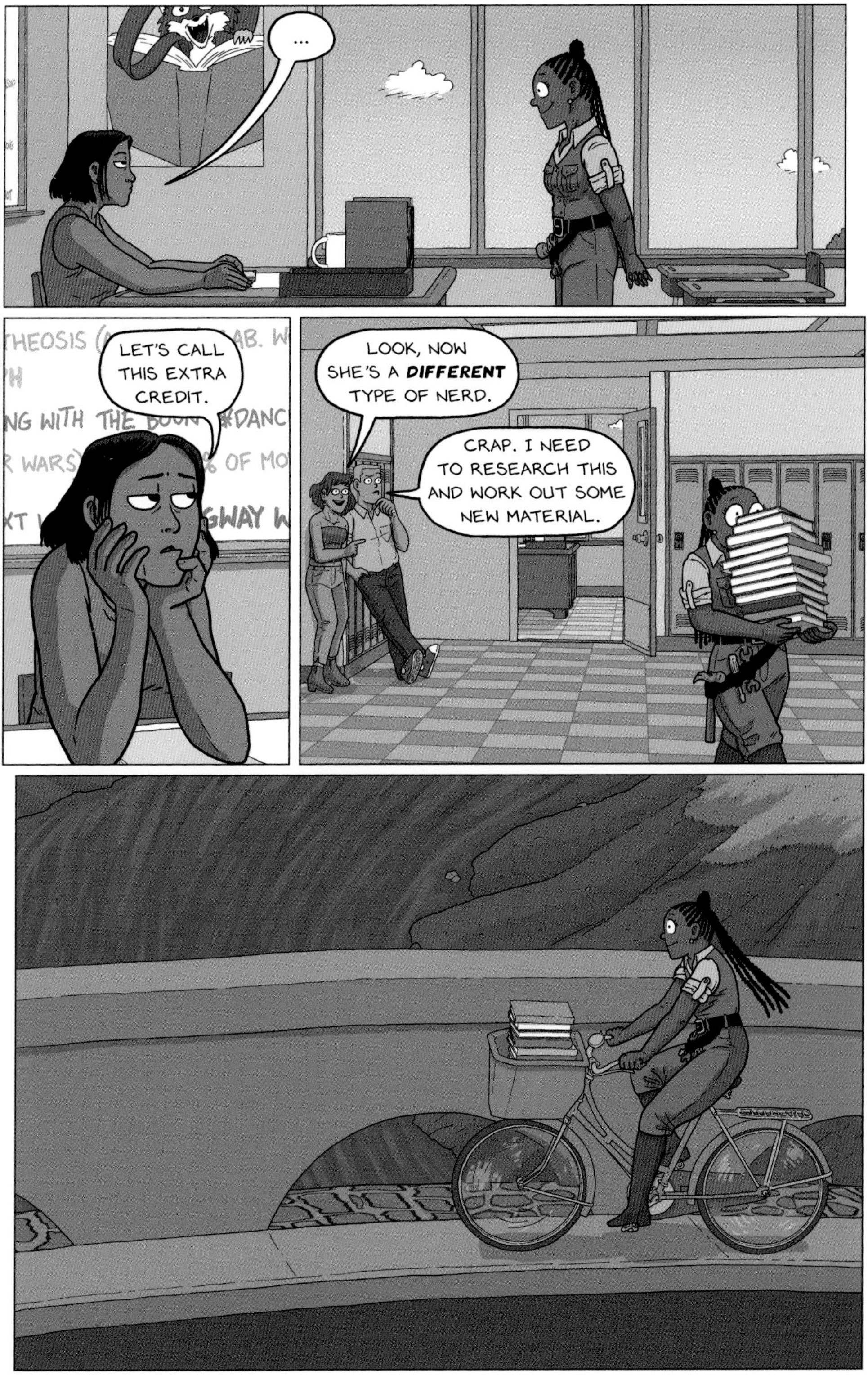
...
LET'S CALL THIS EXTRA CREDIT.
LOOK, NOW SHE'S A **DIFFERENT** TYPE OF NERD.
CRAP. I NEED TO RESEARCH THIS AND WORK OUT SOME NEW MATERIAL.

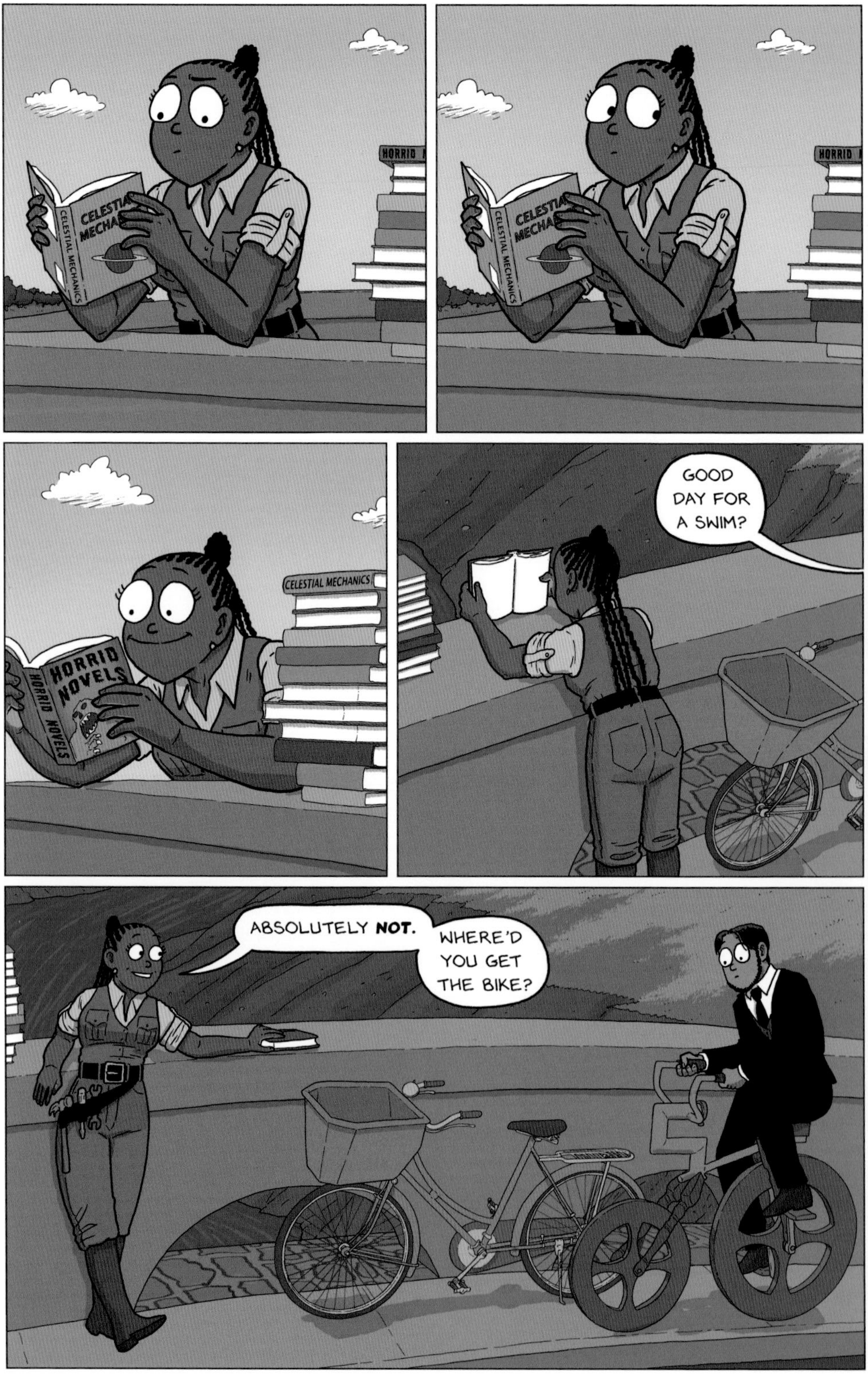
CELESTIAL MECHANICS
HORRID NOVELS
GOOD DAY FOR A SWIM?
ABSOLUTELY **NOT.**
WHERE'D YOU GET THE BIKE?

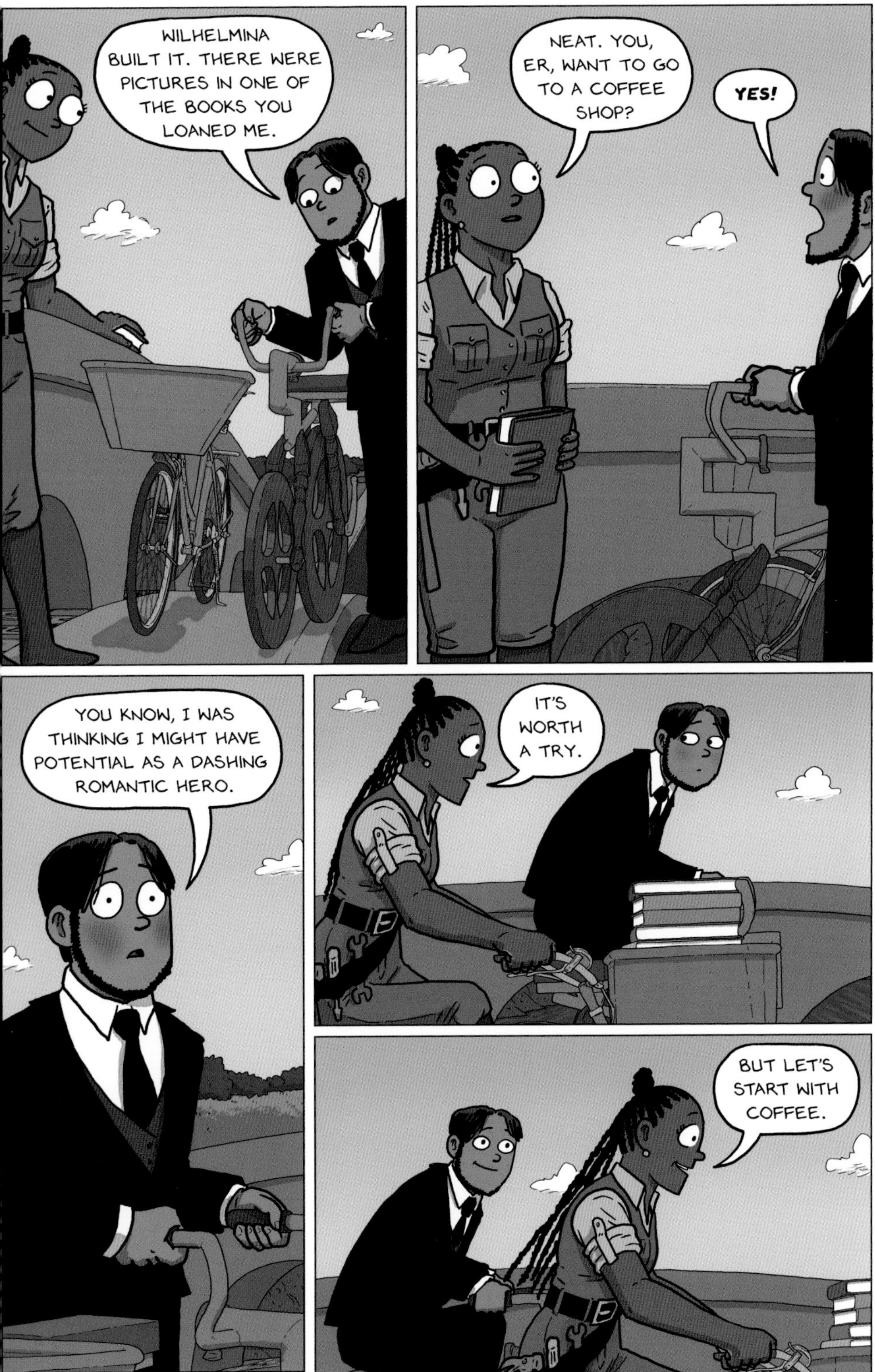
WILHELMINA BUILT IT. THERE WERE PICTURES IN ONE OF THE BOOKS YOU LOANED ME.
NEAT. YOU, ER, WANT TO GO TO A COFFEE SHOP?
YES!
YOU KNOW, I WAS THINKING I MIGHT HAVE POTENTIAL AS A DASHING ROMANTIC HERO.
IT'S WORTH A TRY.
BUT LET'S START WITH COFFEE.

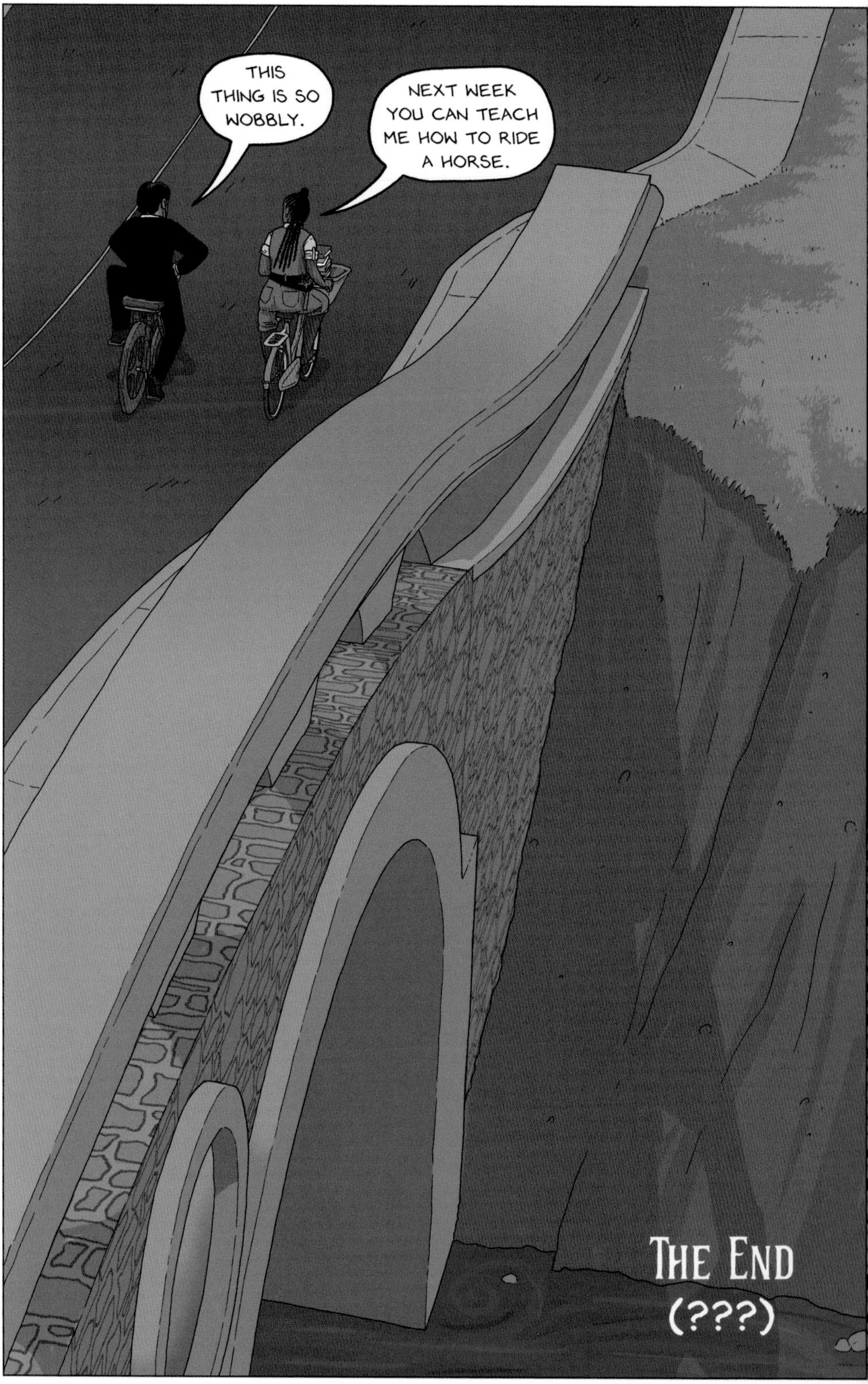
THIS THING IS SO WOBBLY.
NEXT WEEK YOU CAN TEACH ME HOW TO RIDE A HORSE.
THE END
(???)

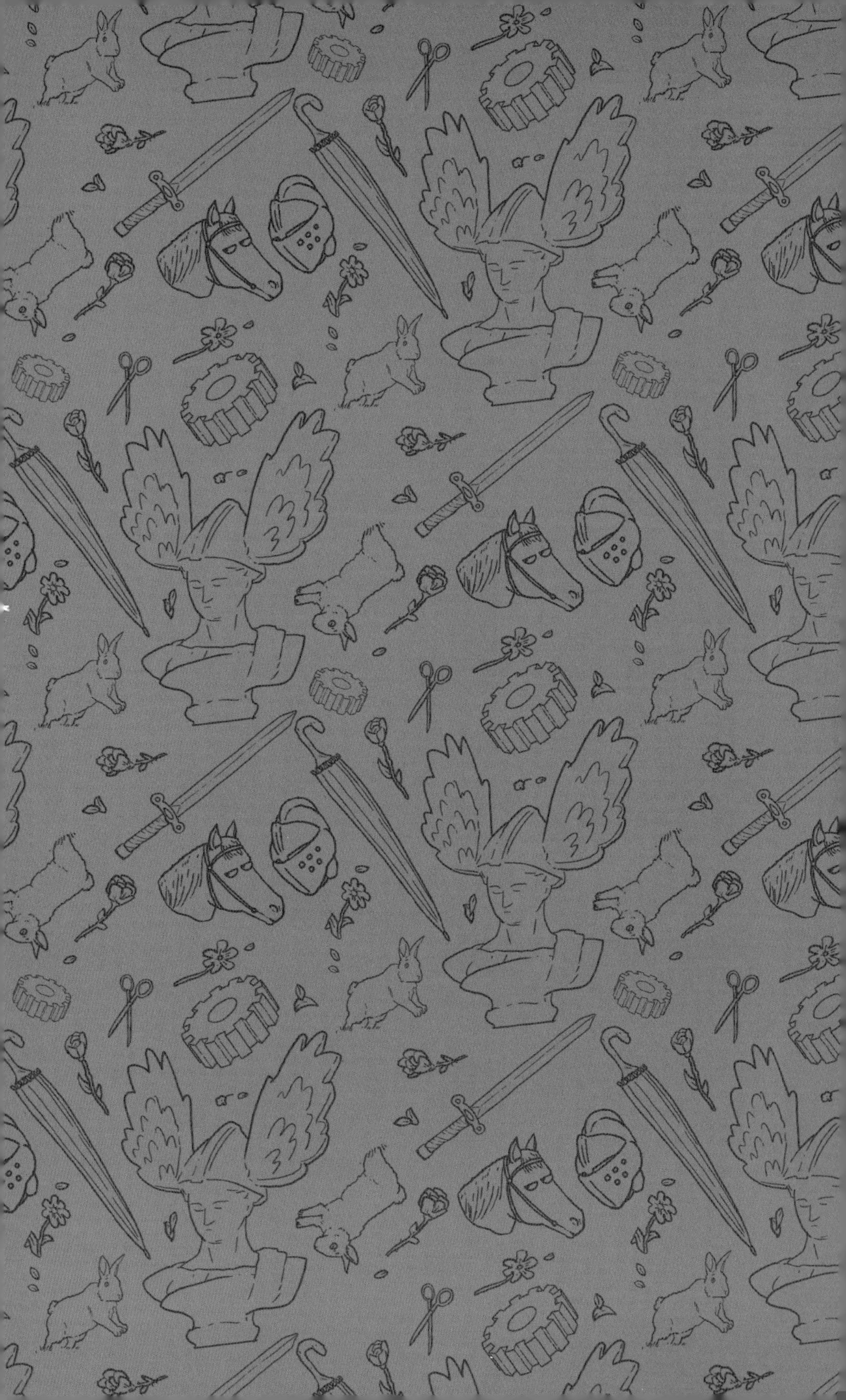

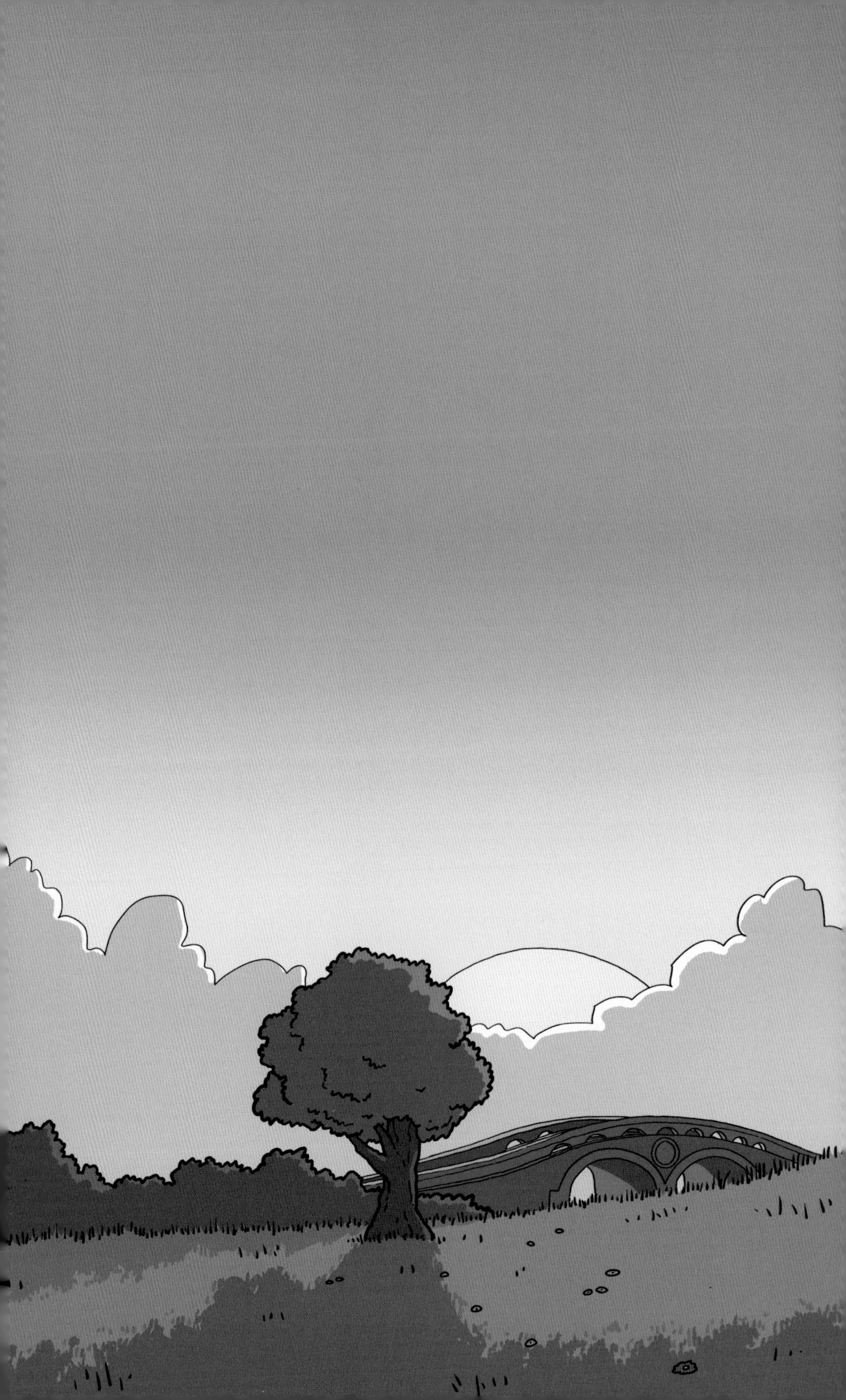

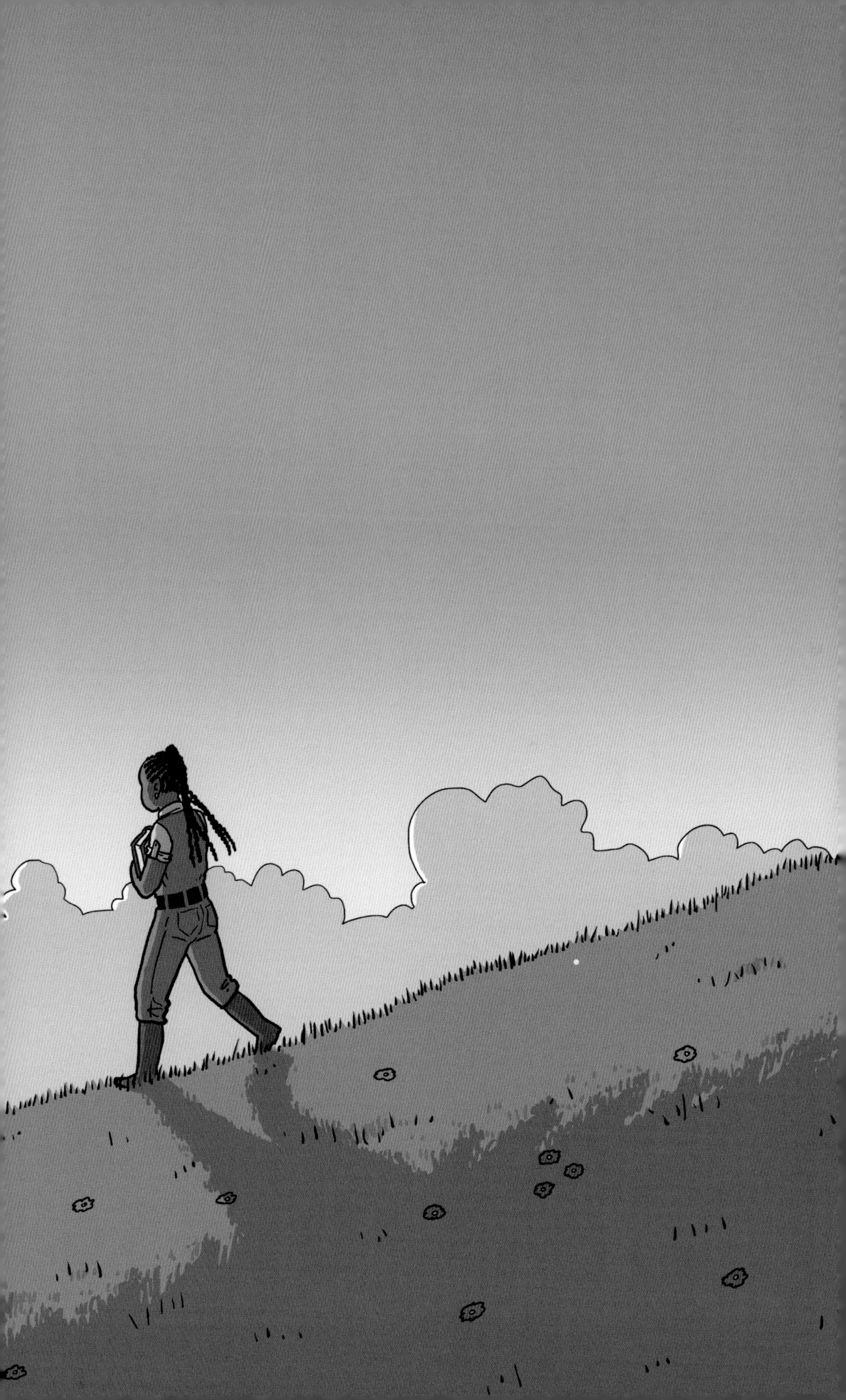

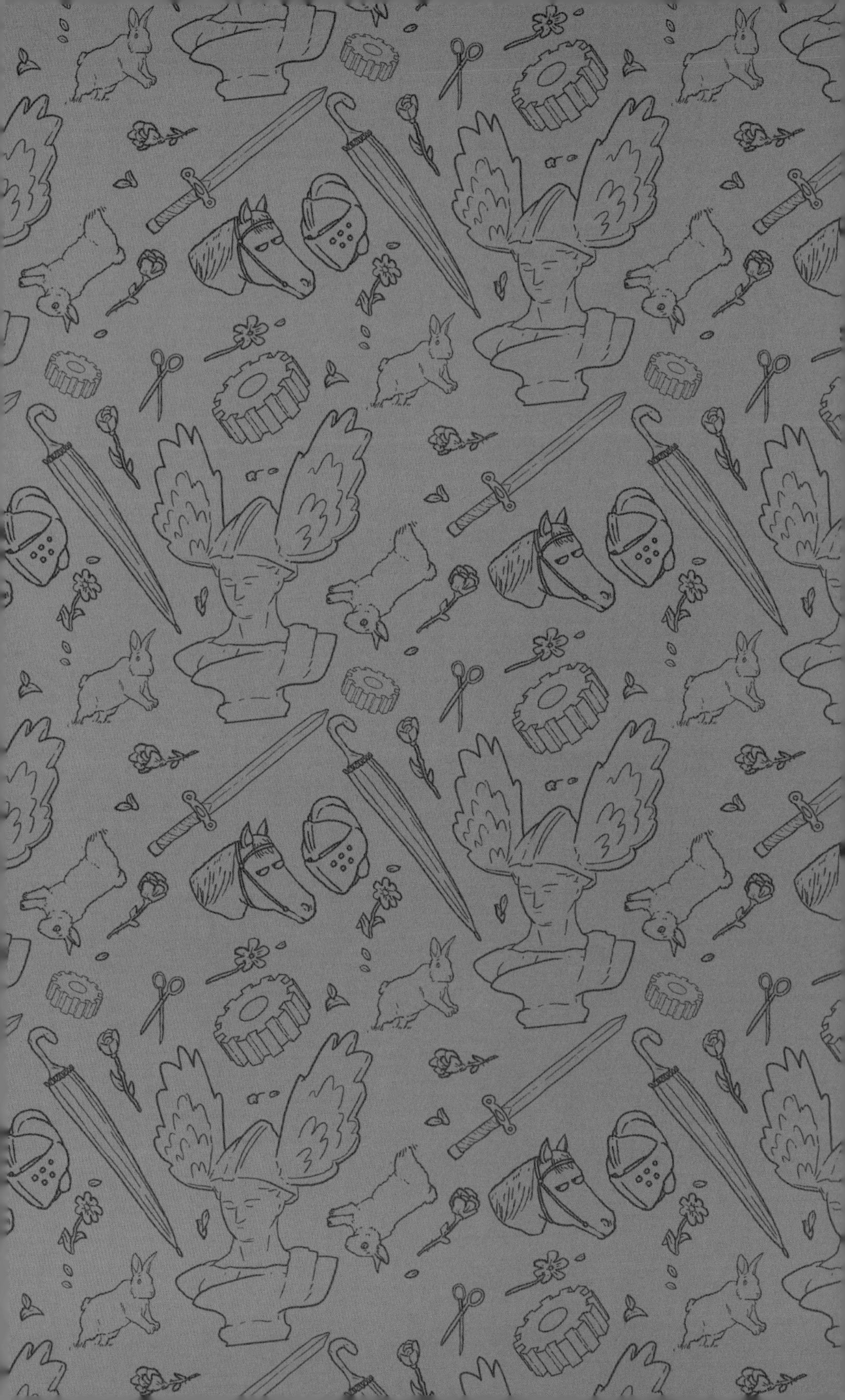